Knightly Obsession

Kofoworola Laiyemo

AuthorHouse™ UK Ltd.
500 Avebury Boulevard
Central Milton Keynes, MK9 2BE
www.authorhouse.co.uk
Phone: 08001974150

This book is a work of fiction. People, places, events, and situations are the product of the author's imagination. Any resemblance to actual persons, living or dead, or historical events, is purely coincidental.

© 2010 Kofoworola Laiyemo. All rights reserved.

No part of this book may be reproduced, stored in a retrieval system, or transmitted by any means without the written permission of the author.

First published by AuthorHouse 5/6/2010

ISBN: 978-1-4490-7978-9 (sc)

The right of Kofoworola Laiyemo to be identified as the author of this work has been asserted by her in accordance with the Copyright, Designs and Patents Act 1988.

This book is printed on acid-free paper.

For Olanrewaju Oluyemi,
Because he truly cares
…and he believes.

Acknowledgments

My Gratitude goes to the entire staff of AuthorHouse Publishers, most especially Rafiq Hudda (who I always refer to as my wealthy companion); to Elaine Sinfield and to Hannah Dibley, for without their professional help and constant support this book would not have gone into publication.

I wish to say a Big 'Thank You' to Hayley Sherman for her invaluable contributions to the success of this project.

I wish to express my appreciation to Betty Ansell for her timely advice in the course of publishing this book.

I also wish to thank my parents, Mr and Mrs Samson 'Lolu Laiyemo for giving me the formal education I needed to propel me forward in life.

My profound gratitude also goes to Mr Olanrewaju Oluyemi who has been a source of inspiration to me, as well as being my emotional, psychological and financial backbone. Without him, my dream of becoming a writer would always remain just a dream.

Finally, my greatest thanks go to God Almighty for making my life a success.

Prologue

Alex Tucker (Jnr.) sat on the edge of his bed; his right palm beneath his chin, his thumb occasionally kneading his lips as if that gesture would give him at least a clue to the riddle on the ground. He was alone in the room, the room that had been his since he was born. His face was contorted in confusion and total bewilderment. He had been like this for sometime, close to five hours; in fact, he had been like that since his father, or rather his uncle, broke the news of his paternity to him earlier that day.

As much as he tried to take it all in, he found it increasingly hard to; the more he tried the more confusing and unbelievable it was.

He looked at his father's – his uncle's – picture hanging proudly on the wall opposite him. He loved the man... God Almighty, how he loved this man; the man he had known all his life as his father; the man he had called Daddy; the man he was emotionally attached to; the man he had always looked up to for guidance and comfort all his dear happy life; his loving and gracious Daddy... only to be told this morning that he was not the man who had actually fathered him. No, 'fathered' was not the word, 'procreate' was more like it – he was told this morning that the man had not actually procreated him.

Alan Tucker had been a father to him, not just in many ways, but in all ways.

Alex turned his head slightly sideways and gazed at the only other picture in the room – the picture he had taken with his father – no, with his uncle (when in God's earth would he begin to accept the truth, the truth that his beloved father had, overnight, 'transformed' into his uncle?) when he was twenty-three. It had been his graduation from the law school – his call to bar.

He had graduated with first-class honours in law from Oxford University and then he had proceeded to the law school where he also graduated with a first-class.

In the picture on the wall opposite him, he was dressed in a lawyer's suit and Alan Tucker, dressed in an expensive Hugo Boss suit, stood proudly beside him. In fact, Alan's arm was around Alex's shoulder, 'to show the whole world that Alex is my son,' he had joked that day.

Alex remembered that the photographer had then replied that Alan Tucker did not need to prove that Alex was his son. For Alex was a younger version of Alan Tucker's sixty year old self. That had been four years ago. To think now that the relationship they had had together, the inexplicable and uncommon father-son affection that they had shared between them all his life, had been nothing but an illusion; nothing but a farce.

Alex Tucker tried to remember how it had all started. 'How did it all start?' he asked, looking at the picture as if he expected some reply from it. The picture did not reply. He lay down on the bed, his torso stretched to both ends of the king-sized bed, for he was a very tall man; his palms were intertwined beneath his head. He tried to recollect what exactly he had been discussing with his uncle, what exactly he had said that had made his uncle come into his apartment in the wee hours to divulge such a fearful secret; a secret he had kept from him since he was born; a secret which, according to his uncle, he had had no intention of telling him till his dying day.

Suddenly, he remembered it all. It had all started the day after he proposed to his main girlfriend. His main girlfriend, Nike, was a black girl of Nigerian origin, who was born in Britain.

Alex had three girlfriends, two of them he had met ever before he met Nike. He had met Alice, then Clarida, then Nike, in that order. He had always known Alice; in fact, one could say he had known her all his life. Clarida, he had met when he had a disagreement with Alice, and he was contemplating leaving her for good, and Nike, he had met when he had a heated argument with Clarida, and he had left her house and gone to a bar to have a chilled beer to cool off. He had met them like that – in that order.

When Alex proposed marriage to Nike, he had expected her to agree to the proposal immediately. He had expected her to be excited about it even; at least that was what his other girlfriends wanted; they would have practically jumped at his proposal, but trust Nike to be different from other girls. Nike had a unique quality about her that had never ceased to intrigue Alex. She was so independent, so insouciant about life. It was that quality, Alex knew, that would always draw him to Nike like bees to a honeycomb.

It had been shortly after one of their rigorous sex sessions, and they were still basking in the euphoria of it, that he had decided to propose marriage to her. It wasn't that he loved her – no, he definitely did not – he just loved her intense beauty; and he loved her dynamism, the energy she exuded in everything she did, especially the energy she exuded in bed. Nike always gave him good sex. Alex smiled briefly, despite himself.

The day he had proposed to her, they had just had what could best be described as a 'wildfire sex'. Nike, as usual, had taken him to depths he did not know he could reach. It was Boxing Day and they had gone to see a movie together – a horror movie titled *Black Christmas*. Nike loved horror movies. The excitement, the suspense, the fright, the sadness and the accompanying tears always made her sexual drive soar – that was what she told him and he believed it; for anytime they went back home after seeing a horror movie, Nike always made him cry out of sheer pleasure of her love-making. That particular Boxing Day, they had gone back to the pad Nike shared with her friend, Tonia. It was a nice two-bedroom apartment on Jamaica road in Bermondsey, overlooking the tower bridge. Nike's friend, Tonia, a pretty, petite blond girl who seemed to spend more time at the gym than anywhere else, had gone to her boyfriend's house for the weekend.

'She seldom stays home now that her wedding is coming up.' Nike had told him this one day, when he had asked after her after not seeing her for three months. Alex did not really care if Tonia spent her entire life on the rooftop. Tonia was not particularly friendly, just polite. She was not his type. She was the type of a person with a smile that Alex considered a 'manufactured smile'. She always had a smile for him whenever he saw her; the only problem was that her smile did not always reach her eyes. She appeared to Alex as someone who never trusted anyone. Alex's previous attempts at trying to strike a conversation with her had always met a dead end. Even his jokes had not gone an inch with her and, boy, he was good at jokes; he knew that and he knew that girls knew it too. However, Tonia always managed to converse with him with a nod, and if he was lucky, with a 'yes' or a 'no' – no more, no less! Alex sometimes wondered if Tonia's fiancée was something of a puppet; someone who hardly talked; someone with no sense of humour, like Tonia. Anyway, on this particular day, Alex was most grateful that Tonia had made herself absent; the last thing he needed was a pretty face with a gloomy disposition.

Nike was an only child but she had mentioned something about having two younger brothers who suffered from some sickle cell disease which could have been prevented if her parents had taken the pains to have their blood group checked before they got married. That was the way Nike had put it. She had told him in no unmistaken terms that if he wouldn't agree to go for the blood test, she would not agree to marry him.

The following day, Alex had gone ahead to have the blood test; and the test had confirmed Alex to carry the sickle cell genotype. He was said to have the AS genotype, and O positive phenotype.

The doctor had explained to Alex that he was a general donor, which posed no problem, but the doctor had advised that he should never have children with a woman who had the AS genotype, as this might result in him having sickly children with SS genotype.

Alex had left the hospital and gone straight home. He had gone to his father's wing of the huge house they shared. There, he met his father seated before a piano, rehearsing the song he would sing with the church choir the next Sunday.

Alex had waited until Alan finished the song before saying a word to him.

Alan Tucker had such a good voice and, as usual, Alex had been mesmerised by the melodious way his father sang.

When the song ended, Alan Tucker turned to Alex and smiled.

'What brings you to my wing at this time of the day, son?' asked Alan, smiling warmly at Alex. His handsome, kindly face shone with the deep affection he felt towards Alex.

Alex smiled back. The warmth they shared between them was electrifying.

Alan Tucker stretched out a hand towards Alex and in a low voice, reminiscent of one talking to his beloved baby, he said, 'Come here and have a seat, son.'

Alex strolled over to where Alan sat and picked up a coffee table from beside the piano. He sat on the table and crossed his legs in front of him. Suddenly, his gaze was averted to the only photograph in the living room, the photograph of his grandfather, Sir Alexander Tucker Snr.

Any time Alex came into the living room, which doubled as his father's rehearsal room, he was always entranced by the huge picture of his grandfather. What captivated him most was not just the handsomeness of his grandfather, but the striking resemblance between the three men who made up the three filial generations.

Beside his grandfather's portrait was his mother's picture. Alex's mother was a beautiful woman with strong facial features. In the picture, she had a determined expression and her jaw seemed jut out. She was a picture of a woman who held her own; a woman who refused to be dictated to. Alex had been told that his mother had suddenly disappeared when he was barely two years old, and she had never been found. He sometimes wondered if she was still alive.

Although Alex had never seen his grandmother's picture, Alan had described her as a very beautiful woman of a mixed origin: half Greek and half English.

Alan had never mentioned anything about a blood disorder to him; now as he studied the pictures hanging on the walls in front of him, he could not help but wonder from whom he had inherited the blood disorder.

'You seem a little troubled, son. What could be the problem?' said Alan aloud, cutting into Alex's thoughts.

Alex looked away from the wall and into the eyes of Alan. 'Why didn't you tell me you carry the sickle cell genotype, Dad?' he asked without preamble.

Alan Tucker was taken aback; the smile slowly faded from his face. He had not expected the question from Alex and he was not prepared for it.

'I don't carry a sickle cell genotype,' he replied tersely.

'Then how come I do?' asked Alex. 'Or was it my mother who had it?'

Alan Tucker looked at him sharply. He wondered how Alex discovered he had the sickle cell blood in him. *Had the boy been digging where he shouldn't?* He sincerely prayed he hadn't; he sincerely hoped Alex would come to no harm.

Alan shut his eyes. 'How did you find out you had the sickle cell gene?' he asked.

'I'm dating a certain lady whose name is Nike,' began Alex. He looked at Alan, who still had his eyes shut. Alex could not determine what was going on in his father's mind. He very much hated to hurt him. He had not introduced Nike to his father before he proposed to her. He had done it in the heat of the moment. What he had planned was to bring Nike to see his father, Reverend Alan Tucker, after they had tied the knot at the registry. Nike was very beautiful and worldly wise and he was not very sure his father, who was known to be holy and deeply religious, would approve of her.

'Go ahead,' said Alan Tucker tersely; the smile had suddenly faded from his mouth and he looked withdrawn.

'Well,' Alex began uncertainly. 'Well I… Well I proposed to her and she insisted I went for a blood test to determine our compatibility. She told me something about her two younger brothers going through some sickle cell trauma years ago, and she would like to prevent that from happening to our children in future.'

Alan Tucker opened his eyes then looked directly at Alex and, for the first time since he recognised Alan as his father, Alex Tucker felt scared of him. Alan Tucker had an expression that was not determinable to Alex; his blue-coloured pupils had turned quite dark, and he looked liked he was in a trance.

Alex waited for his father to talk; he dreaded the next words his father would utter. He hoped his father was not about to drop a *bombshell* on him.

'You must stop seeing that girl at once!' Alan commanded; his tone had changed from being warm to being quite coarse.

Alex felt his tense muscles relaxing. He had expected to hear something more terrible. Leaving Nike should really not be a problem; after all, he was not really sure of his love for her. He had good sex with her, yes he did, but he was not sure he felt anything deeper than lust for her. But there was still an issue to be sorted out and that was the issue of his blood group.

'Dad,' he said, 'I have not come to you because of Nike. I have come to ask you how we could end up with different blood genotypes.'

Alan Tucker sighed deeply. 'This is not a matter to be discussed now,' he said at last. 'Go back to your wing, and in the morning, I will come and discuss some things with you.'

Alex knew better than to argue with his dad. Although, Alan had been a loving dad all his life, he had come to realise that questioning Alan on certain issues would only be likened to taking water out of a brick wall.

'Alright, Dad,' said Alex, 'see you in the morning.'

'Son,' Alan called after him as he turned to leave.

Alex turned back to his dad.

'Yes Dad,' he said.

'You must stop seeing that lady at once!'

True to his promise, Alan Tucker had come to see Alex in his wing of the huge house in the wee hours of the morning.

Alan had come through a single door that connected the two wings together. As far as Alex knew, the door had never been opened save for now. He knew instantly that what his father had come to tell him that morning was something very serious.

Alex was ready to hear whatever his father had to say; besides, he had not slept a wink since the day before and the earlier they had this issue resolved the better.

Alex and Alan sat opposite each other on each of the two chairs in the sitting room.

Alex tensed up, bracing himself for the news.

And then it came.

'I'm not your biological father,' Alan blurted out.

Alex felt he had not heard right.

'What?' he exclaimed. 'What did you say, Dad?'

'I said I'm not your biological father,' repeated Alan sadly.

Alex was stupefied. For some minutes, he could not say a word. He just looked at his father, flabbergasted. He had thought he was prepared to hear what his father had come to tell him, but he was not prepared for this.

How come Reverend Alan Tucker was not his real father? They both shared the same surname and they both looked so much alike. By the way, if Alan was not his father, then who was?

'Who's my father?' asked Alex quietly.

'Your father, Rory, was my brother; he was my younger half-brother,' replied Alan.

'How... How come you never told me this, Dad?' asked Alex; he felt shocked to his bone marrow.

'Because I was trying to protect you from whoever killed your father,' replied Alan.

Alex pondered on this for a while then he felt he had to ask a question.

'Did you bother to find out who killed my father?' he asked Alan.

'Oh yes,' Alan replied. 'We tried to find out. The police tried their best. I even hired some private detectives, but all our efforts at finding out who killed Rory proved abortive. It was while we were at it that your grandmother, who happened to be my step-mother, was murdered.'

At that moment, Alex felt a pain searing through his guts.

'So, my grandmother was also murdered?' he managed to ask.

'Yes,' replied Alan painfully. 'She died of food poisoning right inside this house. I was away with my father on a missionary trip to the United States at the time. We had to be called back from our trip. Her killer was never found!'

Alan looked at Alex; his eye welling up with tears as he said, 'Your grandfather died from the shock of the two deaths.'

Alex had gone quiet; he was trying to come to terms with the gruesome murders of two people in a family-his family. His heart suddenly went out to Alan; his eyes misted over. Alan must have felt very frightened because of what happened to members of his family. That must have been why he never told him a thing until now.

'Your mother's sudden disappearance was linked to the murders of your father and your grandmother, but up till now, no one has been arrested,' Alan continued as tears trickled down his handsome face.

Alex went over to him and brushed away the tears with his fingers.

'I'm sorry, Dad,' he said simply.

However, he wondered why none of the killers had been arrested. His instinct as a lawyer told him the killers might be people who knew the family well; maybe someone who was close to the family let out secrets to the killers.

'Do you think someone who's close to the family might be behind this?' Alex asked Alan cautiously.

Alan pondered this for a while before replying. 'At some point, the police thought the killings might be linked with my elder brother, Jamie.'

'You had another brother apart from my father?' asked Alex with utter incredulity.

Alan looked at Alex, who was totally confused now, and smiled sadly.

'Although, I never told you this,' said Alan, 'my father had a son before me. His name was Jamie. When our mother died, Jamie could not come to terms with her death. Over the years, Jamie became completely transformed. He went from a quiet, studious boy to a cannabis smoking truant, and he was always getting into fights with people. But he managed to hide his cannabis smoking habits from our father for a long time.'

Alan studied Alex's expression; it was now deadpan. He wished he could read his thoughts, but he found he couldn't. Alan continued his story anyway.

'Jamie was caught smoking cannabis by your grandmother three months after she came into this home, and your grandmother told our father. Our father – because he was vying for the post of a knight in the church and did not want his name rubbed in the mud – decided to hide Jamie away from home. So he thought it best to send him to rehab. Jamie hated every minute he spent there, and he always blamed your grandmother for it. Three months later, he came home from rehab and his relationship with Dorothy degenerated.

They had an argument one day and a physical squabble ensued. Dorothy had to call the police and Jamie was taken away. I was not present at the time, but Dorothy claimed Jamie tried to strangle her. Jamie, who was nineteen then, spent six months in prison before he was released. However, our father, Sir Alexander Tucker, had publicly disowned him before then. He would not let him back into the house.'

Alan looked at Alex for a long time. Alex was silent; he was listening with rapt attention.

'I remember the last statement Jamie made before he left this house; he said to Dorothy, "I swear you'll regret this, you bitch!"

Three months after he left the house, Jamie sent me a letter informing me that he was getting married and that was the last I heard from him. He has never been seen since then,' concluded Alan.

'Do you think that Jamie might be respons–' began Alex, but Alan cut him short.

'No,' said Alan. 'You see, Jamie was a rough kind of guy quite all right, but he had a soft heart deep within him. I do not think he could hurt a fly. He was just hurting from the death of our mother. Besides, the police searched everywhere in their bid to find Jamie, but he was never found. He seemed to have disappeared into thin air!' Alan looked straight into Alex's eyes before saying, 'I'm one hundred per cent sure that Jamie had no hand in all that happened.'

Alex went quiet again. If Alan Tucker thought his brother, Jamie, was innocent then he probably was *innocent*. After all, Alan had known every member of the family personally.

However, he supposed that whoever the murderer or *murderers* were, they must be very powerful and influential people in the society; *or how else could they still remain at large?*

Alan sniffed and looked at Alex through tear-filled eyes, then he blurted out, 'You got the AS genotype from your grandmother, Lady Dorothy Tucker!'

Alex nodded. He had suddenly forgotten the main reason why Alan had come to tell him the story of the family. For some reason, Alex felt that carrying the sickle cell genotype was no longer important. What was paramount now was to find out the killers of his father and grandmother, and probably his mother, and bring them all to book.

As if Alan was reading his thoughts, he spoke; 'Son, don't you ever dare look for the murderers. You might lose your life in the process.' Fresh tears began to well up in Alan's eyes as he said to Alex, 'I don't want to lose you, son.'

Alex could not bear to see Alan hurt so much. Although Alex had barely known his parents and grandparents, he knew what impact losing them all would have had on Alan and he decided not to pursue the matter any more; he would let sleeping dogs lie and hopefully, Alan would be healed of all the hurt he felt at the demise of the people he had lived with and loved so much.

Before Alan left Alex's apartment that morning, he said to Alex, 'Son, please steer clear of that Nike lady. She's not good for you.'

Now, as Alex pondered the sad news of his family, he wondered if he would ever set eyes on their murderers. He sincerely hoped some inspector would dig up the case again and seek the criminals out; then he would have satisfaction in seeing them spend the rest of their miserable lives in jail.

But would that ever happen? Would he live to see his family's murderers brought to book?

Chapter 1

Great Britain, fourth of September, nineteen sixty-one

Alexander Tucker, a religious, kind-hearted and God-fearing man, was being bestowed the highly esteemed crown of the knight of John Wesley.

Alan Tucker looked on in great wonder as the procession of the crowning of his father started. The ceremony had begun with the singing of the hymn, *Stand up, stand up for Jesus, ye soldiers of the cross.*

All the congregation of the church rose to the singing and Alan Tucker rose and sang with them. He was oblivious of everything around him including his brother, Rory, and his step-mother Dorothy, who was Rory's mother. His eyes were fixed on his father who he adored with the whole of his heart. He looked on with pride as his father was beckoned to kneel in front of the altar to receive the blessing of the priest.

Alexander Tucker rose to his full height of six feet two inches, an epitome of a real knight, and walked along the aisle with humility to the altar. He was fully clothed in a knight's regalia. All eyes were fixed on him as he knelt before the priest for his consecration and dedication to knighthood. As Alexander Tucker rose to his full height, the Bishop, who had been standing near the priest throughout the prayer time, presented the sword of the knight along with the shield to him and dubbed him by striking a blow with the flat of the hand on the side of the sword that had just been given to him. Immediately afterwards, the Bishop announced in a loud clear voice, 'I now dub thee Sir Knight'. The sponsors then put spurs on the knight and his sword was girded on; and then the fanfare began.

Throughout the fanfare, Alan Tucker's eyes never left his father. His admiration for his father's achievement and especially the respect accorded him was there for all to see. At some point during the ceremony, he caught his step mum looking at him. He stared right back. There had never been any love lost between the two of them since his father married her; and most especially since Jamie left the home. They just pretended to get along for his father's sake. They both loved Sir Alexander Tucker dearly. Moreover, he had his little brother, whom he loved dearly, to consider. Since Rory was born, they had taken to each other like two peas in a pod. Alan had helped bathe Rory; he had helped to feed him; he had been the one who took him to day care before going to school and picked him up after. The love and the care that Alan Tucker showed young Rory Tucker as he grew up did much to endear his stepmother to him.

However, several months after Rory was born, the doubt she had always had towards Alan became more intense. To Mrs Dorothy Tucker, Alan Tucker was a hypocrite. He had those shifty eyes that suggested mischief. Although, she had never seen Alan in any mischief, she found it difficult to trust him like she would her own son. When she discovered that Jamie, Sir Alexander Tucker's first son who had now permanently been cut off the family inheritance, was into hard drugs, Mrs Dorothy Tucker had kept a watchful eye on Alan Tucker as well. However, Alan's character had been flawless up till date. She had to give him credit for that.

It was not that she hated any of her husband's children, but she was trying to avoid a repetition of her bitter experience as a child. Her own mother had re-married soon after her divorce from her father when she was thirteen, and all had gone well between her and her step-father for one year. However, her step-father started smoking cannabis soon after the birth of her younger brother, and one day, after a session with cannabis, he had tried to rape her. Her step-father would have actually succeeded in his *ignoble venture* but for the timely intervention of a neighbour.

Although she had been rescued unharmed, that experience would remain with Dorothy for the rest of her life. She became paranoid and weary of anyone who indulged in drugs. That was the reason why she had insisted Jamie be taken far away from her and that was the main reason why her husband had sent him to rehab. But Jamie had come out all the worse for it, and he had threatened to strangle her; and he had ended up being disowned by her husband. Jamie had also been given a restraining order never to come within distance of where the family stayed.

Dorothy regretted the fact that Jamie could no longer come near the home, but she was fearful of him getting near her or her son. She would rather he remained far away from her.

Instinctively, Dorothy had turned her attention on Alan, the second son. She had secretly watched his every move and mannerism; but nothing in his movement or his mannerisms suggested mischief or moral bankruptcy.

Most times, a force she could not quite understand always made her gaze at Alan and a nagging feeling would visit her; and coupled with it, her heart would start thumping as if it was going to jump into her mouth in second. She couldn't place this feeling; she just could not put her finger on exactly what it was that Alan Tucker was doing wrong, but this feeling just would not go away.

On the home front, Alan was a perfect son to her husband and he was more than a perfect brother to her son Rory. She did not need to be told that he loved Rory with all his heart.

Dorothy decided to allow the love that her stepson had for her son to supersede any grudge she felt for him; moreover, she had been made to understand ever since she got married to Alexander Tucker that Alan Tucker was the apple of her husband's eye; Alan had always been a preferred child to his brother Jamie, whom her husband had disowned a few months before Rory was born.

Sir Alexander Tucker believed Alan was a saint, and nothing she or any other person said against him would register with Sir Alexander Tucker. It would just go in through one ear and out the other.

Several times, Dorothy made up her mind to let sleeping dogs lie, but however much she tried to get the nagging suspicions she had for Alan away from her mind, she still felt it lurked somewhere deep within her.

Now, as their eyes met, the suspicions resurfaced, not unaccompanied with the thumping of her heart. She took a sip of the orange juice placed before her to calm her nerves. The thumping reduced to a quiet regular thud. She forced a smile to her lips as Alan met her gaze steadily.

Alan smiled back; the smile did not reach his eyes.

Several seats from where the Tucker family sat, Jamie Tucker sat amongst some of the guests at the reception. He was in a hooded top and he wore a dark pair of goggles. No one seemed to take notice of him as he sat there and watched the whole ceremony. From time to time, he wiped the tears which streamed down his face from the base of his goggles with a dark handkerchief.

At a point during the ceremony, all the guests stood up and glasses were raised in honour of Sir Alexander Tucker as a toast was made.

'To Sir Alexander Tucker; for a successful knighthood,' chorused the guests.

Jamie Tucker also stood up and raised a glass in the direction of Dorothy Tucker. 'This is to you, Mrs Dorothy Tucker; for your successful transition to the pit of hell!' he whispered.

Chapter 2

London, Great Britain, Twenty-fourth of November, Nineteen Eighty-Two.

Mark sat opposite the boss with great unease. He had always been afraid of the boss ever since they were in high school. Now that he had been to college and dropped out, he was still afraid of the boss. However much he had tried to dissociate himself from the boss, he still felt associated with him in one way or another. The boss always had a hold over him.

He remembered the saga that had put him in this vulnerable position, and the usual feeling of hatred that he felt towards himself over the stupid mistake he had made was all the more overwhelming. He cursed himself for ever more for allowing the boss to put him in such a tight corner. Initially, he had thought that his secret was dead and buried and he had escaped being punished, when the boss had helped him dispose of his step-brother's lifeless body and an innocent man had been jailed for his death, but as the months rolled into years and the years into more years, he had come to accept the fact that, though the secret was buried to the whole world, it was still very much alive to the boss and wherever Mark went, he felt the shadow of what he had done hover around him; it was like an open carcass that oozed a nasty smell around him; it was just that the smell was perceived by none other than the boss and Mark himself.

After he was discharged and acquitted by the jury, with lack of evidence to jail him, he had gone to a nearby park where he sat with three of his friends, discussing the court proceedings and how extremely lucky he was to have had a narrow escape. As he walked home that evening, he suddenly felt a tap on his shoulder. He turned to see a young man in a hooded jacket behind him. Before he could ask who he was, the young man slipped a note into his hand, patted his shoulder and walked off without saying a word. Still overwhelmed by the fact that he had walked free from court, and eternally grateful to the boss for the clean job he had done to ensure he was not sent to jail, he opened the letter excitedly.

See me in my office in thirty minutes.

Signed,
The Boss.

Although the wordings were simple and harmless, Mark could not help but feel an invincible note of warning in the letter. He sensed danger. He felt a chill run down his spine. The thrill he had been feeling ever since he walked out of the courtroom suddenly disappeared, only to be replaced by a throbbing fear. Although, he was free from the shackles of the law, he knew deep down that he would never be free from the invisible chains with which he had been bound to the commands of the boss.

He was aware of the location of the office. In fact, he had been taken there when he needed help to dispose of his step-brother's corpse. With trepidation, he had immediately gone to the office which was situated in the underground basement of a council accommodation in Peckham. To the boss, thirty minutes was *thirty minutes* – not a minute more, not a minute less.

Only few people knew the location of the office; and they were actually connected to the boss. It was actually an abandoned underground car park area of a block of council flats. When Mark got to the front of the council buildings, he checked the time on his watch. It said 9.04p.m., a good twenty four minutes before he should actually get there. He immediately turned away and decided to stall for time by walking down the street adjacent to where the office was located. At 9.15p.m., he was back to where he had met the man in the hooded jacket earlier and he started walking towards the office of the boss. The nine minutes remaining would suffice for the distance he would have to cover to get to the office of the boss. He made to open the gate that led to the underground car park but found that it was locked.

How on earth did the boss expect him to get through this damned gate? He muttered to himself. Suddenly he felt a tap on his shoulder and he froze. The tap was very similar to the one he had got earlier. How did whoever it was know he was there? Surely, he was being monitored. He was really scared. He made to turn around to see who it was that tapped him but the hooded man spoke, 'Don't turn around; you're being watched.'

By who? He wanted to ask but he was too scared to, so he kept quiet.

'Turn left,' said the hooded man. 'We've lost a lot of time; the boss will really be mad.'

Mark turned left and saw a narrow pathway that he had not noticed the first time he came here. He wondered why he had not noticed the path earlier. *I was probably too upset over my brother's death*, he reasoned.

The boss was seated on a chair behind a worn table in the dingy dilapidated room that was his office when they came in.

'Leave us!' commanded the boss and the man in the hood left immediately.

'I have a simple job for you,' said the boss without any reference to the court case.

Mark was silent; he had learned from his first meeting with the boss that he must not talk unless he had the permission to do so.

'I want you to get rid of a man,' said the boss.

Mark was alarmed; the boss gave him a look that dared him to speak, then he continued, 'I have a plan laid down to make the job easy for you.' He passed Mark a sheet of paper.

'Read that when you get home and make sure that no one; not a single soul gets wind of it,' the boss said casually but Mark could detect the note of warning in his speech. Even though his case had been thrown out of court, the evidence still lay somewhere in the coffer of the boss; he only had to open his mouth and Mark would be re-arrested, the case would be re-opened and the boss would make sure that the jigsaw puzzle that had made the case watery enough to be thrown out of court would automatically fall into place, and Mark would face the music. He would definitely be given life without parole and his life would be finished. Mark shivered visibly.

'Are you ok?' asked the boss and Mark was brought back to the present.

'I'm fine, thank you,' said Mark, but he did not feel fine; he felt so sick that he began to sweat. He felt like passing wind but he held it back; he was not so sure what might upset the boss.

The boss gave a slight smile and said to Mark, 'Now, I want a clean job. You will be working with two other guys. My boys will dispose of the body when you're done.' He waited for that to sink in, and then he said with concern, 'I hope you're comfortable with the assignment Mark.'

On impulse, Mark shook his head in the negative and immediately, he regretted his action. The boss noticed his reaction and he gently reached for a drawer on the side of the table before him. He opened the drawer and brought out a huge file from it. As he was about to place the file on the table, some pictures dropped from the file onto the floor. Mark's eyes instinctively flew to the pictures and he froze. What he saw in the picture made him sweat more profusely and the fart he had been trying very hard to hold back escaped.

In the picture, he seemed to be dragging his dead brother's body as blood trickled down the side of his face. Mark's face was so clearly shown in the picture that he wondered how and when it was taken. *It must have taken an expert photographer to take that picture,* Mark reasoned. He knew very well that the picture was enough evidence to nail him.

Mark wondered if he had done the right thing by soliciting for the assistance of the boss to dispose off his brother's body. He wondered if he would not have been better off giving himself up; after all, he had killed his brother by mistake. They had been involved in a scuffle over a lady and one thing had led to another; he had found himself stabbing his brother in his face and in his stomach. His brother had died instantly. His initial decision was to call 999 and give himself up but he had chickened out at the last minute.

Aiden, who was his best friend and who had witnessed the whole fight had introduced him to the boss. One week after the incident, Aiden had been found dead in his flat with his throat slashed, and the police had not been able to charge anyone for his death. The evidence they gathered had been *inconclusive*.

Now, as Mark remembered his friend Aiden, he was sure that the boss was not unconnected with his death. Sweat poured down his face, and he could actually smell his own sweat. His bowels contracted; he felt like going to the toilet, but he managed to remain seated.

The boss was watching Mark's reaction and he was clearly amused. *This fool must think I'm a fool,* he thought.

'Now I really hope you are comfortable with the little assignment Mark,' said the boss.

Mark was speechless; he was still baffled at how the boss had come about the picture. He had no camera on him when they disposed of the body; *or so he thought.* He became confused.

'Why are you looking at the floor?' asked the boss innocently; then he followed Mark's gaze to the picture.

'Oh that?' he said and bent to pick the picture. 'Forget about it; it's a forgone issue,' he said casually as he put the picture back in the file and the file back in the drawer.

Mark knew that the boss was lying; it was not a forgone issue and all the drama he had displayed had been intentional; the boss had actually made him see the picture as a reminder that Mark was indebted to him.

Mark looked into the boss' eyes, and what he saw in them sent a chill down his spine. The boss' eyes told him that what Mark did to his brother would not be forgotten in a very long time!

'Consider it done, boss,' said Mark.

'Good!' said the boss, 'I always knew you were a good boy. That's why I have decided to keep you as my permanent staff.'

'I do not wish to be your permanent staff, boss,' said Mark impulsively; not minding the fact that the boss might be angered at his outburst. *They were age-mates after all!* 'I wish to be able to live my own life,' he finished lamely.

'Of course you do,' said the boss icily. 'You have a right to live your own life, Mark; only you will have to choose to live it with me, or live it in jail.' Before Mark could say a word, the boss said quietly, 'After all, you killed your brother.'

Once again, Mark had been reminded that although he had escaped jail in court, he would never be able to wriggle free of the iron fetters that the boss had bound him with. He felt he had to ask a question.

'Can I ask a question boss?' he said.

'Go ahead,' replied the boss coolly.

'Who exactly is this man? What is he to you, boss?'

'He is my brother!' replied the boss.

Chapter 3

London, Great Britain, First of December, Nineteen Eighty-Two

Rory Tucker got into the sleek Ford Civic car that his father, Sir Alexander Tucker, had given him as a gift for his twenty-first birthday. Since the day his father presented him with the car, Rory had gone everywhere with it; proudly showing it off to his friends and telling whoever cared to listen, how lucky he was to have a generous father.

As he drove along the highway, Rory could not help but feel extremely lucky to have come from a privileged background. More importantly, he felt luckier to have a close-knit, loving family around him. Apart from his father, Sir Alexander Tucker, his other hero in life was his beloved brother, Alan Tucker. He loved Alan with the whole of his heart, and he knew that Alan loved him too. In fact, Alan had treated him more like a son rather than a brother, ever since he was born. This was not surprising, since there was a seventeen year difference between them.

Rory's mother, Lady Dorothy Tucker, was a woman who was not only physically gorgeous, but was beautiful at heart. She would go out of her way to help those in need; she had donated gifts and cash to several charities and she had been personally involved in several charitable organisations, promoting better life for the less privileged in third world countries, while taking care not to neglect the needs of her family. Simply put, Lady Dorothy Tucker was the best mother anybody could wish for.

Rory's sister-in-law, Roberta, was a warm and loving woman who would be prepared to pluck out her very own eyes just to make Rory happy; and she had a beautiful, sharp minded two year old son named Alexander Tucker Jnr., who always made Rory's heart melt with joy anytime he saw him.

This afternoon, Rory had an appointment with his beloved brother for a game of horse-racing. Rory was not really particular about the game, but he liked being in his brother's company. Alan was surely an interesting character. Apart from always being the caring, loving brother, he always made Rory laugh; he made Rory feel that there was not a care in the world.

Alan was not one who liked to be delayed when it came to the game of horse-racing. Next to wanting to be a knight, horse-racing was his only other passion in life. Rory smiled happily and pressed on the accelerator; life was sweet for him. He felt very happy with life.

Suddenly, a Peugeot 505 shot forward from behind him, overtaking him with full speed. Rory's heart flew to his mouth; he suddenly pressed on the brake to avoid collision with the car. As he did so, another car, which was far bigger than Rory's, came from the right hand side and crashed into Rory car. Rory jerked forward and tried to manoeuvre the car to the left. As he turned the steering to the left, a jeep came along at top speed, hitting Rory's car twice.

The impact of the collision forced Rory's car to somersault; and then, before an ambulance arrived, the car burst into flames.

In all the ensuing mayhem, the driver of the Peugeot 505 saloon car retrieved a camcorder from the glove compartment in his car and began to film the whole scenario.

Rory suffered first degree burns, and two hours later, he was pronounced dead at the hospital.

Later in the evening, Andy quietly came into the office of the boss, and without as much as saying a word, he handed the camcorder to the boss. The boss collected the recording equipment from Andy and jerked his head in the direction of the exit.

Andy left the boss' office as quietly as he had come in.

When he was sure that Andy had disappeared down the hallway, the boss took the camcorder and pressed the 'on' button. Then he sat back in his chair and watched the whole scene from when the jeep hit Rory's car, to when the ambulance crew came to take Rory away. He saw how Rory's body was terribly marred by the fire, and he decided that his target could not escape death.

'Bloody son of a bitch!' he said.

Mark had carried out that *assignment*, and all had been well. Three years had passed since then and, although he had had no contact with the boss until now, he always knew that the boss' eyes were on him. Should the boss have any need for him, he only had to snap his fingers and Mark would be expected to come running to him, as he had come running now.

Mark sat tensely in the shabby office, looking all but relaxed. The trepidation he had always felt any time he was in the presence of the dreaded boss was clearly written all over him, and not unaccompanied by the palpitation of his heart. In the last three years, he had dreaded being called upon by the boss to carry out another of his vicious assignments. For the past three years, he had dreaded this day. He willed his nerves to be calm, but he felt more agitated by the minute. He wished the boss would just stop looking at him with those shrewd, evil, beady pair of eyes and say whatever he had summoned him for so they could get things over and done with.

'How are you, Mark?' asked the boss at last. 'It's been what... three years since I last saw you, hasn't it, Mark?'

Mark knew that the boss did not care how he was; neither did he care if they had not seen each other for a hundred years. What the boss always cared about was to be obeyed. Mark answered anyway.

'Yes it has, boss,' he said.

'Good, now there's a little job I would like you to do for me,' said the boss.

Mark was tense. As far as the boss was concerned, shedding innocent blood was a little thing – it was as little as *little* can be. He wondered who the boss wanted him to get rid of next. He still carried the guilt of the man he had killed for him.

'I want you to bear a false witness in court,' said the boss, cutting into his thoughts. Mark was surprised to find himself feel relieved. It was probably because this particular job involved no bloodshed. However, he made an attempt at wriggling free from the assignment.

'You see, boss, I've started going to church and I have been taught the commandments of God. *One of those commandments is thou shall not bear false witness against thy neighbour.*'

The boss looked at Mark for a while, and then he burst into a hysterical laughter. After the laughter subsided, the boss said to Mark, 'For your own good, Mark, I would advise that you stopped going to church. You don't belong there.' His face suddenly became dangerously serious as he said to Mark, 'You belong to me!'

Before Mark got home later that day, he made up his mind to detach himself from the claws of the boss permanently. He had five days before he was scheduled for the court appearance. He had enough time to carry out his plan.

When he got to his house, he brought out an atlas from a drawer and studied it. He frantically searched for a continent that the boss and his cohorts would never assume he would go. His eye caught the continent of Africa.

That must be it, he thought excitedly. With his hand, he traced the map of Africa until he got to Nigeria, then he stopped. *Nigeria!* He had heard so much about the country, including the fact there was so much crude oil there. Perhaps he could find his way to the oil rigs and with very little effort, make a living for himself in the oil industry. He could eventually become an exporter of crude oil. He could be rich in no time. He decided to go to Nigeria.

Mark packed a few belongings and took his British passport, and with the help of a friend who was married to a Nigerian woman, he was able to secure a visa to Nigeria in three days.

As the aeroplane flew over the Atlantic, Mark felt an immense joy. He thought of how easy his friend's wife had secured him a Nigerian visa; he could not believe his luck. He was finally rid of the boss; they would never meet again. He rested his head against the headrest and dosed off into a contended sleep.

In a dilapidated building, in the suburb of Peckham, in the United Kingdom, the boss picked up the note that was dropped into his office; it read:

The plane took off at ten thirty this morning. Right now, he should be flying over the Atlantic. He is expected in Nigeria approximately six hours after take off.

Though the letter was unsigned, the boss knew where it came from. He had trailed Mark's movement ever since he left his office four days before. Mark had decided to run away from him; as far away as possible. That was why he had gone to Africa.

Thirty minutes later, Andy came into the office wearing his usual dark hooded top.

'Our target has gone to Nigeria in West Africa; spread your tentacles there. Get a Nigerian detective and put him on our payroll. Mark should be monitored from the airport in Nigeria. We must keep our tabs on him for as long as need be,' said the boss.

'Alright boss,' said Andy without hesitation. He hated Mark with a passion; he wanted to know when Mark would be eradicated.

'When will he join the others in the grave, boss?' he asked respectfully.

The boss was silent for a while before replying tersely, 'When he decides to open his mouth!'

Chapter 4

Three years after Rory's demise, Sir Alexander Tucker got an invitation to attend a conference with the archbishop in Arizona. On this occasion, he decided to take his son, Alan (who was married with a five year old son, Alexander junior), along with him.

Alan was ecstatic; he would not come short of doing anything that would make him follow in his father's footsteps. Alan had, on several occasions, boasted to whomever it might concern, that he, like his father, would one day become a knight of John Wesley.

On the night prior to their travelling, a very strange thing happened in the Tucker household; it was to change the fate of every member of the household forever!

It was two o'clock in the morning. The boss crept into Sir Alexander Tucker's dinning room as noiselessly as he could. He had opened the door that led to the building with a master key. The boss had a master key for every house he chose to operate in. He tip-toed into the kitchen which was adjacent to the dinning area and opened the refrigerator and there it was… He saw the juice drink that was Dorothy Tucker's favourite and without much ado, he brought out the syringe that had been filled with a clear poisonous liquid. He checked it once to confirm that the poisonous liquid was still in the transparent plastic base of the syringe; then he promptly injected it into the carton of orange juice. He closed the refrigerator as quietly as he had opened it and tip-toed out of the house the way he had come in. When he was outside the building, he heaved a sigh of relief. He was not aware that he had been holding his breath until now. He knew for sure that Mrs Dorothy Tucker would have a drink from the carton of chilled orange juice the following morning, and he smiled happily. His mission had been accomplished.

At 2.15a.m., Mrs Dorothy Tucker sat up suddenly. She thought she had heard some movements in the dinning area. She crept out of bed so she would not wake her husband from sleep. He had a long journey ahead of him the next day and the least she could do was allow him a good night's rest. She quietly walked through the sitting room, into the dinning area and switched on the light. Everything was as she had left it before going to bed. She had probably been imagining things. She put the light off and went back to sleep.

Five hours later, Mrs Dorothy Tucker woke up to find that her husband had gone. She saw a piece of paper peeping from underneath the pillow on which her husband had slept and she pulled it out. Her husband had scribbled some endearments on the paper for her and he had written that he did not wake her up because he wanted her to have a good sleep. He had explained in the note that he had to catch the early morning flight to Arizona in the United States with her step-son, Alan, and that he would see her in five days time. She smiled warmly; her husband was an excellent lover. Even at his slightly old age, he was very romantic. She decided to place a call through to Roberta at the other wing of the house. She wanted to know if all went well with Alan. They had somehow patched things up between them and since the death of Rory, Alan her step-son had been more than helpful. He was always calling her and buying her gifts. Her reservations about him had almost disappeared; she even felt she was beginning to love him as her own son. She picked up the house telephone and placed the call to Roberta.

'Hello, Alan Tucker's residence,' answered Roberta sleepily.

'Hi Roberta, darling. I was just wondering if Alan was okay before he travelled with his father this morning,' she said cheerfully.

'Yes, he's fine thank you, Lady Tucker,' said Roberta but her tone depicted that she did not really care.

Dorothy had sensed a rising hostility between Alan and his wife since they had their son Alexander Jnr., who was now five years old, but she had decided to mind her own business. Some sleeping dogs were better left asleep.

'Alright darling, talk to you later,' she said to Roberta, but she got no reply; she only heard Roberta's faint snoring. She shrugged and replaced the receiver. Then she walked to the kitchen and opened the refrigerator. She found the juice drink as she had left it the night before, only this time, it was very chilled. She loved having chilled orange juice when she woke up every morning. She picked a glass from a cupboard and poured herself a generous glass of orange juice. She took a sip and thought that it tasted a little bit different. She looked at the carton from which she had poured the juice and checked the expiry date; it had not expired.

Maybe it's just a different flavour, she thought and shrugged. She put the carton of juice back in the refrigerator. She lifted the glass to her lips and drank the whole juice in three gulps. Satisfied, she put the empty glass in the kitchen sink and went back to sleep.

Mrs Dorothy Tucker never woke up from her sleep.

Sir Alexander Tucker sat motionless throughout his wife's funeral. As the priest narrated his wife's beautiful life and prayed for her soul to rest in peace, Sir Alexander Tucker's mind travelled far away. His mind was actually with his dearly beloved wife, Dorothy; not as a dead woman, but as a healthy and living woman. Sir Alexander Tucker found it difficult to accept his wife's death. His younger son, Rory, had died three years earlier in a tragic motor accident at a young age of twenty-one. His son's death had hit him badly but he had learned to cope with it. What he might not be able to cope with was the death of his wife. He wondered who would have poisoned his wife. She was such a lovely woman; and she was loved by everyone.

Although the coroner had recorded a verdict of suicide by food poisoning, Sir Alexander Tucker refused to believe that his wife had actually committed suicide. She had been terribly saddened because of Rory's demise quite all right, but Dorothy had not shown any signs that she intended to commit suicide. She had even started to cheer up in the last couple of years before she died, and more so, the relationship between her and Alan had greatly improved. In fact, Sir Alexander Tucker had been very happy that his wife and his son had become the best of friends. How he wished Alan, his beloved son, had not travelled on that missionary journey with him. He wished Alan had been at home with the remaining members of the Tucker family; maybe his wife's death would have somehow been prevented; maybe his beloved wife would not have died.

When Alan got married to Roberta, Sir Alexander Tucker had simply extended the mansion they lived in and he had given Alan and Roberta a whole wing of the house. Only a door separated his wing from Alan's. He had always wanted to be in close proximity to Alan since his mother died; and more especially since he disowned Jamie his eldest son; and Alan, who had grown to adore his father, had always done everything possible to win his father's accolades.

When Roberta gave birth to a son, Alan had named him Alexander (Jnr.) after his grandfather, and he had promptly made Rory the child's godfather.

A few years ago, when Sir Alexander Tucker was made a knight, Alan had expressed his wish to be a knight as well and his father had given him his full support. His son Alan had involved himself in the activities of the church with utmost passion. The night before his wife died, he had travelled with his son to a parish of their church in the United States. The plane had barely landed when they received a call that his wife was at the hospital. Alan had suggested that they came back immediately and when they got to the hospital, he was told that she had died.

Suddenly, he felt a slight pressure on his arm and he was brought back to the present. He looked sideways and noticed that Alan had placed his hand on his arm reassuringly.

'Don't worry, Dad, I'll make sure we find her killer; I'll make sure they are brought to book.' He whispered into his ear.

But Sir Alexander Tucker had not waited for his wife's killers to be found. He had died of a heart attack in the middle of the night.

Chapter 5

Nigeria, West Africa

An angry King had just heard the saddest news of his life: his only son was getting married to a lady from the town of his arch-enemy!

He paced up and down his sitting room, trying to understand why his son would defy his long standing orders and associate with the camp of his enemy. *Why?* No being in the whole town of Illudun would dare go against the rules of the king; it was tantamount to poking a finger into the King's eyes; it was simply a sacrilege. But, alas, the King's own son and heir apparent to the throne of the land had just announced his intention to commit the worst sacrilege imaginable.

King Oba Adeogun abruptly stopped pacing the length and breath of the private sitting room in his palace and looked at his son, his face flushed with intense fury.

'I'm ashamed of you. I'm grossly ashamed of you Leke… and to think that you came out of my loins? It's totally unbelievable,' Oba Adeogun, the king of Iludun land in the western part of Nigeria, West Africa, said angrily to his son, Leke. It was nineteen eighty-five. Leke had taken his girlfriend, Amarachi, who Leke fondly called Ama, to meet his father. He had had a premonition that his father would not approve of his choice; only he did not expect this outburst, this uncontrollable fury, and in the presence of Ama too. He would have expected his father, King Oba Adeogun, popularly known in the town as King Oba, to have exercised a little bit of discretion, despite his reservations about his choice of a wife; but then, King Oba was not known to be able to show any discretion when he was angry; his impatience and subsequent annoyance with anyone who chose to be disobedient to his rules left so much to be desired.

Leke looked at his father in the face; probably for the first time in his life. He used to be afraid of his father but not anymore. He was an adult now – a twenty-four year old adult. He could now look at his father straight in the eye without flinching. His father had always been a harsh man. He was what everybody called 'a no-nonsense man'. The fact that he was the King of the whole town did not help matters. King Oba Adeogun ruled his household and the entire Iludun community with an iron fist.

King Oba Adeogun was a perfectionist to the core. He did not entertain any form of error from anyone, be it his subjects or his children. He was also very unforgiving – a fact that was very obvious to all and sundry. King Oba Adeogun was a fierce and fearsome warrior before he was made a King in the town. The fact that he fought boldly against the Ibos in the Biafran war of nineteen sixty-seven was no news even to the little children of the town. The fact that he had not forgiven the Ibos in respect of the war was also no news. It was a salient rule in the town of Iludun that there would not be any relationship of any kind between an indigene of Iludun and the Ibos, especially those who live in Alugu land. It was a rule that no Ibo was welcome in the town and any indigene of Iludun seen associating with any Ibo would automatically be ostracised and regarded as an outcast in the community; and every other person in the community would have nothing, absolutely nothing, to do with the 'outcast'. To think now that Leke, the King's very own son, would dare to bring an Ibo girl home as an intended bride, was beyond the King's imagination. It was an abomination to the King; and it was an abomination to the whole town. Leke knew this and he saw it in his father's eyes. He saw the fury, the ever green malice – the malice of nineteen sixty-seven, which had taken deep roots in his father's soul. He met his father's gaze unflinchingly and spoke in a clear, steady voice (which was a surprise even to himself).

Leke said to his father; 'Father, Ama is my choice, Ibo lady or not. I love Ama from the depths of my soul. All my life, I have done your bidding; I have always pleased you. Now I desire to be treated as the adult that I am. I am a complete grown up man and I should be given the credence that I know what I want from life. You have lived your life bearing a grudge of almost twenty years even against people who were not there when you fought the war. I cannot control your feelings, Father, but I can choose to take charge of mine and channel them towards loving anybody I choose to love. In my case, Father, love has prevailed over war.' Leke finished, his eyes imploring, his heart wishing desperately for his father to understand.

His father did not understand.

'You're a fool,' King Oba said. 'You're an incredible fool and I'm ashamed to have you as my son – my *heir*.' He looked at his son to see any reaction to that. There was none. Leke just looked resignedly at his father. King Oba Adeogun continued, 'From now henceforth, you shall cease to be my son. You shall cease to be an heir to the throne. You have lost your rights to the throne and you shall cease to come into my presence until you come back to your senses and let go of this Ibo girl. You are now banished from my presence.'

Leke looked around the sitting room, which was just one out of many others in the palace; it reeked of wealth – solid wealth. Every item was made of gold and silver; of expensive velvet and leather; of expensive woodworks and ornaments; from the royal seat to the well laid rug; from the chandeliers to the tables, chairs, frames and antiques; from wall to wall, everything reeked of class, of m-o-n-e-y.

Leke thought about his father's numerous investments, which, according to the law of the land, he would ultimately take over and be in control of in the event of his father's demise; he thought about all the cars which consisted of two Rolls-Royces, a Lamborghini, a Porsche, a Chrysler jeep, two Mercedes Benz saloon cars among others; he thought about the vast wealth, the fat account his father had been building for him but which he was not yet a signatory to until his father, who was usually not easily impressed, became satisfied that he, Leke was mature enough to control an enormous wealth. A voice asked him if he was ready to give up all of those because of Ama. *I would give it all up for her*, he decided stubbornly within himself, even though he knew that with only his degree certificate and almost nothing in the way of personal finance that could be attributed to him, his future seemed – what had one of his lecturer's in the university called it? – Inauspicious. His lecturer, professor G.M. Giles, popularly known as G.M.G., had called him into his office one day and had lambasted him over his poor grades, calling him a layabout and telling him in no unmistaken terms that he was a sorry case.

Now, Leke said to his father, 'Father, if my getting married to Ama will make me forfeit my right to the throne and all its attendant wealth then I'm obliged to give it up. You can give it to the next person in line. If my love for Ama is beyond your understanding, then you can lump it, Dad,' Leke finished angrily, pulling Ama up from the chair she had been sitting on, nervously twiddling her thumbs together. Ama had witnessed the whole episode – the bitter exchange between father and son all because of her – and she felt very uncomfortable. She felt very scared. All she wanted to do was to leave the palace and the entire town and not go back there. She would have decided to leave Leke but for the pregnancy. *The pregnancy for God's sake.* She was three weeks pregnant and she did not want to have a fatherless child. Hot tears sprung to her eyes and cascaded down her beautiful face. Leke saw this and kissed her on both cheeks and ushered her towards the door.

King Oba could not believe what was happening before his eyes. He could not believe that Leke could talk back at him. *What effrontery!* 'I disown you Leke. From now on, you cease to be my son. You're not my son,' he shouted at their retreating backs. They did not look back. King Oba threw down his staff of authority and angrily kicked a coffee table. The coffee table fell onto its side and broke.

King Oba turned to his personal guard who had been standing there, unmoving, just like a statue, and said to him, 'Get me my lawyer, and do it fast. Tell him I wish to see him immediately.'

'Yes your highness,' said the guard, who immediately went to the telephone and dialled the lawyer's number.

The lawyer came five minutes later. He was immediately ushered into the King's personal chambers. The King was seated in his royal seat, his staff of authority in his left hand and his right hand placed under his chin. He looked more than angry – he looked irate. The lawyer knew immediately that all was not well; however, he could not fathom why he was uncharacteristically summoned into the king's presence. The King's countenance filled him with foreboding. He prostrated flatly in front of the King in the usual traditional salute to the King of a Yoruba land. As the lawyer got up, the King blurted out, without a preamble, 'I want Leke cut out of my will immediately. He will not have a share in my fortune. I will not have anything to do with him or his generation ever again.'

The lawyer stood mouth agape. He could not believe what he had just heard.

Leke pulled up in front of the *Flamingo* guest house just on the outskirts of the town. He would rent the guest house for Ama and himself until he could decide what he would do with his life. He looked at Ama who had been quiet throughout their entire journey.

'Are you alright?' he asked.

Ama burst into fresh tears. Leke cradled her head on his chest. 'It's alright, darling. Everything is going to be alright,' He cooed into her ear (although he was not convinced about that himself). Ama did not stop crying; she wet his shirt with her tears.

Leke made another attempt at consoling her. He said to her, 'You know what? We will go ahead with the wedding, my father's consent or not. I've got my degree and I can always get a job to support us. Believe me, when our baby is born, I am pretty sure my father will have a change of heart. He will come running to us, begging for our forgiveness; he has always wanted grandchildren, you know. Ours is going to be his first grandchild and I'm sure that it's going to be a very beautiful baby… as beautiful as you.' That seemed to do the magic. Ama stopped crying, she wiped her tears with the handkerchief in Leke's breast pocket, sniffed and asked Leke hopefully, 'Are you really sure of that?'

'Really sure of what? That I will get a job or that we will have a beautiful baby?'

'No, that… that your father will accept me when we have our baby.'

'Of course he will. He'll come running to us.'

Two weeks after Leke left his father's palace, he came across an advert in the local newspaper for a job in a construction company based in Lagos. He decided to try it out. He had little or no hope of being employed but he decided to travel to Lagos anyway. He had nothing apart from transportation and accommodation money to lose.

The following morning, he said a cheerful bye-bye to Ama, who was a little bleary eyed from crying herself to sleep the previous night (Leke was beginning to get fed up with her cries but he understood what she considered her plight; what with her being an orphan with nobody except him to turn to). He got into his car and set out for Lagos, which was about three hours drive from their abode. He got to Lagos at mid-afternoon. The first thing he did was to look around for a cheap hotel. He got one that was neat and affordable and promptly checked in. Then, his search for a job began in earnest. He called up companies who had placed adverts in newspapers and posters, and he drove around the streets of Lagos, looking for offices with vacancies. He posted and submitted application letters and after two weeks, he began to get results.

There was a particular interview he had been called to attend at a construction company two weeks after he started looking for work. Leke dressed immaculately before going for that interview. After assuring himself for the twentieth time that he looked good enough to eat, he set out for the interview.

At the interview, he was seated confidently opposite the panel of interviewers and they had passed his curriculum vitae (which he had attached to his certificate) around like they were passing round a piece of poisoned meat. They were clearly not impressed. Leke didn't expect them to be impressed. He had gotten a lousy pass degree from the university. In fact, he was not supposed to have graduated from the university that academic year; he was just lucky to be one of the students that were allowed to be given a 'leave to leave' the university so as to 'thin down' the population of 'unwanted students'; students who did not bring glory to the prestigious university; students who did not fail enough to be expelled, but at the same time, who did not do well enough to make the university want to retain them. Of course, the authorities knew too well that no employer in his right mind would want to take on a graduate with an ordinary pass degree; definitely not in Nigeria anyway. The degree was meant to tell the prospective employer everything that the university authorities could not personally say about the degree holder, and that was simply, *'The bearer of this degree is a lay-about and we had to send him off our university to weed off the chaff from the flowers; employing this person would ultimately be to your company's peril and we therefore, take no responsibility for any adverse consequences'.* It was an unwritten code and Leke knew it. He also knew that all employers knew it too.

It was not that Leke could not have done better; it was just that he was so comfortable that he became thick-headed at school. He had everything money could buy and he had enough money, more money than was reasonably necessary for a student to have, and he very much threw his weight around. He partied hard throughout his years in school while his academics suffered and he could not exactly be bothered because, at the back of his mind, he always felt that he would never need to go searching for a job. Everything had been established for him; what with his father's numerous companies and investments and the eventuality of him becoming the future King. Leke had always felt he did not need to struggle to make an impressive grade; besides, who did he need to impress anyway? He had always thought he would one day become someone people were going to fall over themselves to impress, so he had just 'glided' his way though the university and come out with a pass degree. He, however, did not foresee that he would be disowned by his father and that everything he had would be taken away from him. Now, as he sat opposite the panel of interviewers, Leke did not have to be told that his application was going to be turned down. It was registered on the face of each and every one of them. They were just thinking of how best to discard him.

Well, I'm definitely not going to allow you do that in a hurry, Leke thought to himself. He looked at the attractive lady who was introduced earlier as the managing director of the company. The managing director had the look of utter disgust. Leke knew what she was thinking:

Obviously I am not going to allow this misfit into my establishment. I cannot allow the company I laboured so hard to build to crumble like a pack of cards by a mediocre. Leke decided to work on her. He looked directly at the lady and tried to give her one of his charming smiles – the one he used whenever he cared to make an impression; the smile carried a mischievous twinkle to his right eye. That smile had always worked like magic on ladies. It made his face go soft and it gave him an air of confidence all at once. Leke was a handsome man, but whenever he smiled, he looked angelic and it had, oftentimes, worked on women especially. He hoped it would work this time. The managing director, however, was thinking, *I prefer brains to beauty, brother, so that charm won't work with me.*

But Leke was thinking, *you're very lucky I'm now married; three months ago, sister, I would have brought you down from your high horse with a good fuck; then you'd have been eating out of my palms.*

Two weeks later, Leke got a job with the Lagos state ministry. Two months after he got the job, Leke made arrangements for them to travel to the United Kingdom through his office, the office of external affairs. Even though he had been disowned by his father, the King, he had used his father's name to obtain favours while he was on the quest for a good job and he had obtained enormous favours. He made sure he chipped in his background and made emphasis on the fact that he was a prince – King Oba Adeogun's son for that matter. The only thing he did not mention was that he had been disowned by his father. *Once a prince, always a prince*, he always said to himself to allay any guilt that arose within him anytime he used his father's name to obtain favours. He was offered a job in all the establishments he applied to.

He decided to take the job with the ministry of external affairs and two months later, he got a transfer to work with the Nigerian High Commission in the United Kingdom, courtesy of his father's name. He was going to the United Kingdom for the first time not as a common visitor, but as an expatriate – and not without the attendant pomp and pageantry, he thought within himself; not without the attendant dignity and honour. He smiled; his future was not inauspicious after all. His future was bright!

Chapter 6

As the aeroplane touched down on the tarmac at the Heathrow airport in London, Leke felt elated; he felt he had left all his troubles behind in Nigeria. In his mind's eye, he looked into the future with enthusiasm. He sighed with relief as he took his wife by the hand and led her out of the aeroplane. Had he known what fate had in store for him, he would have retraced his steps!

Leke found it very easy to settle down in the United Kingdom. He thoroughly enjoyed his job with the Nigerian High Commission on Fleet Street. He did not allow his wife to do any work apart from attending to her own needs. He brought her gifts everyday, and made sure she was always happy. She soon forgot her troubles; she forgot that she had been orphaned at a tender age of seven; she forgot all the rejections she suffered from members of her father's family and members of her mother's family as well; she forgot that she had had to grow up in an orphanage where there was really no close family unit; she forgot that she had no family she could truly call her own until she met Leke; she forgot the rejection she suffered in the hands of her father-in-law, whom she desperately wanted to be accepted by. She started to believe that when she gave birth to her baby (whom she desperately hoped would turn out a baby boy), her father-in-law would have a change of heart and accept her as the mother of a potential heir to the throne. She was very much aware that Leke was the only son the King had; she was aware that all the others were daughters and therefore, they were of no consequence to the continuity of King Oba Adeogun's lineage on the throne. She was aware that King Oba Adeogun's other children would have no claim to the throne in the event of the King's demise. She was very much aware that if Leke remained disowned, and the King had neither a son nor a grandson, the throne would be taken over by another family apart from King Oba Adeogun's family and she was finally aware that King Oba Adeogun was very determined to keep the throne in his lineage permanently. She reasoned that Leke had been very correct when he told her that King Oba Adeogun had just let his fury and grudge against her tribe override his sense of reasoning. She assured herself that things would change for the better when she gave birth to her son; after all, it would be the King's first grandson; the King would definitely weigh his gains against his losses, and choose to have her, the mother of the future King, who would guarantee the throne for his lineage, as his daughter-in-law indeed and in truth.

In the fourth month of her pregnancy, Ama had gone to have a scan to determine the sex of the baby. She could not wait till the day she would have her baby; she wanted to know her fate. She silently prayed for a boy as she lay down on the examination bed; she prayed still as the cream was applied to her belly; she fervently prayed as she was asked to watch the monitor, where a computer graphic of her beloved baby would appear and she would be able to determine the sex of her baby herself.

The midwife noticed her anxiety and told her to relax. 'It doesn't matter what the sex of the child is you know,' the nurse told her conversationally. 'I personally don't do a scan. I love all my kids with the same measure, boy or girl, it doesn't matter,' she finished softly.

It does matter in my own case; it really matters for the security of my future, thought Ama. But she said nothing, she only smiled nervously.

It was to her dismay when, after a considerable time, the sex of the baby could not be determined. The baby determinedly put his or her legs tightly together, and all efforts at making it change positions proved futile. The midwife tickled Ama's tummy; she gently poked and coaxed; she did everything humanly possible so the baby would move, but surprisingly, it did not move. It just wouldn't budge. After a few more minutes, Ama was advised to come back for a repeat scan a month later.

Ama went back a month later and this time around, the baby turned its back to the screen. The sex of the baby could still not be determined. Ama cursed under her breath. The midwife heard it and, taking a deep breath, gave Ama the same advice she had given her the first time they had done the scan. 'Go home and hope to have a healthy baby, darling; that's all that matters.'

Ama nodded resignedly, she slowly took off the hospital gown and slipped on her dress. Then she picked up her bag, smiled sadly at the midwife and without saying one more word, started towards the door. The midwife stared at Ama's slumped shoulders until she closed the door behind her quietly. The midwife could not decipher why the young lady was so desperate to know the sex of her child. She was indeed an experienced nurse. She had worked at the hospital for twenty-three years and in all the years that she had worked as a nurse and then as a midwife, she had come to accept that black women always preferred male children over female ones; it was simply the culture. 'Where I come from, male children are simply more important than female ones.' That was the way one of her patients had simply summarised it. That was why she had not bothered to tell Ama that, with the experience she had acquired over the years as a professional nurse, she was one hundred per cent positive that Ama was going to have a baby girl!

Ama had her baby in the month of September, nineteen eighty-five. Immediately the baby came; she was wrapped in a white, warm towel and placed in Ama's arms by a smiling nurse who thought Ama was a very fortunate woman to have laboured for so little time, to have had an almost painless labour, and to have a baby so beautiful to hold. As soon as Ama held the baby, she tugged a little at the towel in which the baby was wrapped and pushing the tiny legs apart, peered at the genitals. It was a girl. Ama was not only sad – she was despondent. As Ama held the baby in her arms for the first time, the doctors and nurses came around to take a look at the baby.

'Oh my! She's gorgeous,' a trainee doctor exclaimed.

'Such a beautiful bundle,' one of the nurses cooed.

'She's the most beautiful little thing I've seen in a while,' another said.

But Ama said nothing. She had mixed feelings about the baby she held in her arms. Her baby was extremely beautiful; yes she was, and Ama felt proud to be a mother for the first time in her life. She felt happy to have brought another human being into the world; she felt so different all of a sudden; the life of a being was now entrusted in her hands; she felt very responsible. However, she felt a little dismayed because it was a girl. How she wished she had had a son. Then, she would have been the happiest woman in the whole wide world. Now, she did not know whether she should feel happy or not. She thought about her father-in-law; she thought about the throne. Would she ever be formally accepted into the King's family? Would she ever be loved by the king? Definitely, the birth of her daughter could not secure a grain of sand for her in the King's vineyard. She suddenly felt threatened. She was not sure what the future held in store for her. She was scared.

Leke came in two hours after Ama gave birth to their daughter. As soon as he heard the news, he flew back to London from Scotland and he went straight to the hospital from the airport. As soon as he saw the baby, hot tears of joy rushed down his eyes. He could not stop looking at her even as he talked to Ama. He kissed the baby several times before he gave Ama a kiss. Ama took notice of this and she was surprised at the feeling of jealousy that arose within her. She thought she deserved more attention from her husband. She felt rejected. An eerie feeling engulfed her. Leke was now rejecting her, just like everyone else she had ever known had rejected her and, ironically, the cause of the rejection she now suffered from her husband, the only person who had ever truly loved and understood her, was her own baby, the baby she had carried in her womb for nine months; the baby she had given birth to in pain and difficulty; the baby that had chosen to come into the world not as a boy that she so much wanted, but as a bloody girl.

Leke was not aware of what was going through Ama's mind. He was too overjoyed to notice her sadness. He touched the baby's face; he touched her eyes, her cheeks and her nose; he gently ran his fingers through her hair; he checked her hands, her feet; he touched her ears; he looked deeply into her eyes. 'Don't you think that our daughter has got the most lovely eyes in the world, Ama?' he said without looking at her.

Ama did not answer. Leke did not notice her silence. He went on: 'And the nose; she's got a lovely pointed nose, and she's got pink lips and her hair's so full and long and black. She's simply gorgeous. Ama, please give me a more beautiful word than gorgeous, 'cos that's what our baby deserves. She's more gorgeous than gorgeous.' Ama did not say a word; Leke still did not notice her silence.

'My baby's so lovely,' he went on. 'She's the best thing that has happened to my life. Thank you my dear Ama for giving me such a wonderful daughter. She's going to be the centre of my life, my soul and my very existence,' Leke rambled on innocently, but with every endearment Leke showered on the baby, with every sentence he made, with every word he said, he seemed to thrust a sword deeper into Ama's heart. By the time Leke paused for breath, the feeling of jealousy that Ama initially had for her daughter had metamorphosed into something more unpalatable, something very bitter; she could actually taste the bitterness; she hated her baby with a passion!

Three days after Ama had her baby, she was discharged from the hospital and Leke was on hand to take them home. As soon as they got out of the car, Leke promptly went to the back seat, unfastened the baby strap and gently lifted the baby out of her seat, then he ran into the house, cooing sweet things into the baby's ears and leaving Ama standing beside the car, a deathly expression on her face.

The baby was named Nike, which meant 'care' in Leke's mother tongue. Ama couldn't be bothered to give her a name. She refused to breast feed her and she refused to play with her. As far as Ama was concerned, her baby, Nike was an enemy!

Chapter 7

Nike grew up a daddy's girl and just a little more than a total stranger to her mother.

Leke was not very happy with the way his wife treated Nike. To Leke, Ama's relationship with their daughter as the little girl grew up was not a mother-daughter relationship but more like a rival-to-rival relationship.

Ama was not bothered if their daughter ate a balanced meal or not; she was not bothered if her clothes were warm enough or not; she would not bathe her and she would not look after her health. She became outrightly hostile towards her own daughter. Leke found Ama's character very strange. A few times, he made an attempt to ask her why she could not be bothered about Nike's general welfare, but all he got were either vague answers or outright insults.

Over the years, an emotional gap had been created between Leke and Ama, and the gap widened as the years passed. The warmth and love they once shared had dwindled considerably. Their sex life became drab and Leke gradually became weary of Ama. The only joy he had in their marriage was their daughter and the only hope he had for the survival of the marriage entirely lay with the very existence of Nike.

When Nike was two years old, Ama gave birth to a set of twin baby boys. Leke saw the way Ama took to the boys immediately. She almost worshiped them. Leke wondered why Ama could not show the same degree of love toward their daughter, who was beginning to avoid any form of contact with her mother. Nike always preferred to be with Leke in his study and she preferred to go out with him than to stay with her mother in the house.

When Nike was three years old and old enough to attend nursery, Leke employed a live-in nanny, who was a middle aged widow with kindly eyes. She immediately took to Nike and showed her the love and care that her mother denied her. She had no child of her own before her husband died, and Nike became a surrogate child for her. She thought Ama was ungratefully lucky to have such a beautiful and intelligent child.

When Nike started school, it was the nanny, whom Nike fondly called Aunty Margaret, who made sure that her uniform was neat and well ironed; it was Aunty Margaret who made her breakfast and packed her lunch; it was Aunty Margaret who was there to welcome her back from school, and it was Aunty Margaret who helped with her homework. As the years went by, Ama was almost non-existent in Nike's life. She was always in the nursery, attending to the twins. Nike began to think less of her mother. However much she loved to be close to her brothers, she was always afraid of going near them to avoid being castigated by her mother. Because she totally avoided her mother, she totally avoided her brothers.

Leke loved taking his daughter to the park. He enjoyed the greenery, the horticulture and the fresh air; more importantly, he enjoyed his daughter's company more than he enjoyed Ama's. He was sad to think that things had broken down irreparably between himself and his wife.

One bright Saturday morning, when Nike was five years old, Leke took her to the park as he had been doing since she was three. Leke held Nike by the hand and they both strolled contentedly all around the park. Nike loved this moment; she loved being with her dad; she loved being outside the home, where her mother's shadow of hostility was not cast upon her. Leke decided they should take a break and as they sat on a bench placed under a tree in the park, Nike felt she should ask the question that had been bothering her young mind. She saw the way her friend's mothers showed so much love to her friends and she heard her classmates talk often about how much they loved their mothers; Nike could not bring herself to say anything about her own mother; over time, she learned to keep quiet; whenever she was asked questions about her mum she talked about her lovely father instead. One day, her best friend, Jasmine, asked her innocently, 'Nike, haven't you got a mum?'

'Oh yes I have,' replied Nike immediately. 'Why do you ask?' she said.

'Because you never talk about her. You always talk about your daddy,' came her friend's reply.

Nike refrained from telling her friend the truth about her mother; she did not want to be treated as strange; she did not want to be the odd one out. Rather, in her mind's eye, she replaced her mother with Aunty Margaret and she would tell her friends whatever it was Aunty Margaret did for her. To Nike, Aunty Margaret was her own dear mum. She would say to her friends, 'Oh, my mum bought me a green coloured frock yesterday,' or 'I went with my mum to McDonald's last week, you know,' and she would smile sadly.

However, deep down, she knew that something was just not right. *Why would Aunty Margaret love her whilst her own mother hated her so much?*

'Dad, why does mum hate me so much?' she asked her father suddenly.

Shocked by the statement from a mere five year old girl, Leke quickly made to allay such a thought from her, 'She doesn't hate you, darling. She's just under pressure because of the twins,' he told her gently, cradling her head against him.

'Yes she does. She hates me but loves my brothers,' said Nike stubbornly, tears were pouring down her face.

'She loves you, my dear, and so does Daddy; Daddy loves you very much, and don't you ever forget that,' said Leke, wiping off her tears. Nike innocently nodded in agreement. 'That's my girl. Now let us go have some ice-cream and then we'll go get something from Burger King; and after that we'll go to the movies. We'll watch your favourite cartoon there.'

Nike shrieked with joy and hugged her father tightly; her mother's hostility towards her totally forgotten at that moment.

'Thanks Dad. I love you, Dad,' she said sincerely.

Leke was moved to tears; he swallowed the tears that were threatening to choke him. Right there and then, he resolved to fill the motherly void that had been created in Nike by Ama.

'I love you too, child,' he said.

Nike was brilliant at school. She was always in the first position in her class. One day, when Nike was in grade two in the primary school, her head-teacher called her father for a chat.

'I must congratulate you, Mr Adeogun, on the exceptional performance of your daughter,' the head teacher said after the usual pleasantries. 'I must say that with her brilliance, the sky will be the limit for Nike,' he concluded.

Leke was very proud of his daughter.

One day, Ama told Leke the plans she had been nursing since the arrival of the twins.

'I wish to take the twins to see your father in Nigeria,' she said to Leke.

'Why would you do that?' asked Leke, absentmindedly.

'I assume your father would be happy to see my twin boys. At least he would be assured that his generation would forever lay claim to the throne.'

'I see,' said Leke sarcastically. 'And I assume that's why you've only shown deep hatred to your own daughter ever since you had her. To you, Nike is a female offspring and so, cannot guarantee you a seat in my father's kingdom. I'm beginning to have the feeling that you married me for what you could get out of me. You married me for fame. You greatly amaze me, Ama,' Leke finished angrily.

'That's not true and you know it,' shouted Ama.

'Why, may I humbly ask, do you not show the same amount of care you give the boys to Nike?' asked Leke, his voice still laden with sarcasm.

'Because you have proved to me in more than one way that Nike is more important to you than I am. Since she was born, you've never cared about me; you never cared to listen to my feelings. You practically transferred your love to her,' said Ama defiantly.

'Are you telling me that you're jealous of your own daughter?' said Leke. He was really astonished. 'You must be crazy. You must be stark raving mad,' he said as he stood up to leave the room, but before he left he said to Ama, 'Please let this be the last time you would ever mention my father and his damned throne in my presence. As far as I'm concerned, I am no longer his son; and as for the royalty, the Illudun community can stuff it up his arse when he dies.'

Ama knew that Leke was serious and it meant that she had lost all hope of popularity. She remembered her days at the orphanage; she remembered her struggles; she remembered the shame and reproach; she remembered her best friend, Olivia, who was adopted when they were barely teenagers. She had always counted Olivia to be a very lucky girl. Olivia was not as pretty as she was; she was not even half as pretty as Ama, but she had always gotten her way under any circumstances. Olivia had such an innocent look that made everyone want to love and protect her always; and she had been adopted into a very wealthy family. Before Olivia was taken away from the orphanage, Ama and Olivia had been inseparable; they simply did everything together; and they shared their dreams, their hopes and their aspirations together. A week before Olivia went away, the Reverend mother, Martha, had called them both and had broken the news to them in her usual kindly manner. The realisation dawned on the two girls that they were going to be separated forever and they cried. All the reassurances the Reverend mother gave them seemed to fall on deaf ears. The Reverend mother sighed resignedly; she understood the feeling of the girls. Since they had been brought into the home, they had been like two peas in a pod. Separating them at this stage of their lives would create a void in their hearts. She could only wish that Ama would be as lucky as Olivia. She wished Ama would get adopted into a wealthy, loving family as Olivia had.

The morning Olivia was going away, she had hugged Ama tightly and told her she hoped that Ama too would be whisked away by a lovely family like she had. She had promised Ama that she would write often.

She never did!

Ama could not help the feeling of betrayal she had nursed towards Olivia. Olivia had been adopted into a rich family, and because she was enjoying so much luxury, she had totally forgotten Ama. Ama resolved right there and then to be successful at all costs. She would be so rich and one day, she would see Olivia again and she would ignore her; just as she, Ama, had been ignored. Being wealthy and famous became an obsession for Ama. So when Leke, a handsome and wealthy prince, came her way many years later, she knew without an iota of doubt that her dreams were about to be fulfilled. She had made sure she got pregnant for Leke and she had made sure she put up her best behaviour for him until he had taken her to his father; and then her dreams had been shattered. Leke's father, King Oba Adeogun, had stated solemnly that he would not have anything to with Ama or her generation. He had disinherited his own son, who happened to be the only son he had. But Ama was very much aware of the tradition of the land. The King could only be succeeded by a son. If the King had no son to put forward, then he would relinquish the rights to the throne along with a substantial part of the King's fortune to another family, who would be chosen by the *oracle*. Ama knew that the King would do everything in his might to prevent this from happening. She was also aware that after Leke's mother's death, the king had married four women in a bid to have a son who would be an alternative heir to the throne; but all his efforts to have another son proved futile. The King's four wives had all had daughters.

    Ama had reasoned that the king would have a change of heart and revoke his pronouncement over Leke if she could bear a son; at least that would secure him the throne, and Ama had borne two sons; her hope of becoming a queen had been rekindled. But now, Leke was bent on shattering her hopes yet again. Ama would not be allowed into the King's presence unless she had the King's permission and she could not have the king's permission unless she went through Leke. Leke had sworn never to see his father, not even on his dying day. She thought of what to do; she came to a lock jam. She cried.

    Later that night, as Leke lay on the bed beside Ama, sleep seemed to have eluded him. He tossed and turned restlessly on the bed, replaying the discussion he had with Ama earlier that day in his mind. Everything Ama had said pointed to the fact that she did not care about Nike.

    Suddenly, a fearful thought crossed his mind.

    What would happen to his beloved daughter if he suddenly dropped dead?

    Leke shuddered at the thought. He had, upon his demise, willed everything he possessed to Ama. That was when the going was good between them. He had willed Ama his shares and assets and properties, thinking that she would take care of their children if he was the one who died first. Now he was not so sure Ama would take care of Nike upon his death. Although he was not planning to die soon, he did not want to take chances. He was sure the twins would be well cared for by Ama, should anything happen to him, but he could not say the same for Nike. He looked at Ama sleeping soundly beside him and made a mental note to make some changes to his will. He had made a resolution to give their three children the best of everything in life. He did not want any of them to lack anything even if he suddenly dropped dead!

When Nike was in her fourth year in the primary school, something extraordinary happened.

Mr Mann, a teacher who was regarded as exceptional in his profession, was transferred to Nike's school. It took Mr Mann only a few weeks to notice Nike's exceptional intelligence. He saw Nike as way above her classmates in all things. The way she wrote, her intelligence at answering questions, the way she reasoned, her manner of speech and her general comportment in class did not go unnoticed to the experienced eyes of Nike's new teacher.

In all his years of teaching, Mr Mann had come across several kinds of pupils. Amongst them, he had seen brilliant pupils, and he had seen very brilliant ones; however, he could not remember coming across any as brilliant as Nike Adeogun. The pupil was one that could best be described as 'magic'. She was way ahead of her class. He felt that Nike being in grade four in that school was definitely a waste of talent; he felt she deserved better. He resolved to do something about it.

One day, Mr Mann went to the head teacher's office.

'I notice an exceptional pupil in year four,' said Mr Mann without preamble.

'That must be Nike Adeogun,' said the head teacher without the slightest hesitation.

'Exactly; Nike Adeogun is her name and I would very much like to make a suggestion,' said Mr Mann.

'I'm listening,' said the head teacher with rapt attention.

'Well, I would suggest she sat for the forth-coming entrance examination with the sixth year students.'

'I... er, I... er,' the head teacher stuttered, then he found the right words after a while, 'As much as I consider Nike Adeogun's performance as highly encouraging, I don't think your request would be possible under the present circumstances,' he paused to let that sink in and then he quickly went on. 'I don't wish to offend you Mr Mann, neither do I want to prove difficult, but as you well know, such a thing has never for once been heard to have happened, not in this school, nor in another,' the head teacher finished lamely. He did not want to upset Mr Mann, for he knew that when he was transferred to his school, he came so he could be an asset. Mr Mann knew it too. He knew that the head teacher would not want him to leave the school, so he decided to take advantage of the knowledge...

In the month of September, Nike Adeogun sat for the entrance examination with the sixth year students and when the results were posted, Mr Mann was not surprised to see that the best results went to none other than Nike Adeogun.

That same year, Nike Adeogun was given a scholarship to attend the London Oratory; and that same year, Leke Adeogun, prompted by an occurrence in his best friend's household, made a decision to change his daughter's life for good. ..

Leke had paid a visit to his friend, Anthony Asante one bright sunny morning. He was in a very good mood. His beloved daughter, Nike, had just gained admission into one of the best secondary schools in London at the tender age of nine. His daughter was a genius; and being the father of a genius was not a common thing.

As Leke stepped into his friend's apartment, the sight that greeted him was not what he would have dreamt of in his entire life. He watched spellbound as his dear friend, Anthony, was being led away by three policemen. *What!* His friend was even in handcuffs. He looked at Anthony's wife, Mercy, who had her head deeply buried in her palms and was sobbing her heart out; then his gaze fell on their daughter, Marlene. She was standing with arms akimbo and looking at her father's retreating back with an expression Leke could best describe as defiance. She was a short, stout plain looking black girl, who always had a smirk on her face. *Short woman devil* – that was what her father called her. Marlene's slightly bulging tummy and swollen face did not escape Leke's notice. Marlene had always been an obstinate girl and Anthony had relayed his fears over her future to Leke times without number. 'I fear that daughter of mine would get into some sort of trouble one day,' Anthony would exclaim, 'she's getting more and more obstinate and nonchalant about her life by the minute. I'm really, really scared she wouldn't make it y'know,' Anthony would sigh. Leke soon got bored of Anthony's seeming pessimism over his daughter. He could not fathom why a father would always be so negative about his daughter. His own Nike was a perfect child and he did not understand why any other child could be otherwise. However, as he watched Marlene's demeanour whilst taking a good look at her bulging tummy, he could only hope that the girl was not pregnant; he sincerely hoped that she had simply over-eaten. *But why would Anthony be arrested; and why would Mercy be crying so much? What the hell could be going on here?,* he thought to himself.

'What the hell's happening here? He asked aloud. Mercy looked up in surprise. She had just noticed that there was someone else other than her immediate family and the policemen in the living room.

'Oh I'm so glad you're here, Leke,' she exclaimed amidst tears. 'They've taken him away. I couldn't bear to look at him. I… couldn't bear to look at them all. He's gonna be charged to court… he's… he's gonna be charged for assault and he's gonna go to jail. My husband's gonna go to jail… Oh my God, I can't bear it. I couldn't bear to see him go,' she wailed.

'Calm down,' said Leke. 'Now why would Anthony be arrested by the police?'

'Because he hit Marlene,' said Mercy uncomfortably. 'She… she got pregnant you see, and… and he, he couldn't take it. He got angry and one thing led to another and he… he hit her.'

So she had not over-eaten after all. She was pregnant. Marlene was PREGNANT. Leke made a quick mental calculation of Marlene's age – thirteen! Who would dare impregnate a thirteen year old girl? *The bastard should be arrested and sent to jail.*

'…So Marlene called the police and got her father arrested. Now he'll be sent to jail.'

For a second, the unthinkable came into Leke's heart and he quickly dispensed it. His friend definitely couldn't be responsible for his own daughter's pregnancy. His friend was *not insane.* But why would Anthony get arrested? To Leke, simply beating a child is not enough to warrant the father's arrest. In Africa where he came from, if a child misbehaved, she got flogged. In Africa, the slogan was always *spare the rod and spoil the child. So why would Anthony get the handcuffs?*

'Surely Anthony's not…' Leke began to say uncomfortably…

Mercy looked at Leke hopefully. 'Anthony's not what?' she asked, then went on. 'D'you really think Anthony's not going to jail for hitting Marleene? That boy should have been arrested instead of my husband,' she sobbed.

Leke sighed with relief; *of course his friend was not a pervert.* Marlene's words, however, almost jolted Leke out of his skin.

'Dad surely deserved what he got. Oh yes he did. I hope he rots in jail while I enjoy my life with Rudolph. Next time, he'll think twice before he lays his filthy hands on me; and that's if there's gonna be a next time, 'cos I'm going to live with Rudolph 'cos we love each other and he's going to be the father of my baby.' And with that, she stormed out of the house.

Leke could not believe the cheek of it. Marleene had actually called the police on her own father, just because he expressed his displeasure at her getting pregnant. And to rub insult on the injury, she had the audacity to say she was going to live with the boy who got her pregnant. Now, he was beginning to understand his friend's constant fears over his daughter. The only irony was that his friend, Anthony, seemed to have gotten into more trouble than his daughter. His thoughts quickly went to his own daughter, Nike. Although she was just nine years old (a good four years younger than Marleene and far too young to even have a boyfriend), he could not but experience a strange fear creeping up in him. He did not want his daughter to end up like Marleene – loose, nonchalant, obnoxious and totally incorrigible. He made a firm resolve never to allow Nike to lead the same path as Marlene. Without deigning a look at the still sobbing Mercy, he strolled out of his friend's apartment; his resolution had brought forth a plan he intended to carry out.

'Gentlemen, you don't understand how important it is for me to take my child to Africa to further her studies,' Leke said to the head teacher and Mr Mann. He was seated opposite the two men in a way that made him feel like he was a mere student facing a school disciplinary panel, while, indeed, he had simply gone to Nike's school to tell the head teacher of his intention to withdraw his daughter from the school and have her transferred to a boarding school in Africa. However, all his pleas for the head teacher and the highly respected Mr Mann to reason with him seemed to fall on deaf ears. He made a last attempt at making them see reason with him: 'Of course, gentlemen, you must agree with me that under the present circumstances, it is highly imperative that I give my daughter the necessary upbringing to ensure that she does not go astray.'

'Bullshit!' shouted Mr Mann suddenly. 'Absolute nonsense! You mean you expect me to sit back and allow my toil' (he laid good emphasis on '*my toil*' by pointing to himself), 'my effort on that girl to go to waste?'

The head teacher looked at Mr Adeogun; he was very angry. He could not believe why the father of the most brilliant girl in his school could wish to throw his daughter's bright future away. Leke Adeogun looked at Mr Mann seated beside him; he almost shivered. Mr Mann, unlike the head teacher, did not look angry – he looked murderous.

'Now hold on a minute,' said Leke, jumping to his feet; he was really angry now; he was angry with the head teacher; he was angry with Mr Mann and he was angry with the whole school for trying to dictate what to do with his child. He was the father of his child and he very much intended to tell them so.

'I'm the father of Nike Adeogun and I'm sure I'm in the best position to know what's right for her. I am seizing this opportunity to officially inform you that come next term, my daughter would be going to school in my native Africa… in Nigeria to be precise,' said Leke to the two men, and he quickly added emphatically, 'with or without your permission.' And with that, he stormed out of the head teacher's office.

Chapter 8

On the seventh of September, nineteen ninety-four, Nike arrived at the Blueberry comprehensive boarding school in Lagos, Nigeria, West Africa, accompanied by her father.

After arranging Nike's accommodation in one of the school dormitories, Leke took her to the principal's office.

'My name is Leke Adeogun and this is my very brilliant daughter, Nike,' Leke began after the usual handshake.

'You're very welcome,' said the principal, who was a short, stoutly-built man with eyes that depicted some sort of internal frustration, 'you're very much welcome indeed. I've read about your daughter's exceptional brilliance in the papers and I assure you that she'll have the best time here in this school. You'll never regret your decision to bring her here, and by the way, my name is Diran Lucas,' he finished enthusiastically.

Leke felt that the principal was too eager to please – and that spelt mischief. To Leke, Mr Lucas did not exactly look like a professional teacher and he did not like the way he had said *bring her here* as if he had brought his daughter to a remand home and not a prestigious secondary school. However, he liked the fact that the principal was aware of his daughter's exceptional brilliance; he felt very proud; he felt that his daughter was already a champion even before she was fully registered in the school; his ego got the better of him and he decided to make Nike stay.

Nike's first year at the Blueberry secondary school went smoothly, with Nike coming tops in her class. Her second year in the school was better, and her third year was even better than her second.

News of her brilliance soon spread throughout the whole school and the neighbouring schools. Nike became very popular. Everyone, including older students in higher classes, wanted to be her friend. Many boys wanted to date her. Many showered her with little gifts students could only afford. Nike was very pleasant to everyone but that was as far as it went. She was aware that her father wanted the best for her in terms of discipline; that was why he had taken her from a school in the United Kingdom to Africa. She had promised her father that she would try her best to exhibit what he called an *exemplary character*, and that included keeping up her excellent academic performance and, more importantly, to shy away from any intimacy with the opposite sex. Nike had taken her father's advice to heart. She was her daddy's girl; her daddy was her star and she would do anything within her power to please him.

Leke made sure that he visited Nike at the school six times in a year – thrice during the official mid-term breaks in each term and the other times, during the long vacations. Leke would pick her up from the school on the first day of the break which was usually a Friday, and they would drive down to The Grand Hotel located on the outskirts of the school. Leke usually reserved a room for Nike, and another room for himself. He reasoned that Nike was no longer a little girl and she now deserved some privacy. Nike told her father that she preferred to remain in Nigeria even when the school was on a long break. This was due to the fact that there was no love lost between herself and her mother. Aunty Margaret had long gone from their home. Ama had fired her the same week Nike went to the boarding school in Africa.

There was a certain boy who was a student at Blueberry secondary school along with Nike. His name was Tokunboh Martins and he was popularly known as Toks. Tokunboh was a quiet, gentle boy from a wealthy home, and he was very studious. When he was in his fifth and the last year in the secondary school, he was made the year's school head boy because of his academic excellence.

Tokunboh had fallen in love with Nike right from the moment he set his eyes on her. She was in her second year in the school while he was in the fourth year when he noticed her. He was originally taken in by her exceptional beauty, and then he had noticed that she was exceptionally brilliant, and he had fallen in love with her. He also noticed that Nike was quite different from all other girls; she kept herself from the wiles of the dangerous boys in and out of the school. She had no boyfriend and she was always with her books. Tokunboh liked Nike's attitude; he loved her charisma. It showed they could blend together, for he hated loose girls; he hated girls with easy virtue. However, because Tokunboh felt that Nike was still too young to understand what it meant to be in love, he had decided to wait a little longer before he revealed his feelings for her, although, he secretly kept a close watch on her. It would really hurt him if she was misled to fall prey to the unscrupulous boys in the school.

So, when Nike was in her third year in the school, she was surprised to receive a note from the highly esteemed head boy of the school. A girl called Shade, who was in the same class and the same dormitory as Nike, had brought the note to her. Shade had woken Nike up from a siesta and giggling excitedly, had placed the sealed note into Nike's hand and urged her to open it. Shade was known for her frivolity and she was one who always found everything funny – she would even find something to laugh about in the most saddening incident.

Now, as she gave the note to Nike, she said to her laughingly, 'He sent a note to her, through *moi*, and *her's* gonna open it for us to read; it shall be the beginning of a love story, and they shall live happily ever after,' she finished, making choreographic demonstrations.

Nike hated being roused from sleep, but she laughed despite herself; no one could get angry with Shade for long. However, she wondered why the head boy would send her a note. *It was probably a note of warning*, she reasoned. In the school, the head-boy and the head-girl were revered generally by the other students. They were treated with the kind of respect usually accorded teachers, and whatever decision they made pertaining a student usually held water and Nike did not want to be in the head-boy's wrong books. *But what had she done wrong?* She asked herself. She quickly opened the envelope. It was better to know what she'd actually done wrong than to be kept in suspense. As she opened the letter, she saw Shade peering to read the contents and she laughingly shooed her away.

'Okay, Okay, we shall all see when the time comes. No one can hide such things for long you know?' said Shade, and with that, she winked at Nike teasingly and made an exit from the room. Nike opened the letter and began to read, and then after a while she burst out laughing; Shade had been correct, it was indeed a love professing letter.

It read:

> *Ever since I set my eyes on you, I have thought of none other but you.*
> *When I look at you, I see a hidden jewel.*
> *Please give me half a chance in your life. I want us to share a part of each other forever.*
> Yours
> *Toks.*

Nike found it very strange that the head-boy should show an interest in her. It was very strange indeed, for Toks was not known to be interested in boy-girl affairs. He was admired by many girls. They all wanted to date him. Some wanted him for his looks, some for his brilliance and many for his money. But Nike was not interested in the head-boy, neither was she interested in any boy for that matter. She remembered her promise to her father. She would gently decline the head-boy's request, as she had done to others.

She picked up a piece of paper and a pen and she wrote a note to the head-boy…

Chapter 9

In the United Kingdom, Ama sat in the office of Doctor Tom Thomas in a children's hospital. Her twin sons had developed a high temperature overnight. She had administered all the medication she could think of on them but things did not just improve. The twins had writhed in pain and cried all night. At five o'clock in the morning, Ama could take it no more. She called the ambulance and five minutes later, they were in the paediatric ward of the general hospital.

When the twins had received medical treatment and the temperature had normalised, Ama had immediately placed a call to Leke, who had gone on a holiday alone to the United States of America. The line was engaged; she tried it once more, it went to an answering machine. She left a message for Leke to call her as soon as possible; before she dropped the line, she added that she had called regarding the twins. *Just so he would take her seriously*, she reasoned sadly. She waited for some minutes and then she dialled the number again; again the answering machine came on. She cut the line immediately; there was no point leaving another message. She would try to call him again later. Even though their marriage was now almost non-existent, they had mutually agreed to stay together because of the children. They usually did things differently and overtime, communication between them had reduced to a mere 'hi, how are the children?'

She admitted now that she needed Leke more than ever before.

'I'm so sorry, Mrs Adeogun; after conducting extensive tests, we found out that the twins have a blood disorder called sickle cell disease. Their blood type is SS. However, what I find very baffling is the fact that the twins did not exhibit the symptoms when they were much younger,' said Doctor Thomas.

Ama understood what sickle cell disease was. She had just not deemed it necessary to take precautions against it before getting pregnant. She was too obsessed with wanting to get rich and famous. Now, the children she had relied upon to ensure she got to the royal seat were sickly, and their survival was not guaranteed. How she wished Nike was the child plagued with the SS syndrome and not her boys.

'You see, Mrs Adeogun, sickle cell anaemia is a blood disorder that is common among Africans and–' said Doctor Thomas in a bid to proffer explanation on why the twins came about the sickle cell anaemia disease, but Ama cut him short.

'I know what sickle cell disease is, Doctor, but what I wish to know is if my babies will live long.' She almost added *long enough to know their grandfather – the king* but she bit back the remark; and instead asked, 'What are their chances of survival?'

'Well, at the moment, I would say they have a 20 per cent chance of survival.' Ama's shoulders sagged; she bent her head and sobbed quietly. *Why should she have it so rough in life? It was simply not fair.*

Doctor Thomas saw Ama's reaction and he quickly went on, 'However, we could carry out a surgery on the twins; although, it is quite expensive. It basically involves a blood transfusion. Literally, the blood in their bodies would be drained away and new blood would be transfused into their bodies, then their chances of survival would be very high.'

For the first time that morning, Ama looked hopeful.

She got home that evening feeling very tired and drained. She put the twins to sleep and checked their temperature by placing the back of her hand on their necks and bodies. Satisfied, she turned the lights out and went into the adjoining bathroom. She blocked the plughole and turned on the tap. As the water ran, she poured some liquid soap into the bath and watched as clear, bright, scently foam covered the surface of the water. She turned off the tap after a while and wrapped her hair with a white fluffy towel. She removed her clothes and gingerly stepped into the bath. She felt her tense muscles relax as her whole body was fully soaked in the warm bubble bath. Within minutes, she had dozed off.

Thirty minutes later, she was woken up by the shrill of the telephone. She quickly jumped out of the bath and put on her bath robe. She was surprised that she could actually dose off in the bath. She ran to the bedroom and picked up the telephone.

'Hello, this is the Adeogun's residence,' she said yawning.

'What's wrong with my sons?' asked Leke without any preamble; his voice was very hoarse.

'They've been very sick. The doctor told me they need to have an operation–'

'What exactly is wrong with them?' Leke cut in; he was alarmed.

'They have sickle cell anaemia; the doctor said–'

'I'm on my way home,' said Leke and the line went dead. Ama looked at the telephone receiver for a considerable time before gently replacing it on the cradle. Leke had only asked after the children. He had not bothered to ask her how she had coped with them since morning; he had only been concerned about the kids. Ama knew that if Leke had his way, he would not utter a word to her at all. *Where had her loving husband gone?* She desperately wanted her husband back. She sat on the bed and tried to remember when their marriage began to hit the rocks. Her mind told her it was the moment she gave birth to Nike. Nike had come and stolen her husband's love from her; Nike had come and she had lost her position in Leke's heart; she had lost her marriage and the love of her husband and more importantly, she had lost her right as the prospective queen of Illudun land. She hated Nike with a raw passion.

Ama fell asleep on the huge bed beside her sons and dreamt of Iludun land. She saw herself presenting her babies to King Oba Adeogun. She was dressed as a queen and she had a crown on her head. She had on elegant purple attire and she had royal beads on her neck. Leke was holding her hand and smiling at her. He was dressed like a king. Her boys were looking radiant. Suddenly, the king lifted his crown from his head and as he was about to place it on Leke's head, Ama woke up to the loud shrill of the bell.

Leke pressed the bell for the fifteenth time. Because he had been unable to speak with Ama on the telephone back in the United States, he had packed his belongings in a hurry and had forgotten to take his set of keys from his apartment in the United States. As he was about to press the bell for the sixteenth time, Ama opened the door.

'I'm so sorry I did not hear the bell,' she said but Leke did not answer her. He brushed past her and ran upstairs to the room the twins usually slept in. He did not see them in there. He ran to the bedroom he still shared with Ama and found the kids deeply asleep on the huge bed. He rushed to them, picked one of them and hugged him to his bosom; with the other hand, he picked the other twin; but he had a feeling that something was amiss. Neither of the twins had made a sound. He quickly put the second twin on the bed and placed a hand on the body of the first twin. It felt cold. Alarmed, he looked down at the other twin and placed a hand on his forehead. It was very cold. One after the other, he felt their pulses; there were none. He knew that the inevitable had happened; he did not need a doctor's confirmation. His experience with the red-cross during his national service year in Nigeria was enough for him to know what had happened to his lovely sons.

Ama sensed something wrong and rushed to where Leke stood, holding one of the twins in one arm, while his other hand was placed on the arm of the other twin. Leke turned to look at Ama for a long time before he uttered his first sentence since he came in that morning.

'Our sons are dead.'

Ama knew what that meant.

Our marriage is over.

Ama screamed and she was soon engulfed in a black cloud.

Chapter 10

Blueberry Secondary School, Nigeria, West Africa

'Attention everybody! Attention everybody! The attention of Miss Nike Adeogun is needed at the school reception. The attention of Miss Nike Adeogun is needed at the school reception please!'

Nike listened to the announcement once again.

'Miss Nike Adeogun, please report to the school reception urgently,' came the announcement again.

Nike dropped the book she was reading on the floor. She was seated on a pavement at the back of the girls' dormitory in the school. The back of the dormitory had been her secret library for some months now. Any time she wanted to get away from the hassles of the other students, the pavement at back of the girls' dormitory became her place of solitude. There, she could read her books without being disturbed. She knew without a doubt that for her to have been called through the public address system, something very serious had happened. But she could not decipher what was in the offing. She picked up her book from the floor and ran towards the school reception.

She got to the reception, panting heavily. A man was standing before the receptionist; his back was turned to the door. Nike needed no one to tell her that the man standing with his back turned to her was her father.

'Daddy!' she exclaimed and ran to him. Her father turned around and scooped her up in a warm embrace. 'Oh, Daddy,' said Nike. 'Daddy, I'm so glad to see you; what a great surprise... I mean it's not holiday yet,' she finished, still locked in an embrace with her dad. She was, however, worried about her dad. She knew without being told that something was definitely wrong. Her daddy's face looked drawn and he looked very emaciated.

'I'm glad to see you too, Nike; I'm really glad to set my eyes on you,' said Leke. He was not aware that he was holding onto Nike too tightly until Nike spoke again.

'Is something wrong, Daddy?' asked Nike; she was terrified. Fear and sadness were boldly written on her daddy's face; that was very much unlike her strong, jovial daddy. Leke breathed in heavily, then he looked down at

Nike and said tersely, 'Nike, I need to talk to you privately. I've already taken permission from the school to excuse you for the day. Let's get out of here.'

'Alright Dad,' said Nike. She turned and waved at the school receptionist, who had been watching the whole scenario with keen interest, then she followed her dad out of the reception.

They got to The Grand Hotel and this time, Leke paid for just one room and ordered some food and soft drinks.

'You will be going back to school today,' he explained as he sat down tiredly on the two-seater leather sofa placed adjacent to the bed. He removed his tie and rested his head on the head rest. He soon closed his eyes and after a few minutes, Nike thought her father was asleep. She went over to where he sat and shook him.

'Dad, what exactly is the matter? You've been sad and a little quiet all day,' she said.

Leke opened his eyes; he looked very tired. He looked at Nike for a few seconds then, with his right hand, he motioned for Nike to sit beside him. Nike sat beside her father.

'Nike, although you'll forever be my baby, I wish to let you know that you're no longer a kid,' Leke began and Nike nodded anxiously. Leke continued, 'Something terrible happened back in England and I wish to tell you in person; that's why I had to fly all the way here to see you.'

'What happened, Dad?' asked Nike. She was really alarmed; she was very afraid.

'The twins are dead!' said Leke flatly.

'What? The Twins? Dead?' said Nike. She buried her face in her hands as hot tears began to trickle down her face. She was not very close to the twins; the circumstances between her mother and herself had prevented her from getting close to her brothers, but they were her brothers anyway, and she had loved them dearly. More importantly, they were her father's kids, and they had been family to her. Now that they were dead, the only person she could actually call family was her father. Her mother had never written her a single word since she came to school in Africa. All her letters to her had not been replied, and whenever she had asked after her, her father had always given a vague reply. She knew that there was no love lost between them and over the years, she had stopped asking after her mum.

Leke placed his hand across his daughter's shoulders and pulled her to himself; and they cried together. In the midst of their sobs, Leke briefly explained to Nike how the twins died. He told her the autopsy report which determined that, although the twins had had sickle cell anaemia, the direct cause of their death had been an overdose of painkillers. He explained to her that the twins had initially been given some medications which Ama had not disclosed to the doctor; and the medication had reacted with the doctor's treatment. The twins had gone into a coma in the middle of the night and they had died before Leke got back to the house in the morning. In his narration, Leke deliberately omitted how Ama had subsequently been arrested and charged with manslaughter. He did not tell her how he had spent so much money to hire a lawyer, who fought tooth and nail to get Ama off the hook. Ama had eventually been acquitted because the lawyer had been able to prove beyond all reasonable doubt, that Ama had suffered temporary insanity resulting from her childhood trauma, marital problems and the twins' poor health. The lawyer was able to establish and convince the court that Ama had not deliberately killed her children. Ama was discharged and acquitted; but she was also referred to a mental home for medical treatment.

Leke felt that the death of the twins was enough bad news for a girl of thirteen; telling her that her mother had been taken to a mental home might be too much for her to bear. However, he decided to break one more piece of sad news to her. He felt she deserved to know; at lease for posterity's sake.

'Nike, I want you to know that…' Leke began. Suddenly, the doorbell rang. Leke quickly dried his face with a handkerchief and went to answer the door.

'Room service,' said the waiter who was carrying a big tray with covered dishes and soft drinks. Leke collected the tray of food from him, said thanks and closed the door.

'You must be starving,' he said to Nike who was still sobbing. He opened a can of soft drink and gave it to her. She took a sip and put the can down.

'I don't want to eat,' she said as Leke opened a dish of fried rice. 'I'm not hungry.' Leke understood her lack of appetite. He did not feel hungry himself, so he covered the dish with the lid. He went back to sit beside Nike and took both of her hands in both of his.

'Stop crying my child,' he said as he took a napkin and wiped tears off her face.

'There's something I wish to tell you Nike… Your mother and I are getting a divorce!' said Leke tersely; he was holding his breath. Nike stopped crying immediately. She raised her eyes and looked at her dad.

'Is that what you really want, Dad?' she asked.

'That's what I really want,' said Leke, exhaling deeply. 'I'm sure I'll be better off without her in my life.'

Nike agreed with her dad completely. She thought they should have got divorced sooner. She would stick with her dad whatever decision he took as long as he was happy with it. She put her hands around her father's neck and kissed him on the cheek.

'I'm with you, Dad; whatever decision you take, I'm with you all the way!' she said.

Leke left the hotel early the following morning. His flight back to the United Kingdom was scheduled for 10a.m. He checked his watch as he drove out of the hotel premises. He had two hours before he was due to check in at the airport, but he had a dilemma. The car he was driving was a hired one and he was expected to return it to the car hire service before heading for the airport. He made a mental calculation of the time it would take him to get to the company and he decided that it would take him roughly one hour, thirty minutes, taking into consideration the heavy traffic hold-up peculiar to Lagos roads. He pressed on the car accelerator and increased his speed; he did not want to miss his flight. As he manoeuvred a bend, a trailer carrying several logs of wood appeared before him. It was coming from the opposite direction at top speed, and then it swerved to the lane where Leke was. Leke saw it and quickly pressed on the brake; but he was too late; his speed was too high to accommodate the sudden brake. The lorry rammed into his small car head on, making Leke's car stop abruptly. This forced the car travelling behind Leke to crash into his car from the back. The resultant effect was a series of cars crashing into one another, thereby causing a bloody jam. In the ensuing chaos, onlookers looked in horror as glass splinters flew in all directions. Ambulance crews were called to the scene and immediately, the paramedics set to work. As dead bodies were pulled out of some cars, several casualties were taken into ambulances and driven straight to hospital. When the paramedics got to Leke's car, they found that the car door did not need to be opened. The door was already severed from the body of the totally crumpled car, and Leke was bent over the steering wheel as blood gushed out of his forehead.

Twenty minutes later, Leke Adeogun was pronounced dead at the general hospital.

At the same time Leke Adeogun died, Nike sat in class three of Blueberry secondary school receiving her first lesson for the day. She sat in the front row as usual and pretended to listen to the teacher as he explained Newton's laws of motion.

Nike appeared to be paying attention to what the teacher was saying but her mind was not in the classroom. Her eyes were totally fixed on the teacher but she was not looking at him; she was looking through him. She saw her dad – her dearly beloved dad – as she had left him in the hotel room the day before and her heart went out to him.

'Poor Dad!' She muttered under her breath; he must be going through *hell*. With the twins now gone, she knew that her mum would try her very best to make life a living hell for her dad. She was glad that her dad had finally

made a decision to divorce her mother; she felt it was the best decision her dad had ever made.

But what would become of you? a voice within her asked. She immediately shelved the question. There was no question of what would become of her. She knew without a doubt that her father would make adequate provision for her. Her father would make sure she never lacked anything. Her future was secure as far as funds were concerned. Her father loved her dearly and she knew it.

Just then, the school porter came into the classroom. He walked straight to the teacher and whispered in his ear then he went out as quietly as he had come in. The teacher cleared his throat and called Nike's name. Hearing her name being called brought back Nike from her musing. She stood up on impulse and said 'Here sir!' She had no inkling of why the teacher had singled her out of the whole class. She hoped that the teacher had not noticed that she was not concentrating on the lecture.

The teacher looked at Nike with pity and he told her to go and see the principal immediately.

'Yes sir!' said Nike as she dashed out of the classroom. *Maybe her father had come back to her*, she thought. Maybe he had come to discuss her future with her. She got to the principal's office and she was motioned to have a seat.

'I'm sorry to announce that your father is dead, Nike,' the principal said flatly. 'He died this morning in a car accident along the expressway.'

'No!' shouted Nike. She stood up from her chair. 'My father's not dead. My father cannot die. I saw him yesterday, and he promised to come back to see me. Maybe you're mistaken sir. It was my twin brothers who died and not my father. My father came to give me the news yesterday…' Nike rambled on.

'Calm down, Nike. Calm down,' said the principal. He stood up and came to where Nike stood; then he gently took her hands and covered them with his. 'I know the news must be a great shock to you. But I must let you know that your father died on his way to the airport this morning. The hospital authorities were able to contact the school because they saw a card with your name and school boldly written on it in his breast pocket. Since you both bear the same surname, they assumed you must be his relation. That was why they sent someone to the school to inform me.'

Nike wished she was dreaming. She closed her eyes and willed herself to wake up from this nightmare. She imagined that she was still in the class, receiving a physics lecture. She imagined that the principal standing before her and telling her that her father had passed away was not real; she imagined it was all a farce; the mist would blow away and she would be told that her dad was still alive and not dead. When she opened her eyes, the principal had not disappeared; he was looking at her with an expression of concern.

'I'm so sorry, Nike, but you know, sometimes life's like that – very unpredictable,' said the Principal and Nike knew that what was happening was real. It was not a farce and her beloved dad was truly dead. She felt herself shivering; her head felt very heavy and she thought it would fall off her neck. Her legs suddenly felt too light to withstand her weight and they wobbled. The principal was quick to support her. She fell into his arms and lost consciousness.

Two days after Nike went into a coma, she woke up on a hospital bed. Everywhere was strange to her; she felt dizzy and she thought she was in a haze. She closed her eyes and slowly opened them again. Her view became clearer. She noticed that she was not alone in the room; someone was with her. He was seated on a chair beside her and he was reading a book. As if by telepathy, her companion looked at her and their eyes met. He was none other than Tokunboh Martins – the incumbent head boy of Blueberry secondary school.

'You're awake, Nike. You're awake. Oh! I'm so glad you're awake,' whispered Tokunboh excitedly. He got up from his chair and knelt beside her. 'I've been praying for you ever since you were hospitalised. Are you okay? Are you hungry? Shall I call the doctor?' he asked her in his excitement. But Nike did not answer. After a while, she gave him a very faint smile and drifted back to sleep.

Tokunboh got up and ran out of the room. On his way to the doctor's office, he bumped into a nurse.

'Sister, sister,' he cried, 'she's awake. She's awake.'

'Who's awake?' asked the nurse confusedly.

'Nike Adeogun, the girl from Blueberry secondary school.'

'Oh! That must be the girl in ward 2,' said the nurse and she ran to Nike's room with Tokunboh trailing behind her excitedly.

The nurse met Nike sleeping. She removed her stethoscope from around her neck and placed it on Nike's chest. There was a ray of hope in her expression. Next, she pressed her fingers to Nike's wrists and, at the same time, she placed the stethoscope on her neck. After a little time, she replaced the stethoscope around her neck. She gave a sigh and turned to Tokunboh who was anxiously waiting for what the nurse had to say. The nurse smiled warmly at Tokunboh before asking him, 'What are you to the lady? A brother?'

'No I... I... er,' stammered Tokunboh before he replied carefully, 'I'm just a friend.' He hoped to high heavens that he was able to mask the love he harboured in his heart for Nike. It was supposed to be secret. Love affairs and boy-girl relationships were totally forbidden by the school and if authorities in the school got wind of such activities, the students involved would be expelled. Tokunboh did not want any trouble for himself but he would always put his life down to protect Nike – that was the kind of love he had for her. So, as he replied the nurse, he tried to make his expression void of any emotion.

The nurse smiled and winked at Tokunboh before saying, 'If you're just a friend to her, then you must be a very special friend. I hope she realises this when she wakes up.' Then she walked out of the ward.

Tokunboh always made it a point of duty to bring food, chocolates and fresh flowers for Nike after school every day after she was admitted into the hospital. The cooked food normally went untouched and was eventually thrown away by the hospital staff. The chocolates, however, were kept on a table beside Nike's bed, while the flowers withered away without Nike having an opportunity to admire or perceive their fine scent. This did not deter Tokunboh from bringing Nike more food and chocolates and more fresh flowers each time he came around.

The day after Nike woke up from her coma, Tokunboh went to the hospital with a basket full of food and chocolates and, of course, a bunch of fresh flowers. He knelt beside Nike's bed as he usually did and brought the flowers to her nostrils.

'I know you can hear me, my love,' he said with deep emotion, 'I know deep down inside me that you can hear me. I've brought you fresh flowers again today; and I'll be the happiest person on earth if you can savour the scent of these flowers and open your eyes. My love, I wish above all things that you would open your eyes and look at me now.'

As if by magic, at that instant, Nike's eyelids flew open. She gazed into Tokunboh's eyes as she struggled for her vision to be focused. There was a haze all over the room and around Tokunboh as she opened her eyes, making her vision blurred. The haze gradually disappeared and she was able to make out Tokunboh's features. When her vision steadied, she recognised Tokunboh instantly and she gave him a weak smile. She tried to broaden her smile to show him that she appreciated his visit, but her muscles were tense and she was so tired, she only managed to retain the weakest of all smiles. But Tokunboh was happy with it. He beamed and clasped her hands in his.

'Oh I love you, Nike. I'm very glad you're alive. Today, you've made me the happiest person on earth… Now talk to me; tell me you love me.'

Nike opened her mouth and the first sentence she uttered in three days was, 'I'm hungry.' The words were so faint; Tokunboh had to read her lips to hear them. He got up immediately and served her a meal of curry rice that he had brought for her. Nike took a spoon from the basket and struggled to scoop rice into it. She had been fed intravenously since she came to the hospital. The drip had been attached to her right hand and being a right-handed person, she was finding it difficult to feed herself. Tokunboh noticed this and took the spoon from her. He gave her the first spoon of rice – her first spoon of real food in many days– and watched her eat it slowly; then he pierced a sachet of lucozade drink with a straw and offered it to her. She took a sip and shook her head in the negative when he prompted her to have some more. Tokunboh scooped some more rice with the spoon and as he took it to Nike's mouth, the nurse he had seen the day before entered the ward; this time with a doctor. The nurse cleared her throat and winked at Tokunboh again before saying jovially, 'young man, you must be a very friendly friend to the lady, I must say. You truly deserve every degree of love the lady has to offer.'

Tokunboh laughed cheerily and the doctor grinned but Nike looked confused; she did not understand what the nurse meant by her statement. Reading her expression, the nurse went over to Nike and, patting her gently on her shoulder, said to her, 'this young man has been with you every single day since you came here. If my husband had been half as nice as he is, I would not have left him.'

The next morning, before lessons began, Tokunboh went to see Nike at the hospital. This time there was a simple note stuck in the bunch of flowers he brought. He saw Nike sleeping peacefully on the bed. He tiptoed towards her and gently placed the bunch of flowers beside her. He looked around to ensure that no one else was in the room and gave her a warm kiss on the lips.

'Welcome back to this bright happy world,' he whispered before he quietly left the room. When he got to the door, he hesitated, turned around and blew the still-sleeping Nike a silent kiss before he closed the door behind him.

Nike woke up to the fine aroma of roses and orchids. She picked up the flowers and put them to her nostrils. She smiled happily as she savoured the nice scent. Suddenly, a little note dropped from the bunch of flowers in her hand and she hastily picked it up.

It read:

Get well soon,
We have a whole life ahead of us.
Love
Toks.

Warm tears sprang to her eyes as she read the note over and over again. She felt the deep love Tokunboh had for her oozing out of the wordings of the note. Even though her dad had unexpectedly passed onto the world beyond, fate had brought her much love through Tokunboh Martins. However, the loyalty she had for her dad made her resolve never to return Tokunboh's love. Although her dad was no more, she still felt fiercely attached to him. She did not want anything to come between her and her dad. She knew that wherever her dad was, he still loved her deeply and she would not allow another man's love come in between what she shared with her beloved dad.

Nike was discharged from the hospital five days after she was hospitalised. Tokunboh came with the school driver in the school van to take her back to the school.

'Hey sunshine,' he said to her. 'You're leaving this place today which makes it the second best day of my life,' he finished and chuckled; then he looked at Nike who had a puzzled expression, and asked her seriously, 'Do you know the best day of my life?'

Nike shook her head in the negative. Tokunboh looked into her eyes and held her hand gently before saying with all sincerity, 'It was the day I met you!'

Nike was deeply touched; she smiled at Tokunboh albeit uncomfortably. She knew that Tokunboh had been there for her in her time of need. He had gone a long way to prove his love for her and she was about to deny him that love. She knew she owed Tokunboh so much but she remembered her dad's wish for her not to get involved in any love affair and she was not about to disobey her dad even in death.

The driver dropped her at the principal's office and Tokunbo went with her to see the principal.

'You're very much welcome back to the world,' said the principal to Nike as soon as they entered his office.

'Thank you, sir,' said Nike respectfully.

'It's alright,' said the principal and then he went on. 'In spite of the fact that the doctor has certified you well enough to attend lessons, I want to give you three days rest before you actually start attending classes.' The principal smiled warmly at Tokunboh and continued, 'Young Mr Martins here has promised to help you with your studies towards the up-coming examinations should there be a need. We have made photocopies of all the lessons you missed while at the hospital.'

'Thank you, sir,' said Nike again.

'You may leave now,' said the principal.

Three days later, Nike started classes in earnest and Tokunboh was on hand to make sure she adjusted well with her lessons. They usually studied together after school hours and Tokunboh was always eager to explain things to her. Soon, they were as inseparable as two peas in a pod. Some students became friendlier to them while other students began sniggering at them. There was a particular student in the school whose name was Tunde Oka. Tunde Oka was known in the school as a truant and the school thug, whose only grace for remaining in the school were the numerous *largesse* the principal constantly received from his father. Tunde Oka knew that the principal secretly took bribes from his father, and he would always use this as an advantage to ensure he remained in the school for as long as he so wished.

Tunde Oka particularly hated Tokunboh Martins for various reasons. Tokunboh was everything he wished he were; Tokunboh was handsome; he was from a very wealthy background and most importantly, he had the friendship of the most beautiful girl in the school; he had the friendship of Nike Adeogun who had politely rebuffed his own friendly gestures on several occasions. Each time Tunde Oka saw Tokunboh with Nike, it took all his resilience not to strike them dead. However, neither Tokunboh nor Nike knew that they had an enemy that nobody ever wished to have.

On their way back from the school library late one Saturday evening, Nike decided to tell Tokunboh what had been on her mind since she left the hospital.

'Tokunboh,' she began, 'you know I appreciate all that you've done for me, don't you?'

Tokunboh nodded quietly; his heart was beating fast. He sensed the discomfort that Nike felt as she spoke. He hoped she was not about to tell him that their friendship was over; he hoped she was not about to tell him that his life was over.

'Well Tokunboh, well…' said Nike as she looked into Tokunboh's eyes almost pleadingly.

Tokunboh was silent; he wanted Nike to say whatever it was that was bothering her without him interfering.

'Well you see, Tokunboh,' said Nike again, and then she continued with obvious difficulty, '…Well, I just want you to know that I'm still morning my father's death and I would like to keep his memory living. I am not ready to go into a relationship with you or with any other person.'

Tokunboh closed his eyes for a moment to keep back the tears that were threatening to well up in them. After a while, he opened his eyes and took Nike's right hand in his. He sighed deeply before saying with all sincerity, 'I love you very much, Nike, and I promise never to hurt you in any way. I know that your father's death has created a void in you. Please let me fill that void; let me make you happy again.'

Nike was moved to tears by the display of affection, but she was adamant in her decision. Tokunboh saw this in her expression and said to her, 'I've got plans for us, Nike. I'll study to become a medical doctor; I'll be a plastic surgeon and I'm going to make lots of money working on celebrities overseas. I'm going to build you a mansion and buy you the most expensive cars and jewelleries. We'll have lots and lots of kids and we'll be happy forever… I promise you nothing but happiness, Nike; believe me. Just give me a chance to prove myself,' Tokunboh finished, desperately searching her eyes for an emotion that might give him a flicker of hope.

Nike looked away from him; she did not want to betray any emotions in Tokunboh's presence. She knew deep within her that she had fallen in love with him; she fell in love with him the day he fed her at the hospital. But what would her father have said?

Her father's image suddenly flashed in her mind's eye and she remembered her promise to her father. She looked at Tokunboh as hot tears fell freely from her eyes.

'I'm sorry, Tokunboh,' she said tearfully. 'I'm afraid I can't.' And with that, she left Tokunboh and walked slowly to her dormitory.

Tokunboh watched her walk away and that day became a very sad day for him; Nike had just told him his life was over!

Chapter 11

The examinations came and went. The results came out and Nike was promoted to class four. Meanwhile, Tokunboh had written his General Certificate Examination and passed with flying colours. Officially, he was a graduate of Blueberry Secondary school.

One of the regulations of the Blueberry secondary school was that school fees, along with the boarding fees for a session, had to be paid at the last term of the previous session immediately after the examinations and before the holidays began.

A day before the school went on the official holiday, Nike was summoned to the principal's office.

'I'm afraid you're the only student in the entire school whose school and boarding fees have not been paid,' said the principal to Nike as soon as she took a seat opposite him.

Nike buried her head in her hands. This subject had been bothering her since her father death; she was only hoping that, one way or the other, her mother would shoulder the responsibility of taking care of her schooling; at least till she graduated from the secondary school. Her mother had not called her since her father died two months before; neither had she replied to her letters.

She looked up at the principal. The principal started leafing through the sheets of papers on his table as he spoke again. 'As you are well aware, Miss Adeogun, the law of the school stipulates that if a student fails to pay the school the full amount of levy before the stipulated time, the student in question must leave the school.' He let that sink in, and then he continued, 'In view of the recent sad occurrences, the school authorities have decided to give you two weeks to pay your fees. The school bursar will be around to attend to you when the holidays begin. In the event of you not being able to pay the required fees, you shall have to leave the school.'

Nike nodded slowly before saying, 'I wish to express my profound gratitude, sir, for the two weeks of grace given to me to pay up and I promise to do so before the end of the two-week period.'

'Good,' said the principal. 'You may now leave.'

As Nike left the principal's office, her legs seemed to wobble. She held onto a chair to steady herself before walking out of the office.

'Poor girl,' said the principal sympathetically. He would have helped her personally, but he had a large family to feed; although the salary he received as the principal of the prestigious Blueberry private secondary school was quite huge, it was a meagre sum when it came to the upkeep of his three wives and sixteen children. That was why he secretly took bribes from the parents of some students who needed one favour or the other from him. He had always defended his actions by reasoning that all the bribes he took were meant to augment his salary.

When Nike left the office of the principal, she headed straight to the girls' dormitory.

'When are you going home, Nike?' asked Belinda who was her bunk mate. Nike did not have a home, at least not in Nigeria since her father's demise. She did not have any money to rent a hotel as her father used to do in those days and she did not have money to travel back to the United Kingdom. She was dead broke, *as broke as a church rat*, they say. But she was not prepared to bare her burdens for all to see.

'I'll be going home tomorrow,' she lied.

'But all other students are leaving today. The school will officially close for holiday tomorrow and not a single soul will be in the dormitory; it's better you pack your things and leave with the rest of us today,' Belinda cajoled. But Nike shook her head and forced a smile to her lips.

'I'll go home tomorrow; there are a few things I'd like to put in place before I leave.'

'Okay, suit yourself,' said Belinda as she moved to the wardrobe to pack the remaining of her belongings.

When all the girls had gone, Nike got up from her bunk and wandered outside the dormitory. She strolled aimlessly around the nearly deserted school for a while then, feeling tired, she went to sit on the pavement surrounding the school library.

At that moment, Tokunboh came out of the library. He had packed his bags and gone home the previous day, but then he had come back to do some reading at the library. Since Nike declined his *proposal*, he had seen very little of her. He oftentimes felt that she was deliberately avoiding him. The few times he had the opportunity to glimpse her were either during the morning assembly, when no one was allowed to speak to one another except teachers, or when he walked past her classroom whenever she was receiving lectures. Now he was surprised to see her around when other students were no longer in the school premises; and she was sitting on a pavement, obviously deep in thought.

'Nike,' he called out to her.

Nike jumped; she came back to the present and hastily stood up.

'Hi Tokunboh,' she said, feeling sheepish. 'I didn't know you were still around.'

'That's because you never cared to know,' he replied gently, the love he still felt for Nike shining through his eyes. Nike slowly directed her gaze to the ground. With his right thumb and forefingers, Tokunboh gently raised her chin so that she looked at him.

'Why are you still in school, Nike?' he asked her gently.

Nike was silent for a while; her mind raced as she searched it for what to say.

'Well I... I... er,' she stammered.

'Don't lie to me, Nike,' said Tokunboh painfully. 'Why are you still around?'

Nike decided to tell the truth, 'Because I have no money to go home!'

'Where is your home?' Tokunboh asked with concern.

'In the United Kingdom.'

'And your mum – why hasn't she sent for you?'

There was no point telling lies to cover her mother's uncaring attitude.

'I don't know. I've not heard from her since... since my father died,' replied Nike sincerely. Tokunboh looked at her for a while and then he asked the question that popped into his mind when Nike said she had not heard from her mother since her dad's demise.

'Have your school fees been paid, Nike?'

Nike was silent.

'Tell me the truth,' demanded Tokunboh. 'Have your school fees been paid?'

Nike shook her head and burst into tears. Tokunboh dropped the books he was holding on the floor and took her in a warm embrace.

'Sshh, baby sshh,' he said. 'I'll sort you out.' After a while, he looked at Nike, dried her tears with his hands and said to her, 'Let's go,' as he bent down to pick up his books.

'Let's go where?' asked Nike confusedly.

'Let's go to my house,' said Tokunboh as he pulled her along.

'B... but I can't go to your house,' said Nike fearfully. 'What about your parents?'

'My parents are fine,' replied Tokunboh. 'My father's the nicest human being on earth. You will like him; you'll see,' Tokunboh finished reassuringly. But Nike still hesitated.

'What about your mother?' she asked.

'My mother has no choice than to obey my father. She's very submissive to my dad. Whatever my dad says in the house holds water.'

Tokunboh followed Nike to the girl's dormitory and stood outside the building while Nike went in to pack her belongings. When she came outside, Tokunboh picked up her two bags and they headed towards the school gate.

When they got to the entrance of the school, Tokunboh flagged down a taxi.

'Could you please take us to the Martins Villa?' he asked the cab man briskly. The cabman nodded and asked them to enter the taxi. There was no one in Lagos who did not know the location of the huge mansion called the 'Martins Villa'. However, only a privileged few were allowed in. He wondered what these two young people were going there for. He demanded his fare as they were settled in his car and Tokunboh promptly paid the amount which Nike considered a little exorbitant for a taxi ride. She wondered how Tokunboh could have paid so much money without blinking an eyelid.

The taxi man dropped them in front of the Matins Villa in Victoria Island and sped off.

Tokunboh carried Nike's bag to the main gate. Nike followed him hesitantly.

'What are we doing here, Tokunboh?' asked Nike fearfully. 'I mean this is supposed to be the house of the Nigerian Petroleum minister. What are we doing in the house of the petroleum minister, Tokunboh?'

'You wait and see,' Tokunboh replied teasingly. He dipped his hand into the breast pocket of his shirt and brought out a plastic card. This, he slotted into a hole on the side of the huge gate. The gate opened immediately. Nike stood stupefied. She had never seen a house as big and as beautiful in her life.

'Come on,' urged Tokunboh laughingly. 'I want you to meet my parents. We haven't got the whole day.' When he saw that Nike was reluctant to go into the compound with him, he took her hand and pulled her in.

Once inside the compound, a uniformed guard stood to attention and gave Tokunboh a salute. Nike was more than impressed – she was flabbergasted. She began to suspect that Tokunboh was the son of the renowned Nigerian minister of petroleum. If that was the case, Tokunboh must be swimming in *pure, natural wealth*! She should have guessed all along; Tokunboh was posh and cool and collected and he shared a surname with the Petroleum minister. She should have known all these years.

Dummy! she chided herself silently.

'Hello Ali,' Tokunboh greeted the guard cheerfully. 'How are you today?' he asked him.

'I'm fine thank you, sir!' replied the guard as he took Nike's bags from Tokunboh.

'Is Daddy in?' Tokunboh asked him.

'Yes sir!' replied the guard as he handed Nike's bags to a servant who had come out to greet Tokunboh and his guest.

Nike marvelled as she was led into the fully air-conditioned house. They came into a big sitting room and Tokunboh asked her to sit while he went upstairs to call his parents.

Nike sat awkwardly in one of the huge black leather sofas in the obviously expensively decorated sitting room. Tokunboh laughed and told her to relax. 'No one is going to swallow you up here. My family is a friendly one,' he said as he ran up the staircase leading to his parent's private sitting room.

Nike tried to relax but she couldn't. She shifted to the edge of the huge sofa and looked around the sitting room. There was only one picture hanging on the wall of the sitting room and it was placed directly opposite her; it was the picture of Tokunboh. In the picture, Tokunboh wore a dark blue suit and a bow tie. He looked so handsome and mature the way he posed in the picture and he seemed to be smiling down at her. Her heart swelled with pride with the thought that Tokunboh had chosen her to be his girlfriend despite his handsomeness and wealthy family.

Just then, Tokunboh came down the stairs with his parents in tow. Nike got up and curtsied to Tokunboh's parents by kneeling in front of them in the *Yoruba* traditional way.

Tokunboh's father pulled Nike up and hugged her. Nike liked him instantly. Tokunboh had been right about his dad. Sir Fola Martins, the honourable minister of petroleum in Nigeria, was indeed a very pleasant man.

'You are very much welcome to our home,' said Sir Fola Martins as he released Nike from his embrace.

'Thank you very much, sir,' said Nike. 'I feel honoured to be let into your presence.'

'Oh that's okay, my dear,' said Sir Martins carefreely and then he said, 'Please meet my lovely wife, Mrs Yetunde Martins.'

'I'm pleased to meet you madam,' said Nike respectfully, but she got no reply. Mrs Martins managed a stiff smile and nodded curtly at her.

Nike felt terrified. Mrs Martins was indeed a tall, lovely woman and Nike immediately saw in her where Tokunboh had got his beauty from; but she was certain that the woman had no liking for her.

'Dad, Nike will be staying with us till she goes back home,' Tokunboh informed his father.

'That's alright with me,' said his father.

'And where is her home,' asked Mrs Martins, speaking for the first time since she saw Nike.

'She lives in the United Kingdom with her mum; but after the demise of her father, she has been in a slight financial difficulty. That's why I have requested Dad to finance her studies till she leaves school.'

'I see,' said Mrs Martins coolly.

'There should be no problem with that, my dear,' said Sir Fola Martins to Nike. 'Tokunboh has explained your situation to me and I am ready to finance your education to any level.'

Nike was overjoyed; she could not believe her luck.

'Thank you very much, sir,' she said. 'I really appreciate your help, sir,' and as an after thought, she turned to Mrs Martins and said to her, 'Thank you very much, madam. I'm very grateful.'

Mrs Martins only nodded coolly and gave Nike a scornful look.

'Toks, my dear, remind me later to arrange a travel ticket to the United Kingdom for your friend,' Sir Fola Martins said to Tokunboh.

'Thanks a lot, Dad,' said Tokunboh to his dad happily. 'I love you, Dad; you're the best.'

'That's alright. Now I want you to feel at home and make yourself happy. My wife and I are due to attend a political gathering in thirty minutes,' Sir Fola Martins said to Nike and he moved towards the exit of the house. His wife followed in his wake, but not before she gave Nike a frighteningly cold stare.

'See, I told you they'll accept you right away,' declared Tokunboh excitedly.

Nike hesitated, then she said to Tokunboh, 'your dad likes me but I'm not quite certain your mum does.'

'Forget about my mum; she can be fussy at times but, as I told you earlier, it's whatever my dad decides that becomes the law in this house. Besides, give my mum some time; when she sees that you're such a nice and intelligent girl, she'll come round and you two will be the best of friends.'

At two o'clock in the afternoon, a servant came and announced that lunch was ready.

'Thank you, Salome,' said Tokunboh to the servant, then he pulled Nike to her feet.

They had lunch on the patio. Nike could not remember when last she had such a sumptuous meal. They had baked vegetables with creamed prawns for starters. Afterwards, they were served fried rice and grilled chicken with *moin-moin* on the side as the main course. The desert was fruit salad topped with ice-cream. After the meal, Nike felt so full, she thought she might not be able to get up from her seat.

'Get up, lazy bones,' Tokunboh told her playfully. 'I want to show you around the house; I want you to be familiar with the house we will eventually live in as a husband and his wife in the very near future.'

Nike poked him in the ribs playfully. 'Whatever gave you the impression that I want to be your wife,' she said.

Tokunboh's expression suddenly got serious.

'I will marry you, Nike,' he said simply.

'Is that a proposal?' asked Nike. She felt they were both too young to be engaged in this kind of love game.

'It's not a proposal yet,' Tokunboh told her. 'It's an affirmation.'

Nike felt uncomfortable with the discussion. 'Tokunboh,' she began earnestly, 'I really don't feel the time is ripe for us to go into a serious relationship; I mean, you're just fifteen and I am barely fourteen years old. Don't you think that we're rushing things? You might meet another girl when you're a bit older and get over the crush you have for me.'

Tokunboh tilted her face to meet his before saying, 'Read my lips, Nike; I promise you this day, that I will never love anyone else but you. What I feel for you is a deep and unending love and not a crush. I've had my own share of girls before I met you – many girls have thrown themselves at me – but since I could read my a, b, c, I must confess that I have never felt this way with any other girl. I love you Nike and don't you ever forget that.'

Nike remained silent; she was overwhelmed by Tokunboh's profession of love. She felt a warm sensation rising up within her. It was a nice feeling. Tokunboh decided to change the subject. It would be better if he gave her time. He understood her indecision; her late father had justifiably warned her against the wiles of men. It would take him a long while to convince her that he was different from other men as far as Nike was concerned and he was prepared to wait.

'Come on, let me show you round the house,' he said as he took her hand in his. She followed him willingly. Tokunboh showed her around the edifice beginning from the apartment downstairs, which Tokunboh told her he mainly used. One after the other, he showed her every room there; they went to the kitchen, the guest rooms and the computer room. Nike noticed that each room was adequately furnished to match its purpose. She also noticed that all the rooms were tastefully furnished.

'Where are your siblings?' Nike asked curiously.

'I'm an only child,' replied Tokunboh flatly.

'Oh,' said Nike. 'I'm sorry.'

'You shouldn't be; it's not your fault,' Tokunboh replied grinning. Next, they climbed the staircase and Nike was dumbstruck by the sheer opulence that met her. She had never seen a sitting room as big in her life.

'This sitting room is actually reserved for my parents and a few important guests, especially their political friends,' Tokunboh explained. Nike was taken in by the expensive paintings on the wall, the decorations, the scently plants and the beautiful chandeliers and sculptures made from marbles.

'This is beautiful,' Nike said breathlessly.

'Thank you,' said Tokunboh modestly.

Nike loved Tokunboh majorly for one thing; he had everything going for him and he stood to inherit an enormous wealth, yet he was not proud. He always carried himself with modesty. He was definitely not a spoilt little Richie-rich.

Tokunboh led her onto the balcony which overlooked the swimming pool in the compound. The swimming pool was open and rays of sun reflected on the water, making the water glimmer in the bright sunlight. There were beautiful plants and flowers surrounding the swimming pool. Nike could not believe the magic of it. It was indeed a beautiful sight to behold.

'Oh my,' she cried 'Can I see the swimming pool, please?'

'Of course you can,' said Tokunboh as he led her back downstairs.

He handed her a pair of bathroom slippers for more comfort. Nike removed her shoes and slipped them on. Hand in hand, they went outside the house. They walked past the servants' quarters at the back of the building and past the array of expensive cars parked in a shed, towards the swimming pool. There, Nike stooped low and made ripples in the water. Suddenly, she scooped some water with her hand and threw it at Tokunboh playfully. Tokunboh wiped his face with the back of his hand and pretended to be angry. Suddenly, he gave Nike a push. Although, the push was gentle enough, Nike lost her balance anyway and found herself in the pool, struggling to stay on top of the water.

'Naughty boy,' she called out to Tokunboh who was laughing at her. Tokunboh removed his shirt and shoes and joined her in the pool. They laughed and played together in the pool until it was time for dinner.

After dinner, Tokunboh showed Nike to her room and gave her a kiss on her mouth.

'I had such a wonderful day. Thank you, Nike,' he said and left the room.

When Tokunboh had gone, Nike touched her mouth; Tokunboh's mouth had felt so warm against hers that she wished the kiss had lingered.

'That was nice,' she said aloud before laying on the bed.

As she lay on the bed, she thought of Tokunboh; she thought of the happiness he gave her. She thought of all he had done for her and she thought of all his promises to her. But most of all, she thought of the love he had for her. Surely, no other boy would do all that Tokunboh had done for a girl without being in love with her. Even though he was a few rooms away from her, she missed him terribly. She had to restrain herself from going to look for him. She took a pillow and hugged it tightly. She wished Tokunboh was in the room with her. Momentarily, she thought of her father; she was not sure how he would feel if he were seeing her now.

'I can't help it dad; please forgive me,' she said aloud.

She was not sure her father heard her and even if he heard her, she was not certain she had his approval; but one thing she was certain of was that she had fallen hopelessly in love with Tokunboh Martins.

The next morning, Tokunboh came into the room carrying their breakfast tray.

'Wakie, wakie, sleeping beauty,' he said jovially as he entered the room. Nike woke up to the lovely smell of toast, fried eggs, bacon and steaming coffee. When Nike opened her eyes, the sweet aroma of the food suddenly made her hungry. Tokunboh was dressed as a chef; he wore a white apron over his casual shirt and a pair of jeans trousers. He also had a chef's hat on his head and a large spoon in his free hand. As soon as Nike opened her eyes, Tokunboh touched his forehead with the large spoon and made a mock salute. 'May I have the pleasure of personally serving you breakfast, oh my lovely princess?' he declared, laughing. Nike burst into laughter. Tokunboh was indeed an interesting character, she thought. She got up from the bed and gave Tokunboh a kiss on the lips. Tokunboh stood for a while, his expression getting serious, and then he gently laid the breakfast tray on a bedside table before taking Nike in his arms. He bent slowly and gave her a long kiss. Nike enjoyed the kiss; she felt fulfilled. All of a sudden, she realised that her nightwear was slightly open at the top and she quickly hugged it close to herself. Even though, she was in her early teens, her breasts were fully developed and she was not ready to bare them for any man to see.

Tokunboh laughed at her gesture.

'Don't worry, I didn't see anything,' he said teasingly.

Nike poked him in his ribs and ran to the adjoining bathroom.

'Your food is getting cold, madam,' shouted Tokunboh from the bedroom.

'Give me a sec,' said Nike, 'I usually brush my teeth before I eat.'

They had breakfast together in the room. After breakfast, Tokunboh presented Nike with a ticket to the United Kingdom. He also presented her with receipts stating that her school fees had been paid for two sessions running. Nike was overjoyed. 'Thank you, darling,' she said without thinking. 'Thank you very much.'

'Never mind; besides, I'm glad to be your darling,' said Tokunboh grinning.

Nike gave him a funny look. 'Tokunboh you're so naughty. I didn't mean it that way.'

'Really? Then my heart is broken,' said Tokunboh, still grinning. All of a sudden, his expression changed; he drew Nike close to him and they were soon locked in a passionate kiss.

After a while, Tokunboh's mother's image flashed through Nike's mind. She remembered the cold stare Mrs Martins gave her the day before and she pushed Tokunboh away from her.

'What's the matter?' asked Tokunboh concernedly.

'Y… your mum,' stammered Nike.

'My parents travelled to Abu Dhabi this morning. My father has official matters to discuss with some business associates there, and he requested that my mum followed him. From what I gathered, they will be there for a week and afterwards they will be in the United States for a two week break.' Tokunboh was thoughtful for a while, and then he asked Nike quietly, 'Nike, why are you so afraid of my mum? She's an *angel* you know.'

Nike was silent; *if Tokunboh's mum was an angel, she must be an angel of evil*, she thought to herself. But it was obvious Tokunboh did not know this or, if he knew, he pretended not to know. *She was his mum after all!*

Tokunboh looked at Nike, oblivious of what she was thinking about his mother, and he gently pulled her back in his embrace.

An hour later, Nike was crying as her head was buried on Tokunboh's chest. She felt so ashamed of herself. She did not quite remember how it happened; one thing had led to another during the kiss and they had found themselves on the bed naked; they had both got carried away and they had made love. The realisation of what she had done hit her when she felt the pain of Tokunboh's thrust within her. She screamed from the intense pain she experienced and pushed Tokunboh away. She felt as if raw chilli had been poured into her. *Is this how sex is?* she wondered. *Why do people get so excited about it then? Why do girls in the school talk so much about it?*

'I'm so sorry Nike,' Tokunboh told her after a while. 'I guess I forgot that you're… well that you're a virgin; I got carried away.'

Nike covered her mouth with her hand and, still sobbing, she ran into the bathroom and closed the door behind her, oblivious of the blood stain on the bedspread.

She sat on the edge of the huge bath and cried some more. She closed her eyes and remembered her promise to her father.

'Forgive me, Father, for I have broken my promise to you; if you can hear me where you are, I want you to forgive me please,' she said earnestly. However, she did not feel forgiven. She cried some more. After a while, she quietened and stepped into the bath. That was when she noticed the blood stains on her lap. She closed her eyes and tried to shut out the memory of what she had done – she couldn't. The memory of what she had done with Tokunboh was still very fresh in her mind. She turned on the shower and scrubbed herself thoroughly. She found that that helped a bit. She slowly got out of the bath and towelled herself dry. She knew without a doubt that Tokunboh was still in the room, waiting for her. She dreaded facing him. *How would he view her now? A cheap girl? More importantly, how would the world view her? A slut? Would she look different now that she was no longer a virgin? Would people notice the difference in her?* She studied herself in the lengthy bathroom mirror. Nothing had changed in her, except of course, her eyes were a bit swollen from her weeping. She turned to go back into the room but she suddenly stopped in her tracks. *Would Tokunboh still be in love with her? Would he still treat her with so much care as he had been doing now that he had gotten what other boys had always wanted? She was not so sure.* Bracing herself, she opened the bathroom door and entered the room. What she saw gave her the shock of her life.

Tokunboh was on his knees with an open little box in his hand. Inside the box stood a glittering diamond ring. The three words Tokunboh uttered erased all the guilt and the doubts that Nike had been feeling.

'Marry me, Nike,' said Tokunboh simply.

The pleasant feeling returned to Nike's stomach.

'I bought this ring when you were at the hospital,' continued Tokunboh. 'I would have presented it to you some time ago, but you seemed not to have made up your mind about me. I've been waiting for the day you will say yes. Now that you find me worthy of your beautiful body, kindly find me worthy to be your life partner. Please tell me you will marry me, Nike,' he pleaded.

'But we can't get married now; we are underage,' Nike said to Tokunboh.

'We are not getting married now,' said Tokunboh, 'but with this ring, I wish to profess my eternal love for you. I will wait for you, Nike. I will wait till you are eighteen and we will get married right away. Believe me, Nike; we shall live happily ever after.'

Nike was gobsmacked. Here she was thinking that Tokunboh would fall out of love for her; *after all*, she had given him what she cherished most; she had given him what she promised her dear dad that she would keep until her wedding night. Had her father not warned her that a boy would immediately fall out of his professed *love* for her, should she give him her *honour*? But here was Tokunboh, loving her all the more for it. She did not know what to say. But Tokunboh was still on his knees waiting for her reply.

'Well, what do you say?' he asked.

Nike smiled.

'Yes,' she said at last.

Tokunboh heaved a sigh of relief; smiling happily, he stood up and removed the ring from its case. Lifting up Nike's left palm, he slipped the diamond ring on her middle finger. Then, they became locked in a passionate kiss.

Later that night, they made love again and Nike was surprised to find herself responding to Tokunboh's love-making. He prompted and she responded; he sought and she gave. Later, as she lay in his embrace, she could not believe the magic of it. It was so much unlike the first time; this time, it was so pleasant that Nike felt she had been to paradise and had come back. Now she knew why people got excited over it. It was definitely worth all the excitement!

'Are you all right?' asked Tokunboh.

Nike nodded happily and fell into a deep contented sleep.

The next morning, Tokunboh went with the family driver in one of the Mercedes Benz cars parked in the compound to drop Nike off at the airport.

As Nike went to board the aeroplane, Tokunboh waved at her. Nike felt so sad. She was missing him already. She would rather be with Tokunboh than go to the United Kingdom to see her mum. But Tokunboh had insisted that she went.

'Go and make peace with your mum,' he had told her. 'You have both lost so much in so little time and it'll be good for her to know that you care.'

Chapter 12

Great Britain

Alice looked at Alex lovingly as he taught her the *Pythagoras Theorem*. Her concentration was not on whatever Alex was teaching her; her concentration was on Alex himself.

Within a couple of weeks, Alice who was known to be a loner, had found love with Alex.

Alice and Alex had grown up in the same neighbourhood in the London Borough of Camden. Her parents had been very strict, religious people who seemed to be wary of 'the youths of today', as they always called young people. Her father had actually been a vicar at the local Methodist Church in the neighbourhood and her mother had been a grade two teacher in the school they attended.

Alex was three years ahead of Alice, both in age and in school. However, Alex had always found Alice to be an intriguing person; not the way anyone would have thought, but the other way round. To Alex, Alice was too pious, too proper, too religious, too slow; it was unbelievable. All these traits were not immediately apparent to all and sundry unless one got close to her, and that was almost impossible. Alice was not allowed close to any other person apart from Alex. Her parents were overly protective of her. According to them, they were trying to protect her from the 'wiles of the devil'. Their belief was always that 'bad company corrupts good manners', and their belief was also that all the 'youths of today' were bad company, apart from Alex of course.

However, they could vouch for Alex only because they could vouch for his father; they knew and trusted his father. Their family had been friends; Alex's dad, Alan Tucker, had been a worker at the same church the Palmers attended. He had combined choir leading with managing the treasury of the church and it was in the records of the church that he had done so without blemish. He was blameless. Alan Tucker could not afford to be otherwise; his biggest dream in life was to become the Knight of John Wesley.

Alice was known to be an introvert. She made no friends in school and she had none in the neighbourhood. Her strict upbringing left no room for her to develop any kind of relationship. She was too shy to talk to people. She always looked downwards as she walked so as to avoid being smiled at or being greeted. Her classmates soon began to avoid her; students in the school never bothered to approach her for friendship.

One day, she decided to take a lonely path home from school. The lonely path was actually a narrow way created by some labourers at the back of a construction site for their convenience. A sign had been placed on the wall of the site warning children and adults off the premises because there could be sparks emanating from works going on in the site, and this could be hazardous to passers-by. Unknown to Alice and many others, the lonely path had become a haven to some hooligans and people who were into drug business.

It had rained terribly and there had been a terrible traffic hold-up due to a public diversion. Alice had waited at the bus stop with the other students for a while but the buses were not forthcoming. Alice was in a hurry to get home. It was her fourteenth birthday and in the Palmers' household birthdays were always special. It was one of the rare occasions that the Palmers dined out. Although, no other person was usually invited, Alice always liked the feeling. They usually went to real adult restaurants and they ate meals like celebrities, and Alice could order anything she wished. It was the only time that Alice was allowed to make a choice; it made her feel grown-up. Alice could not wait to get home, change into proper clothes and go on a dinner date with her parents, and she had decided to take the lonely path home.

Although, she had been warned several times by her parents, just as the parents of other students had warned their kids to avoid the lonely path, she had decided to take just this one risk. She would walk through as fast as she could and in no time she would be at home, she reasoned. When she got to the middle of the path, she heard whistles and calls from behind her. She decided to ignore them.

'Hey Jack, there goes the lonely cat,' said a voice from behind her.

'Oh yeah!' exclaimed another. 'Lets go see what she can offer.'

Scared out of her wits, she quickened her steps; but before she got to the middle of the road, two firm hands grabbed her on each shoulder and she was pulled back the way she had come. However much she cried out for help, her yells seemed to be blown away by the air, never to be heard by a living soul. One of her two assailants suddenly covered her mouth with his large hand, while the other fiddled with her blouse. All Alice's pleas for them to leave her alone fell on deaf ears.

At that moment, Alex was walking back to the college. It would be more appropriate to say that he was racing back to the college. The college was situated very near to Alice's secondary school from where Alex had graduated.

He had forgotten an important letter in his drawer. The letter which was meant for his father, had been given to him by the college principal. Alex was not privy to the content of the letter but it had been given to him with a warning by the college principal that the information contained in the letter must reach his father that evening; and he had forgotten it in his drawer. He had football practice that evening and he very much hated to be delayed. He checked his wrist watch; he had roughly forty-five minutes to get to the football stadium. If he could run as fast as his legs could carry him, he would make it to the college, pick up his father's letter, run back home, deliver the letter to his father and make it to the football pitch in good time.

However, as he got to the bend that led to the school, he thought he heard some noise but he decided to disregard it; he could not afford to let anything distract him. However, the noise got a little louder and he stopped in his tracks and looked back towards the direction where the noise came from. He spotted two men dragging a lady towards the back of a van and he raced towards the van. Much to his chagrin, he noticed that the two men were actually assaulting a lady. He ran faster as he made his right hand into a fist, leaving his thumb pointed. He got to the scene and without thinking twice, he jabbed his pointed thumb into the bottom of one of the two assailants. The man gave a yelp and held his left buttock with his hand, spontaneously letting go of Alice. Alex did not allow him to get over the pain; he kicked him in the groin. The man gave a big shout and doubled over, holding his manhood; his pupils rolled to the side of his nose as his knees wobbled and he went down, still holding his manhood.

The second man rushed at Alex, who proved to be quicker than him. Before the man got to him, Alex bent and scooped a handful of sand in his hand; this he threw at the other assailant, specifically aiming at his eyes. He got the target; the man screamed and rubbed his eyes profusely with his two hands. While he was still trying to clear his eyes of sand grains, Alex rushed at him, raised his right leg and gave him a double kick in his belly. The man gave a groan and fainted. The other man got up and disappeared down an alley, still holding unto his manhood.

Alex rushed to the victim and to his surprise, he found that the lady he had just saved was none other but Alice Palmers. He pulled her up from where she sat crying and after comforting her, he reproved her gently for daring to take the lonely path home. He gently led Alice away from the area.

When they were at a safe distance from the lonely path, he placed his thumb under her chin and gently raised up her head. He asked her to promise him that she would never take the lonely path home again. But Alice said nothing; when she raised her eyes to his, the look in them told Alex that she would be eternally grateful to him.

The two families had become quite close as a result of their engagements in church activities. Frederick, who was simply called Fred, and Gladys Palmers, who were the parents of Alice, made sure that Alice, who was their only child, attended church regularly; and that was about the only social life she was allowed to have. Alice was made to live a sheltered life. Alice sang in the choir which Alex's father mastered. They always had a choir practice every Wednesday and Saturday, and after each choir practice, Alan usually took Alice in his car and he would drop her off at her house. Sometimes, Alex went with him to say hello to the Palmers; sometimes, he went alone. There, he helped Alice with her homework; and there, Alex discovered that Alice was not too bright a girl; it took her a bit more time than normal to grasp anything; although, he never showed this to her, nor did he tell her so. Alice was, however, very eager to learn. Anytime he came around, she would rush downstairs into the sitting room where he was with her homework and he would coach her. He took time out to explain things to her; he answered all her questions, even if he felt that those questions were sometimes dumb! This gesture endeared him to Alice's parents. Soon, they began to trust him enough to leave him alone with her while they went out. They had come to trust him very much and to regard him as a pious and harmless young fellow as opposed to the 'youths of today'.

One month after the incident on the lonely path, Alex had gone to the Palmers' home and he had met Alice all alone in the house.

'Your mum and dad gone out?' he had asked Alice

'Yes, Mum has gone to visit Dad in the hospital. Dad's having his heart checked out,' replied Alice.

'Oh!' was all Alex said. He sat down uncomfortably. Ever since he had been coming to the Palmers', today was the first day he would be alone with Alice in their home.

Alice sat awkwardly opposite him for a while, then she took the remote control of the television and began to fiddle with the buttons.

'Do you… do you care for a drink?' she asked awkwardly after a while.

'No thanks,' said Alex. He was looking at Alice as if he was seeing her for the first time. She was a big girl – a little too big for her age; that was why Alex had never been able to come to terms with why Alice could be so timid. The big girls he knew took advantage of their bigness and bullied other girls. But not Alice; she was so shy; she could not look anyone in the face. Her awkwardness somehow made him amused.

Alice shifted her feet and Alex's eyes were drawn to them. To his surprise, Alex realised for the first time that Alice had the cutest feet he had ever seen. They were slim and tanned and her toe nails were well pedicured. It was as though they had been cut from someone else and glued to Alice's legs. Alex slowly traced his eyes back to Alice's torso, and to her face, and a strange feeling stirred within him. He had never sat so closely to Alice alone until now; that was probably why he had never noticed that Alice, in her awkwardness and voluptuousness, possessed a kind of beauty, hidden to many. Alex wondered what she would feel like in his arms. He definitely was no green horn when it came to sex, but Alice was of a different breed; she was of a different orientation from the girls he had dated. Alice was brought up to shy away from people – *except him of course!* He knew without a doubt that she had never done *it!* He suddenly felt like touching her; he felt like *discovering* her femininity.

Suddenly, Alice looked up and caught Alex looking at her and her cheeks burned. She immediately looked down at her interlocked fingers which were trembling visibly. A chuckle escaped from Alex and Alice covered her face with her trembling hands; she got up and made to run into her room. But she had to run past Alex to get to her room. As she did so, Alex caught her and pulled her towards him; and they were soon embraced in a warm kiss. Alex chuckled some more at Alice's clumsiness at kissing. He had not expected her to know how to kiss and he was not disappointed. All the same, he found it very amusing that Alice kept her upper and lower teeth firmly shut as they kissed. He promised within himself to teach her. With his tongue, he prodded her to open her mouth and respond to his kiss. After a while, nature seemed to take its course and Alex found Alice responding to him like a *pro*.

Alice was soon lost in Alex's world. As much as she wanted to stop what was happening, she had lost the will power to do so. Several times during the lovemaking, her mind actually told her to stop, but she found herself responding to Alex in an action that she could only dream of. She had overheard girls in her school discussing what was now happening to her but she had not understood how exactly it was until now. She could not even believe she could overcome her shyness in Alex's arms. She chose to disregard what her mind was telling her, and she decided to enjoy the magic that was happening to her.

Alex slowly tucked out her blouse form her skirt and ran a hand up to her breasts. Alice moaned with pleasure as Alex softly kneaded her breasts. This was sheer paradise; and to think that she had been missing out on this for so long.

Satisfied and proud of himself for being able to arouse so much emotion in a girl that boys had likened to a *brick-wall*, Alex decided to go a step further. He shifted a bit and started unbuttoning Alice's blouse…

It was hours after Alex had left that Alice came back from paradise and into reality. She had been made a woman by Alex. She could not believe she had actually done it. It had happened at a time she had not planned it to happen. *What would her parents say if they got wind of it?* She became scared; butterflies rose from the pit of her stomach. She quickly got up from the chair and gave herself a thorough wash, hoping to death that her parents would not notice the change in her.

Alice's parents did not notice the change in her until two months later; but then it was too late. Alice was already pregnant. She had not seen her period for two months and she had been too scared to tell her mother. The thought that she could be pregnant had crossed her mind several times, and several times she had waved it aside. *She couldn't be pregnant,* she thought. She had only done it once. The girls in her school had sex a million times and they had never mentioned being pregnant.

But one day, she was preparing dinner with her mother in the kitchen, when her mother took a critical look at her and blurted out without a preamble, 'Alice, I hope you're not pregnant.'

Alice's heart jumped to her mouth; she almost fainted. 'N… no… no, I'm not preg… pregnant. How can I be, Mother?' she stammered, looking everywhere but at her mother.

'You tell me,' replied her mother with her eyes still scrutinising her. She was looking at Alice sternly, with a fat hand akimbo and the other hand holding a big spoon with which she constantly stirred the soup in the huge pot placed on the gas cooker.

'I sincerely hope you're not pregnant Alice, because if you are, I'll personally wring your neck,' said Mrs Palmers.

Alice felt like peeing on the floor; she thought her life had come to an end.

'When last did you see your period?' asked her mum and Alice jumped.

'I er… I… I er. I saw it last on Saturday,' she lied.

But her mother saw through her lie. She saw it written all over her daughter's face that she had been up to something forbidden.

'We'll go see the doctor tomorrow morning,' she said with finality.

'What?' asked Alice, clearly alarmed.

'Are you deaf?' shouted her mother. 'I said we'll go for a pregnancy test tomorrow morning, and heaven help you if you're actually pregnant.'

Chapter 13

'I'm afraid your daughter's pregnant!' declared the doctor.

The Palmers were seated before the doctor in his office when the doctor broke the news. Alice looked down at the floor of the surgery as tears flowed freely down her eyes. Reverend Palmers took off his glasses and wiped his face with the back of his hand. The air-conditioning in the room was obviously not enough to withstand his sudden perspiration.

'You mean my own daughter is pregnant out of wedlock?' asked Reverend Palmers after a while.

'I know how you feel,' said the doctor sympathetically, 'but it's surely not the end of the road for her. She can still pick up the pieces of her life and get back on track. I can introduce her to—'

Reverend Palmers did not let the doctor finish his sentence. He squeezed the pair of glasses in his hand until they cracked and shattered; but Reverend Palmers took no notice of what he had done. He suddenly got up from his chair and turned on Alice.

'Did you hear what the doctor said?' he yelled down at her. Alice shivered and curled into a ball on her seat. 'He said you can still pick up the pieces of your life,' continued Reverend Palmers, his voice rising with the utterance of every word. 'Do you know what that means?' Reverend Palmers bellowed. 'It means that your life is now in pieces; it means that your life has been shattered; it means that you're ruined.'

The doctor quickly interjected.

'No, Mr Palmers, that's not what I meant…' he began, but Reverend Palmers had started breathing hard. Soon, he held his chest as he gasped for breath. The doctor quickly summoned two nurses in, and Reverend Palmers was wheeled out of the office and into a ward. By the time Reverend Palmers was administered the first series of medication, he had gone into a coma. That evening, Reverend Palmers was transferred to the general hospital not far from the neighbourhood.

Reverend Palmers died three days later at the general hospital.

The burial ceremony had been low-key, with only the church vicar and very few church people in attendance. Alice noted that Alex and his dad were conspicuously absent. She wondered why they had refused to attend the burial of her father despite the close friendship between their families. She wondered if Alex knew the cause of her father's death; she wondered if he was trying to avoid her; if he was trying to avoid smearing himself with the stigma that seemed to engulf her as the days passed.

But would Alex's father cast her away as well? she wondered. She raised up her head and looked around the auditorium where the burial ceremony took place. Everyone sat bleary eyed as the priest poured encomiums on the remains of her father. Her mother sat at the front pew, surrounded by friends and well-wishers. Alice felt as though, they were only present, not because of her, but for her mum. How she wished Alex could at least be there for her; she needed all the strength he could offer her now. She felt so neglected, so alone, she cried.

At the funeral reception, her mouth had felt so bitter that she could not take a bite of any of the food that was served. She had looked on forlornly as guests paid condolence to her mother, while she had been deliberately ignored. It was very obvious that news had quickly spread that she had *killed* her father.

No one had bothered to say hello to her; and no one had asked her how she was faring. She was, however, aware that some of the guests stole glances at her when they thought she was not looking; and whenever her eyes met some of the guests', they quickly looked away. Throughout the ceremony, Alice was avoided like a common plague. Alice felt she should have been the one lying in the grave and not her father. She felt she did not deserve to be alive.

The day after the burial of Reverend Palmers, Mrs Palmers packed a few belongings and scribbled a note on a piece of paper. This, she placed on Alice's bed as she slept and tiptoed out of the room. She had made up her mind to leave the United Kingdom for good, and she did not want her mind changed by Alice. As far as she was concerned, Alice had deprived her of the two things that mattered most in her life – her husband and her pride. She had always taken immense pride in the fact that she was able to bring Alice up in the most decent of ways, and she had dreamt and boasted that her daughter would be the first virgin bride in this day and age. But Alice had gone ahead and shattered her dreams; Alice had nipped her pride in the bud by getting pregnant, and she had *murdered* her husband in the process. Since the death of her husband, she had hardly spoken a word to Alice; she had not even bothered to ask who was responsible for her pregnancy. Mrs Palmers knew she would never forgive her daughter for what she had done.

Before Mrs Palmers left the apartment, she took a good look around the sitting room. It was devoid of anything that could remind anyone that she had a daughter called Alice. She had destroyed all the photographs that used to hang on the walls of the sitting room; and she had destroyed all the family pictures that she kept for so long. There was no point carrying the reminder of the grief caused by Alice. In her mind, she had disowned Alice; Alice was no longer her daughter. She would go far away, as far as Thailand, and she would start a new life there; her life in the United Kingdom, along with the dream she had woven round her family, totally forgotten. For a fleeting moment, memories of her husband and the happy times they shared crossed her mind, and she quickly banished them. If she was to start a new life, it had got to be now!

Alice, in turn, had tried her best to avoid her mother. After the demise of her father, she had gone into her mother's room to plead for forgiveness; to explain to her mother that she had made the *terrible mistake* only once, but her mother had simply shouted at her to get lost and she had thrown her huge, heavy Scholl shoes at her. Alice had been quick to take a dive, and the shoes had landed on the wall behind her. Alice had fearfully run into her room and shut herself up and, experiencing intense guilt over what had happened to their once closely knit family, she had buried her head in a pillow and cried her eyes out. She had afterwards, tried to avoid her mother right until the day her father was laid to rest.

As she woke up from her deeply troubled slumber the day after the burial, she was greeted by the note her mother left her. The note read:

By the time you read this note, I'll be very far away from you. You have succeeded in killing my husband and shattering my dreams in life. I hope you live the rest of your miserable life without me. Don't ever try to look for me, because you will never find me!

Alice rubbed her already swollen eyes with her hands and read the note again. The words coldly stared back at her. As she read the note once more, each word seemed to slice into her flesh and puncture her heart. Slowly, the intensity of those words dawned on Alice. For the first time in her life, she was on her own. She had no family; she had no friends. She was now all alone in the whole wide world. Once again, she broke down and cried. Alice cried and cried till it was evening time and then she fell asleep.

At six o'clock the following morning, she woke up famished. She realised she had not had anything to eat since her father's burial. Even then, she had only managed a cup of tea and a couple of crackers, which she had vomited right after she swallowed the last crumb of biscuit.

She slowly got up from the bed and walked into the sitting room. The sight she met in the sitting room took her aback. The walls were devoid of the family photographs which used to hang proudly on them; the flower vases had gone and the electronics have been disconnected. Alice grimaced at the lumps of electrical wire lying haphazardly around the sitting room. Everywhere looked so untidy; Alice wondered how her mother had got the time to turn the sitting room upside down.

Sighing deeply, Alice left the sitting room and wondered into the kitchen. There, she met the shocker of her life. Not only was the refrigerator disconnected, there was not a grain of food in it. Her mother had made sure that she had wiped the kitchen clean of everything edible. Even the dustbin had been wiped clean. Alice found it difficult to imagine her mother would wish her to die of starvation. She felt a burning pain in her heart; she wanted to cry; she wished she could cry to ease up the pain, but she couldn't. Her tear-well seemed to have dried up suddenly. She rubbed her burning eyes with her hands until they hurt.

She strode out of the kitchen and walked towards the room her parents had once slept in. After a moment of hesitation, she quietly opened the door and peeped into the room. She saw that the bed had been stripped of the bed sheet and, resisting the urge to go inside the room to find out if her mother had indeed packed all her belongings, she gently stepped back and closed the door. There was no need going in to see things for herself. It would only hurt all the more. She slowly walked back to the sitting room and sat down.

Now that her home had been stripped of all that made it a home, and she technically had no parents to care for her, her only option was to walk right into a foster home and hand herself over for adoption or something. Despite herself, she almost chuckled at the thought. It sounded so ridiculous. However, considering the situation she found herself in at the moment, giving herself over for adoption was the only solution that came to mind; after all, she was still a minor. She was just not sure she could find a family that would be willing to adopt her along with her pregnancy. *Pregnancy!* In her distress, she had almost forgotten that she was pregnant. Her hand immediately flew to her stomach. With her fore-finger, she pressed it a little and then she applied a bit more pressure; she felt no pain. She somehow did not feel pregnant. She sighed deeply. From the information she gathered, it would be a few months before she started showing. *But would she keep the baby? Was she ready to be a mother?* How she wished Alex was around; how she longed for his presence, his strength. She didn't think Alex should ignore her as others had done. After all, he had made her pregnant. He had put her in the family way and made himself very much at large. That was why he had not come for her father's burial. At that moment, she could not decide which hurt most – her father's death or Alex's betrayal.

Suddenly, her stomach rumbled and she was reminded of the hunger that was eating at her. She decided to walk down to the nearest Tesco store to get something to eat; *maybe some sandwiches or a ready made salad*. She hoped the food would settle in her stomach when she ate. These days, she was finding it more difficult to hold food down.

She got up from the chair and walked slowly to her room. Once in her room, she opened a bedside drawer and brought out her purse. There she found a ten pound note. She remembered the note had been given to her by her dad before he died. It was part of her weekly allowance. Holding the ten pound note firmly in her hand, the reality of what happened suddenly dawned heavily on her. Now that her dad was dead, it might take a very long time before she ever saw another ten pound note.

Clasping the money firmly in her right hand, she left the building and walked down the road, towards Tesco Express.

As she turned into a street, she heard her name from behind. She became very frightened and on impulse, she began to walk faster. But whoever wanted her attention seemed to be bent on getting it. Alice heard footsteps just behind her and without looking back, she broke into a run. But a hand caught her before she could run far.

'Hey Alice. It's me, Alex; what's up with you?'

Alice froze and turned around to look into the eyes of the only person she had been thinking of since she lost her virginity. She could not believe her eyes. In her wildest dreams, she never thought she would come face to face with Alex, ever again. She just thought he had done his deed and simply absconded. Now as she looked up at his young, handsome, tanned face, she knew without a single doubt that Alex had not run away. He had probably gone on holiday somewhere. However dumb she thought she sounded, she said the first thing that came to her mind, 'Alex, is it really you?'

Alex chuckled before replying, 'Of course, it's really me. What's been happening to you? And why were you walking to so fast?'

'I'm going down to the stores to get something to eat. I've not had anything to eat since…' Alice faltered. Alex grinned.

'Don't tell me your dear mama did not cook. When did you start eating out, dear mummy's pet?' asked Alex grinning.

'My mum's gone,' said Alice simply. She looked everywhere but at Alex as she said this. She still felt she was the cause of everything that had happened to her family, including her mother's sudden disappearance.

Alex's smile slowly faded; his expression turned into a confused one.

'What d'you mean your mum's gone?' he asked. 'Where's she gone to?'

Alice looked uncomfortable. 'I don't know,' she said, 'honestly, I don't'.

Alex was all the more confused. 'What d'you mean you don't know?' he asked. 'What's happened to your family?'

'My father died,' said Alice simply and she burst into tears.

'What!' exclaimed Alex. 'What happened? I mean, how did he die?'

'I… I... caused it,' sobbed Alice. 'I'm the cause of everything. I should be dead.'

Alex pulled her towards him; he was still confused. *How could Alice be the cause of her father's death?* As far as he knew, Alice was a very good girl. She could not have shot or stabbed her father, *or could she?*

'How were you the cause of your father's death?' he asked her gently.

Alice sniffed once and looked up at Alex. 'I'm pregnant, Alex,' she said simply.

'Holy shit!' Alex swore as he suddenly pushed Alice away from him as if she had suddenly turned into a heap of burning coals; and then he put forth his hand to steady her, so she did not fall from the pressure of his push.

'How… how did it happen?' he managed to ask her after a few minutes; but he already knew the answer. He was responsible for Alice's pregnancy. He had impregnated her when he had slept with her on the couch in their home. He cursed himself for allowing a moment of lust to ruin things; *and boy*, he had really ruined things. He sighed deeply and then he looked at Alice and said the first comforting words Alice had heard since the death of her father. 'Alice, we have to talk.'

Chapter 14

The British Airways Plane touched down at Heathrow airport, London, exactly six hours after it took off from Mur'tala Mohammed Airport in Lagos Nigeria.

After Nike was cleared by the airport immigration, she went immediately to the taxi rank and took a cab home.

She got to the house she had lived in with her parents until she was nine years old. She looked at the front of the house and felt that nothing seemed to have changed since the last time she had come on holiday. She remembered her father telling her that he had bought the house on mortgage from the landlord some time ago. She wondered who paid the mortgage now that her dad was dead. She could not remember her mother ever going out to work. Her dad had always provided for her even when things where not going on smoothly between them. Her beloved dad had worked so hard to provide for them all and her mum had only repaid him by giving him tough times. She had always nagged him and she seemed to be very unhappy that they were in the United Kingdom and not in some royal household in an old town in Nigeria.

She had asked her dad, one day, what the fuss was all about and her dad had simply told her that he was from a royal family somewhere in the western part of Nigeria, and that her mum believed they should go back and assume their rightful place. Her father had waved off further questions about his origin and he had told her never ever to think about it; and she had obeyed him. As far as Nike was concerned, her daddy was never wrong!

Now, as she stood in front of the house, she wondered how her mother would receive her. Would she be happy to see her? Would she embrace her? Would she tell her that she had missed her so much and was glad she had come home?

Nike doubted it all.

She walked slowly to the door and pressed the bell. She waited for sometime and pressed the bell again but she got no reply. After pressing the bell for the third time, she turned away from the building. Maybe her mum was not in. She decided to go look for a bed and breakfast lodge somewhere and come back the next day. She had enough money to cover the expense, courtesy of Tokunboh Martins.

As she made to leave, the door to the flat opened and there stood her mother in the doorway. Her mother was wearing very flimsy lingerie and it was obvious that she wore nothing else underneath it. Surprisingly, Nike was glad to see her. Not minding the apparent look of surprise on her mother's face, Nike ran to hug her. Her mother did not hug her back. Nike pulled back from her uncomfortably.

'I've missed you mum; I'm sorry about Dad's death,' she said after a while, '....and about the twins, of course,' she added hastily. She knew her mother loved the twins dearly; it was like they were her life; the reason for her existence.

Ama had not expected anyone to come looking for her. Ever since she was certified well enough and discharged from the mental hospital, nobody had come looking for her. Her friends had totally deserted her and neighbours had avoided her like a plague. She had found solace only in the arms of a young Englishman she had met at a club a month before, and she had eventually succeeded in persuading him to move in with her.

'I didn't know you were coming,' said her mother flatly, as she gave way for Nike to pass. Nike went into the house and pulled her traveller's bag after her.

'I'm so sorry for not writing to inform you beforehand; but then you never replied any of my letters to you,' said Nike hesitantly. She studied her mother's demeanour; her mother seemed to be edgy. *Wasn't she happy to see her at all?* Nike thought she should tell her that they had to bury the hatchet and become one family again, since they now had only each other. She would tell her about Tokunboh later. She smiled when she thought of Tokunboh. It was a nice feeling to be in love, and she felt it would be equally nice to have an older person, such as her mother, to share the experience with. More than ever before, she felt she needed parental guidance. Her life had changed drastically and dramatically since the death of her father two months before. She would plead with her mother on her knees *if need be*, and tell her to accept her as her child for the first time. As she opened her mouth to talk to her mum, a huge Englishman with tattoos all over his body, who looked like he was in his mid-twenties, came down the stairs. He was totally naked!

'What's been holding you back, love?' said the man said as he descended the stairs. 'Come back to bed.'

Nike stood transfixed. Her mother had been cheating on her father in her father's house, with a man almost young enough to be her son! It was totally incredible! She could not believe that her mother could actually have a lover. Her dad was barely two months dead and her mother did not have the decency to at least mourn his death for a considerable length of time. She gave her mother a damning look.

Just then, the man noticed that they had company and he quickly covered his manhood with his hands. He was clearly embarrassed; his cheeks burned. He turned and ran back up the stairs, oblivious of his exposed scrotum dangling behind him as he ran. In his haste, he had totally forgotten to cover his backside.

Ordinarily, Nike would have found the whole scenario very funny, but in this case, there was nothing to laugh about. Even though her dad was dead, she still felt that her mother was cheating on him. *At least, she should respect his memory, which is still very fresh*, she thought. She did not think she could ever forgive her mother for what she had done.

'Mum, how could you do this to Dad?' she asked her mum angrily. 'Why are you doing this to us?'

'Why am I doing what?' asked Ama unconcernedly, she had suddenly regained her confidence now that her deed had come out in the open.

'You damn well know what I'm talking about,' shouted Nike.

'Shut up,' shouted Ama. 'Just you shut the hell up. You just can't come into my house and yell at me.'

'It's my father's house too,' said Nike tearfully. 'I have a right to it as much as you do.'

'Not any more, my dear,' said Ama cynically. 'The will has been read and your father gave everything to me. I own this house now; I own everything!' She smiled at Nike but her expression clearly showed that she hated her with a passion. She continued after a while, 'I guess your father had always wanted to change his will and give everything to you; he had given me the signs and made suggestions to that effect, but for one reason or the other, the poor fellow did not do it before he died.' She looked at Nike who had a murderous expression and laughed diabolically before saying, 'that leaves me in custody of all that your father, who happened to be my beloved husband, left behind.'

Nike was dumbstruck; she could not believe what her mother was saying. When she eventually found her voice, she asked in a quiet voice, 'and where does that leave me?'

Ama gave a throaty laugh before replying her mockingly, 'that leaves you with nothing.' She said it with a quiet voice that was laden with obvious mockery, and she laughed at her own joke.

'How could you be this heartless, Mum?' Nike asked her mum. Her actions were totally unbelievable; she began to doubt if this woman standing before her was actually her mother.

'You know something,' her mother said. 'I sometimes have the conviction that you're not my real daughter. Sometimes, I think that my real baby was swapped at the hospital. How else could you have stolen my husband's love from me?'

Nike looked at her mum, totally confused. Her mother went on, 'Because of you, Leke refused to reconcile with his father, the King, thereby depriving me of the right to the throne.'

Nike was all the more confused. 'What are you talking about mum?' she asked quietly.

'Oh, you mean dear Daddy never told you anything about that? It's better you go and ask him what I'm talking about. As for me, I have a new life to enjoy with my prince charming upstairs.' And with that, Ama pushed Nike out of the apartment and threw her bag after her. Before she closed the door, she told her, 'I'll advise you not to hope for a part of anything that belonged to your father. You will not lay your fingers on even a penny!'

Ama slammed the door in Nike's face and went upstairs to her lover.

'I'm so sorry, darling,' she said as she got into the bed she had once shared with Leke, and was now sharing with her huge lover, Bernard. She looked up at his flushed face, which still registered embarrassment over what happened a few minutes before. His face, which had a tinge of redness to it, had actually creased into a deep frown. Ama pulled back the duvet covering Bernard and held his huge phallus in her hand. She studied his face intently as she began to caress his manhood. In the twinkling of an eye, the redness on Bernard's face disappeared and his frown began to decrease as he twisted and jerked and moaned loudly; and Ama smiled with pleasure. Satisfied that she had Bernard back in the *mood*, Ama asked him in her most sexy voice, 'Now where were we before we were rudely interrupted?'

Nike picked her bag from the ground and left without looking at the house. Now that it belonged to her mother, as she had claimed, she felt no more affiliation towards it. She walked slowly towards the high street, wondering what she should do next. She walked past a police station and stopped. She wondered if it would be a wise decision to go in and report her plight and immediately decided against it. Her mum would be arrested for child neglect or cruelty or both, and the next moment, the story would be published in newspapers. She did not want any scandal attached to her father's name. She had a fierce desire to protect her father's image, even though he was dead. She checked the time; it was twenty-five minutes past five in the evening. If she could get to the airport in time, she could catch the next flight back to Nigeria. There was no point staying in the United Kingdom, where she no longer had family. Tokunboh was the only family she now had in the whole wide world and he was in Nigeria. Thankfully, she had an open ticket and that meant she could go back to Nigeria that same day. She would be better off with him, she decided.

She walked to the bus stop and took a bus to the train station. Two hours later, she was back at Heathrow Airport.

When she got to the immigration clearance, she gave the officer on duty her passport. The officer checked the passport thoroughly. She leafed through every page of the passport, while looking at Nike intermittently.

'You are a British Citizen,' affirmed the officer.

Obviously.

'Yes,' said Nike impatiently. She badly wanted to ask the officer why she should be delayed with stupid questions.

'May I know why you've decided to go back to Nigeria today?' asked the clearance officer suspiciously.

'It's an open ticket,' replied Nike coolly, 'I suppose I could travel anytime with it.'

'I observed that already,' said the officer equally coolly. She was having suspicions about Nike's journey. Why would a teenager arrive into the United Kingdom and wish to travel back to where she had come from the same day? She posed the question on her mind.

'Why would you come here from far away Africa today and wish to travel back today?'

Nike tried to avoid any form of scandal; more importantly, she did not want to be associated with her mother, so she lied.

'I had not seen nor heard from my mum since my father passed away a few months ago; so I decided to come and see if she was alright. I got here, only to be told that she had gone to Africa to see me. I only got to speak with her today. I miss her a lot and I can't wait to see her.'

The officer studied Nike for a long time, then her facial muscles seemed to relax. She suddenly smiled at Nike and gave her a pass.

Nike got back to Nigeria at 2.00a.m., Nigerian time. She walked to a telephone booth, dropped a few coins into it and dialled a number.

'Hello, this is the Martins' villa,' came a sleepy, masculine voice.

'Hello, can I speak to Tokunboh Martins please?' said Nike.

'May I know who is speaking please?' asked the man at the other end.

'My name is Nike Adeogun,' replied Nike patiently.

The man knew who Nike was. She was the girl that had been kissing master Tokunboh by the swimming pool two days before.

'Hang on a second while I put you through,' said the man.

Nike only had to wait for ten seconds before Tokunboh's clear voice came on the line.

'What happened? Where are you calling from?' he asked concernedly.

'I'm back in Nigeria; I'm at the Mur'tala Mohammed airport. I'll explain everything when I get back to the house,' said Nike.

'Just hang in there,' Tokunboh told her as he got up from the bed. 'I'll be there in thirty minutes.'

Nike thought she ought to apologise to him. 'Tokunboh, I'm awfully sorry for the inconv–' she began, but the line had gone dead. She gently replaced the receiver and went to a well-lit area of the airport to wait for Tokunboh.

Tokunboh came to pick her up with the family driver forty-five minutes after he spoke to Nike.

'I'm so sorry we're late, darling. There was a diversion on our way and–'

'Sshh,' Nike cautioned, 'I'm supposed to be the one who owes you an apology.'

When they got home, Tokunboh made Nike a cup of hot tea and she narrated everything she encountered with her mother to him.

Later, as they slept in Tokunboh's room, Tokunboh reiterated his promise to make sure that she never lacked anything.

The holidays went by quickly and it was time for Nike to return to school. As she packed her belongings, including the numerous groceries Tokunboh had bought for her, she cried.

'Don't worry, I chose to attend the University of Lagos in this town so I'll be close to you,' Tokunboh assured her. 'You don't have to worry over a thing. You just have to snap your beautiful fingers and I'll be right by your side,' he said, pulling her close to him.

Nike sniffed.

'Promise me you'll write often and you'll come and visit me,' she said.

'I promise,' said Tokunboh, and they were soon engaged in a long kiss.

Chapter 15

Sir Fola Martins and his wife returned from the United States three days after Nike left for school.

The day after they came back, Tokunboh went to his parents and requested to talk to them. When they were all seated, Tokunboh narrated Nike's story as she had told him. He requested that his parents accept her as a child because she was no different from an orphan.

Tokunboh's father was deeply moved with compassion for Nike, but his wife wasn't. She really didn't care if Nike died and went to hell. As far she was concerned, the girl was nothing but a cheap gold-digger. She asked the question that she had wanted to ask ever since Tokunboh told them that Nike's mother had rejected her.

'Does that mean she slept here in this house throughout her holiday?'

'Yes,' admitted Tokunboh, but he quickly added, 'but she did not sleep in my room. She slept in a different room far away from me.'

His mother gave him a look that said she did not believe him.

Tokunboh did not care what his mother thought.

'It's alright,' said Sir Fola Martins. 'I remember when I was a little boy myself; things were so terrible for my parents that I had to drop out of the secondary school twice for lack of funds before I won a scholarship to study overseas. That is why I'm always eager to help those in need. I know how it is to be poor. Tell your friend to get in touch with me anytime she needs anything.'

Tokunboh was so grateful; he went to hug his dad.

'Thanks Dad,' he said. 'I appreciate you, Dad. You're the best dad in the world.' He gave his mother a kiss and made to leave the sitting room; but before he left, his father said to him, 'Tokunboh, please be careful. I know you're a very sensible boy but still, I want you to be careful. I understand how it could be between a boy and a girl.'

'I totally understand you, Dad,' said Tokunboh. 'I promise I won't let you down.'

When Tokunboh was in his room, his mother came in without knocking on the door and sat on his bed.

'Tokunboh, did you use a condom with her?' she asked him without preamble.

Tokunboh paused from what he was doing on the computer and feigned ignorance of what his mum had implied.

'Use a condom with whom?' he asked his mum innocently.

'With that Nike girl,' said his mum flatly.

Tokunboh turned away from the computer and looked at his mum straight in the face. He knew that his mother had always meant well for him, no matter what she did or did not do, but right now, she was beginning to get on his nerves.

'Why would I use a condom with her, mum?' he asked her calmly, his voice laden with anger.

'Oh come off it,' said his mum. 'I'm not a kid. A boy does not stay with a girl for a whole three weeks without something happening. Now, I do not care what happened, all I care about is your welfare. Tell me Tokunboh, did you use a condom?'

'I don't know what you're talking about,' said Tokunboh. He tried to avoid his mother's glare by turning back to the computer. But his mother said to him, 'Tokunboh, you know young girls of nowadays cannot be trusted. They sleep around and carry diseases around and I don't want–'

Tokunboh was livid; he was really angry at his mother's subtle inference to Nike as a wayward girl. 'Oh for God's sake mum. Nike's not like other girls. I met her, a virgin,' he shouted. Suddenly, he realised what he had done; he had unknowingly let the cat out of the bag. He almost hated his mum for putting him in such a tight corner.

'Look mum,' he said, trying to be calm. 'I love that girl, can't you see? The earlier you accepted her as your prospective daughter-in-law, the better for all of us,' he said with finality.

Mrs Martins saw her son's determination and decided to change tactics. She knew Tokunboh could be very stubborn when it came to something he believed in; besides, she loved him dearly and it hurt her to see him upset. She would get rid of the *brat* from his life secretly; after all, she was the one and only Mrs Yetunde Martins.

'That's alright Tokunboh,' she said. 'If you really love her, I guess I have to accept her.'

Tokunboh smiled. He had always thought his mum would come round and fall in love with Nike as he had done. He got up from the chair and hugged his mum tightly.

'Thanks Mum. I love you Mum,' he said, and his mother smiled. The smile did not reach her eyes.

One week later, Mrs Martins went into Tokunboh's room and informed him that he would be travelling to the United States for his university degree the following week.

'I've always wanted you to be a graduate of Yale,' she said brightly.

Tokunboh was agitated.

'What happens to Nike?' he asked.

'I knew you would come to that,' said his mother sweetly. 'I have made provisions for her to join you in the school when she leaves the secondary school; there, you can study together and get married immediately after your studies. After all, she has less than two years to go and I will definitely make sure she visits you in the United States as often as possible until she joins you there finally.'

Tokunboh relaxed; what his mother said made sense to him. His mother had great plans for Nike and himself. *God bless her.*

'God bless you, Mum,' he said and gave her a peck on her cheek.

'That's alright,' said Mrs Martins.

A thought crossed Tokunboh's mind. 'Mum, can I make a request?'

'Go ahead,' said his mum eagerly.

'Can I send letters to Nike when I'm in the states through you? You know the school screens every letter addressed to every student in the school and I don't want Nike to be in trouble with the authorities. You know my letters to her may contain some things the school would frown at,' Tokunboh said jovially.

'Of course, you can send her letters through me. You know I will deliver them to her immediately,' said Mrs Martins. She was pleasantly surprised. *This was going to be much easier than she thought. Tokunboh could keep sending the letters and she would keep destroying them.*

'I must see Nike today to tell her the good news,' said Tokunboh excitedly.

His mother totally agreed with him.

The week after he had the discussion with his mother, Tokunboh went to the United States of America to enrol as a medical student at the University of Yale.

His mother had gone with her personal chauffeur to the airport to see him off.

When she got back to the house, she opened her bag and brought out the letter Tokunboh had sent to Nike through her. It read:

My love,

As I explained to you before now, I'm on my way to the United States. As I write this note, my heart bleeds. I indeed crave your love, your touch and your whole being; but I'm happy in the knowledge that you will be with me in the United States very soon. My mum has assured me that.

As I promised you earlier, I shall write you every week. My mum will deliver the letters to you.

As I count the days remaining for us to be together, let my love be with you.

With Love,
Tokunboh.

Mrs Martins sniggered and tore the letter to pieces. She would take care of the brat called Nike when the time was ripe.

Chapter 16

Great Britain, Alan Tucker's residence

Alan Tucker entered the sitting room unannounced and stood rigid. The sight before him was one that he had hoped he would never behold.

Alex and Alice were locked in a compromising position on the three seater couch in the sitting room.

Alan had been suspecting a relationship between the two ever since Alex persuaded him to take Alice into the house. What he had not expected was that Alice, who had very strict parentage, could go this far with a man.

Now, as Alan Tucker stood, looking at the two shocked lovers with their sweaty, naked bodies intertwined, he knew he had to make a fast decision so his image with the church would not be tarnished.

'Alex, we have to talk,' he said tersely and left the sitting room.

Chapter 17

Nigeria, West Africa

One day, three weeks after Tokunboh left for the United States of America, Nike woke up from her bunk in the school feeling dizzy. Luckily, it was a Saturday and there would be no classes that day. She looked around the dormitory. Everybody was asleep. The students were normally given liberty on weekends to wake up later than usual. She gently got up from her bed and went to the bathroom to wash her face. As she bent her head over the sink, she felt nausea rising within her. She opened her mouth and threw up. Each time she raised her head, the nausea came, and she quickly bent her head over the sink again. The vomiting went on for a long time and she had to keep her head bent. When she was at it, Shade came into the bathroom. She studied Nike for a long time, and when Nike finally raised her head, she told her bluntly, 'You are pregnant, Nike.'

'What?' yelled Nike, alarmed. She knew what led to pregnancy and she knew she had done it, but for God's sake, she did not want to get pregnant.

'Don't yell at me,' said Shade mockingly. 'After all, I wasn't there when you were doing *it*.'

Nike was in no mood for Shade's jokes. She hoped to high heavens that she was not pregnant. The only person who could be responsible had travelled out of the country and she had not received a single letter from him as he had promised, and she was beginning to get worried. Besides, she was running out of funds and each time she went to the Martins' Villa to see Tokunboh's parents, she was told that they had travelled. She had so many problems to tackle and the last thing she needed right now was to get pregnant.

'Are… are you sure of what you've said?' she asked Shade fearfully.

'I'm as sure as hell is real, babe,' replied Shade mockingly, and before Nike could speak, she went on, 'believe me girl, I've been there several times and, as they say, experience is the best teacher. I've got pregnant so many times that I can tell when a girl is one day pregnant. You are very pregnant, Nike,' she asserted authoritatively.

'It can't be possible,' said Nike quietly.

'What do you mean, it's not possible?' asked Shade. 'You want to tell me that you didn't do it?'

But Nike ignored her. 'This shouldn't happen to me this time,' she moaned. 'Oh God, what am I supposed to do?' she cried and buried her head in her hands.

'You don't have to ask God what you're supposed to do,' said Shade irritably. 'After all, God did not ask you to do it.' Shade was obviously relishing this moment. She loved teasing people even when the situation called for seriousness. As far as Shade was concerned, life was sweet whatever happens and there was always a way out of every problem. To Shade, no real problem existed in this sweet world. Besides, Nike's predicament was no problem at all; she definitely knew who was responsible for her pregnancy, *and boy, wasn't his father loaded?*

'Have you told the father?' she asked Nike.

'Have I told whose father?' Nike countered. She was bewildered.

'The father of your baby of course; I mean the most honourable Tockunboh Martins,' said Shade.

'You're crazy,' replied Nike. 'How can you be so sure that I'm pregnant. You're not a doctor, so I don't believe you.' And with that, Nike left the bathroom. Shade laughed after her. 'You don't believe me now, but you will believe me when the time comes,' she said.

Nike did not go back to the room after she left the bathroom; rather, she went to the back of the dormitory and sat on the pavement where she normally studied. This time, she was in no mood to read any book; she was frightened. All Shade had said in the bathroom had really scared the wits out of her. *Could she really be pregnant?* She began to count with her fingers – *one, two, three, four, five*. It had been five weeks since she last saw her monthly period. She was supposed to have seen her period a week ago, and she hadn't. She was more than frightened now; she was agitated. She began to perspire. *What if she was really pregnant? What would she do? How could she be sure she was pregnant in the first place?*

If she was to confirm anything, she had to make a visit to the school hospital; but she knew very well that before she would leave the hospital that day, the report would be on the principal's table. It was the norm that the hospital sent reports concerning any student of the school for the principal to deliberate on; and if she was indeed found to be pregnant, she would be out of the school before she blinked an eyelid. The school hospital was definitely out of it!

She thought of sneaking out of the school to do the test at another hospital in a far location. *That must be the solution*, she thought. She still had some money left from the amount Tokunboh and his dad gave her as pocket money. The next weekend would be the school open day and she would be free to leave the school compound without anybody batting an eyelid. She would go and do the test secretly and she would give a fake name at the hospital for security, she decided.

Two weeks after she went for the pregnancy test, Nike sat in her usual hiding place at the back of the girls' dormitory, her pregnancy test result in her hand. The test result read positive; she was indeed pregnant!

She was at a loss for what to do. She had not received a single letter from Tokunboh ever since he left for the United States of America. She could not bring herself to face his mother. She had noticed Mrs Martins' reservation towards her. In fact, she could swear that Mrs Martins hated her guts. She only pretended otherwise whenever Tokunboh or his father was around. She decided to seek advice from Shade. Despite her crazy attributes, Shade always seemed to have a solution for every problem.

'You have to go and see his mother of course,' said Shade without hesitation.

'But–' began Nike, but Shade did not let her finish.

'There're no buts,' she said. 'You're carrying her son's baby; you're carrying her grandchild. That should be enough to make her love you if she has any conscience. And besides, you said Tokunboh is her only child didn't you?'

'Yes, he is,' said Nike.

'Good, that makes it all the more easy,' said Shade with confidence. 'Every woman wants more than one child to carry her name. She'll be more than happy to receive you!'

Nike got to the Martins' villa the next Saturday morning. With trepidation, she filled out the visitor's form required by the security guard and waited for Mrs Martins to summon her in.

Alli recognised Nike as the girl that Master Tokunboh had brought home several weeks before, but since he was not in, the girl had to follow the normal visitor's protocol at the Martins' villa otherwise his job would be on the line.

The form was sent into the house and Nike waited at the reception outside the mansion. While she waited, she fearfully twiddled her fingers until they hurt. She could not help being scared. If Sir Martins had been in the house, she would have been a bit comforted but she had been told right from the minute she got there that Sir Martins was not at home. That meant she had to see his wife, Mrs Yetunde Martins, or go back wherever she came from. She had decided to see Mrs Martins. There was no point delaying the inevitable. The earlier the iron lady knew that she had her grandchild growing in her womb, the better; besides, she might use this opportunity to ask after Tokunboh. So, she had waited.

'Please come with me, miss,' a servant said to her suddenly.

Nike felt her heart jump to her mouth. Her stomach began to churn as she followed the servant into the beautiful mansion. She tried to brace herself for whatever the iron lady had to say. She knew that whatever it was, it would either make or mar her future!

Nike was taken to the visitors' sitting room by the servant. She remembered that Tokunboh had shown her the sitting room the first time she had been to the house.

'Good luck!' the servant whispered and quietly left. She knew that Nike must be experiencing some problem pertaining to Mrs Martins' son and she was not ready to witness Mrs Martins' reaction to it.

Mrs Martins was seated on one of the leather sofas in the visitors' sitting room. Nike stood before her, shivering. She assessed Nike scornfully from her head to her shoes before saying tersely, 'And what can I do for you, young lady?'

Nike was surprised that Tokunboh mum's had spoken to her as if she was seeing her for the first time. *Or had she forgotten who she was?*

'My name is Nike Adeogun; I'm… I'm Tokunboh's… I'm Tokunboh's friend,' she stammered. She was not sure if Tokunboh had told his mother about them.

Mrs Martins looked at Nike more scornfully, then she said sarcastically, 'Really, I never knew you thought I may have lost my memory; that's why you had to re-introduce yourself to me.'

'No madam,' said Nike hastily. 'I never thought such a thing, but–'

'Then tell me what the hell brought you here and stop wasting my time,' shouted Mrs Martins.

Nike was visibly shaken. But there was no point beating about the bush. She swallowed hard.

'I'm… I'm pregnant, madam,' she said.

Mrs Martins looked at her for an uncomfortably long moment before bursting into a raucous laughter.

'You're pregnant?' she said finally, and before Nike could say a word, she asked her, 'By whom? By my son of course!' she mocked, and then she laughed some more. She laughed so hard, tears poured down her face.

Nike stood there, wishing the floor would open up and swallow her; she couldn't stand this woman's savagery.

After a while, Mrs Martins took a handkerchief and dried her tears. She got up from her seat and went to the bar on a corner of the sitting room. There, she poured herself a shot of whisky which she swallowed in a gulp. With a stiff, cynical smile on her face, she looked at Nike for a long, uncomfortable moment. Nike looked at Mrs Martins through the blur of her tears, her eyes desperately pleading for her to try and understand her plight, to have mercy on her.

'You're a fool,' blurted Mrs Martins.

Nike cringed.

'You're a big, worthless fool,' continued Mrs Martins.

She poured herself another shot of whisky and went to sit where she had sat before. She stretched her legs on a coffee table before her and took a sip from her drink.

Nike looked at the floor. She could not bring herself to look at Mrs Martins.

'How old are you, young lady?' asked Mrs Martins suddenly.

'I'm… I'm fourteen,' said Nike fearfully.

'You're fourteen, and you feel you're old enough to open your legs for a man?' said Mrs Martins; it was as if she spat the question at Nike.

Nike remained silent.

'Young lady,' continued Mrs Martins as if Nike had no name. 'You have no home training. Some children are said to lack adequate home training, but I must tell you that you've got none at all. Your father and mother did not train you at all.'

Nike saw red at the subtle insult Mrs Martins passed on her father. At that moment, she hated Mrs Martins with a passion; she did not mind that she was Tokunboh's mother. But she kept quiet. She was in Mrs Martins house and she was the one who needed her help. Besides, she could not blame Mrs Martins altogether. Her father had warned her against what led her into this *mess*; she was the one who had not listened. She was the one who had got carried away and stupidly landed in trouble.

'Now get out of my house,' shouted Mrs Martins; she looked like she might strangle something any moment.

Nike turned around and ran.

'Wait there, young lady,' shouted Mrs Martins before Nike could make her full exit.

Nike turned to face her.

'Make sure that you never, ever mention to anyone that my son is the father of that bastard you're carrying; and don't you ever come anywhere near this house again. Do you understand?'

Nike felt choked by the tears welling up within her. She covered her mouth with her hand to keep back the sobs that threatened to escape from it.

'Now run along, you miserable slut,' yelled Mrs Martins, unmindful of Nike's tearful state.

Nike ran out as fast as her legs could carry her.

'So the bitch sent you away,' said Shade angrily.

Nike nodded. She was still in tears. They were seated on the pavement in her secret rendezvous, away from the prying eyes of other students. Nike had taken Shade there to narrate the outcome of her meeting with Mrs Martins. She felt she had to tell Shade everything; she could not think of a single solution to her problem. She was relying entirely on Shade to proffer a solution fast; otherwise, she would be sent out of the school when she began to show.

'The woman must be very heartless and wicked and cruel and... in fact, she must be a very bad witch!' said Shade vehemently.

Nike said nothing; she had nothing to say.

After a while, Shade snapped her fingers. Nike looked at her hopefully.

'There could be a solution after all,' Shade told her happily.

'What is it? What is the solution?' asked Nike expectantly.

Shade smiled slowly as she said to her, 'The only solution lies with none other but the notorious Tunde Oka!'

'What?!' exclaimed Nike. Shade had just mentioned the name of one student that other students in the school did their best to avoid. *How could the notorious Tunde Oka proffer a solution to her problem?* Nike felt deflated; she regretted coming to Shade for advice.

Chapter 18

As soon as Nike had left the Martin's Villa, Mrs Martins picked up the intercom and spoke to the security guard, 'Alli, never allow that girl into this house again, do you understand?' she said.

'Yes madam,' said the security guard respectfully.

'Good,' said Mrs Martins and the intercom went off.

Next, Mrs Martins picked up the telephone and put a call through to Blueberry Secondary school.

In the reception of the Blueberry Secondary school, the school secretary was typing out some letters when the telephone rang. She hesitated before picking it up. She hoped it was not the principal calling to ask for the first draft of the letters he had dictated to her earlier. The school intercom system was under repairs and any time the principal wanted to give her a message, he used the telephone. Much to her chagrin, the principal seemed to enjoy calling her on the telephone even when the message he had for her was totally unnecessary. *The man can so be impossible*, she thought.

The telephone rang again and she it picked up with reluctance.

'Hello, this is Blueberry—'

'Put me through to Lucas now,' came the terse voice at the other end of the telephone.

The school secretary stood at attention. She recognised Mrs Martin's voice; but then everyone working with the school recognised Mrs Martin's voice.

'Certainly Mrs Martins,' she said and put the call through to the principal's extension.

'Mrs Martins is on the line, sir,' she said to Mr Lucas, the principal and quickly dropped the line. She did not want Mr Lucas to cajole her into lying to the iron lady that he was not around. Everyone tried to avoid Mrs Martins. She hoped Mr Lucas was not in some trouble.

'Hello madam, Lucas on the line,' said Mr Lucas fearfully; he was fidgeting with his tie as he spoke. He wondered what on earth would prompt Mrs Martins to want to speak with him.

'See me in my house immediately,' said Mrs Martins and the line went off. Mr Lucas looked at the telephone receiver and his hands shook terribly. He could not fathom why Mrs Martins wanted his presence in her home, but whatever it was, he knew it would be an unpleasant matter.

Mrs Martins was the chairperson of the board of directors of the Blueberry Secondary school. In fact, rumour had it that she owned over eighty per cent of the shares of the prestigious school. Mrs Martins commanded much respect even among the members of the board of directors of the school. As far as the school was concerned, it was Mrs Martins who called the shots.

Mr Lucas was particularly fearful of Mrs Martins because she was the one who had brought him out of total obscurity, and made him the principal of Blueberry Secondary school. Mrs Martins had told him in no mistaken terms that he, Mr Lucas, was grossly indebted to her. To Mrs Martins, Mr Lucas was no more than an errand boy. She had blackmailed him into submitting to her will a couple of times, and she had exploited his position as the principal of the school to intimidate the children of her opponents any time and any way she wanted. A few times, he had been made to expel some students from the school in an unjustifiable manner. Mr Lucas felt he had no choice but to obey the iron lady. After all, he had many mouths to feed.

Sighing, he picked up the telephone and made a call through to the school secretary.

'Get me the school driver,' he ordered.

Ten minutes later, the school driver came in and off they went to the Martin's villa.

They got to the Martin's villa thirty minutes after Mrs Martin's call to the principal; after showing the security guard his personal identity, he was ushered into the compound, whilst the school driver was left behind in the school van.

As soon as he was in the compound of the big mansion, a butler was on hand to take him to Mrs Martins.

'This way,' said the uniformed butler, and with obvious trepidation, Mr Lucas followed him. The butler did not envy Mr Lucas; nobody working for Mrs Martins ever wished to find himself in her black books.

When they got to the Martin's private sitting room, the door seemed to open of its own volition and they both went in. Mrs Martins was seated on one of the large, expensive sofas in the sitting room, opposite a giant television set. She had a glass of whisky in her hand and a half-filled bottle of the whisky on the coffee table beside her. She directed Mr Lucas to a seat. Mr Lucas promptly sat down as far away from her as possible.

'You may leave now,' she said to the butler who eagerly scurried away.

Mr Lucas looked down at his own shoes; he was very frightened. Mrs Martins studied Mr Lucas for a while; she liked what she saw. She liked instilling fear into her subjects. She took a sip from her glass and cleared her throat. Mr Lucas stiffened but he remained silent. His reaction did not go unnoticed by Mrs Martins. She smiled.

'There's a girl in the school called Nike Adeogun,' she said suddenly.

Mr Lucas remembered the girl immediately. 'Yes madam,' he said quickly. He had noted the close relationship between Nike and Tokunboh Martins, who happened to be Mrs Martin's son. He was also aware that her school fees and school levies were being paid by the honourable minister of Petroleum, who happened to be Mrs Martin's husband. Surely, this must be some kind of good news. He went on to give the low-down on the student without being asked to. 'She's a very intelligent girl in the school; she's almost as intelligent as your lovely son Tokunboh Martins,' he said happily, laying emphasis on the word *almost*. There was no harm giving accolades to Mrs Martins' son. She was very proud of her son and the praise would make her happy, so he went on, oblivious of the irritated look Mrs Martins gave him, 'You see, madam,' he said. 'Tokunboh, your son, was a great asset to the school till he graduated, and Nike is following in his footsteps. It's just a pity that she lost her dad a few months ago but Tokunboh was–'

Mrs Martins had had enough. 'Will you shut the hell up,' she yelled at Mr Lucas. 'Who asked you for a dissertation on the girl and my son?'

Mr Lucas kept quiet immediately. He directed his gaze to the floor once again. Mrs Martins went on, 'What I summoned you here for is that I want you to stop the friendship between my son and that girl.'

Mr Lucas looked up slowly. 'How… how will I do that?' he asked hesitantly, 'Tokunboh is no longer in the school and…'

'That's where I was coming to,' said Mrs Martins thoughtfully. 'You see, I want you to make her write Tokunboh a letter…'

Later that day, Nike was summoned into the principal's office. Her heart skipped a few beats when Belinda came to inform her that she was wanted by the principal. As she left the library and slowly walked towards the principal's office, she knew what she was going there to do; she was going to the principal's office to receive her letter of expulsion from the school. She was a hundred per cent sure that Mrs Martins had reported her to the principal; she had definitely informed the principal that she was pregnant. Her life as a student of Blueberry Secondary School was definitely over.

As she sat in the principal's office, she braced herself for the judgment that was about to befall her. However, she was surprised when the principal passed her a pen and a piece of paper and told her that he was going to dictate a letter for her to write down.

Was she expected to write out her own expulsion letter? She took the pen and paper and waited for the principal to start dictating.

The principal opened his mouth and began:

Dear Tokunboh,
  I am very pleased to inform you that I am no longer in love with you.
  I must confess that I was never in love with you; I was rather in love with your father's money...

Nike stopped writing; she suddenly realised what was happening. The principal had been given orders to force her to write a letter of denial to Tokunboh under duress; and she was being forced to tell lies upon herself in the process. She resolved not to go on with the letter. She dropped the pen on the paper and looked at the principal unflinchingly.

'I'm not going on with this,' she said determinedly. 'I'm not going to tell lies against myself; and I'm definitely not going to break Tokunboh's heart.'

The principal looked at her for a moment, then he gave a short mirthless laugh.

'Of course you're going to break his heart, my dear,' he said to her. 'You know why you're going to break his heart? Because his mother said so!'

Nike had already known that Mrs Martins was behind all this. The principal was only carrying out the instructions she gave him. But writing that letter, she knew would break Tokunboh's heart and she couldn't do that to him; he had given her so much.

The principal went on, 'You're going to do as I say. The letter must arrive at the United States of America by DHL first thing on Monday morning; in fact, Tokunboh must have read it by noon on Monday, so that leaves you with no option but to write it now!'

'No, I will not. I will not write the letter; I will not break Tokunboh's heart,' said Nike stubbornly.

'You want to prove stubborn with me, not so?' the principal asked, obviously frustrated. Then, he went on when Nike remained adamant. 'You know the terms and conditions of the school. No student is allowed to be in any close relationship with the opposite sex, and you have the audacity to go against the law of the school and also tell it to my face.'

Suddenly, the principal stood up and left the office. He soon returned with four male teachers. Before Nike could fathom what was actually happening, the teachers had grabbed her by her hands and feet and laid her flat on the principal's table. A female teacher came in with a big cane and gave Nike a stinging lash of the cane on her back. Nike cried out in pain. She wrestled in vain to be free from the hold of the male teachers. They seemed to have pinned her down on the table with a force beyond the ordinary. She could not even move a muscle. The female teacher gave her more strokes of the cane; some fell on her back, while most fell on her buttocks.

Nike tried to endure the flogging for a while; she gritted her teeth and yelled in pain. After some time, she could not take the torment any longer; she cried out loud that she would write the letter. The flogging stopped instantly.

The principal ordered all the teachers to excuse them and asked Nike to sit on the chair in front of him. Nike sat down on the chair but she quickly stood up again. The chair felt too hot for her to sit on; her buttocks were definitely bloated from the numerous strokes of cane she had received. The principal did not care whether she wrote the letter while standing or flying. All he wanted was for her to write that letter so he could deliver it to Mrs Martins that same day. He looked at Nike sternly and ordered her to start writing while he dictated.

Weeping loudly, Nike picked up the pen and bending over the principal's table, she wrote profusely…

…Now that you're out of my life, I want you to stay permanently out!

I do not want you to think about me, because I am definitely not thinking of you.

I also want you to stop writing me letters, because I detest reading them.

Whilst hoping that our paths would never cross again, I wish you all the best in your future endeavours.

Nike's heart seemed to bleed with every word she was made to write. Every word seemed to rub raw chilli on the wound she had sustained from the flogging she received from the teachers. It got to a point that she could not decide what gave her more pain between the physical beatings she had received earlier or the emotional torture she was experiencing from what the principal was making her do. What made her angrier was the fact that Tokunboh had written her letters as he had promised, and those letters had just not been delivered to her. The principal had not given her the address that this letter was going; otherwise, she would have tried to remember it and she would have written another letter to Tokunboh that would eventually counter what she had been made to write under duress.

After a while, the principal was satisfied. Dictating the exact words, he made her round up the letter and collected it from Nike; then he ordered her out of his office, but not before warning her never to mention the letter or its contents to anyone.

Nike tried to run out of the office but her movement was slowed down by the pain she was feeling in her buttocks.

When she was finally out of the principal's office, a thought came to her mind. Why had the principal not mentioned anything about the pregnancy? She had not even been told to write it down in her letter to Tokunboh. *What was Mrs Martins up to?*

She did not know what Mrs Martins would do next; but then no one ever knew what Mrs Martins could do next. That was why people who knew her well enough always tried their best to avoid getting into her trap, except her husband and her son of course. She respected her husband because his political status gave her power, and she loved her only son more than life itself, and she would do anything within her means to protect his interest.

When Mrs Martins read the letter that Nike had been forced to write, she kissed it and said to Mr Lucas, 'Bravo Lucas, well done indeed! You have proven yourself to be a loyal person to me and a smart one *after all*.

If Mr Lucas ever sensed the sarcasm in her praise to him, he chose to ignore it. *He had no choice really.*

'You shall receive a package soon for a job well done,' said Mrs Martins finally.

'Thank you, madam,' Mr Lucas said happily.

When Mr Lucas had gone, Mrs Martins poured herself a shot of brandy. She had deliberately omitted the pregnancy part when she discussed Nike with Mr Lucas. Obviously, the girl would wish to terminate the pregnancy in order to continue her schooling, especially since her school fees had been paid for on a platter of gold. In the process of aborting the pregnancy, anything – anything at *all* – could go wrong and the less anybody knew that she was aware of it, the better for her social image. She could always deny having anything to do with the stupid pregnancy; it would only be the girl's word against hers, and she was sure that if anything, the principal would defend her with confidence. She did not want any scandal attached to her or her son in any way. As she took a sip of brandy from her glass, she could not help but praise her own ingenuity.

Back in the dormitory, Nike asked Shade quietly, 'How will I contact Tunde Oka without anyone ever knowing?'

Shade grinned, 'Now I know you mean business,' she said as she pulled Nike out of the building towards their secret rendezvous. She could not afford to talk about Tunde Oka in the presence of the other girls. Anybody who had the misfortune of being associated with the notorious Tunde Oka risked being ostracised by the other students. Nike followed her meekly. Now that she had been forced out of Tokunboh's life, the best thing to do was to get rid of the pregnancy and carry on with her life.

'Now, I will take you to Tunde Oka's hideout, but I must warn you that you have to comply with whatever he tells you to do. Tunde Oka can be… well, he can be demanding.'

'I don't understand,' said Nike, totally confused. 'What would Tunde Oka demand from me? money?'

Shade hesitated before answering, 'Well, it could be money and he could request that you paid him back in kind.'

Nike was more confused, 'pay in kind?' she asked. 'How do I pay in kind?'

'Well you… he may…' Shade stammered and looked at Nike uncomfortably.

Nike was impatient. 'He may do what?' she asked.

'He may request that he sleeps with you!'

'What!' exclaimed Nike. 'Over my dead body, I will not.' Nike tried to remember Tunde Oka as he was normally seen. He was a huge, black, ugly boy whose hair always looked like it was badly in need of a comb. She couldn't imagine him to be better looking than that; she shuddered visibly.

'I can't stand the guy,' she said to Shade. 'If not for the fact that I need those tablets urgently, I would not be caught dead talking with him.'

Shade was thoughtful for a while, then she said, 'Okay, okay, I'll talk to him. I'll plead with him to leave you alone. Tunde and I have come a long way and he listens to me.'

'Better,' said Nike gratefully. 'I just can't allow that swine to come anywhere near me.'

Shade was not very sure that she could prevent the *swine* from getting anywhere near Nike; she could not prevent him from sleeping with the other girls she had taken to him for help, but in the case of Nike, who was still somewhat a daddy's girl, she could try and persuade Tunde Oka to let her be; she would just try.

Shade led Nike past the girls' dormitory and past the boys' dormitory into a thick bush behind the school premises. They got to a ramshackle hut which looked like it was hastily built with rusted corrugated iron sheets.

Shade turned and whispered to Nike to be polite to Tunde when they entered the hut. Tunde was not known to be a level headed human being, least of all, when he was angered.

Nike nodded fearfully and followed Shade into the little hut. They met Tunde Oka seated on a large stone inside the hut with his back turned to the exit. He was smoking what looked like weed, heavily. Nike covered her nose with her hand to shut out the smell of whatever it was that Tunde Oka was smoking; she did not succeed.

'What brings you to my domain, Shade?' said Tunde Oka without turning to look at the two girls. He looked straight ahead of him as he intermittently puffed on the weed he was smoking. Looking at him, no one would believe he was a student, much less a student of the prestigious Blueberry Secondary School. Tunde Oka indeed, looked like a village tout and he should have been expelled for his notorious activities in the school but his father's wealth had ensured his continuity as a student of the school.

'Tunde, my friend needs your help; she's pregnant and she needs to flush it out before the school authorities get wind of it,' Shade told him pleadingly.

For the first time, Tunde Oka turned to look at the girls. He saw Nike and his blood chilled. So the insolent bitch, who had rebuffed his romantic gesture, had finally landed herself in a big mess and had come looking for him to rescue her. *Her boyfriend had obviously forgotten her the moment he got to the United States.*

'The drugs are not here with me,' he said coolly. 'Let your friend stay here while I go get them; meanwhile, you may leave,' he told Shade.

Nike was very scared; she did not want to be left in this lonely place with the notorious Tunde Oka. Shade, sensing her fear, moved close to her and reassured her by patting her on the shoulder.

'You'll be fine, trust me, you will,' Shade whispered to her, then she moved close to Tunde and whispered something into his ear. Nike guessed she must be telling him that she preferred to pay in cash and not in *kind*.

Tunde nodded shortly and Shade patted Nike's shoulder one more time before letting herself out of the hut.

When Tunde saw that Shade was well out of sight, he stood up from where he sat and walked towards Nike.

'So you want me to clear up the mess that my enemy created?' he asked her gruffly.

Nike did not reply; she was too scared to speak.

Tunde Oka laughed softly, then all of a sudden, he gave Nike a blinding slap across her face. Nike fell onto the ground and groaned in pain. She tried to get up so she could run away, but she was too slow, and she was too weak to defend herself. Tunde Oka pushed her to the ground and removed his belt from his waist. As he unbuttoned his trousers, Nike struggled to get up but Tunde Oka bent and pinned down her hand with his knee, while he slid down his trousers.

'Don't be stupid,' cried Nike; she was deeply in pain from where Tunde Oka's knee sunk into her flesh. 'Please don't be a monster,' she said. 'Don't violate me.'

But Tunde Oka was past caring; he pulled up her skirt, tore her underwear and forcefully had her right there on the ground. Nike cried out in pain as Tunde Oka vehemently pushed into her. As far as Nike was concerned, her whole world had ended.

When he was done, Tunde Oka lifted Nike up with one hand and pushed her out of the little hut. Nike fell on the ground outside the hut and winced. She was lucky that she had not landed on the ground with her head.

After a while, Nike gathered the remaining strength left in her and limped towards the school. She was unmindful of the thick, dark blood trailing her as she went.

It had got very dark by the time she got to the school compound. She went straight to the teachers' block of flats and located the principal's apartment. Gathering all the strength in her, she knocked on the principal's door.

'Who the hell's knocking on my door so vehemently,' the principal asked from behind the closed door.

'It's me, Nike Adeogun,' said Nike weakly.

The door opened immediately.

'I've been raped,' she managed to say before collapsing into the principal's arms.

When she woke up at the school hospital the following day, a young, handsome doctor was injecting a liquid substance into the drip that was attached to her hand. She had never met the doctor before.

The doctor smiled warmly at her when he noticed that she was awake.

'I am Doctor Wale Macauley, and I am standing in for the hospital doctor, who is away on holiday,' the doctor introduced himself.

Nike nodded and lowered her eyelids; she could not bring herself to look at the young doctor; he must think she was very wayward.

But the doctor did not think so. 'How're you doing, lady?' he asked her kindly.

Nike felt she was doing really badly. Her body ached all over. The thought of being raped had caused a psychological, emotional and mental damage in her. She knew that the damage would never be rectified; not while she was alive anyway. She thought about her whole life and burst into tears. The doctor gave her a reassuring pat on the back and said to her, 'Don't worry. I know how you feel; you'll be alright. I'll personally make sure you're fine. I'll refer you for psychotherapy and in no time, you'll forget the sad experience. It could happen to anyone you know?'

Nike felt it couldn't happen to anyone; it had happened to her because she had stupidly asked for it. If she had listened to her father in the first place, she would not have gotten pregnant and she would not have gone to seek remedy from Tunde Oka.

She burst into fresh tears.

Just then, the principal walked in. He looked very angry.

'Who raped you, Nike?' he asked as soon as he was in the room.

'I'm afraid this is no time to ask such questions,' said the doctor to the principal. 'The girl is clearly upset. It's better for you to question her when she's fully recovered. At this stage, she might not even remember the full details.'

The principal was thoughtful for a while then he nodded slowly in agreement to the doctor's suggestion.

'Can I have a word with you in my office?' the doctor asked the principal.

'Sure,' said the principal, 'why not?' He followed the doctor to his office and closed the door firmly behind him when he entered the office.

'Please have a seat, Mr...' said the doctor.

'Mr Lucas,' said the principal as he took a seat opposite the doctor.

'Yes, Mr Lucas; I am Doctor Wale Macauley.'

The two men shook hands and they went quiet for a while. Doctor Macauley cleared his throat after a while and began hesitantly, 'Where are the girl's parents?'

'Her father's dead and I don't know anything about her mother,' replied Mr Lucas impatiently, and then he went on, 'You can tell me what the problem is doctor. You can tell me anything in confidence. Besides, the school regulation stipulates that the principal or his representative, as the case may be, must be made aware of any health problems a student might suffer at any point in time for posterity's sake.'

'I already know about the regulation, but I asked for any of her parents because what I'm about to say will not affect the girl in question presently, but it might affect her greatly in future.'

'You can tell it to me,' said Mr Lucas, he was getting curious by the minute.

The doctor looked at Mr Lucas for a while before saying slowly, 'I'm afraid the girl's womb is damaged!'

Mr Lucas was dumbfounded. *What has a girl being raped got to do with her womb being damaged?*

'I don't understand, sir,' he said to the doctor at last. 'Could you please shed more light on things?'

'She was pregnant when she was raped,' the doctor began.

Mr Lucas looked deeply shocked. Surely, Nike did not get pregnant when she was raped a few hours ago; at least his little knowledge of biology told him so, and besides, he was the husband of three wives and the father of many children, plus he had concubines all over the place, so he should know. A name came to his mind, *Tokunboh Martins! Could that be the reason why Mrs Martins was so adamant at separating the two lovers all of a sudden?* Mr Lucas shivered visibly.

'You see, she had received a lot of beatings and kicks before she got raped, and her womb got ruptured in the process. We had to carry out a D & C to remove the dead foetus and we also had to remove the womb to prevent further damage to other organs.' The doctor paused for that to sink in, then he threw in the bombshell, 'Nike Adeogun will never be able to bear a child in her life!'

Mr Lucas remained thoughtful for a long time. He was not particularly saddened by the fact that Nike would be barren for the rest of her life; he was scared of the story leaking to the entire school, and to the ears of the board of directors of the school. If the story did leak, he might be considered an incompetent principal, who could not ensure the best behaviour and safety of his female students. His career would definitely be threatened and Mrs Martins might not lift a finger to protect him. She would rather save her image first. Mrs Yetunde Martins was not a woman who handled anything that might mar her social status with light fingers.

'We have performed a series of tests on the girl to ensure that she has not contacted any kind of sexually transmitted disease and I am pleased to inform you that she's free from STDs,' the doctor went on but Mr Lucas was no longer listening; different thoughts ran wildly in his mind; they were not unconnected with how he could bury the news of what had happened to Nike.

'Excuse me, Doctor,' he said finally. 'I must get back to the school immediately. I have some pressing things to attend to.'

'Certainly, Mr Lucas,' said the doctor as he stood up, 'I would suggest that the lady stayed with us for a few days more. This would enable us to monitor her progress.'

Mr Lucas would have preferred the hospital management to detain Nike there for the rest of her life. The problem emanating from the girl was beginning to get overbearing. He shook hands with the doctor and hurriedly left the hospital premises.

When he got back to his office, he saw a note on the floor and he picked it up. The note simply read:

> *I did it – I mean the rape part and not the pregnancy part – but let me warn you that if anybody hears about it, then you*

should consider all your secrets out in the open. My lovely dad would not want me roped into any scandal; I hope you know what that means.

Signed,
Tunde Oka.

Mr Lucas sat heavily on the chair. He should have guessed all along that Tunde Oka was behind the rape. However, his hands were heavily tied. He was indebted in several ways to Tunde Oka's father. He had collected bribes from him severally on the account that his son would remain in the school, no matter the amount of atrocity he committed. He had been made to cover Tunde Oka's several nefarious activities because of the greed for money. Now, he could not wriggle out of Tunde Oka's web because his father would not take kindly to it. Tunde Oka's father could be as ruthless as, or even more ruthless than, the son. *Like father, like son, they say!*

At the end of the day, Mr Lucas decided that Nike would be sent away from the school without anyone knowing why. *After all, he had many mouths to feed!*

That evening, Mr Lucas paid a visit to Nike at the hospital. When he entered Nike's room, he shut the door firmly behind him and without directly looking at Nike, who sat on the bed with her hand fixed to a drip, he gave her a stern warning never to divulge any information about her rapist to anyone; not even the hospital staff; otherwise, she would have to leave the school.

Nike knew why the principal had given her that warning. He was afraid of the notorious Tunde Oka and his father. *It was indeed an unjust world!*

Since Nike had been admitted into the hospital, the school had not made provision for her meals. Doctor Macauley had made it a point of duty to check on Nike regularly, even when it was not really necessary, and each time he came, he brought with him groceries and other necessary edibles. Every time he went on his ward rounds, which was mostly twice a day, he made sure he came into Nike's room to have a chat. Nike noticed that all the time Doctor Macauley came to see her, he never asked her how she got pregnant; neither did he ask how she got raped. The only time he had mentioned calling in the police on the matter was so that her rapist would be prosecuted and Nike had vehemently declined. The doctor had asked why, but she had refused to say anything more about the issue. She was afraid of telling him that the principal had threatened her to absolute silence over the issue.

Doctor Macauley had relented in persuading her to report the case in the long run but not before he gave her the assurance that she could always call on him for assistance should she change her mind over the issue.

Doctor Macauley, who was not more than twenty-six years old, had treated Nike more like he would treat his kid sister than a patient. He was very concerned about her plight. His opinion was that the troubles the young lady had gone through in so little time was too much for a girl her age. He could not bring himself to blame her for her mistakes because he understood the fact that, in Africa, if a girl should have the misfortune of losing a parent, some circumstances beyond her control might push her into doing things she would never have dreamt of. When he lost his parents at the tender age of ten, his elder sister, who was then eighteen, had had to drop out of school and become an 'escort' girl just to send him to school. He knew that being an escort girl in a night club in the part of the country they lived in, was prostitution in the real sense of the word, but they had been left with no choice. When their parents died, the extended family had turned their backs on them and it was as if the whole world had shut them out. But his sister was determined to send him to school, come rain or shine, and she had achieved her aim.

During his housemanship, he had sworn to work very hard as a doctor and become successful; then he would *polish* up his dear sister, who had sacrificed all she had so he could go to school. He swore to take her out of the shameful profession she was engaged in and build an empire for her. However, his sister had not lived to reap the benefits of her hard work on him. She had been shot by a stray bullet on one of her usual outings a day before his graduation, and she had died instantly. He still carried the guilt of his sister's death up till today. He made a resolution to set up a charity for orphans in his sister's memory.

The day he heard Nike's story, he likened her to his sister and made a decision never to allow her go through what his sister went through. He decided to be there for her through thick and thin.

Two days after Mr Lucas warned Nike to keep quiet over the rape case, he came back to see her. This time, he held a brown envelope in his hand and a traveller's bag was slung over his shoulder. Nike had just finished a breakfast of cornflakes provided by Doctor Wale Macauley. When Mr Lucas came into the room, her heart did a summersault. Since she had been on admission at the hospital, she had come to realise that Mr Lucas' visit spelt nothing but doom for her.

Mr Lucas placed the traveller's bag before Nike and dropped the brown envelope on the bed beside her.

'I have come to take you away from the hospital,' he said to Nike. 'I have discussed at length with the doctor in charge and he has certified you well enough to leave this hospital.'

'The doctor did not tell me that I would be discharged to today,' said Nike doubtfully. Doctor Macauley had told her he would be attending a medical conference that day but he had not mentioned her likelihood of being discharged.

'The doctor need not tell you anything; I'm the principal of the school and in view of that fact, I take the overall decisions on every student in the school. In about two hours from now, the school driver will be here to take you away from this hospital,' said Mr Lucas with finality. The look he gave Nike dared her to protest against his decision.

Mr Lucas had actually gone to the most senior doctor in the hospital the previous evening, and he had lied to him that Nike's mother had requested that her daughter should be sent to the United Kingdom for further treatment. He had even forged a letter to that effect; the doctor had obliged after Mr Lucas agreed to sign a form authorising him to discharge Nike from the hospital.

Nike knew better than to protest to the idea of the principal sending her away from the school. She had no alibi anyway. She had violated the rules of the school by getting pregnant in the first place and she deserved to be expelled from the school. Besides, if she wanted to pursue the rape case, she knew the principal well enough to determine that her complaints would eventually be swept under the carpets and the law suit would only bring her sordid past to the limelight. Everyone in the school and in the neighbourhood would suddenly be made aware that she had gotten pregnant and was raped with her pregnancy; and in the long run, Tunde Oka, who was her rapist, would be roaming the streets as free as a bird. The principal was crafty and he would do all in his power to ensure that only his wish was done. Apart from that, where would she, a lonely orphan, get enough money for a law suit? Deciding that the stress and the agony of a law suit would be too much for her to bear, she decided to take the principal's instructions. She would go away and find a means to survive; probably get a job somewhere.

On his way out of the hospital, Mr Lucas bumped into Nurse Bola in the hospital lounge and he scribbled a hasty note and placed it in her hand. Nurse Bola was one of his numerous girlfriends and she adored him so much, she was always eager to do his biddings. In the note, Mr Lucas had asked Nurse Bola to get him Nike's file with its entire contents by early morning.

The file reached him at his home at 6.30 a.m. the following day. Mr Lucas had gone into the bush behind the staff quarters and set fire to the file. He stood by until the file and its contents burned to ashes.

Now, he was very sure that no future investigator would be able to dig up anything on the girl that he had tricked the hospital doctor to discharge; and more importantly, all evidences that might incriminate Tunde Oka, who happened to be the son of his benefactor, had been destroyed.

Exactly two hours after Mr Lucas left the hospital, the school driver came to pick Nike up. As she picked up the traveller's bag which contained all her belongings, she wished Doctor Macauley had not gone for a meeting that day. She was afraid she would never see him again.

After putting her luggage in the back of the van, she sat beside the driver at the front, and the driver sped off. They drove on in silence for about one hour and all of a sudden, the driver took a sharp turn to the right and drove into a lonely road.

The driver looked around as if he wanted to make sure that no one was following the van, then he looked at Nike thoughtfully for a few seconds. 'I have heard of your pitiful story and I feel much pity for you,' the driver said to Nike.

Nike was silent. She was tired of people hearing her story. All she wanted to do was get away from the school which was her past and start a new life somewhere.

'I want to help you,' said the driver suddenly.

Nike looked up at him; she could not fathom how a mere driver, who was probably a family man on a meagre salary, would help her.

'You see,' continued the driver, 'that stupid principal has instructed me to drop you off far away from the school. In fact, he instructed me to drop you off somewhere that will be difficult for you to trace your way back to the school.'

Nike was shocked; she did not know why the principal would want her to get lost in the world.

'You see,' said the driver reflectively. 'The principal has dipped his hands in a pot that is too hot for him to handle; and the more you're seen around, the higher the chances that he may not come out of the tangle he is in alive. If you're still seen around, the principal might be caught by his own clique of evil doers, or he might be caught by the federal authorities; so he has instructed me to take you to far away Illudun land.'

Nike did not understand what the driver was saying and she was very much afraid to ask him to make her understand. She felt that the driver might unearth things that were better buried. She had so much trouble to handle; she did not want to add the principal's headache to it. *Besides, where the hell was Illudun land?*

'I will not take you to Illudun land,' the driver said with finality. 'You will remain with my cousin in Lagos. He's a very nice guy; he'll take care of you till you're able to get your bearing. You see, I feel you'll be better off in Lagos, where you've lived all your life, than go to Illudun land, where all you'll see will be strange people with strange culture. I promise you'll be fine staying with my cousin, Maxwell.'

Nike felt she had no choice, wherever she was made to stay. She had very little money left and she had no roof over her head.

'Thank you very much,' she said to the driver, 'I'm very grateful to you. I really am.'

'That's alright,' said the driver, 'but you must promise me you'll be a very good girl; stay away from boys and focus on how to set your life straight.'

'I will,' said Nike. 'I promise'.

'And one more thing, you must also promise never to venture near the Blueberry Secondary school again. It will do us both a lot of good if you stayed away for a long time.'

'I will,' said Nike. 'I promise'.

It was dark by the time they got to Palmgrove Estate, where Maxwell lived. Maxwell had obviously been expecting them, for as soon as they got to the door of the rented two bed apartment, he opened the door and came out to meet them.

'Hello Dandou, Dandou,' he shouted as he hugged the school driver.

'I've told you to stop calling me Dandou,' said the driver, rolling his eyes exasperatedly. 'My name is David, and it's about time you stopped calling me Dandou, okay?'

'Alright Dandou,' said Maxwell cheerfully. 'I'll remember that next time.' Then turning to Nike, Maxwell said cheerfully, 'And who is this little damsel with you, Dandou?'

David sighed, frustrated; he was fed up of Maxwell calling him Dandou and he was tired of correcting him every time over the nickname. Maxwell had called him 'Dandou' ever since they were kids and he thought that by now Maxwell should have jettisoned the nickname that he so much hated, but it seemed that with Maxwell, David had no choice but to stick with it. He grimaced any time he remembered how he had come about that nickname. Maxwell and himself were both fourteen and in the secondary school then. It so happened that Maxwell had taken him along with a group of friends after school one day, and they had somehow gotten themselves in a silly game of cigarette smoking. They had a competition on who could smoke the most cigarettes at a time.

Maxwell had immediately brought out ten packets of Dandou cigarettes and the boys in the group except Maxwell, who happened to be the judge, had taken a packet each. David, who was the most familiar with cigarette smoking, had placed three cigarettes in his mouth and then he had gone ahead to light them. In that manner, David had smoked the whole packet of cigarettes to the amazement of the other boys. Having unanimously been crowned the champion of the game that day, he had been carried shoulder high in the sky with the last three sticks of cigarettes still burning in his mouth. The uproar had made the neighbours call in the police.

When the boys saw the police, they had scampered away, dropping David to the ground. The other boys, including Maxwell, were able to escape the police, while David, who was in pain from the impact of his bottom hitting the ground, had been arrested with the cigarettes butts, half-smoked cigarettes and the cigarette packs lying all around him.

To make matters worse, it came to light when he got to the police station that the ten packets of Dandou cigarettes that Maxwell had given the boys had been reported stolen. David had spent three months in a remand home and when he was released, he had earned the nickname 'Dandou'. What irked him most was that his cousin, Maxwell, who had been the orchestrator of his arrest and his getting locked away, had also made the nickname stick with him wherever he went.

Maxwell was, however, a person one could not get angry with for long. Despite his unscrupulous character, Maxwell was witty, sharp and generous; he soon warmed his way back into David's heart when he offered to pay his school leaving examination fees after David lost his parents in a plane crash.

Out of curiosity and caution, David had asked Maxwell where he had gotten the money from.

'I stole it from my father,' was Maxwell's blunt reply.

David knew that Maxwell was telling the truth, but he had no choice, so he had collected the money and he had forgiven Maxwell for the suffering he had caused him previously.

Now, what David had come to see his cousin Maxwell for was to seek his favour; he was there to crave his indulgence by requesting him to accommodate a total stranger, since taking Nike into his own home might spell trouble for her in more ways than one. His wife was not receptive and she could make life a living hell for Nike. Besides, if she ever got wind of Nike's story, she could report her to the principal of the school where he worked and the consequences could be dire.

In view of all the reasons, David thought it best to overlook Maxwell's exuberance and beg him to accommodate Nike; besides, Maxwell was very kind-hearted and always ready to help anyone in need, even if he had to play the part of Robin Hood – stealing from the rich to give to the poor.

Maxwell stepped away from the entrance of his house and let David and Nike in before he followed suit.

Nike looked around the sitting room awkwardly. She was very sure that Maxwell lived alone. There were no pictures on the walls; not even a picture of a living being and the whole sitting room, although neat and tidy enough, somehow lacked the touch of a woman. She thought she might not be able to live comfortably with a man who had no wife and no children. *What if he raped her just like Tunde Oka had done?* She was beginning to think of how to reject David's offer of her living with his cousin, when she heard Maxwell speak.

'Sit down and be comfortable Nike, I'm not going to eat you,' said Maxwell, clearly amused. 'My Dandou here has instructed me to take care of you as I would my very own sister and I want to assure you that I'm going to do just that; I'm going to treat you as the kid sister I never had.'

On hearing that, Nike relaxed and sat on the couch. She suddenly felt assured that she would not be assaulted by this guy and with time, she would forget the trauma she had just gone through. She would learn to pick up the pieces of her life and make something worthwhile from it. She looked up and smiled at Maxwell timidly.

'Thank you very much,' she said.

'That's my girl,' said Maxwell cheerfully and he went into the kitchen to make them a nice dinner.

After dinner, David left and Nike's new life in Maxwell's house began in earnest.

Chapter 19

Connecticut, United States of America

On Monday morning, in the United States of America, about eight hours after Nike Adeogun received a letter of rustication from the school, Tokunboh Martins received a letter from DHL. He checked it and saw that it was from Nike Adeogun in Nigeria. He flushed with excitement. He happily signed the duplicate and handed it to the DHL man.

'Thanks a lot,' he said politely and closed the door. This was the first letter he had received from Nike after so long. He was beginning to wonder why she had refused to reply his numerous letters. With hands trembling with excitement, he ripped the parcel open and brought out the letter. Then, he gently opened it and read.

Slowly, the smile on his face changed to a look of surprise, then shock, then total shock and then, finally, to outrage. He checked the handwriting; it was definitely that of Nike. He could not be mistaken. How could Nike write him such a letter after what they shared, after the love she had professed for him?

'There must be something amiss,' he said loudly. 'Something is definitely wrong!' Nike just couldn't do this to him; not after what they had been through together. He decided to place a call to Nigeria to find out what exactly the problem was. He hurriedly slipped out of his pyjamas and put on a pair of jeans and a T-shirt and ran outside, wearing a pair of bathroom slippers. He did not mind the biting cold he felt as he ran to the nearest store to buy a calling card.

'Can I have an international calling card please?' he asked the shop attendant when he got to the grocery store.

'Certainly,' said the shop attendant and he promptly gave him a card.

Tokunboh paid and left; he did not hear the shop attendant calling him to come back for his change. Tokunboh got back to his house as fast as he could and, picking up the telephone receiver on the corner of the living room, he punched some numbers as fast as he could. After a while, his mother's voice came on the line.

'Hello my darling son,' cooed Mrs Martins into her cell phone; she knew immediately that the caller was her son Tokunboh; apart from her husband, only Tokunboh knew the number of her special cellular phone.

But Tokunboh was in no mood for endearments.

'Mum, where's Nike?' he asked rather harshly.

'Oh you mean that girl?' his mum asked scornfully. 'I didn't want to tell you this before now, but I guess it'd be better to let the cat out of the bag. Tokunboh, I caught Nike in a compromising position with a boy in a hotel room; and that was after she had collected so much money from your father and me. I personally made it a point of duty to visit her in the school every weekend so I could give her money. Luckily, one of my aides, who had been watching her movements, gave me a tip-off and I went there one day to see things for myself. Tokunboh, I've warned you before, but you didn't listen to me; you know girls these days can never be trusted.'

'I don't believe you,' yelled Tokunboh into the phone. 'Nike's not that type of a girl; she's a good girl; something must be amiss; there must be a mix up somewhere.'

Mrs Martins tried to stay calm; betraying her emotions would only make Tokunboh suspicious. But Tokunboh had already begun to suspect foul play.

'You're sure there's nothing phony about the letter I received this morning?' he asked his mum.

Mrs Martins feigned a slight annoyance. 'What do you mean by that, Tokunboh? What letter?' she asked.

'I mean are you sure that you do not have a hand in all this? Mum, I know you. I know what you can do to achieve whatever cause you believe in,' said Tokunboh accusingly.

His mother began to sob; she was happy that Tokunboh could not see that she was faking it. Tokunboh was confused. The only time his mother had cried was when he threatened to leave home at the age of eleven. That was the day he knew that even his mother was capable of crying. *Could she be telling the truth about Nike?*

'It's alright, Mum,' he said softly this time. 'I'll call the school to find out what this is all about.'

His mother was quick to protest.

'No! No! You shouldn't do that,' she said. 'I mean I don't think it would be a wise idea to call the school. You know, if you call the school, you might be putting her in trouble.'

'Alright mum, I will not call the school,' Tokunboh lied; he still suspected that his mother had a hand in all that happened. More so, his mum's sudden concern for Nike's wellbeing in the school, despite her so-called infidelity, gave room for suspicion. His mother was never known to be concerned about anyone except her husband and her only son. He decided to call the school anyway. He could pretend to the school's receptionist that he was Nike's distant cousin calling from abroad.

'Bye, Mum. I love you, Mum,' he said to his mum and hung up the phone. Next, he dialled the telephone number of Blueberry Secondary School. The call went directly to the receptionist's desk.

'Hello, this is Blueberry Secondary School. Can I help you?' answered the receptionist.

'Hello, I'm a cousin to Nike Adeogun. I'm calling from the United States. Can I speak with her urgently please,' said Tokunboh tensely; his heart was beating very fast.

The receptionist, who doubled as the secretary of the school, remembered the girl instantly. She was the girl the principal had given a letter of expulsion while still on admission at the hospital. She knew about this because she had personally typed out the expulsion letter. Now, she felt that there was no need to lie about the girl's whereabouts.

'Nike's Adeogun is not in the school,' she said.

Tokunboh was alarmed.

'Why?' he wanted to know. 'Why should she not be in school on a Monday morning?'

'Because she has been expelled,' said the receptionist.

The news was a blow to Tokunboh; *what could Nike have done?*

'What did she do?' he asked the secretary calmly.

The receptionist had become impatient. 'I don't know,' she said, 'and I'll appreciate it if I could go back to my work; I'm very busy; please excuse me.' And with that, she hung up the telephone.

Tokunboh sat staring at the receiver for a long time, then he decided to call his mum again to find out if she had heard the news he was just hearing.

'Hello darling,' said Mrs Martins when he heard Tokunboh's voice for the second time that day.

'Mum, did you know that Nike had been rusticated from the school?' asked Tokunboh without mincing words.

Has she? Lucas is really proving himself as her worthy servant. She silently blessed Lucas. The man was beginning to get smart.

'Yes Tokunboh, I knew that. You see, she confessed to the principal that she was pregnant by a fellow school mate and…'

Tokunboh felt his world had ended. *Nike, pregnant by a fellow school mate? Was that possible? Could he actually be responsible for the pregnancy?* But Nike had never mentioned any pregnancy to him before he left, neither had she written it in the letter she sent him. He remembered the letter and he felt very sad. *So Nike could betray his trust in her?*

'Hello! Hello, Tokunboh. Are you still there?' yelled Mrs Martins from the other end of the telephone. But Tokunboh was no longer listening. He slowly dropped the receiver on its cradle and slumped on the chair beside him. Suddenly, he cried out in a very loud voice, 'How could you do this to me Nike? Why, Nike? Why?'

Just then, Ryan Thomas, Tokunboh's flatmate entered the flat.

'What's the problem, man?' asked Ryan in his usual boisterous tone. Tokunboh did not answer him. He was not happy that Ryan had seen him in this state. Ryan had told him times without number not to trust Nike so much. He had advised him to enjoy life the way *he* did; but Tokunboh had always waved him away.

Ryan, who was a twenty-one year old student at the college where Tokunboh was studying to gain access to Yale university, was never known to be sad; he believed in living life to the full. Tokunboh had always detested what he considered Ryan's reckless way of living. He engaged in different kinds of orgies. He had once been caught, pants down, with one of his girlfriend's mothers!

Ryan's slogan in life was always, 'Live your life and be happy; you never know when you'll die!' Ryan had even introduced a pretty blonde lady to Tokunboh one evening.

'Hey man,' he had said to Tokunboh. 'I've got a hot-blooded chick for you to spend the night with; and believe me man, you talk of any bedroom antics; you can bet she's got it!' Ryan had winked at him and urged him to spend the night with the lady; but Tokunboh had smiled and declined the offer.

'What the hell d'you mean you're not interested in her, man?' Ryan had asked him angrily. 'Why don't you want the chick, she's pretty, isn't she?'

The lady was pretty quite all right; in fact, she was very pretty but she was not Nike Adeogun, and Tokunboh had told Ryan so.

'What the heck d'you mean she's not Nike, man?' Ryan had drawled. 'Don't be so stupid man. For all you know, your chick in Nigeria might be with another man right now.'

Tokunboh had laughed and told Ryan that Nike could not do such a thing; and then, he had gone outside, leaving Ryan and the pretty blonde lady in the flat.

Now, as he sat on the couch with his eyes swollen from so much crying, he had to admit that Ryan had been right after all. While he was in the United States thinking about Nike, she was busy frolicking with another man even to the point of getting impregnated by him.

Tokunboh bent his head and cried like a baby.

'It's alright, man,' said Ryan as he went over to Tokunboh. As he bent to pat him on the back, he saw a letter popping out of the breast pocket of his T-shirt. Guessing that might be the cause of Tokunboh's misery, he promptly took the letter and read it.

After he had finished reading it, he looked at Tokunboh with his mouth wide open. He had heard so much about this Nike Adeogun *chick* from Tokunboh; he had heard how she was caring and faithful and loving and so on and so forth. What he had not heard from Tokunboh, however, was that the chick was capable of writing this nasty note. *Could it be a mistake?*

'Is there a mistake somewhere, man? Or is what I'm seeing here actually what it is?' he asked Tokunboh.

Tokunboh remained silent; he could not bring himself to speak. After some time, his emotions got the better of him and he burst into tears again. Ryan was bemused; in all his twenty-one years on earth, he had never seen a man cry until now. Even when his late father was shot by his mother after she caught him in bed with her sister, he had found it difficult to shed a tear even at his burial. He was rather happy that his father had lived his life and had been happy till he died. His father had died doing what he loved most – and that was having a good *fuck*. To Ryan, that was what life was all about – booze, sex and rock 'n' roll!

Now, he was finding it terribly difficult to understand how Tokunboh could cry over a woman. As far as he was concerned, a woman was no more than a piece of arse. Why Tokunboh would cry over a piece of arse was far beyond his understanding.

'Look Tokunboh; this Nike chick has gone astray, so why don't you get another piece of arse? I can get you two, maybe three, at once if you want.'

Tokunboh stopped crying and gave Ryan a murderous look. 'I don't want anyone else apart from Nike,' he said. 'And I would appreciate it very much if you stopped referring to Nike as *a piece of arse*.' With that, Tokunboh stood up, went into his room and shut the door behind him.

Ryan was not angry with Tokunboh; he was just confused at his reaction to his offer; he honestly didn't know what he had said or done wrong.

Tokunboh skipped lectures for the rest of the week. He did not go out and he did not have his bath. He hardly drank and he seldom ate. All entreaties by Ryan to make him go out of the flat and treat himself to a nice time, met a brick wall. Ryan took time off his studies to fix meals for Tokunboh but all the meals usually went uneaten. Tokunboh only survived on light yoghurt and a few crackers daily. By the end of that week, Tokunboh looked so gaunt, Ryan greatly feared for his life.

On Saturday evening, Ryan made up his mind to change Tokunboh's mood.

Before he got home that evening, he went to pick one of his numerous girlfriends. He met another lady in his girlfriend's flat and when Ryan laid out the plans he had for that evening, it took him half a minute to persuade his girlfriend's friend to go with them. *She will do a lot to bring my dear friend, Tokunboh back to his senses*, he thought to himself.

But one thing kept bothering him as he drove home; *How the hell could he get Tokunboh to play ball?*

Before they got to the flat, Ryan knew exactly what he would do to get his dear friend out of his misery and straight into bed with the hot chick he had got for him.

When they got to the house, they found Tokunboh sleeping on the couch in the living room. Tokunboh woke up from his slumber as soon as they all came into the room. He assessed them all and, assuming Ryan had come home to engage in a threesome as usual, he got up and made to leave but Ryan stopped him from moving any further by standing in his way.

'Hey Man,' said Ryan. 'I'm sick and tired of you going about your life like a living ghost. For God's sake, get real man. Forget about that good for nothing bitch and move on with your damned life man. Take it or leave it, you're going out with us tonight.'

Tokunboh shook his head vigorously. 'I'm not going anywhere with you,' he said determinedly.

'Oh yes you are,' yelled Ryan.

'Oh no I'm not,' Tokunboh yelled back. 'You can't control my life you know. You've got your life to live and I've got mine to live; so leave me the hell alone.'

Ryan was frustrated. His friend was wallowing away in self pity over a lady who was obviously not worth it and all he was trying to do was help. In just one week, Tokunboh had become a shadow of himself and he couldn't sit back and watch him kill himself. He decided on a more subtle approach.

'Look man,' he said, placing his hand on Tokunboh's shoulder. 'I want the best for you. Can't you see? It breaks my heart to see you so sad. I wanna to take you out, just this once, and if you don't enjoy yourself, believe me, I'll bring you right back; believe me, man, I will.'

Tokunboh thought about this for a while. For once, Ryan had given him the option of returning to the flat if he did not fancy the club. That sounded a little bit okay and it might, indeed, ease the emotional pain he was feeling. He agreed to go out with them.

'Gee man,' cried Ryan happily. 'Now you're on the right track.' Ryan knew that he had just been able to scale the first and the least difficult hurdle.

There was no way on earth he could get Tokunboh to sleep with the *chick* he had got for him without assistance. He remembered the pills he had bought from a friend. They were always handy anytime he had need of them. He might as well use them on Tokunboh tonight to get him in the *mood*.

'Before we all go out,' he said to them all, 'we must share a drink to celebrate Tokunboh's change of heart.'

They all agreed to a drink. Tokunboh thought there was no harm in sharing a drink with them as long as it was not alcoholic. He did not wish to get drunk and fall into a ditch at the end of the day, just as Ryan and his friends had done several times.

Ryan dashed to the kitchen, opened the refrigerator and brought out a big bottle of coca-cola. He opened a cupboard and brought out four glass cups and, making sure that one of the glass cups had a slightly different design at the base, he laid them on a big serving tray. He poured a generous amount of the dark coloured drink in each glass and, looking around to make sure he was not being watched, he dipped his hand into his trouser pocket and brought out a little grey coloured plastic container. He opened the container and smiled to himself. The drugs in the plastic container were a mixture of morphine and ecstasy. Anytime he took a tablet of each drug, he felt relaxed and in the mood.

Ryan tilted the plastic over the glass of coca-cola with the different design. As he tilted it, one of the ladies called out his name. Hearing his name made him jump. Although, he had intended to drop one of each of the pills in the drink, his hand had shaken terribly when his name had been called and four pills had popped into the drink.

'Shit!' he cursed. He quickly rushed to the cupboard and brought out another glass. He did not want Tokunboh to take an overdose of the drugs; he knew how fatal it could be. At that moment, Tokunboh came into the kitchen and picked up the tray with the drinks on it.

'The ladies are waiting for you,' he said to Ryan. 'What have you been doing?'

Ryan felt uncomfortable. He thought of a way to change the drugged drink without Tokunboh suspecting that he wanted to drug him. He surely did not want Tokunboh to call the police on him.

'I'm trying to change one of the drinks. I think something fell into it,' he said vainly.

'Which one of the drinks?' Tokunboh asked, looking at the four glasses he was carrying.

Ryan rushed to him and took the glass with the drugged drink in it.

'This one,' he said and moved toward the sink, but Tokunboh hastily collected the drink from him.

'I see nothing wrong with the drink; you just want to cause a delay so we would go to the club very late and come back much later. I know your game, Ryan, and I've beaten you at it,' he said winking and to Ryan's horror, he raised the glass to his lips and gulped the whole drink down his throat. He set down the glass and licked his lips.

'Thanks Ryan,' he said. 'That was nice.'

Ryan was stupefied; he had just committed raw murder! His first thought was to call the ambulance, but that would give him away. Tokunboh would know he had laced his drink with drugs and the police would be called in. He would be arrested and sent to jail. On the other hand, if he didn't call the ambulance right away, Tokunboh may have a seizure or die; or he may have a seizure *and* die. And then the police would be called in to investigate and they would eventually nail him and he would still be arrested and sent to jail. He might probably be placed on a death row or…

Suddenly, Tokunboh started laughing. He was laughing so loudly that the two ladies were forced to come to the kitchen. When Tokunboh saw them, he took their hands and they formed a circle and he began to sing and dance. He was dancing so hard and laughing so hard that the girls responded to him on impulse.

'What did you do to transform him so easily?' one of the ladies asked Ryan, who still stood transfixed.

'You must be a genius; I like this,' said the other lady to Ryan.

Those words were very calming to Ryan and he was beginning to think that Tokunboh would be alright as soon as the effect of the drug wore off.

All of a sudden, Tokunboh yanked his hands away from the circle and fell on the floor. The ladies fell down with him; they were clearly enjoying Tokunboh's demonstrations. It took them a long time to notice the foam that had begun to build up in Tokunboh's mouth. By the time the ladies knew what was actually happening to Tokunboh, he had begun to shriek in pain and writhe on the floor.

'Call the ambulance at once,' yelled Ryan's girlfriend.

Without thinking twice, Ryan rushed to the telephone and dialled 911.

By the time the ambulance arrived at the scene, Tokunboh was dead.

The police were called to the scene and Ryan and the ladies were promptly arrested.

Chapter 20

Nigeria, The Martins' Residence

Mrs Martins was watching the NTA news at seven when a call came to her cellular phone. She answered it immediately.

'Hello, my darling son,' she said sweetly.

'Sorry ma'am, this is not your son calling,' said a voice very different from that of Tokunboh. Mrs Martins sat up; she was alarmed. The only two people who knew this particular cell phone number were her husband and Tokunboh. *Had Tokunboh been kidnapped? What ransom could they want? Why would her son be kidnapped?*

'Who are you then?' she shouted into the phone.

'Well ma'am, I am a member of staff at the Yale New Haven hospital, Connecticut, where your son is. We found your number in his diary and we thought we should call,' said the voice at the other end.

'My own son in the hospital?' yelled Mrs Martins.

The man at the other end of the phone grimaced at the piercing pitch of Mrs Martins' voice.

'I'm afraid your son is…' he began to explain, but then he heard a single click at the other end. Mrs Martins had hung up the phone.

Mrs Martins picked the home telephone and placed a call to her travel agency.

'I need a first class ticket to the United States right away,' she said to the agent.

'It's going to be an impromptu booking, madam,' said the agent hesitantly. 'I'm afraid it'll cost you…'

'I do not care how much it's going to cost me; just book me onto the next available flight to the United States immediately; one of my aides will be coming to pick up the ticket in a few minutes,' yelled Mrs Martins into the phone.

The agent winced and rubbed his ear; he hated dealing with Mrs Martins.

'Right ma'am,' he said and the line went dead.

Three hours later, Mrs Martins was on a flight heading for the United States of America.

'Your son died from an overdose of a combination of ecstasy and a morphine commonly called oramorph,' an elderly doctor explained to Mrs Martins.

Mrs Martins had arrived in New York in the early hours of Tuesday and, without caring to check into the hotel that had been booked on her behalf, she had taken the little travellers' bag that she had packed hastily and had taken a taxi to the Yale New Haven hospital in Connecticut.

Mrs Martins had requested to see her son immediately and she had been taken to the morgue, where her son lay. She had seen her son lying peacefully in the morgue and she had touched his cold face. She could not believe that her son was really dead. Since she had Tokunboh, her life had revolved around him. Anything she had ever done had one motive behind it – Tokunboh's well-being. Tokunboh gave her the utmost joy in life and, as a son, she had brought him up with the hope that, one day, he would take over her husband's numerous businesses since he was the only heir to the Martins Empire; but Tokunboh had died and all her dreams, her hopes in life, had been totally shattered. She had been too numb to cry when she saw Tokunboh's dead body; she just stood rooted to the spot, wishing Tokunboh would suddenly stand up and tell her it was all a farce; that he was not really dead.

But she knew that Tokunboh was dead; her baby was dead and she seemed to have lost everything she had worked for all her life.

After a few minutes, the kindly hospital staff, who had taken her to the morgue, had gently guided her out and taken her to the elderly doctor who had confirmed Tokunboh's death at the hospital.

Now, as the doctor explained the circumstances surrounding Tokunboh's death to her, she could not help the hot tears that flowed freely down her face. She placed her head in both of her hands as she listened to the doctor.

'We were reliably informed that the culprit, who laced your son's drink with the harmful drug, has been arrested and he will be charged to court soon. We could make arrangements for you to attend the hearing and probably attest to how decent and well brought up your son was. I presume that will go a long way…,' the doctor was saying.

But Mrs Martins was not interested in the hearing; she was more interested in the culprit following her son to the world beyond. Any other punishment would not suffice for her son's death. However, her powerful *tentacles* did not extend to the United States of America and she had no choice but to allow the law to take its course.

As she sat there, listening to the doctor, a name dropped in her mind. Nike Adeogun! *Had the girl not come to inform her that she was pregnant by Tokunboh?* That meant she could still have a grandson to call her own; she could have a grandchild to carry on the Martins' name. She should not have sent the girl away the day she came to tell her the *good news*, she thought. For the first time in her life, she regretted her actions. She hoped to the high heavens that the girl had not decided to terminate the pregnancy. Instead of waiting around for a court case that would not bring Tokunboh back to life, she could do all in her power to save his unborn child. At least, that would guarantee her not losing at both ends.

Mrs Martins left the doctor's office with a strong determination to accomplish her new mission.

After making arrangements for Tokunboh's body to be sent back to Nigeria, Mrs Martins took a flight back to Nigeria. She would search for Nike Adeogun and she would make sure she found her; she would bring her home and make her comfortable until she gave birth to Tokunboh's baby, her very own grandchild, then she would officially adopt the baby. She knew that Nike would be too happy to give up her baby to her, considering her dire circumstances. *Had Tokunboh not told her that the girl had no father, and that her mother had disowned her or something?*

Mrs Martins knew that Nike would indeed have no choice but to hand her baby over to her; at least, she would be assured that her baby would be guaranteed a far better life than she had. Mrs Martins would only take the baby and then Nike Adeogun could go to the pit of hell for all she cared. She only hoped the baby would be a son. She really needed a boy to carry on the Martins' great name.

'Mrs Martins is on the line, sir,' said the school receptionist.

'Sure,' said Mr Lucas. For the first time in history, he was glad to speak with Mrs Martins. He was very sure that she would appreciate the work he had done to ensure that Nike's getting pregnant by Tokunboh was a thing of the past.

'Hello, madam. Mr Lucas on the line,' he said confidently.

'Let me see you in my house right away,' said Mrs Martins curtly and the line went dead.

Mr Lucas sat confidently on the sofa in the visitor's sitting area at the Martins villa. This time, he was not looking at his shoes; he looked up and he looked directly at Mrs Martins, his face flushed with happiness. He was so sure to get a double bonus from the *iron lady* for a job well done.

Mrs Martins looked agitated. She paced about the sitting room for a while, then she went over to the bar and poured herself a stiff shot of brandy. She did not offer Mr Lucas a drink. Mr Lucas did not really mind that. The financial reward he was expecting from Mrs Martins was better than any amount of drink she could offer him.

Mrs Martins went to sit directly opposite Mr Lucas and asked him pointedly, 'Where is Nike Adeogun?'

Mr Lucas cleared his throat before answering, 'I have sent her away, but not before I made sure that pregnancy was flushed out of her system. I really did a good job on that, madam. No one would know that your son was ever connected with that pregnancy. I have even destroyed her file at the hospital. Right now, she has no record at the school hospital,' he finished with dignity.

Mrs Martins choked on the brandy she was drinking. Mr Lucas felt she was clearly overjoyed. He adjusted his tie and grinned up at Mrs Martins happily.

Suddenly, Mrs Martins threw the brandy remaining in the wine glass at his face. Mr Lucas winced and wiped his face with a handkerchief. He looked down at the white shirt; it was coloured brown where the drink had poured.

Mr Lucas was confused; he thought Mrs Martins should be grateful for the job he had done.

'So you had the audacity to abort my grandchild?' Mrs Martins asked him. 'You terminated the life of my grandchild? My only hope of carrying on the Martins' prestigious name has been aborted by you and you have the guts – you have the effrontery – to come and say it to me?'

Now he understood. Had he known why Mrs Martins had wanted to see Nike Adeogun, he would not have taken responsibility for her miscarriage.

He noticed Mrs Martins' fists had curled into hard balls, her eyes glittered menacingly; Mr Lucas thought she might get up from her seat in a minute and strangle him herself. He quickly bent his head to avoid her hateful glare.

In a bid to save his face and his image with the iron lady, he decided to tell the truth. He looked up slowly and told her the truth. 'Actually madam, I was not responsible for the girl's miscarriage. A boy called Tunde Oka was responsible. He raped the girl when she was still pregnant with your grandson and she lost the pregnancy afterwards. It's a pity that her file has been destroyed but I still have the letter from Tunde Oka in which he confirmed raping her. Besides, you can ask the doctor on duty that day–'

Mrs Martins had heard enough. 'Get me the letter from the so-called Tunde Oka,' she said. 'I'll make my own investigations and if your accusation is true, then someone's got to be castrated.'

Mr Lucas was relieved. He had been successful at his own gambit; he had successfully shifted the blame on Tunde Oka. Tunde Oka and his dangerous father could go ahead and face the equally dangerous and more powerful Mrs Yetunde Martins.

'Very well, madam,' he said as he stood up to leave.

'Lucas,' Mrs Martins called as he got to the door; he turned back to face her.

'Yes madam,' he said.

Mrs Martins looked at Mr Lucas straight in the face before saying through gritted teeth, 'When you're coming with Tunde Oka's letter, please bring along a copy of your resignation letter as well!'

When Mr Lucas had gone, Mrs Martins brought out her other cell phone and dialled some numbers. After a little delay, a strong, coarse, male voice came on the line.

'Hello madam,' said the male voice.

'Pablo, I have an urgent assignment for you; there's a certain boy by the name of Tunde Oka, who decided to wipe out my generation. I want you to make a scapegoat out of him!'

'Right ma'am,' said Pablo and the line went dead.

Pablo puffed deeply on the wrap of marijuana in his hand and blew a thick cloud of smoke into the air. Through the haze of smoke, he looked at his two partners in *crime*, who were slumped lazily on the well-worn couch in the shabbily decorated large sitting-room, drinking locally brewed gin. They were all secretly on the iron lady's payroll and her generosity to them knew no bounds. However, it had been a while since they carried out an assignment for her and they were beginning to get bored. Their speciality was blood shedding and Pablo, who was the head of the gang, knew that *madam* would not call him unless someone had actually stepped on her toes till they bled. He hoped to have a field day doing this particular job for her.

He smiled at his partners, 'The iron lady has a little job for us,' he said.

Two days later, Tunde Oka's dead body was seen hanging from a tall tree within the school premises; he had been castrated. A placard was firmly pasted on his chest and a simple sentence was boldly written on it for all to see – it read:

A simple message for other bad boys!

Chapter 21

Great Britain, the Tucker's residence

Alexander Tucker Jnr. got to the house he had been born in and which he now shared with his father, Alan Tucker. He had barely known his mother before she disappeared mysteriously one fateful morning, when he was just two years old. He gently slotted the key into the key-hole on door of the wing of the house that was allocated to him when he turned eighteen, and let himself in.

He went to the bar at the end of the large sitting room and poured himself a stiff shot of whiskey. He was not exactly an alcohol drinker; in fact, he seldom drank whiskey except on days he was stressed out – just like today. Today, Alice Palmers had called, and as usual, she had professed her deep love for Alex. She had told him she was counting the number of days remaining for them to get married and live happily ever after.

'Yeah Right!' Alex had muttered under his breath; *Alice was surely living in wonderland!*

Alan had transferred Alice to far away Leeds and placed her in a private school after he caught them both in a compromising position in the sitting room of the Tucker's huge mansion.

After Alice's father died and her mother went away, Alan Tucker had been granted temporary legal custody of Alice Palmers until she turned eighteen, primarily because of the closeness between the two families, and secondly because Alan Tucker was known in the neighbourhood as an upright and God-fearing man.

But the secret relationship that had been formed between Alex and Alice had continued even when she moved into the Tucker's residence. They had not been discreet enough, and Alan Tucker had caught them having sex.

Alice had immediately been transferred from London to a private school in Leeds, so that the two *lovebirds* would not see each other again.

Alice had proceeded to a college in Leeds and dropped out, and Alex had finished college and gone to Oxford University to study law.

However, Alice could not let go of Alex; he was her first and only boyfriend, and since Alice had lived a sheltered life since she was born, she had become emotionally dependent on Alex. To Alice, Alex Tucker would always be the only man for her.

When Alice turned eighteen and independent of Alan Tucker, she had transferred herself back to London, where she got a job as a bar attendant at a local pub. With her meagre salary, she had been able to secure a room in a multi-occupant apartment in the suburbs of Peckham, and she had decided to wait for Alex until he would graduate from law school, secure a good job and get married to her.

However, Alex Tucker was no longer interested in Alice. The day they had made love for the first time as teenagers, he had simply been sowing his wild oats. Besides, after his father had caught them having sex on the couch in his sitting room a few years ago, Alex had promised Alan that he would never have any intimate relationship with Alice again.

Although, Alex had on several occasions, wanted to call it quits with Alice, he had always stopped short of telling her so. Alex knew that the reason for his reluctance was not far-fetched. He somehow blamed himself as the orchestrator of Alice's situation. Alice and Alex had come a long way, and Alice had naturally assumed that they would eventually get married. Alex felt so sorry that he was going to cut her expectations short.

'Alice,' Alex said aloud, even though he was the only one in the sitting room, 'I'm sorry we have to call it quits soon; I'm no longer interested in you.'

Alex closed his eyes painfully; how he wished it was that easy to say to Alice!

Chapter 22

Nigeria, West Africa

As the years went by, Nike found out that Maxwell was into big time fraud. He was into duping wealthy individuals and defrauding banks and finance houses. Overtime, he taught Nike the rudiments of his job.

'If you want to succeed in life, you must be bold and you must take risks,' he would say to Nike. 'Money, they say, is in the mouth of a lion, and if you must take it out by force, you must be very wise, very smart and very cunning!'

Nike spent four years in Maxwell's home before he deemed her old enough to be trained in his line of business. Nike, at eighteen, could be mistaken for a woman in her mid-twenties. She was tall and voluptuous with full-rounded breasts and she was very beautiful.

Right from the time she started living with Maxwell, she had been tutored on how to walk, talk and behave like a mature lady. Maxwell had taught her how to speak confidently and fearlessly; and most of all, Maxwell had taught her how to manipulate every situation to her advantage.

'You must always be in charge; you must take charge; you must always be on top of every situation, even if it means you stepping on toes!' Maxwell would lecture.

Nike had listened and digested all Maxwell taught her, but she had never really needed to explore the advice until after her eighteenth birthday.

The day after Nike's eighteenth birthday, Maxwell came into the kitchen where Nike sat at the tiny dinning table having a late dinner.

'Hello, Nike. How y'doing?' he said.

Nike looked up and swallowed the morsel of ground rice in her mouth and smiled at him.

'I'm fine thank you, brother,' she replied.

'Good,' said Maxwell. 'Now I have an errand that you have to run for me tomorrow morning.'

Nike continued eating. 'What errand?' she asked, chewing a juicy piece of fried meat. It would not be the first errand she would run for Maxwell; and as her life had turned out, it would surely not be the last. But Maxwell's expression this night was a little bit strange. Nike could not read it. Maxwell suddenly dropped two envelopes on the dinning table beside Nike's plate of food.

'Nike, this errand is a serious one. It's going to determine how your future will unfold,' he said, and when he saw that Nike looked very confused, he decided to expatiate further. 'What I mean is; the errand you're going to run for me tomorrow is a very important one and it's going to either make or mar your future!'

In the four years that she had lived with Maxwell, Nike had grown to be very fond of him; almost like she had been fond of her father. Maxwell had proven to her in no mistaken terms that he was the big brother she had always longed to have. In all her four years in his house, Maxwell had never looked upon her as a girl he might want to have any affair with. He had soon doused her initial suspicions about why he had decided to accommodate her, and she had found herself settling down to a life as Maxwell's baby sister. She had never disobeyed him and she had always sought his advice on matters that were beyond her capabilities.

Maxwell had enrolled her in a public secondary school a year after she was rusticated from the Blueberry secondary school, and she had passed her examinations with flying colours. She had made her intentions of pursuing a university degree known to Maxwell the same year she passed out of the secondary school, but Maxwell had waved her dream aside.

'To be smart in this world, you do not really need a university degree,' Maxwell had intoned, 'all you need is your brain and your smartness.'

Maxwell had confused Nike with that particular statement, but she had decided to let the matter rest. Besides, obtaining a university degree was a very expensive venture, and Nike was not certain how buoyant Maxwell was. He had done so much for her, and the least she could do was bother him with school fees.

After that discussion, Maxwell never broached the subject before her, neither did he put her to any trade. Everyday, Nike woke up, did her chores in the house, ate and slept. Although, she sometimes wondered what the future had in store for her, she never bothered to ask Maxwell for more than he was willing to give her.

Maxwell, however, made sure Nike never lacked anything. He bought her clothes, shoes and accessories, and he bought her toiletries. As the years went by, Nike soon forgot all about her future; she began to live for the present. She had a good life and she had a good brother; whatever the future had in store for her could not be better than what she had at the moment; and she was very much content with what she had at the moment. She had been content with what life had brought her – until now.

As she studied the envelopes suspiciously, she began to have the feeling that the time had come for Maxwell to inculcate her into his line of business. She suddenly felt scared. She knew what Maxwell did for a living and she always prayed, day and night, that he would never be caught. Maxwell's arrest would be a disaster for her; in fact, it would put her life in jeopardy; it would turn her whole life upside down. So she had prayed for Maxwell's success at every dubious transaction he made. And she had hoped she would never have to join him in his *business*.

Now, the time she had dreaded for four years had suddenly come. Her mouth suddenly went dry; her stomach turned; she felt like vomiting. Suddenly, she stood up, ran to the bathroom, bent over the water closet and puked. As she did so, she felt Maxwell standing behind her. After a while, Maxwell gently came behind her and rested his hands on her shoulders; and then, he gently guided her to the wash basin and washed her face.

'I know how you feel,' he said to her when she was relaxed. 'You feel scared; you feel nervous, not so?'

Nike was too weak to speak; she only nodded in the affirmative.

Maxwell smiled. 'I'm your brother,' he said, 'I can't lead you to your downfall. Do you believe me?'

Nike nodded again.

'Good,' said Maxwell. 'Now you will go and carry out that job and I will be with you all the way. It's about time you started making your own money!'

Nike had gone to the bank the following morning with the confidence that Maxwell had instilled in her. Maxwell had given her adequate instructions on how to talk to the cashier, what to say to the manager and how to behave in his presence when she eventually saw him.

'You just get him to counter-sign the agreement and I shall take care of the rest,' he had told her.

Nike adjusted the tight-fitting skirt she was wearing, so that the slit on the side of the skirt opened a little bit wider to reveal a clear, smooth thigh. She was dressed not as the teenager that she was, but as a more mature woman. Maxwell had seen to that aspect of her appearance. He had given her tips on how to dress to look like a confident adult the night before and Nike was really beginning to feel like one.

'Be calm and confident,' Maxwell had told her repeatedly. 'Walk, talk and act like the business woman that you are!'

Nike entered the bank building with her heart in her mouth. Her heart began to beat very fast and her jugular vein pounded away as she approached the cashier. *Be calm*, she cautioned herself inaudibly; *remember you're a confident business lady; be calm and confident.*

'I am Dr. Matilda Malomo, the M.D. of Matmal stationeries,' she said to the beautiful cashier, trying to exude confidence. 'May I see the manager, Mr Soji Thomas?'

The receptionist looked at Nike for a longer time than necessary; it was as if she was trying to determine Nike's real age. Nike's legs began to wobble as she stood in front of the cashier. She thought she would break down in tears if the cashier looked at her for five seconds more.

'Do you have an appointment ma'am?' asked the receptionist at last. She was, however, still sceptical.

Nike liked the way she had been refered to as *ma'am*. It boosted her confidence.

'Sure,' she said, 'my P.A., Mr Maxwell Dogu, booked an appointment with Mr Thomas last week.' Nike produced a complimentary card, which the receptionist collected and studied for a long time. Satisfied at last, she returned the card to Nike, smiled and asked her to have a seat; then she picked up a telephone, dialled a few numbers and spoke into it.

Nike sat opposite the receptionist and clasped her trembling hands together on her lap. Through the corner of her eye, she spotted an exit different from the main entrance. She should be ready to make a bolt in the event of the police getting involved.

'Miss Malomo, you can go in to see Mr Thomas now,' said the receptionist with a pleasant smile.

'Thank you,' said Nike sweetly. 'By the way, which way is it?'

'First floor, third room on the right,' said the receptionist without looking at her. She was reading the mail that a courier had just dropped on her table.

Nike walked gingerly to the first floor. She got to the door marked 'Manager' and adjusted her blouse, making sure that the top hem of the blouse revealed the cleavage of her beautiful breasts. Maxwell had told her that the manager had a soft spot for beautiful women, especially those with lovely cleavage in the right places. Given that alone, Nike felt she shouldn't have much difficulty in getting the manager's attention. Nike knew she was beautiful, despite her weight. She had received calls, whispers and love letters from the men and boys wanting to date her, but she had declined all advances. She had had enough heartache from the opposite sex to last her two lifetimes!

Besides, Maxwell had hammered it into her that she would be better off using her physical assets to con men into doing anything she wanted. But Maxwell had warned her never to allow any man to get her into bed in the process. She had been taught how to lead a man on until she got whatever she wanted without letting him touch her skin; and she had brought all that she had learnt from Maxwell to see the manager of one of the most prestigious banks in the town.

Nike knocked gently on the manager's door and waited until she heard 'Come in'. She opened the door and went into the office. The manager stood up as Nike entered his office.

'My, my! Maxwell never told me his M.D. was as young and beautiful as you,' said the manager as he offered Nike a hand.

Nike shook hands with him and sat down on the chair he offered her.

When the manager had gone to sit in the chair opposite her, Nike crossed her legs in front of her. The slit on the skirt opened wider as she did this, revealing a smooth, attractive thigh. The gesture did not go unnoticed by the manager. The manager shifted in his chair and adjusted his tie. He tried to concentrate on Nike's face, which was exquisite anyway.

'Mrs Malomo…' began the manager.

'Miss Malomo,' cut in Nike suggestively.

'Accept my apologies, Miss Malomo,' said the manager uncomfortably. 'I… er. I have perused the proposal and quotations submitted by your P.A. for the supply of stationery and printed receipts, but I'm afraid your company is–'

'My company is the only one with a long history of meeting targets,' Nike cut in, giving the manager a very sexy smile.

The manager shifted uncomfortably in his chair and pretending to look through her proposal once again, he said, 'Miss Malomo, you couldn't be so sure of that; this bank has a long-standing relationship with one of your competitors and–'

'And I'm prepared to make a long standing relationship with you; this is a little business transaction compared to what my company does, and all I'm asking for is a little opportunity to show you how nice I really am,' said Nike as she got up from the chair and leaned over the table, so that her top revealed a substantial part of her curvy breasts.

The manager's eyes darted to Nike's breasts. He blinked twice, adjusted his eyes glasses and cleared his throat before saying, 'Well Miss Malomo, you see…' The manager paused as Nike stood and walked round the table to where he sat.

Nike sat on the edge of the table, just in front of the manager. She pulled her legs to make the slit on her skirt wider; wide enough to reveal more of her left thigh and brushing her right leg against the manager's thigh, she said sultrily, 'Believe me, Mr Thomas, starting a business relationship with me will be the best thing you will ever do in your life. My company will satisfy your bank in official matters and I will satisfy you in personal ones; that I promise.'

Nike winked and the manager smiled.

Miss Malomo's offer was not lost on him!

Nike got home with the signed proposal and the cheque for the advance payment for the supply of stationeries.

Maxwell studied the documents, kissed them one after the other and gave Nike a huge hug.

'Well done, my girl,' he said. 'Well done!' He made a move towards the kitchen, which doubled as his study, then he thought of something and turning back to Nike; he said seriously, 'Nike, I hope you did not do anything with the bastard.'

Nike chuckled and feigned ignorance of what Maxwell meant.

'Anything like what?' she asked.

'You damned well know what I'm talking about, Nike. I hope Thomas did not as much as touch your skin with his lecherous hands,' replied Maxwell. The smile on his face had disappeared and he was on the verge of becoming really angry. He had promised David that he would protect Nike in every way he could, especially when it came to men who may try to exploit her womanhood; and he was not about to renege on that promise.

Nike laughed aloud as she saw Maxwell's countenance. 'Of course not. I did not allow him to come anywhere near me,' she said and then getting serious, she said, 'Maxwell, you have thought me well; and I have learnt very well!'

Maxwell broke into a smile and said to her, 'Sister, you and I are going to make it together. Together, we will beat the world; together, we will make it big.'

Nike felt she had to ask Maxwell what he was going to do about the stationery supplies.

'Maxwell, how are we going to execute the project?' she asked cautiously.

'What project?' asked Maxwell bemusedly.

'I mean the supply of stationery.'

'There aren't going to be any supplies,' he said.

Nike was scared. 'But what if the police get involved? What are we going to do?' she asked.

Maxwell chuckled then. 'You still have a lot to learn, dear sister,' he said. 'There isn't going to be any police.' Seeing Nike's puzzled expression, he added, 'You see sister, everything in that proposal is a scam; the company, the address, the company registration number; everything is a farce. No one on this earth can trace our whereabouts.'

'What about the cheque?' Nike asked unconvincingly.

'We'll go cash it tomorrow morning,' replied Maxwell.

'And then?'

'And then we'll put the matter to rest!'

Chapter 23

Great Britain

Alice left the hospital feeling a bit light-headed. She had just had an abortion. That was the second baby she would be terminating in her life. She called a taxi and as she got into the car, she gave the driver her home address.

Her home was a room in a multi-occupant apartment in Peckham; she hoped her co-tenants were not in; especially a lady called Phillippa, who had made it a point of duty to check in on her all the time, even at odd hours. Alice knew that Phillippa was just trying to be friendly, but she really did not appreciate having her privacy intruded upon; more especially now that she just wanted to be left alone.

As soon as she got into her room, she locked the door securely and went to lie on the bed, wishing desperately that she could fall asleep. But sleep eluded her. She tossed and turned on the bed for a couple of hours, thinking about her life so far.

When she got pregnant for the first time at the age of fourteen, Alex had taken her to the hospital where she had an abortion; and Alex had paid for it. Afterwards, Alex had convinced his father to take Alice into their home.

Alan Tucker had taken Alice in and he had been very kind to her. He had treated her like a daughter and all had been well until the fateful day Reverend Alan Tucker had caught her and Alex having sex in the sitting room.

Reverend Tucker had promptly made a decision to take Alice to a boarding school, where she would be very far away from Alex. Alice had gone to a boarding school in Leeds, and her education had been paid for by Alan Tucker. She graduated from the school, and then, she had proceeded to a college in Leeds. She had left the college without any certificate or results to show for it, and she had come back to London and taken up a job, serving drinks in a bar. Alice and Alex had resumed their relationship then.

Now, at twenty-one, Alice had been careless again and she had become pregnant with Alex's child. When she informed Alex, he had simply blown his top, called her stupid and he had left her in anger.

Alex had returned the following morning with a sum of five hundred pounds for the termination of the pregnancy and he had warned her never to get pregnant again or she should consider their relationship over. Alex had also taken her to the local pharmacy and bought her enough birth-control pills to last a life time!

What Alice could not understand was why Alex was so much against her getting pregnant.

Alex was twenty-four and he had already graduated from the University as a lawyer. Alice had naturally assumed that they would get married and raise a family. But Alex had never proposed to her, and he had never talked about marriage with her.

Alice sighed. She badly wanted someone to talk to; she badly needed her mother.

She started crying.

Chapter 24

Nigeria, West Africa

Maxwell came into the kitchen and found Nike there.

'I've got a big assignment for you,' he told Nike without preamble.

'I'm listening,' said Nike absentmindedly, biting into a spicy, vegetable spring roll. Over a span of two years, she had carried out several *assignments* for Maxwell and she was now very used to them. As far as Maxwell was concerned, any fraudulent activity they carried out was merely an *assignment*.

'This job's going to be a little bit tougher than the other ones,' said Maxwell thoughtfully as he sat on the dining chair.

Nike, who was already seated at the dinning table, shrugged carefreely and buttered a piece of toast. The scam she had pulled off at the bank had given her a lot of confidence. She felt she would do better than Maxwell would expect in any other task he gave her. She took a bite of the bread, chewed it a little, swallowed it and then she took a sip of the steaming black coffee in the mug beside her plate before answering, 'What job?'

Maxwell looked at Nike who was munching away unperturbed. He knew he would find it difficult to convince her of the need to pull off this particular scam. It involved the use of weapons.

'We're going to rob a bank,' blurted out Maxwell.

Nike spewed out the coffee in her mouth and the lukewarm liquid splashed on Maxwell's face. He patiently wiped it with a napkin.

'I'm... I'm so sorry Maxwell. I didn't mean to...' Nike began to apologise.

'It's alright,' said Maxwell pleasantly, 'it was not exactly your fault.' He looked at Nike for a long time. Nike's head was bent. She did not like the term that Maxwell had used. She did not like the term '*Rob a bank*'. It depicted them as robbers and she did not like being tagged a thief. What would her father have done if he were alive to see his beloved daughter paraded on the television as a robber? What would the world think of her? What if she was caught and charged to court and sentenced to prison or, worse still, sentenced to death? She shuddered visibly.

'Are you alright?' asked Maxwell after a while.

Nike cleared her throat noisily before answering in a barely audible voice, 'Maxwell, I… I don't like to be a thief. I don't want to be called a thief. I… I don't want to be killed.'

'No one has called you a thief and nobody will ever call you one; and you will not be killed; you will not even be arrested… not as long as I live,' said Maxwell gently.

Nike looked up suddenly. Her half-eaten bread and her coffee, which had now turned fairly cold, were clearly forgotten at that moment.

'But how can you expect us to go rob a bank successfully? What if we're caught?' she asked fearfully.

'Now come on, baby. Come on,' said Maxwell impatiently. 'You don't think that I would lead you into trouble, do you?'

Nike shook her head in the negative. 'No, I don't,' she said.

'Good,' said Maxwell. 'Now, here's the plan….'

At exactly eleven fifteen a.m. the following day, they were seated outside the bank in a white Mercedes Benz. A minute later, Maxwell checked his watch. It said eleven sixteen a.m.

Nike felt her heart beating faster with every passing minute. She wished it was twelve thirty p.m., the time, according to their laid out plan, they were expected to be on their way home after the successful operation.

At eleven thirty a.m., Maxwell motioned for them to step out of the car. Nike opened the door and got down from the car. She was putting on a dark skirt suit, tailored to fit. She looked every inch the business tycoon she was portrayed to be.

Maxwell was also dressed smartly in a navy blue suit and expensive leather shoes. He was supposed to be Nike's business partner.

With her heart in her mouth, Nike followed Maxwell to the boot of the car. Maxwell deftly opened the boot and pulled out the heavy briefcase that contained stacks of fake US dollars in various denominations. Then he locked the car securely and nodded to Nike. Together, they walked towards the entrance of the bank's building.

When they got to the reception, Nike noticed that the Newgen bank was far bigger than many she had seen. Security guards were positioned at strategic places in the bank. The serene atmosphere gave Nike cold feet. But for her loyalty and gratitude towards Maxwell, she would simply have turned back and run out of the building.

'Good afternoon, madam,' said Maxwell pleasantly to a receptionist.

The receptionist looked up and seeming to judge their appearance, she replied equally pleasantly, 'Good afternoon, lady and gentleman. How can I help you?'

Nike noticed that the receptionist was looking directly at Maxwell as she talked. It was not surprising; Maxwell was a naturally good-looking man; he had taken extra time with his dressing that morning and it was beginning to have a positive impact on people of the opposite sex. Nike smiled, despite herself.

'We'd like to see the manager of the branch please,' said Maxwell very sweetly.

The receptionist looked sceptical for a moment. 'Do you have an appointment to see him?' she asked.

'Actually we don't, but we've got a very private and confidential matter to discuss with him,' replied Maxwell, his tone very professional now. 'And we believe that the bank will have a lot to benefit from our discussion,' Maxwell finished, as he placed the suitcase on the reception desk. Maxwell fiddled with the buttons and after a while, the briefcase opened to reveal a stash of dollar notes.

'You see what I mean?' asked Maxwell, smiling.

The receptionist's eyes almost popped out of their sockets as she sighted the money.

'I see what you mean,' she said. 'Kindly come with me; I shall personally take you to see the manager.'

The office of the manager was located on the first floor of the bank building. The receptionist led them up a spiral shaped staircase and down a narrow corridor. She stopped in front of a door marked 'Operations Manager'. The receptionist pressed a few buttons on the door and waited. A few minutes later, the door opened to let them in. The receptionist turned around and smiled warmly at the two important guests to the bank before going in. She stepped aside to let Maxwell and Nike in before closing the door gently until she heard a click on the door.

Nike looked round the tiny office and decided that it was the office of the secretary to the manager. At a corner of the office, there was a door marked 'Operations Manager'. Just outside the door, a security guard stood unmoving – just like a statue.

Nike was amazed at the tight security that surrounded the manager. She was all the more doubtful of the success of their mission. She began to sweat a little.

They were met by the manager's young, petite, bespectacled secretary, who looked up wearily from a computer as they entered the office.

'Good morning, Chito. What brings you here today?' asked the secretary.

Chito, the receptionist, smiled brightly, and with a voice laced with immense pride, said to the secretary, 'Rosemary, I have with me two very important guests here and I'll like to personally take them to see the manager.'

Rosemary scoffed and looked at the three with a frown. Nike hoped Rosemary would not be a hard nut to crack. She darted her eyes sideways to see Maxwell's reaction. Maxwell looked straight at the secretary. He was an epitome of self confidence.

'You know very well that is not the protocol,' said Rosemary. 'In fact, Chito, I must let you know that you have behaved very unprofessionally this morning.' And before Chito could reply, Rosemary went on, 'I'm afraid, you'll all have to fill out a form while I check if the manager is in.'

Chito gave a short laugh and then she said to Rosemary pleasantly, 'Of course the manager's in and you know it, Rosemary.'

Rosemary gasped; her glasses almost fell off her face. If she were to tell Chito that her utterances depicted a total lack of tact and common sense, she would be making a grave understatement. She thought of words that would hit Chito where it hurt, without creating a bad impression for herself before the visitors, but before she found her voice, Chito went on. 'These two are very important visitors and they are here to transact a very important business with the manager.' With that, she jerked her head towards the briefcase Maxwell was carrying.

Maxwell deftly placed the briefcase on the table and opened it. For the second time that morning, the secretary gasped. All protocols clearly forgotten, she said sweetly to Maxwell and Nike, 'Please sit down, gentleman and lady. I'll personally go in to inform the manager of your presence.'

Nike heaved a sigh of relief; the initial hurdle had been scaled.

Maxwell closed the briefcase and they both sat down in the seats provided by the secretary. Six minutes later, they were ushered into the presence of the manager. The door clicked shut as the secretary stepped outside.

Unlike Nike's expectations, the manager was a stout looking man with short, stubby fingers. He lacked the posture and charisma of a person that commanded so much respect within the bank. As they entered his office, the manager stood up and went to Maxwell and Nike with his right hand extended for a handshake.

'Good morning. I am Mr Dede Cole. My secretary has explained your mission. I'm very pleased that you came here; I can assure you that you have come to the right place,' said the manager as he shook hands with Maxwell. He turned to Nike, took her extended hand in his short, fat one and lifted it to his lips.

As the manger kissed Nike's hand, Maxwell thought of a way to dispatch the burly security guard who seemed to be looming over all of them. He could do without having to engage a far bigger man than he was in combat. The man could even have a real gun hiding somewhere in his pocket.

'May we have a private audience with you, Mr Cole?' asked Maxwell professionally. 'The business we have come to transact with you involves an amount so heavy you might personally wish to benefit from it.'

Mr Cole wasted no second to think it over. Over the years that he had been a manger at the prestigious bank, he had, on many occasions, done what he called *private practices* with several individuals, exploiting the bank's money at his disposal. As a result of his illegal practices within the bank, his liquid cash and assets far exceeded those of the three directors of the bank put together. He was not about to let go of this golden opportunity to make more money.

Looking grimly at the security man standing near the exit of his office, he shouted, 'Get out!'

Without any hesitation, the security man turned around and scurried out of the office.

When the manager heard the click of the shut door, he went to the door and turned the handle. Satisfied that the door was securely locked and everyone else was out of earshot, he smiled and turned back to face Maxwell and Nike.

'Lady and gentleman, may we now proceed with the—' began the manager, but before he could finish his sentence, Maxwell had strolled over to him and given him a punch on the side of his head.

The manger fell to the floor and winced, holding his head in his hands.

Maxwell quickly pulled out a gun and squatted in front of the manager.

'Any noise from you and you'll be long forgotten; you know what I mean?' said Maxwell quietly.

The manager nodded vigorously; his lips quivered but no words came out of them. He looked at the gun pointing directly at him and he shivered visibly.

'Good,' said Maxwell. 'Now I want you to cooperate fully with us; and when I say fully, I mean fully. Do you get the gist?' said Maxwell; his face had contorted into a deep frown.

The manager nodded again, and again no words came out of his mouth. Nike could not blame him. Maxwell painted a picture of ruthlessness. If she had not known who Maxwell actually was, she would have been sent into jitters herself.

'Good,' said Maxwell again. 'Now I want you to listen carefully, so we don't have to go over the instructions again. We have already wasted a lot of time with your stupid protocol officers.'

The manager nodded again. Maxwell continued, 'Now before we embark on the transactions, let me quickly explain things to you.'

Maxwell nodded at Nike, who immediately opened her purse and brought out a syringe filled with a red liquid. This she handed to Maxwell who, after taking it from her with his left hand, smiled wickedly at the manager.

'What is this?' Maxwell asked the manger politely.

The manager quivered and spoke in a coarse, fearful whisper. 'A… a syringe.'

Maxwell gave a short laugh before saying to him, 'You're very correct in calling it a syringe. But let me inform you that this is not an ordinary syringe. It contains a substance that has the potential of killing a human being within two seconds.' Maxwell let that sink in and then he continued. 'Now, I don't suppose you'll be stupid enough to opt for this deadly substance to be injected into you. I want you to think about all the properties you have acquired; think about your family – your wife and kids. Think about how they'll suffer at my hands when you die. Now do you feel me?'

The manager nodded vigorously.

'Good,' said Maxwell. 'You see the briefcase in front of us? It contains thirty thousand fake American dollars. Now I want you to get up and place a call to whichever office handles money in your bank and tell them to bring you five million naira cash, all in the highest denomination. Then, you'll be kind enough to empty the briefcase and fill it up with the money ordered. Got it?'

The manager nodded.

'Now get up,' ordered Maxwell.

The manager scrambled to his feet.

Maxwell got up too and with the gun still pointing towards the manger and the syringe still in his left hand, he followed the manger to his desk.

As the manger got to the desk, Maxwell stopped him from sitting on his chair. Rather, he passed him the telephone and asked him to speak into it as calmly as he normally spoke.

'Remember, I want no games,' said Maxwell.

The manager nodded, picked up the receiver, dialled a number and spoke calmly into the phone; he was not oblivious of the mouth of the gun pressing against his thigh.

'Tell him not to bother coming into your office when he brings the money,' whispered Maxwell. 'Tell him to just push the bag in and leave.'

The manager nodded.

'Don't bother coming into my office; just push the bag in and leave,' he said.

Twenty minutes later, the bag was pushed into the manager's office.

After hearing the click of the door as it was shut, Maxwell gestured for Nike to open it. It was filled with bundles of crisp naira notes.

Maxwell smiled; Nike smiled too.

'Now get to work,' Maxwell ordered.

With the gun now pointing to the manger's neck, he set to work. He emptied the briefcase that Maxwell had brought in and filled it up with the bank's notes. That done, Maxwell handed the syringe to Nike and shut the briefcase. Next, he went over to the manger and did a search on him. He emptied his pockets of his two mobile phones and a pager. These, he placed on the table and turned to the manger.

'Now, you're going to take this briefcase to the car downstairs and while you're at it, you must smile and inform anyone you meet that you're going with us to your headquarters to finish the business. Got it?'

The manger nodded. 'Got it', he said, as he carried the heavy briefcase.

'Good,' said Maxwell. 'Now move.'

Nike moved to the manager's left side and curled her arm with his so that the syringe was positioned between her palm and the manager's hand.

Maxwell stood on the manager's right, the gun clearly hidden in his trouser pocket and together, they left the office.

The security man stood up as they entered the secretary's office. He did not look at any three of them. He looked past them and straight ahead. For the first time in his official life, the dreaded Mr Dede Cole wished he had not been so tough on his staff that they feared looking directly at him.

As they passed his secretary, he decided to make an eye contact with her with the hope that she might guess he was in deep trouble.

'We're going to finish our business transactions at the headquarters,' he said, with a frozen smile on his lips. He blinked several times as he talked, hoping to the high heavens that Rosemary would notice something wrong and call for help.

Rosemary was happy that, for the first time since she had come to work with Mr Dede Cole, the manager was smiling and winking at her.

The normally grim-faced and rigid Mr Dede Cole must be experiencing pure joy from the business that was brought to him on a platter of gold, she thought.

She rolled her eyes and winked right back.

Smiling pleasantly at the manager, she replied, 'Have a nice trip, sir.'

She looked at Maxwell and Nike simultaneously and said to them, 'Thanks for coming to transact business with us.'

Maxwell smiled; Nike smiled too.

'It's been a pleasure,' they chorused.

Maintaining a very pleasant disposition, they led the manager, who still had a frozen smile on his lips, out of the bank and into their car.

Maxwell sat behind the wheels and Nike sat beside the manager at the back. The briefcase was placed on the manager's lap.

Maxwell passed Nike the gun.

'Blow his head off if he dares to make a sound,' he said.

Nike pointed the gun at the manager as the dark tinted windows of the car were wound up.

Maxwell drove for twenty five minutes, then he turned into a bush and stopped abruptly.

'I don't think we'll be needing your services from now on,' he said, turning to the manager. 'It has been nice doing business with you, sir,' Maxwell mocked. Then he opened his side of the door and got out of the car. He went round to open the door for the manager and ordered him to get out. Then he opened the briefcase and brought out two bundles of notes. He shut the briefcase and closed the door. Then he went round to the driver seat and once again, he got behind the wheels.

Before he drove off, he threw the two bundles of naira notes to the manager who was standing, numbed from the realisation of what had happened to him.

'This should tide you over till you find another job,' he said laughing and he drove off. Ten minutes later, Maxwell packed the car and told Nike to get down.

'Why?' asked Nike confusedly.

'Because the police might now be looking for a white saloon car with a man and a lady in it,' replied Maxwell patiently. 'Having come this far, we cannot afford to take any risks.'

'Oh,' was all Nike could say as she followed Maxwell to a parked BMW jeep.

They got home at twelve thirty-five in the afternoon.

'Not a bad calculation,' said Maxwell to no one in particular.

Nike thought Maxwell was a genius; she marvelled at his ingenuity. But there was a question she had wanted to ask ever since Maxwell brought out the syringe.

'Max, I know the gun was a farce, but what was actually in that syringe?' she asked.

Maxwell laughed before replying, 'pure, undiluted strawberry juice!'

After that particular scam had been successfully pulled off, there was no turning back for Nike. Under the tutelage of Maxwell, she pulled off credit card fraud, money laundering and printing of fake receipts and forms. Together, Maxwell and Nike defrauded corporate organisations and individuals, especially expatriates. Whenever it was absolutely necessary, she flaunted her beautiful body for men to see, teasing them with it; prompting them to desire it, to ask for a taste, and when she was able to secure what she wanted, she absconded without letting the men see as much as her underwear.

Nike became very smart and worldly-wise. She outsmarted every man that came her way, leaving them with emotional bruises and financial drain.

Nike grew to become a very beautiful and confident woman. As she grew, she lost her baby fat; and by the time she was twenty-one years old, she had metamorphosed into a gracefully slim and strikingly beautiful *mermaid*. She had a strikingly beautiful face with a pointed nose, beautiful full lips and high cheekbones. Her flawless, lucid complexion made her skin look like butter melting on cocoa-butter. She had the right curves in the right places, making her figure look like a perfect *eight*. Every man she met fell in love with her; but she never gave in to their advances. She had not forgotten the pain that falling in love brought her; and she could never forget what she suffered in the hands of the notorious Tunde Oka.

Apart from Maxwell, Nike could never bring herself to trust any man again!

Chapter 25

The month Nike turned twenty-two, something happened that turned her life around.

She had gone out to secure a *business deal* that fateful day and she had returned home, happy in the knowledge that the deal had clicked just the way Maxwell had predicted that morning before she left home.

As she got into the compound that housed the flat she shared with Maxwell, she suddenly had an eerie feeling; it was as if something terrible had happened, but she could not place a finger on what was actually amiss. She got to the front door of the flat they lived in and saw that the glass door had been smashed and the flat had been broken into.

She went to the door and peeped through the smashed glass; what she saw scared the living daylights out of her. She saw through the rough hole that the whole sitting room had been turned upside-down. *What could have happened in the few hours that she had been away? And where was Maxwell?* She sincerely hoped nothing was wrong with him.

Just then, a neighbour came to her, bearing an envelope in his hand. As he got to where Nike was, he extended the envelope to her. Nike took it and hastily opened it.

It was a letter from Maxwell; it read:

My dear Nike,

I have been arrested by the state security service men. Everything we worked hard for has been confiscated; but I SHALL BE BACK! That I promise.

I advise you to steer clear of our home for the meantime. Better still, please travel back to the United Kingdom and start a new life there, while I fight for my freedom here. I have given Tony your British passport and the little money I could salvage from the house. This should tide you over till you can find your way back to the U.K.

Anywhere you find yourself in life, always remember to keep your dignity; and as it was from the beginning, let my love remain with you.

Your brother,
Maxwell.

Nike read the letter from Maxwell for the third time as tears poured down her face. She turned and looked at the flat she had lived in with Maxwell for eight years. The flat that had housed her and given her protection from the wicked world for eight years had just been smashed and her wall of protection had been smashed along with it. She had been ousted from her life of comfort and contentment in the twinkling of an eye. Worst of all, Maxwell had been taken away and she no longer had a brother to turn to; she no longer had a shoulder to cry on; her guiding angel had been arrested and once again, she was left alone in the whole wide wicked world.

She looked ahead of her – far away into the fast darkening sky – and she saw a bleak future; she looked back at the house she had lived eight happy years in, and she saw her happy past disappearing into thin air.

All of a sudden, she felt very frightened; all the confidence that Maxwell had built in her seemed to have evaporated and everything she had achieved in the years she had been with Maxwell all seemed to have been a sweet dream. Now, she was wide awake; she had awoken from that sweet dream and the bitter reality of life was slowly engulfing her. She remembered her past; she remembered all that had brought her to Maxwell in the first place and she felt so empty; she felt so wasted that she broke down and cried.

She walked past her neighbour Tony, who could only mouth the words 'Sorry Nike' as she walked away from the house and from the entire compound.

As Nike walked along, she thought of what to do next; *where would she go? Where should she go? Who should she turn to?* She definitely would not go back to the United Kingdom; she did not want to bump into her mother. They were better off a far distance away from each other.

She opened the envelope which contained her passport and counted the little money that Maxwell had given her. It was barely enough to cover hotel housing and feeding expenses for two weeks. She knew she had to get a normal job to survive. For the first time since she started living with Maxwell, she regretted not furthering her education to a degree level. In this country, only graduates were guaranteed decent jobs except when their parents were highly connected. Nike felt she had all odds against her; she was not a graduate and she had no parents to connect her with any decent job. The only connections she had were with Maxwell's friends who were fraudsters like Maxwell, and Nike had tacitly made up her mind to leave their kind of profession for good. There was no point working herself to the bone to acquire so much wealth, only for some state security men, who had no inkling how much sweat and careful planning and intelligence she had to employ to earn the money, to confiscate everything and cart it away into government coffers.

As she turned into a street, she saw a sign-board that read:
Dancers wanted; training will be given.

She stopped short and read the advert again. She looked up and noticed that the building on which the sign had been posted was a club.

Alright, she could do with dancing for a short period of time. There should be no harm in that, she thought and went inside the club.

A small man with tiny eyes, a high forehead and a bald patch in the middle of his head was behind the bar, cleaning glasses, as Nike entered the club.

'Hello,' she said carefully. 'My name is Nike. I saw the advert for a dancer outside and I wish to apply. May I see the manager in charge please?'

The man looked up from a glass he was polishing and sized Nike up with his eyes. He seemed to like what he saw because he suddenly broke into a smile and smacked his lips as if he had just swallowed a delicious lobster.

Nike felt irritated by the man's actions, but she kept quiet, trying not to show her ire.

'I'm the manager in charge,' said the man and he smacked his lips once again.

'Thank you,' said Nike. 'How may I apply sir?'

The man smacked his lips again; Nike felt like spitting in his face, but she kept her cool. *After all, she needed his favour.*

'You need not apply,' said the man. 'You're employed.'

Nike could not believe her luck.

'Pardon?' she said.

The man grinned.

'I said you're employed,' he said. 'Come, I'll show you to your room. By the way, you will be living in one of the rooms in the quarters at the back of the building.'

Just as well, thought Nike, she had no where to lay her head!

'Thank you, sir,' she said.

'Call me Calculous,' said the man. 'Everybody does, you know.'

Nike wanted to laugh, but her situation made her unable to. The laughter eventually came out in a weak smile.

She allowed Calculous to lead her out of the bar to the backyard. When they got to the quarters, Nike almost cried for the sheer horrible sight. *Dirty* did not begin to describe the environment. Unwashed plates were scattered in several places and rodents played around the whole area. Nike cringed; she felt goose pimples on her skin. Fate had unkindly taken her out of a nice comfortable apartment and brought her into this ramshackle piece of accommodation. Life was indeed *unfair!*

Calculous opened a door and ushered her in. Nike went into the small room and saw a very fat lady with a pretty face, smoking on the couch.

'Zazza,' shouted Calculous. 'I thought I told you times without number never to smoke in the room.'

The lady jumped and quickly dropped cigarette on the floor and rubbed it vigorously with her shoe. 'I'm sorry, Calculous. It won't happen again,' she said.

Calculous wagged a finger at her angrily as he said, 'Let this be the last time I will warn you.'

'Right Calculous,' said Zazza as she crossed her hands obediently behind her back.

'Meet Nike,' said Calculous to Zazza. 'She's our new dancer. Please make her comfortable and let her in on all we do here as she starts work today.' And with that, Calculous left.

Nike looked around the room; various underwear and dresses were draped all over the room – on the bed, on the chair with cracked legs and on the faded standing mirror. She did not think she would ever feel comfortable in this shabby ramshackle room. However, she had a burning question to ask.

'Why did Calculous enter this room without knocking?' Nike asked Zazza after she was sure that Calculous was out of earshot.

Zazza shrugged before replying, 'That's what you get if you work for Calculous. He barges into our rooms any time and any how he deems fit.'

Nike was furious. 'But that's not decent,' she said. 'You ladies should call him to order!'

Zazza studied her for a while and then she burst out laughing. 'You mean we should call him to order and lose our jobs? You must be kidding,' said Zazza when her laughter subsided.

But Nike was still angry. 'What if he rapes you girls?' she asked Zazza.

Zazza looked at Nike for a long time then she smiled and said simply, 'He can't!'

Nike was confused. 'What do you mean *he can't?*' she asked Zazza

'He can't do it,' replied Zazza.

'He can't do what?'

This time Zazza rolled her eyes exasperatedly before answering. 'He's an *impo!*'

Nike was still confused. 'What do you mean he's an *impo?*' she asked innocently.

Zazza's eyes danced with mirth as she replied, 'Calculous is impotent!'

'Oh!' was all Nike could say. She was clearly embarrassed by the news.

Zazza saw her embarrassment and laughed again. 'You seem to be from a very nice and decent background,' she said at last. 'May I ask what brings you here?'

Nike thought for a while. Maxwell had taught her never to divulge information about herself to anyone, much less a complete stranger. *Never let anyone be able to read you like a book*, Maxwell had told her. Tears welled up in her eyes when she remembered Maxwell.

'It's a long story,' she said to Zazza.

'I understand,' said Zazza sympathetically. 'Everybody has a story to tell.'

'Zazza,' said Nike, 'why do people call the manager Calculous?'

Zazza shrugged again. 'I don't know,' she said, 'but I suspect that the name is supposed to be an irony; the guy cannot calculate one plus one and get the correct answer. He had to employ his nephew to do all the calculations for him.'

'Oh I see,' said Nike.

'I'm glad you see,' said Zazza teasingly. 'Now let's prepare for tonight's session; we don't want to keep our customers waiting.'

Back at the bar, Calculous was behind the counter imagining things he knew were outrightly impossible. He was imagining himself in bed with the new dancer. He imagined they were making love and she was screaming out her head for the sheer pleasure he was giving her.

As his imaginations got wilder, Calculous began to feel horny. His hands immediately flew to his crotch; he zipped down his trousers and held his limp phallus in his right hand. It was as limp as ever. Calculous cursed. He cursed the day he decided to abscond with the wife of his former boss. That fateful day, he had packed his belongings out of the accommodation his former boss had given him and he had moved everything into the back of the van owned by his boss. His boss' wife, who had been his lover since the year he came to work for her husband, and whom he had had sex with every time his boss was not around, had hatched a plan for them to run away and live together somewhere very far away from Lagos, where they all lived. Calculous had agreed to the plan without any hesitation. He did not stop for a moment to think about his own wife and the little boy she had for him. His boss' wife was very good in bed, and more importantly, he had eyes on the huge amount of money that his boss' wife was able to siphon out of the joint account she shared with her husband.

Calculous had driven the van and they had travelled a few kilometres to the outskirts of Lagos when his mistress suddenly zipped down his trousers and bent her head over his crotch. Calculous lost concentration and he lost control of the vehicle. The van skidded off the road and crashed into a pillar on the side of the road. The impact of the crash made his lover, who had not bothered to use a seat-belt, jerk forward, hitting her head on the dashboard. She died instantly.

Calculous had been rescued out of the crushed van alive, but his penis had been severed from his body. It took four hours for surgeons to operate on his dismembered organ and sew it back in place. After a few days, a doctor told him the worst news of his life.

'You'll only be able to pass urine with your penis,' the doctor had told Calculous. 'I'm afraid you'll have to forget using it for any other activity!'

The doctor had been right; since the accident, Calculous never had any problem using the urinal, but he had never been able to make his phallus turgid. He had soon lost all his concubines and he had no choice but to go into compulsory celibacy.

Over the years, Calculous had wondered several times if he was not better off dead; maybe the doctors should not have fought so hard to save his life; maybe they should have just let him slip off into eternity. At least, his pride would have been saved then; no living being would know that he had lost the use of his manhood.

Now, as he day-dreamt about the new dancer he had just acquired, he desperately wished he could have a *taste* of the beautiful lady; he desperately willed his manhood to come to life; he pressed and cajoled; he prompted and caressed, but nothing happened. His penis lay limp in his hand.

Frustrated, he held it up and with his left fist and with his right one, he punched it several times.

'*Damn you! Damn you! Damn you!*' he said.

Back in the dancers' quarters, Zazza stood back to admire her handiwork. She had dressed Nike up in a dancer's costume similar to hers and she had applied a generous amount of her make-up on the new dancer.

'Wow! You look gorgeous,' she enthused, as she re-adjusted the yellow and gold ribbons in Nike's hair.

Nike stood up from the chair she had been sitting on while Zazza fixed ribbons to her hair. Mouthing a big 'thank you' to Zazza, she went to stand before the only mirror in the room. Although, the full length mirror was quite old and tainted with a huge crack in the middle, Nike could still make out how she looked. She looked at her reflection and hated herself. She thought she looked like a young, cheap prostitute. She was wearing a gold coloured, tight fitting blouse which did not reach her navel. Her navel had been adorned with a gold-plated ring and she had to put on a matching gold-coloured mini skirt, which barely covered her behind. Overall, Nike felt that her dressing left very little to the imagination; she felt disgusted! And to make matters worse, she was donned up in ridiculously huge gold-plated earrings and gold and yellow coloured ribbons. Nike thought the accessories only made her look like a stray child. Twenty-four hours ago, it would not have appeared to her in her wildest dreams that she would ever be dressed up in such a shameful manner.

But life sure had a way of springing up surprises on people!

At least, this job would go a long way to tide her over until she was able to determine what next to do with her life; and besides, this hell hole would give her a respite from the State Security men who had taken Maxwell away. Who knows, they might be looking her as well. Sighing, Nike turned away from the mirror and went back to Zazza.

Zazza read her expression and said to her, 'Why, don't you like your costume?'

Nike was about to answer her when the door opened and a very thin, black lady with a gold canine entered the room. Nike noticed that the newcomer was dressed in a similar fashion to Zazza and herself. *She must be one of the dancers*, she decided.

'Zazza, are you not ready yet?' said the lady as she came into the room. Both Zazza and Nike turned to look at the lady and before they could speak, the lady whistled and went to Nike. She held Nike by the waist and said in a very sexy voice, 'My, my, aren't you beautiful.'

Nike said nothing; she tried to wriggle free from the lady's hold, but the lady had a firm grip on her waist. Suddenly, the lady's hand flew to Nike's breast and on impulse, Nike slapped it away.

'Don't mind Sussie,' said Zazza to Nike. 'She's one hell of a girl who is struggling with determining her sexuality.'

Sussie giggled and winked at Nike, who only gave her a cold stare.

Zazza noticed the hostility from Nike and made to patch things up between the two ladies.

'Nike, meet Sussie,' she said to Nike and turning to Sussie, she said, 'Sussie, meet Nike, our new dancer and friend; and please, Nike is just a friend to you Sussie, nothing more, nothing less, got that?'

'Got it,' replied Sussie and then she gave Nike one of her notorious winks.

Nike nodded curtly and turned to Zazza. 'Now shall we move to the dance floor?' she said.

'Certainly,' said Zazza amiably. 'After you, girls.'

The club dance hall was filled with people by the time the dance-girls got there. As they were ushered in, the crowd clapped and cheered and whistled; and flowers were thrown at the dance-girls. Nike cringed and almost bolted but she managed to draw comfort from Zazza's reassuring smile.

'This is what you should expect all the time,' Zazza whispered in her ear. 'It's no big deal.'

Nike nodded and followed Zazza and Sussie to the stage.

Suddenly, the stage was brightly illuminated and the girls were in the full glare of the cheering crowd.

'Just follow my footsteps. Do whatever I do,' Zazza whispered to Nike again. 'Before you know it, you will be a perfect dancer.'

Zazza was right; after taking a few clumsy steps, Nike started gyrating to the rhythm of the music. She found out how easy it was to be a dancer and she was actually beginning to enjoy it when the music suddenly stopped. They went for a thirty minute recess and they came back to start another dance session. This time around, Nike did not need to copy Zazza's dance steps. She wriggled her body and her buttocks perfectly to the music.

The ladies danced until the early hours of the morning and by the time the music finally ended, Nike was worn out and famished.

The crowd cheered loudly and the ladies disappeared backstage.

The ladies went to the dancers' quarters through an exit at the backstage. Zazza and Nike went into their room and Sussie went ahead to an adjoining room, but not before she had given Nike a wink.

Nike immediately looked away as Sussie winked at her.

Once they were in the room, Nike pulled off her costume and accessories and changed into the dress she had worn to the club the day before. She made a mental note to ask Zazza for a loan later in the day, so she could go to the market and buy a few clothes.

'Did you enjoy yourself?' asked Zazza pleasantly. After dancing through the night, she did not look a bit tired. Nike thought she must have been doing the job for a very long time.

'It was ok, but is that all there is to it?' Nike asked Zazza.

'Officially, yes, but it could be more difficult than this.'

'How do you mean?' asked Nike confusedly.

Zazza was thoughtful for a while before answering. 'You see, Calculous sometimes expects us to perform some underground jobs.'

'And what might they be?' asked Nike suspiciously.

'What I mean is that… you see… sometimes we are required to do some *extra-curricula* activities to earn more money for Calculous and in return, we get a handsome commission.'

Nike suspected foul play, but she hoped what she was thinking was not what Zazza was saying, because if it was, she would be out of the door before Calculous could say *Nike*.

'Can you please be more explicit?' she asked Zazza irritably. But before Zazza could reply, Sussie came through the door. 'Calculous would like to see Nike,' she announced, winking at Nike.

Zazza looked at Nike sadly, then she stood up from her seat. She knew why Calculous had summoned Nike to his office, but she did not know how to tell it to the new novice. 'Come with me,' she said simply.

Nike picked up her bag which contained her passport and the money Maxwell had given her and followed Zazza out of the room. They both went to a little office and Zazza knocked on the door.

'Come in,' shouted Calculous from behind the closed door.

Zazza opened the door and went in, pulling Nike after her.

Calculous was sitting behind a desk that was piled high with dirty newspapers and old, rusty books. A distinguished looking elderly man was seated on the chair opposite Calculous, puffing on a thick cigar. Nike noticed that the man was expensively dressed in a white lace outfit and he had a velvet cap on. He looked rich.

What could such a distinguished looking man be doing in a night club with someone like Calculous? Nike wondered, but decided it was none of her business; she was there to work and earn a living – that was all!

There were no seats available for Nike and Zazza, so they stood like obedient servants before Calculous.

'You danced amazingly well, Nike,' said Calculous.

'Thank you,' said Nike.

'This gentleman here, Chief Miye, saw you dancing and he has requested your company tonight,' said Calculous.

Nike looked at Chief Miye, who was smiling lazily at her amidst the haze of smoke emanating from his Cigar.

Nike hated Chief Miye instantly. She knew what Calculous meant by requesting her to keep the man's company. She was a dancer, not a prostitute, and she determined to tell him so.

'I'm a dancer, not a... a companion,' said Nike; she could not bring herself to mention the word *prostitute*.

Calculous looked angry. 'Didn't Zazza explain things to you?' he began, but Chief Miye cut in.

'Don't worry, my dear,' said Chief Miye. 'I'll make you very happy; that is in cash and in kind; I'll give you lots of money to compliment your beauty.'

Suddenly Chief Miye got up and pulled Nike to him. Nike pulled back and gave him a blinding slap across his face.

Calculous was shocked; Chief Miye was stunned; in all his years of patronising the club, he had not seen a girl with such effrontery. He touched his face which still stung from the impact of the slap, then he looked at Nike with his mouth hanging open from the sheer shock of what had happened.

After a while, Calculous recovered from shock and he stood up angrily. 'You are fired!' he shouted at Nike. 'Get the hell out of here before I beat you blue and black.'

Nike did not wait for Calculous to beat her. She turned around and without deigning Zazza as much as a look, walked out of the office and out of the club.

Before Nike walked to the main road, she had made up her mind to pursue the only other option in life. She would pick up the remaining piece of her life and go back to the United Kingdom!

With the little money she had, she took a bus to the British High Commission in Victoria Island. There, she met an officer who was kind and polite to her.

She swallowed hard and explained herself to the officer. The officer heard her story and deftly saw to it that necessary papers were processed for her to travel back to Great Britain. An accommodation was given to her at the High Commission's guest house and the next day, she was put on a plane going to Heathrow Airport, Great Britain.

Chapter 26

Great Britain

The boss looked at the picture of his late wife for a long time. It was almost twenty-four years since she died. His wife was the only woman he had ever loved; she was the only woman he had sacrificed so much for and she had betrayed his love.

She had cheated on him with his brother – *his very own brother* – and she had had to go with him. One thing the boss didn't share with anyone was his woman. His brother had incurred his wrath by committing the abominable and he had had to pay the penalty. He would not have killed his wife if she had not threatened to expose him to the world. He remembered the way she had died and closed his eyes to shut out the sordid memory. His hands shook terribly and the picture fell off his hands onto the carpeted floor.

After a while, he opened his eyes and the memory was still there, fresh as ever. That fateful morning, his wife had come into the bedroom they shared and had said the words which made him realise that walls indeed had ears.

'Did you kill your brother?' his wife had asked him.

The boss had instantly made an innocent face as he shook his head in the negative. He had always found it very easy to register innocence in his expression even in the presence of a vicious interrogator. His ability to be resilient and hold his own even under threat had always been a plus for him. However, his innocent expression did not cut ice with his wife; she knew him too well to believe he did not have a hand in the death of his brother – the only man she had fallen in love with; the man she had genuinely shared her heart and her body with; the man who was the father of her beloved son – her only child.

'I'll make sure you're exposed, you sludge,' his wife had said before the boss could respond to her accusation. 'I'll tell the whole world who you really are. I'll tell them you're nothing but a bloody murderer.'

'Now wait a minute, woman–' began the boss.

'No, you wait a minute,' interrupted his wife vehemently. 'You wait a frigging minute. I'll not stand here and allow you to lie to me. I know what you've been up to right from the start. Oh yes I do. I just put up with you all these years so I could be close to your brother.'

The boss' eyes had turned spooky but his wife did not mind; she went on, yelling at the top of her voice. 'I have loved your brother ever since I gave him his first kiss.'

The boss' spooky expression suddenly changed into a dangerous one, but his wife was past caring.

'Oh yes I did,' she said, clearly enjoying the emotional pain she was causing her husband.

'You want to know something else?' she went on. 'I disvirgined your brother! Oh yes I did. He lost his virginity to me.'

The boss had slapped her then. He slapped her so hard she went flying across the room and into the adjoining bathroom. The boss had known that his wife was cheating on him with his brother and his plan was to get rid of his brother and make the affair a secret to the world; but his wife's next words changed his plans.

'I will blow it out to the whole world that your brother was a better lover and I will proclaim it to all and sundry that our baby really belonged to your brother.'

And the boss had known that his wife had to go. The scandal she was threatening him with would be too much for him to face. Granted, he could wriggle his way out of any terrible situation, and he was proud of his ingenuity, but he knew that the smear would be rubbed on the minds of some people; especially those that portrayed him as blemish-free. He did not want a single doubt to arise when the time came for him to be voted into their midst.

He tied his screaming wife up in the bathroom and gagged her with a towel until midnight.

At exactly 12.01 the following morning, he went into the bathroom to untie her. He had met his wife crouched on the floor of the bathroom, tired and withdrawn, and he had cried for her. He hated to see her suffer so much, but his reputation in the community was more important than his wife. He removed the towel from her mouth and bent to kiss her but his wife spat in his face. He quickly stuffed the towel back into her mouth and stood up.

'You know I love you,' he said to her sadly, 'but I'm afraid you have to go. I just can't let you tarnish my good image with the public; you understand what I mean?' he asked her pleadingly. His wife gave no reply; she could not give any reply. She only gave him a damning look. In fact, the look she gave him made the boss realise that she hated him with all her heart.

The boss slowly opened a bottle filled with a stinging liquid and lifted it to her nostrils. She fell asleep instantly. The boss gently lifted her up and carried her down the stairs, through the door and into a car that had never been seen around the house before. Then he got behind the wheel of the car and drove her to the sacred place he had driven so many others to; and his wife had remained dumb ever since.

Now, as he held the picture of his beloved wife in his hands, he could not help but shed tears, just as he had shed tears for her on every anniversary of her death.

Chapter 27

London, Great Britain

On a hot Saturday afternoon, in the week that Nike came to finally settle in the United Kingdom, she fell into a deep slumber and she had a dream. In the dream, she was putting on the loveliest wedding gown she had ever seen. She was standing before the priest, beaming with smiles. She had never felt so happy all her life.

Her bride groom, who stood with her before the priest, was tall and dark and handsome, and he had curly hair. Nike particularly took note of her groom's hair and she wondered for a second where her husband got the curly hair from; but she was happy with it anyway.

'Who gives this woman's hand in marriage to this man?' asked the priest.

When nobody stood up, the priest asked again, 'Who gives this woman's hand in marriage to this man?'

Still, there was total silence.

The priest asked for the third time, 'Who gives this woman's hand in marriage to this man?'

A slight murmur arose within the congregation; Nike was beginning to get agitated. Suddenly, her father stood up, 'I do,' he said in his clear, smooth voice.

Nike breathed deeply as her father came forward. But when she turned to look at her father, his face suddenly changed to that of Tokunboh Martins. In her confusion, she looked at her bride groom standing beside her; he was none other but Tokunboh Martins. She frantically looked at her father again, he was still Tokunboh Martins. She screamed and the shrill of her voice woke her from her deep slumber.

'Oh God, so I have just been dreaming,' she muttered to herself while panting heavily. She took a towel from the towel rack on the wall and dried the sweat that had broken out on her body.

Why would she dream about her father and Tokunboh Martins after such a long time? And the dream was so vivid, it looked real. She at least knew her father was dead; *God bless his soul; but what about Tokunboh Martins?* She did not know where he was or what he was doing at the moment. *Was he married? Was he thinking of her? Had he dreamt of her as she had of him?*

She remembered him telling her that he would become a doctor. *Not just a doctor, but a successful one*, he had told her. He had promised to marry her one day and take care of her needs. He had told her she would not need to work for a single day. He was going to build a house for her and buy her expensive clothes and jewellery, and she knew he had meant every single word. She knew he had meant to keep his promises to her; after all, as a mere secondary school student, he had made sure that her school fees had been paid and he had given her money out of the pocket money his father gave him.

Nike looked around her ramshackle room. The house was actually a shared apartment and there were four other co-tenants living in the same house. That meant she had to share the toilets and the bathroom with people who were no more than strangers to her. Although, she was grateful to the council for providing a roof over her head by paying her landlord her housing benefits, and she was grateful that she did not starve, she still felt poor. If she had Tokunboh in her life, she would at least have acquired better things in life, she reasoned. Tokunboh came from a very rich family and he was not stingy. Maybe the dream she had was cupid's way of telling her to look for Tokunboh; to look for the love of her life.

'I must find Tokunboh Martins,' she said aloud. 'At least, I owe him some explanations. I know he will understand my dilemma and he will forgive me; and we will live together happily ever after!'

She laughed at her own expression and got up from the bed.

She had learned of the Yahoo messenger before she came to England. Maybe if she searched around for a cyber café and logged on a computer, she would create an e-mail address and she would be able to locate Tokunboh Martins through the Yahoo messenger.

Satisfied with her *intelligent reasoning*, she hastily got dressed and left the house. She located a cyber café half a mile from where she lived. She went in and saw a young shop attendant sorting out calling cards behind a desk.

'Can I make use of one of your computers for an hour please?' she said to the attendant.

'Of course, miss. It'll cost you a pound an hour, miss,' replied the man.

Nike gave him one pound and went to sit as she was directed.

She logged on to the computer with the number on the piece of paper and quickly signed onto a yahoo account using the e-mail address Nikeadeogun@yahoo.com.

That done, she went straight to the Yahoo messenger and clicked on it. She searched for names beginning with Tok. She remembered that Tokunboh had loved being called Toks way back in school, and she presumed that he would still choose to go by that name; as they say, *old habits die hard.*

Soon enough, she found several names beginning with Tok. She went through them and coincidentally, she came across a Tokunboh Martins. Excited, she posted the bearer of the name a note which read:

Hello, this is Nike Adeogun. Are you indeed Tokunboh Martins formerly of Blueberry Secondary school?

In the poorest part of Harlem in New York City, in the United States of America, Tokunboh Martins – a notorious thirty-six year old playboy – was surfing the internet in the comfort – or more appropriately, in the discomfort – of his dingy, shabby-looking studio apartment, when he received a message on the Yahoo messenger from a certain Nike Adeogun. Although he had lived in the slum of Harlem for twenty-two years, he was familiar with Nigerian names. He knew very well that Nike was a girl's name. Even though he did not have an inkling who Nike Adeogun was (in fact, he was very sure that he had never met her), he was ready to play ball. *She could turn out to be a good lay!,* he said aloud before replying her.

Yes of course, I am Tokunboh Martins of the Blueberry Secondary school. How are you Nike? How'r you doing?

Nike was overjoyed. She shrieked with excitement, oblivious to the reproving stare from the other computer users around her. She wrote:

Long time no see, Tokunboh; I've really missed you. What have you been up to?

Nothing much. I've missed you too Nike, Tokunboh hastily wrote back. *This was going to be an easy catch,* he thought and grinned. He received a reply immediately.

Are you a medical doctor now, Tokunboh? Do you remember your promises – the mansion you were going to build, the clothes and the jewellery? Do you remember, Tokunboh?

Tokunboh did not remember promising any lady anything; in fact, in all his life, he had never promised any lady anything better than a good fuck!

Of course I remember, darling. I remember all the promises. You know I'm a man of my word.

Nike was very happy. This gentleman had called her by one of the endearments that Tokunboh had used for her in those good old days and he had said that he was a man of his word (Tokunboh Martins definitely was a man of his word); that had erased all the doubts in her. Surely, he must be Tokunboh Martins; he must be her Tokunboh Martins.

I know that, of course. Remember you paid my school fees in those days?

'Pssh!' said Tokunboh aloud. 'Nonsense! The actual Tokunboh Martins this lady is looking for must be stupid or *very* stupid.' In all his years as a Casanova, he had never bought more than a handkerchief for a lady. It only took him a couple of lies and confessions of love, which of course he never meant, to get a lady. Come what may, after all the lies and pretence, he always got to eat the apple of the descendants of Eve and before they could call Tokunboh, he had left them and gone to look for another prey.

Yes I know that, darling, and it was nothing really. It was my pleasure doing it, wrote Tokunboh.

But why would a guy pay for a lady's school fees? He thought. *Had the lady no parents?* He decided to find out.

How are your parents, Nike? Tokunboh wrote and that came to be his greatest undoing!

Nike blinked twice when she saw the last message from Tokunboh Martins. *What the hell had he meant by how are your parents? Didn't he remember that her dad was dead and that she was not on talking terms with her mum?* A bell of caution rang within her. She decided to put this man to a test. Who knows, he might well be a bloody impostor.

Desperately wishing he would pass her simple test, Nike wrote carefully: *Is your father a politician Tokunboh?*

When Tokunboh saw the message, he burst out in a raucous laughter. He laughed so loud and so hard, tears poured down his face. He laughed till he could laugh no more. *His own father, a politician? Hell would rather freeze over!* His father was known to be a professional jail-bird there in Harlem, New York city. Since Tokunboh learned how to call 'daddy', his father had gone in and out of jail for one offence or the other, as often as the president of the United States went in and out of the White House. Tokunboh had never known his father with any particular job except, of course, street gambling, binge drinking and going to jail. However, he knew that telling this lady called Nike the truth about his dad would be tantamount to rubbing himself in the mud before her. He was very much aware that girls absolutely loved wealth and stardom; and that meant girls absolutely loved to be lied to, so he wrote a lie:

Of course, my father is a renowned politician!
What was the post your father held last? Nike wrote back.

Tokunboh thought fast about what to write. He did not know what post the other Tokunboh's dad held, but it would do him no harm if he could boost his own father's profile to a level that a responsible, ambitious and hardworking black man in the United States could reach; so he wrote:

My father was the Governor of New York City!

Nike was furious. There was no point sending further messages to this bloody impostor. She had been deceived by a man yet again. The idiot had been deceiving her all along.

'Shit!' she swore.

The lady who sat browsing the internet beside Nike heard her swear and looking at her with obvious disgust; she shifted her chair away from her.

Nike deleted Tokunboh from her yahoo messenger list and got up from her chair. She left the cyber café without logging herself off the computer system.

As she walked back to her apartment, she was convinced that she would never see Tokunboh Martins again. Nobody had told her this, but she knew it by intuition.

Back in Harlem, Tokunboh's smile slowly faded as he found himself permanently logged off Nike Adeogun's Yahoo messenger list. He had just lost a very juicy apple!

Chapter 28

Nike hated male chauvinists; Leonard Conrad was definitely one. Nike watched with disgust as he boasted of his numerous conquests over the female gender to his friends, intermittently taking chunky bites from the abnormally large sandwich he was holding.

'Tell you what,' said Leonard to his friends, 'girls are not different from cows. They are very dumb. Once they know you're loaded, they run after you at the snap of your fingers. I just get them into my bed like that.'

Leonard demonstrated how easily he got ladies into his bed by snapping his middle finger against his thumb.

'…And when I'm through with them, I send them away,' Leonard proudly told his friends.

'I enjoy breaking young girls' hearts; its boosts my ego,' Leonard laughed.

Nike felt anger burning inside her at what Leonard was saying about the female gender. It was just not *fair*. She noted that Leonard was on his fifth sandwich since she entered the cafe. *No wonder he's so fat,* She thought to herself. Nike did not fancy fat men. The only attribute she would accord 'Leo the boaster', as she silently tagged him, was his height. He had a good height for a man, although he did not look particularly striking. He was devoid of a face that would make a female want to look at him twice. He was not good-looking, far from it, but he was not altogether ugly. He was just 'Leo the boaster'.

'The last girl I had crawled on her knees begging me after I had conquered her and told her that I no longer had any use of her. I threw her out of my house and shut the door,' Leonard continued, laughing hysterically.

Nike was beginning to wonder what all those women that Leonard claimed to have 'conquered' saw in him, when someone at the table made a statement that made her cringe with furious anger.

'You've not done a good job of it, Leo,' said the little man with wispy hair. 'I would have had her and her mother at the same time. They would have both fallen for me like overripe apples – both of them; but no, not you; you only got the daughter, not the mother. Y'know what, Leo, don't start thinking you're a superhero, 'cos you're definitely not. Your mum's fucking rich, that's why the girls follow you, but I've got the charm,' the wispy-haired man said with obvious relish.

Nike assessed him from head to toe; she could not help but think that the girls he claimed to have had were either straight from the psychiatry or *dead*. *How on earth would any decent girl have even a fling with a man like that?* Nike thought to herself. The wispy-haired guy was not only ugly, he looked poor. He was too short for a man. Nike assessed his height; at most, he would be five foot no inches. He was also very skinny – ungraciously skinny as if *he was suffering from kwashiorkor*, Nike thought. He sure reminded her of an insect called cricket. She burst into laughter.

As she did so, all the men at Leo the boaster's table turned in her direction. The wispy-haired man was the first to talk to her. 'Care to join in the fun, babe? We could give you a nice time afterwards. We sure gonna have *a loooong foursome night*,' he finished, winking at her. Nike felt like spitting in his face, but she kept her cool.

'It's alright, Johnnie, I'll handle her myself. I'm the boss in this gathering. I foot the bill and whatever I say goes,' said Leo the boaster, taking a mouthful of the bogus sandwich he was holding.

Aha! Johnnie, Nike thought, *Johnnie's his name – Johnnie the cricket.*

'But–' started Johnnie.

But Leo quickly cut in. 'Y'know what they say about he who pays the piper…?'

Nike took in Leo the boaster's expression; it had a tone of warning to it. Obviously, the stupid fellas depended on him for survival. *Well we'll see about Leo the 'rich' boaster,* Nike thought.

'I spoke to the lady first,' said Johnnie resignedly; his shoulders had suddenly sagged.

'And I said No!' shouted Leo.

Nike could not believe the stupidity of them all. How on earth could they be fighting over a lady who had not uttered a single word to them? *Were they for real?*

It had been over a year since Nike had returned to settle in the United Kingdom and in all the months she had spent in the U.K, she had not met anyone as stupid as Leonard and his friends.

Suddenly the third man in the group, who had only been laughing, spoke up in a voice so quiet it was barely audible to Nike, 'I think Leonard's right. Let him have the girl and let each of us listen to how he conquered her over a bottle of beer afterwards.'

So they had conquered her already! Nike could not believe the cheek of it.

'The name's Leo, Billy,' said Leo angrily. 'Leo! Leo! Leo! My name's bloody Leo and I am the lion of this goddamned den. I've told you several times never the hell to call me Leonard. When on earth are you going to stop being dumb?'

'Sorry Leo,' said Billy almost fearfully.

The third one's Billy then – Billy the laughing jackass.

'Better,' said Leo with raw pride. 'So I take it it's now agreed that the lady's mine.'

Not so fast darling, Nike told him in her mind. *I promise to take you on a looooong journey; a journey you'll never forget in your life!* She made a resolve right there and then to deal with the fools. '*Idiots*', she muttered under her breath. The men did not hear her.

'Always remember guys, I am the king of this group. After all, I pay the bills…' Leo continued proudly, but Nike was no longer listening; she was thinking about how to deal with them; she was thinking about what journey to take them on.

A statement came to her mind suddenly. Whoever was it that said that *To defeat a group of villains, break the leader first?* Nike could not remember who said it, but she borrowed a leaf from the saying. She looked at the group, her eyes met those of the leader; her eyes bored into his and he thought, *I've got you already beautiful lady; from the look on your face, I know I have you.*

He smiled.

But Nike thought, *I'll show you what it means to disrespect a lady. Get ready to go to the dungeons of hell; and if you come back, you would have learned to respect a lady – that is if you come back.*

She smiled.

Nike spent the whole night thinking about Leo and his group. She had been insulted by the whole lot and she would be damned if she would let it pass. She sought revenge with the whole of her being. She remembered Maxwell; she remembered all her escapades with him and she remembered all he had taught her.

Could she borrow a leaf from all she had learnt from Maxwell so she could teach the proud son of a bitch called Leo a bitter lesson? Nike wished she could contact Maxwell right away. How she wished Maxwell had not gone to jail. From her calculations, Maxwell should have spent a year and a month in jail, serving a sentence for fraud. She thought of calling one of his friends but decided against it. She did not trust Maxwell's friends. They were prone to duping anybody that made the mistake of crossing their path, and Nike did not believe she would be exempted.

Over the years, she had come to trust nobody except Maxwell.

What if Maxwell was out of jail? a little voice from within her asked.

Nike stopped to think about it and then she sighed sadly. *That could only happen in fairy tales*, she said loudly. What happened to Maxwell over a year ago was definitely no fairy tale; Maxwell had been arrested and sentenced to five years in jail for his fraudulent activities and from what Nike heard, he would be made to serve at least two and a half years in prison.

As Nike relived happy memories of her years in Maxwell's house, she felt heaviness in her heart. Apart from her late father and Tokunboh Martins, the only other person that had genuinely had interest in her welfare and happiness was Maxwell.

She wondered what Maxwell would look like now. She was sure he would look so gaunt and underfed. It was a well known fact that the Nigerian prison system was not just a place for correction, but a place where prisoners had a taste of hell on earth. She felt so sorry that Maxwell had to go to such a place. Worst still, all Maxwell had ever worked for in his life had been confiscated and withdrawn from him. She wondered what had become of the flat Maxwell bought. Maybe it had been taken over by the government as well. She was suddenly curious.

She brought out her mobile phone and dialled the landline. She could never forget Maxwell's telephone number. She knew it by heart.

Nike waited and after a while, she heard a ringing tone. Her heart skipped a beat. She had not expected the telephone to ring. She wondered who could be living in Maxwell's house. Then she heard a husky, male voice on the other side of the line.

'Hello,' said the voice.

Nike recognised Maxwell's voice instantly.

'Maxwell, is that you?' she asked excitedly.

'Yes, it's me,' replied Maxwell wearily, 'and who's this?'

'It's me, Nike,' answered Nike breathlessly.

'Nike!' shouted Maxwell into the phone.

'Yes, Maxwell, it's me, Nike.'

'Nike, oh my dear Nike; I've been looking for you all over the place. Where are you calling from?'

'I'm calling from London. When and how did you get out of jail, Maxwell?'

'I got out of jail last month; a new governor was elected and I was given a state pardon, *period*,' replied Maxwell. 'Now I want to know what's been happening to my baby. Are you okay?'

'Yes I'm okay,' replied Nike, then she remembered Leo the boaster. 'Well not really,' she said.

'Tell me what the problem is,' said Maxwell, very much attentive. 'Big brother Maxwell is very much around and well now.'

Nike was overjoyed. Now, she could put Leo where he belonged. She trusted Maxwell to sort something out.

'Well you see Maxwell, there's a certain guy here in London who, because he's got a wealthy mother, has decided to insult me and I want to teach him the lesson of his life.'

At the other end, Maxwell smiled warmly and stroked his newly cultivated moustache. He liked what he was hearing. Since he got out of jail, he had been hard of cash. He could stage a big come back with this bloke with a rich mum. 'Listen carefully,' he said. 'I want you to make friends with this guy, but remember to keep your dignity. Just make friends with him long enough to get necessary details off him, then, you leave the rest to me.'

Nike beamed. 'Okay, Maxwell,' she said. 'How do you want me to go about it?'

Maxwell smiled and stroked his moustache again before answering. 'Now you listen carefully…'

The following evening, Nike had gone to the café and she had sat and ordered a cup of tea. She sipped the tea and waited patiently, wishing Leo the boaster would come.

Leo the boaster came.

Nike was happy, but she hid her happiness behind a serious expression. She looked around for a newspaper, saw one, picked it up and began to scan through it.

Leonard saw Nike and smacked his lips. He had come to the café deliberately in the hope that the beautiful, black lady would be there.

He confidently moved to where Nike sat and placed a large hand on the table.

'Hello, lady. May I join you?' said Leonard.

Nike stopped reading the newspaper and looked up. 'Oh yes you can,' she said sweetly.

Leonard pulled back a chair beside Nike and sat down. However, he felt uncomfortable as his huge tummy pressed against the table.

Nike watched, greatly amused as Leo struggled to adjust himself to a sitting position.

'Why don't you pull your chair further away from the table?' Nike asked.

Leo gave her a huge smile then he said cheerily, 'You're right; I need to pull back my seat.'

He stood up and pulled back the chair further away from the table so that the space between the chair and the table could accommodate his large frame, before sitting down on it with a loud thud. Nike struggled to suppress the laughter that welled up within her.

Leo was surely a dumb person, ripping him of a large chunk of his inheritance would definitely be a breeze.

'So, where were we?' asked Leo confidently.

'We were trying to create a space for your large tummy,' replied Nike.

Leo laughed very loudly. He thought Nike was very funny. 'You're a very funny lady,' he said to Nike.

Nike grinned. 'Thank you,' she said.

Leo looked around the restaurant as if he actually owned the place, then turning to Nike; he said with a huge smile, 'Now, shall I order you a huge sandwich?'

Two huge sandwiches were brought for each of them by the café owner. Nike thought that those particular sandwiches of such massive sizes were specially made for Leo by the café owner because he knew who he was.

Within minutes, Leo wolfed down his sandwich and asked for more. She managed to eat a quarter of her own sandwich and she pushed her plate away. Leo saw this and promptly picked up the partly-eaten sandwich on Nike's plate and munched away.

Nike watched with a keen interest as he ate. She could not believe a normal human being would have such a large appetite for food.

After dinner, Leo offered to pay the bill.

'My mum's very rich, you know,' he said to Nike as he gave a waiter some money. 'When my mum dies, I stand to inherit a few millions, so money is not my problem. It's how to spend it that is the problem,' Leo finished, grinning. His experience with ladies told him they all liked money and the same experience told him that he had already won the heart of Nike.

Nike looked at him and grinned too. She had never seen such a stupid man in her life!

For two weeks, Leo and Nike regularly had lunch at the café.

One day, two weeks after they became friends, Leo invited Nike to his home.

This was it! Nike thought that the game was just about to begin. She smiled warmly at Leo and said sultrily, 'Yes please, I'll like to go to your home.'

'I must warn you though – my house is a very big and beautiful one; I'm sure you've never seen anything like it. I don't want you to be surprised when you get there,' said Leo, grinning proudly.

Nike pursed her lips angrily; she felt like twisting Leo's fat neck to his back. She could not begin to imagine how a man could be so vain. But she held herself in check. She had a game plan to strip Leo of all that he had and she could not afford to destroy her plans for him by getting angry.

Nike forced a smile to her lips.

Leo drove Nike to his house in Hampstead Heath. It was a huge, Victorian house surrounded by beautiful horticulture and it had a swimming pool. Leo led the way into the house and Nike was ushered into a huge sitting room that was decorated with different expensive antiques and furniture. The house was indeed as beautiful as Leo had described it.

'Is the house really yours or your mother's?' she asked pleasantly.

'It's actually my mother's for now, but it'll be mine as soon as my mother dies,' answered Leo. He saw a questioning look in her eyes, and he decided to expand. 'My mum's got a condition called fibromyalgia and she also has multiple myeloma that's become resistant to treatment,' said Leo sadly. But then his face brightened up as he said, 'I'm her only child and she's shown me a copy of her will already. I stand to inherit all her millions and the five houses she's got. She's even made me a co-signatory to all of her accounts. She opened a separate account for me and placed five million pounds in it; but every month, she requests to see the balance on the account. I guess she's trying to see how I'm going to manage her estate when I eventually take over. I have not spent a penny of the money. The interest just accumulates. I'll show her how smart and very prudent I am until she dies and then I'll spend all the money however I wish.'

'Oh, I see,' said Nike.

'You better see,' said Leo. 'You're looking at a multi-millionaire in the making. It's better you become my girl and give the whole of yourself to me now; otherwise, you'll be a loser when I'm in control of my mother's wealth.'

Nike opened her mouth and wanted to give Leo a tongue-lashing but she quickly closed it back; the time was not ripe to teach Leo a lesson.

'When is your mum going to die?' she asked instead.

Leo shrugged. 'The doctors have given her a few months, six at the most. Most times, she lies on her bed in her room upstairs.' answered Leo.

Nike made a quick mental calculation. She had less than six months to carry out her plan. She hadn't envisaged that Leo's mother would die that soon. She had to call Maxwell and inform him of this development later in the day.

Smiling up at Leo, she moved closer to him and touched his groin. Leo gave a sharp breath as he felt blood rush down his crotch. With one large hand, he pulled Nike towards him; placing his lips firmly on hers, he kissed her deeply, forcing her mouth open with his tongue as his male hardness pressed against her.

Nike cringed visibly; she hated guys whose breath stank. Leo's breath stank terribly; it stank of a bad combination of garlic, stale sandwich and cigarette smoke. She pulled away from Leo.

Managing a weak smile, she said to him, 'Leo, I have to be sure of all you told me before I commit myself to you. I have to be sure you can take very good care of me – of my needs.'

Leo smiled slowly. All ladies were the same and Nike was no different. The girls he had in the past were all after his money. But he had enticed them with it until he got them in his bed and then he had left them without giving them a penny of his wealth. He was about to do the same with Nike.

'How else do you want me to prove my vast wealth to you?' he asked her, still feeling the heat in his groin.

Nike thought for a while before answering him. 'I want you to show me your bank statement. I want to be sure you really have that money in your account; I want to be sure that you're not just blabbing.'

Leo was happy with what he had heard. He was happy that Nike had not asked for much. If his bank statement was what she needed to get in his bed, he would readily provide it for her, and then they would get it over and done with. There were other ladies out there, waiting to be conquered!

Leo ran up the stairs into his bedroom. Soon, he was back with a copy of his bank statement and a cheque book. These he showed to Nike proudly. 'I have brought along my chequebook too, so you'll be double sure that the money in the account is actually mine,' he said, grinning.

Nike took the cheque book and flipped through it. As she did so, a bank card dropped from the pages of the cheque book. Nike picked it up and handed it to Leo. She noticed that Leo had written only one cheque since the chequebook was issued. The counterfeit part of that particular cheque was still attached to the chequebook.

Nike noticed Leo's signature. Interestingly, it looked too complicated to memorise. She would need to have a copy with which she could practice a forged signature. She would have to find a way of obtaining a copy of Leo's cheque with his signature on it. She smiled as she handed back the chequebook and bank statement to Leo. Leo dropped the documents, including the bank card onto a chair nearby and pulled Nike to himself again. Nike obliged him a kiss for half a second before pulling back from him.

'What's the problem now?' asked Leo confusedly. 'You've seen concrete evidence of my wealth, haven't you?'

'Yes I… yes I have,' Nike stammered.

She thought frantically of a way to divert Leo's attention from the documents he had just dropped on the chair. 'I feel very thirsty,' she said to Leo. 'Can I have a glass of water please?'

Leo dashed into the kitchen to fetch a glass of water. He badly wanted to continue where he had stopped.

When she was sure that Leo had disappeared from the sitting room, Nike quickly went into action. Picking up the cheque book from the chair, she ripped off the little page which had Leo's signature on it and then she ripped the first page off the cheque book, frantically hoping that Leo would not notice this while she was still in his house. She took the bank statement and copied Leo's full address onto the back of the cheque she had torn out of the cheque book. She also turned Leo's bank card over and wrote the sixteen digits on the front of the card beside the address. Next, she turned the bank card to the other side and wrote down the three-digit number at the back of it. As she wrote down the last number, she heard Leo's footsteps. She quickly opened her bag, dropped the pieces of papers into it and crossed her legs, trying to relax.

'There you go, my sweet girl,' said Leo as he handed a glass of water to Nike. When he was in the kitchen, pouring the water into the glass, an idea had struck him. Nike was proving too difficult for him; he wanted to get things over and done with, so he had decided to make things fast for both of them.

Leo had opened a plastic bottle he secretly kept in a cupboard in the kitchen and he had dropped a tablet of ecstasy into the glass of water and waited for it to dissolve into the clear liquid.

This should get her in the mood fast, he reasoned.

'Thanks,' said Nike as she took the glass from Leo.

As she put the glass to her lips, an image of Tunde Oka flashed before her. She remembered her resolve never to trust any man again; she remembered Maxwell's several warnings to her. She looked up at Leo's grinning face. She wouldn't put anything past him.

Nike put the glass of water on the coffee table and pretended to be in pain. She held her tummy and bent low.

'What's the problem now?' Leo asked her, clearly alarmed.

'I… I… I'm in severe pain. I think I should leave now. I… I have to go home straight away.'

Leo was very unhappy. All his efforts at getting Nike into his bed that day were about to be wasted. He made a desperate attempt at getting Nike to have a drink of water.

'Why don't you drink the water; it will make you better,' he said.

'No, I'll be better off at home. I'll see you later,' said Nike as she got up from the chair and walked towards the door, still holding her tummy.

Leo watched sadly as Nike opened the door and walked out of his house.

When Nike got to her house, she picked up her mobile phone and placed a call to Maxwell in Nigeria.

Maxwell's voice came on the line immediately.

Nike explained all that transpired between herself and Leo that day.

Maxwell listened carefully as Nike talked. When she had finished her narration, Maxwell told her calmly, 'Send me all the documents you were able to get from the fool. I assure you that in two months time, he's going to declare bankruptcy.'

Nike believed Maxwell; she believed Maxwell was capable of doing whatever he set his heart to do. But she was scared. She was scared of what might become of her when Leo found out what she had done.

'What if Leo finds out and gets me arrested?' she asked Maxwell fearfully.

Maxwell laughed before answering, 'He won't get you arrested.'

'How are you so sure of that, Maxwell?'

'Because you are going to get the fool arrested first!'

Chapter 29

Nigeria, West Africa

The documents arrived at Maxwell's secret office two days later. Maxwell opened the envelope which contained Leo's cheque, complete with his address and signature, and studied it for a while.

'This should be an easy job,' he said aloud. He went to sit at his desk and promptly opened his computer. Rubbing his hands together excitedly, he set to work.

Three weeks later, the five million pounds in Leonard Conrad's account had depleted to a mere five hundred pounds; and by the end of the month, the account read a miserable five pounds and eighty-one pence only.

Maxwell bought a shop in a shopping complex not far from his office and put all the goods he had bought on the internet with Leo's money up for sale at a discount of forty per cent. The goods were cleared off within a week!

By the end of the month, Maxwell had made 5.5 million pounds in total. He sent a silent blessing to Nike. She had got him back on his feet. But there was still a job to do; they had to send Leo to prison.

He placed a call to Nike…

Chapter 30

Great Britain

One evening, Nike invited Leo to her apartment. She looked very sexy in a skimpy halter-neck and a mini skirt. She wore a black pair of high heeled shoes to match.

When Leo saw her, his breath caught in his throat. He wanted Nike badly; but he could not fathom why she was playing hard to get.

As soon as Leo entered Nike's room, she blurted out, 'Some people told me you're merely deceiving me.'

Leo looked at her exasperatedly. 'What do you mean?' he asked.

'I was told you do not have a share in your mother's will. How am I supposed to be sure that I'll be well taken care of when she dies?'

Leo swore under his breath. He could not believe Nike could be so greedy. Besides, whoever told her he was ready to spend a penny of his mother's money on her anyway? He just wanted to fuck her and dump her – *that's all*.

But Nike had taken him to so much trouble just because he wished to get her in his bed. He wanted to teach her a lesson she would never forget. He wanted to sleep with her and blow it to the world; he wanted to make mockery of her, so he decided to play it cool.

'How do you want me to prove myself this time?' he asked wearily.

Nike smiled and slowly loosened the tie of her blouse. The blouse fell to her waist revealing two big but firm, lovely breasts with taut nipples.

Leo stood, mesmerised. In all his promiscuous life, he had never seen breasts so big and so beautiful. He smacked his lips; he wished he could have a taste.

'All this and more will be yours, if you could just convince me you're a signatory to one of your mother's accounts by taking me to her bank and withdrawing some money from it.'

Leo shifted his feet uncomfortably. 'But that would be difficult,' he said. 'My mother has to countersign the cheque before I can withdraw money from her account.'

Nike moved closer to him and brushed her breast against his nose. 'Surely, you can do anything to have these, can't you? Besides, you would be putting the money back into the account immediately. I just want to be sure you have a stake in your mother's estate.'

Leo nodded.

'It's a deal,' he said.

The following morning, Nike got dressed carefully. She wore a grey skirt suit and a white shirt underneath it. She wanted to give an impression of a responsible woman before the police.

She got to the police station and requested to see an officer. A pleasant, petite police woman smiled at her and asked her name.

'Miss Nike Adeogun,' said Nike.

The policewoman entered it into the computer. Next, Nike was asked her date of birth, which she promptly gave. The policewoman entered this into the computer as well.

'May I know why you have come?' the policewoman asked Nike politely.

'I have come to lodge a complaint. Actually, as a law abiding citizen of this great country, I have come to report a possible murder case,' said Nike calmly.

The policewoman braced up; she was now at alert. She opened a drawer, brought out a tape recorder and pressed the record button. The tape began to roll.

'Can you please be more explicit?' said the policewoman to Nike.

'Certainly madam,' said Nike. 'I've got this boyfriend who's got a very sick mother. The doctors think that the woman will die in a few months time.'

Nike paused for breath. The policewoman was listening attentively; her expression was deadpan. Nike went on. 'It so happens that my boyfriend's got greedy; he wants his mother dead any moment from now. In fact, he's told me that his mother would die before this week runs out.'

Nike forced tears to her eyelids as she continued, 'I don't want the poor woman to die. She has suffered for too long; she doesn't deserve to die.'

The policewoman passed Nike a tissue. Nike took it and wiped tears off her face, thankful of the training she received from Maxwell a few years ago. She sniffed and thanked the policewoman.

'It's alright,' said the policewoman. 'Now may I know the name of your boyfriend and if possible, his mother?'

'My boyfriend's name is Leonard Conrad, popularly called Leo, and his mother's name is Mrs Margarette Conrad.'

The policewoman recognised the name at once. Mrs Margarette Conrad was a London businesswoman, who had a multi-million pound empire. She also knew of the woman's ill health. She believed Nike totally. But she had to know why Nike had taken the pains to come and report her boyfriend to the police. Some other girl might get greedy and go along with the evil plan of her boyfriend, with the intention of spending the money they would accrue together.

'I quite appreciate your courage in coming to report an intended evil, but why would you go to so much length to do this?' she asked Nike calmly.

Nike had a ready answer; she had pre-empted the question herself.

'I found out that my boyfriend spent the five million pounds largesse he got from his mother to furnish two houses he bought for a lady in Nigeria, and I feel hurt that he could cheat on me. In fact, Leonard's so broke, he's thinking of going to the bank today to collect some money from one of his mother's account on which he is a co-signatory. He told me he would forge her signature.'

The policewoman nodded when she heard this.

'Can you tell me the name of the bank?' she asked.

'Of course,' said Nike and she gave her the name of the bank. 'He told me he would be there later today at two o'clock.'

At two p.m. later that day, Leo was arrested at the bank as he tendered the cheque with the forged signature of his mother. That week, he was charged to court for forgery with intent to defraud and intended murder. Leo realised he had been set up.

'The bitch set me up,' he swore. 'I'll make sure she pays for it.'

After all the evidence was gathered, Leonard Conrad was found guilty of ten counts of forgery with intent to defraud and intent to commit murder. He was sentenced to three years imprisonment.

On the day Leonard's judgement was given, Nike was praised by the presiding judge for her good conscience and courage to report the intentions of Leonard before he could actualise his evil plans.

As Leonard was led away in handcuffs, Nike whispered to him, 'This is for all the ladies you've conquered!'

Leonard Conrad did not hear her; he only heard his heart telling him to kill Nike whenever he came out of jail.

Daniel Tompkins, one of Leonard's loyal friends was present throughout the court trial. He was the only person who believed Leo's assertion that Nike had pressured him to do all he did. He wished Nike would rot in the pit of hell.

The next morning, the news was in all newspapers and the television. Leonard Conrad was broadcast as a criminal while Nike was painted a heroine.

In the confines of her room, Leo's mother sat in a wheelchair and listened to the story of her son's incarceration on the television. Thirty minutes later, she called in her lawyers and changed her will. She willed everything she had upon her death to charity and left nothing for her son, Leonard. As far as she was concerned, Leonard was not a worthy son!

As Nike was going home from an outing, her mobile phone rang. She picked it. It was Maxwell from Nigeria.
'Hello,' she said.
'Nike, I forgot to tell you this earlier; you must not return to wherever you're residing at the moment. Under no circumstances must you go back there. Look for an alternative accommodation for your own safety.' And Maxwell hung up.
Nike looked at the phone in her hand; and then, she looked straight ahead of her. Maxwell was right; Maxwell was always right. But she had not envisaged it would come to this. Where the hell would she go?
As Nike walked slowly to the bus stop, deeply in thought, a gentleman in a dark suit, wearing tinted sun goggles spoke into his mobile phone.
'I think we've found the girl,' he said.

Chapter 31

In a restaurant not far away from the bus stop, Alex Tucker sat at a table, sipping orange juice. He had just had an argument with his second girlfriend, Clarida. As much as he liked Clarida, especially for her intelligence, he was beginning to get frustrated over her constant insistence on getting married to him.

Alex had met Clarida the day he had had an argument with his first real girlfriend, Alice Palmers. Alice had gotten pregnant with his child for the second time and she had refused to go for an abortion. She had insisted that they got married straight away and Alex had angrily left her apartment. He had bumped into Clarida as he walked to the car park and he had recognised her as his favourite newscaster on television. Alex had always secretly admired Clarida and he was not about to let go of an opportunity to get to know her personally. Alex had put up his charm and exchanged pleasantries with Clarida. She had given him her business card and taken his number. They had dinner the next day and a relationship had begun. But two months into the relationship, Clarida had started hinting that she wanted a husband and especially a father for her daughter. And their relationship had begun to wane. Alex felt he was not ready for marriage yet; he was just in his twenties and he felt he still had his young years to enjoy before he tied himself to a particular woman.

Today, he had gone to see Clarida at lunchtime and she had broached the subject of marriage again. Again, Alex had told her he was not yet ready for marriage and Clarida had flown into a rage, calling him an irresponsible man.

Alex had angrily walked away from her home and he was now in the restaurant to cool off. As he sipped his drink, he knew it was about time he told the two women in his life he was no longer interested in them!

Nike got to the bus stop and stood there as several buses passed. She was in total confusion for what to do. She did not want to go back to the police to seek accommodation. She had accomplished what she had initially set out to do in Leonard Conrad's life and she did not want to be reminded of it. Being accommodated by the police would always remind her of Leo. Suddenly, she began to feel hunger pangs. She remembered that she had not had any food since the previous day.

She turned around and went to the nearest restaurant. She did not see the man in the dark suit, wearing a pair of tinted sun goggles following her. But he was behind her and he followed her into the restaurant.

Nike sat at a table and ordered lunch. It was served to her within twenty minutes. As soon as she began to eat, she heard a man's voice beside her.

'Can I join you, lady?' said the man.

Nike cursed; she did not want any company right now, much less a man's company. She looked up at the man. He was a tall Englishman with sun bleached hair. And he was smiling down at her behind a pair of sun goggles. Nike wished he would kindly remove his damned goggles. It was not sunny inside the restaurant after all!

'Only if you would remove your sun goggles,' she said.

'Thank you,' said the man as he took off his sun goggles and sat in a chair opposite Nike. He thought that the King's granddaughter, at least, had a sense of humour, very much unlike her grandfather, the King.

There was an awkward silence. Nike shrugged and continued eating. She had not invited him to her table; she was not about to start a conversation with him.

'You're a princess,' said the man suddenly.

Nike halted the fork with the scoop of rice midway between her plate and her mouth. Slowly, she put the fork down.

'What did you say?' she asked the man calmly.

'You're the granddaughter of a wealthy and powerful King in Nigeria, and he wishes to see you.'

Nike remembered that her mother had mentioned something like that. But she did not know this man, she had never seen him in her life. By the way, how could an Englishman know her background in Nigeria so well?

'Who are you?' she asked him cautiously.

'I am Detective John Bryant. I'm working in conjunction with my partner in Nigeria. Your grandfather hired us to find you.'

Nike was deep in thought. She did not know whether to believe this man; yet she wondered how he could know so much about her if he had not been sent by her grandfather.

'Princess Nike Adeogun, I am persuaded to believe you hold the key to your grandfather's successful rule in your town,' said Detective Bryant.

Nike jerked up her head then. *How could she hold the key to her grandfather's successful rule? Hadn't he been ruling his people before she was born?* A warning bell rang within her. This man could be a criminal, a molester, a pervert. *He could have been sent to her by Leo's friends.* Nike was scared.

'Since I was born, I have never had a grandparent; my so-called grandfather has been absent in my life, *all my life*. Now that I am old enough to care for myself, I do not need him in my life. Now you run along and tell him that,' she said calmly.

Detective Bryant was silent for a while, then he said, 'Your grandfather needs you…'

'Get lost!' shouted Nike.

'Okay, Okay,' said detective Bryant. 'I'll take my leave. But if you ever change your mind in the future, here's my card. You can call me on that number.' Detective Bryant dropped his complimentary card on the table before Nike and left.

Nike picked up the card and read it. The card showed that the gentleman was truly a detective. But it could have been forged, she reasoned.

'May I have the honour of joining you, my princess?' Nike heard a voice say.

'I said get lost!' she yelled before looking up. She thought the detective had come back.

But Nike looked up and looked into the eyes of the most handsome Englishman she had ever seen.

Alex Tucker's attention had been drawn to Nike's table when she had yelled at Detective Bryant. He had looked at her and he had been attracted to her immense beauty. Alice and Clarida totally forgotten at the moment, he had stood up from his chair as soon as the man in the dark suit left and he had strolled over to where Nike sat.

'I'm sorry,' said Nike, clearly embarrassed by her utterance. 'I… I thought… Never mind. You may sit down,' she said lamely.

Alex sat down on the chair that Detective Bryant had just vacated. 'My name is Alex, Alex Tucker,' said Alex, offering his hand for a handshake.

Nike took it and tried to smile. All she had been through since morning, especially what Detective Bryant had just told her, were taking their toll on her. She managed a weak smile anyway. Alex Tucker looked pleasant enough and he was, indeed, very handsome.

'My name is Nike,' she said, 'Nike Adeogun.'

Alex kissed her soft, warm hand and lifted up his eyes. 'Do you know that the happiest day in my life is today? Because today is the day I met you!'

When Alex made that statement, Tokinboh's face immediately flashed before Nike. Tokunboh Martins was the only man who had ever made that statement to her; and now, this man called Alex Tucker had made the same statement. Instinctively, Nike knew she would eventually become Alex Tucker's girlfriend!

That night, after Alex had left, Nike checked into a hotel. She lived in the hotel for two whole weeks before deciding to look for proper accommodation. Maxwell sent her money everyday from Nigeria. Although, she had willingly given Maxwell all the money they were able to siphon from Leo's account, Maxwell had insisted on giving Nike a million pounds from the money. He usually sent her a small amount of the money on a regular basis.

'I don't want anyone to cast suspicions on you,' Maxwell had explained to her. Nike knew she would be eternally grateful to Maxwell for being there for her through thick and thin.

Nike picked up a newspaper and went through it. Luckily, she found a couple of adverts for landlords who wanted tenants. She called the number on the first advert she saw.

After a few rings, a lady's voice came on the line. Nike liked the voice instantly.

A meeting was arranged for two p.m. at the house in Bermondsey.

Nike was not late for the meeting. She knocked on the door and a very pretty blonde lady answered it.

'Hi, my name is Tonia,' said the blonde lady. She recognised Nike instantly. She was the lady she had read about in the newspaper. She was the lady who saved an old woman from being murdered by her son. She decided to offer Nike accommodation if she liked the house.

'I bought the house a few weeks ago and I have a phobia of living alone,' she explained to Nike.

Nike liked the house instantly; it was very neat and tidy, she could not believe her luck. Besides, she liked Tonia. She felt they would get along fine.

'I'll take it,' she said to Tonia.

Two weeks passed before Nike saw Detective John Bryant again. This time around, he came knocking on her door. Nike opened the door and gasped when she saw the detective.

How had he known where she lived? She was about to close the door on him but Detective Bryant put a foot in the way.

'If you do not leave now, I'll have no choice but to call the police,' said Nike through gritted teeth.

'Please hear me out,' said Detective Bryant. 'I'm not an impostor as you think. I am here on the wishes of your grandfather. He truly wishes to see you before he dies. It's very important he sees you. There's a lot you need to know about your life.'

That got Nike's attention. There was really a lot she needed to know concerning her life. What her mother had mentioned about her royal background still rang a bell. Besides, hearing that she still had a family, a blood relative somewhere, brought a nice feeling to her heart. She would call Maxwell in Nigeria and ask him to find out if Detective John Bryant was actually telling her the truth.

'Do you know my grandfather's residence in Nigeria?' she asked Detective Bryant.

For the first time that morning, Detective Bryant smiled. The smile lit up his face. 'Your grandfather is a goldfish in Illudun land. He has no hiding place,' he said.

When Detective Bryant had left, Nike called Maxwell.

'Please, Maxwell, there's a certain detective who keeps telling me that I have a grandfather who is a king in Illudun land. Could you possibly find out for me if he's telling the truth?'

'Of course I will,' replied Maxwell.

'Thanks a lot, Maxwell,' said Nike gratefully. 'What would I do without you?'

'You're welcome anytime,' replied Maxwell.

The next day, Maxwell called Nike.

'Detective Bryant was right,' he said. 'The king of Illudun land is truly your grandfather. In fact, I am right here in his palace. I'm standing beside him.'

For the first time in her life, Nike spoke with her grandfather, King Oba Adeogun.

Life indeed was a game. She had suddenly been *upgraded* from *nothing* to a wealthy *princess,* in the twinkling of an eye.

That month, Nike travelled to Nigeria and, accompanied by Maxwell, she went to Illudun land to see her grandfather for the first time in her life.

Nike arrived at her grandfather's palace at noon, the day after she got to Nigeria. She marvelled at the beautiful mansion that was her grandfather's palace with the array of cars and servants, and exquisite decor everywhere.

This was the life she had been missing all her life!

Nike felt that the King had some explanations to give her; she wanted to know why he had not bothered to contact her father all the years he was alive; she wanted to know why the King had decided to contact her now.

In the evening, the King took Nike for a walk in the palace compound. As they walked along, the King told her about her father, Leke Adeogun;

he told her about his childhood days. He told her how much he had loved him and he told her why he had disowned him when he had married her mother.

They got to a huge conservatory with pots of beautiful flowers and the King ushered her in. It was very cool inside the conservatory. Nike felt relaxed.

They sat down, and the King told her the story of the Nigerian civil war. He told her how his father's house had been destroyed by the Ibos; he told her how he lost all his siblings in the war.

Nike watched her grandfather as he talked with pain. She felt she understood why he had opposed her father's marriage to her mother. She felt no anger towards the old man. Rather, she was beginning to form a bond with him. She thought her grandfather was a kind-hearted old man, who only wanted to preserve the law he had made in his kingdom.

'I heard about my son's death, but where is your mother?' the King asked suddenly.

'She… she's dead too,' Nike lied. However, she felt no remorse or guilt over the lie. As far as Nike was concerned, her mother was as good as dead.

'I'm so sorry,' said the King as a tear trickled down his face. 'I'm so sorry for all the pain you must have gone through as an orphan.'

'It's alright, Granddad,' said Nike. 'At least, we have each other now.'

The King was thoughtful for a while, then he looked at Nike and said to her calmly, 'Nike, I want you to get married soon and have a son, who would succeed me. It's very important that you do that soon.'

Nike agreed with her grandfather completely. She knew the old man regretted his actions toward her father in those days and she would do anything to stop him regretting any further; she knew the old man was suffering from the loss of his only son and she would do anything to make her grandfather happy.

She promised to work on giving her grandfather a great-grandson as soon she found a suitable partner. She did not want to tell her grandfather about Alex Tucker yet. She only just met the guy.

Nike enjoyed her stay in her grandfather's palace. She was pampered and treated as the princess that she really was. But she had to go back the United Kingdom soon. She had already lied to her grandfather that she was a student at the university, studying medicine. She did not want her grandfather to think that her father had not given her the right direction in life.

One week after Nike visited Illudun land, she left for the United Kingdom.

Chapter 32

United Kingdom

Alex and Nike regularly kept in touch. Six months into their relationship, they became very intimate. Alex saw more of Nike than Alice and Clarida. They went for picnics and dined together regularly and, often times, they went to the movies together. After each outing, they usually retired to Nike's apartment for *good sex*. What intrigued Alex most about Nike was that she loved horror movies.

'Horror movies makes me feel horny,' she had told him one day. Truly, after they had watched a horror movie, Nike performed better in bed. Alex did not mind watching horror movies with Nike.

On Christmas Eve, they had gone to see *Black Christmas* and they had gone to Nike's apartment afterwards. Nike opened the door of the flat and let Alex in before securely locking the door after her. Nike always securely locked the door. 'Not my fault; just can't let go of my African experience,' Nike had told him one day. 'In Africa, one couldn't be careful enough,' she had added in a way of explanation. Alex did not ask for further explanation. He drew her close to himself and gave her a long kiss on her lovely mouth. When he started unbuttoning her lovely silk blouse, she held his hands in both of hers and said huskily, her eyes dark and seductive, 'Not yet my darling, let me show you how to be loved by a real African princess; let me treat you like an African prince.' And she led him into the bedroom. Alex noticed a bottle of red wine placed on the dressing table beside the four-poster bed. *The bitch had this all planned eh! Well I'm all ready babe,* Alex thought and smiled. He was excited. Nike pushed him on the bed and unbuttoned her blouse to reveal a pair of full golden brown breasts with taut nipples – she had no brassiere on. She slipped off her skirt to reveal the firmest, most beautiful pair of thighs Alex had ever set his lustful eyes on – she had no underwear on. Alex's eyes roamed over her greedily, starting from her full, well-rounded breasts to her firm, flat stomach and to the dark triangle between her legs. Alex felt hot adrenalin rush to his groin. He must admit that Nike, above all others, always made him feel this way, even when he was not initially in the mood. He made to reach for her but she pushed him back onto the bed. She lay on top of him, her eyes, darkened with pure lust, fixed firmly on his face. She reached for the red wine and uncorked it. Alex thought she wanted them to be drunk on the wine before getting into the real act. Alex did not really care for wine; he was impatient. However, he waited for her to take a swig of the wine.

I'm ready to do it your way, babe, as long as it leads me to your paradise. Alex smiled. Nike had something else in mind though; she, instead, poured a little of the wine down the hollow between her breast and snuggled up to him, placing her chest on his mouth. *Ah! She wanted to play naughty.* Alex liked naughty girls. He licked up the wine that had run up to the base of her abdomen, and then he licked further. Each gesture he made elicited a groan from Nike; each groan becoming more audible by the second. Nike just managed to place the wine bottle on her dressing table before pulling Alex on top of her. Alex was ready. He thrust into her with such force that Nike gripped him hard on both shoulders. Her nails sank into his flesh. Alex felt no pain.

Just then, it started snowing outside. London weather had always intrigued Alex as incredibly unpredictable – as unpredictable as Nike's love-making. At the moment, however, Alex couldn't be bothered about London weather; his focus was on Nike's love-making. As the snowfall got deeper outside with everywhere whitening up, Alex thrust deeper inside, with everywhere in the room reverberating with the rhythm of their love-making. Suddenly, Nike changed the position and the rhythm changed and so also the reverberations. Alex became unaware of everything else. He was in *paradise*. After a long while, the snowfall outside dwindled and then the snow stopped falling altogether just as the reverberations in the room, on Jamaica road in Bermondsey, dwindled and stopped altogether.

As they lay, sated in an embrace, Alex could still not believe the magic of it. He was not a greenhorn as far as anything – anything at all – that could go on between a man and a woman was concerned (in fact, he was well known to ladies as a notorious play boy); however, he was yet to meet a lady who could beat Nike in the act of love-making – he could bet his bank account on it. He had heard of girls you could take home to mama and those you couldn't. He knew that Nike was one of the latter, not the former. But he wasn't about to let go of her.

Alex remembered the conversation he had with Daniel Tompkins, who was Nike's former neighbour. Alex had gone to have a drink with Daniel on a cool Saturday afternoon two weeks after he met Nike. Alex had ordered a beer and Daniel, a coke. As they sat at the table, they saw Nike come in. She had looked around the bar as if she was actually looking for someone and she saw them. Alex had waved to her in a gesture of invitation to join them but she had merely waved at them briefly and had hurriedly left the bar.

Daniel had looked at her retreating back with an inscrutable expression until she was well out of sight, and then he had turned to Alex and asked inquisitively, 'You have something on the lady?'

Alex did not answer. He hated inquisitions and Daniel was very inquisitive. Daniel was known as 'the great adviser'. He was wise in his own eyes. He was only twenty-eight, just a year older than Alex himself but he always behaved like he was Alex's grandfather. Daniel had gotten married to his childhood sweetheart, Emily, when he was twenty-one and Emily was nineteen and they had three daughters to show for it – Helen, Jenny and Beth – who were six, four and two respectively. Daniel was very proud of himself. Alex was very sorry for him. He thought he had no life! It was said that life began at forty; but to Alex, Daniel's life had ended – or almost ended – before he was thirty. He had so many responsibilities, so many mouths to feed on his meagre salary.

Daniel was not born with a silver spoon as Alex was. His father, Eric Tompkins, was a small time carpenter who was suffering from drug addiction and alcoholism. It was not that Eric had always been addicted to drugs and alcohol, no, he had not. He was a responsible line manager, working for British Telecom and earning an admirable salary. He had met and married Daniel's mother Gladys, who happened to be his immediate boss. Mrs Gladys Tompkins resigned from her job to be a doting full-time housewife to Eric. Daniel, who was the first child, was born that same year and two years later, they had Daniel's sister, Mary. They had their four other children in quick succession with just one year gap between each child and the next, beginning with Mary. After the arrival of the third child, Eric got a second job in order to care for his growing family. Despite his busy schedule with so many children to care for, Eric found the time once a year to whisk Gladys away on a holiday, leaving the children with an agency nanny. It was obvious to everyone who knew the Tompkins that they were still very much in love. One day, when Daniel was seventeen years old, his mother received an urgent call from her G.P. The results of the tests conducted on her were out and she needed to go to the hospital.

'I'm very sorry, Mrs. Tompkins,' the Doctor said uneasily, 'the tests carried out on you show you have ovarian cancer.'

Mrs Tompkins closed her eyes to keep them from shedding tears. She was a strong woman, she thought to herself. She had been through too many troubles in her life to let a common infection with an ovary weigh her down. Besides, she could get the damned ovary removed immediately; she was thankful for advanced medicine.

'How soon can we get the operation done?' She asked the doctor confidently.

'I'm so sorry, Mrs Tompkins. The cancer has spread beyond an operable stage; in fact, give or take, we would say you have two weeks to live. I'm really sorry madam, but that's the situation here.'

Mrs Tompkins' confidence broke then. She couldn't stop the tears pouring down her face. The doctor wrote down some prescriptions and handed the paper to her. She took it and, without looking at the content, dropped it in her handbag. She got up and managed a faint 'Thanks' to the doctor before leaving the hospital. By the time she got to her house, she had made a firm decision to solve her problem permanently.

Eric Tompkins woke up the following day to find his wife still sleeping. Surprised at this, he checked the bedside clock; the time was seven-thirty in the morning.

'This is strange,' he muttered to himself. Since he married his wife, he had always known her to be an early riser. She usually got up to make sure everything was set for him to go to work; she usually packed his breakfast and lunch; and she usually made sure his clothes were already ironed and his shoes ready to be worn. But that morning, Gladys had done none of those. Eric immediately sensed something was terribly wrong. Maybe his wife had taken ill. He placed the back of his palm on her neck. It felt cold. He lifted her hand; it fell back limply. He checked her pulse; there was none. He was about to call the ambulance when a pack of tablets fell from underneath the pillow. He picked it up and read the label. It read:

> *One tablet to be taken three times daily. Do not exceed the stated dose. Keep out of reach of children.*

He checked the content of the pack; fourteen tablets were missing out of twenty-four. His premonition that something was wrong instantly became a reality. Something was terribly wrong; he bent down and pushed open her eyelids; his wife's lifeless pupils stared back at him. He knew without doubt what had happened; his beloved wife was dead – stone dead.

Eric Tompkins took to the bottle from then on. He quit his job and got married to alcohol. From morning till night, he drank himself to stupor. Most of the responsibility of the whole family fell on Daniel. Daniel grew up fast. Three weeks after his wife died, Eric Tompkins was found on his bed, as cold as death; the pack of tablets he found under his wife's pillow three weeks earlier was firmly clutched in his left palm. Daniel gently took the pack from his father's hand and checked the content; the pack was empty. The children were already expecting his death; the only shock was that it came sooner than they had expected. Eric Tompkins was laid to rest beside his wife and Daniel became fully responsible for the upkeep of the family.

Everybody who knew them was well aware that Daniel and his siblings lived a precarious existence. Daniel had practically sent himself to school and he lived on grants throughout his time at college. He could not go further to university like Alex did, so he had promptly gotten a job as a trainee plumber in a construction company, with the hope of climbing up the ladder to the top one day. He had such perseverance. Alex had no such perseverance. Alex preferred to start at the top – whatever he did, he must start at the top and have the best. There was also enough money (family money) at Alex's disposal, so Alex had gone on to university, read law and he had graduated with first class honours!

Alex felt that Daniel's struggles and hard experiences of life had turned him into what he had become – a young old man. Daniel always had advice for everyone. He would always warn everyone of an unforeseen danger or the other and try to provide a solution to it even though there might be no danger after all. Daniel also had a pleasant but sober disposition to life. He did not like to offend anybody. If he found that any of his advice (albeit numerous and unsolicited for) did not go well with whomever he was rendering it to, he usually looked for a way to douse the anger or animosity his advice might have caused. He would try and give a compliment, even if it was unsuitable. Consequently, unbeknown to Daniel, everyone tried to avoid him.

However, on this occasion, Alex knew he could not avoid Daniel, so he tried to avoid the question by calling on the waiter to bring the bill. Alex paid for both their drinks and Daniel said thank you. Daniel waited for a moment then said again, 'I asked if you've got an eye on the lady.'

Alex saw red. *You sure are an incorrigibly nosey fellow,* he thought but said nothing. Moreover, he did not have something on the lady yet; he was still trying to woo her and he did not wish to *spill the beans* before they were *ready to eat*. Alex concentrated on his drink.

Daniel saw his reluctance to talk about it; he shrugged and went on anyway: 'Saw you chatting her up the other time and I really feel I should give you a warning. You know, me and you are best friends.'

Alex did not know that they were best friends. Daniel continued, 'You know there are ladies you could take home to mama and there are some you couldn't.' He paused and waited for Alex's reaction. There was none. Alex's face was deadpan. Daniel went on anyway, 'Well I must tell you that Nike is not the type of a girl you can take home to mama. That lady did not only eat the forbidden fruit in the Garden of Eden, she ate the whole goddamned tree!'

Alex had had enough. He couldn't stand this badmouthing. He got up abruptly and slammed his cup of unfinished beer on the table; part of the beer splashed on to the table and on Daniel's shirt. If Alex saw this, he couldn't be bothered to proffer any apology; he was too angry to do so.

Alex said through clenched teeth, 'You put a lid on it, you fucking hold it right there. I never asked you for the lady's C.V., neither do I want any advice on any lady. If you've got your belly full of words of wisdom that nobody wants to listen to anyway, you can gorge them out and stuff them back down your fucking throat.' Alex looked down at Daniel with pure disdain. Daniel flinched and grimaced at those words. He had not expected such a torrent of venomous words from Alex. In fact, Alex had never spoken to him in such a tone. Daniel felt sorry that he had invoked Alex's wrath; he did not like to offend anyone. He tried patching things up by changing the subject.

'I'm sorry,' he said and after a while, 'Thanks for the coke, it was a very nice drink,' he finished lamely.

Alex rolled his eyes in exasperation; he wanted to tell Daniel that he did not manufacture the Coca-cola, he wanted to tell Daniel to simply get lost and leave him alone but he held himself in check; there was no point aggravating matters; the guy was already feeling sorry and almost ready to cry. Plus, he noticed that the white shirt Daniel had on had turned brown where his drink had poured and he had offered no apology; that should be enough retaliation.

Alex simply walked out of the bar, leaving Daniel staring after him.

Daniel really felt sorry that he had angered his dear friend, Alex, but he felt more sorry that Alex had not waited to hear the rest of the story. He had wanted to tell him how Nike had sent one of his very many close friends, Leonard Conrad, to prison.

Now as he lay beside Nike, dear old Daniel and his words of wisdom clearly forgotten, Alex felt an overwhelming need to possess her forever. Although he had talked about them living together on a few occasions, Nike had always brushed the idea aside, *for reasons best known to her,* she had always said. Alex felt within him that she was faithful to him; but he couldn't rule out a possibility that she could decide to leave him for good whenever she deemed it fit. Nike was not especially an emotional person. She was independent, carefree and firm and she reasoned like a man. Alex liked independent women, not the kind of women who 'police' their men around and cry all the time. Alex had a deep feeling that Nike had an inkling that he was not faithful to her, but she feigned ignorance of this; the only give-away was the subtle warning about STDs and the need to 'cover up', that she gave sometimes. Alex liked Nike for all of this and more.

Now, Alex felt the urge to keep her with him permanently and then he proposed.

'Will you marry me, Nike?' he said suddenly.

'Hmm, what? What did you say?' Nike was roused from her slight slumber, for she was almost falling into a satisfied sleep.

'I said marry me, Nike.'

She raised her head to look at him, saw the seriousness in his expression and burst out laughing.

'What's funny?' Alex asked, slightly confused and slightly amused.

'Me, marry you? Whoever told you I was interested in marrying you?'

'Other girls would jump at this. What do you take yourself for, Proudie?' Alex asked her jokingly, playfully poking at her ribs. He knew deep down within him that he did not really care if Nike accepted or refused to be his wife, he just liked sex with her and he liked her company. She did not complicate his life. He had sometimes wondered why all other ladies could not be like Nike – unpretentious: always going for what she wanted at any time she wanted it. Other girls would initially pretend to hate what they actually wanted and had been actually craving for – *me*, Alex thought and smiled.

Nike saw the smile. She had always known that Alex was full of himself. Granted, he was what anyone would call a ladies man, what with his good height of six foot two and a fine build. He had dark hair and unbelievably blue eyes. He had a finely chiselled nose and a mouth that made you want to kiss him all the time. He was also blessed with incredibly long eye lashes that added a feminine touch to his masculinity.

Nike always managed to restrain herself from showing him how attractive she found him. She knew other girls would fall over themselves to get his attention but not her – *not Nike*, she affirmed within herself. She was different and she would tell it to him. She would tell him he had better come off his high horse because his proud talk would not work with her.

'You had better come off your high horse because your proud talk won't work with me,' she told him. 'I am not other girls,' she finished emphatically.

'I'm not sitting on any horse and definitely not on a high one. I'm humbly lying on your bed and asking you to marry me,' Alex finished with a mock bow.

Nike was about to say something then she looked at him with a look that she would ordinarily give a dunce and said, 'Okay, okay. Since you think you are the best thing that recently happened to humanity, and if I decide to marry you now, where's the ring?'

Alex looked sheepish for a second but he said quickly, 'I'll get that later. But can we make do with this for now?' he said teasingly, then he took the wrapper that fell off the cover of the wine bottle, made it into a tiny string and wound it around her third left finger. By the time he had finished doing this, he was laughing hysterically at his own joke. 'I am a weirdo; we're both weirdoes you know? That's why we should marry each other – we fit!' Alex said, still laughing.

Nike took a pillow and hit him several times. 'You silly cow,' she said. 'You abnormal, silly cow. You are the first and probably the last man to propose to a lady with a wine wrapper for a ring. You are impossible,' Nike finished, laughing. Alex pulled her towards him and the snow began falling again.

Meanwhile, in a studio apartment in the very suburb of Brixton, Alice sat on the only seat in the room. Her head was well-rested on the headrest. Her eyes were closed, but every now and then, a tear escaped from either of her eyelids. Every now and then, she wiped the tear from her eyes with the back of her hand as if to shut out the unbearable fact that Alex had lied to her yet again. She knew that Alex was with another woman; he never told her that he had other girls but she knew it. She just had no courage to leave. However much this knowledge made her so sad, she was afraid to lose Alex. He was the only man she had ever been close to; the only man she had ever known; the only man that had shown any interest in her; the only man she ever wanted to be with. She was content to let sleeping dogs lie. She cuddled a teddy that had been given to her by Alex several years ago. The teddy was tattered and looked pitiable. There were signs of sewing, mending and re-sewing on the teddy but Alice just wouldn't throw it away. It was actually the first gift that was given to her by Alex. Any time she missed Alex, the teddy always served as a substitute. The teddy served as a solace to her whenever she could not find Alex – like now.

Alex had promised her that they would be together all through the festive period but he seemed to have disappeared into thin air now. She had called his mobile phone several times and left messages. She had even dared to go and enquire about him at his office (this she knew would have made Alex irate if he had seen her) but the two times she had been there, she did not go beyond seeing his secretary who very politely told her that Alex was on a short vacation and that the office was not in any position to divulge his whereabouts.

Alice had the feeling that the secretary knew where Alex was, for she thought she saw guilt written all over her face the second time she went to the office. *Maybe the secretary was one of Alex's lovers; maybe they were sleeping together.* Alice quickly jettisoned the thought as it came to her mind. *Don't be absurd*, she reprimanded herself. *Alex would not go to such a level as to sleep with his secretary.* She was not surprised at her own fierce defence of Alex; she had always defended Alex's unpalatable acts towards her even before he deemed it fit to come over to her to give an explanation. *Alex was just too busy to come to her*, she thought to herself. *Busy doing what?* came a small voice deep within her.

She had no answer to that.

Alex left Nike's apartment and came back in the evening; he had gone to buy a diamond engagement ring!

In the evening Alex and Nike made love again. After the fierce lovemaking, Alex proposed to Nike again; he looked serious this time. He opened the box which contained the diamond ring and said to her, 'Nike, please marry me.'

Nike looked at the ring for a long time; she liked diamonds. *After all, diamonds, they say, are a girl's best friend.* She wanted to marry Alex, but she did not want to make the mistake her parents made.

'We have to go for a blood test,' she said.

'What?' said Alex, laughing. 'Don't worry about that. We're already sleeping together.'

Nike had a serious expression. 'I'm not referring to what you think,' she said. 'Before we can get married, I need to be sure that your genotype is not AS.'

Alex was quiet for a while. 'Why?' he asked quietly at last.

'You see, Alex, I desire to have children in future and if we're supposed to be married, I must be sure that our children would not end up dead like my younger brothers.'

'I still don't understand,' said Alex.

'My younger brothers died of a preventable disease known as sickle cell disease and I wish to prevent that from happening to my kids in future,' said Nike determinedly.

Chapter 33

Out of curiosity, Alex had gone for the blood test and it was confirmed that he actually had an AS genotype.

'That means you are highly likely to have a child or children with SS genotype with a partner who has an AS genotype,' the doctor had explained to Alex.

Alex remembered that Nike had told him she had the AS genotype. He did not remember his father ever telling him there was anything like that in the Tucker blood. He felt he needed to have a heart to heart talk with his father.

When he got to his father's wing of the house they shared, Alex met him seated before a piano, rehearsing the song he would sing with the church choir the following Sunday. Alex had waited until Alan finished the song before saying a word to him. Alan Tucker had such a good voice and as usual, Alex had been mesmerised by the melodious way his father sang. When the song ended, Alan Tucker turned to Alex and smiled.

'What brings you to my wing at this time of the day, son?' Alan smiled warmly at Alex. His handsome, kindly face shone with the deep affection he felt towards Alex.

Alex smiled back. The warmth they shared between them was electrifying.

Alan Tucker stretched out a hand towards Alex and in a low voice, reminiscent of one talking to his beloved baby, he said, 'Come here and have a seat, son.'

Alex strolled over to where Alan sat and picked up a coffee table from beside the piano. He sat on the table and crossed his legs in front of him. Suddenly, his gaze was averted to the only photograph in the living room, the photograph of his grandfather, Sir Alexander Tucker Snr. Beside his grandfather's picture was his mother's picture. Alex's mother was a beautiful woman with strong facial features. In the picture, she had a determined expression and her jaw seemed to jut out. She was a picture of a woman who held her own; a woman who refused to be dictated to. Alex had been told that her mother had suddenly disappeared when he was barely two years old and she had never been found. He sometimes wondered if she was still alive.

Although Alex had never seen his grandmother's picture, Alan had described her as a very beautiful woman of mixed origin – half Greek and half English.

Alan had never mentioned anything about a blood disorder to him. Now, as he studied the pictures hanging on the walls in front of him, he could not help but wonder from whom he had inherited the blood disorder.

'You seem a little troubled, son. What could be the problem?' said Alan aloud, cutting into Alex's thoughts.

Alex looked away from the wall and he looked into the eyes of Alan.

'Why didn't you tell me you carry the sickle cell genotype dad?' he asked without preamble.

Alan Tucker was taken aback; the smile slowly faded from his face. He had not expected the question from Alex and he was not prepared for it.

'I do not carry a sickle cell genotype,' he replied tersely.

'Then how come I do?' asked Alex. 'Or was it my mother who had it?'

Alan Tucker looked at him sharply. He wondered how Alex discovered he had the sickle cell blood in him. *Had the boy been digging where he shouldn't?* He sincerely prayed he hadn't; he sincerely hoped Alex would come to no harm.

Alan shut his eyes.

'How did you find out you had the sickle cell gene?' he asked.

'I'm dating a certain lady whose name is Nike,' began Alex. He looked at Alan, who still had his eyes shut. Alex could not determine what was going on in his father's mind. He very much hated to hurt him. He had not introduced Nike to his father before he proposed to her. He had done it in the heat of the moment. What he had planned was to bring Nike to see his father, Reverend Alan Tucker, after they had tied the knot at the registry. Nike was very beautiful and worldly-wise and he was not very sure his father, Alan, who was known to be holy and deeply religious, would approve of her.

'Go ahead,' said Alan Tucker tersely; the smile had suddenly faded from his mouth and he looked withdrawn.

'Well,' Alex began uncertainly. 'Well I… well I proposed to her and she insisted I went for a blood test to determine our compatibility. She told me her two brothers died of sickle cell disease, and she would like to prevent that from happening to our children in future.'

Alan Tucker opened his eyes, then he looked directly at Alex and for the first time since he recognised Alan as his father, Alex Tucker felt scared of him. Alan Tucker had an expression that was not determinable to Alex; his blue-coloured pupils had turned quite dark and he looked liked he was in a trance.

Alex waited for his father to talk; he dreaded the next words his father would utter. He hoped his father was not about to drop a *bombshell* on him.

'You must stop seeing that girl at once!' Alan commanded; his tone had changed from being warm to being quite coarse.

Alex felt his tense muscles relaxing. He had expected to hear something more terrible. Leaving Nike should really not be a problem; after all, he was not really sure of his love for her. He had good sex with her – yes, he did – but he was not sure he felt anything deeper than lust for her.

But there was still an issue to be sorted out and that was the issue of his blood group.

'Dad,' he said, 'I have not come to you because of Nike; I have come to ask you how we could end up with different blood genotypes.'

Alan Tucker sighed deeply.

'This is not a matter to be discussed now,' he said at last. 'Go back to your wing and in the morning, I will come and discuss some things with you.'

Alex knew better than to argue with his dad. Although Alan had been a loving dad all his life, he had come to realise that questioning Alan on certain issues would only be likened to taking water out of a brick wall.

'Alright Dad,' said Alex. 'See you in the morning.'

'Son,' Alan called after him as he turned to leave.

Alex turned back to his dad.

'Yes Dad,' he said.

'You must stop seeing that lady at once!'

Alan Tucker had come to see Alex in his wing of the huge house in the wee hours of the morning. Alan had come through a single door that connected the two wings together. As far as Alex knew, the door had never been opened save for now; he knew instantly that what his father had come to tell him that morning was something very serious.

Alex was ready to hear whatever his father had to say; besides, he had not slept a wink since the day before and the earlier they had this issue resolved, the better.

Alex and Alan sat opposite each other on each of the two chairs in the room.

Alex tensed up, bracing himself for the news.

And then it came.

'I'm not your biological father,' Alan blurted out.

Alex felt he had not heard right. 'What?' he exclaimed. 'What did you say, Dad?'

'I said I'm not your biological father,' repeated Alan sadly.

Alex was stupefied. For some minutes, he could not say a word. He just looked at his father, flabbergasted. He had thought he was prepared to hear what his father had come to tell him, but he was not prepared for this.

How come Reverend Alan Tucker was not his real father? They both shared the same surname and they both looked so much alike. By the way, if Alan was not his father, then who was?

'Who's my father?' asked Alex quietly.

'Your father, Rory, was my brother; he was my younger half-brother,' replied Alan.

'How… How come you never told me this dad?' asked Alex; he felt shocked to his bone marrow.

'Because I was trying to protect you from whoever killed your father,' replied Alan.

Alex pondered on this for a while then he felt he had to ask a question.

'Did you bother to find out who killed my father?' he asked Alan.

'Oh yes,' Alan replied. 'We tried to find out and the police tried their best. I even hired some private detectives, but all our efforts at finding out who killed Rory proved abortive. It was while we were at it that your grandmother, who happened to be my step-mother, was murdered.'

At that moment, Alex felt a pain searing through his guts.

'So, my grandmother was also murdered?' he managed to ask.

'Yes,' replied Alan painfully. 'She died of food poisoning right inside this house. I was away with my father, who was your grandfather, on a missionary trip to the United States at the time. We had to be called back form our trip. Her killer was never found!' Alan looked at Alex; his eye welling up with tears as he said, 'Your grandfather died from the shock of the two deaths.'

Alex had gone quiet; he was trying to come to terms with the gruesome murders of two people in a family. His heart suddenly went out to Alan; his eyes misted over. Alan must have felt very frightened because of what had happened to members of his family. That must have been why he never told him a thing until now.

'Your mother's sudden disappearance was linked to the murderers of your father and your grandmother, but up till now no one has been arrested,' Alan continued as tears tricked down his handsome face. Alex went over to him and brushed away the tears with his fingers.

'I'm sorry, Dad,' he said simply.

However, he wondered why none of these killers had been arrested till date. His instinct as a lawyer told him the killers might be some people who knew the family; maybe someone who was close to the family let out secrets to the killers.

'Do you think someone who's close to the family might be behind this?' Alex asked Alan cautiously.

Alan pondered on this for a while before replying, 'At some point, the police thought the killings might be linked with my elder brother, Jamie.'

'You had another brother apart from my father?' asked Alex with utter incredulity.

Alan looked at Alex, who was totally confused now and smiled sadly.

'Although, I never told you this,' said Alan, 'my father had a son before me. His name was Jamie. When our mother died, Jamie could not come to terms with her death. Over the years, Jamie became completely transformed. He went from a quiet, studious boy to a cannabis smoking truant and he was always getting into fights with people. But he managed to hide his cannabis smoking habits from our father for a long time.'

Alan studied Alex's expression; it was now deadpan. He wished he could read his thoughts, but he found he couldn't. Alan continued his story anyway. 'Jamie was caught smoking cannabis by your grandmother three months after she came into this home and your grandmother told our father. Our father, because he was vying for the post of a knight in the church and did not want his name rubbed in the mud, decided to hide Jamie away from home. So he thought it best to send him to rehab. Jamie hated every minute he spent there and he always blamed your grandmother for it. Three months later, he came home from rehab and his relationship with Dorothy degenerated.

They had an argument one day and a physical squabble ensued. Dorothy had to call the police and Jamie was taken away. I was not present at the time, but Dorothy claimed Jamie tried to strangle her. Jamie who was nineteen then, spent six months in prison before he was released.

However, our father had publicly disowned him before then. He would not let him back into the house.'

Alan looked at Alex for a long time. Alex was silent; he was listening with rapt attention.

'I remember the last statement Jamie made before he left this house; he said to Dorothy, "I swear you'll regret this, you bitch!"

'Although, three months after he left the house, Jamie sent me a letter informing me that he was getting married; and that was the last I heard from him. He had never been seen since then,' concluded Alan.

'Do you think that Jamie might be respons–' began Alex, but Alan cut him short.

'No,' said Alan. 'You see, Jamie was a rough kind of guy quite all right, but he had a soft heart deep within him; I do not think he could hurt a fly. He was just hurting from the death of our mother. Besides, the police searched everywhere in their bid to find Jamie, but he was never found. He seemed to have disappeared into thin air!' Alan looked straight into Alex's eyes before saying, 'I'm one hundred per cent sure that Jamie had no hand in all that happened.'

Alex went quiet again. If Alan Tucker thought his brother, Jamie, was innocent then he probably was *innocent*. After all, Alan had known every member of the family personally. However, he supposed that whoever the murderer or *murderers* were, they must be very powerful and influential people in the society; *or how else could they still remain at large?*

Alan sniffed and looked at Alex through tear-filled eyes then he blurted out, 'You got the AS genotype from your grandmother, Lady Dorothy Tucker!'

Alex nodded. He had suddenly forgotten the main reason why Alan had come to tell him the story of the family. For some reason, Alex felt that carrying the sickle cell genotype was no longer important. What was paramount now was to find out the killers of his father and grandmother, and probably his mother, and bring them all to book.

As if Alan was reading his thoughts, he spoke, 'Son, don't you ever dare look for the murderers. You might lose your life in the process.'

Fresh tears began to well up in Alan's eyes as he said to Alex, 'I don't want to lose you, son.'

And Alex had decided to drop the case; he could not bear to see Alan hurt so much. Although, Alex had barely known his parents and grandparents, he knew what impact losing them all would have had on Alan. He decided not to pursue the matter any more; he would let sleeping dogs lie and hopefully, Alan would be healed of all the hurt he felt at the demise of the people he had lived with and loved so much.

Before Alan left Alex's apartment that morning, he said to Alex, 'Son, please steer clear of that Nike lady. She's not good for you!'

Chapter 34

Nike came in one day and found the flat she shared with Tonia in state of disarray. There was a half-packed traveller's bag on the leather sofa; a make-up bag was placed beside the bag and there was a toothbrush falling out of the make-up bag. A pair of shoes that she recognised belonged to Tonia lay on the rug as if they had been kicked off her feet in a hurry and there were the remains of a broken wine glass and a broken wine bottle on the floor and splinters of glass all over the floor. Tonia ordinarily would not leave the sitting room in such a mess. Tonia, unlike Nike, was very neat and orderly. Nike's first thought was that the flat had been burgled; although that was very unlikely, Nike could not rule out the possibility. *Was Tonia hurt?* Nike panicked. She moved back towards the door for safety and she took out her mobile phone to dial 999 when she heard a faint sound. She listened carefully and the sound became louder; it was a sound of racking sobs. Nike stopped short and then she tiptoed towards the direction of the sound, frantically looking around to see if there was an intruder in the house. The sound was coming form Tonia's room. Nike knocked softly on Tonia's door. There was no reply. She knocked again, loudly this time and when she got no reply, she opened the door gently and peeped into the room. She saw Tonia sitting on the beautifully carpeted floor of her bedroom, beside the bed, crying her eyes out. Her head was rested against the edge of the bed and she was holding a tissue which she occasionally used to dap at her eyes which had been made sore and puffy by her incessant crying.

Confident that there was no intruder in the house after all – at least not at the moment – Nike opened the door wider and went inside the room. She looked around the beautifully decorated room (which was a far cry from her own room which was always in a state of disarray) for a second, wondering what could have upset the normally composed Tonia – the cool and collected Tonia. Nike had always wondered if Tonia had any cause to worry about anything in life. Tonia seldom laughed, but then she was seldom downcast. In fact, Nike had never seen her downcast, not until now anyway. She really wondered what was amiss. Tonia seemed to have everything going for her; she was pretty – as pretty as the word can be – she had a good job, was from a good and respectable family and, most importantly, she was in a great relationship… *and she had not lived a lousy life like she, Nike, had,* Nike thought to herself. So what could be the problem? There was an unwritten agreement between them to respect each other's privacy always, not to pry into each other's affairs unless otherwise invited, but then this was the first time Nike had witnessed Tonia in this state and besides, curiosity got the better of her and she decided to pry. She cleared her throat loudly for attention and Tonia looked up startled. She quickly dabbed at her eyes with the tissue she was holding and made an unsuccessful attempt at a smile.

'I didn't hear you come in,' she said faintly.

'I didn't expect you to…' Nike replied. 'You were busy crying.'

Tonia was silent.

Nike made an attempt to get her into a lighter mood and she said, 'Now tell Aunty Nike what the matter is and we'll see what we can do. You know she'll so full of wisdom, she can always get your milk back from the cat who stole it.' Her little joke did not achieve anything; rather Tonia burst into fresh tears. 'Now tell me what the matter is so we'll know how to thrash it out. You know, a problem shared is half solved they say,' Nike said seriously.

Tonia sniffed, coughed a little and then blew her nose before answering in a muffled tone, 'Benjamin has left me.'

'What? What did you say? I did not hear you properly, please speak louder.'

Tonia spoke louder, 'Benjamin has left me.'

Nike had heard her properly the first time but she wanted to be sure of what she had heard. Now that she heard it twice she was sure of what she heard but found it unbelievable. *Tonia and Benjamin – the couple of the century; Benjamin has left Tonia;* it was unbelievable. As a couple, they were as perfect as perfect could be. Their wedding was just two weeks away and all arrangements had been made towards its success. Nike knew that much, for she had gone with Tonia to choose her wedding dress and she had been pinned down to be the chief bridesmaid. She had gone with Tonia to make the booking with the wedding planner – the most expensive around. She was there when Tonia had given the cashier at the office of the wedding planner the cheque for the deposit, which was no small amount (although, Tonia had mentioned the fact that the cheque had been issued by Benjamin); She was there when Tonia called to book for a course on how to have a successful marriage; she was there when… The list was endless.

'What happened?' Nike asked calmly. Tonia sniffed one more time, wiped the tears off her face with the back of her hand and adjusted herself on the floor of the bedroom so that her back was resting against the edge of the bed. Nike saw this and sat on the floor too. She wanted Tonia to feel that she had a best friend in her, a friend who was willing to bear everything with her, a friend who was willing to climb mountains with her and descend into the valleys with her, a friend who would sit on the floor because she was sitting on the floor. Nike curled her knees under her chin, crossed her hands across her legs and waited curiously. Tonia said, 'Do you remember Brian McGregor? The... the popular one?' she added rather uncomfortably when she saw no sign of recognition registered on Nike's face.

Nike remembered Brian McGregor instantly. 'You mean the notorious Brian McGregor of the 'Wild Rockers'? Of course I know him. Last time I heard, he was in prison doing time for drug trafficking and murder,' Nike said, looking at Tonia with a puzzled expression. She was really curious now but she decided against pressing for more information. She did not want to appear eager to hear the story. That might put Tonia off telling her anything more. Tonia was not ordinarily given to many words and in the years that they had been staying together as flatmates, Nike knew that Tonia was easily put off with long discussions. While waiting for Tonia to compose herself, she tried to find a link between Brian McGregor's incarceration several years ago and Tonia's predicament now and she failed totally. She looked at the pieces of used tissues heaped at Tonia's feet and she guessed that Brian McGregor was probably related to Tonia. Maybe he was her cousin. Nike could not imagine Brian McGregor to be anything other than that to Tonia – her cousin. She could not even begin to imagine that they were friends – Tonia and Brian McGregor! It was simply laughable. Tonia was too posh, too polished, too sophisticated to have any relationship (apart from a filial one which in that case, Tonia wouldn't be able to do anything to change), even if it was platonic, with Brian McGregor. Tonia and the unscrupulous Brian McGregor of the 'Wild Rockers' were simply worlds apart. Nike tried to remember Brian McGregor the way he had been shown on T.V. and the newspapers before he was locked away – long, bleached dirty-looking hair, a big round shaped earring in his right ear and a smaller one of similar shape in his left ear. He was a huge muscular man who was dressed in an expensive tattered pair of jeans and an expensive shirt that looked so tight on him it seemed to want to burst at the seams. Nike could even remember the tabloid headline in one of the newspapers: 'Evil Boss of the notorious 'Wild Rockers' gets his due'. *But why would Benjamin leave Tonia now because of Brian McGregor's problem? And why was it now that Tonia and Benjamin had to split over Brian McGregor; after several months of courtship and all those wedding preparations?* The only other logical explanation was that Benjamin thought that Tonia was Brian McGregor's girlfriend before he went to prison. Nike almost laughed out loud at the thought. It was just impossible. *Brian McGregor definitely couldn't have been Tonia's boyfriend.*

'Brian McGregor was my boyfriend,' Tonia blurted out.

Nike almost choked on her own saliva. 'What? Brian McGregor? Your boyfriend?' Nike could not imagine Tonia and the ruffian together. She almost gave a laugh but she managed to retain her caring, sober look. This was going to be an interesting story and Nike would not want to spoil things by laughing at her friend. *Tonia and Brian McGregor – together? How interesting.*

'How… how did it happen?' Nike managed to ask, while trying to stifle a chuckle.

Tonia started explaining, albeit incoherently, 'It… it was many years ago. I was fifteen and in the secondary school. I was naïve and I was besotted with him. He was so full of life and so popular. He was every girl's dream and he had chosen me. We were always together and he lavished so much attention on me. I was proud to be his girl. The relationship lasted for one month and… and…'

'No! Wait,' Nike cut her short. She did not want to miss out on any part of the story. 'How and where on the earth's surface did you meet Brian McGregor? Under what circumstances did you two meet? Start right from the beginning.'

Tonia blew her nose one more time, cleared her throat and told her the story right from the beginning…

Chapter 35

Tonia was an only child, born into a rich family. She lacked nothing that money could buy as a young girl. Her father, Doctor Philip Saunders, was a neuro-surgeon who spent most of his time either at the hospital or at the medical research centre. He was a renowned and well-respected medical practitioner and he was dedicated to his job. He was a quiet, gentle and very reserved man and Tonia grew to respect and love him even though she did not see much of him when she was growing up. Tonia's mother, Beatrice, on the other hand, was a model, a top fashion designer and a socialite who was full of glamour and pride. Beatrice was a very beautiful woman and she knew it. She was always elegantly dressed without a strand of her hair out of place. This was not only because Beatrice was conscious of the cameras following her everywhere she went; Beatrice was inherently glamorous and wherever she was, she desired to be the centre of attraction. She enjoyed being attended to and she carried herself with pride. Her gait never went unnoticed.

Beatrice tried to inculcate her traits into her daughter at a very early age – as early as six years old. She would always watch Tonia carefully as she ate, talked and walked. 'Walk smartly,' she would shout at Tonia. 'Ladies do not walk sluggishly'; 'Stand straight, ladies do not slouch'; 'Eat healthily, and use the appropriate cutleries to eat, you could find yourself in front of the cameras in the near future, especially as you are my very own daughter,' Beatrice would say with self pride, laying a salient emphasis on the word *my*. On and on the corrections went; and on and on the chastisement went. Tonia bore the unnecessary chastisement and unnecessary corrections until she got to year eleven in the secondary school and then her boring, comfortable life was changed drastically.

Tonia had attended the best nursery and the best primary school in London – her mother made sure of that. However, when she was about to go to the secondary school, her father had a change of heart.

'I think Tonia should go to a public secondary school for a change,' said Philip Saunders to his wife. His wife, Beatrice, choked on the expensive red wine she was sipping. She coughed so hard, the glass of wine she was holding shook and the wine spilled onto the expensive white sofa on which she had been reclining. She placed the glass of wine on the coffee table that was beside the sofa and stubbed out the half-smoked cigarette she was holding in the other hand by dipping it into the wine glass; her sophistication and polished manners apparently forgotten.

'What the hell do you mean Phillip?' she said, jumping off the sofa; her breathing was laboured. 'You mean the daughter of Beatrice Saunders, *my very own daughter*, should mingle with the dregs of society? You mean you intend to send my daughter to a bloody school where she would have no choice but to wine and dine with the children of nonentities, where she would sit and study in the same classrooms with never-do-wells?' Before Phillip could utter a word in reply, Beatrice continued. 'Absolute nonsense! It won't happen, not in this life and not in the life after,' she finished vehemently. Her chest heaving up and down so much that thoughts of her collapsing crossed Phillip's mind for a fleeting moment.

'Please listen to me, Beatrice,' said Phillip in his usual quiet voice. 'I want the best for our daughter. I do not wish her any hurt in life, but you would agree with me that life is all about ups and downs and diversities. I want my daughter to know what life is all about.'

'I can teach her what life is all about,' Beatrice cut in, but Phillip went on as if she had not spoken.

'How else do you think Tonia will know about life if she does not go through life itself? I want Tonia to see all sides to life; I want her to know what it is like with other people. You never know what her future career will demand. Who knows, she may find herself vying for a ministerial post in future. Tell me how she would be able to win the hearts of the common man without actually knowing what it is like to be common. What promises would she give? Would they believe her? How would she be able to relate to the common man if all her life she had been wrapped up in a cotton wool of luxury? Remember, Beatrice, experience is always the best teacher they say,' Doctor Saunders finished, hoping his wife would see reason with him.

His wife finally saw reason with him but only because he had mentioned the probability that Tonia would one day become a minister in future. Beatrice Saunders was surely not one to disregard any avenue to become famous and in command of things. She relished the thought that, one day, she would become a mother to a cabinet minister. She smiled warmly; Phillip Saunders heaved a sigh of relief. What he had thought would be a mini world war had been just a storm in a tea-cup.

Beatrice had agreed for Tonia to attend the public secondary school only on the condition that she would be chauffeur-driven in one of their expensive cars to and from the school. The daughter of Beatrice Saunders must always stand out among others.

It was when Tonia was in year eleven that two girls got transferred from a school in the United States of America to Tonia's school in Great Britain. The two girls (who were actually a couple of years older than the other students in year eleven) had been studying their new environment carefully since they came to the school. They had watched the boys and the girls of their new school closely. They watched the way they interacted with one another; they saw the way the boys dated the girls, the way a boy would always hang out with a girl, shower her with little gifts that only school children could afford, gifts like cakes, chocolates and sweets and at most, little teddies; they saw the way a girl would flush with pride and immense joy at the new gift she had just acquired from her boyfriend and they usually heard how a girl would brag about such gifts to her friends – they were greatly amused. As far as they were concerned, the other students' apparent naivety was totally unbelievable. The two new students thought that they had been transferred to a school where every student was just developing 'milk teeth' and they felt like big aunties to them all; or how else would one explain the enthusiasm at being given sweets and teddies as gifts or how, in fact, a fifteen year old girl would choose to date or go out with a fellow classmate. To the new girls, this was totally ridiculous. They wondered if those boys and girls in their class who were dating each other actually knew what to do with each other when they were alone together.

As the two girls walked to the bus stop to catch a bus home from school one bright sunny afternoon, the shorter one of the two, whose name was Jessica, said to the other one, whose name was Fantasia, 'Do you think, Fantasia, that the boys in our class know where to insert their little dicks when they are with their girlfriends?'

A black elderly woman who appeared to be in her late sixties looked sharply at the girl who had uttered what she considered a vulgar statement, shook her head and said loud enough for the girls to hear, 'The world has really become a spoilt place. Kids who should be talking about school and grades are talking adult talks. What is this world really coming to?' she asked no one in particular and then she quickly moved away from the girls. If Jessica and Fantasia heard what the elderly woman said, they appeared to take no notice. Jessica continued, 'Take little Freddie and Rosemary for instance' (to Jessica and Fantasia, everyone in their class was 'little'). 'Do you think they even do anything together? Freddie is so shy he could barely look at anyone straight in the eye'.

'That's what I sometimes wonder too,' Fantasia chuckled and they both laughed at what they considered the total 'silliness' of their new classmates. Where they came from in the United States, fifteen year old girls, who considered themselves big girls, who were 'worth their onions', usually went out with rich older men – men who had achieved substantial 'something' in life, men with class and money. As they talked and waited for the bus to arrive, they spotted a shiny silver-coloured Porsche speed by. They both noticed the young girl seated at the *owner's corner* of the Porsche. Jessica, who was the more outspoken of the two, jerked her head at the car which had just sped by.

'Did you see Cinderella?,' she asked.

Fantasia had indeed seen the impressive Porsche and she had indeed seen Tonia in it. The two girls had both noticed that, while the other students either walked home or made use of public transportation to get home from school, the quiet girl who they both knew as Tonia and who they had unanimously nicknamed 'Cinderella', was usually chauffeur-driven home. They also noticed that Cinderella usually went home in no small car. She always went home in a Chrysler Jeep or a Porsche, like she did that day.

'Her folks must really be in a hell of money,' Jessica enthused admiringly. 'They must be fucking rich,' she said.

Fantasia just nodded in agreement. She was no longer with Jessica. Physically – yes – she was still at the miserable bus stop, waiting for the miserable bus to arrive, but her mind was far away; her mind was with Tonia in the attractive Porsche car, travelling with her to her home, wherever the rich girl lived. Fantasia decided right there and then that she would penetrate Tonia's world and see what she could get out of it. It was not fair that while others barely had enough, a little girl, just one girl, should have everything others like Jessica and Fantasia herself could only dream of. It was just not fair. So, as Jessica rambled on about how she imagined how very rich Tonia's family would be, Fantasia began to form a plan…

The next morning, Fantasia saw Tonia alighting from the Porsche that had come to pick up her from school the previous day and she ran out to meet her, cheerfully greeting her as if they had been friends for a long time.

'Hi, Tonia darling. How are you today? I've been waiting for you for quite some time. Why have you come late this morning?'

Tonia looked at her and then she turned her head and looked behind her to see if the weird girl who had come running towards her was actually talking to someone else behind her. Tonia saw no one behind her and she knew that

Fantasia had actually been talking to her. Tonia looked at her sceptically, for she had never spoken a word to either the girl or her friend before. Tonia had always regarded the two with suspicion. To Tonia, they looked very worldly-wise; to Tonia, they looked so out of place among the other students; to Tonia, they seemed to have seen everything, been everywhere, have wandered to the ends of the earth, even up to the great Marianna Trench and further, looking for who they could devour, just like the devil; to Tonia, they were certainly not the sort of girls her parents would love to see her mingle with; so she had always deliberately avoided them. She always made sure not to sit anywhere near them in class and whenever they were in the school canteen for lunch, she would always look out for a table that was very far away from where the girls were sitting.

Now, Tonia wondered why one of the two girls would come to her to say such endearing words to her as if that was the normal thing they did everyday. Tonia smiled at Fantasia cautiously and extended her hand to her for a handshake. Fantasia, however, moved closer to her and gave her a bear hug.

'It's so good to see you this morning, Antonia darling. Come on let's go to the class before lessons begin.'

Tonia was flabbergasted. She did not like this; she did not like it at all and the fact that Fantasia had called her by her full name did not appeal to Tonia. Tonia hated to be called Antonia (Her aunt whom she hated dearly was called Antonia and she did her best not to be associated with her). She did not want to be friends with this Fantasia girl at all. She pulled away from her stiffly but politely, said bye to the chauffeur, who obviously had been watching the *drama* with interest, and quickly walked ahead of Fantasia. Fantasia smiled, she did not care if Tonia wanted to be friends with her or not; she had made an impression on the dummy that drove her everywhere. She had even called 'Cinderella' by her full name to show how very close their friendship was. Come what may, he would be a witness to the fact that she was Tonia's very good friend, for only good friends greeted each other with such endearments. She looked at the chauffeur and smiled warmly at him. She needed her face to register in his memory. The chauffeur smiled back. He was thinking, *so, the lonely Tonia has got a friend after all. That's really nice.* Then he got into the car and drove off.

Fantasia smiled again. Plan A was successful. Plan B was in the making. There was a look of triumph on her face as she quickly walked towards the classroom. *Fantasia, you're a very smart girl, very smart indeed*, she said within herself as she went into the classroom.

That morning, as she received her first lessons, Tonia wondered why one of the two girls, who did not ordinarily talk to or mingle with any other students in their class, would choose to embarrass her by hugging and embracing her in the presence of everyone, including her driver. She felt that there must be more to it. Was it a ploy? Could she want money? Tonia would not put anything past either of the two girls. They always appeared like they were up to some mischief. Tonia decided to try and keep the two of them further from her than ever.

As the students filed out of their various classrooms for lunch, Jessica and Fantasia followed Tonia to her table. They observed once again that the table had a space and a seat for only one other person. Every student in the school was not oblivious to the fact that Tonia was a loner – probably a snob and she did all her best to remain so. She mingled with no one either in the classroom or in the canteen and everyone had learned over time to let her be. However, Fantasia was determined not to let her be. She had a mission to accomplish in Tonia's life and she was determined to do just that. Fantasia quickly sat down on the vacant seat placed at Tonia's table and instructed Jessica to get a chair from another table and join them. Tonia was miffed but she decided not to utter a word. The best answer for a fool – or fools as the case was – was silence. She ate on in silence, cautiously watching the two nuisances, wondering what they were actually up to. *God, how she detested these girls.* Tonia felt that by now, the two girls ought to know that she was not ready to be their friend – not now and definitely not in future. *How wrong she was!*

While they were eating, Fantasia and Jessica tried all they could to get Tonia to converse with them to no avail. 'I've always liked quiet people with class you know,' said Fantasia to Jessica.

'Me too,' said Jessica, looking at Tonia and willing her to say something to break the ice.   Tonia said nothing.

'I like Antonia's driver. He's a real cool dude,' Fantasia said to Jessica again, silently daring Tonia to challenge her. Tonia said nothing. She was getting really angry now. Firstly, she did not like to be called Antonia and secondly, she did not like the implication of closeness between Fantasia – and anybody for that matter – and herself. But Jessica was really interested now. She was not aware that her friend had gone as far as knowing someone that was close to their dear *Cinderella*. Jessica's eyes widened for real as she asked Fantasia, 'Have you met him? When did you meet him? Was he nice?'

'Of course. He's a nice hunk of a gentleman,' replied Fantasia. She was trying not to look at Tonia however much she desperately wanted to watch her reaction.

'Really?' said Jessica, eyes glowing. She had suddenly forgotten that they were playing games with Tonia. 'Tell me something, when do I get to meet him?' she asked interestedly. To Jessica, a man was a man no matter what his status was in life. What mattered was that he should have enough dough to spend on her, especially for food, and more importantly, he should have the libido to satisfy her ravenous sexual appetite; and from what she had heard of Tonia's driver, he should be capable of both tasks.

Tonia felt disgusted listening to them. She could not fathom why on earth the two girls would drool over her chauffeur. She got up abruptly and without saying a word to either of them, left the table, her food only half eaten. She did not hear Fantasia's subtle reference to her father...

Chapter 36

Benjamin Walters looked on forlornly at the remains of his father, Sir Alfred Walters, in the hearse. It had been two weeks since his father's demise but he still found it unimaginable that his father was gone; gone to be seen no more; but more terrifying was the fact that his father had committed suicide. His father had shot himself in his study that Monday morning, two weeks ago. The single bullet had pierced his head and ripped his brains apart. He had died instantly. Right now, the wound in his father's head was blocked with cotton wool which had turned from white to crimson due to the rush of blood from his brains onto the cotton. There was a bustle of activities all around him but Benjamin was oblivious to all of them. His mind went back to his father lying in the coffin, stone dead. A month before, his father had been very much alive, vibrant and vying for the post of the Mayor of London. He had gone about his campaign with vigour and enthusiasm and he had won the hearts of many. A month ago, almost all fingers had virtually pointed to his father as the next Mayor of London. It was simply inevitable that Sir Alfred Walters would become the next Mayor. Everyone knew it; his enemies knew it. However, unfortunately for Sir Alfred Walters and fortunately for his enemies, there was a sudden twist of fate. An upcoming journalist had stumbled upon Sir Alfred Walters' sordid past. The journalist had somehow come up with the fact that, in his younger days, Sir Alfred Walters had been a notorious drug baron in Australia and he had done time in an Australian jail for rape. The prosecutors had been able to nail him for rape but he had narrowly escaped jail for drug offences due to lack of concrete evidence and the power of money. The journalist had painted a picture of a dangerous criminal who was not given adequate justice back in Australia. There were enough jail pictures to suffice. Benjamin Walters could still remember the tabloid; 'From Prison to the Mayoral seat – a Possibility?' Sir Alfred Walters' opponents had quickly taken advantage of the news and support for his father had promptly gone on the decline. Although the story was a big break for the journalist, it was a big brokenness for Sir Alfred Walters and his entire family. Benjamin had seen his father's shoulders sag; he had watched his father's admirable vivacity fast become something of the past. His father had withdrawn from the Mayoral race and he seemed to go into hibernation. In the weeks leading to his death, only his family had access to him. Sir Alfred Walters had simply withdrawn from public life. But the newspapers wouldn't let him be. They kept asking questions, digging deeper into his past, making ambiguous insinuations and writing about him in derision. The Walters household were well aware that the rivals were behind the propaganda. What beat everyone in that family was how the story managed to come out in the first place, for it had been seen to that Sir Walters had gotten a new identity altogether while in Europe.

In the days that preceded his death, Sir Alfred Walters had taken to the bottle. He had simply drunken himself to stupor. All efforts of his household to get him to seek help proved abortive. On Monday morning, exactly two weeks before, Benjamin had received an urgent call in his office and he had rushed home to find his father lying in a pool of his own blood, a pistol in his limp hand. His father had shot himself out of the shame his past had brought him. His father's enemies had succeeded!

Now, as Benjamin looked at the preacher saying the necessary good things he felt he had to say about his father (even though, he was not looking convinced himself), deliberately leaving out what had actually caused his death, Benjamin made a resolution in his mind. He was going to run for the Mayoral seat in the very near future. He was going to be what his father had wanted to be; he was going to be the Mayor of London for his father and he was never going to let anything – anything at all – taint his image!

Chapter 37

Fantasia watched from her classroom window as the hunky chauffeur opened the door for Tonia to get down from the owner's corner of the Mercedes Benz. She did not rush out to meet them this time. She had another plan up her sleeve. She decided that if she was going to achieve her ultimate goal in Tonia's life, she had better become her friend. She watched as Tonia walked towards the classroom and as soon as she saw her enter the building, she quickly got down from the table she was sitting on and positioned herself neatly on the chair beside the one everybody knew Tonia always sat on. Tonia walked into the classroom and, as soon as she saw that one of the two girls she had come to hate with a passion would be sitting close to her should she choose to sit in her normal position, she quickly turned left and took a seat at the far end of the classroom – very far away from Fantasia. She did not mind the fact that, since she started that particular class, she would not be sitting in her favourite chair.   Fantasia noticed with dismay that Tonia was pointedly avoiding her and she decided to let it be for now. 'But not for long, babe,' she said very determinedly under her breath.

During lunch, Fantasia called Jessica and let her in on her plans. They watched as Tonia entered the school canteen and looked around. Satisfied that there was no sign of her two 'stalkers', she went to get her food, found a table with a single seat and gingerly sat down to eat. No sooner had she sat down than they appeared by her side like magic; one on her right and the other on her left. She almost screamed. She had had enough and she was about to tell them so, when Fantasia raised her hand in a gesture for Tonia not to say anything. The two girls brought two chairs to Tonia's table and sat down with her. Looking directly at Tonia, Fantasia said to her, 'I know you despise Jessica and myself, Tonia, and I know your hatred for us may not be unfounded given the fact that you don't know the facts about us.' She tried to put up an innocent expression. Tonia picked up her cutlery and started eating; she'd rather these girls left her alone; she was not interested in any facts about them. Fantasia saw that Tonia was not really interested in what she was saying then she went on. 'Jessica and I were born into very wealthy homes; far wealthier homes than you can ever imagine.' She let that sink in. Tonia said nothing. Jessica nodded in the affirmative to buttress what Fantasia was saying.

Fantasia continued. 'Our fathers were business partners who were in the oil and gas business in the United Sates. You know, the importation of crude oil from Africa and the Middle East and the supply of refined petroleum and its products to the third world countries,' Jessica nodded again, this time, vigorously. Fantasia noticed that Tonia was beginning to show a flicker of interest in her story and encouraged by that, she went on. 'Our families were close family friends, who usually took holidays together. We've been to several places all around the world, haven't we, Jessica?' Fantasia turned to Jessica who immediately said 'yes' and nodded even more vigorously. Fantasia went on uninhibited. 'We've been to the Bahamas; we've been to Barbados and the island of Trinidad and Tobago. We've been to Saudi Arabia, to Morocco in Egypt. We've been to Kenya in Africa. Oh my God, you should see the zoos, the wildlife. Have you been to Africa, Tonia?' she asked Tonia, who shook her head in the negative. Jessica was impressed at the flawlessness of Fantasia's lies. It was simply amazing. *This girl must be a genius*, she thought. She was very proud of herself for having a genius as a best friend. She made sure that Tonia was not looking in her direction and gave Fantasia a quick thumbs-up with both of her thumbs and blew her a silent kiss.

Fantasia smiled and went on happily, knowing fully well that she now had Tonia's rapt attention. 'We've had a good life – me and Jessica – we've really had a wonderful life.' She paused and pretended to reflect on *the good old times*, then suddenly her expression changed into a pained one. She gave Tonia a sad look and went on quietly. 'It so happened that one day Jessica's dad was kidnapped and killed. No ransom asked. No explanation offered.' Jessica nodded in total agreement; it was just as well, for since she was born, she had not known any particular man she could call 'Daddy' and really mean it. She had had several 'fathers' who were actually her mother's boyfriends. Her mother had changed men just as often as Tonia's mother probably changed clothes. Jessica had soon learnt to adjust to one man as she had learnt to adjust to the previous one in her mother's life and they had all been called 'Dad'; that was a rule laid down by her mother and that was a rule she had had to follow if she wanted to continually have food in her belly and a place to lay her head.

Jessica brought her mind back to the present and heard Fantasia telling Tonia that her own father had panicked after Jessica's brother had been killed as well and fearing for the two girls' safety, he had arranged for the them to travel to the U.K. to continue their studies. *The bitch,* Jessica thought, *so it was Jessica's family who should be murdered like chickens and Fantasia's family left intact.* Jessica was beginning to get angry with Fantasia for dragging her 'image' in the mud and painting herself in pure white. She had even succeeded in making Tonia believe that they – Fantasia and her father (who happened to be a penniless drunkard back in the farms of Alabama) – were Jessica's knights in shinning armour. However, she could not argue with Fantasia right in the presence of Tonia. That would ruin things. She would have to leave the argument for later. Besides, Fantasia was doing a good job on Tonia, despite everything. She, therefore, started nodding once more. She was, however, not fully aware of what Fantasia was saying at the moment.

Fantasia nearly cursed. She felt like slicing Jessica's fat head off her shoulders to stop her from nodding like a fool. She had just asked her if she thought her father was stupid for sending them abroad to study and she was nodding like the agama lizard she had seen on an African documentary on the television. Fantasia was, however, grateful that Tonia had not bothered to deign Jessica a look; she looked on at Fantasia with undivided attention. By the time Fantasia finished telling Tonia her story, she and Jessica had secured a place for friendship in Tonia's heart. Plan B had worked; it was time for the real action!

When the chauffeur came to pick Tonia up after school hours that day, she said an inaudible bye-bye to Fantasia and Jessica before getting into the car; and she waved as the car drove past them at the bus stop.

'It's working, Fantasia. She's finally accepted us as good friends. Oh you're a genius, Fantasia,' said Jessica enthusiastically.

Fantasia, however, was not satisfied. She had a deep frown on her face when she said absent-mindedly, 'No, I'm not; not yet anyway. She hasn't fully accepted us as friends.'

'What do you mean she hasn't fully accepted us?' Jessica was confused. *Didn't Tonia just wave at them?*

'Cos if we were really her friends, we would be riding in that carriage with her, you dummy.'

'Oh,' was all Jessica could say. She could not imagine the two of them in the same car as *Cinderella*. That would simply amount to biting off more than they could chew. But Fantasia had begun to devise a plan. She would get into Tonia's world at all costs. As she pondered how to go about this, a name and the surname sprang to her mind. Brian McGregor!

'Brian McGregor.'

Fantasia smiled. 'Hello Brian. It's me. Fantasy.' To Brian, Fantasia was always Fantasy. That was his pet name for her. As Jessica had always relied on her wisdom for survival, she had always relied on Brian McGregor for wisdom, advice and money for survival. She had, in turn, always done his bidding; whatever Brian wanted her to do, she always did. She had the assurance that she would always be covered no matter what he put her up to and Brian could always pull her out of any danger. He had the name and he had the money!

Immediately his name came to her mind at the bus stop. She had looked around for a telephone booth, saw one and excused herself from Jessica before walking briskly towards it. Out of sheer habit, she looked around to be sure that no one was watching her before opening the door of the phone booth and entering it. She was aware that Jessica was watching her, wondering what she was up to this time. She would explain to the dumb girl later that she had an urgent business to transact. As she dialled Brian's phone number, she fervently hoped that he was not in his studio; he never picked up calls when he was busy in his studio. She was very happy when he had picked up her call on the third ring. Now, as Brian heard her voice, he knew that there was something urgent she wanted him to fix; Fantasy would not ordinarily called him at two o'clock in the afternoon. If she just wanted fun, she always called late in the evenings.

'Hullo, Fantasy,' Brian McGregor said brightly. 'Good to hear your voice.'

'See Brian, I haven't got much money on me, so I'll make this snappy. I happen to have a very hot chick for you and her father's loaded.'

Brian smiled broadly; Fantasia heard the smile.

'What do you want from me, Fantasy?' asked Brian at last.

'First, you must promise to reimburse me for this phone call; you know I'm only a school girl.'

'I promise,' Brian said impatiently. 'Now what is it?'

'As I was saying, she's swimming in the quid. You know, Porsche today, Mercedes Benz, tomorrow, a Rolls Royce the day after, a Lamborghini the day after, a…' Fantasia was too excited to stop; she also did not care any more about the cost of the phone call; she was going to be reimbursed.

'Cut it, cut it, cut it. I catch your drift. Now will you please go straight to the point.'

Fantasia went straight to the point. She told him everything about Tonia, how far she had gone with her and what she wanted him to do for her.

'Smart girl, really smart girl that you are, Fantasy.'

Fantasia smiled. It was a very nice feeling to be called 'smart' by Brian McGregor.

'Now listen carefully,' said Brian. 'Invite her to a party and…'

Fantasia listened to Brian's instructions with rapt attention and by the time he finished, she was totally convinced she already had Tonia in her pouch.

'Thanks a lot Brian. You are the best,' she said gratefully and went on. 'By the way, when I said earlier that she was a hot chick, I meant she's still a virgin.'

Brian loved virgins; they still had 'it' very tight and he always loved the feeling. Besides, he loved the idea of being the first to 'snap' them open; it always gave him a pleasurable feeling – it made him feel like a hero.

'My dear Fantastic Fantasy,' he said licking his lips with pleasure so much so that Fantasia heard, 'has anyone ever told you that you're the smartest girl in the world?'

'Thanks Brian.' Fantasia understood what Brian meant. Brian knew that Fantasia understood what he meant. If she was able to 'get' Tonia, she would be the seventh virgin that Fantasia would pimp for Brian. Her job was just to introduce the lady formally to him and he would do the rest. Brian was not a greenhorn when it came to wooing ladies; he knew how to pamper them and he pampered them silly. He, however, liked them young so he could groom them to his taste and mould them into whatever he wanted them to be. Brian sometimes wondered how some men found it difficult to get ladies into their bed. To Brian McGregor, that was the easiest thing in the world. He did not force the ladies to do what he wanted; the ladies usually begged for it in the end. Brian McGregor knew how to make a lady feel loved; he could make a lady feel like she was the best thing that recently happened to the world; he would buy gifts, pull out a chair for the lady when they went on a date, spend a fortune on her and in the end the lady usually 'opened up' without any inhibitions. The only sad thing about Brian McGregor was that he soon got tired of the lady he was at one time 'drooling' over and when her time was really 'up', he would begin to do the reverse of what he did to woo her – it was that simple. The lady would get so angry and leave him alone. Some very angry ones usually cursed and cursed some more, but Brian wouldn't be bothered – he had already got what he wanted and by the time he was through with one, another was in the pipeline!

'Do you go to parties Tonia?' Fantasia asked Tonia brightly, the following week in class.

'Of course I do,' replied Tonia bemusedly. *Who doesn't go to parties in this world?*

'I mean real parties,' said Fantasia (she was happy that Tonia now spoke with her without the usual guardedness). 'Do you attend real parties?'

'What do you mean real parties?' asked Tonia wearily.

'Okay, let's put it this way: do you attend parties alone, unsupervised by mum and dad?'

'Of course I do; I attend family parties and friend's parties,' replied Tonia indignantly.

'You mean parties organised by your parents' friends for their kids? Get real Tonia. It's about time you grew up. You're not growing any younger you know.'

'What are you talking about, Fantasia?' asked Tonia confusedly.

'I'm talking about you growing up fast; I'm taking about you blending with the people in this jet age; I'm talking about you knowing what's happening in the world.'

Fantasia saw confusion all the more registered on Tonia's face and said coolly, 'Tonia, let me ask you a direct question. When was the last time you went to an adult's gathering, like a night club for instance?'

'I'm only fifteen and still too young to do anything without my parents' authority.'

'Parental authority my foot,' Fantasia scoffed. 'Of course you're not too young. You're a big girl and your parents do not want you to realise it quickly because they revel in the power they wield over you. You should put a stop to all this babyishness; your parents want you to be forever dependent on them, emotionally and in every other way, because it is always an ego booster for a human being to have control over another; it's just bloody human nature.'

Tonia said nothing. She was deep in thought. She remembered her mother – her bossy nature. She remembered the way her mother breathed down her neck all the time, always correcting her every move. *Fantasia must be right*, she thought.

'Tell you what, Tonia,' Fantasia continued. 'Imagine you found yourself in my situation – rich parents, had every thing I ever wanted. I had servants who attended to my beck and call, but all of a sudden, in the twinkling of an eye, I was dumped in a foreign land, very far away from my beautiful home, far away from all comfort, just so I could be safe. My father had to bring Jessica and me over here to hide us from his business enemies. Of course my father can always afford to bring us to school in a Rolls-Royce but for the enemies; they'd find us out sooner than we expected. That's why we have to live like miserable peasants. It's all a pretence you know. We have to lie low.' Fantasia paused to see if her assertion had any effect on Tonia. Tonia was very near to tears.

Satisfied that her story was producing a desirable effect, Fantasia went on. 'Now, Tonia, I wish to let you know that it's not easy to adjust to a sudden change from a way of living to another; what will I compare it to?' She pretended to think for a while, whilst looking towards the ceiling with a finger to the right side of her head then she continued. 'It's like a new born baby bird being ousted from a bed of very soft, warm grass that its mother prepared for it and dumped in a cold, thick, huge forest. There's very little chance of it surviving.'

'What are trying to tell me, Fantasia?' asked Tonia innocently.

'All I'm saying is that you have to prepare for anything to happen in life. You need a wealth of experience to tackle anything that comes your way and you need to gain those experiences right from now. Imagine if your parents were no more. You have no friends to turn to, you're not even sure who likes you because you're so much into yourself.'

If her parents were dead. Tonia had never thought of that happening. She felt alarmed. Fantasia saw that. She was pleased with herself.

'Now I'm not saying your parents would die soon. God forbid that,' she said, as if she meant it, but she really didn't care if Tonia's parents breathed their last breath right that minute. 'But of course you know that these things happen,' she went on soberly then paused for the enormity of that to sink in and continued. 'So, my dear, all I'm saying is be prepared for anything; that's how Jessica and I have survived till this date and besides, Tonia, life is too short not to enjoy it; before you know it, you're forty, then fifty, then eighty, probably ninety and if you're damn lucky, a hundred… and then you're dead. Of what use would your dead body be to you? None, of course. So, my dear, you need to start enjoying your life from now. Make life sweet for yourself; there's a thousand and one nice things out there that you're missing out on. Trust me, life is very much sweeter than you can ever imagine and besides, there's nothing as interesting as gaining full control of your own life; try it and see.' Fantasia felt exhausted now. She had thought too much and said so much just to change Tonia's rather frigid way of living. *Tonia must definitely pay for this*, she thought within herself.

'I get what you mean,' Tonia said. She was beginning to feel like she had been caged all her life and that she had missed out on interesting things. 'But how do I go about enjoying my life? My parents would not even hear of me going out alone; they would skin me alive,' she said miserably.

'Relax,' said Fantasia. 'I will help you grow up. We're friends now, aren't we?'

Tonia nodded, 'Of course we are.' She was not totally convinced.

'Good. I want you to look into your future and see a mature, independent woman, who has full control of her life; that's what I'm going to turn you into,' Fantasia promised Tonia, but there was a strange expression on her face; she had a far away look that was almost frightening.

Tonia flicked her fingers before Fantasia's eyes several times to bring her back to the present, but Fantasia was not looking at Tonia; she was looking past her. She was looking at her own past, very far away in the suburbs of Alabama…

Chapter 38

Fantasia, unlike Jessica, her next door neighbour who had no particular father, had a father, a mother, two brothers and a pet dog that was called puppy.

The family were not exactly the poorest in the neighbourhood but, at the same time, they just managed to scrape three meals a day. Her father, Henry, was a factory worker, who worked hard to cater for the needs of his family. He did not want his wife to work and he did not allow his children to go into any part-time work. 'Your education is very important to me. I want you all to have all the degrees that I couldn't have. I promise to send you all to the university to attain any height that can be attained in this world,' their father would say to all three of his kids determinedly.

When Fantasia's two brothers were in their first year at the university and Fantasia was in her first year in the secondary school, their father lost his job. There were job cuts at the factory and he was made redundant. All attempts at getting another job proved futile. His pay-off quickly went before he could think of what to do; the meagre amount paid to him by the company was met with a backlog of debts and bills to be paid, and with the constant demands of the whole family to cope with, Henry Peters soon lost all hope in life. He became moody most of the time. It soon affected the way he related to his family. He became more reserved by the minute. Any attempt by his children, especially Fantasia, to strike a conversation with their beloved dad was always met with a gentle, but withdrawn, yes or no.

One bright summer evening, precisely two years after her father lost his job at the factory, Fantasia rushed home from school and found her father fast asleep and snoring on the couch. In her excitement, she rushed to him and shook him awake. 'Daddy, Daddy. I came first in my class,' she said proudly, jumping up and down in her excited state. Henry was happy that his daughter had kept her promise to come tops in her class; he was, however, sad that he could not keep his part of the bargain; he could not afford to buy her the bicycle he promised. He had no money. He just smiled sadly at his daughter and, without uttering a word, went back to sleep. Fantasia looked at her father; her shoulders suddenly sagged. She looked deflated. The Daddy she had always known would have scooped her up in a very huge embrace and taken her out for a nice treat – and he would have bought the promised bicycle for her before they came home. She could not fathom what had transformed her beloved Daddy into someone who didn't care what happened to her. As much as she tried to understand what was happening, the reasoning eluded her. God, she wanted her dear Daddy back. She squeezed her report sheet into a ball and with hot tears running down her eyes, turned and walked away sadly. After that day, she never brought another report card to her father and from that day onwards, her grades plummeted. But Fantasia was not bothered.

One week later, her two brothers, Tyrone and Kirk came home from school unexpectedly.
'Why are you back so early? It's not holiday yet, is it?' their mother, Sonia, asked them, but she could sense why already, so when she heard her older son explain to her that they had chosen to drop out of school for lack of funds, she just shrugged and went into her room.
Fantasia saw little of her brothers as the months went by. Two years after they came home, she stopped seeing them altogether. Every time she enquired about them, she was met with vague answers from her mum and no answer from her dad.
As she grew up, she learned not to ask questions that would not be answered anyway. She assumed that her brothers had just drifted away. She soon began to live without thinking about them.
When she was fourteen years old, she became so used to living alone with her parents and the dog that she was beginning to think that she was probably an only child right from the beginning. She sometimes thought that the presence of her two brothers in the house a few years before might have been just an illusion. Sometime in the future, she would learn that the thought of her brothers being an illusion was just a method her mind naturally devised to cope with the absence of her brothers in her life and to cope with the fact that her parents thought it not of any importance to search for them.
One day, when Fantasia was fourteen years old, something happened in her home and this occurrence changed her life for ever.
She was seated in her daddy's favourite couch watching a programme on television. The programme soon ended and she switched the channel to a more interesting channel. Paddy Moore's show was on. She had heard her friends talk about Paddy Moore's show and she was curious to know what the usual excitement that went with the show was all about, so she decided to

watch the show. She, however, could not believe her eyes when she saw two women fighting over a man. They fought so hard that one of the women had her dress torn.

'So what the hell's the big deal? Men and women fight over one another everyday,' she said aloud to no one in particular because no one was in the house. Thinking it was going to be a boring programme after all, she was about to go over to the television to press the button that would switch it off when her eye caught the dress of one of the women on the show. It was actually the woman that had her dress torn at the top by the more aggressive woman. She could see the woman's left breast popping out of her torn dress, although the authorities of the show had made an effort to make the view less conspicuous. Fantasia would have laughed for the sheer stupidity of the women, who she thought had the kind of decency that left so much to be desired, if she hadn't recognised the dress worn by the woman who had her left breast hanging out.

Wait a minute; that looks like mum dress, she said to herself doubtfully then she took a closer look. Yes, it was indeed her mum's dress. She knew this because it was her mum's favourite dress. It was bought for her by her dad in the good old days. She had heard her mum say times without number that the dress was very expensive and her dad had to save for it over a period of time. It was the only good dress her mum now had (she had sold others to keep body and soul together). She wore it to occasions that mattered. She wore it to festivals, funerals and birthdays. The dress had become a party uniform for Fantasia's mother. The dress was so much known to all the villagers that knew her mum that a woman once joked, on one of their outings, that the dress could not be stolen by anyone for it would quickly be fished out because no one else had a similar dress.

Now, as Fantasia looked at the dress, she was ninety-nine per cent certain that it belonged to her mother. But how could her mother's beloved dress be stolen without her knowledge? She wished the face of the woman wearing it would not be so obscure. Suddenly, the other woman moved slightly to the side, so that the woman who was putting on her mother's dress now faced the audience. She was holding the torn part of her dress together with her left hand and cursing and swearing and pointing at the other woman. Fantasia squinted to see who the woman actually was – she was none other than her own mother!

Fantasia almost fainted; it was simply unbelievable. How on earth could her mother fight on national television with another woman over a man? Her mother was fighting for another woman's husband. That meant her mother was cheating on her father. *The slut.* Fantasia spat on the floor. God, it was so appalling – it stank. She was not sure what her dad's reaction would be if he heard. She pondered whether to tell him or not. She had become so distant to her dad over the years that she could not predict what his reaction would be if she told him. Maybe she should keep quiet and pretend not to know. No! She would not keep quiet about it, she decided. She could not do this to her dad. She still loved her dad dearly despite everything. She would let him know and stand by him, no matter what decision he took. She did not mind not living with her mother in the case of a divorce.

As she sat thinking about the whole saga, her father came home, swearing and cursing profusely. 'Fucking, useless woman,' he said. 'They are all the same,' he continued when he saw Fantasia. 'Women – they are all fucking whores. The whole lot of them should be executed.' Henry was sweating profusely and his breath stank; he smelled of alcohol all over. But Fantasia did not mind that her father stank of alcohol; she went over to him to comfort him, but she was surprised at how fiercely her father shoved her away. He pushed her so hard, she landed against a table. She cried out in pain. That was the first real pain Fantasia experienced in her life and she resolved never to forget it for the rest of her life. She held her buttock where it was badly hit by the table and was still screaming in pain when her father came over and kicked her several times on the other buttock with his boots.

'Daughter of a slut,' he said, now kicking her all over. He couldn't care less where his boot landed on Fantasia's body. Fantasia covered her head and coiled up into a ball to protect herself from much injury. 'I married your mother with my goddamn money,' Henry spat out angrily and continued. 'But she chose to be a whore even up to the TV house. You're all shameless bitches, all you women. I hate you, do you hear me? I hate you. I hate you. I hate you.' Henry stopped kicking Fantasia as suddenly as he had started and spat on her before leaving the house.

When she later woke up at the hospital, Fantasia did not know how she got there, but however she had got there, she was grateful to be there. She thought it was better than where she was before. She touched her face – it hurt. She gently traced her fingers to her cheeks and her cheekbones; she felt a burning sensation in them. She touched her lips; they were swollen. She tried to lick them to soothe the pain and tasted dry blood. She discovered she could not twist her body. She looked downwards; her chest was swathed in heavy bandages. She groaned painfully. Where was everyone? She had not seen her mother, neither had she seen her father. Strangely, she still loved him. Her mind had already made an excuse for his behaviour. Maybe he was too angry to realise that it was actually his beloved Fantasia he kicked around and not her mother. Everyone who knew their family had always called her a *carbon copy* of her mother. Maybe her father mistook both of them for each other in his fury. She was convinced that her father would come round and, with deep regret for what he had done to her, he would come to her at the hospital and he would say sorry and she would forgive him and they would embrace each other and everything would go back to normal; everything would even go back to when her father still had his job, when her brothers were still around, when there was peace and happiness in the house. She became more hopeful as her thoughts tended towards great optimism; *Maybe there had never been any show on the television; maybe her mother had never been on that show on the television; maybe the woman she (and obviously, her father) had seen was another woman and not her mother after all. Maybe it had all been a farce…*

She, however, knew that what had happened had not been a farce and that her mother had actually been on TV and had caused her the misery and the pain she was now in.

Fantasia's mother entered the hospital ward with a swollen eye and a bandage around her head.

'I was able to escape before your father could do much damage on me,' said her mother when their eyes met. 'You don't have to say anything, darling,' her mother continued. 'I know you're in so much pain. Your father has sent me packing. He said he would commit murder if you and I came near the house. He said you look like me and he does not want to be reminded of me anytime he saw you.'

But why mother? Why did you do it? Fantasia tried to talk aloud but she sounded incoherent; her words just came out in grunts. She was in so much pain. But her mother somehow had a telepathic sense of what she was thinking and she gave an explanation to what she knew her daughter was trying to ask her.

'I had to do it to make the family stay alive and when I say family, you should know that includes you, your father and the dog,' said Sonia self-righteously. 'I got the money to feed you all from Brigitte's husband.' Sonia let Fantasia absorb that then she went on. 'The only mistake I made was that I hadn't envisaged Brigitte would find out about us. I just got a letter inviting me to the show; I didn't have a clue why. I found out when I got there. They're all bitches, the whole lot of them, including the host,' Sonia finished vehemently.

No, you're the bitch mother, Fantasia wanted to say but she kept quiet to keep herself from experiencing more pain.

Her mother went on. 'You and I will live together when you're discharged. Don't worry, we will make it,' she said confidently.

I don't want to live with you; you're nothing but a cheap whore, Fantasia wanted to shout, but she could not.

The doctor came in then. He checked Fantasia's pulse, her heart beat, her legs, her head and then he looked at her file. 'You're a very lucky young lady,' said the doctor. Fantasia did not feel lucky. 'The x-ray shows that you have just a couple of broken ribs.'

Fantasia felt that all her ribs had been pulled out and replaced with hard steel.

The doctor went on. 'But you do not have a fractured skull and more importantly, there's no internal bleeding,' he smiled warmly at Fantasia and continued. 'In a few weeks, you should be out of here and resting at home.'

Fantasia's heart skipped a bit at the thought of going home. She did not want to go home and more fearfully, she did not know where 'home' was.

The doctor smiled at Sonia warmly and asked her how she was faring. She smiled back and told him her condition was improving. 'Please do not hesitate to call on me if you need any help,' the doctor said and started towards the door. When he got to the door, he turned back and said rather firmly, 'and that includes if you need any help with fixing that good-for-nothing husband of yours; I shall be glad to see him eternally jailed for what he did to you and your daughter.' And with that, he strolled out of the room.

Fantasia looked at her mother intently; she did not want any charge brought against her father; she still loved him dearly, despite what he had done. Sonia read her daughter's expression and understood it; she did not want her father jailed. She decided not to press any charges. Sonia knew that her daughter had always had a special love for her husband, Henry. She knew that Fantasia loved them both, but she had always loved her father more. Sonia had never felt any jealousy over this. What she did not realise was that right from the moment her daughter saw her fighting over a man on television, whatever love her daughter had felt for her had faded out, only to be replaced with a very intense hatred.

Fantasia spent five weeks in the hospital before she was discharged. On the day of her discharge, her mother came in a taxi to pick her up. Although her mother had visited her every day at the hospital, the hatred that Fantasia had for her had not diminished, it had in fact increased with every visit. Fantasia felt very dismayed that throughout her stay at the hospital, her father did not deem it fit to visit her – not even once.

It's not fair, Fantasia thought one day. After all, it was not her fault that her mother chose to cheat on him. She resolved to go over to her father as soon as she left the hospital and make him see reason with her. She was determined to win back his love so she could move in with him. They would start a new life all over again, without her mother of course!

When they got to the new accommodation her mother managed to secure for both of them, Fantasia looked around the dingy, poorly-furnished apartment with pure distaste clearly written all over her face.

'This is the best thing I can afford for now,' said Sonia as a way of explanation, then she quickly went on, 'but don't you worry, I'll get us a better place before you know it and we'll both live happily ever after.'

'How will you afford a new place?' Fantasia asked bitingly. 'I guess it would be from the proceeds of your prostitution businesses.'

Sonia flinched. She could not believe her daughter would talk to her in such a derogatory manner. Tears sprung to her eyes as she said to her daughter, 'That's not fair. You should try and understand my situation. I did what I had to do to keep the family out of starvation.'

'No, you did what you had to do to gratify your whoring emotions,' said Fantasia, her eyes filled with loathe. 'The last time I checked, a more sensible woman would take up a decent job to feed her family instead of stooping so low as to be a whore.'

'I'm not a whore,' shouted Sonia, 'and I take exception to you calling me that. If you must know, I applied for jobs everywhere–'

'And you could not get any,' Fantasia cut in, 'not even a cleaning job in a goddamned factory. Please! Give me a break! Give your flimsy excuse to the next fool.' And with that, Fantasia walked out of the door leaving her mother nervously twiddling her thumbs as tears poured down her eyes.

Fantasia nervously knocked on her father's door gently at first. She heard no response. She knocked gently one more time. She got no answer, then she knocked loudly, then louder and she still got no answer.

Where could Dad have gone? she wondered. She checked her watch; it was eleven o'clock in the morning. Had her dad gotten a new job? Maybe he had gone to work. Happy with the thought, she decided to wait for her father. She looked around, saw a big stone and carried it to the front porch. No sooner had she sat down than her father emerged from somewhere behind the house, pathetically drunk.

Fantasia could not believe the sight that met her – *her father? Drunk?* It was simply unbelievable. *What could have gotten Dad into this?* she wondered. *Her dear dad who never so much as touched alcohol.* Her heart swarmed with pity for her dad. *He must be taking my mother's unfaithfulness so hard*, she thought as she stood up to go and meet her father who was staggering towards her. Before she could get to him, her father stumbled on a stone and fell. She rushed to his side and held his hand to pull him up.

'Get away from me, you child of a whore,' Henry shouted at her, 'and don't you dare come near me. Go to your slut of a mother. I shall not see you both anymore,' Henry finished, slurring his words. He got up to his feet unsteadily and walked towards the door of the house. Fantasia followed him.

'I said stay away from me, girl. I'll kill you if you come near me,' Henry warned his daughter vehemently and then he staggered to the door. Fantasia followed him still.

Henry opened the door and went into the house. As he made to close the door, Fantasia put a foot in the doorway and with eyes pleading, she said to her father, 'Dad, please let me live with you.'

But Henry pushed his daughter so hard, she fell to the floor. 'You shall not live with me; not now, not ever. I never, ever wish to set my eyes on you again. Go live with your slut of a mother. I have the dog to keep me company for the rest of my life.' And with that, he slammed the door, leaving Fantasia still lying on the floor, her body, heavily bruised and dusted with sand.

After a while, Fantasia stood up and brushed sand off her dress. She looked at the closed door to her father's little house for a few seconds then she turned abruptly and limped back to her mother's apartment.

Living with a slut is better than having nowhere at all to live, she reasoned.

Living with her mother proved to be a very difficult task for Fantasia. As the days rolled into months and the months rolled into years (precisely two years after she moved in with her mother), their mother-daughter relationship had degenerated so much that Fantasia and her mother became strangers to each other. They merely said a stiff hello whenever they could not help bumping into each other.

Fantasia watched with utter dismay, as her mother went out with a different man each day of the week. She heard her mother's telephone conversations with her friends from her room and even though she hated her mother's chosen profession, she couldn't help but respect her expertise on how she extorted money from the men she went out with.

'You remember the day I fixed an appointment with Bob the carpenter?' her mother would coo into the phone enthusiastically as she relayed her escapades to her friends. 'Good, I had totally forgotten to tell Harry the engineer not to come over. As we were having it' (to Sonia, sex was always 'it' and Fantasia always knew what she meant by 'it') 'Harry came knocking on the door. Of course I know how Harry knocks – slowly but determinedly, three knocks at a time until the door is opened. I know the way they all knock on my door – that's why I don't have a bell… Of course… trust Sonia, the smart one,' she would laugh throatily, and then she would continue excitedly, 'I immediately released Bob, he yelped and I got off him. I gave an excuse that the postman had brought the important mail I had been expecting. Then

I went to open the door for Harry but I did not let him come in. I told him that my daughter was at home and very ill and she did not want to see anyone but her beloved mother.'

That always made Fantasia cringe with fury. It took all her willpower not give her mother some neck wringing. She always had no choice but to listen to her mother relate her escapades in her rather loud tone.

'You know Fantasia and all my men don't get along,' Sonia would continue enthusiastically. 'Harry, you know, is a nice man who is always willing to help; so I seized the opportunity and asked him for some money to take my daughter to the hospital before she dies and you know what? He gave me enough money to take her to the hospital and to also set up health insurance for both of us and then I gently shooed him away with a promise to call him as soon as my daughter was well… That's me – Sonia the smart one.' And then Sonia would laugh hysterically and puff deeply on a cigarette. Feeling proud of her wisdom, she would continue, 'Of course I went straight to Bob but not before I had sprinkled some onion juice into my eyes… Of course it hurt but it was worth it. I went to Bob crying and I told him that I just received a letter from my mortgage company stating that my flat was going to be repossessed if I didn't do something urgently. You know Bob is dumb and he will always be dumb. I promised him a nice blow job and he gave me a cheque to clear his one month salary… What? Of course I gave him the blow job after I received the cheque, then I kissed him good-bye and shooed him away. I didn't want Ricco to meet him in my bedroom.' Then she would laugh more hysterically before dropping the phone and then picking it up again, she would call another friend. 'Hello Joycee. Sorry I couldn't finish my story the other time… hmn… Where was I?… Yes, the man I spent the night with at the Ritz Hotel in New York last month; very stingy but trust Sonia the smart one, I got all the dough I wanted from him. I'll tell you how I did it…' and on and on she would talk, laughing excitedly at intervals and puffing fiercely on a cigarette after each laugh until Fantasia could take no more.

At this juncture, Fantasia always had no choice but to leave the flat and go outside for a walk or for a breath of fresh air. Each time she went out of the flat, a thought always sprang to Fantasia's mind: *Her poor dad had been right; she was the child of a whore!*

Fantasia also noted that all her mother's lovers were fully loaded. According to her mother, the slogan was always was, *cash in hand, back to the ground.* Soon enough, Sonia bought a nice comfortable flat for both of them in the neighbourhood. To Sonia, life was becoming sweeter; her troubles were way behind her, but to Fantasia, life was becoming more unbearable by the day; after so long, she was still struggling to come to terms with the fact that her mother had to lay her back down in order to get money to care for them. To her, all those men who had sex with her mother were mere violators of her mother's body; they were destroyers of her mother and destroyers of both their lives. Even after all those months, she could not bear the thought of other men going into her mother. As the men came and went, one after the other, Fantasia felt more and more frustrated. She resolved never in her life to follow in her mother's footsteps. She mentally counted the years left for her to turn eighteen, when she would be legally allowed to work. *Not long at all – in a few months, in just a very few months.* She resolved to get a job, any job at all would do as long as she still had her pride and dignity as a virtuous lady; not a job like her mother's, she reasoned with distaste. She would work hard as hell, save up some money and leave her mother for good. She would enrol in a school (probably an evening school), and work part-time. She pictured herself as a mature young adult, a successful business magnate with a conglomerate of companies under her control. *She was going to make it; she was going to be successful!,* she resolved fiercely.

One week after her resolution, Fantasia came home from school and found nothing to eat. There was nothing in the fridge, nothing in the cupboards and nothing the kitchen. Although she was very hungry, her pride got the better of her and she decided against going to her mum to ask for food or money for food. She went to bed hungry. The following day, there was still nothing edible in the house, but by this time, the hunger she felt was really serious; she felt her intestines were being torn apart. She ran to the sitting room where her mother was reclining on the sofa with a bottle of beer and a magazine and asked her why the whole house was devoid of food. Her mother gave her a steady look before replying tersely, 'Since you have made up your mind not to appreciate the things I do for you, I suggest you go out and find a means of livelihood for yourself. Then you'll realise my worth.'

Having said that, Sonia turned her gaze back at the magazine she was holding and began leafing through the pages.

Fantasia stared at her mother in utter surprise. 'Let me remind you that I'm still a teenager. In fact, I'm sixteen years old in case you've lost your memory. Surely, you wouldn't expect me to go out there and become a bloody prostitute like you,' she spat at her mother.

'That's exactly what I expect you to do – become a bloody prostitute like me, if that's the way you wish to put it,' her mother said in her still steady voice, never for once, looking up from the magazine she was reading.

'Fine,' said Fantasia, 'I will not stoop low to beg you for food. I will struggle and make it on my own. And by the way, I wish to let you know that from now henceforth, you cease to be my mother and I cease to be your daughter,' she added as she stormed out of the sitting room. Sonia did not look up from the magazine she was reading and she never gave her daughter a reply. In her mind, she thought that if Fantasia suffered a little, she would realise how hard it was for her to get money to put food on their table and to buy clothes to cover their backs. She felt that Fantasia would come to appreciate her and she would come begging her. Fantasia never did!

As she walked out of the house after changing into an old pair of jeans and sweater, Fantasia could think of nowhere in particular that she should go. She was so sure that everyone in the neighbourhood knew her story. As she passed people on the way, she felt them pointing invisible accusing fingers at her and saying to one another that the child of the village whore was passing by. She felt famished but she could not summon up the courage to beg for food. She found herself walking towards the local bar. She did not know why her legs were adamant to lead her to the bar, but she knew in her heart that her mind had registered the fact that if there was any place in the world her dad would be found in, it was the bar; so she allowed her legs to lead while she simply obeyed. After all, her father would not deny her food, she reasoned.

When she got to the bar, she entered it with wobbly legs. This would be the very first time she would enter a bar and she had a foreboding about meeting her dad after their last encounter at his house a couple of years before. She shuddered as she remembered the scene. *But surely, time would have eased the pain in her father's heart a little*, she reasoned with herself. Surely, her father would experience some joy at seeing his only child after such a long time. Surely her father wouldn't deny her food.

As soon as she entered the bar, she spotted her father at a table in the midst of his friends, drinking away. She started walking towards him with trepidation but before she got to him, she was stopped by a bar attendant who told her she was not allowed in because she was still considered underage. She knew quite well that even if she was not underage, the barman would still have preferred her not to come near his property. He would have been better off without Sonia's daughter coming in to 'disgust' his customers. Despite the fact that Henry had assaulted his family and had turned himself into a drunkard, the villagers' sympathy was still very much with him. People quickly gave the only tenable excuse for Henry's sudden transformation – his bad, cheating wife – and Fantasia always had to carry the stigma of her mother's infidelity.

'I wish to see my father. I'm very hungry and I wish to see him for some food,' Fantasia explained to the barman.

But before the barman could reply her, Henry shouted from where he was seated, 'What are you doing with that daughter of a bitch? I asked you to bring me another beer and not to talk with that daughter of a whore.'

The whole group burst into laughter. Fantasia burst into tears. She covered her face with both of her hands and rushed out of the bar. She was never to come into contact with her father again.

As Fantasia ran out of the bar, she bumped into a man who immediately put out his hands to steady her. 'Y'alright young lady?' the man asked in a concerned tone; he was trying to look at her face as he held her in his hands. Fantasia decidedly hid her face from him by looking sideways and trying to free herself from the man's grip. It was better he didn't see her face and realise who she was for she could not bear another ridicule; she had had enough in one day to last her a lifetime. Her actions, however, seemed to arouse the man's curiosity. He determinedly but gently pulled her face towards him so he could get a better view of her. Fantasia closed her eyes so he could not look into them. She knew that the man knew who she was now. She waited for the usual laughter and insults that seemed to follow her around like a stigma nowadays. She got none. Instead, the man asked again in a concerned voice, 'Sure y're alright?'

Fantasia knew instantly that he was not from her neighbourhood. In fact, the man was not an American. Fantasia knew this from his accent. His next sentence to her proved him to be a Briton. 'Where were you rushing off to, young lady? And why are you crying?'

Why was she crying? Definitely, her secret was not open to this gentleman. He was a total stranger to the town. She thought it better to get away very fast before he knew who she was. She wriggled herself free from his grip and ran away as fast as she could, leaving the man staring confusedly after her. No sooner had she left him than she started feeling the hunger pangs that had brought her to the bar in the first place; only this time the hunger was so fierce she was forced to stop and hold her tummy. She bent her head in agony. She decided that it was better to get away from the stranger before she caused another scene. It would be only a matter of time before someone who knew her would walk by and introduce her to the stranger – in a very unpalatable manner of course. With that thought in mind, she walked on slowly, clutching her stomach with her hand and fully aware that the stranger was still staring after her. She suddenly felt a sharp pain at the base of her stomach and she yelled out in pain. The stranger was very quick to come to her aid. He ran to her and lifted her up as if she was a piece of cloth and without asking her further questions, carried her to his van. When he got to his van, he carried her on his shoulder and with his free hand, he opened the door. He gently lifted her onto the back seat of the van and sat beside her before asking her for the third time if she was alright. She wished she had the strength to say 'yes' but she didn't. Besides, what was the point of telling lies to this stranger? He would soon discover the truth about her. She told him the truth.

'I'm hungry,' she said faintly. She was weak from the lack of food in her belly and from her experience in the bar. She half expected the stranger to start raining abuses on her and to push her out of his van. Her experiences in life had turned her into a pessimist. She had, long ago, stopped expecting anybody to be kind to her, not in the least this stranger who knew nothing about her except the fact that she was hungry. But before she could say another word, the stranger told her to remain seated where she was and got out of the van. Fantasia saw him disappear down the road. Her mind told her to get out of the van with dignity before the stranger came and threw her out himself.

The stranger came back before she made up her mind. He was carrying two packs of meals and some fruits in a little basket. What she saw made Fantasia decide to stay put. No sooner had he dropped the packs onto the seat beside her than Fantasia grabbed one, opened it and began to eat. Within minutes, she had finished a double sized burger, fries and two pieces of chicken; then she took an apple from the fruit basket and began to munch it noisily. When that was finished, she took a banana, peeled it and began to eat. All the while, the stranger looked on in wonder. He was trying very hard to decide why a girl, so young and so beautiful, could be so hungry. *Where was she from? What was her background? Had she no parents?* He had no answers to all the questions; however, curiosity got the better of him and he decided to ask the girl for the answers. But before he could speak, he saw the girl lick each finger on her right hand noisily, one after the other, then she took the last fruit in the basket – a plum. She took a bite whilst eyeing the other pack of food in the stranger's hand. He noticed this and promptly handed it to her. 'You may as well have this,' he said. 'I presume you need it more than I do.'

The girl grabbed it and said 'Thank you,' before popping the remaining bit of plum into her mouth. After she swallowed the last bit of the plum, she began to open the pack that the stranger had given her, but she stopped and pondered for a while before folding the top of the pack to close it. 'That'll go a long way to save me from hunger tomorrow,' she said to no one in particular. But the stranger heard and he took the opportunity to ask questions.

'Where're you from, young lady? Who exactly are you?'

'Believe me, sir, you don't want to know,' said Fantasia without looking at the stranger. She made a firm resolve not to cry.

The stranger studied her for a while. He noticed her twitching lips and he saw that her fingers were trembling. Fantasia was very much aware that the stranger was studying her. She fervently hoped that she had no visible signs of being her mother's daughter. She hoped the stranger would not see the stigma that oozed from her wherever she went and that he would not recognise her as the much-hated daughter of a slut.

'You're the...' the stranger began to say but stopped short as he saw the girl stiffen. 'What exactly is the matter with you, my darling?' he asked her, very much concerned now.

'What were you about to say?' Fantasia said, still looking uptight. She interlocked her fingers in an attempt to keep them from trembling.

'I was about to say that you're the most beautiful girl I've seen around here,' said the stranger sincerely. The lady deeply heaved a sigh of relief. The stranger saw this and clasping her hands in his, said to her, 'See, my name is Brian McGregor. I'm a pop artist from London in the United Kingdom and I'm here to perform a gig. I'm afraid time is running out and I've got to meet my mates in roughly thirty minutes. Whatever the problem is, you can tell me. I promise to be discreet about it if that's what you're afraid of.'

'I...er... I don't know where to start...' Fantasia began.

'Well you can start by telling me your name,' said Brian kindly.

'My name is Fantasia,' said Fantasia.

'And where do you live?'

'I live with my mother.'

'And your dad?'

'Separated from my mum.'

Brian appraised her from her dark, lovely hair which was tied in a bun, to the well-worn shoes she wore. He took note of her slimness, her very young face and her overall look and he decided that she was a mere teenager; in fact, she looked liked she was just at the prime of her teens. To Brian, Fantasia could not be more than thirteen, fourteen at the most.

'I take it then that you're underage.'

'What do you mean underage?' asked Fantasia cautiously.

'I mean you're supposed to be under care of either or both of your parents. You're not supposed to be out here, starving to death. Do you mind telling me what exactly is the problem here? I could be of help you know.'

As Fantasia opened her mouth, a statement rang repeatedly in her mind...

I suggest you go and find a means of livelihood... find a means of livelihood... find a means of...

She shut her eyes tightly and clasped her head in her hands and pressed hard to shut out the memory of what her mother had told her.

Brian McGregor was alarmed. 'Are you alright?' he asked.

'I... I'm fine,' she said. 'It's just that I just developed a headache.'

'Do you want me to take you home?'

'I have no home,' she blurted out without thinking.

'What?'

She quickly thought of what to say.

Find a means of livelihood… find a means of livelihood.

Well it was about time she did just that and what other way could she start than to hook up with this kind-hearted man who had come to save her from obvious starvation; this man who was her knight in shining armour. But who would dare have anything to do with an underage girl? Surely this man would not desire to sniff the air of a jail. She feigned a smile and said,

'I mean I have lived with my mother up until now.'

Brian was very confused. 'What happened now? I mean why are you not with her now?'

'Because she died. She… she died last week.'

'I'm so sorry,' said Brian. He did not know what else to say then he remembered that she had told him earlier that she still had a father.

'Why not go live with your dad?' he asked her hopefully.

'My dad would not want to see me,' she said truthfully. *At least that was true.* She could not bear to frame her father's death. She still loved him despite all he did to her. She mentally made an excuse for his behaviour as she had always done. *Her father was hurting!*

'And why would your father not want to see you?' asked Brian curiously.

Fantasia cleared her throat. *This is where the real lies have to begin*, she told herself silently. *Fantasia be very careful; whatever you say from now henceforth will either make or break you.*

'You see,' she began and looked at Brian intently as if to draw some inspiration from him, and then she continued. 'You see, my father did not approve of my marriage to Tyler. He swore never to have anything to do with me if I went ahead to marry him.'

Brian was surprised. 'Are you married?'

'Yes.'

'May I ask how old you are then?'

Fantasia thought frantically. Anything between eighteen (which was a legally acceptable for a lady to get married) and twenty would do. Anything above that and the stranger would not believe her.

'Nineteen,' she said.

'Are… are you sure?'

Fantasia feigned annoyance. 'What do you mean *am I sure?*' she asked.

'I didn't mean to be rude but you look way too young to be nineteen. I would have bet my life on fifteen or sixteen at most,' said Brian. He did not look totally convinced that the lady talking to him was the actual age she had told him.

Fantasia was shocked at his accuracy; she was actually sixteen years old but she shrugged carefreely. 'Suit yourself. You can believe whatever you want. I've told you my age. It's left for you to choose to believe it or not; even my mother looked younger than me before she died,' she finished, pretending not to be concerned. Something within her mind told her that if she showed this man how desperate it was for her to convince him she was not underage; his suspicions would be all the more aroused. Whoever said that life itself was a lesson and that experience was the best teacher was very correct.

She looked at Brian from the corner of her eyes and tried to read his expression. He looked undecided. She was, however, prepared for his next question.

'Where is your husband?'

'He's dead,' she said sadly. *Experience was really the best teacher.* 'He died two months ago. That was why I had to go live with my mother in the first place.'

'I'm so sorry,' was all Brian could say.

After the initial tale of lies had been said, a torrent of more lies seemed to have been opened in Fantasia's mind. She delivered answers to questions she knew Brian would naturally wish to ask, but was probably afraid to ask or felt too sorry to ask.

'You see,' she continued. 'My husband and I worked so hard to make a living. It's just that…' She pretended to sob a little; Brian offered her a handkerchief. 'Thank you,' she said and went on. 'It's just that, my husband was so ill he could not get a good job. He developed this heart problem that refused to leave him. All our savings went into funding his treatment. At the end he…' She sobbed some more. 'He died,' she finished, blowing her nose into the handkerchief that Brian had given her.

'I'm so sorry,' said Brian. Just then, his alarm beeped. 'Shit!' he cursed. 'I really must go now. My boys would be waiting for me at the club now. I… er. I don't know what you would like to do though,' he said, looking at her sceptically.

'Fine, I'll go with you,' said Fantasia.

'But you can't go with me,' Brian started to protest, 'I…'

But Fantasia was already out of the van. 'Oh yes I will. I'll go anywhere with you. After all, I'm an adult.'

Brian McGregor thought for a while then he shrugged, went ahead of Fantasia and motioned for her to follow suit by jerking his head towards the direction in which he was heading. Fantasia seized the opportunity to assess Brian McGregor. He was tall and huge and his clothes hung on him rather too tightly. He looked like he was in his mid-thirties, maybe thirty-four. He was blonde and his long greasy hair was tied at the back with a black ribbon. Fantasia thought that his hair was too greasy and his overall outlook did not exactly depict him as a very decent man. Although Fantasia was looking at his back, she remembered he had a round face, high cheekbones and a little *goatee*. Fantasia could do with the beard but what irked her was his hair. If only he could cut his *damned* hair and reduce the amount of grease in it, he would at least be attractive enough. However, he had been her knight in shining armour. He had saved her from the pangs of hunger. In the good old days, her father used to say *no one should judge a book by its cover, it was the content that mattered*. Fantasia felt even if she were to place a judgement on Brian McGregor by the way he looked, she would be left with no other choice than to go with him; at least, she would be guaranteed some loaf on her table and a little change in her pocket. She had found a way to earn a living. Fantasia had come to learn from living with her mother that in life, there was no such thing as a free gift; one had to sacrifice something to gain another. She remembered her mother's slogan: *money in the hand, back on the bed*. Fantasia was prepared to do just that.

Before they got to the bar, Fantasia had made mental calculations on how to spend the money she would eventually accrue from Brian McGregor. She would move out of her mother's flat and out of her mother's life for good. She would eventually move out of the neighbourhood and begin a new life altogether. She would not be a prostitute like her mother though, she would only stick with Brian McGregor and perhaps, they would eventually marry and she would be able to mould him into what she really wanted him to be.

How wrong could she be!

Things started to go wrong as soon as they got to the bar. Fantasia saw Brian stop in front of the bar that she had run away from a couple of hours earlier. She was very sure that her father would still be there, drinking away his life. In fact, her father would be in a pathetic state of drunken stupor by now. She stopped abruptly and thought very fast.

'Ouch!' she yelped, holding her tummy.

'What is it? What's the matter with you?' asked Brian. He looked alarmed as he rushed to Fantasia.

'I've got tummy ache,' Fantasia groaned.

Brian held her close to himself. 'What do you want me to do?' he asked as he checked his watch. The time was nine thirty-five p.m.; he was really running out of time. He had to make a last minute preparation with the other members of the band before the gig. He looked at Fantasia; she was now doubled over with her hand still on her tummy.

'Please can I go back to the van? I think I'd rather wait for you there,' she said to Brian with a grimace.

God, this girl is impossible. Is she for real?, thought Brian who was beginning to doubt Fantasia's sanity now.

'Look, why don't I just drop you somewhere safe… perhaps the hospital–' he began to say but Fantasia cut him short.

'No!' she yelled. 'I'm not going to the hospital. It's just a minor ache. It will subside as soon as I get some rest. I'll wait for you in your van.'

Brian hesitated for a few seconds then he shrugged and started towards the van. He did not trust her enough to give her the key to the van. He would open the van, settle her in and go back with the key. That way, she would not be able to run away with his van.

Brian came back to the van in the wee hours of the next morning and found Fantasia fast asleep in the back of the van. He knew the girl would still be there, so he had despatched the band members to their respective rooms in the hotel he had booked.

He dipped his hand into his trouser pocket and brought out the key. He tried to open the van as quietly as he could but Fantasia woke up the minute he turned the key in the hole.

'Sorry for waking you up,' he said as he got into the van.

'It's alright,' Fantasia yawned.

'When are we going home?' she asked as she stretched her muscles.

'When are *we* going home, you say?' asked Brian. 'What do you mean, when are we going home? We're not going home together are we?'

'Of course we are,' replied Fantasia determinedly. 'I have no home to go to; wherever you sleep tonight, there I will sleep also.'

Brian thought for a few seconds that Fantasia probably was fresh from a mental hospital. He had never encountered such a human being since he had been coming to perform gigs in Alabama. He thought of a way to send her away without causing a scene. Who knows, the girl might get very desperate and rope him into something terrible. If he had to send her away, he had to play it cool.

'Look, why don't we look around and rent some place for you tonight; I'll pay the rent and we can both go our separate ways. How about that?' he said.

Fantasia was in deep thought. She had found a good catch who was in a good position to fend for her and she was not about to let him go. However, if she protested, he might decide to pull her out of his van and drive off then she would lose him for good. She would go along with his plans to get her a place in the neighbourhood and if she played her cards right, she could get herself a place in his bed and in his heart, not only tonight, but forever.

Only if she played her cards right; after all, she was not the daughter of Sonia the harlot for nothing!

'Yes, thank you,' she said and smiled up at Brian.

Brian was relieved. He smiled back tiredly and slotted the key into the ignition. Fantasia looked for the seatbelt and fastened it around her as Brian revved up the engine and sped off.

They found a guest house a few miles from where they had parked and they got out of the van. When they were outside, Fantasia staggered tiredly towards the guest house and Brian had to hold her to prevent her from falling. Fantasia snuggled against him and as they went along, Brian became more conscious of her body. He decided not to have anything to do with the lady. This was not his home country and he couldn't afford to get in trouble in a foreign land.

Brian got a room, said goodbye to her and made to leave the guest house. But Fantasia pulled him back and feigning severe tiredness, she pleaded with him to take her to the room. Brian hesitated for a few seconds then he shrugged. There was no harm in taking her to the room and turning right back, *or was there?*

They got into the room and Brian said to her, 'Well now that you're in the comfort of the room, I wish to take a leave.'

Fantasia pulled him towards her and held onto him. Now was the moment she had been waiting for. Now was the time to play her game. She was Sonia's daughter, *wasn't she?*

'I fell in love with you the moment I saw you,' she lied. 'I really want you,' she said, holding onto him tightly.

Brian stood there uncomfortably. He was at a loss for what to do.

Fantasia tried to remember her mother's escapades with men; she tried to remember how she described her means of hooking men and bringing them into her nest. She gently brushed a hand over Brian's crotch; she felt him respond immediately. She smiled. Her little seduction had worked; she had to give it to her mother; *Sonia the smart one was simply a genius!*

Fantasia tried to pull out more seductive antics from what she could recollect of her mother's ideas. She looked up at Brian seductively as she unzipped his trousers. Brian was finding it increasingly difficult to remain in control of his body. His mind told him to flee, but his body refused to move. After a while, Brian lost total control of his body. Soon, they were in the well laid bed and Brian became lost in Fantasia's world.

Afterwards, Brian looked at Fantasia, who had rested her head in the crook of his elbow and asked her gently, 'Why did you lie to me, Fantasia?'

Fantasia had tried to hide the pain she felt as they made love; she did not want Brian to know it was her first time. But obviously, he had known. She tried to feign ignorance of what Brian meant.

'What do you mean *why did I lie to you?*' she countered, trying to avert her eyes from Brian's gaze.

Brian turned her face up so she looked directly at him.

'You know what I mean, Fantasia,' he said gently still. 'Why didn't you tell me you were a virgin?'

Fantasia was silent.

'That means the story you wove around yourself was nothing but… well… nothing but a woven story. Fantasia, please, I want you to tell me who you really are. I don't want trouble with the police.'

'You will not be in trouble with anyone, I promise,' said Fantasia. She got up and kissed him deeply and Brian found himself responding.

Soon, they were making love again.

Fantasia woke up at ten-thirty in the morning and the first thing she noticed was Brian's absence. She sat up and looked around quickly. She wondered where Brian had gone. *Or had it all been a dream? A mirage? – but what about the love making, the cuddling, the intimacy?* Of course she hadn't been dreaming it all. She touched her crotch and smiled.

She was now a woman; she had been made a woman by a man who was no more than a total stranger to her. Surprisingly, she did not regret any of her actions in the course of night. The stranger had been kind to her and she had no misgivings about giving him her virginity. She looked around for a sign that Brian was still around somewhere, probably in the bathroom or at the reception downstairs, but there was none. She became alarmed. Had the man had his fill of her and decided to leave without causing a stir. *No he wouldn't dare! I will find him, wherever he is and I will bring him back to me. He shall be mine forever,* she decided and jumped off the bed. As she got up from the bed, a paper fell from her body to the floor. She picked it up and read:

Hello stranger,

I've got a gig somewhere in town this afternoon and I must rush over to the other members of the group for a little rehearsal before it starts.

Please wait for me. We need to talk.

I have paid for a few more days, so you can relax while you wait.

Fantasia relaxed and waited for him to come back; she had nothing else to do. She knew without a single doubt in her mind that her mother would not remember she had any daughter. She might as well enjoy herself here at the guest house.

She picked up the intercom and ordered a sumptuous meal and then she turned on the television and waited for the meal to arrive. She grinned broadly as she realised that she was now assured a daily meal. Being smart was what the world entailed.

Brian came back to the guest house at three-fifteen a.m. the following day. Expectedly, Fantasia was wide awake by the time he opened the door of the suite. She had done nothing the whole day apart from eating, drinking and sleeping. Several times that day, Fantasia wondered how she could have been so blind not to know that there was a better life outside struggling to live. She made a permanent decision to hook up with Brian forever, so that she would never have to struggle for anything in her life.

When Brian stepped into the room, Fantasia got up from the bed, jumped into his arms, and they became locked in a long passionate kiss.

Fantasia stayed at the guest house with Brian for two more days before she agreed to take him to see her mother. On a promise that he would keep her story secret, and that nothing she said would douse their relationship, Fantasia had reluctantly told Brian everything about her mother. However, she had kept her father's drunkenness a secret.

When they got to the little cottage she lived in with her mother until she met Brian McGregor, she hesitated for a few seconds before knocking on the door.

Sonia opened the door immediately. She took a good look at Fantasia and her guest and decided that her daughter had made good her promise. She had found a man-friend for herself!

Sadly, Sonia turned around, went back into the house and into her room without uttering a word to either of them.

Fantasia pulled Brian into the house and shut the door behind them. She took Brian to the little living room and asked him to have a seat. Brian sat down on the well-worn couch which had been purchased second-hand by the former owner before Sonia eventually bought it.

'Was that your mum?' he asked Fantasia knowingly.

'Yes,' said Fantasia flatly.

Then, after a moment, she asked him, 'Do you want a drink or something?'

'No, not at all. I'm fine,' Brian was very quick to answer. 'Besides, I have to get going now; I... er... I... er, have something to do in town,' he lied.

Fantasia understood why Brian was in a hurry to leave; he didn't like her mother's attitude. She was thankful that she had told Brian all about her mother, especially her *loathsome* attitude, before they came.

She stood up with Brain and followed him outside the house.

When they were well out of earshot, Brian held Fantasia's hands gently and sighed deeply.

'Look, Fantasy, I don't think this is going to work,' he said uncomfortably.

Fantasia gave him a daring look and then she said in a dangerously low voice, 'I hope you're not trying to leave me; don't even dare to Brian. Remember your promise to me; for better for worse, we'll stick together.'

Brian did not remember making such a promise to Fantasia. In the few days that he had known her, he had somehow developed a liking for her; besides, he enjoyed making love with her. She was very fresh and he liked that. However, he was scared of her mother and more importantly, he was scared because of her age. Legally, she was a minor and he did not want trouble with the law. Although, Fantasia had told him that her mother did not give a damn about her and she wouldn't be bothered if she absconded with him, he still felt that their relationship was wrong and he desperately wanted out! He looked at Fantasia and he saw the determination in her expression. He knew how difficult it would be to convince her that their relationship was doomed right from the onset. He desperately thought of a way to wriggle out of the tangle.

Play it softly, deceive her if you can, his instincts told him.

'Look, Fantasy, I must admit that I have fallen in love with you; I fell in love with you the moment I... the moment we made love,' he began and seeing Fantasia's frown disappear, he went on, 'but we must play this game softly. I'll arrange for you to come with me to the United Kingdom next week, so we can avoid any problems your mother might decide to pose. At least, no one would recognise you as a minor in the U.K. and we can begin a new life together over there. How about that, darling?'

Fantasia was thoughtful for a while. The idea of going over to the United Kingdom and starting a new life was appealing. She would no longer carry the stigma that had followed her around this goddamned town as the daughter of a whore. She smiled slowly.

'It's a deal,' she said.

Brian was happy for her change of mood.

'You must stay here with your *mama* for a few days while I get things sorted,' he said to her. 'At least she won't be suspicious of our moves if you stay with her.'

Fantasia's face fell.

'It's just for a few days,' Brian coaxed. 'It's not going to be forever, can't you see?'

Fantasia reluctantly agreed to stay with her mother for a few days, while Brian went back to the guest house.

'Only a few days,' she reiterated, 'and you'll come and get me.'

Brian totally agreed with her.

'Only a few days,' he said. 'I cross my heart and hope to die.'

Fantasia stayed in her mother's house for two days afterwards, happily waiting for Brian to come and take her to the United Kingdom. In the days she stayed with her mother, she neither spoke to her nor ate the food her mother bought. She lived totally on the pocket money that Brain had given her the day he had come to the house with her.

On the third day, she had the hunch to go to the hotel and check on Brian. Besides, the money he gave her was fast diminishing and she wanted a top-up.

She got to the guest house at mid-day and went to the attendant on duty.

'I have come to see Brian McGregor,' she told the attendant cheerfully.

'Brian who?' asked the attendant, who was eyeing Fantasia with apparent scorn. He obviously thought Fantasia was one of the call girls, who often came around to *pay homage* to the customers. He usually thought the girls should know better than to frolic with hard-working men for their money.

'Brian McGregor, I've come to see him,' Fantasia replied coolly; her gaze matched that of the attendant with equal disdain.

'I'm sorry, we have no Brian McGregor here,' replied the attendant with disdain.

'Is there a problem?' asked the attendant when he saw the funny look Fantasia gave him.

'You must be joking,' said Fantasia cynically. 'I'm sure you've got a Brian McGregor here. The problem is you don't know your job; whoever employed you in the first place?'

Fantasia moved away from the attending desk and walked towards the staircase leading to the room she had shared with Brian two days before.

'Wait a minute, miss. Where the hell d'you think you're going?' shouted the attendant as he ran after her.

At the foot of the stairs, Fantasia met another man coming downstairs. She recognised him instantly as the man who had attended to Brian and herself the first time they had come to the guest house. She smiled with relief. At least *this one* should be able to get Brian for her.

'Hi, remember me?' she asked him cheerfully.

'Of course I remember you quite well, miss. You were here with Mr McGregor a few days ago.'

Thank goodness! thought Fantasia. *He remembers me quite alright.*

'I'd like to see Brian McGregor,' she told him confidently, but when she saw the confusion registered on the attendant's face, she quickly elaborated. 'You know, the man I came here with.'

'I know the rocker quite alright,' said the man hesitantly, 'but he checked out of here two days ago. Didn't you know?'

Fantasia was agitated. Her scalp suddenly became itchy; she scratched it vigorously.

'Didn't I know what?' she asked, but she already knew the answer; *Didn't I know that Brian McGregor merely deceived me? Didn't I know that he had persuaded me to stay at my mother's house, so he could travel back to the United Kingdom without a tag along? And who happens to be a tag along? ME!*

Fantasia felt like a fool. She turned abruptly and walked towards the exit of the guest house.

'I'm very sorry, miss,' said the attendant.

But Fantasia was already out of the door.

After Brian McGregor left for the United Kingdom, Fantasia lived with her mother for two weeks without any squabbles. She tried her best to avoid her mother as much as she could. She did not eat any food her mother bought and whenever she wasn't in school, she stayed with some girls in the neighbourhood till dawn.

On the first day of the third week, Sonia knocked on Fantasia door.

'Yes, what can I do for you?' Fantasia asked her mother as soon as she opened the door.

'Oh, a whole lot of things,' said Sonia sarcastically. 'How about starting to contribute to the house rent; especially now that you have proved to me that you can take care of yourself?'

Fantasia looked at her mother with apparent disdain and without saying a word to her, she slammed the door shut.

Inside her room, Fantasia rested her frame against the door and sighed deeply. The money Brian had given her had depleted to mere coins, but she had sworn to herself that over her dead body would she stoop to beg her mother for a living. But she did not know who to turn to for help. Her father was definitely out of the question; she dreaded the humiliation he gave her anytime they met.

The only solution that came to mind was that she would have to find another man to replace Brian; and this time, she would be smarter. The man would not know a thing about her. *But where could she find a man at such a short notice?* Her mind went to a night club. If she went to the club, she might be lucky enough to hook up with one of the many rich tourists who went there for recreation.

She took a shower and got dressed carefully. She wore a tight-fitting blouse on a tight-fitting mini-skirt; and standing before a mirror in her room, she made up her face. She brushed her lips with a lipstick of deep red colour then she applied mascara to her eyelashes. Next, she applied some gold-dust to her eyelids. Satisfied that she looked a bit older than her age, she applied blusher lightly to her cheeks. That done, she turned several times, checking her overall appearance. Judging that something was just not right, she turned to face the mirror fully and then she knew. Her tight fitting clothes revealed too much of her youthfulness. She needed something to make her look bigger. She opened her wardrobe and frantically searched for a big blouse. She found a loose-fitting blouse that her mother had bought for her in the days she was trying to make their mother-daughter relationship work. The blouse was one of the numerous gifts that her mother had bought her and she had rejected. She had actually cut many of the dresses her mother bought in those days to pieces and thrown them in the trash can for her mother to see. She did not know why she had not meted out the same fate to this particular blouse. Apart from the fact that she had resolved never to wear any dress that her mother bought with the money she got from her numerous men-friends, she particularly hated this blouse. She was, however, thankful that, for whatever reason, she had not thrown it away.

She brought out the blouse, quickly ironed it and put on. It fitted perfectly with her short skirt. It made her appear quite older. But her chest needed some touch up. She quickly dashed to her drawer and pulled out a pair of black socks. These, she stuffed into her brassiere, one after the other. Then she put on a pair of high heeled shoes and stepped back from the mirror to admire her handiwork. A confident, mature-looking woman stared right back at her.

Totally satisfied with the way she looked, she marched confidently out of her room, past her mother, who looked stunned at her appearance, and out of the house.

She got to the club at midnight. Luckily for her, the night club bouncer was in a deep conversation with his colleague when she got there. Fantasia smiled sweetly at them and for a moment, she pretended to look for her identity in her purse. After a while, the bouncer impatiently waved her in and continued his conversation.

Fantasia could not believe her luck. She went into the club, hoping to the high heavens that no one would recognise her.

Once inside the club, she scanned the dimly-lit place, frantically searching for a familiar face. Satisfied that no one would recognise her, she walked slowly to the bar and ordered a beer.

She sat there, drinking beer for about thirty minutes before a man came to her.

'Hello lady,' said the man as he came close to Fantasia. 'Can I buy you another drink?' Fantasia hated him immediately. Not only was he shabbily dressed, his breath stank and he staggered even as he tried to sit. *He wouldn't do for me*, thought Fantasia. She wanted a man who was sober and who would be interested in furthering their relationship beyond the bar. She was not at the bar for a one night stand. She was not Sonia the harlot.

Fantasia regarded the man with disgust and kept mum. Suddenly, the man belched loudly and Fantasia stood up with irritation. Leaving her beer half drunk, she walked towards the ladies. The ladies should serve as her hide out from the drunken man, she reasoned. By the time she came back, he should have wandered off.

However, the drunken man stood up from his chair and followed her.

'Hello, lady. I fancy you very much and I just wanna know you better,' he said as he gripped her hand. Fantasia yanked her hand off his and pushed him. The man staggered and lost his balance. But before he fell to the ground, he held onto a man who was dancing and launched after Fantasia. Fantasia backed away from him but the man was undeterred. He went after Fantasia with a drunken determination. But before he got to her, the man whom he had held onto for balance held him by his collar and yanked him towards the door.

'You don't disrespect a lady, mister,' he said to the drunk as he pushed him. The drunk fell to the floor.

As two security men struggled to get the drunk out of the club, Fantasia's rescuer went over to her and whispered in her ear, 'Don't worry, babe, I'll take care of you.'

Fantasia fell for him immediately.

'Let's get out of here,' she said to him as she pulled him towards the exit. She did not want an interrogation that might expose her for who she really was.

Once they were outside, Fantasia breathed fresh air into her lungs, grateful that she had escaped a scandal. Her rescuer looked at her curiously.

After a moment, she stretched forth her hand and introduced herself. 'Hi, my name is Fantasia. Who are you?'

'Call me Toby,' said the man, who was still assessing Fantasia. He could not make out who she was. In all his many years of patronising the night club, he had not seen a lady so young and so fresh. She was somehow different from the women who usually came to the club. There was something different about her. Toby could swear she was not a regular customer at the club. He wanted to know her better.

Fantasia forced a smile to her lips. 'I really fancy you, you know?' she said.

'Me too,' replied Toby.

It was obvious to Fantasia that Toby was not a man of many words. Anyway, that did not really matter. What mattered most was how much he was worth. She assessed him from head to toe. He looked neat enough in a white Tommy shirt, decent blue jeans and a pair of crocodile skin shoes. Fantasia also noticed that his watch was nice enough. He should be loaded, she thought.

Fantasia smiled again. 'I'm happy you came to my rescue back there, you know,' she said.

'Me too,' said Toby. 'I'm happy too.'

'I really want to show my appreciation. Your place or mine?'

Toby grinned.

'My place wouldn't be comfortable,' he said. 'You know how it can be with the woman; your place would be nice. That is if you don't mind'.

'Of course, I don't,' said Fantasia. 'Do you drive?'

'Yes.'

'Come on then,' said Fantasia.

Toby obliged willingly.

They got to Fantasia's little cottage at two o'clock in the morning. Fantasia opened the door with her spare key and let Toby in before following him into the sitting room. As she stepped into the sitting room, she stopped in her tracks. Her mother was lying in the only three-seater couch in the room, her eyes fixed on Toby.

'Where have you been Fantasia?' asked Sonia; she was still staring at Toby.

'None of your business,' said Fantasia as she pulled Toby out of the sitting room, along the corridor and into her room.

When they were in her room, Fantasia slammed the door shut and locked it from within.

Toby looked uncomfortable as Fantasia undressed in his presence. He now knew who Fantasia was; she was the daughter of the unpopular Sonia, whom no one wanted to be friends with. That wasn't what bothered him though. What really bothered him was Fantasia's age. She could be a minor for all he knew. He surely did not want to go to jail again.

'I don't think this is…' he began to say, but Fantasia stretched and placed a forefinger on his mouth.

'Don't worry about a thing. You won't regret coming with me tonight… I promise you, you'll be fine; I cross my heart…' she said as she pulled him towards the bed.

When they got to the bed, Fantasia bent low and slowly unzipped his jeans trousers. As Toby's jeans slid to the floor, Toby lost his willpower. Fantasia quickly slid down his boxer shorts and caught his turgid penis in both of her hands. Toby became lost in her world.

Sonia sat still in the three-seater couch throughout the night. She had mixed feelings about Fantasia's escapades with men. As far as she knew, Fantasia had had two men in a few weeks. She had lofty dreams for Fantasia. When her two sons had been killed in Thailand in a shoot-out involving rival drug squads, she had made a silent vow to make Fantasia's life better than her brothers'. But Fantasia had not given her the opportunity. She had condemned her in every way possible. And now…? Well, now Fantasia was following in her own footsteps. Fantasia was fast turning into exactly what she had always condemned her of. *Or had she pushed her daughter to the limits?* Sonia felt very guilty. She had not meant to push Fantasia so hard; she had just wanted her to realise how tough the world outside was. She had wanted Fantasia to appreciate her efforts at clothing her, providing shelter for both of them and putting food on their table. But Fantasia had either not got the message or she had got the message wrong! Instead of being grateful to her, Fantasia, in her stubbornness and her thirst for vengeance over the shame that she thought her mother had inflicted on the family, had gone out and hooked up with men.

Sonia winced; her daughter was now a woman and she had lost her totally. She had a good mind to call in the police and request an arrest of the hunky man that had followed her into the house, just like she had the urge to call for the arrest of the other man that had come earlier. But she knew that would be dragging her daughter's image further in the mud. The scandal might be too much for her to bear and she dreaded the consequences.

Suddenly, Sonia heard groans and cries of pleasure from Fantasia's bedroom.

She broke down and wept.

At nine o'clock in the morning, Sonia heard footsteps in the corridor and she knew that they belonged to Fantasia and her *guest*. She closed her eyes and pretended to be asleep. She heard some chuckles along the corridor and then she heard the front door open and close; she then heard Fantasia come into the sitting room and felt a bundle of currency drop on her chest. She was forced to open her eyes.

'I knew you were not sleeping,' said Fantasia mockingly. 'I just hope we didn't really disturb you in the night. That's my share of the rent for the month.'

And she turned around and left.

Sonia picked up the bundle of notes and leafed through it as she thought of how to make Fantasia stop frolicking with men for money. An idea slowly came to her mind, but she wasn't sure it would be the best. She wasn't sure she should do it.

The mother-daughter relationship between Fantasia and her mother went from bad to worse, and from worse to the worst as the months rolled by. As if on cue, Fantasia made sure Toby never came to the house she lived in with her mother after that first time. They either met in the guest house down town or they met in his friend's houses. And Toby delivered. He took care of her basic needs and Fantasia never asked for more than she needed to survive. She really liked Toby. He was nice and he seemed to care. The only snag in their relationship was that Fantasia was the second woman. Toby had told her right from the beginning that he had a fiancée and he could never marry Fantasia. Fantasia had decided to stick with him partly because nice guys were difficult to come by, especially if you were Sonia's daughter, and because of the money Toby spent on her.

Moreover, Fantasia had graduated from high school with a high degree of failure and she was not thinking about going to college, at least not yet. What was uppermost in her mind was to turn eighteen, go out and get a job and move out of her mother's life for good.

Toby's relationship with Fantasia went well for a year. The day that Fantasia turned seventeen, Jessica, who was her next door neighbour and a daughter to her mother's best friend, had come visiting. After having tea and biscuits with Jessica, Fantasia had suggested that they both went to the movies. Fantasia was proud of her income and she happily boasted about her ability to foot the bills to the admiring Jessica as they went along.

Jessica was Fantasia's only friend. Fate had somehow brought them close because of their respective situations. While Fantasia hated her mother for her relationship with different men, Jessica lived in constant fear of her mother and her numerous boyfriends. What Fantasia found funny in Jessica's case was that she was mandated to call all her mother's boyfriends 'Daddy' and anytime they came calling, Jessica was to stay outside the house until they finished their *mission* with her mother.

Today, Jessica's mother was with one of her *daddies*, and she had been mandated as usual to stay outside the house until her mother said she could go in. However, Jessica was thrilled to be going to the cinema with Fantasia, whom she had come to adore and whom she looked up to.

At twelve noon, Toby left his house with the gift he had bought for Fantasia. The previous day, he had remembered that Fantasia had mentioned her birthday to him earlier in their relationship and he planned to give her a surprise gift.

He had gone into a shop and bought her a beautiful make-up set. This, he wrapped in a shiny wrapping paper and attached a lovely birthday card to it.

He had called Fantasia's house early in the morning. Her mother had told him nicely on the telephone that she was still sleeping and he had been assured that Fantasia would be indoors throughout the day.

He got to Fantasia's house at one-fifteen p.m. and gently knocked on the door. The door opened immediately.

'Hello, nice to see you again,' said Sonia sweetly.

'Nice to see you too, Sonia,' said Toby.

'Do come in, darling,' said Sonia as she stepped aside to allow Toby in.

'Oh you brought a gift, how sweet of you,' said Sonia as she led Toby to the sitting room.

'May I see Fantasia please?' said Toby once he was seated.

'Oh, Fantasia has gone out with her boyfriend,' replied Sonia. 'I suppose she wasn't expecting you today.'

The wrapped gift dropped from Toby's hand. All the while, he had been thinking he was the only boyfriend Fantasia had.

'B... Boyfriend?' he stammered. 'Does she... Does she have another...?'

'Oh darling,' said Sonia and she stroked Toby's hair seductively. 'I suppose she didn't tell you about her other boyfriends then? Oh poor darling.'

Toby sat on the couch motionless; he was lost in deep thought. *How could Fantasia be cheating on him without letting him know?* After all, he had always been truthful to her. No wonder she did not mind when he told her about his fiancée. *Could she be going out with me for money then?*

'Of course, it's for your money. What did you think?' said Sonia and Toby knew he had voiced out his thoughts.

'Sorry Sonia,' he said and stood up. 'I guess I have to get going.'

'Oh no, not yet,' said Sonia, standing up. 'I know how you feel darling. Please let me ease your pain.'

Toby stood rigid. In his confused state, he allowed Sonia to undress him down to his underwear. He did not protest as Sonia led him to her bedroom; he was too confused and too shocked to protest.

Fantasia came back with Jessica at three o'clock. When she noticed the heap of male clothes on the floor, she pulled Jessica away from the sitting room and towards her own room. She wasn't about to let Jessica witness how men *roughened* her mother up. As they passed her mother's room, Fantasia heard a familiar voice and she froze on impulse. The voice – the passionate groan – was too familiar for her not to recognise. She had heard that groan two days before, when she had spent quality time with Toby.

After a while, she could not take the suspense any more and an inexplicable force suddenly drew her hand towards the door knob. She turned the knob and pushed the door open.

She stood mouth agape as she witnessed the unthinkable. Her mother was making love with her boyfriend. Once more, Sonia had proved to Fantasia that she was an incorrigible whore! If Sonia was not her mother, Fantasia would have arranged for her to disappear into thin air. But blood, they say, was thicker than water and that was Sonia's saving grace. Fantasia shut the door and left the house in anger. Jessica followed her out. She had seen what her friend Fantasia saw and she felt very sorry for her. She did not know what to do to comfort her except to follow her wherever she went; after all, her mother would be very mad if she went home at that moment; she was still very much busy with one of her *daddies*. In future, Fantasia would realise that in Jessica, she had a friend who would not leave her in her time of need.

Fantasia walked aimlessly for a long time and Jessica walked aimlessly with her. Fantasia was lost in thought all the while they walked. She hated her mother with a passion. The more they lived together, the more intense the hatred became and she had to do something about it really fast!

As they walked along the road leading to the guest house, Fantasia thought she saw a familiar figure just a few feet beyond them. She squinted and with her left palm, she guarded her eyes from the rays of the sun so she could make out who the figure was. As her gaze focused on the man, only one name came to her mind – Brian McGregor! Yes, that must be him; she definitely could not be mistaken. The man she was seeing entering the guest house, where she had been made a woman, was no one but Brian McGregor. Without thinking, she quickened her steps and Jessica followed her.

As Brian got to the foot of the stairs, Fantasia caught up with him.

'Who are we seeing here?' she said with obvious sarcasm. 'The notorious Brain McGregor.'

Brian flinched and stiffened; he recognised the voice quite all right. He would recognise that voice anywhere, any time. He had come to Alabama the night before to perform a gig at the club on a special invitation. The money offered him by the club owner had been so attractive, he couldn't refuse the offer. He had hoped to the high heavens that fate would not bring him face to face with Fantasia. But here he was in the same guest house he had brought her to the previous year, face to face with her. Fate sure knew how to play its games.

He turned round and forced a grin.

'Hello, Fantasy,' he said. 'Long time no see.'

Fantasia shot out her hand and dealt him a punch on his thigh.

Brian held her hand and shook her.

'Hold it right there, young lady,' he said. 'What's the matter with you?'

'What's the matter with me, you ask?' said Fantasia cynically. 'You used me, you dumped me and you ran away and now you ask me what the matter is with me. You despicable idiot. You traitor, you…'

Brain looked around them; they had drawn the attention of the people in the guest house reception. He surely did not want a scandal.

'Look, why don't we both go to my suite and we'll sort this out amicably,' he said. 'I've got my reasons you know.' And then he bent his head low and whispered into Fantasia's ear, 'Now we do not want our names on the local tabloids tomorrow; I suppose your mother's unpalatable image should be enough cause for concern, don't you think so?'

Fantasia was forced to remember her mother's betrayal and her features softened. She wanted to get away from her mother – as far away as the sky was from the earth. She was lost in thought for a while. After a careful thought, she consented to allow Brian to lead them to his suite. Brian would definitely be in a position to help her get away from the United States and settle her in his country; only this time, she would be smart enough to make him fulfil his promise to her.

Brian did not renege on his promise this time, but not after he had made Jessica his lover as well. Brian had rented them all a secret little cottage from an old farmer downtown until he was able to make arrangements for the two girls to be *smuggled* into Europe.

Brian had somehow got some passports for them and they had travelled under the names of Mary and Kathy Granger. He had then taken them into the United Kingdom as his band maids, who he had employed while in the republic of Ireland. Before they entered Europe, he schooled them on how to answer possible questions they may be asked by immigration and they had been given clearance.

When they got to the United Kingdom, Brian had taught them how to go about seeking asylum as underage students while, at the same time, hammering it into them never to mention his name at any point during the interview.

After a lengthy legal proceeding, Fantasia and Jessica had eventually been granted right to stay in the United Kingdom on grounds that they were underage and lost in a foreign country. Brian had, afterwards, encouraged the two girls to go to school and that was how they found themselves in the same school as Tonia.

Fantasia and Jessica had soon made friends with some girls in their neighbourhood. Five of them Fantasia had pimped for Brian in exchange for money. Fantasia did not mind sharing Brian with a few other girls as long as he gave her any amount of money she asked for. The way her life had turned out, Fantasia would do anything for money!

As the months went by, Brian introduced Fantasia and Jessica into the world of drugs. The two girls became agents of drug sale and apart from the little financial reward they got from Brian, Fantasia and Jessica also got free cocaine for themselves.

A month after Fantasia, Jessica and Tonia became *close* friends, Fantasia invited Tonia out for an overnight party.

'I would have loved to, but my parents will never allow me out of their sight for the whole night,' said Tonia.

'I know that,' replied Fantasia, 'but I also know that you're a smart girl. You'll know how to manoeuvre your way around your parents, won't you?'

'No I won't,' Tonia said honestly and as her mother's constant stern expression flashed before her mind's eye, she bit down on her lower lip and said fearfully, 'I can't.'

Fantasia sighed. She hoped Tonia would not be a hard nut to crack. She would have suggested to Tonia to run away but Brian, she was sure, would have none of it; he would not want to get into trouble with the law for *kidnapping* an underage girl. An idea sprang up within her and she pondered on it until a possible plan slowly unfolded before her…

The next morning, Fantasia went to sit near Tonia in class. Tonia gave her a bright smile, much to the surprise of the students who witnessed it. Tonia's smiles came very rare, but the more surprising thing was that she had actually smiled at a girl commonly known for her notoriety.

'Good morning, Tonia my friend. How are you today?' asked Fantasia breezily. The greeting was not so much meant for Tonia as it was for the rest of the class. She had intended for everyone to notice the friendship she had struck with the richest *snob* in the school. Her intentions did not go unnoticed. Every student in the classroom left all they were doing and gaped at the two new friends. How Fantasia had been able to strike a close relationship with the highly esteemed student was beyond their imagination. And to cap it all, Tonia replied, albeit quietly, 'I'm fine thank you.'

Fantasia looked around and smiled at the other students with pride boldly written all over her face and then she turned back to Tonia and slipped a note into Tonia's hands.

Without a glance at the note, Tonia opened her bag and promptly dropped the note inside it.

'That's the plan,' whispered Fantasia as the teacher for the morning lessons came in.

After school hours, Tonia's driver came to pick her up. When she was comfortably seated at the back of the car, Tonia brought out the note that Fantasia had given her in the morning and read:

Tell your folks that as from now henceforth, you'll be attending extra classes in view of taking the final exams. A letter from the school will be ready tomorrow morning to convince your parents of this. I broke into the principal's office yesterday and I was able to get the school's stamp.

NB: please tear this note into shreds and throw away.

Fantasia read the note for the third time. Each time she read, a cold feeling crawled up her spine. She did not like Fantasia's plan. She had a foreboding that her parents would find out the truth someday, somehow, or worse still, something terrible might happen to her.

But Fantasia had told her she was missing out on life. Fantasia had brought out the curiosity in her when she told her that there was more to life than being driven everywhere by a driver. Since the day she had that discussion with Fantasia, Tonia had felt a yearning within her. It was a yearning that needed to be satisfied; a yearning that prodded her to go beyond the confines of her parents' home and explore the other side of life. She wanted to be free from her lacklustre existence; she wanted to see what Fantasia had described as the *real life* had got to offer her.

She decided to go along with Fantasia's plan!

The next day, Tonia assured Fantasia that she would go all the way with her plans but she voiced out her scepticism.

Fantasia laughed at Tonia's innocence and assured her that all would be well.

'But what if my parents contact the school authorities?' asked Tonia doubtfully.

'No, they won't,' replied Fantasia confidently. 'I have taken care of that. The letter I will give you will suffice. I have even forged the principal's signature to that effect.'

Tonia was marvelled. She had thought Fantasia was very smart and now she was beginning to admire Fantasia's intelligence. She thought Fantasia was *cool*.

'But what if somebody or the school authority notices that my chauffeur has suddenly stopped coming to pick me up at school; won't they inform my parents?'

'Your chauffeur will not stop coming to pick you up,' replied Fantasia, her eyes dancing with the excitement welling up within her. She saw Tonia's confusion and she decided to explain things to her. 'You see, Tonia,' she began. 'I have arranged with a good and wealthy friend of mine to pick you up in his very nice car after school hours, so we can always go and catch some fun and when it is almost time for your chauffeur to come and pick you up, my friend will drop you outside the school gates. To everyone in the school, you'll still get picked up at the right time after school hours, only you'll have a new driver!'

Having said that, Fantasia gave Tonia the forged letter with the school stamp on it, informing all parents of the tutorial organised by the school for students in year eleven.

As Tonia read the letter, she noticed the principal's signature and she wondered if the principal had not actually signed it. She marvelled at Fantasia's ingenuity.

The following Monday, at exactly the same time that Tonia's chauffeur was known to pick her up from school, Brian McGregor came to pick Tonia up in his brand new Cherokee jeep and drove her straight to his house.

Brian's house was a modest, tastefully-furnished, five bedroom duplex. Although, it was not comparable to Tonia's parents' house, it was a suitable apartment anyway. A huge, modern piano was placed in a corner of the sitting room and the settee was made of expensive leather. The blue colour of the rug matched with the blue painted walls and the overall effect was dully attractive.

Fantasia and Jessica were already in the house, waiting for Tonia. By the time she arrived with Brian, proper introductions were made between Brian and Tonia. From then on, a relationship struck between Tonia and Brian McGregor.

Brian gave Tonia all the care and attention she could only dream of. He related with her not as a child like her parents did, but as a woman – as his woman. He bought her gifts and expensive clothes which she kept at his house and changed into whenever Brian took her to his home.

Brian took her out to movies and to good restaurants and treated her like a queen. Tonia had never been treated like a queen before. She had always been under her mother's scrutiny and her father's gentle admonitions. With Brian, however, Tonia felt mature; she felt she had suddenly grown up and she was enjoying every minute of it. Fantasia's plan had worked well and Tonia soon fell head over heels in love with Brian McGregor.

Two weeks after Tonia met Brain McGregor, she lost her virginity to him. It was on a rainy day and Brian had gone to pick her up from school as usual.

'We will not go out to dinner today,' said Brian as they got into his house. 'Fantasy and Jessica will not be here today and I want us to be together.'

He removed Tonia's jacket and hung it on the jacket rack in the corridor and for the first time, he pulled Tonia into his arms and kissed her on the mouth. He stepped back and watched her reaction. Tonia's eyes were closed and she seemed to have enjoyed it. Brian was surprised to discover he actually cared to see Tonia's reaction to his kiss. He had a feeling that he was half in love with her. Tonia was very much unlike Fantasia and Jessica. Tonia was polished and very sophisticated and he respected that in her. The way she talked and the way she comported herself whenever she was with him spelt complete innocence and decency. He was surprised to be thinking of not wanting to hurt Tonia. If Tonia was not underage, he would have publicly declared his love for her. He decided to wait three more years and then he would be confident enough to ask for her hand in marriage. For now, the *sneaky* relationship they had would suffice. With his hands, he gently prodded Tonia to open her eyes and he looked deeply into them.

'Shall I?' he asked gently, almost whispering.

Tonia nodded. She had heard Fantasia and Jessica talk so much of this experience and she was eager to discover it. Besides, she was in love with Brian and above every other thing in the world, she would love to share this first experience with him.

Brian bent his head and gave Tonia a long, full kiss and then he bent his huge frame, picked her up in his arms and carried her upstairs to his bedroom…

The relationship went smoothly for two more weeks until the day after Tonia's final school examinations.

Tonia decided to give Brian a surprise visit. Her father had travelled to Canada for a medical conference and her mother had gone to Brazil for a modelling shoot. It was her chauffeur's day off and Tonia had the opportunity to leave the house unsupervised. She called a cab and within minutes, she was in front of Brian McGregor's residence. She had the spare key that Brian had given her and excitedly, she slotted it into the keyhole, opened the door and entered the house.

She looked around the sitting room and to her amazement, she saw clothes draped all over the settee. She picked up one of the clothes and noticed it was a female top. The excitement she felt died down, only to be replaced by a note of warning.

Was Brian cheating on her? She doubted it. Brian McGregor had professed his deep love for her times without number and she believed him. Brian could not be cheating on her; *or could he?*

She decided to find out for herself. With trepidation, she ran up the staircase and without bothering to knock, she opened the door to Brian's bedroom and went inside the room. The sight that met her was to leave a scar on her heart for the rest of her life. There, on the bed, Fantasia sat on Brian's crotch. They were totally naked and panting heavily. They were both oblivious of Tonia standing there, mouth agape, until Tonia found her voice and screamed.

Brian opened his eyes, saw Tonia and immediately pushed Fantasia away.

'Holy shit!' he swore as he got up from the bed. But before he reached Tonia, she turned around and ran out of the room and out of the house.

As he ran after her, Brian tried to mumble an explanation. 'Tonia, please come back. It's not what you think. Tonia, let me explain…'

But Tonia was already out of the door. Brain almost ran after her but he stopped as he got to the door. He did not want to cause a scandal and if people saw him running after a girl, stark naked, he would surely make a tabloid the following day. Tonia got home and cried herself to sleep. She could not cope with Brian's betrayal. She could not imagine that he could cheat on her with her best friend. She even wondered if what she had seen was real. How could Brain and Fantasia, the only two people she trusted in the whole wide world, do this to her?

She buried her head in a pillow and cried some more. Tonia cried until she became sick.

By the time her parents returned home a few weeks later, Tonia looked so pale and dehydrated, she had to be taken to the hospital. While at the hospital, she was constantly visited by a psychologist recommended by her doctor.

Tonia spent three months at the hospital before she was deemed fit enough to return home.

Chapter 39

Fantasia slotted her spare key into the key-hole and the door to Brian McGregor's house opened swiftly. It had been three months since Tonia broke up with Brian and it had been three months of bliss for Fantasia. She had been able to divert the attention Brian accorded Tonia back to herself. She had noticed that Brian was beginning to fall in love with Tonia and she had been jealous. She had gotten Tonia and Brian involved with each other because she knew that the gesture would earn her more money from Brian. Falling in love was definitely not part of the bargain. To say she was happy when Tonia had broken up with Brian after she walked in on them would be an understatement. Fantasia was outrightly overjoyed!

Fantasia giggled ecstatically and opened the door wider to let Jessica in before she followed in her wake. Fantasia was now the only lady in the whole world who had a spare key to Brian McGregor's house and she was proud of it. Earlier that evening, Brian had called her on her home telephone at the flat he rented for her, and he had invited her over. Brian had moved Fantasia and Jessica out of the government apartment soon after Jessica and herself were granted asylum and he had gotten them a rented apartment in order to have free, uninhibited access to them. With the girls living alone, Brian had reasoned that he could do whatever he felt like with them and no one would complain about it. 'Nobody will accuse me of shagging under-aged girls,' he had told them laughingly on the day he moved them into the flat.

Now, as Fantasia and Jessica entered Brian's house, Jessica went into the kitchen to get some food to eat. 'I'm famished,' she said as she began opening cupboards and the fridge.

'You're always famished,' said Fantasia. 'That's why you're fat.'

Jessica was not as bothered about her weight as she was about food. She did not joke with food, so she shrugged at what Fantasia said and kept on munching what she had rustled together from the refrigerator.

Fantasia wandered into the bedroom. She sat gingerly on the bed and put her nose very close to the pillow. She smelled Brian's favourite perfume. Brian

McGregor might look scruffy on the outside but Fantasia knew he had class. He always used very expensive stuff like expensive perfumes and aftershave; he also wore expensive shoes and clothes. He had the money. She was aware that Brian's main source of income was his hard drugs deals and not the music he was into. His band was just trying hard to be successful, thus, the other members, oblivious to what Brian was really into, had to depend on Brian for finance. The edge Brian had over the others promptly made him the head of the band.

Fantasia hugged the pillow to her bosom. She wanted to feel Brian before he came home. He had told her earlier that he had some businesses to attend to. Fantasia had instantly understood what he meant. She had come with Jessica to wait for him. She knew they were going to have *a good time* that night. That was not the first time they would be having a threesome. Fantasia could not wait.

'Remember, I want no stories. It's either the real stuff or nothing,' said the African foreign affairs minister, laying much emphasis on 'nothing'.

'The real stuff or nothing, of course,' said Brian. He knew what the minister meant by 'nothing'. He meant 'no money'; he meant if Brian did not get him the real cocaine in its purest form, which all barons knew was very hard to come by, then Brian McGregor should forget about the money promised. Brian McGregor could not forget about the money. It was three times the money he ordinarily should have charged. He knew that the minister was dearly in need of the illegal 'stuff', so he had charged him dearly and the minister had agreed to pay. Brian did not stop to wonder where the minister would get such an amount of money; he knew most African politicians stole from their government; he knew that was the norm, so Brian was not bothered about where the minister would get the money from, or whether he would pay when the goods were delivered. He was positive that the minister would pay because he knew that the minister had embezzled enough money from his government.

Because he was very sure of getting the exorbitant amount of money he had billed the minister, Brian had gone an extra mile to purchase the much desired class A drug. He had combed the length and breath of all barons' domain; he had cajoled, bribed, threatened and had come up with forty kilograms of the cocaine in its purest form. When he was eventually handed the drug, he had carried out some tests and convinced he had the right stuff, had happily paid the agent. He had carried it home and hid it in the briefcase in his room. Before calling Fantasia, he had brought out the cocaine he was going to give Fantasia and Jessica before their round of orgy began and kept it underneath the bed. Fantasia loved having a fix of cocaine before sex. She told him it made her feel so high, she could do any 'style'. Brian always loved her styles, so he always made sure some cocaine was on hand to make her high.   At four o'clock that afternoon, he had got a text from a certain Mr 'D' to give him a call. He knew the certain Mr 'D' was the minister for foreign affairs from a country in Africa. He always chose a letter to identify himself any time he sent a text. *This minister could not be too careful*, Brian thought. Brian never called his 'business partners' at his home; who knows, his home could be bugged at any time so he had gone to a booth very far away from his house and made the phone call.

Before he went out, he had opened his briefcase and brought out the contents. He checked the cocaine for the tenth time since he bought it; he was almost tempted to sniff some. Satisfied that the minister would be very impressed with him and happily pay him the amount he had requested for, he had placed the bag of cocaine back into the briefcase and closed it. In his frenzy, he forgot to lock the briefcase securely as he normally did; as he placed the briefcase in its rightful position, it snapped open. Brian did not notice this. He hastily draped a cloth over the briefcase. *Just to make it less conspicuous*, he thought and then he went out to make the phone call. He did not want to keep the foreign minister waiting.

As Brian drove back home after his conversation with the foreign minister, he laughed hysterically. That evening, he was going to be catapulted financially from one level to a greater one.

Fantasia got up from the bed and started ransacking Brian's drawers for some money. She always stole money from him any time she visited and if Brian had taken any notice, he had never asked her about it. Knowing fully well that Jessica was still eating in the kitchen downstairs, she confidently searched everywhere for money. Save for some discarded coins, there was no money in Brian's drawers. Fantasia did not want coins; they were of no use to her – she wanted notes. She wanted some Pound Stirling. She opened Brian's wardrobe and searched his trouser pockets; she found eighty pounds in twenty pound notes. Encouraged, she searched some more, making a mental note to leave all the clothes as she found them in the end. As she was searching a shirt pocket, she caught a glimpse of a cloth draped over an object. Curiosity getting the best of her, she dropped the shirt she was holding and deftly moved to where her eyes had directed her. She carefully removed the cloth that was used to cover the object and stared, mouth agape at the white substance in the suitcase that lay half open on the floor of the room. She bent to pick up the suitcase. It felt heavy. She carried it and dropped it onto the bed and opened it widely. She could not believe what she was seeing. *Where had Brian gotten so much coke from?* She looked at the substance closely and immediately knew from experience that it was the real stuff, the expensive one. She could not believe her luck. She blew the air a loving kiss. 'That's for you, Brian,' she said loudly. 'Wherever you are, take this kiss as a token of my thanks. You are the best.'

She arranged a sizeable measure of the cocaine in two lines on the top of the bed side drawer, placed the bag containing the remaining cocaine back in the briefcase rather untidily and carried it back to where it was before. She went back to the bed side drawer and rubbed her palms together excitedly before taking a line up her right nostril. She tilted her head from one side to the other to make sure it settled in her brain. 'Good stuff,' she said to herself. Then she sniffed the other line of cocaine up her left nostril and repeated the same process. 'Very good stuff,' she said. Gladly satisfied, she slumped happily on the bed and waited impatiently for Brian's return. The threesome was going to be more than good; it would be awesome; it would be fierce; it was definitely going to be out of this world. She felt very horny all of a sudden; she felt her loins tingle; she felt wet. *Where the hell was Brian?* She momentarily closed her eyes and reeled in the effect of the cocaine on her system.

As she really began to crave for Brian's lovemaking, he entered the room without knocking. The first item that caught Brian's eye was the cocaine on top of the bed side drawer. He was alarmed; he hoped it was not the minister's 'coke'. He remembered placing the bag of cocaine in his secure briefcase and relaxed a little. He silently gave thanks for his wisdom at keeping the minister's stuff away from where Fantasia or Jessica might see it; he was going to make a fortune this night.

'Oh darling, you're back,' Fantasia said. She had woken up from her slight slumber. 'I've been craving for you, darling. I feel so horny. I can't wait,' she said as she stretched out her hand towards him. 'Come,' she commanded.

Brian smiled, but before he went to her, he decided to check out his 'gold mine', as he had come to call the minister's bag of cocaine, and make sure that it was still intact. It wasn't. 'What!' Brian exclaimed when he saw the cocaine spilling out of the bag in the opened briefcase. 'What happened to this bag? What the hell have you done, Fantasy?' he crossed over to where Fantasia was, roughly pulled her from the bed and shaking her vigorously, asked her how on earth she was able to open his briefcase. But Fantasia was no longer herself; the cocaine she had taken was really taking its toll. With her eyes half closed, she tried to focus her gaze on Brian; she couldn't. Her vision was blurred. 'I s s-saw y-your brief- briefc-case and I o-pened and I… and I t-took the *coke*. It was g-good stuff, re-ally g-good stuff,' she said, slurring her words. She was incoherent, but Brian managed to understand what she said. He felt ruined; this girl had ruined his chance of making money that night and she had probably ruined his chances of making money from the minister forever. How would he be able to convince him that his lover had stumbled upon the drugs and taken some; even the dumbest creature wouldn't believe the story. Besides, the minister had made it clear to him that he wanted the real stuff and he wanted the right amount; he had made it clear that he would settle for nothing less; *Or nothing*. He remembered the money. *Or nothing*. He could not afford to lose that much money. He looked at Fantasia grinning at him sheepishly with her bleary eyes trying very hard to focus on him. He hated her with a passion.

'Let's start to fuck, Brian,' Fantasia said to him. 'I feel like a real good fuck,' she finished, still grinning.

The stupid bitch, Brian thought. With all the strength he could muster, Brian hit her across the face with the back of his free hand. The force pulled her out of his grip, onto the bed. Fantasia yelled with pain. In her drug-induced stupor, Fantasia did not fully understand what was happening to her; she assumed Brian was just trying to have a wild sex, but she was experiencing too much pain from Brian's *foreplay*. She resolved to tell him gently that he should take it easy on her; after all, she was all his to have at any time he wanted. She, however, felt too weak to speak. Brian lifted her up from the bed and gave her a punch on the side of her face. Fantasia fainted. The sheepish smile, although looking a bit frozen, was still registered on her face.

'Bitch!' Brian yelled, lifting her up again. Because he was very angry, he did not notice that she had fainted. With all his strength, he threw her against the wall; her body hit the wall and landed heavily on the edge of the bed. The sharp pointed end of the wooden bed-stand hit Fantasia on her neck, very close to the base of her head. A measure of the sharp edge of the bed sunk into her neck, piercing a jugular vein. Thick blood gushed out from her neck onto the floor and some of the blood splashed on the bed and the wall. Fantasia died, still smiling.

Jessica was eating a piece of water melon. She had finished eating a huge meal of fried chips, three fried eggs, four croissants, cheese, tomato, ham and mushroom pizza; and a huge piece of Madeira cake. In short, she had eaten a part of everything she found in the refrigerator. She was now having some fruits for dessert. She liked having fruits after every meal; she usually had fruits eight times a day!

Jessica was about to take the second bite of water melon when she heard a noise. She stopped mid-way so she could listen properly. The noise was coming from the bedroom upstairs. *Fantasia,* she thought. She had not heard her voice since she went into the bedroom upstairs. She had been busy eating away. She never missed the opportunity to have a full belly anytime they came to Brian's house. There was always so much to eat and she took advantage of it. She cherished food as Fantasia cherished sex. It was not that she did not enjoy sex; she very much enjoyed it; she particularly enjoyed any sexual activity that Fantasia participated in. Fantasia was creative, wild and funny. The girl was simply fantastic; and she was her mentor. However, given a choice between sex and food, she would gladly choose food, *any fucking time*! That was the reason she had dodged behind the refrigerator when she had earlier noticed Brian come into the house. She had wanted to finish the meal she was having and have her belly full of the delicious things she was consuming before going upstairs to join him and Fantasia.

Now, as she checked her wrist watch, she noticed that the time had really flown since she saw Brian go upstairs. *What could be happening in the bedroom upstairs?*, she wondered. In normal circumstances, Fantasia would have come into the kitchen and dragged her upstairs for some *fun*, at the same time berating her for her uncontrollable consumption of food. But none of that had happened. This was very strange. Could it be that Fantasia and Brian had gotten carried away and had decided to leave her out of the action? *Very unlikely,* she reasoned. Fantasia would not do that. Fantasia had never done that. She felt uneasy. She hoped nothing bad had happened to Fantasia. She did not know what she would do without Fantasia.

Dropping the partly-eaten water-melon on the dining table, she ran upstairs to see what might be happening. The door was left ajar. She pushed it widely open and entered the room. The sight that met her almost made her drop dead. She took in the sight; the blood splattered all over the bed and all over the rugged floor. She saw Fantasia's blood splashed on the wall and she saw Fantasia lying lifeless on the floor where she had fallen beside the bed. She blanched and looked up at Brian, who was panting heavily. Heavy sweat was dripping from his face, his neck and his hands. Jessica saw blood on his hands. She made her conclusions.

'You skunk,' she yelled at Brian. 'You miserable sludge. You killed her. You killed my best friend. You killed Fantasia. I'll make you pay for this. I'll sure make you pay dearly for this. I'm gonna tell the whole world you're a bloody killer. I'll tell them you killed my best friend,' Jessica yelled, her tone rising with every sentence she made. She went to Brian and started punching and kicking him with her hands and feet. Brian held her two hands in his and pushing her down on the bed beside Fantasia's dead body, told her in a calm but dangerous voice to keep quiet if she did not desire to join her best friend wherever she was. Jessica cried all the more. She kicked Brian with her bare foot. 'Leave me alone, you murderer, I'm going to tell; I'll tell the whole world you killed my best friend,' she cried.

'Now put a lid on it. Just keep your filthy mouth well shut and let me think of how to dispose of this body so none of us gets in trouble. You know I could easily rope you in,' Brian said desperately, trying to make Jessica reason with him. But Jessica was beyond reasoning; she was in a terrible state of hysteria. She yelled all the more. Brian felt disturbed by her increasing yells. He covered her mouth to keep her from yelling more. Jessica bit his palm with all her four canines. Brian yelped in pain. He quickly removed his palm from Jessica's mouth. Jessica yelled more. Brian lost control and out of sheer desperation, he clasped his big palm on Jessica's throat to stifle the sound she was making, lowering her onto the bed as he did so. Jessica choked. She wanted to cry out but she could not. She wrestled with Brian and tried to take his hand off her neck but Brian was too strong for her. His hand gripped her neck firmly. Jessica felt her stomach begin to churn; she felt like throwing up, but the food would not go beyond her throat; Brian's grip on her neck was too strong. She willed the food to stay back in her tummy to ease the discomfort. She tried to twist her neck to the side in order to let in a bit of air to her lungs and she felt her neck break. She looked at Brian in the face and as her spirit ebbed away, her cold eyes clearly told him that she wished him a more painful death than the one she was experiencing at that moment.

Jessica died with her eyes wide open, the fierce hatred she felt for Brian McGregor, eternally registered in them.

Satisfied that Jessica would remain dumb for the rest of her life, Brian McGregor stood up from her and looked around the room.

'*Shit!*' He muttered. The room was a big mess. He had better dispose of the bodies before anybody got wind of it.

But it was too late. His neighbour, Mrs Blunt, a fifty-eight year old widow, had gotten wind of it; in fact, she had witnessed the whole episode from when Jessica started yelling at Brian McGregor till the time he clasped his palm around her throat and lowered her onto the bed. Mrs Blunt did not deliberately witness what happened in Brian's house, she had just witnessed it by mistake. Her bathroom window was directly facing Brian McGregor's bedroom window and to protect both her own privacy and Brian McGregor's, she had always kept her bathroom window shut. By the way, she did not have an ounce of liking for her neighbour; he had always seemed notorious to her and he looked like a ruffian; thus, the less she saw of him, the better for her. But her niece, Andrea, had visited from the university the previous day and had stayed overnight. Andrea had opened the bathroom window after she had a bath that morning, with the promise that she would close it later.

'It is just to let out the steam,' she had explained to Mrs Blunt. Obviously she had forgotten to close the window before she left the house that morning.

As Mrs Blunt walked into the bathroom that morning, the first thing she noticed was the open window. She stretched her hand and made to close the window when she heard someone screaming from the next building. She could not resist the urge to look towards Brian McGregor's window; she looked at it and saw a fat lady yelling at her neighbour, who was looking rather strange. At first, she thought it was one of the usual brawls between lovers and she wanted to ignore what she was seeing. However, her instincts told her that what was happening was no ordinary brawl; so she had stayed and watched curiously for a while. When she saw Brian McGregor's hand tightly clasped around the girl's throat, she had dashed out of the bathroom, ran to her bedroom and dialled 999.

As Brian McGregor made to lift Fantasia's dead body up from the floor, he heard police siren. He stopped short. Definitely, no one knew what had happened yet; definitely, the police could not have come looking for him, he reasoned.

But the police had come looking for him.

The woman that had called in had told the police that it was likely that a murder was going on in the house next to hers and she had given her address and the address of the suspected murderer. The police had acted fast and rounded Brian McGregor up immediately but it was too late. The damage – or damages – had been done.

'Brian McGregor, we know you're in there. You are advised to come outside and surrender yourself to the police right away,' a policeman bellowed into a megaphone outside; Brian McGregor stood rigid, fresh outbreak of thick sweat appeared on his forehead. *How had the police known?* he wondered. *They say walls had ears*; Brian believed the saying now.

Suddenly, he heard a deafening sound – his front door had been broken into. Before he could react, two policemen had come into the room. Brian automatically raised his two hands in surrender. One of the two policemen quickly moved to where he was and placed handcuffs on his hands.

'You're under arrest,' the other policeman said. 'You have the right to remain silent, but anything you say can and will be used against you in a court of law.'

Brian said nothing; he was too tired to say anything. Besides, he knew there was nothing he could say – he had no alibi. All the evidence was there for all to see. He watched resignedly as the policeman who had handcuffed him began to take pictures.

A month later, Brian McGregor was given two life sentences for the two murders he committed and he was also given a nine year jail term for drug peddling. The policemen had found drug-weighing machines and lots of kilos of class A drugs all around his house.

Two life sentences and nine years in prison without a hope for parole! Brian McGregor was convinced he was going to die in prison.

Brian McGregor was surrounded by a crowd of people from all walks of life, especially cameramen, journalists and reporters as he was led to prison in handcuffs. He did not respond to the torrent of questions they all asked him as he was led along.

'Why did you do it?' a reporter asked. Brian did not answer. He could not answer the question. He had asked himself the same question in his solitary moments and had gotten no answer.

'We heard all of you were best of friends; how come you killed them?' another asked.

'Those poor girls were so young. Don't you feel lucky that there was no separate charge against you for being a paedophile?' another asked still.

'So, what do you intend doing with the rest of your life in prison?'

'I bet you will miss young girls and drugs.'

'Are you happy, sad or very sad?'

And on and on and on the questions went, some questions were logical, some challenging, some spiteful and some out-rightly silly. But Brian had no answer to any of them. He just looked ahead; he looked into his future in prison. His future looked very bleak.

'Have you lost your tongue?' another reporter asked bitingly.

'Do you feel ashamed of yourself, Mr. McGregor?' another asked before he entered the high security prison van that was to take him to prison. He was never to come back to the outside world.

Tonia had watched the whole trial on the television. Although she had split from Brian McGregor four months before his incarceration, she still felt emotional about what had happened. She was especially surprised that Brian had killed the two people closest to him. She was surprised that Fantasia and Jessica had died – just like that. She still found the whole saga very hard to believe. She had been hurt at Fantasia's betrayal, yes, but she still grieved for her at her death. She grieved also for Jessica; the dull, fat Jessica who had lived and died for her friend, Fantasia. She, however, could not decide what emotion she felt for Brian. What he did to her still hurt badly. She would never forget it.

Seven years later, Tonia, now a graduate of business administration from Cambridge University, met Benjamin Walters at a conference for stockbrokers. It was seven years after Sir Alfred Walters' demise. Benjamin, who had taken over his father's business empire, had attended the same conference.

One year after they met, Benjamin Walters and Tonia started making marriage plans. For the first time since she was hurt by Brian McGregor, Tonia fell in love again. She was so besotted by Benjamin that she allowed herself to be carried along with every plan that Benjamin lay ahead for their future together. She supported his ambition of becoming the next Mayor of London and she attended all the classes he organised to prepare her for the task of being the wife of a public figure. Tonia's love for Benjamin knew no bounds and it showed in whatever she did.

Two weeks before their wedding, Benjamin Walters called Tonia on the phone and called off the wedding.

'I happened to stumble on a confirmed story about you and the notorious Brian McGregor,' Benjamin had said and before Tonia could confirm or deny it, he went on. 'I'm sorry. I can't marry anyone who has frolicked with a criminal in the past. It would jeopardise my political ambitions.'

And Benjamin Walters hung up.

Once again, Tonia had loved and lost; she felt her whole world collapse around her.

Before Tonia finished telling Nike the bit she knew of the whole story, Nike was fuming with anger. She was so angry she felt bile rise within her. She looked at Tonia, whose tears had dried on her pretty face. Tonia was someone who always looked pretty whatever emotion besieged her and now was not an exception. Tonia was indeed a pretty girl. However, Tonia's prettiness was not what was uppermost on Nike's mind; in fact, her mind was filled with only one thing – vengeance!

Chapter 40

Benjamin Walters sat rigidly in his office. He was staring into space but he was actually seeing nothing. Several thoughts had crossed his mind since he broke up with Tonia. *Why had I met Tonia at all? What if I had refused the invitation to the damned conference where I met the bitch? Why didn't I take enough time to dig into her filthy past before I became entangled with the scheming bitch? Why did I believe that she had a flawless life just because she is the highly esteemed Doctor Phillip Saunders' offspring? What if...?* He did not hear his secretary come in.

The secretary once again coughed for attention. Benjamin looked up and bellowed at her, 'What is it now, Freda?' He continued without waiting for a reply, 'Can't I just have some peace?'

Freda was unperturbed. She was used to her boss' foul moods. She told him he had a visitor who had refused to book an appointment to see him some other time. 'Sir, your visitor maintains that you've got more to gain from her visit than you or anyone could ever imagine. She claims it has something to do with your political ambitions.'

On hearing that, Benjamin's eyes came alive for the first time that morning. Anything to do with his political ambition was worth his attention. He switched his mind off Tonia and asked for the lady to be brought in to see him.

'Certainly Sir,' the secretary replied and marched out of the office.

Nike came in a minute later.

'Hello, Benjamin. How are you today?' Nike said sultrily as the secretary closed the door after ushering her into Benjamin's office.

Benjamin looked up from the file placed on his table. He looked shocked to see Nike standing in his office. It was clearly registered on his face that Nike was the last person he wanted to see and that was if he wanted to see her at all. His next words confirmed this.

'My secretary told me I was expecting–'

'An important visitor who will enhance your political career?' Nike interjected before Benjamin found the right adjective to use and then she continued in her sultry tone as she gingerly sat down on the chair opposite Benjamin, without being invited to sit. She was wearing a tight-fitting blouse which left very little to the imagination as far as her firm, full breasts were concerned. Added to her beautiful face and excellent shape, Nike's breasts were one of her main assets. She was one of those rare ladies that were blessed with breasts that stood full, firm and attractive without the need of a brassiere. Any red blooded man would have taken a very long look but not Benjamin – at least not in the mood that he was in at that moment. He was still smarting from the *disgrace* Tonia had put him through. He was finished with Tonia and anything to do with her, and the least person he wanted to see was the lady seated opposite him. He had always had his misgivings about her and right now, he had a mind of personally throwing her out of his office, but he had his political career to consider. He certainly did not want the ever-nosey press to associate him with any form of violence. Besides, this *twat* was not worth his rubbing his image to the ground over. He decided that he would patiently listen to whatever bunkum she came to say and then he would politely send her away with a subtle threat of possible litigation should she step her foot anywhere near him or anything that concerned him again. He, however, hoped he would not have to resort to litigation of any kind, much less with a woman who, he was convinced, had no reputation to write home about.

He had broken up with Tonia with a mutual agreement that neither of them would spill out any details about their separation. He was convinced that Tonia knew better than to go to the press because they both knew that she had as much to lose as much as he did. Tonia was a very private person who had a despicable past that she would rather not let the world know about, so she had readily agreed to the common excuse of 'irreconcilable differences' should she be questioned by anyone, especially the press, about their sudden break-up in future, for they both knew that it was inevitable that the news would be out eventually. He was only being careful not to let anything cause a dent in his political career. He had made her understand that he was doing all this to protect her image as the daughter of the renowned surgeon who, it was rumoured, had been pinned down to be the next health minister, or would Tonia rather let out a secret she had successfully guarded from the world, to jeopardise his father's ministerial post? She had sadly but eagerly promised him that she would not tell a living soul about their break-up.

'I heard about you and Tonia's break-up; Tonia told me everything,' Nike said, jolting Benjamin back to the present.

So Tonia had opened her filthy mouth to this equally good for nothing bitch. How dare she?

'She did?' he said, his face red from burning anger. Although, he was struggling not to show his fury, he determined to show Tonia, as soon as he could, how dangerous it was to open her mouth when she would have done best to keep it shut – and tightly too. He decided to send her a letter through his solicitor to show her how serious he was about her having to keep the matter a secret. Nike's next words, however, caught him off guard.

'She did and I think you did the right thing by sending her away. She's not good enough for you. She's never been good enough for you anyway,' Nike finished, giving Benjamin a seductive look.

'Really?' Benjamin said, for the first time showing a flicker of interest in Nike.

'Really. And I've always wanted to let you in on her secret. It's only that you've never shown any liking for me,' Nike finished, giving Benjamin an innocent look.

'I'm awfully sorry about that. It was not intentional. Do accept my profound apology.'

'Oh it's alright. You're forgiven. Let's look for a way forward now or don't you think so?', Nike said suggestively with a mischievous twinkle in her eye.

If Benjamin noticed the twinkle, he pretended not to. He, however, couldn't resist the temptation to ask the question he felt was relevant to him. He tried to sound casual when he said, 'Of course I do think so and I do appreciate your coming to see me, but if you don't mind my asking, how much of Tonia's secret do you really know?' Benjamin silently prayed that Nike did not know much.

'Oh lots. I know much more than you do.'

Benjamin's heart sank. He thought Tonia's mouth needed a heavy padlock fitted in.

'You see,' Nike continued, 'I've got lots of things to tell you about Tonia, but this is neither the time nor the place.'

Benjamin did not really want to know anything further about Tonia; he had known enough to last him a lifetime. However, he was curious to find out if Nike was the only one who knew anything about Tonia's sordid past apart from himself, or if several others knew; so he said, as politely and as uninterestedly as he could, 'Do you, by any chance, know if Tonia has talked to any other person? I mean anyone apart from you?'

'That is exactly why I have come to see you. I've come so that we can both map out how the secret will not turn into a big scandal.'

Benjamin looked alarmed; Nike was pleased with the effect her words were having on him. She went on, 'As you and I know, any scandal, of whatever nature, will certainly have a not so desirable effect on your highly esteemed person and of course, more importantly, on your admirable political standing,' she finished, laying emphasis on the two words she knew were the most important to Benjamin at the moment – Political Standing.

Benjamin dreaded to hear whatever Nike had to say to him. He had a foreboding that whatever Nike had come to discuss with him was going to put him in a delicate position. He had always regarded Nike with scepticism; there was something about her that made her look untrustworthy. That was the main reason why he had encouraged Tonia to stay as far away from her as possible, especially when he felt certain that he was going to marry Tonia. That was why Tonia spent more of her time at his place and not at the flat she shared with Nike. He had thought he could inculcate in Tonia, the ethics of being a wife to a political figure. He had even gone to the extent of enrolling her in a course so she could be well-groomed on how to behave in a comely manner, in a manner befitting for a mayor to be; and the *silly bitch* had gone on to pour all his efforts on her down the drain.

'What exactly do you want from me?' he asked Nike at last, albeit reluctantly.

'Do you mean what exactly do I want to give to you? Let's fix dinner for Wednesday. Shall we say 7p.m?'

Benjamin checked his diary. He was fully booked for Wednesday. 'Sorry. I'm fully booked for Wednesday. How about tonight, 7p.m?

'Sorry I'm fully booked for tonight,' Nike replied coolly without checking any diary. She had no diary to check. *You are not the only one who can be busy, darling*, she thought within herself. 'How about Thursday, 7p.m?'

Benjamin knew she was playing games with him. But he also knew she really had something to tell him. He agreed to dinner on Thursday night without consulting his diary this time. Any plans he had could be shifted to another time. Besides, there was no point making plans that could crumble within a twinkling of an eye if he was not careful enough to fill all loopholes.

'Thursday, 7 p.m. then; deal?'

'Deal!'

Chapter 41

Thursday evening came very fast. Nike took time with her dressing that evening. She wore a cool white evening dress that was a calming contrast to her bronze complexion, and she wore a pair of silver, high heeled sandals to compliment the dress.

Benjamin was already seated at a table by the time Nike got to the restaurant. She spotted Benjamin immediately and she walked towards his table.

Benjamin stood up immediately when he saw Nike. He pulled out a chair for her and waited for her to sit.

If Nike had not heard how Benjamin jilted Tonia, she would have thought Benjamin was a perfect gentleman, but the way he had dumped her friend and flatmate did not depict him to be a gentleman. Nike resolved never to allow Benjamin's pretence to douse the vengeance she planned to mete out on Benjamin. However, she would play along with Benjamin until the right time came.

Nike allowed Benjamin to order their meal. They had little talks here and there as they ate. Throughout the meal, Nike was aware that Benjamin was watching her; he was watching her every movement.

Nike gave Tonia a silent salute for putting up with a man like Benjamin for so long. She could not imagine herself being Benjamin's girlfriend for one day; he would have driven her nuts.

'So what is it you have come to discuss with me?' Benjamin asked over a glass of wine.

'Do you want to listen to Tonia's past or do you want to hear how I can help you win the mayoral election?' Nike asked.

Benjamin was silent for a while. He reasoned that whatever was between himself and Tonia was over and done with. He no longer needed to be saddled with her past. However, since his father died without securing the mayoral seat, his life long ambition was to become the Mayor of London in his stead and he was prepared to give it whatever it took.

'Let's leave Tonia aside and concentrate on the upcoming mayoral elections,' said Benjamin at last. 'Now, what is your master plan?' asked Benjamin

Nike smiled. 'I'm sure you're aware that London is the most diverse and multi-cultural city in the U.K. Not so?'

Benjamin nodded impatiently; he was curious to hear what that had got to do with Nike. 'Are you aware that during elections, foreigners are mostly ignored,' asked Nike.

Benjamin shook his head this time; he was getting really impatient now.

'Well, I can make sure all persons of colour living in London cast their votes for you,' said Nike.

Benjamin grinned, despite his impatience with this lady. *This lady must be insane*; he thought.

'How is that possible?' he asked at last, looking serious now.

'It's very possible,' Nike replied. 'But first, we have to get engaged.'

Benjamin looked at Nike as if she had just gone insane and burst out laughing. 'Have you come to waste my time?' he asked her. He was sure that Nike was a lady who did not enjoy a comfortable balance of her mentality and he wished he could tell her so. But he had to be careful with any words he uttered; he did not want aspersions to be cast on his image, especially now that the election was fast approaching.

'I'm dead serious,' Nike said calmly. 'I've got a checkmate up my sleeve.'

Benjamin studied Nike and noticed she was serious. Out of curiosity, he asked Nike a simple question. 'What exactly do you have up your sleeve?'

Nike smiled confidently before she answered him. 'Benjamin, here is the game plan…'

After dinner, they went out to the car park. Benjamin offered to drop Nike off at home but she declined. *Tonia might be home and it would not be fair on her part if she saw her alighting from Benjamin's car*, she thought.

'Thanks, but never mind. I'll call a cab,' she said and gave Benjamin a huge smile.

Benjamin shrugged and got into his car. He waved at Nike once and sped off. He had deliberately come without his chauffeur. He did not want anyone to associate him with Nike until he found out who she actually was. After driving a considerable distance away from Nike, he found a lonely street and pulled over. He brought out his mobile and called a line.

'Hello, Detective Ranee on the line,' a voice said.

'Ranee, please I need a file on a lady called Nike Adeogun. More importantly, I need to know if she has been involved in any public scandal; whether published or unpublished,' Benjamin spoke into the mobile phone.

'Right, Benjamin,' said Detective Ranee. 'Anything else?'

'Not for now,' said Benjamin. He closed the flap of the phone and thought about the discussion he had with Nike. The lady had given him a brilliant idea quite alright. London was a multicultural community and the number of ethnic minorities was fast increasing by the day. His opponent, Fred Edwards, was an Englishman just like him; but Fred Edwards was the incumbent Mayor of London and so had the power of incumbency. It was a known fact that the Mayor had a lot of avenues to make free adverts at his disposal, such as bill boards, the tubes and the underground stations. Benjamin knew that the Mayor had an edge over him in the upcoming elections and if he was to make headway, he had to explore all avenues possible and one of the avenues would be to be liked and accepted by the vast minority groups as well as the English people, as Nike had rightly pointed out. But first he had to prove that he was not biased and what better way could he do that than to marry one of them?

But Nike had to prove herself beyond all doubts that she was up to the task. He would put Nike to a few tests and if she was intelligent enough to pass his test, there would be a deal! But first, he had to be sure that Nike had no skeletons in her cupboard as Tonia had.

The file arrived in his office three days later; it was marked, 'Very Private'.

Benjamin closed the door of his office shut and hastily opened the file. There, he saw that Nike had not had any scandal with any authority. In fact, she had once received a commendation from the London Metropolitan Police for helping them arrest and prosecute a notorious fraudster named Leonard Conrad. The detective's findings had further noted that Nike Adeogun was the granddaughter of a powerful king in far away Africa. The only hitch in Nike's past was that she could not complete her secondary school education in the Blueberry Secondary School in Nigeria, due to an injury. The nature of the injury had remained obscure, even to Ranee's contacts in Nigeria.

Detective Ranee had made a little note at the base of the report, asking Benjamin to revert to him if he wanted to know the exact nature of the injury. Benjamin made a mental note to find that out from Nike herself. What he had read about the lady was enough. He did not think she would rub his prestige in the mud as Tonia had.

'What injury did you sustain at the Blueberry Secondary School?' he asked Nike over dinner the following day.

Nike was obviously taken aback. She had to give it to Benjamin; she almost clapped for him. She had somehow not envisaged him going behind her to dig into her past. But then, she should have expected it, she thought; especially after what he went through with Tonia. She made a mental note to be careful with Benjamin in future; the guy was simply intelligent; he was very smart indeed.

'I was involved in a car accident that rendered me paralysed for a long time,' Nike said unflinchingly, looking directly at Benjamin.

Benjamin suddenly felt sorry for her.

'Oh, I'm so sorry,' said Benjamin sincerely, then, 'How did you get well?' he asked gently.

'My grandfather called in some traditional healers in his community where he is a King and they did the healing,' said Nike. She had deliberately mentioned the kingship of her grandfather because she knew that Benjamin must have been informed.

'I see,' said Benjamin. He wondered why that had not been recorded but decided to wave it. *Sustaining an injury was not a crime.* 'Won't you ask me how I got to know so much about you?' he asked her in a friendly tone.

Nike scooped some lamb stew into her mouth and shrugged carefreely before answering him, 'There's no need for me to ask. I always knew you would find out,' she lied.

The campaign began in earnest that month. Nike worked tirelessly among the African people and the Asian people living in London to secure popularity for Benjamin. She distributed pamphlets assuring them better recognition with the British government should they vote for Benjamin Walters as the next Mayor of London. She made them realise the love that Benjamin had for the minority groups in London and by the end of the month, the polls rated Benjamin as the more loved mayoral candidate among the minority groups in London.

Benjamin read the report from the comfort of his sitting room and smiled. Nike had indeed proved herself; she had put the kettle to the boil. The deal was definitely on!

Chapter 42

Vanessa Wellington slid beside Tonia in the BMW convertible and passed one of the two milkshakes she had bought at McDonald's to her.

'Thanks,' said Tonia before she took a sip.

'You're welcome.' Vanessa looked at Tonia for a while and pondered whether she should divulge what had been bothering her for some time – for two weeks to be precise. She had gone to Oxford Street for some shopping to give her wardrobe a make-over when she saw Benjamin in his favourite Porsche. She was about to swear silently at him for causing her best friend so much misery when she caught a glimpse of a black lady sitting beside him. In all the months she had known Benjamin since she decided to reside in the United Kingdom permanently, she had not had any reason to associate Benjamin with any people of colour, much less a black woman. She was even beginning to think that Benjamin had reservations towards blacks. For him to be seen gallivanting around with a black woman aroused curiosity in Vanessa. Determined to get to the root of the matter, she crossed over to the other side of the road and using the mammoth crowd of people going about their different businesses as cover, she followed his car all the way to their destination. She was very thankful to whatever had caused a slight traffic hold-up to occur that day. Because of the hold-up, she was able to trail Benjamin's car to the Chinese eatery located on New Oxford Street. Forgetting that she had parked her own car on Regent Street which was a considerable distance from where she now was, she waited until she was certain that they would have settled down in the restaurant before she followed them in. She picked a table four seats across from them and looking around, spotted a newspaper on the table two spaces from her. Reasoning within herself that the newspaper would effectively serve as cover while she watched them, she stretched behind her without actually getting up to pick the paper. While she did this, the chair shifted noisily and she quickly sat back in the chair. The sound made Benjamin and the lady look in her direction curiously. Vanessa quickly bent her head and pretended to study the menu. When she was satisfied that the couple she had taken the arduous task (even though it was unsolicited for) upon herself to investigate, had settled down to their meal, she quietly walked to the serving area and ordered a simple meal of noodles, baked beans and stir fry. She was not particularly hungry; she was just there as an unofficial detective. As she went back to her table, she picked up the newspaper she had earlier tried to get. If she had known that Benjamin did not recognise her, she would not have gone to so much trouble; she would have sat in her chair and studied the two of them without any inhibitions.

Two minutes after she sat down, she saw Benjamin lean across the table he shared with the black lady; she also watched the black lady tilt her head towards him and Benjamin whispered something that was very inaudible in her ear. Whatever he had said to her erupted a deep throaty laughter from the lady. Vanessa had a feeling that what Benjamin told the lady must have been one of the usual jokes that new lovers shared, besides, why did he have to whisper into her ear? Why couldn't he speak up so everyone would hear what he had to say if there really were no skeletons in their cupboards?

Vanessa, therefore, took her mobile phone and pretending to fiddle with it, pressed her finger on the camera button and clicked away. Satisfied that she had enough evidence in her mobile phone, she got up twenty minutes later and walked out of the restaurant, her food cold and untouched.

Now, as she relayed her findings to Tonia, she watched Tonia's expression change from surprise, to outright disbelief, when Vanessa showed her the first picture – the picture of Benjamin leaning across the table to whisper things into Nike's ear. Then Tonia's expression changed into outrage when she saw some of the other pictures – the picture of Benjamin and Nike clicking their wine glasses, the picture of Benjamin touching Nike's hair, the picture of Benjamin actually giving her a peck, the picture of Benjamin laughingly sharing a lobster with Nike, the picture of Benjamin… Tonia had had enough. She threw the pictures on the floor of the car. Vanessa did not expect Tonia to be capable of flying into such rage; the Tonia she had always known was calm and collected, always able to take control of her feelings in whatever pressing situation she might find herself in.

Vanessa was very grateful that Tonia had not started driving. They had decided to finish their milkshakes before moving on. Now Tonia felt the milkshake turn sour in her mouth; she threw it on the ground, rested her head on the stirring wheel and began to sob quietly.

'Do you want me to drive?' Vanessa asked, concerned. She regretted telling Tonia the outcome of her investigation. *I should have kept it to myself,* she reasoned within herself. Now she'd made a mess of the whole situation.

'I trusted her, Vanessa. I really trusted the bitch,' Tonia spat.

Vanessa was shocked to hear Tonia swear. She had never heard any foul word from Tonia all her life. Tonia had been brought up in a home where swearing was forbidden. She did not know what to say, so she kept quiet while Tonia narrated how she had been good to Nike, how she had taken her in when she had an accommodation problem, how she had made her to pay only the minimum amount of rent, how she, Tonia, had taken it upon herself to pay the extra bills – council tax, water rates, gas bill, etc. On and on she went until she became exhausted. By the time she finished telling her story, Vanessa had only one piece of advice she could give Tonia and she gave it to her.

Chapter 43

Nike was in a state of extreme happiness as Benjamin dropped her off in front of her flat. Benjamin had given her a kiss that day, the first real kiss and not just the usual peck on the cheek or the slight grazing of his lips on hers to show appreciation to her for all she was doing towards the success of his career. It was not the fact that Benjamin kissed her that made Nike so happy, but the fact that her efforts at getting him seduced was beginning to yield good results. She had purposed in her mind that she was not going to sleep with him – no, she definitely wouldn't, she had already told him that she was a virgin and she was pretty sure he had believed her. Nike hated the idea of 'opening up' for two men in the same period; she felt it would make her feel like a slut. Besides, she still reasoned that Alex was still very much in her life even though they had not come in contact with each other for three months. She had decided to stop seeing Alex for the period she would be with Benjamin until she was able to take revenge on him for what he did to Tonia. She would lead Benjamin on and on and on till she achieved her main objective in his life, which was the only reason she had come into his life in the first place. She could only hope that Alex would understand should she deem it fit to explain everything to him later on. The thought of what she had planned for Benjamin filled her with immense excitement.

Still in her state of euphoria, Nike opened the door to the flat that she had shared with Tonia and almost bumped into her.

'Hi Tonia, how are you doing today?' she asked Tonia brightly.

'I'm doing splendidly, just like you would love me to do,' replied Tonia coldly, blocking the way so Nike could not go in. Nike looked beyond Tonia and to her amazement, she saw some of her belongings including her portraits and the pictures that she had neatly hung on the wall in the sitting room, lying on the floor of the sitting room.

'What the hell's going on here, Tonia?' Nike demanded to know.

Tonia said nothing but she remained where she was.

'Tonia, I demand to know what's going on. Why are my things lying around the sitting room?'

'Your things are lying around the sitting room because you chose to lie around the whole city of London with Benjamin, you miserable slut,' Tonia shot at her.

'Now come. I won't have you call me names, Tonia. I'm not a slu–'

'Oh, yes you are and I'll call you whatever I want. This is my house and since you have chosen to betray my trust in–'

'Enough!' Nike was furious now. She couldn't be bothered with what Tonia felt at this point; she had no right to throw her things out no matter how betrayed she felt. 'It's your house quite all right,' she continued angrily. 'You bought it but I pay for the room I live in, got it? You've no right to...?'

'I've got every right to do what I want in my house. Now, I want you to pack your things and move out this night.'

'You can't do that, Tonia. The law says–'

'Oh don't even go there, 'cos if you want to go there, we can go there.'

Nike knew what Tonia meant. She had no tenancy agreement with Tonia. Tonia could always claim that Nike was an intruder or that she had overstayed her welcome. She had never bothered to ask Tonia for a receipt any time she paid her rent because of the cordial relationship between them; there was no evidence that she paid any rent in the house; besides, Nike was too tired to argue any further. She decided to pack her things and leave.

She saw a hotel two yards from Tonia's flat and went in to enquire about a room. When she entered the hotel lobby, a bored-looking receptionist quickly got up and gave her a watery smile.

'Good evening, madam. May I help you?' she asked Nike, looking at her hastily packed bags with suspicion.

'Yes, please can I have a room for two weeks?'

'Certainly. Do you have a reservation?'

'No, I don't but I need a room urgently, please.'

'Certainly, madam, can I see your passport please?'

'My what?'

'Your passport madam,' said the lady, still looking at Nike with suspicion.

'Look, I have just been sent away from my home; I had to pack my bags in haste. I can't say for sure where my passport can be right now.' Nike noticed the receptionist looking at her more suspiciously and went on hastily, 'Look, let me have the room for this night, I promise to get the passport down to you first thing tomorrow morning.'

'I'm sorry, madam, that would be against our rules and regulations. I would need a form of identification in other to book you in.'

'Well I have no form of identification. What do you expect me to do?', asked Nike irritably.

'Get your passport,' replied the lady determinedly.

'I'm sure you heard me correctly when I told you I couldn't find my passport.' Nike was about to add *or are you deaf?* but she held herself in check.

'You can get a police report,' the receptionist advised.

'What?' Nike could not believe what she had heard – the incredulity of it. She said, 'You must be joking. You want me to get a police report just to get a room at this time of the day?' She checked her watch and said tersely, 'eleven-thirty p.m.; I mean, this is ridiculous.'

The receptionist was not bothered. She shrugged, sat down on her chair and started clicking away at her computer.

'Well, what do you say?' asked Nike hopefully after waiting for a few minutes.

'I said show your passport or a police report,' said the lady firmly.

'And I'm telling you for the umpteenth time that that would not be possible,' said Nike and trying with great difficulty to exercise patience, she went on. 'By the way, what have you been doing on the computer, I thought you were attending to me?'

'No, I was playing a game,' the lady said without looking away from the computer.

Nike almost exploded. 'You mean you left me, a potential customer standing before you while you play a silly game? This must be some sort of a big joke.'

The lady clicked on, unperturbed. She did not respond to what Nike said, neither did she look up from her computer. She later heard Nike storm out of the hotel lobby, swearing profusely at her and promising to report her to the hotel authorities. The receptionist did not care; this was her fourth job in six months and she had been looking for an excuse to stop working permanently. The only reason she was working was because her boyfriend, Frank, whom she was living with, had insisted that she had to work as long as there was still someone out there who was willing to employ her.

Nike marched out of the hotel, dragging her belongings after her. She did not mind the fact that some of her clothes were almost spilling out of the big bag she dragged along with her left hand.

She walked a considerable distance further from the hotel before noticing another one. She started walking towards it but stopped short midway. *What if she encountered the same scene she had encountered earlier on?* She was too tired to go through all that argument one more time. She thought of what to do, who she could squat with overnight. Benjamin was out of the question. She had told him she bought the house with Tonia because of their long standing friendship. One name sprang to her mind suddenly – Alex! She dialled a cab office and requested to be taken to Alex Tucker's residence on Goldhurst Terrace, NW6.

Alex was surprised to see Nike on his doorstep so late in the night.

'What are you doing here so late in the night Nike?' he asked, standing at the door with arms folded across his chest.

'Alex, please, I'm very tired. Could you just allow me in first and then I will explain later,' Nike said. She looked so worn out. She felt like fainting. She put her luggage on the porch and rested her frame against the fence.

Alex had learned to be suspicious of Nike's moves over the months that he had known her. He looked at her wearily, taking in her scruffy looks and her rough looking baggage and asked her, 'Nike what's happened to you? What have you been up to?'

Nike almost screamed at him out of frustration. She, however, decided to play it softly with him. She made as if she was about to fall. Alex immediately stretched out his hand and caught her. 'Are you okay?' he asked. He very much wanted to hold her in his arms forever. He missed her so much. For three months, all his efforts at seeing Nike had been futile. She had not picked his numerous telephone calls, and she was never at home when he called at her house. Besides, he had heard of her relationship with the politician called Benjamin Walters. He certainly would not want to admit another man's woman into his house.

Nike shook her head in the negative to the question Alex asked. 'No, I'm not okay', she said, 'I'd really be pleased if you could just allow me in so I can rest my feet. I'm really tired and unwell.'

'Do you want me to call an ambulance?' asked Alex; he was very much concerned now.

'No!' Nike shouted. 'You will do no such thing. Just let me in and I'll explain. Please.' She closed her eyes and made to fall off Alex's hands. Alex gripped her firmly. He bent low and carried her into the house. His mind told him to retrace his steps before it was too late but he followed his heart which still harboured his love for Nike. His feelings for Nike were so deep, he could not refuse her any help.

Chapter 44

Alex sat on the couch facing the television in the sitting room. He held a Sky remote control in his hand but the television was not on. Alex was in no mood to watch the television or to do anything else for that matter. He was troubled over two things. Firstly, he had heard of Nike's frolics with Benjamin Walters, the mayoral aspirant. Secondly, he still hadn't been able to locate the killers of his father and grandmother, and probably his mother. Alex considered the two problems and decided that Nike was the direct and remote cause of the two consecutively. If he hadn't set his eyes on the bitch, he would not have known that the life he had been living was a farce and *as they say, what you don't know cannot kill you.* Nike was the one who had persuaded him to go for the damned test that had revealed his true parentage and the same Nike had callously dumped him for her best friend's former fiancé. To think that she had the cheek to come knocking on his door for a roof over her head was the height of it. Alex could not fathom why he had admitted her in; he did not want to admit to his love for her for, at the base of his heart, he knew he had developed a soft spot for her. Now, Alex regretted the day he met Nike. She had breezed into his life, managed to turn it upside down and had breezed out of it – just like that! Alex decided to allow Nike to stay for the two weeks they both agreed on and then on the last day, on or before twelve midnight, she had to get out of his house and his life – and stay out!

A week after Nike started living in Alex's apartment she woke up one day with a pleasurable feeling. She wondered what could have erupted such a feeling of absolute joy in her that morning, for as far as she could remember, she always woke up on the wrong side of the bed. She paused for a moment to remember what had happened the previous day, and then she smiled. Benjamin had handed her a shopping voucher for the sum of five thousand pounds.

'Buy a new wardrobe; you're going to be part of my entourage during my campaign for the next four weeks and as you well know, we don't want you to dress up, looking hungry,' he had said to her with outright insolence as he handed her the voucher. She had wondered then, what Benjamin would have thought of her had he known how bulky her account was, for Nike still had a sizeable chunk of the money she was able to stash away from the Leonard Conrad saga; plus her grandfather, thinking that she was a student in the United Kingdom studying medicine, always made sure he transferred a generous amount of money, befitting a student from a very rich home, into her account every month. She had taken the salient insult Benjamin had passed to her that morning in her stride and strode out of his office. The five thousand pound largesse would compensate her for the insult. She, however, couldn't help but feel that the arrogant man had a touch of generosity despite himself.

Nike had taken a taxi to Harrods for a nice shopping. She had bought everything from designer suits and shoes to designer underwear and designer trinkets and designer goggles. Everything she bought had a taste of class to it. By the time she left Harrods, she had exhausted the whole five thousand pounds!

Still smiling, she got up gingerly from the bed and checked herself in the standing mirror placed near the bedside drawer. She would have preferred a mirror with a well-decorated frame and not one with a dull wooden frame like the one she was looking into. She made a mental note to tell Alex to change it immediately. She had to feel comfortable and very welcome for the short period she was allowed to stay in his house. Satisfied that her eyes were not puffy and her face was not showing any signs of tiredness, she put on her bathrobe and walked into the en-suite bathroom. While in the shower, she lathered her entire body and let the cool water cascade onto her lovely face and body. She thoroughly enjoyed every minute of it. Thirty minutes later, she stepped out of the shower and into the bedroom. She dried herself and lavished an expensive Chanel cream all over her body before opening her wardrobe to select the best clothes to wear to the meeting she was going to attend with Benjamin at ten o'clock. She saw an array of expensive clothes – clothes she had bought the previous day. She chose a beige Hugo Boss skirt suit and a cream coloured blouse. She chose a matching pair of earrings and a matching pair of beige Christian Louboutin shoes to go with the suit. She applied moderate makeup – pink lipstick, mascara and slight blusher. She checked her eyebrows; they were well shaped and perfectly thickened. When she eventually finished dressing up, she made a last appraisal of herself in the standing mirror. She liked what she saw. *Who says beauty and brains don't go hand in hand?* She blew herself a kiss, picked up her purse and turned to leave the room. She opened the door and nearly bumped into Alex who was slouched against the door ledge.

'What... what are you doing here? Don't tell me you've started sneaking up on me. By the way, for how long have you been standing by my door,' Nike managed to say after regaining her composure.

Alex said nothing for a while, although he very much wanted to remind her that the house, including the door she called hers, was his. He wanted to tell her that her sudden relationship with the politician had taken him by surprise and had hurt him deeply. He wanted to tell her he had been standing by the door for approximately forty-five minutes, waiting for her to step through it so they could have a long talk. He wanted to tell her that since he met her, all she had done to him was to turn his beautiful life upside down. He wanted to tell her to get the hell out of his house. He wanted to tell her to get lost. But he just looked at her from head to toe, taking in her dressing, taking in her beauty. *God she was achingly beautiful.* Alex felt a rush of adrenalin to his loins. He felt his maleness hardening. Nike had always had that effect on him whether she was fully dressed or fully naked; she had the same effect on him whether she was dressed in office clothes or lingerie; he knew she would have that effect on him even if she was dressed in a sack-cloth with ashes in her hair!

Alex felt like taking Nike in his arms just like he used to, and locking her in there forever with the belief that nothing was amiss. But he knew something was amiss. He knew everything was amiss. Nike was now going out with Benjamin Walters. She would never be his again.

'Is it because of the blood test?' Alex blurted out suddenly.

'What? What are you talking about?' asked Nike.

'Of course you damned well know what I'm talking about and don't you go pretending about it all,' shouted Alex angrily. The handsomeness of his face was slightly dimmed by the puffiness of his eyes. His hair was dishevelled and his cheeks were flushed. It was obvious he had not slept a wink throughout the night.

'Do you love him, Nike?' he asked quietly.

'Oh, don't be absurd,' said Nike uneasily. She did not know what else to say. She felt deeply pained to see Alex this way but she would be damned if she would let him know that. She looked at everything else but Alex.

Alex moved an inch closer to her and with the tip of his thumb and forefinger, held her chin and tilted her face so that she was looking at nothing else but him. He looked directly into her eyes and asked, albeit quietly, 'Do you love him that much, Nike? Do you love him enough to throw everything we had, everything we shared, down the drain? Is it the power? Are you so power thirsty? Or is he that good in bed?'

When Nike did not answer, Alex went on sadly, 'Or is it because you feel that because we both have the sickle cell genotype, there's no future for us.

There's definitely more to life than having children you know. Think about the fun, the laughter; think about us; think about what we—'

Just then, a car horn beeped downstairs. It was the cab man Nike had requested earlier on; she always went around in cabs and the bills were always paid by Benjamin. She did not want Benjamin to know that she could afford a car; that would have to be a gift from him in the near future.

'I'm sorry,' said Nike, trying not to look directly at Alex. 'The cab man has come for me; I'm really sorry, I really am,' Nike said lamely and fled, leaving Alex sadly staring after her.

Chapter 45

Alice was pregnant again. She was alone in her room as had become the norm these days. Phillippa, her next door neighbour, who had made friends with her the week she moved into this multi-occupant apartment, had introduced several potential boyfriends to her. She had rejected them all. She had explained to Phillippa each time that she had eyes only for Alex. Phillippa had condemned her one day, calling her the biggest fool on earth and she had also called Alex an *asshole*. Alice had been able to bear the insults Phillippa hurled at her, but she had not been able to condone the one she had hurled at Alex.

Alice had flipped and gone on to defend Alex; she had told Phillippa that she took exception to what she said about Alex. Even though, it was an obvious fact that Alex was not a faithful lover, Alice loved him so much she could not allow anyone, not in the least Phillippa, to insult him.

Phillippa's anger had matched Alice's and she had poured a torrent of swear words on Alex. Afterwards, the two friends had vowed never to have anything to do with each other again.

Since she had severed friendship with Phillippa, Alice had turned into a recluse. She had no family, she had no friends and worst of all, she had lost Alex. She knew that her getting pregnant was all her fault. She had made the mistake of missing a pill whilst being fully aware that her fertility rate was higher than normal. She had rushed to take a morning-after pill five days after she last had sex with Alex but by then it had been too late. Although it was her fault that she forgot to take the pill at the right time, she couldn't help but think that her not remembering to take the pill was partly Alex's fault. He had not bothered to come to see her and whenever he bothered to answer her calls, he had given vague excuses for not calling her or going over to her place to visit her. It was as if their relationship was dead or worse still; it was as if Alice was forcing herself on him. Alice had the feeling that Alex no longer had any feelings for her; he was just trying not to hurt her. She also had the feeling that he had another girlfriend but she tried desperately to shelve the feeling;

she couldn't bear the thought and she couldn't leave Alex either. He was the first and the only man she had known all her life and she couldn't imagine life without Alex. So, it was with great exhilaration that she received Alex when he visited her one day and told her he was there to spend the night and also make up for lost times. She couldn't believe her luck. Little did she know that Alex had had an argument with Clarida and since Nike was then at large, the only person he felt he could seek refuge in was Alice. It took nothing but a little attention to please Alice. She never asked to be taken out to dinner or cinema; she never asked to go on a vacation with Alex; she never asked for anything but to be told the three most deceiving words, '*I love you*'. She was content with those words and as soon as Alex saw her, he said to her, 'I love you, Alice,' and she forgot all the pains he had put her through; she forgot that he had refused to answer her calls on many occasions; she forgot that this was the first time in two and a half months Alex would deem it fit to call on her. She was so besotted by the fact that Alex would actually spend the night with her that she forgot to take any precaution against pregnancy.

Alex told her a lot of jokes; they laughed, ordered pizza, ate, danced together to some music in the room, showered together and one thing led to another before the end of that evening and they made love.

And they made love again, three times during the night before the day broke.

When Alex was leaving that morning, Alice felt so sad she started crying. Alex tenderly kissed away her tears with a promise to always call her and to return the next weekend to spend two days with her. Alex knew that would not happen; in fact, he knew he would not see Alice again for a long time.

It was five days later, when Alice discovered she had almost depleted her vitamin supplements and she had gone to the pharmacy to get some, that she caught a glimpse of the morning after pill. Then she remembered. In her euphoria at seeing Alex, she had completely forgotten to take the pill. The vitamins she had gone to buy completely forgotten, she had bought the morning after pill and rushed home. She had taken one tablet with water, frantically hoping that she was not already pregnant. Alex had told her not to become pregnant again after he took her for the second abortion and bought her enough contraceptive pills to last a year. He had also warned her that if she got pregnant one more time, she should consider their relationship over. She did not want that to happen.

One week after Alex visited her, she soon forgot all about her worry over pregnancy. Another worry had superseded that – she had not seen or heard from Alex.

Two weeks after she took the morning after pills, she felt a throbbing pain at the base of her stomach. Thinking it was the normal period pain, she had happily taken two paracetamol which had proved to her in earlier times to combat period pains. However, the pain refused to subside this time. She had taken a further two tablets and taken a rest. The pain increased and she did not see her period. She became afraid. She rushed down to the pharmacy to buy a pregnancy testing kit. She fearfully did the test, frantically hoping for a negative result. The test proved positive. She nearly fainted. She decided to disregard the result and go for a test at the hospital. She was given an appointment in two days to come back for the result. In the two days prior to hearing the result, Alice lost weight due to fear and worry. She could not bear to lose Alex. She saw the doctor studying his computer that day, a deep frown edged between his eyebrows; she hoped her worst fear would not be confirmed.

'I'm afraid you are pregnant,' said the doctor.

Her worst fear had just been confirmed!

It took Alice two days to make up her mind on what to do. She called the cab office and requested to be taken to Goldhurst Terrace, Kilburn, NW6.

The driver, who was obviously a chatter box, talked all the way to Alex's apartment but Alice hardly heard what he was saying.

'You know, London weather is very poor,' he said, and continued when Alice didn't respond, 'I don't like summer. I don't like the winter. I don't like the autumn. I don't like the spring.' Alice kept mum. She was tired of foreigners complaining about London weather. For God's sake, couldn't they talk about more interesting things like life and love... and Alex?

'...I don't like the snow and I don't like it when it's too sunny,' the driver continued, oblivious to Alice's silence. 'London definitely has all extremes,' he said.

Alice sat in the back of the cab with her heart in her mouth. She knew that Alex would be highly upset over two things. Firstly, she had not been invited to his house and Alex detested her visiting his house without being invited. The second and more fearful thing was that she was pregnant again. She knew that Alex would hit the roof should she let him in on her situation. However, she felt she had to do the right thing by telling him anyway; after all, it was his baby. Besides, she could persuade him to marry her. They were adults; they'd been adults for long and Alex was rich. He could take care of the family. Her reasoning gave her a bolt of confidence.

However, as the cab man parked in front of the house, Alice's heart skipped a bit. She paid the driver and with great trepidation, got out of the cab.

Alice stood before the massive building and appeared to study it for a while then, feet wobbly, she went to the front door of Alex's wing of the house and nervously pressed the bell. She waited for two minutes before pressing the bell the second time. *Was he not in?* It was a Sunday evening and from what she knew about Alex, he did not usually go to the club on Sunday evenings. He usually spent Sunday evenings preparing for work the next day. At least that was what he had told her. She had assumed he would be at home and since he had refused to answer her numerous calls, she had taken the boldness to check on him in his home. She was about to press the bell the third time when the door opened and she saw herself looking into the eyes of the most beautiful lady she had ever seen. Not only was she beautiful, Alice noticed that the lady had a very lovely shape and she was wearing a negligee underneath her housecoat!

'Yes, can I help?' said the lady icily, her cold eyes boring into Alice's soft, fearful ones.

Alice felt her throat go dry. *A woman was living with Alex!*

After a minute, when Alice had said nothing, the lady folded her hands across her full chest and leaning against the door ledge, continued in her icy tone. 'Perhaps, you'll excuse me if you've got nothing to say. As you can see, I have just woken up from a siesta and I have a busy evening ahead; the last thing I need is some lazy *mug* knocking on doors, looking for who will give her the next meal.' Nike knew that the woman standing before her was not a beggar. She had inkling that she was one of Alex's numerous girlfriends. However, she thought this plain, round woman standing before her was not really Alex's type. Nike studied her from top to bottom; she studied the scarf on the woman's head, the conservative blouse she wore, the long, flared skirt and the slightly high heeled shoes. She looked so soft, so homely; Nike almost felt pity for her. She couldn't decipher what on earth Alex was doing with her; she was definitely not his type. *He's got other girls besides you, Nike. Trust me, he's not good for you.* She tried to remember who had said it. *Or had she been thinking it?* Before she could remember, Alice uttered her first sentence since she got there.

'My name is Alice. I'm so s… sorry to bother you. Are you Alex's f… friend or something?' Alice couldn't help stammering even though she tried to remain calm.

'No, I'm not,' Nike replied pejoratively. She let that sink in and lips pursed, she went on.   'I'm more than a friend to Alex. I'm his fiancée.'

'His what?' Alice couldn't stop her lips from trembling. She bit down hard on her bottom lip to keep them from trembling; she bit so hard, she tasted blood.

'His fi-an-cée,' Nike said slowly, looking down on Alice as if she was talking to a five year old child, 'as in Alex and I are going to get married.'

Alice turned white. 'I… er. I… er. I'm sorry to come here. I never knew Alex had another woman…'

'You are the other woman,' Nike interjected. 'I am the main woman. How on earth did you expect Alex to be serious with someone like you? Get real, babe. We're not in the seventeenth century; the world has definitely moved on.'

Alice felt hot tears cascade down her face. She did not bother to wipe them off. She felt she was in a nightmare and she desperately needed to be woken up. How could Alex do this to her? She had practically lived her life for him. She frantically searched her mind for something to say; something that would make this woman, who claimed to be Alex's fiancée, understand how she felt for Alex. She desperately sought to elicit sympathy from this lady; after all, she needed Alex more than any other person could, especially as she was carrying his baby. Maybe she could persuade the lady to change her mind and leave Alex for her.

'I… er… I'm pregnant for Alex,' she said, eyes pleading.

Nike was unperturbed. 'Oh really,' she said mockingly. 'It's just as well as I'm pregnant too.'

'Preg… Pregnant?' Alice asked.

'Yes pregnant; as in I'm going to have Alex's baby!' replied Nike scornfully.

Alice felt her throat begin to tighten. She felt a rush of blood to her brain so much so that her head began to pound hard. She put her forefingers to her temples to suppress the pounding she was feeling in her head. What was happening was too much for her to take in. How long had this lady been Alex's girlfriend? More importantly, how could Alex go to the extent of getting another woman pregnant when he had told Alice more times than one that he was not ready to father a child yet? He had even made Alice abort a child for him twice. Was it now possible for Alex to impregnate another woman and not insist that she abort the pregnancy as well? She began to feel an intense headache. She thought she might faint. She closed her eyes for a moment to stop the tears from flowing. Hot tears rushed down her cheeks anyway. She searched her mind frantically for what to say and she uttered the first sentence that came to her mind. 'How… How did it happen?' she managed to ask.

Nike gave a short laugh before answering sarcastically, 'You want to know how it happened? He put his *dick* inside my *pussy* several times – that's how it happened. How did yours happen?' she finished bitingly.

Alice closed her eyes again. She could not believe this was happening to her. She could not believe Alex would ever let her down. She had always had the nagging fear that Alex was probably cheating on her, but she had always banished the thought from her mind. Now that the constant fear that had besieged her for so long had apparently become reality, she still found it difficult to believe; she desperately hoped she was dreaming. She wished someone would wake her up from this nasty dream. She opened her eyes, expecting to see that the lady had actually been an illusion; expecting to see Alex instead of that lady. Instead, she saw the lady looking at her spookily. She felt the hatred in the lady's eyes boring into hers. She was at a loss for what to do.

The lady spoke again, her voice filled with loathe. 'You may be idle but I'm afraid I'm not. Excuse me.'

Nike began to close the door but then she remembered something, turned around and looked at Alice straight in the eyes before saying, 'Oh, a word of advice; if I were you, I'd take care of that 'thing' growing in my belly; it could prevent you from getting another man. The choice is yours though, either way you choose to have it, I wish to remind you that you have lost big time. Have a good day.' And with that, Nike slammed the door loudly, leaving Alice gaping at the closed door.

Clarida had not seen Alex for a long time. The last time he came over, they had settled their differences and he had promised to be back the following weekend to take her and her daughter, Melissa, to the London eye. She really wanted to settle down with Alex permanently so that her daughter could have a father, albeit a surrogate one, to look up to. All her life, she had never desired anything more than getting married to Alex. However, anytime she broached the subject, Alex had always been evasive. It had actually been the cause of their constant arguments. She had made resolutions several times to take things easy with Alex and she had broken the resolution several times. Alex was simply proving difficult. At first, she had thought he was so shy, he found it difficult to propose to her and she had promptly done the proposal. She did not belong to the school of thought that a lady should wait for the man to propose. To Clarida, that was archaic and besides, she did not have enough patience to wait, so one day, as they were having dinner at a restaurant, Clarida had looked at Alex as lovingly as she could and with a sultry voice, had proposed to Alex.

'I want to spend the rest of my life with you, Alex,' she had said. 'We could be together forever without you having to come to my house once a while. You will be a father to Melissa and we will all live happily ever after,' she concluded happily.

Alex had looked shocked, then bemused, then angry all in a matter of seconds. He had replied, trying to control his temper, 'That seems to be the problem with you, Clarida. You're bossy and domineering. I do not need that, you know. If I ever wanted to get married to you, I would request that you kindly give me the honour of doing the proposal.' The suggestion in the words he had used was not lost on Clarida. *If I ever wanted to get married to you. Could he have someone else in his life?* Clarida quickly banished the thought from her mind. *Impossible!* Although she was busy most times, she had never had any reason to suspect Alex of infidelity. Until recently, he had kept all his promises to her. he had always come around; he had always remembered her birthdays, save for Valentines and Christmas days which he had told her he did not believe in; he had spent quality time with her whenever he could get away from work and more importantly, he got along with Melissa. No! Alex couldn't be cheating on her. *Alex belongs to me alone*, she said to herself fiercely. She could not bear the thought of sharing him with another woman. It was not that she loved Alex with all her heart. She wanted a permanent bed-mate that she could trust and more importantly, she wanted a father for Melissa. She stopped believing in love after she caught Melissa's father sleeping with her best friend. She had walked out of the matrimonial house, never to go back even after several pleadings from Melissa's dad. She was not one of the women who had the ability to share her man. Afterwards, she had two other relationships which had ended on the same note – the men cheated on her. She was not heartbroken though because she had not gone into the relationships with her heart. She fiercely guarded her heart from being broken once again. The day she met Alex for the first time, she had liked him immediately. She liked his wit, his charm and more importantly, she liked his looks. Alex was a man a lady would always be proud to be with in public; moreover, apart from his stubbornness, he was kind-hearted. He was kind to her and he was kind to Melissa. She had decided to get married to Alex because of all these reasons and because he was rich. She earned a very nice package as a broadcaster with Sky Television and she would not want to fall prey to a gold-digger who would only be interested in her as a meal-ticket. With Alex, she knew that would not be the case.

After a subdued argument, Alex had got up from the table and simply walked out of the restaurant, his food hardly touched. Clarida had taken a taxi home. She had been deeply hurt over the way Alex had treated her. When he did not bother to call her, she had called him after a few days and Alex had visited her with twelve red roses and a bottle of champagne for her. He had also bought a big teddy for Melissa. They had laughed together when Melissa ecstatically carried the teddy that was bigger than her tiny four year old frame upstairs. They had watched with tenderness and loving smiles as she struggled with every step upstairs. They had dinner indoors and made love. Alex had left the following day with a promise to come back to see her the following weekend. Alex did not fulfil his promise. Clarida called his mobile several times but he did not answer any of her calls, neither did he bother to return them. She waited for a week and afraid that something terrible had happened to him, she decided to visit his home.

That Sunday evening, she left her tastefully furnished four bedroom-duplex in Hampstead and drove to the mansion in Goldhurst Terrace., NW6 in Kilburn. She seldom visited Alex's home. He was seldom home. The mutual arrangement they had was that he should always visit her at home. Now, as she drove towards Kilburn, she hoped to meet Alex at home.

Nike was still fuming as she got dressed that Sunday evening. As soon as she got rid of *Alice in wonderland,* she dashed off to the bathroom to give herself a cold shower, thinking the cold water would douse her anger. It didn't. She couldn't stop thinking about Alex's betrayal. She knew Alex was a womaniser; she knew he was an incorrigible play boy. What she couldn't believe was that Alex could go as far as getting another woman pregnant and the *stupid* woman had the nerve to visit his home when she was very much around. She could not believe the effrontery. Alex must have encouraged her to do so, maybe to arouse her jealousy. She thought it a good thing that she had lied to the daft Alice that she was pregnant also and it was even a better thing that Alice had swallowed it hook, line and sinker. At least, that would guarantee that she would not venture near the house again. Whatever she wanted, she could do with her pregnancy. Nike couldn't care less. However, she thought of a way to get back at Alex. He must definitely pay for this.

Just then, her phone rang. She looked at it to see who was calling. It was Benjamin. *Fuck Benjamin.* She was too angry to travel around London with Benjamin. Let him do his campaign for that day without her. She had a more pressing matter to deal with. She had Alex to deal with! Her mobile phone stopped ringing after a minute and twenty-nine seconds. The phone made a sound to tell her that Benjamin had left her a message. She did not bother to listen to it. Two minutes after her mobile phone stopped ringing, the doorbell rang. She stood rigid for a while. *Had Benjamin decided to come for her?* She could not remember giving Benjamin her *temporary* home address. She had deliberately kept it from him. She did not want a meeting to take place between Benjamin and Alex. She knew they were both quick tempered and if she did not prevent a meeting between the two, the unpleasant meeting between George Walker Bush (Senior and Junior) and Saddam Hussein would be child's play compared to it. She waited a while; the bell rang for the fourth time. She knew it couldn't be Alex, for he had his own key to let himself in. The door bell rang for the fifth time. Nike decided to go and see who it was who wouldn't let her have some peace in her *home,* even if it was her temporary abode. She prepared herself to give whoever it was some telling off. She silently sharpened her tongue for a confrontation. She opened the front door as the door bell rang for the sixth time. If she had expected anyone to be at the door, it was not who she saw standing at the door. She recognised her immediately. She was her favourite newscaster, Clarida. She had always liked her eloquence and confidence on television. She sincerely hoped she was not one of Alex's girlfriends. She sincerely hoped she was not one of her rivals. Clarida's first words to her made her peeved.

'I'm Alex's girlfriend. May I know who you are?'

At that moment, Clarida ceased to be Nike's favourite. From that moment onwards, Nike hated Clarida. She was disappointed that Clarida's mannerism was a far cry from how she was portrayed on television. She thought of what to say to upset her – to break her confidence.

'You must be Chlamydia. I see you on TV all the time. Not much of a newsreader, are you?' said Nike, her eyes blazing.

Clarida's face registered shock at the name Nike called her. She flushed with anger. 'The name is Clarida, darling, and not… what you just called me,' she said scornfully; she could not bring herself to say Chlamydia.

'Oh I see,' said Nike coolly, 'and what brings you to my doorstep?'

'*Your* doorstep? This is supposed to be my boyfriend's house.'

'And you're supposed to be having a laugh,' Nike said cynically and went on. 'Alex and I are engaged,' she finished, raising her left hand for Clarida to see the ring on her third finger. It was actually the ring Benjamin had given her for their engagement; *but it would suffice for this purpose*, Nike thought. She actually enjoyed watching Clarida's reaction. Clarida's face was drained of all colour. To say she looked absolutely shocked would be an understatement.

'That can't be true. Alex belongs to me. He told me so several times,' Clarida said furiously. She was almost yelling.

'Please keep your voice low sweetheart,' said Nike mockingly and then she continued. 'You know something, watching you on T.V., no one would believe you could be so dumb. Couldn't you just ponder for a while within your small mind, why on earth Alex would invite me and not you to live with him if you're so sure he belongs to you? You will agree with me that Alex has never wanted anything to do with you apart from the occasional fuck you give each other. It's me he wants to spend the rest of his life with, not you,' said Nike cuttingly, laying emphasis on the *me* and the *you* by pointing to herself whenever she said 'me' and pointing at Clarida when she said 'you'.

Clarida almost exploded. 'You're just a farce. There must be something amiss,' she said through gritted teeth.

'You're the something that's amiss. Now, I'd be very grateful if you made yourself at large, Chlamydia.'

'I'm Clarida,' Clarida shouted.

'If you don't get going now, I'll be obliged to call the police. You and I know very well that we don't really want your name to be in the tabloids tomorrow morning, or do we?' Nike began to make some shadow writing and continued. 'Just imagine the caption, *Popular News reader arrested for trespassing and fighting over big time lawyer's cock!* How about that darling?' she finished mockingly.

At that, Clarida gasped. She couldn't believe the vulgarity of the lady standing before her. Moreover, she really did not want any scandal attached to her name. She had an admirable career to protect and she had pride. She decided to deal with Alex himself when next they met; she really had no business with this *tramp* standing at the door. Without saying one more word, she turned around and started walking away, her fury reflecting in the way her stilettos clicked loudly with each step she took.

'Goodbye Chlamydia,' Nike called after her.

Clarida felt herself stiffen; she clenched her fists and gritted her teeth. It was all she could do not to turn back and give her a punch.

Alex slotted his key in the key-hole of the front door to his house at exactly eleven-thirty p.m. that day. He had deliberately stayed out late in order to avoid bumping into Nike. He had taken a decision to avoid her until the time was ripe for her to leave his house. He had given her two weeks to find accommodation and he was not going to allow her to stay a day more. He made a mental calculation of when he expected Nike to be out of his house. *Three days time – not later than twelve midnight.* He knew from experience that as long as she was indoors, Nike would never wait till eleven-thirty before she turned in for the night. He opened the door, switched on the light and stopped short. Nike was lying on the couch, facing the ceiling.

'What are you doing here in the dark?' he asked.

'And how's that supposed to be your business?', Nike replied tersely.

'You don't answer my question with another, got it?' said Alex irritably.

'No, I don't get it and I don't get how you could question me about Benjamin while you frolic around with two other women, you skunk,' said Nike angrily, sitting up.

'What do you mean *frolic around with two other women?*' Alex asked suspiciously. From experience, he couldn't put anything past Nike; however, he couldn't help wondering if and how on earth she knew about the other women in his life.

Nike got up from the couch and stood near it, arms akimbo. She was determined to level it up with Alex. That was why she had waited for him to come back. She had taken several cups of strong, black coffee to keep her awake. She knew Alex meant for her to have gone to bed before he came in – *the idiot.*

Alex asked her again, albeit cautiously this time, 'I just asked you a question, Nike, and I need an answer right now; what did you mean when you said I was frolicking with two women?'

'Oh, you want to start playing dumb with me now? How very smart,' said Nike, her voice filled with sarcasm.

'Cut the crap and answer my question, Nike. I'm beginning to lose my patience.'

'Which is just as well,' retorted Nike and continued angrily, 'I lost my patience with you a long time before now. I lost a bit of my patience with you when I met your first concubine and then I lost all of my patience with you when your second concubine came on the scene. You should be ashamed of yourself. You despicable swine. You don't even discriminate – fat, slim, tall and short, whichever one goes and here you were chastising me over Benjamin the other day. What do you take me for?'

'Hold it right there would you? Just hold it for a minute. What crap are you saying for God's sake? What the hell are you talking about? I would be lying if I said I understood any of these jargons. Could you please arrange the jigsaw puzzle and let me in on what you're driving at?'

Nike slowly clapped three times in mock applause. 'Well done Mr. Denzel Washington; or should I call you Tom Cruise? or Brad Pitt? You really should have tried your filthy hands at acting you know? Then, you would have known what I'm driving at. Your great pretence beats my imagination. Alexander Tucker, you are a genius.'

Alex had had enough. He strode to where she was and, grabbing her hand so tightly she almost screamed, he yelled at her, 'Will you let me in on what's going on? What the hell have you been up to, Nike?'

'You mean what the hell have *you* been up to, Alex,' Nike said scornfully and then she went on. 'You are the one who was careless and indecent enough to have a fat slob and the arrogant bitch as concubines. Now you let go of my hand, idiot.'

Alex immediately released her hand. He knew instantly who she was referring to. 'How did you meet Alice and Clarida?' he asked quietly.

'Oh, so you know at long last, what I'm talking about,' said Nike mockingly. 'Thank goodness.'

'I said cut the crap and tell me how the hell you met Alice and Clarida,' Alex shouted at her impatiently.

'They came here looking for you, lover boy. That's how I met them; that's how I met the two of them. God knows how many more are still coming. You are a sorry case, Alex. You are a despicable male slut.'

Alex slapped her hard on the face then.

Hot tears sprung to her eye; she kept them from falling. She had not cried since her father's death and she was not about to start now. Not even Alex would make her cry. She made a silent resolve to make Alex pay dearly for slapping her. The only other person who had slapped her in her life was her mother and she had never forgiven her for it. She was not about to forgive Alex for slapping her either; he would surely pay for it, she promised herself, rubbing her face stoically.

Alex looked at the hand he had used to slap her. He could not believe what he had just done. *Had he just slapped Nike?* He moved to her side and attempted to pull her towards him. She pushed him away.

'I'm sorry, Nike. I didn't mean to do that. I don't know what got over me. I must be going bananas or something. He lowered himself and knelt down on one knee. Nike felt touched but she did not show it. She maintained her angry composure.

'Nike, please forgive me,' pleaded Alex, still on his knee.

'I've forgiven you,' said Nike.

'Permit me to get up,' said Alex innocently.

Nike felt her head swell; she relished this moment very much. She looked down at Alex, trying very hard to maintain her expression of disdain.

'Get up,' she said, trying very hard not to smile.

Alex got up and pulled Nike into his arms. 'I've missed you, Nike. I've really missed you. I missed your touch, your charm, your love-making.'

Nike felt her heart melt; she was sure that Alex would forever have that effect on her. She looked up at Alex with soft eyes, the immense liking she felt for Alex clearly evident on her face.

'What about your *concubines?*' she asked softly.

'What about your…?' Alex could not bring himself to say *lover*. '…What about Benjamin Walters?' Even the name tasted bitter to Alex as he said it. 'What is Benjamin to you Nike?'

'He's nothing to me. He's just… We're just business partners.'

'That's a lie,' Alex yelled, his voice laced with pure jealousy. 'Don't lie to me Nike,' he said painfully. 'It'll hurt me if you do.' After a few seconds, Alex asked her hesitantly, 'Is Benjamin Walters your lover?'

Nike was quick to reply. 'No.'

'And you expect me to believe that?'

'Suit yourself. Believe anything you want. I don't need you to trust me. And by the way, who the hell are you to question me? If you should ever want to point accusing fingers, why not direct them to yourself. Talk of the pot calling the kettle black,' said Nike, her anger rising. She pushed Alex away from her now.

Alex thought for a while before saying quietly, 'I knew Alice and Clarida before I met you, Nike. I left them when I thought… When I was so damned sure you would marry me; but then, you refused my marriage proposal and then you seemed to vanish from the surface of the earth. I had no choice but to…' Alex faltered and Nike completed his sentence.

'But to go back and fuck them.'

'You are *fucking* Benjamin too,' Alex accused her.

'No I'm not,' shouted Nike. 'Benjamin has not so much as seen my underwear.'

Alex looked at Nike's left hand; he concentrated on the third one.

'Where did you get the ring from? He gave it to you didn't he?'

Nike fiddled with the ring Benjamin had given her. She could not tell Alex what she had laid up for Benjamin; he would not believe her.

'It's a stunt. It's not real,' she said.

'Like hell it's a stunt. Feed that to the birds, Nike. Tell your story to the marines. I'm too old in the game and I'm too worldly-wise for cheap lies.'

'Then let's leave it at that. You can believe whatever you want to believe. Now I'll like to go to bed if you don't mind.'

'You must stop seeing Benjamin at once,' Alex said as Nike went past him. She stopped in her tracks and turned to face Alex.

'Says who?' she asked.

'Says me,' said Alex. 'This is my house remember, and as long as you choose to live in it, you must abide by my rules and the first rule is *stop seeing Benjamin*. I hate to imagine you in his arms.'

Nike laughed out very loudly. 'You hate to see me with Benjamin indeed. I'm sure you would hate to see me with any other man. Alex, you're the most unserious human being I've ever come across. But tell you what, I'm not your wife, so I'll do with my life whatever I damned well wish. Get the picture?'

'Then be ready to move out of my house,' said Alex; he knew he was blackmailing her, but he could not help himself.

'It's a pity you have to resort to cheap blackmail but let me remind you that you gave me two weeks to stay in your house and I've got three good days left. A man of your calibre should stick by his word.' And with that, Nike stormed out of the sitting room.

Alex watched her go. He could not decide whether he should be angry or sad. He decided to allow Nike to stay for the remaining three days and then he would personally lead her out of his house and shut her out of his life for good. He knew that would be extremely difficult to achieve but he would do it. Nike had brought him enough heartache to last a lifetime. He knew that he felt something very deep for Nike; however, he sincerely hoped that feeling was not what everyday couples called *love*.

Five hours after Alice left Alex's residence, she woke up in a hospital ward, on a hospital bed. She looked around her room and wondered how she got there. She could not remember. She sat up suddenly. Just then, her eyes caught the dress she wore. It was a hospital gown. She was now very frightened. *What on earth had brought her here?* She frantically hoped she had not caught some bug or *something*. But who would have brought her to a hospital without her knowing it?

Just then, a tall, lanky man with blue eyes and a big smile came into the room.

'Hi there. You're awake. I was almost thinking you'd never wake up,' said the man cheerfully as he came to stand near Alice's bed. 'My name is Jeremy Flanders. Fondly called Professor Flanders by my students,' the man introduced himself kindly. 'I'm the man who was fortunate enough to have hit you with my car; otherwise, I would not have met you, lovely lady,' joked Professor Flanders dryly.

Then Alice remembered everything. She remembered how she had got to the hospital. She had left Alex's house in a haze as the reality of the fact that Alex did not really care about her finally dawned on her. She could not believe that after all she had sacrificed for Alex, he could jilt her for another lady. When she remembered how she had lost her family –her closely knit family – because Alex had got her pregnant, hot tears trickled down her eyes. Everything around her became blurred as she hastily walked away from Alex's house. It was at that moment that she had run into a car that was reversing from a house onto the road and she had been hit by the car.

Although, she insisted that she was fine, the driver of the car had insisted on taking her to the hospital and staying with her until she was certified okay.

Alice had been given a thorough examination by the hospital staff and after being administered some pain relieving tablets, she had been given the all clear.

Professor Flanders had insisted on taking her back to her house. However, she started feeling dizzy as soon as she was settled in Professor Flanders' car. She had to be taken back to the hospital. She was given a bed rest and Alice could only remember the incident up to the moment she dozed off.

Now, as she looked at the smiling Professor, she was eternally grateful that he had stood by her and not run away when he hit her. She was all the more grateful that he was still with her now. She would not have been able to cope with the emotions she was experiencing from Alex's betrayal. She needed someone by her side; she needed a friend to talk to; she needed someone who was kind and who would understand – someone like Professor Jeremy Flanders.

Alice studied Professor Flanders' features. He was tall and he had a kind, bespectacled face. He was good-looking without being overly attractive. He was sort of good-looking in an academic way and he looked very fit, even though he was wearing a shirt, a pair of trousers and a tie.

Alice thought Professor Flanders would be very handsome if he really cared about his looks.

She looked at his warm, smiling face and smiled back.

Chapter 46

It was now two days to the day that Nike was bound to leave Alex's house for good. Simeon O'Neil, Alex's fifteen year old neighbour came knocking on the door. He rang the door-bell several times, then knocked some more. Nike wondered who the hell could be knocking at the door and pressing the bell at the same time. She hoped whoever it was wouldn't turn out to be one of Alex's numerous girlfriends. Ever since those two came around, she had not stopped wondering how many of them Alex actually kept. Sharpening her tongue in readiness for a confrontation, she put on her dressing gown and went to open the door. She met Alex at the door before she got there.

'Scared of confrontations between me and your whores?' she asked Alex mockingly as he opened the door.

Before Alex could respond to her cutting remark, Simeon rushed into the house.

Simeon was used to Alex. They sometimes played chess and computer games together.

'Hello Alex,' Simeon said breezily. 'Good to see you today. How you doing mate?'

Alex was not Simeon's mate in the real sense of the word, but he did not mind. Simeon saw him as a big brother and he loved Simeon as a younger brother.

'What's up Si?' Alex said, as he patted Simeon on the back in a friendly gesture. 'What brings you to my house so late at night? Your mum and dad okay?' asked Alex pleasantly.

'Yeah, sure they are. It's just that I've got into a row with them – especially dad,' replied Simeon as he went to the adjoining kitchen.

Simeon opened the refrigerator and poured himself a tall glass of pineapple juice. He went to a cupboard and took out a pack of cookies. These, he carried back to the sitting room and sat on the couch opposite Alex. He had a bite of cookie, chewed and swallowed it and took a full swig of the pineapple juice before he continued. 'I don't know why the old man chooses to give me a hell of a time; I'm sick and tired of his whining… I'm sick up to here.' With his free hand, Simeon touched his forehead in a bid to show Alex how sick he was of his dad's whining.

Simeon always rowed with his parents, even though it was evident to all and sundry that he loved them dearly. Alex knew that Simeon adored his mother especially; he was just going through the normal adolescent period. Alex remembered some of the disputes he had gone to settle between Simeon and his parents. He remembered when Simeon, even though he was underage, had taken his father's Bentley out with his girlfriend and had crashed it on a pole; he remembered when he had run away from school, only to reappear at the end of the school term with skin so tanned, he looked almost burnt. He had nonchalantly explained that he decided to jet out to Jamaica for a short break. But for Alex's timely intervention, Simeon's father, who was a retired professional boxer, would have dealt his son a deadly punch.

Alex could never forget the day a girl came to Simeon's parents' house, followed by her own parents, and claimed that Simeon had impregnated her. The issue was later settled when another boy from the school was heard boasting to his friends that he had also *had a go* at the girl. DNA tests subsequently established that Simeon was not responsible for the pregnancy and he was subsequently let off the hook.

Alex felt Simeon had done one of those things again, so he asked him wearily, 'What have you been up to this time, Simeon?'

'You see…' Simeon suddenly realised the presence of a lady who he had not seen before and turning to Nike. He said sultrily, 'Sorry miss, excuse my manners. May I have the honour of knowing the most beautiful woman in the world?'

Nike smiled warmly at him. She liked the boy. She like his charm and his wit. He was also good looking, tall, lanky, but a bit too thin, with a dust of freckles around his pointed nose. He had black, curly hair and a face that promised handsomeness in the very near future. She extended her hand to him. 'It's nice meeting you too,' she said.

The boy took her hand, kissed it warmly and bowed slightly before saying, 'Nice meeting you, madam.'

'Let's go upstairs,' said Alex to Simeon, trying to break the impending closeness that was threatening to build up between Simeon and Nike. He did not want any closeness between the two *at all*. Nike spelt trouble and wherever she went, she left an indelible array of problems in her wake. He did not want Nike to land Simeon in trouble and he was determined to make him stay very far away from her.

'It's obvious you don't want your friend to stay close to me. I won't bite him, darling. I don't bite,' Nike teased Alex, her eyes challenging.

'Of course you don't,' said Simeon, oblivious to the tension between the two. 'In fact, you strike me as an angel newly sent from heaven. You're so beautiful, I wish to stay close to you forever; that is if Alex won't mind,' he finished, winking at Alex. He had naturally assumed Nike was Alex's partner. He knew Alex would not mind him joking with his girlfriend even if the jokes were a little bit naughty.

Alex very much wanted to correct the impression but he kept quiet. He did not want to go into an argument with Nike in the presence of Simeon. *The less Simeon knew of the bitch, the better for them all.*

'Thank you, my dear,' said Nike teasingly. 'You're welcome to come and visit me any time.'

'That's very kind of you,' said Simeon. 'You're the kindest angel on earth.'

Alex knew he had to stop the conversation before it got out of control. He cleared his throat and said to Simeon, 'You were saying something about a row with your parents, Si.'

Simeon looked at Alex for a little while, his expression suggested he was struggling to remember what it was he had been telling Alex; then he said, 'Yes, it's about my mum and dad. They have the hunch that I could be a wealthy, popular doctor and that's what they want me to be, period! You know how Dad is – very stubborn and adamant; he never changes his mind once it's made up,' said Simeon with all seriousness, his banter with Nike completely forgotten. He sat down resignedly on the sofa.

'What's wrong with you being a doctor?' Alex asked Simeon, deliberately ignoring Nike, and went on. 'I would say it's one of the most noble professions in the world; and it's better than not being anything.'

Nike knew that Alex's last statement was a jab at her but she let it pass; she already had something up her sleeve for Alex.

'Of course it's a good thing,' said Simeon, 'but can you imagine me ever being a doctor? Me? It's simply incredible.'

'And what's so incredible about that?' asked Alex with a serious tone. 'You can be what you want to be, I would say.'

'Yeah, but you need to get some things right before you can be a doctor; get the picture?'

'Things like what?'

'Things like knowing your damned sciences. I mean knowing them really well. And believe you me, I struggled for four years to cope with chemistry and biology but the more I read those damned subjects, the more the knowledge eludes me.'

'You talked things over with your folks?' asked Alex.

'You bet I have. They just would not listen. They want me to be a doctor – nothing more, nothing less. Mum has always said that she wished to be referred to as the mother of a doctor; you know such vanity.'

'Do you really want to be a doctor, Si, or is it just your mum who wants you to be a doctor? You must really think about this; it's what you want that really counts you know.'

'I would be anything for my mum,' said Simeon. 'I don't mind being a doctor for her; but the problem I've got is knowing my sciences; they're so tough…'

'I can teach you,' Nike interjected, prompting Alex to look at her sharply, his eyes daring. Nike ignored Alex's daring look and continued. 'I can teach you Physics, Chemistry and Biology if you don't mind; and I would also bet that with my coaching, you would come out with an A in all subjects.'

Alex laughed out loud then. How could Nike know anything pertaining to academics? *This must be the greatest joke of all times,* Alex thought.

'Did you go to school, Nike?' he asked without thinking.

If looks could kill, Alex would have dropped dead with the look Nike gave him.

Simeon was beginning to feel uncomfortable. He looked from one to the other and decided that things were not exactly all right between them. He cleared his throat and said uneasily, 'I'd really appreciate it if you could give me some extra lectures on the subjects, miss, and please excuse Alex's manners; he gets touchy sometimes.'

Nike was quick to reply. 'I know he's got a lose nut in his brain.'

Simon was aghast; he looked from Nike to Alex. Alex had a murderous expression; he looked from Alex to Nike; Nike had a spooky expression.

Simon shifted from one foot to the other uncomfortably. He was torn between his loyalty to Alex and his appreciation of Nike's beauty and the academic benefit he was about to gain from her; but before he could utter a word, Alex walked out of the sitting room.

Simeon came back to see Alex the following day and after much pleadings, Alex at last agreed for Nike to give him the extra lessons he so much needed. Alex had insisted that the lessons be conducted in his house, under his roof. He decided to exercise patience and endure a few more weeks living with Nike. He could not afford to allow Nike to get close to the O'Neil's. He could not bring himself to trust Nike not to cause chaos in their home.

Two days later, the science classes started in earnest. Simeon came in two hours after school each day to listen to Nike divulge what she had learnt in school many years ago to him. They had three weeks to cover the three subjects before the examination would begin. Nike made out a timetable for the lectures.

The first week, Nike taught Simeon all he needed to know in Physics. On the first day of the lectures, Nike started by asking, 'Simeon, can you tell me Newton's first law of motion?'

Simeon was taken aback by the question. He had not expected this approach and he had stammered, 'I... er. Newton's first law of motion is... Well... It is...'

Nike quickly went on. 'Newton's first law of motion states that a body continues in its state of rest or of uniform motion unless otherwise acted upon by an external force.' She waited for Simeon to assimilate what she said and then she continued. 'This law of motion is generally regarded as the law of inertia.'

And that had got Simeon's concentration. Alex had been wrong; Nike had indeed been to school and she knew what she was doing. He wished Alex had not gone to work that day; he should have been around to see that his views about Nike had all been wrong. To Simeon, Nike was a woman of excellence. He jettisoned all the doubts that had been created within him by Alex's remarks about Nike; he sat straight and listened attentively.

Nike went on to talk about Newton's other laws of motion and their applications to day to day living. She also talked about velocity and acceleration and force and power, all the while giving Simeon formulae and calculations to buttress her points.

Simeon was very much surprised at Nike's eloquence in the knowledge of the sciences; he found it difficult to believe that Nike was not a real science teacher. What enthralled him mostly was the temerity with which she delivered the lectures. Combined with his admiration of her beauty, Simeon could not help but respect her obvious intellect.

On the second day, Nike taught Simeon all about Static Electricity. She talked about atoms, nucleus and positive and negative electrons. She taught him about electrical conductors and circuits and charge. She taught him Electricity and voltage and waves and tides. They talked about Potential energy and Kinetic energy; and they talked about Temperature and heat transfers. At the end of the lectures for that day, Nike gave Simeon enough homework to keep him busy till the next day.

The following day, Nike marked the homework and she gave him more homework; then they talked about Radioactivity and the Electromagnetic spectrum; and they talked about lenses and Sound and Magnetic fields.

On the third day, Nike taught Simeon Biology. She taught him Cell division and the difference between plants and animal cells. They talked about Osmosis, Digestion and Respiration and their differences. They also talked about the nervous system and hormones and stimulus.

The fourth day, Nike taught him the different types of diseases and their causes. They talked about Evolution and Darwin's theory of evolution; and they treated alleles and inheritance and co-ordination and movement.

The fifth day brought them to the topic of Ecology and co-habitation. Nike taught subjects in commensalisms, parasitology and symbiotic relationships and she gave Simeon some homework to do.

The sixth day was a Saturday, and the subject they discussed was solely Chemistry. They talked about the Nomenclature of compounds and their formations. They treated electrolysis and the formation of Sodium amalgam by the mixture of mercury and sodium in electrolysis. They talked about tin ores and iron ores and they talked about acids and alkalines.

The seventh day was a Sunday, so Alex was at home when Simeon came in. Alex was in his study when Simeon rang the bell. He resisted the urge to go downstairs to open the door. He did not want to get involved in the association between Nike and Simeon. He somehow knew that some calamity was lurking somewhere, waiting for the slightest opportunity to rear its ugly head. He felt that wherever Nike was, calamity would not be far from there. He only wished Simeon's examination would be over pretty quickly and he would be free to get Nike out of his house and permanently out of his life.

Suddenly, he heard Nike speak in a voice that he had not heard her use before. He opened the door of his study slightly so he could catch what she was saying. She was giving Simeon some instructions. Her voice was crystal clear and she spoke with authority. It seemed she was actually making some corrections on Simeon's homework.

Wonders shall never end! Alex muttered to himself. He remained on his seat for a while; however, he badly wanted to see Nike *in action*, so he got up from his seat and went downstairs.

'Our topic for today is the chemistry of hydrocarbons,' he heard Nike say. He was surprised at the seriousness in Nike, so much so that he gave a little chuckle. At that moment, Simeon turned and waved at Alex while giving Nike a thumb up.

Alex stepped into the large living room and pulled out a dining chair beside Simeon. He quietly sat down on the chair and folded his hands across his chest. Nike glanced briefly at Alex and turned back to face Simeon. She adjusted her eye glasses and continued with the lecture she was giving Alex. She had bought the eye glasses prior to the day that lessons were supposed to begin because she wanted to look serious; she had even chosen to dress like a proper teacher so that Simeon would take the lessons seriously. The scheme had worked not only on Simeon, but on Alex as well.

'We shall start by naming the differences between branched chain hydrocarbons and straight chain hydrocarbons…' continued Nike.

Alex watched Nike talk about the chemistry of hydrocarbons with gusto. Even though, Alex, being a lawyer and not a science oriented person, understood very little of all Nike said, he could not help but be impressed with the way she exuded so much confidence and in-depth knowledge of the subject.

At the end of that day, Alex's impression of Nike had metamorphosed completely to something akin to deep respect. He was, after all, proud that Simeon had met Nike in his house.

The following morning, Nike woke up feeling famished. She had skipped dinner the day before because she had lectured Simeon till late in the evening. Now, the hunger pangs she felt were eating at her stomach.

She went into the kitchen and filled the kettle with water; this, she plugged into a socket and walked to the refrigerator. She stopped to read the note that was pasted on the door of the fridge; Alex was reminding her to keep the refrigerator tidy. She burst out laughing. Alex was too tidy for her liking. He was just too fussy over what she considered very unimportant.

Still laughing, she opened the refrigerator and picked out a sandwich and a bottle of apple juice. She bit off a large chunk of the sandwich, chewed for some time and took a leisurely swig from the bottle.

'Bad habit,' she reproved herself. 'Very bad habit; you should have poured it first into a cup.' She wondered what Alex would have done, had he seen her placing the whole bottle into her mouth. She laughed and took one more full swig. 'I bet Alex would have wrung your neck at this, Nike,' she said to herself.

'I bet Alex would have wrung your neck at this!' said Alex, jolting her from her frivolous mood.

Nike turned to face Alex standing in the doorway with his right hand in his trouser pocket and his left hand on the door frame; as she turned, the bottle she had been holding fell to the floor and the clear amber liquid spilled on the carpeted floor. She bent to pick the bottle up and then she turned on Alex.

'Why do you make it a habit of sneaking up on me?' she asked Alex angrily.

'That's because you make it a habit of doing the wrong things,' replied Alex; but he was not looking angry. Rather, he had on a friendly expression.

Alex walked into the kitchen, held Nike by the arms and gave her a kiss on her forehead. He pulled back from her and looked straight into her eyes then he said in a voice laden with emotion, 'Nike, to say that I was greatly impressed with you yesterday would be an understatement you know. You outrightly blew me away. I used to think… Well, I thought…' Alex smiled and took her in his arms. There was no need for him to tell her what he used to think of her; what mattered was what he found out she was. He bent to kiss her but she fended him off with her hand.

Pulling away from him, she said, 'What did you think I was? A cheap tramp who has a pea brain and knows nothing else but to follow men around?'

Alex thought about what Nike said and sighed. 'Yes,' he said sincerely.

Nike looked shocked, then she looked angry and then she looked outraged.

'What?' she said. She had not expected Alex to be so blunt in his reply. *What a cheek*!

'…but I love you all the same; I have always loved you,' continued Alex. 'Marry me, Nike.'

'No!' said Nike and she totally disengaged herself from his embrace. Totally forgetting the hot water in the kettle, she walked out of the kitchen.

The lessons went on throughout the remaining period of two weeks without a hitch.

When his school certificate examinations began, Simeon wrote his examination papers with confidence. He was sure that he would excel in his sciences.

When his results were posted, his scores in the three science subjects were astounding!

Chapter 47

It was eight months and a day since Nike started living in Alex's house as a *temporary* tenant. Although, Nike knew deep down within her that Alex still harboured suspicions about her relationship with Benjamin Walters, they had somehow managed to patch things up between them and tried to co-habit amicably.

This particular day, Nike packed an overnight bag carefully. The following day would be a great day in the journey of her life. Benjamin Walters was going to introduce her formally as his bride to be. Tomorrow, she would meet the high and the mighty in the society. Tomorrow, she would be regarded with respect by all and sundry. Tomorrow, her destiny would change forever. As she zipped up her small overnight bag, she could not help but revel in the glory of it all. Very soon she would be Mrs Benjamin Walters. She smiled.

In the few months that she had been with Benjamin Walters, she had come to understand that there was a special kind of dignity attached to political positions. In the months that she had known Benjamin Walters, she had worked tirelessly to secure a degree of love for him among the Africans and the Asians in the city of London. At least, she had kept that part of their bargain. What she was not sure she really wanted to keep was the other part of the bargain – the marriage part. She knew that Benjamin did not love her. He just wanted to use her to achieve his goal of becoming the Mayor of London. A tiny voice told her that she would be wrong in hating him for that – at least, he had kept his part of the bargain. He had supplied her with all the money she had demanded in the course of the campaign. He had treated her like a true fiancé would treat his fiancée. He had taken her to restaurants and even treated her with courtesy such as pulling out a chair for her at restaurants – all that, despite his obvious arrogance.

Nike had politely attended the secret course on *how to be a celebrity wife* that Benjamin had arranged for her, just like the one he had arranged for Tonia, and she had completed it the week before. Now, Benjamin was ready to introduce her to his political friends. He had invited her over to stay the night in his house. Nike had made it plain to him that there would be no sex before marriage. She had thought of breaking away from him long before now, but she had started enjoying the attendant publicity and dignity that accompanied her relationship with Benjamin and she had delayed carrying out her real plans.

Now, she pondered on her life with Benjamin so far. She had entered into the arranged relationship with him with a plan to take vengeance on him for having treated her best friend shabbily. What she had not bargained for was that she would fall in love with the celebrity image that the relationship would accord her. She did not love Benjamin and she never would, but she had fallen in love with her image. She was torn between her resolution to enact revenge on Tonia's behalf and the luxury she was enjoying. A voice within her told her to go on and enjoy her new found life, which would bring her dignity and respect; after all, the so-called friend she was fighting for, had forced her out of her home and left her in the cold, homeless and abandoned. Another voice within her countered and told her that she would have done the same, or worse, were she in Tonia's shoes; besides, Benjamin would divorce her after four years and leave her emotionally in the cold, perhaps in bitter divorce proceedings; and she would be made out to be a gold-digger. She would be the shamed one of the two. Was *that not the trend with celebrity divorces?* The partner who was regarded as the one who brought in the bread would always earn public pity, while the other partner would be painted as the black sheep and a gold-digger. Benjamin had even made her sign documents that allowed her to take a very small amount of money in the event of their divorce.

Nike sat on the bed and buried her face in her hands. For the first time since her father's death, she was really confused.

The sharp horn of the cab driver brought her back from her musing. She got up from the bed immediately and picked up her bag. Benjamin had told her to pack only very few personal effects. He had told her not to bother with the dress to wear and the shoes to put on.

'They've already been taken care of by the top fashion experts I hired,' he had said. He did not trust Nike to be able to pick the right wear for the right occasion, so he had employed the services of fashion consultants.

'At least it would be better that way than you going to the political gathering to embarrass me,' he had told her in his usual arrogant manner. Nike had borne the caustic remark in her stride. *But for how long would you continue to put up with Benjamin's arrogance? Can you take it for four more weeks not to talk of four years?* A voice within her had asked. She could not provide an answer then and she could not provide an answer now.

She ran towards the door but before she left the house, a thought came to her mind. She went back to the living room, found a pad underneath the television stand and scribbled a quick note for Alex. She stuck the note underneath the television, but changed her mind and took it to the kitchen. Alex would see the note quicker in the kitchen than underneath the television. She stuck it underneath the microwave oven and ran out of the house.

As she ran, she remembered the admonition of one of the coaches Benjamin had got for her.

Don't run, walk gracefully; you're going to be the wife of a Mayor.

Nike felt her head swell with pride. Right there, she decided to go ahead with the marriage. Benjamin Walter's punishment would come in due course.

Nike got down from the cab and paid the driver. She turned around to look at the mansion that housed Benjamin Walters and she hesitated for a moment; *Is this really what you want, Nike? What if things got too hot for you to handle?* asked a tiny voice from within her. She subdued the voice and walked to the door. Before she pressed the bell, the door opened and a smiling lady, who Nike guessed must be in her early forties, came out to welcome her.

'You're welcome, darling,' the lady enthused, 'you're very much welcome here. Mr Walters has been expecting you. We've all been expecting you. I'll be your chaperon for as long as you live here,' said the woman in a slightly accented voice. Nike guessed she must be from somewhere in Eastern Europe. The lady did not offer her a hand; rather, she bowed slightly as she introduced herself. Before Nike could reply, she continued breezily, 'Now, we'll go to your suite and help you change into something suitable before you see Mr Walters.' She took Nike's overnight bag from her without asking for permission to do so.

Nike looked down at her clothes. She wondered what was wrong with what she had put on; she wore an elegant navy blue mini-skirt suit and a cream blouse underneath. *What did this lady mean by change into something suitable?* She checked her shoes to see if she had mistakenly stepped on dog poo. She hadn't. She almost hated the lady standing before her, but she kept herself in check. *It's not her fault*, she reasoned; Benjamin must have given his staff instructions concerning her and one of the ignoble instructions was that she should be *suitably* dressed before she could come into his presence; as if she was some lunatic, who had just been brought from the psychiatry to meet the king. Besides, the phrase, *for as long as you live here* did not go unnoticed with Nike. *Had Benjamin explained the terms and conditions of their marriage to his staff as well?* Benjamin Walters was beginning to annoy her!

Nike looked at the still-smiling lady, who obviously had no inkling of what was going on in her mind, and forced a smile to her lips. The lady seemed friendly enough, so she made an attempt at a conversation.

'My name is Nike and I'm pleased to meet you,' she said.

'Pleased to meet you too, ma'am. Please call me Monica.'

'You have a nice name, Monica,' said Nike.

'Thank you very much, ma'am,' said Monica.

Nike was a bit irritated. 'I'd very much appreciate it if you called me Nike.'

'I'm sorry, ma'am,' said Monica uncomfortably, 'but Mr Walters would not take kindly to it. You understand what I mean?'

She now realised the kind of life she would be living in Benjamin's house. It would be a programmed life. She would not be different from Benjamin's computer. Every member of staff in the house would take care of her as Benjamin's property and Benjamin would be the *computer programmer*. She would be accorded the amount of respect that Benjamin felt was due to her – *no more, no less.* To all intents and purposes, she would be one of Benjamin's personal effects.

'I understand what you mean,' said Nike angrily and she marched into the house.

She marched into a large drawing room. Nike would not have thought in her wildest dreams that the house contained a drawing room that was so large. Nike looked around and she admired what she saw, despite herself. The wall of the drawing room was painted white and decorated with three large paintings that Nike knew must have cost a fortune. She walked over to the largest one of the paintings and traced her hand all over it. It was a painting of the Tower Bridge as it was opening up. Nike was mesmerised by the drawing. It looked so real that, as she studied the mastery of the artwork, Nike imagined she had been catapulted out of Benjamin's residence and onto the Bridge. It was as if she was seeing the great Tower Bridge for the first time. Nike was momentarily taken back to her life in Tonia's house in Bermondsy; she had crossed the Tower Bridge several times in those days and although she had praised intelligence behind its creativity, she had not really appreciated its beauty as it was illuminated in this artwork.

Nike wanted to know who the artist was. As she squinted to read the signature at the base of the artwork, Monica cleared her throat and spoke to her. 'I'm sorry ma'am, but I wish to let you know that we're running late. Mr Walters would like to assess you before the luncheon tomorrow.'

Nike was aghast. She turned away from the painting and turned to Monica.

'What the hell do you mean by Mr Walters would want to *assess* me?' asked Nike, eyes blazing.

Monica cringed visibly; she looked so frightened, she seemed to withdraw into her blouse. But before she could respond, Nike continued furiously, 'Now you listen to me, and listen good; I'm Benjamin's fiancée and we're about to get married; the earlier you realised that and started treating me as Mrs Benjamin Walters and not some other servant in the house, the better for you and the better for your pay slip. Now do you understand?'

'I do understand completely, ma'am,' said Monica confusedly, then she began with obvious reluctance, 'But you see, Mr Walters said…'

'Oh fuck Mr Walters,' shouted Nike with apparent frustration.

Monica looked stunned; nobody ever swore in the house; no one was allowed to swear. She covered her mouth with both of her hands as if the swear words had come out of her own mouth and not Nike's.

But Nike was beyond caring. 'To hell with Mr Walters,' she went on. 'From now henceforth, I demand to be given my own identity and not to be treated as a piece of furniture in Mr Walter's residence. Have I made myself clear?'

'Yes ma'am,' said Monica tearfully.

'Good,' said Nike. 'Now show me the way to my suite. I'll like to freshen up before meeting *my lord the king*,' said Nike sarcastically.

Monica led her out of the drawing room and into a spacious living room. Nike did not wait to admire the expensive décor in the living room. However, she could not but feel the presence of money in the air. There was so much opulence in the whole house, Nike felt choked.

Monica led her to the delicately carpeted staircase and they both climbed the stairs in total silence. At some point, Nike was sorry that she had overreacted and lashed out at Monica. The woman had only been protecting her job. Benjamin should be the victim of her tongue-lashing and not Monica. She looked up at Monica, who was a step ahead of her and her heart went out to her. She had a compulsion to apologise to her but she restrained herself. If she wanted respect from any of Benjamin's staff, she should begin to command it – now!

They got to the head of the stairs and Monica turned right; Nike followed suit. Monica opened the first door on the right and waited for Nike to go into the room and then she followed her in.

Nike looked in awe at the delicately decorated king-sized bed. She looked at the rug on the floor; it was white and fluffy. There was a bedside chest of drawers with different kinds of lavender on top of it. Nike walked to it and picked up a perfume. It was a Hugo Boss xx perfume. She put it down and picked another; it was a Very Valentino perfume. She noticed that all the perfumes were designer labelled. She opened the first drawer and her mouth fell open. Inside the drawer was the most beautiful diamond bracelet she had ever seen. She picked it up and kissed it; she loved diamonds. She was beginning to forgive Benjamin for his sauciness when Monica spoke.

'I'm so sorry, ma'am, but it's time to take a shower. That diamond is for you to wear tomorrow. It was actually bought for the former ma'am but since…' Monica faltered. She should not have made the last statement. *Oh God!* She cried silently, how could she have made such a stupid mistake? She looked at Nike, hoping to the heavens that she had not read a meaning to her last statement. But she had. Nike remembered Tonia and the humiliation she suffered at Benjamin's hands. She remembered what had brought her to Benjamin in the first place. She remembered her resolution to revenge on Tonia's behalf. Her blood boiled over.

Monica noticed this and said, 'Sorry, ma'am,' then she disappeared into one of the array of wardrobes attached to the wall. After a moment, she brought out an evening dress and laid it on the bed. Then she went to the chest of drawers and opened the second drawer. She brought out a cute little purse, a pair of earrings and a matching necklace. These, she lay on the bed beside the evening dress. Next, she opened one of the wardrobes and brought out some underwear.

'These, you will wear today, ma'am,' she said, satisfied with her work.

Nike barely looked at the items. 'Will I have the dignity of being by myself for one moment?' she asked cuttingly.

'Certainly, ma'am. I'll be back in an hour to assess you. Mr Walters will be ready for dinner in an hour and a half,' said Monica and she briskly walked out of the room. She seemed grateful to be rid of Nike for an hour.

Nike waited till the door closed behind Monica before she began to undress. She slowly zipped down her skirt and let it slip to her ankles; then she gingerly stepped out of the heap. Next, she unbuttoned her suit and blouse and piled them onto the skirt before slipping off her underwear. Before she went into the adjoining bathroom, she looked at the pile of used clothing including the underwear that she had just dumped in the middle of the room and a ripple of laughter rose to her throat. For the first time since she met Monica that evening, she saw something humorous and she laughed out loud. She tried to imagine how Monica would feel when she saw that her new ma'am was not nearly half as neat as they would expect Sir Benjamin's bride to be.

'At least, I will enjoy this while it lasts,' she said to herself before she entered the bathroom.

In the bathroom, she made a bubble bath and gingerly stepped into the warm, soapy water. She sat in the bath for longer than she knew was necessary before she stepped out and slowly towelled herself dry. She understood her own game. She was deliberately wasting time. Monica had given her an hour to get dressed and she was bound to prove to her that Nike was not one to be controlled by anyone. After Monica had mentioned *the other ma'am*, Nike had noticed that Monica was not exactly out to be wicked to her, but neither was she totally out to be nice to her; she was neither here nor there; she had merely been carrying out orders handed to her from above. Nike also noticed that the respect she had demanded had met with a form of silent hatred from Monica and she knew automatically that she was going to encounter much difficulty were she to make Monica totally obey her. Benjamin was the one who paid Monica's piper and obviously, Benjamin was the one who dictated the tunes. So, Nike made up her mind to frustrate Monica for as long as she lived in this house.

She came out of the bathroom with her towel wrapped around her and lay on the bed beside the clothing and the jewellery that Monica had neatly laid out for her. With her head turned towards the ceiling, she crossed her legs, waiting for Monica to come back and *assess* her for dinner as she had declared earlier. *Imagine the cheek of it* – she, Nike, would now be assessed like a mannequin.

'Well, we will see about that Monica,' she said aloud and waited; she could not wait to see Monica's reaction to the pile of clothes she had created on the floor and the fact that she was laying on the bed, almost fully undressed.

At exactly one hour after Monica left Nike, she came back into the room and the first thing that came to her attention was the pile of dirty laundry in the middle of the room. The smile on her face became frozen immediately. Nike saw this and almost chuckled; but she kept back the laughter. *Miss or Mrs Monica, as the case may be, must not know that she was playing games with her.*

Monica looked at the bed and saw Nike barefooted and with only her towel wrapped around her. She could not believe the sight that met her. *Hadn't she explained to this moron that Mr Walters would be waiting for her in a few minutes? Mr Walters had been very correct; this lady needed some brushing up.*

She, however, managed to keep on her frozen smile as she spoke to Nike in a clipped tone. 'I'm sorry to say this, ma'am, but Mr Walters will be greatly upset if you're not ready for dinner.'

'I suppose you're my chaperon. Not so?' asked Nike caustically.

'Yes I am. *I am your chaperon,*' said Monica with obvious dignity. She said the statement as if she was introducing herself to Nike as her guardian angel.

'Fine, and I suppose you know your job enough to be able to carry it out to the best of your ability. Not so?' said Nike with obvious sarcasm.

Monica looked so angry, her face burned, but she still kept her frozen smile as she answered tersely. 'Of course, ma'am. I'm able to carry out my job effectively. That's why Mr Walters employed me. I've been chaperon for a lot of celebrities like—'

'I do not care about whomever you've chaperoned in the past. All I know is that I'm not satisfied with your job. I may have to tell Benjamin that I need a change of chaperon,' said Nike cuttingly.

The smile vanished from Monica's face. She looked at Nike for a few seconds before replying in a dangerously low tone. 'You will not do that, ma'am.' Her facial expression was a good match to her voice which was laden with pure hatred.

'Oh, we shall see about that shan't we, darling?' said Nike as she got up from the bed and untied her towel. She tried to guess the amount of money Benjamin paid Monica for the services she was meant to render to her, and she failed; but one thing she knew was that it must be a huge amount of money for Monica to forgo the so-called celebrities and cling desperately onto her.

Nike untied the towel and let it slip down her body. Monica stood, mouth agape. She was mesmerised by Nike's sheer beauty. In all her experience as a chaperon, she had not seen a woman so perfect. Nike was indeed a paragon of beauty; she had the right curves in the right places and there seemed to be nothing out of place on her. She had well-rounded buttocks and her tummy was so flat, she looked like she'd spent all her life at the gym. Monica was especially stupefied by Nike's boobs; they were very big, probably a 40 F, but they were very firm and her nipples jutted out perfectly on them. If Monica had not worked with several people who had gone *under the knife* to acquire different shapes and sizes of breasts; If Monica had not acquired enough experience to be able to distinguish natural breasts from those stuffed with silicone, she would have bet her life that Nike had had a boob job. But she knew without a doubt that Nike's attractive boobs were a natural gift. Her skin was also blemish free and her complexion was so lucid, she looked so blindingly beautiful; Monica felt that it must have taken God a considerable time creating her. *No wonder Mr Walters was bent on getting married to her, despite her character shortcomings*, Monica reasoned. How could someone with apparently no morals, be so physically beautiful? Monica wondered; *it was just not fair.*

Nike knew that Monica was appraising her beauty, or *assessing her beauty* as Monica would say. She always had that effect on people, male or female, big or small. The only difference was the reaction of the people to her beauty. Men always dreamt of getting in-between her legs while fellow women were always riddled with jealousy.

She finally got dressed and Monica helped with her makeup. When she checked her own reflection in the mirror, she liked what she saw. The evening gown greatly accentuated her natural curves and the creaminess of the dress fitted perfectly with her golden brown colour. The beaded necklace and earrings made her dressing so complete; she looked and felt like a queen.

She picked her little purse and made to leave the room but before she got to the door, Monica, who had been quiet for some time, spoke. 'S…orry, ma'am,' she said, and Nike, wondering what she was sorry for this time, turned round to face her. She was beginning to get the feeling that part of the instructions Benjamin laid down was for Monica to apologise to her every second.

'What are you sorry for this time, Monica?' she asked irritably.

'I'm s…so sorry; I don't mean to be rude, but you see, you can't be angry when you go to Mr Walters. He can be quite volatile and he might just assume that… well, he might assume that I've not done a proper job.'

Nike nearly burst into flames of anger. She could not imagine the cheek of it. She knew the two words Monica had left out of her speech – *on you!* Benjamin had instructed them to do a proper job *on her!* Benjamin had obviously cut her an image of a girl who had been picked out of a slum awaiting an *extreme makeover*! She wondered if the damned marriage would eventually take place. She was not so sure!

She decided to reserve her temper for Benjamin; there was no point arguing with a woman who seemed to have been programmed to irritate her.

Monica led her downstairs towards the large drawing room. She walked briskly past the painting that had captured Nike attention earlier in the day and quickly opened a pair of sliding doors with a remote control and they stepped out onto the veranda. There, Nike was stupefied as a beautiful sight greeted her. She glanced around the most beautiful horticulture she had ever set her eyes on. Even in the dimly lit veranda, she could make out the different coloured daffodils and lilies and hibiscus flowers.

Monica walked past the array of flowers, giving Nike absolutely no room to stop and admire them. Suddenly, Monica turned left and another pair of sliding doors opened to let them in. They went in and were met by a Chinese man dressed in a black suit, complete with a white shirt and a black bowtie.

'Hi, Yung Chu,' said Monica. 'How are you today?'

Yung Chu did not reply; he merely bowed deeply to both of them and he led them along the corridor to a large, expensively furnished sitting area. He opened the door and curtsied again.   Monica and Nike entered the sitting area and Yung Chu shut the door firmly behind them. Nike thought all these protocols they had to pass through before she was led into Benjamin's presence very funny. She was not aware that Benjamin had built such an empire for himself. *Very little wonder he was so power crazy; no wonder Monica was so much in awe of him.* So this was what Tonia had been enjoying for a year. Little wonder then that she hardly spent a night in the flat they once shared in Bermondsey. Nike felt she would postpone Benjamin's punishment and stay married to him for the agreed time so she also could enjoy being a queen in Benjamin Walter's kingdom. She was beginning to like the feeling.

Monica pressed a few buttons on the door at the far end of the sitting room and finally, they were ushered into Benjamin's presence. Benjamin was seated with his legs crossed on a large leather sofa and a mobile phone to his right ear. Monica bowed and left immediately. Benjamin motioned for Nike to sit and he continued talking on the mobile phone.

Nike waited till Benjamin snapped the flip of his mobile phone shut before she said angrily, 'What the hell was all that about, Benjamin?'

Benjamin looked at her for a long time before he replied her in a dangerously low voice. 'What the hell was all *what* about?'

'You damn well know what I'm talking about, Benjamin, so cut the pretence,' shouted Nike.

'Young lady, you are not allowed to swear and you are not allowed to shout. I suppose by now, you should have mastered the lessons you were taught. I paid handsomely for those lessons you know?' retorted Benjamin icily.

Nike could not believe the cheek of it. 'What do you take me for? One of your servants?' she said, her eyes blazing. Without waiting for Benjamin to give her a reply, she went on. 'I take exception to being treated as one of your personal effects by your employees; and I assume Monica was strictly acting under your stupid instructions.'

'You may choose to call yourself whatever you like,' said Benjamin, unperturbed, and he continued. 'Officially, you are supposed to be my fiancée; I *employed* you to be my official bride and I believe that I have kept my part of the bargain by giving you a handsome reward. The choice is yours; you either abide by my rules or get sacked,' Benjamin said with apparent finality.

Nike could not believe what Benjamin had just said; she could not believe the cheek of it – the sheer cold bluntness with which Benjamin had just told her the truth about their relationship. Her marriage plans with Benjamin were truly a hoax; it was an agreement between both of them to ensure Benjamin achieved popularity amongst people of colour in his mayoral race, while she got financial buoyancy from Benjamin along with societal respect when she eventually became his first lady, as the wife of the Mayor of London. But at least, as his fiancée, Benjamin ought to ensure she got a high degree of respect from his staff. After all, she had paid her dues; she worked tirelessly for Benjamin to be liked among Africans and Asians.

She managed to put her temper under control before asking calmly, 'If I get sacked, what becomes of my toil, my efforts during your numerous campaigns?'

'It's really up to you, my love,' said Benjamin with sarcasm. 'The ball is in your court; you either take it or leave it. But if you choose to take it, you have to abide by my rules; in this game, Nike, I call the shots.'

Nike gazed at Benjamin spookily; Benjamin's gaze matched hers with equal degree.

Nike was thinking, *if only you knew me very well, Benjamin, you wouldn't mess up with me. You have touched the tail of the lioness; you must surely face the wrath of the lioness.*

As an idea unfolded in Nike's mind, a slow, dangerous smile formed on her lips and lit up her face.

Tomorrow, Benjamin would face the wrath of the Lioness!

Nike dressed up with extra care the next afternoon, mostly because Monica had been fussy over her all day. She had been darting in and out of Nike's room, making sure that nothing –absolutely nothing – went wrong. Nike could not blame her; she had shown Monica times without number that reliability was just not in her diction.

'This is a very special day for Mr Walters,' Monica had told her times without number that day. It was as if she was trying to hammer it into Nike's head that the very best behaviour was expected.

When she got fed up hearing Monica's rhetoric, Nike had replied scornfully that she knew that. She told Monica through gritted teeth that she had known it had to be a very special day since Benjamin had decided to choose that day to officially introduce her to his party members.

Benjamin had called her several times, since the beginning of the week before, to remind her of the need for her to dress in a manner that would *befit* him. She had been attended to by different fashion icons and professionals, who taught her how to dress, speak and behave befittingly as the wife of a very important public figure; and she had gone through the rigours of the numerous training judiciously. She had complied with his all wishes – up until now.

They were due to be at the hotel in an hour. Benjamin had been invited by his political party to a formal dinner and he had decided to seize the opportunity to introduce Nike formally as his bride to be. He had warned that she would be under much scrutiny by his political rivals and supporters. More importantly, he had told her that she had to be perfect because of the press.

Benjamin, himself, was always dressed impeccably with not a single hair on his head out of place. The manner in which he talked in public was exceptional. In the eyes of the public, Benjamin was indeed an epitome of perfection.

Sometimes, Nike wondered what the obsession was all about. One day, she had questioned him about his obsession over dinner and he had brushed her questions aside with diplomacy.

Now, as Nike checked herself in the full length mirror, she almost felt sorry for Benjamin. However, she had made up her mind to carry out the deed and end everything today.

Satisfied that her dressing and composure would not betray what she had in mind, she turned her back to Monica and spread her hands wide for Monica to slip on her fluffy white coat.

Benjamin was seated in the back of the metallic-coloured Bentley by the time she got to the car.

The chauffeur deftly opened the door for her as she stepped outside and he waited for her to settle comfortably beside Benjamin before he gently closed the door. He then got behind the steering wheel and drove smoothly towards the Chancery Court hotel. As the chauffeur drove along, Benjamin seemed to be locked in his own world. He did not say a word to Nike throughout the journey. *All the better*, thought Nike. *Secrets were better kept secret when words were not uttered.*

They arrived at the venue for the dinner at exactly three o'clock. Nike was not surprised to see that tons of journalists, photographers and paparazzi had surrounded the venue. She was, however, grateful for the security arrangements at the venue. With the help of the security personnel, they were able to escape the throng of reporters ready to throw questions at them.

By three-fifteen p.m., they were seated in the dining hall of the hotel. Nike glanced around the hall and took in the different dignitaries who were in attendance. She noticed the incumbent Mayor of London, Mr Fred Edwards, who happened to be Benjamin's running mate and arch enemy. She noticed he was seated as far away from where she and Benjamin sat as possible. She knew without being told that the incumbent Mayor was at the luncheon not to honour Benjamin, but to see his probable *disgrace*.

A press conference had been slated for seven p.m. Then, journalists and people in rival parties would be given the opportunities to throw different questions at Benjamin, ranging from his family background, to his motive for vying for the highly coveted post of the Mayor of London and finally, he would be asked what he intended to do when he got elected into office, *should he* eventually be elected.

Nike knew that Benjamin's rivals were ready with difficult questions and insinuations intended to throw him off balance. Nike also knew for sure that Benjamin was smart and intellectually capable of thwarting all their political gimmicks. What Nike was, however, not sure of was Benjamin's ability to withstand the shocker that she was about to unleash on him!

Nike's eyes shifted from the incumbent mayor and her gaze rested on the wife of the Prime Minister. Although, Benjamin had no cordial relationship with the prime minister, his wife had endeavoured to come and represent her husband anyway. As Nike took in the petite figure sitting on the same table, chatting away with the Mayor, she wondered how the Prime Minister's wife would handle the saga that was about to take place.

Nike quickly scanned the whole dining area with her eyes and she was immensely proud to be seated with such important people in the society. She, a once brutalised and rejected pregnant girl, a very vulnerable girl who had no inkling of what the future held in store for her, was sitting at a table with the high and mighty in the British society. She was moved to tears as she was fleetingly reminded of her past. Even though the relationship between herself and Benjamin was some sort of a hoax, she, and none other, was here to assume the dignity of it. Tonia's tearful face the night Benjamin jilted her suddenly came to mind, and she was torn between making good her resolve to punish Benjamin for what he had done, and foregoing her resolve and playing up her part as Benjamin's intended wife.

Just then, Benjamin leaned towards her, smiling and he whispered something that was only audible to her.

'Why are you looking around like you just arrived from an African jungle? I believe you've had adequate training and I expect you to behave likewise. That's what I paid Monica and the others for, you know.'

Benjamin had whispered to her in his usual arrogant manner and Nike had been rescued from her dilemma. Benjamin had unknowingly given Nike the go-ahead with her resolution to enact revenge on Tonia's behalf.

Nike turned back to Benjamin. Smiling up at him sexily, she intoned, 'It's alright, my darling. You need not worry about me. Monica and the other trainers did a perfect job on me.'

She would play the game with him until the right time came. *It always took two to tango.*

'Then let it reflect in your character,' said Benjamin tersely, but when Nike looked at him, he was still smiling.

Alright buddy, thought Nike, *two can always play the game!*

She smiled back at Benjamin.

Everyone at their table saw their secret exchange of smiles and the whispers they made in each other's ears and they thought them very lucky to be so much in love.

A smartly dressed waiter came to their table to take their orders.

Benjamin opened the menu and quickly scanned through, then he placed his orders. 'I'll have oriental king prawns in filo for starters; and then I'll have

Duckling breast with orange, cranberry and brandy sauce as the main course; and I'll make do with white chocolate and strawberry charlotte as dessert.'

The waiter scribbled away as Benjamin talked. He felt honoured to be serving the proposed Mayor of London; he was a great fan of Benjamin's and he wanted to give him the best service today; he wanted Benjamin to recognise him next time they met and wave at him.

Benjamin waited for the waiter to stop writing; although, he thought he could do better with a smarter waiter.

'Right, sir,' said the waiter at last. 'And for the lady?' he added smilingly, turning to Nike. But Benjamin was quick to answer; he did not trust Nike to pick the right choice.

'Oh, the lady will have the same as–' started Benjamin, but Nike cut him short.

'I'll have chicken paste with chardonnay and cranberry for starters,' she said without deigning a look at Benjamin. She however, sensed the look of warning Benjamin passed her, but she was undeterred. 'I'll have Lamb shank with red wine and Rosemary as the main course; and then I'll settle for the chocolate mousse with Rum Truffle as desert,' she finished, looking directly at the waiter.

'Right miss,' said the waiter and he scampered away.

When the waiter had gone, Benjamin tilted slightly towards Nike and with lips pursed, he said to her, 'You should have allowed me to do that ordering; now everything you ordered has more alcohol content than I want for you; I just hope you'll be sane enough to behave yourself at the end of the meal.'

'Well, we'll see about that,' replied Nike as she forced a smile to her lips.

What she meant by that statement was totally lost on Benjamin.

After dinner, Nike took a glass of champagne and sipped it slowly. Benjamin took out a little piece of paper, scribbled on it and passed it to her.

Nike read the note; it was a note of warning. Benjamin was warning her to stop taking alcohol. However, at that point in time, Nike did not care what Benjamin said or did anymore. She was smarting from the subtle insults that Benjamin had been passing to her. She saw a waiter passing and beckoned to him.

'Yes miss,' said the waiter pleasantly.

'Can I have a glass of Don Perignon please?' she said equally pleasantly.

'Of course, miss,' said the waiter as he promptly placed a glass of champagne in her hand.

'Thanks a lot,' said Nike to the waiter and she gulped the champagne down within seconds. By this time, Benjamin's expression had turned into a murderous one; but Nike was way past caring now. Next, she leaned across the table and picked up a glass of wine that had been placed before the French ambassador to Britain.

'May I have the honour of having your wine please?' she asked the French ambassador. She tried to sound pleasant enough, but her speech had started to slur.

'Certainly,' replied the French ambassador and he deftly passed her the drink.

Nike gulped it down within seconds.

Next, she leaned towards an MP, who was looking at her, clearly amused. Before Nike requested for his wine, he reached for it and gave it to her.

'My pleasure, madam,' said the MP as he handed Nike the drink.

'Th…th… thanks a lot,' said Nike as she took the drink. 'You're the best.'

At this time, all attention was on Benjamin's table. The would-be wife of the proposed mayor was indeed a spectacle to behold.

Benjamin's face was flushed as he took the drink from Nike's hand.

'What the hell do you think you're doing?' he yelled, almost standing up from his chair; he obviously could no longer keep his emotions under control.

'What…what d…do you mean, what the hell am I doing?' asked Nike, her words slurring. 'You asked me to behave myself and that's exactly what I'm doing, you sludge.'

The guests at their table gasped and some guest who sat at other tables close to theirs, laughed; Benjamin sat down in his chair and buried his head in his hands, clearly embarrassed. As if on cue, reporters and photographers came to their table and clicked away.

Some reporters rushed at Nike to interview her.

'Madam, can you say officially, what you are to the proposed mayor, Mr Benjamin Walters?' asked a reporter.

'Oh yes I can,' said Nike sweetly, 'I'm his f… fiancée.'

'Does that mean you're going to be his wife?' asked another.

'Oh yes, *dumbo*,' replied Nike, 'did you go to school at all?'

The reporter, who did not appear angry at Nike, continued his questioning. 'How would you describe the proposed mayor, Mr Benjamin Walters, who happens to be your fiancé?'

Nike belched loudly before answering, 'Oh, he's an arrogant, obnoxious, but generous man; he's even promised me a brand new Mercedes jeep and a mansion in St. John's Wood when he assumes office. Isn't he great?'

'He's very great indeed,' said the reporter; he was clearly amused as he asked further questions. 'May I know where our proposed mayor thinks he'll get the money for the jeep and the mansion he promised you, madam?'

Nike pretended to think deeply about the question. She put a finger to her temple and looked upwards for a while then she looked at the reporter who had asked her the question and shrugged. 'Honestly, I don't know and I don't really care,' she answered. 'You should work that out yourself. Right now, I feel like doing a big fat poo!'

Nike stood up from her chair then. She squeezed past the hoard of photographers and reporters and staggered towards the toilettes; and then, all of a sudden, she broke into a run, farting loudly as she ran along.

Some reporters covered their nostrils with their hands as they ran after her; they were not ready to lose a big fat story!

Nike's actions had caused uproar in the dining hall.

In the ensuing chaos, Benjamin's agent and personal assistant, along with the help of a few policemen, were able to sneak the clearly embarrassed Mr Walters out of the dining hall before the reporters were able to bombard him with questions.

However, only one reaction came from the table of the incumbent Mayor of London; all the guests seated on that table were immensely happy.

Mr Fred Edwards blew a kiss towards the location of the toilets, where Nike had disappeared. He had secured a huge point against his adversary!

Nike got to the door marked 'toilets' at the end of a long corridor that was adjacent to the dining area. She quickly opened the door, went in and shut the door with a loud bang before any of the reporters could follow her in.

Once inside, she bolted the door from behind and rested her frame against it, unmindful of the knocks and shuffling of feet coming from the other side. She quickly thought of how to escape the arena without anyone being aware. In the present circumstance, the main entrance was definitely out of it. She looked up and saw a set of doors on each side of the wall. One was marked 'Gents' with the drawing of a boy beneath it; while the other was marked 'Ladies' with the drawing of a girl in a skirt beneath it. She quickly moved towards the door marked 'Ladies' which she opened and went in. Luckily for her, there was no one in there, but she knew it was just going to be a matter of time before the authorities would force the door she had locked open.

At the right hand side, she saw a door marked 'cloak' and she opened it. Inside the cloak cupboard hung a waitress' uniform and two leather jackets; one was brown and the other was black. She unhooked the black jacket and but it on. The jacket hung loosely on her slim body but she did not mind the fact. She checked her reflection in the mirror and determined that her dress was well hidden underneath the jacket. It was just as well.

Next, she removed the pins that Monica had used to hold her hair in place. She momentarily felt sorry that she had to let go of the fashionable design that Monica had shaped her hair into. However, this was no time for a display of fashion; this was a time for the pursuit of safety!

Next, she opened a tap and buried her head underneath the running water then she wet some tissue and made her face free of all make-up.

Satisfied that it would take a long time for anyone to relate her to the notorious woman that was Benjamin Walter's fiancée (if she still was), she dashed out of the ladies. When she got to the door that led to the ladies and the gents, her mind searched frantically for a way to escape.

After a while, she gently unlocked the door and opened it a little; people still thronged around the door. She quickly clicked it shut, bolted it and ran back to the ladies.

At the ladies, she opened the cupboard marked 'cloak', brought out the waitress' uniform and quickly changed into it. The big uniform hung unflatteringly on her slender body. However, when she checked herself in the mirror, she was sure that no one would know who she was.

On her way out, she picked up a mopping bucket and a mop and opened the door. She stepped aside as reporters rushed past her into the toilets. Satisfied that no one had recognised her, she bent her head, took out the mop from the bucket and scrubbed her way out of the hotel.

Once outside the hotel, she removed her shoes, and leaving the mop on the ground by the entrance of the hotel, she ran as far away from the hotel as her legs could carry her. As she ran, she spotted a black cab parked on the side of the street. She went over to the cab and opened the door. She opened her purse and gave the driver a generous amount of money, then she instructed him to take her to Alex Tucker's residence in Goldhurst Terrace, NW6.

The black cab dropped Nike in front of the house at Goldhurst Terrace at eight thirty-six in the evening. She was grateful that Benjamin was not aware of her abode at the moment; she should have enough time to pack her bags and get out of Alex's house before Benjamin found out where she lived. The way Benjamin looked back at the dinner hall a couple of hours before, she did not expect him to do less than commit murder. But before Benjamin could make mince meat out of her, she would be far away in Africa; not in some jungle, but in the opulence of her grandfather's palace. She would *chill* out there for some months until the news of what she had done died down.

Knowing fully well that Alex would be in his study and even the slightest noise would irritate him, she gently slotted her key into the key-hole and turned the knob slowly and gently. She was tired and she did not want any confrontations with Alex. She planned to go straight to bed after making her face free of all makeup. She hated to go to bed with even the lightest of all makeup. She got into the living room and tiptoed toward her bedroom; but before she got to the door of her bedroom, she heard Alex's voice behind her.

'Why are you prowling around my house like an evil spirit?'

Nike froze for a moment and turned to face Alex. She saw Alex's tired eyes and decided that he had not slept a wink since she left the house the previous day. She felt a little pity for him. He was standing at the bottom of the stairs, one hand holding the banister railing and the other hand was placed akimbo. His shirt was creased and his hair, ruffled.

Nike knew that Alex was definitely taking her supposed relationship with Benjamin Walters a little too hard. She sincerely hoped that there would not be another argument between them; she did not just feel up to it.

'I'm awfully sorry for disturbing your peace this evening,' she said with an attempt at being pleasant. 'I tried not to make a noise but, alas, you've got very sensitive ears, your highness,' she finished, making a mock bow.

Alex saw her ruffled hair and her blouse which appeared to have been hurriedly buttoned. He noticed that the top-most button was not slotted into its rightful button-hole; rather, the second button was fixed into the hole meant for the first. It made the blouse stand on her in a ridiculous fashion. Alex looked at Nike's feet – they were bare. Raw jealousy rose up in him. Nike saw this and wanting to escape further questions which would of course, bring forth heated arguments as usual, she said, 'I might as well go to bed so I don't disturb you further.' And with that, she turned round, opened the door of her bedroom and hurriedly went in. Alex saw the door firmly close shut after Nike and he heard a click as she securely locked the door.

Alex woke up very early the following morning. He had a shower and got dressed hurriedly. He put on a dark blue Hugo Boss suit on a white shirt. He wore a suitable light blue tie and checked his reflection in the bedside mirror; he looked good. He picked up his briefcase and walked out of the room. He was the lawyer in charge of the divorce between Sir Luis Fernando, a Brazilian business mogul and his estranged wife, Ann-Marie. It was a celebrated divorce case which involved a lot of money. It had been rumoured by the media nationwide that the divorce settlement would be the largest to date.

Alex's boss, Sir Richard Stonewall had appointed Alex as the leading barrister in the case. He knew the move was not a result of Sir Stonewall' deep love for him, for Sir Stonewall had never been known to love anybody (he only loved his job and the money it brought him). Alex knew that his appointment was rather a test of his capability as a prospective partner in the law firm. He had made applications severally to become a partner at the firm and he had always received a negative answer from the management on the premise that he had not spent the minimum five years of law practice with the firm.

Alex had waited until he had spent six years with the law firm and then he had made another application. He knew that the management of the firm would not have a tenable excuse to refuse him now. He was a brilliant lawyer with brilliant academic records.

However, Sir Richard Stonewall was not one to offer anyone a position on a platter of gold. His mission statement was always – *You desire it, you work for it!*

And Alex was very much determined to work for it. His firm was representing Sir Luis Fernando and he was the leading lawyer. He had been commissioned to beat down the alimony to the lowest possible amount and Alex was determined to accomplish the assignment. He had arranged a meeting with the lawyers of Mrs Ann-Marie Fernando in respect of the settlement and he knew he must not be late. He checked his watch. The time was six fifteen in the morning. He still had enough time to listen to the weather forecast. He switched on the television and tuned the channel to BBC News.

'…And now the breaking news again,' the newscaster was saying; Alex was anxious to hear the weather forecast. He willed the news reader to skip the breaking news, whatever it was and go straight to how the weather was.

However, the breaking news got Alex rooted to a spot, for before his very eyes, he saw Nike Adeogun drunk and misbehaving on television.

'Mr Benjamin Walters disgraced at a dinner party by his fiancée, Miss Nike Adeogun…' the news reader said before shifting the news to another highlight.

Alex put his briefcase on the sofa and rubbed his eyes with his two hands. He could not believe what he was seeing; neither could he believe what he had heard. *Was Nike crazy?* Alex was not sure whether he should laugh or cry. Nike was surely the limit. *The girl was really crazy,* he thought. *She's gone totally insane.*

Leaving the television on, he left the living room and ran to Nike's room. After the second knock, Nike answered from behind the locked door.

'Who's it?' she asked sleepily.

'It's me. Alex. Please open the door.'

After a while, Alex heard a click and the door opened to reveal a very sleepy Nike in pyjama top and bottom.

'What can I do for you?' Nike asked him, yawning.

Alex brushed past her and entered the room. 'Nike, what happened?' he asked without preamble.

Nike stifled another yawn before answering. 'What do you mean, *what happened?*'

'I mean what happened yesterday at the Chancery Court hotel.'

'Oh, the story's already out isn't it?' asked Nike.

'The story's out and I want to know everything,' said Alex with finality.

Nike told him everything right from the beginning; she told him why she had gone into an arranged relationship with Benjamin Walters and how she had planned and waited all along for the day she would humiliate him, just as he had humiliated her friend and flatmate, Tonia.

By the time Nike got to the end of her story, Alex was having so many hiccups as a result of laughing so much.

'...And now, I have to go hide somewhere until the heat cools down,' Nike finished.

Alex did not want Nike to leave his house; not now that he knew what she had really been up to with Benjamin. Now that he knew he could get her back into his life, he would not be stupid to let her slip through his fingers like she almost did.

'No, no, don't leave,' he said to Nike's surprise. 'I don't want you to leave; I've missed you so much, Nike.' He moved close to her and she walked into his arms. She had definitely missed him too. She raised her head and they were soon locked in a passionate kiss.

When they disengaged, Alex looked deeply into Nike's eyes and said with a voice laden with deep emotion, 'Marry me, Nike.'

Just then the clock in the living room chimed seven o'clock; Alex remembered the meeting he had with Ann-Marie Fernando's lawyers.

'Oops!' he exclaimed. 'I should be on my way now; but Nike, I don't want you to go anywhere. I want you stay to here with me.'

Nike sighed and shook her head. 'I need to go to a big town in Nigeria where my grandfather is the King. At least, I will be assured safety there,' she said.

Alex thought about this for a while; he really could not afford to lose Nike again.

'Alright, I'll go with you,' he said.

Nike looked at him, very surprised.

'Are you sure?' she asked at last.

'Very sure,' replied Alex confidently. 'I'll go to the ends of the earth with you!'

Chapter 48

The meeting between Alex and Mrs Ann-Marie Fernando's lawyers went smoothly. Alex had, in fact, expected more difficulty than the lawyers posed. The meeting had lasted for four hours and after careful and concise deliberations between both parties, it was agreed that the alimony would be settled out of court. A six-figure sum of money was penned down as the money that would eventually be accrued to Mrs Ann-Marie Fernando.

However, a three-week probationary period was agreed upon before the agreement would be signed. Because Mrs Ann-Marie Fernando had always made it clear that she would be content with whatever alimony her lawyers decided on, Alex was one hundred per cent sure that the case had been won. He had been able to beat the alimony down to the barest minimum. Even sir Richard Stonewall could not have done better. Alex was very proud of himself.

'Well done, my boy. Well done,' Sir Richard Stonewall enthused, as he read the report later in the day.

Alex sat proudly on the chair opposite his boss as they discussed the case. Now, he was very sure that Sir Richard Stonewall would append his signature to his application to be made a partner at the law firm.

Before he left Sir Stonewall's office, he decided to make an unusual request.

'Sir, may I take a week's leave from the office starting from next week?'

Sir Stonewall looked up from the report he was studying. He removed the pair of thick rimmed glasses he was wearing from his face before he replied tersely. 'My boy, the job's not completed yet. The deal's yet to be signed; we can't afford to make a costly slip now.'

Sir Stonewall replaced his glasses and continued reading.

'Of course, we can't,' replied Alex. 'But the job's as good as done and I shall be back to sign the deal; I promise.'

Once again, Sir Richard Stonewall removed his thick rimmed spectacles from his face and asked Alex another question, with a little show of concern.

If Alex was insistent on travelling out of the country at this critical time, then the journey must be very important, he thought.

'This trip you're trying to embark on; how important is it to you?'

'Very important, sir,' replied Alex.

Sir Stonewall was thoughtful for a while. He nibbled at the end of his spectacles for a while before asking Alex, 'You think this trip's more important than your career, your prospect as a partner in the firm?'

Alex knew he was being tested and he knew the right answer to give.

'Nothing's as important to me as my career, sir. That's why I've made it mandatory for my fiancée to shelve any further plans with her family and come back to the U.K. with me after one week of our stay in Africa – with or without her family's approval; otherwise, our upcoming marriage would be cancelled.'

Alex watched Sir Stonewall's features relax and he knew he had said the right thing. Sir Stonewall always put his job before anything else. He was known to have been married and divorced three times because he constantly chose his career over his family.

'You're allowed exactly five working days off, starting from the twenty-fourth,' said Sir Stonewall after a while. 'But remember, if you're not back by the end of the week, consider your career with this office over. Is that understood?'

'It's well understood, sir,' replied Alex elatedly. 'Thank you very much.'

It was with some degree of elation that Alex relayed his victory at securing a vacation from his busy office to Nike, despite his tight schedule.

'That means you really want to travel to Nigeria with me,' stated Nike.

'That means I really want to travel anywhere with you,' affirmed Alex, taking her in his arms.

Nike was deeply touched. Alex must really be in love with her to want to travel to a totally unfamiliar continent with her. *Was he really serious about wanting to marry her? Would they be better off married? Would she be happy married to Alex? Would they live happily ever after?*

'Tell me how to go about securing a visa to your country,' said Alex, jolting her out of her reverie.

'That's no problem,' she said. 'We'll go to the Nigerian embassy as a couple and I'll take along the necessary documents. Your visa should be ready within a few days.'

Chapter 49

Nigeria, Africa

Their flight to Nigeria was without turbulence. To Alex, the six-hour journey seemed to drag. However much he loved adventure, this would be his first time on the continent of Africa and he had mixed feelings about the journey he had decided to embark on. His decision had been made on impulse and several times during the journey, he had thought of catching the next available flight back to the United Kingdom as soon as the aeroplane landed at the Murtala Mohammed airport in Lagos. He looked at Nike, who was stretched out on the seat beside him; she was fast asleep with a copy of the novel she had been reading earlier almost dropping off her hand. He took the novel and began to read.

They arrived in Lagos, Nigeria at twelve-thirty p.m., Nigerian time. After the usual hustle and bustle of the immigration procedure at the Murtala Mohammed International airport, they were finally given a pass out of the airport. As soon as they got out of the exit of the airport, they felt a rush of heat beat against their faces. Nike breathed in the air; she felt suddenly refreshed; she was back in good old Africa. Three taxi men rushed at them, begging for their clientele in pidgeon English.

'*Madam, I beg where you want go?*' one man asked.

'*Na me see them first, na me go carry them,*' said another.

'Madam, come inside my taxi. It's the best; very clean; very clean indeed,' said yet another.

Nike assessed the third taxi man from head to toe; he wore a dirty brown T-shirt which Nike was very sure, used to be dark red in colour. The shirt had obviously been worn for several months without being dipped into a bucket of soapy water. The taxi man had on a pair of tattered jeans and a matching pair of tattered bathroom slippers. He was looking very dirty – very dirty indeed – but before Nike could decline his offer, one of the other taxi men shouted.

'Sharrap! I saw them first, so I will carry them first. *Na me go take the hard currency today,*' said the man. With lips pursed and his chocolate-coloured teeth exposed, he clenched his fists and moved viciously towards the dirty looking man.

The dirty looking man, who was obviously bigger and rougher looking, saw this and rushed at him. Before the onlookers could decipher what was actually going on, the man with the chocolate-coloured teeth was on the floor with blood gushing out of his forehead and his mouth; two of his brown teeth lay beside him on the floor.

Alex looked on in horror as a crowd began to gather at the scene. Nike tugged at Alex's shirt and told him to move away from the scene but Alex protested saying they had to call the police. Nike shrugged and moved on; then she stopped and turned back. She shouted at Alex, saying, 'Suit yourself, but don't blame me if you find yourself in a Nigerian jail tonight.' When she saw Alex's hesitation, she quickly added, 'This is not Great Britain, you know?'

Alex moved away quickly; he picked up his traveller's bag and, dragging it behind him, he followed Nike to the airport car park.

'Why would I be jailed for another man's crime?' Alex asked Nike as they pulled their suitcases along the pavement.

'Because in Nigeria, anything can happen,' was all Nike said as she walked on. Her demeanour showed Alex that she was not ready to entertain further questions; so Alex kept quiet and pulled his traveller's bag after Nike.

Before they got to the car park, Nike saw a taxi cab that looked neat enough and she beckoned for the driver to stop. They debated on the price in a language that Alex did not understand and after a while, Nike seemed satisfied and motioned for Alex to take his luggage to the boot of the taxi. The taxi man opened the boot and after stacking in the luggage, shut the boot loudly. The boot opened automatically. He tried to shut it again, and again, the boot opened of its own accord. The taxi man smiled sheepishly at Alex and Nike and said to them, 'Don't worry, everything will be alright.'

He dashed into the car, opened the glove compartment and brought out a long rope. He went to the boot and pulled it open. He passed the end of the rope through an opening in the upper part of the boot and connected it to an opening on the lower part; then he fastened the rope, pulling it as hard as he could. After a while, satisfied that he had done a good job of it, he smiled at Nike and Alex again and said proudly, 'See, I told you that everything would be alright.'

Alex sincerely hoped so. He looked at the boot; it was slightly open and he could partly see their luggage scattered inside it. He feared that the rope would snap open as they went along and their bags would fly out of the boot. He feared mostly for their safety. He expressed his fear to Nike who shrugged and told him they would be fine. She was beginning to lose her patience and all she wanted to do was get away from the airport; and besides, the weather was beginning to get really hot; she could not wait to get to the hotel which she knew would be adequately air-conditioned.

The driver got into the taxi and urged them to get into the back of the taxi. Nike went into the car and waited for Alex to follow suit but Alex didn't. He just stood there, looking gobsmacked. The taxi driver's seat belt was a replica of the rope he had used to hold the boot together. He could not believe what he was seeing. He rubbed his eyes with his hands and opened them; the taxi driver's seat belt was still a rope!

'Alex, get the hell inside the car and let's go,' Nike shouted from inside the taxi.

'No, ma'am,' said Alex determinedly. 'There's no way in hell I will step a foot in this damned taxi… There's absolutely no way.' And with that, he turned to leave. Nike sighed exasperatedly and jumped out of the taxi.

'Alex,' she called out to him. Alex waited and she continued. 'Alex, I'm sick and I'm tired of all this. This is about the best cab around and we've already reached an agreement on the price, which I would say is relatively cheap. Why don't we just take the cab and leave?'

'You mean we should put our damned lives at risk because the damned cab's cheap? I mean, just look at his seat belt.' He pointed at the driver who was looking quite confused, the rope he had converted into a seatbelt tightly fastened diagonally on him. He could not fathom what was amiss. Alex went on, 'does the guy want to commit suicide? No way, babe. Find me a nice cab with a nice seatbelt and a lockable boot and I'll pay for it,' said Alex stubbornly.

Exasperated, Nike ran her hand through her hair and made a last attempt at making Alex see reason with her. 'See, Alex,' she began gently. 'Many of the cab men here are not trustworthy; many have links with unscrupulous people and some of them are actually robbers. The risk with this taxi is very little compared with some other ones with good bodies. Trust me, I've checked the driver out and he seems a nice guy. Believe me, those taxi drivers with good cars may get the money to maintain their cars from dubious means. This is my country and I should know better,' she finished, hoping to heavens that what she said had made an impact on Alex. It had.

Alex thought for a second then he got into the taxi. Nike made a sigh of relief and got in beside him.

When they were comfortably seated at the back of the taxi, the driver sped off. Throughout the journey to the hotel, Alex saw himself tensely holding the edge of the car seat he sat on.

'Relax darling,' said Nike. 'We'll be at the hotel soon and safely too.'

'Like hell we will,' Alex grunted. 'By the way, Nike, don't you have policemen in this country?'

'We do. Why do you ask?'

'How on earth can a car in this condition be on the street? I suppose your policemen don't work.'

Just then, they came to a police checkpoint. The driver wound down the window and spoke rapidly to the policeman who had come to him.

'Can I see your particulars?' asked the policeman.

'Oh yes! Of course,' said the driver as he opened the glove box and brought out a load of crumpled sheets of paper. Before he handed the papers to the police officer, he dipped his hand in his pocket and brought out a wad of notes; this, he placed beneath the stack of papers which he handed to the police officer. The police officer smiled, took the papers with the money and stuffed the notes inside his trouser pocket. Without as much as glancing at the papers, he returned them to the driver.

'Thanks,' said the driver before driving off.

'But that's criminal,' shouted Alex. 'The police officer took a bribe and he didn't look at the man's particulars; we should report this, Nike.'

'Sshh!' said Nike. 'Keep quiet and mind your own business,' said Nike reproachfully.

Alex wanted to make a protest but Nike placed a finger on his mouth.

'Welcome to my country,' she said.

Chapter 50

Great Britain

Professor Jeremy Flanders was a lecturer at City University. He was a professor of micro-biology with a speciality in mycology. He was known to be one of the most brilliant professors in the United Kingdom. Added to his brilliance, he was very kind hearted. He always took time off his heavy duty to attend to the academic needs of his students. His students and colleagues never hesitated to call on him should there be problem they might need his ingenuity at solving. He was one academic who was said to live a triangular life from the classroom to the science laboratory to the bathroom and back to the classroom. He was actively involved in the laboratory aspect of medicine. He cultivated different types of fungi and performed numerous and extensive experiments to find cures for many diseases caused by plant and animal fungi. He became a graduate at the very young age of twenty-one with a first class degree and by the age of twenty-five, he had obtained a PhD. Before he was thirty years old, his name had been included in the prestigious journal of scientists as a formidable mycologist and at the age of thirty-two, he was conferred with the prestigious title of a professor. In spite of all the accolades and honour accorded him wherever he went, Professor Flanders was known to be down to earth and long-suffering. He was liked and admired by all and sundry as a hard working and selfless being. When he was appointed a professor, one of his colleagues rightly pointed out during an oratory on him that his whole life was dedicated to his job and to the service of humanity.

Amidst all the cheer and liking, Professor Jeremy Flanders was a lonely man who had experienced love on the bitter side of life. He had fallen in love with a girl called Laila when he was in high school, and two months into the relationship, it had ended as abruptly as it started. Laila had simply written him a letter after graduating from the school, saying she had fallen in love with someone else.

He had again fallen in love with Margaret, a beautiful petit first year student in the same university he attended, when he was in his third year, and their relationship had lasted for two years. It ended when the lady decided to move back to her native Australia. All his letters to her were returned to sender and his phone calls were not picked up. He soon learnt from a friend, five months after Margaret left for Australia, that the lady was married and pregnant. He refused to believe what his friend told him and he decided to go to Australia and see things for himself. He could not bring himself to accept that Margaret would jilt him after all the love they shared.

That week, he bought a ticket to Australia and the day after he got the ticket he was on a flight to Australia. On the flight, he found excuses for Margaret's refusal to pick up or return his phone calls and her decision to return his numerous letters unread. *Maybe she was busy,* said a voice within him. *But busy doing what?* another countered. *Maybe she died,* said yet another. Jeremy Flanders shivered visibly.

As he stepped out of the lobby after going through immigration clearance, he received answers to all his questions; for before his very eyes, just a few feet from where he stood, he saw Margaret with her protruding tummy, kissing a short, bald man passionately. He stood dumbstruck for a while as he watched his love kiss another man, oblivious of any other being around her. Hot tears trickled down his face as he called out her name. She turned immediately and their eyes met. The first sentence Margaret made confirmed his fears.

'I'm… I'm so sorry, Jerry. I should have told you before now. This… this is my husband.'

Jeremy Flanders looked at the man that Margaret had just introduced to him as her husband. He was short; in fact, he was shorter than Margaret and he was fat. His bald head shone in the bright morning sunlight. The man had a broad smile which only made his ugly face uglier; he was obviously happy with himself for being deemed fit to be a husband to a lady as beautiful as Margaret. *What on earth could make Margaret leave him for a short, ugly man?* Jeremy wondered.

But then he noticed the man's shoes; they looked very expensive. In fact, Jeremy could bet his life those shoes were personalised. He slowly raised his eyes to look at the man's face one more time and as he did so, he took in his appearance; the man wore a very expensive Giorgio Armani suit. Jeremy also noticed a sleek metallic coloured Bentley parked beside the pair and he understood why Margaret had left him for the fat, bald man – money! Pure raw money. The man was obviously stinking rich, Jeremy knew.

Jeremy Flanders looked at Margaret for the last time and without uttering a word to either of them, he turned around and took the next available flight back to England.

After Margaret, Jeremy Flanders resolved never to fall in love again. He dedicated his life to academics and to the service of humanity.

However, when he was twenty-four years old, during his research to obtain his PhD degree, a lady, who was also undertaking research towards obtaining her PhD degree, was transferred to his school. They had been paired together during their research on a project and one thing led to another, Jeremy Flanders found himself falling in love again.

He saw Lillian as a brilliant lady who was as dedicated as himself to the cause of improving humanity. Besides, Lillian was a very beautiful lady; she was tall (almost as tall as Jeremy Flanders, who was six foot two inches in height) and slim and she possessed the kind of intelligence he was yet to see in another woman. Jeremy Flanders felt they belonged to each other. He was sure it would work this time. He proposed to her three months after they met and the wedding bells started ringing. Jeremy Flanders did not want a long courtship; he wanted more commitment from Lillian. He wanted to avoid a repetition of what happened between Margaret and himself. *Once beaten, twice shy,* they say.

But Lillian had run away with his best man on their wedding day!

A letter had been delivered to him in his home that morning as he checked himself in the mirror for the umpteenth time, dressed in his well-tailored wedding suit and a pair of expensive Italian leather shoes. Lillian had explained to him in the letter that she had fallen in love with the best man the moment she set her eyes on him and that she was sorry for the inconvenience she had caused him. And that had been all she wrote.

All efforts at locating her had proved futile. Lillian was no where to be found. She had simply disappeared.

Jeremy Flanders had withdrawn once more into his academic shell after that. He had buried himself into his work until the day he met Alice. Alice was so different from all the ladies he had dated. She was not beautiful, yet you could not call her ugly. She was just… well, faithful, humble, docile Alice.

Since they met on that fateful day she had run into his car, he had felt the need to be with her… to comfort her and to protect her. Although, Alice was voluptuous on the outside, she was very fragile on the inside.

Professor Flanders had taken a special interest in Alice after she told him her story. She had trustingly told him her story from beginning to the end and Jeremy had thought that their lives had some sort of similarities. They had become quite close and five months after they met, they were married. It was a quiet ceremony in a registry attended by only two of Professor Flanders' friends and none of Alice's except Phillippa, who was Alice's on and off friend. Alice had only opted to invite Phillippa to the wedding so she could have a chief bridesmaid.

After the wedding ceremony, they had a quiet dinner – just the two of them – and Professor Flanders had reiterated his promise to Alice to love and cherish her for the rest of his life. He had told her that her baby would be his baby and her life would be his life.

For the first time in Alice's life, she saw a glimmer of hope on the horizon. However, deep down within her, she still felt very much in love with Alex. Much as she tried to hide this fact, Jeremy Flanders knew it. He had known right from the beginning that he would have a difficult time winning Alice's heart totally to himself. He promised to show her all the love and care in the world until she was able to let go of Alex and give her heart totally to him.

He decided to give her time. He decided to give her all the time she needed to realise how much he cared for her.

Chapter 51

Professor Jeremy Flanders picked up the house telephone and dialled 999; he could not remember where he threw his mobile phone during the frenzy that followed when his wife's water broke. As soon as his call came through, he requested for the ambulance service.

'This is Professor Flanders. Could you please come to my house immediately; I'm afraid my wife's in labour.' He gave his address and post code and without waiting for a reply, he dropped the telephone and ran back to the bedroom. He held Alice by the hand and stroked her hair. He bent down and kissed her forehead before crooning in her ear, 'The ambulance will be here soon and you'll be fine, darling.'

She had better be fine, he thought to himself. He squeezed Alice's sweaty hand. *She had better be fine*. He loved her so much and he wanted to spend the rest of his life with her. Alice had gone through so much in her life and he wanted to make it up to her. He would show her love and care all the days of his life. He would make sure she forgot the trauma she had been through. He knew that she was still in love with the man who got her pregnant; that was why she could not bring herself to allow him to make love to her yet. But he resolved to make her happy all the same. He would warm his way into her heart and she would learn to love him. Her child would be his child, and they would…

The ambulance came then. Alice was put on a stretcher and carried into the ambulance. Professor Jeremy Flanders was by her side all the way to the hospital. He was rubbing her hands with his and crooning sweet things into her ear. He noticed that other drivers made way for the ambulance to pass as the siren blew away and he was grateful that he had decided to call the ambulance rather than take Alice to the hospital in his private car.

They got to the hospital fifteen minutes later and Alice was wheeled to the labour ward. Professor Flanders went in with her. He was given medical garments to put on and he went into the changing room. He came out five minutes later, looking like one of the doctors; the only difference was that the colour of his scrubs were blue and not green!

Alice was placed on a hospital bed and told to relax. Professor Flanders silently counted the number of medical professionals attending to Alice. They were six – two doctors and four nurses. Professor Flanders was very sure that Alice would get adequate treatment. *She would be alright*, he assured himself. He watched as a midwife put on a glove and inserted two fingers into Alice. Alice stifled a scream.

Brave girl, thought Professor Flanders.

Twenty-five minutes later, one of the doctors assigned to Alice summoned Professor Flanders into his office.

'I'm afraid your wife is not due to go into labour yet, Professor,' said Doctor Whyte as soon as the door was closed behind them.

'But her water broke before I called the ambulance,' said Professor Flanders.

'That's correct,' replied Dr Whyte, 'but her cervix is not dilated yet, so she's not contracting.' Dr Whyte paused to allow the information to sink in. He looked at Professor Flanders above his thick rimmed glasses. Professor Flanders tried to hide his emotions; he tried to hide his fear. Never had he been so scared in his life; not even when his terminally ill aunt was dying. He waited for the doctor to continue.

'Professor, I'm afraid we have to induce your wife to give birth. We already checked the baby and we fear he might be distressed.'

Professor Flanders thought for a while. 'Will that be okay? Will my wife be alright?' he asked. His expression registered the fear he had been trying to hide.

'Oh yes. Of course she'll be fine,' said the doctor. 'We will, however, need you to sign an agreement for permission to carry out an operation should there be a need for one.'

Doctor Whyte stayed with Professor Flanders as he signed the letter then he collected it and kept it in a drawer. Smiling, he motioned for Professor Flanders to come with him.

Alice was induced with prostaglandin gel the minute the doctor and the professor walked into the labour ward. Six hours later, a second dose of prostaglandin gel was administered on Alice. Thirty minutes later, a drip containing syntocinon was set up and the liquid was passed into Alice's vein.

After a while, the medical personnel gave up hope that Alice would give birth the natural way. Professor Flanders was ushered out of the labour ward as an operating table was wheeled in; but before Professor Flanders got out of the operating room, the baby came. A midwife cried for joy. Professor Flanders ran back to Alice's bedside. He held her hand and stroked her hair.

'You'll be fine,' he said. 'You'll be very fine, I'll make sure of that,' he said fiercely.

When the baby's head was fully out, everyone cried for the sheer miracle of it. Alice was urged to push some more. Although she was getting weaker by the minute, Alice summoned all the strength left in her and pushed.

The baby came out fully then and the placenta followed in its wake. Everyone in the room, especially Professor Flanders, was overjoyed.

'You made it, baby. You made it,' he cried, cradling Alice's head tenderly on his chest.

'Congratulations,' everyone said to her.

Alice could only nod in agreement. She was too weak to say a word.

The baby was wrapped in a soft white towel and placed in her arms. As Alice held him, she experienced mixed feelings. On one hand, she was overjoyed that she had brought a baby into the world. She felt fulfilled; she had, after all, been able to accomplish something in her life. On the other hand, she wished Alex was beside her to see the bundle of joy they had brought to this world together. She felt slightly unhappy. However, when she saw Professor Flanders smiling down at her and her baby, immense pride and joy written all over him, she soon forgot all about Alex and she was filled with happiness.

Suddenly, the baby whimpered, cried a little and went quiet. Everyone stood at attention; a nurse took the baby from Alice and immediately gave him to Doctor Whyte who took one look at the baby and immediately began an emergency resuscitation on him. All hands were on deck as all the medical personnel present fought to revive the baby. Forty-five minutes later, Doctor Whyte announced the saddest news in Alice Flanders' life.

'I'm sorry, we lost him... The baby is dead.'

Alice Flanders screamed and fainted.

Chapter 52

Reverend Alan Tucker sat rigidly amongst the other reverends in the front row of the pew in the church. Reverend Mathew Franklin, who happened to be his arch enemy, was preaching. Alan hated Reverend Mathew Franklin for one thing; *he was too pious*. He made Alan Tucker feel like the devil incarnate. To Reverend Mathew Franklin, going to heaven was always the soul of his messages and everyone who wished to go to heaven must be very holy. To Reverend Tucker, Reverend Franklin was too harsh in his preaching.

Alan Tucker was always reminded of his guilty past anytime Reverend Franklin preached and as usual, he struggled to suppress the guilty conscience that assailed him now.

Well, that was my past, Alan tried to reassure himself. His past was dead and buried. *All things have become new.* He hoped nothing would happen in the present or in the future that would make him dig up his past. He really hoped so and more importantly, he hoped nothing in his past would stop him from achieving his life long dream of becoming a knight of John Wesley. He tried to concentrate on Reverend Franklin's message.

'You must be holy, for God is holy; the bible says, flee all appearances of evil. Be holy for God your father is holy; He'll only listen to your prayers if you're holy; our God hates sin and all sinners shall go to hell.'

Reverend Alan Tucker lifted his face and looked at Reverend Franklin. At some point during the preaching, Reverend Franklin looked down at the row where Reverend Alan Tucker sat and their eyes met. Reverend Franklin fixed his gaze intently on Reverend Tucker as he changed his line of preaching.

'Even if you call yourself a Reverend and you are a sinner, you'll go to hell.' His eyes were still fixed on Reverend Tucker as he continued. 'Even if you're made a knight and you still commit sin, you shall not make heaven; thus says the word of God.'

Reverend Alan Tucker knew that those statements were directed at him. He could not fathom why Reverend Franklin took it upon himself to torment him. He remembered that he had extended an olive branch to Reverend

Franklin by humbly going to him after a church sermon one day and had asked him why he was so cold towards him and he had gotten a vague reply.

'I'm not against you at all, Reverend Tucker,' he had replied condescendingly. 'It's just that I have not received the conviction in my spirit that you are holy enough to be made a knight.' And with that, Reverend Franklin had left without deigning a look at him. Alan Tucker had never felt so embarrassed in his life!

On the day a vote was cast amongst the reverends on who should be chosen as a knight, Reverend Mathew Franklin was the only one who had cast a vote against Reverend Alan Tucker.

Now, as Reverend Mathew Franklin preached, pointedly condemning him in the midst of the whole church, Reverend Alan Tucker resolved to find a permanent solution to the enmity between them.

However, he was reminded of an impending problem that needed his urgent attention. Alex, his nephew had gone to Africa with that *good for nothing* Nike girl. Ironically, they had gone to the only country in Africa that he had warned Alex never to venture near. They had gone to Nigeria. He remembered telling Alex never to have anything to do with the bitch who called herself Nike.

Had the boy no brains at all? Or had he grown so much, he now chose to disobey him at will?

Alan felt his blood boil over by the thought. Alex had never gone against his wish until he met Nike. Now, he had gone to the only place he'd rather he didn't venture near.

Alan's cheeks became flushed with anger. He must find a way to make Alex come back to the United Kingdom immediately.

Reverend Mathew Franklin saw a change in Alan Tucker's countenance and feeling happy that his message was hitting his foe in places he obviously did not like, he continued his speech with vehemence. 'All sinners shall die; all sinners shall die; all sinners shall die…'

But this time, Alan Tucker was no longer interested in Reverend Mathew Franklin and his message; he had a far more pressing need; he had a mission to accomplish.

Chapter 53

The boss sat in his study which was situated in the upper part of his five bedroom mansion in Brighton. It was, in every way, different from the shabby underground compartment that used to be his office in the days of yore; in the days when he had the grace and freedom of youth on his side. His study, which doubled as his secret office, was tastefully furnished. Different kinds of books lined the cabinets built on the walls adjacent to where his table and chair lay. The rug on the floor of the room was cream-coloured and fluffy, with flowery patterns designed on it. The colour of the rug matched perfectly with that of the wall. Although the house was his secret rendezvous, he had bought it in the name of his late wife, whom he had murdered and had disposed of her beautiful body without a single trace. For a second, a fleeting image of his beautiful wife flashed before him. After all these years, he still missed his wife dearly; he missed her beautiful body; he missed her scent, the pleasure she gave him. But she had chosen to give herself to another man and to rub insult on the injury, she had threatened to expose him; she had posed as a threat to his repute and he had to do what he did to protect his good name. He shut his eyes and, rocking to and fro on his leather chair, he pressed his forefingers against his greying temples in a bid to shut out her memory from his mind. After a while, his mind was brought to the present; to the task at hand.

Now he was a sixty-five year old gentleman who had built an enviable reputation for himself over the years. As the years went by, he had less use of the services of his *boys*. He had to call for the murder of two of them and the third one had run away. He had only one of the boys left – Andrew, whom he usually called Andy; the most faithful one of them. He lifted his private mobile and dialled a number; Andy's terse voice came on immediately.

'Yes, Boss,' he said.
'Book me a flight to Nigeria immediately.'
'Yes, Boss.'
'And alert my contacts there. The traitor's days may now be numbered.'
'Yes, Boss.'

Andy was very happy. He had not entirely been satisfied with Mark in far away Africa. In fact, he had suggested to the Boss that he found a means to *waste* the guy when they got wind of him making plans to travel to Nigeria and settle there permanently. The boss had declined then, saying that if Mark kept his mouth shut, they would have no problem. But they had kept a close watch on Mark, unbeknown to him of course, over the years. They had received pictures of Mark as he transformed from a clean shaven man to a heavily bearded tanned looking man and then they had seen his pictures as a grey haired man. He had gained much weight over the years and the pictures of him that they received recently showed him as a happily married man with two kids. They had kept tabs on his family as well.

When Andy expressed his fears over the fact that Mark might tell his wife or any of his children about them, the Boss had dismissed his concern. He had felt that the Boss had developed a soft spot for Mark; and he had hated Mark with a passion. Nothing would make him happier than to see Mark die.

As soon as the Boss had planned to get rid of Mark, Andy had set to work with gusto. From the comfort of his room, he called up all their contacts in Nigeria and told them to get ready for the arrival of the Boss. However, he reminded them of the pact – all actions must be kept secret. Then he lay on his bed and rested his head on the pillow. He put a foot up the wall and took out a wrap of weed from underneath the bed. He lit it and puffed deeply. He slowly exhaled and watched as thick smoke rose from his nostrils and disappeared towards the ceiling. Satisfied, he removed the burning wrap of weed from his mouth and smiled. He sincerely hoped that Mark's death would be a painful one.

Chapter 54

Nigeria, Africa

Nike got up gingerly from the posh master bed in the room allocated to her and Alex at the Sheraton hotel. They had a shower together in the lovely en-suite bathroom after unpacking their bags and they had made passionate love afterwards. Now, as she got up from the bed, she felt a strong hand gently pull her back towards the bed. Before she could make any protest, Alex was on top of her. Her body allowed her to make just a short groan of protest before it began to respond to Alex's love making. Alex had always had that effect on her. She had always seen him as irresistible. Her body would always respond to him even at the oddest moments. Now, as her body succumbed to his rhythm, as they travelled out of planet earth together, Nike felt fulfilled for the second time that day. With each thrust that Alex made, Nike felt her legs go pleasantly weaker. Her head felt lighter one more time and she felt like she was out of this world. He prompted and she yielded; he sought and she gave and after a long while, they climaxed together and they came back to planet earth, happy and deeply satisfied.

Alex woke up with a start. He looked at Nike, who was still sleeping peacefully beside him and he gently removed his hand from beneath her head. Everywhere was quiet except from the slight snoring coming from Nike. He stretched over her and drew the window curtains beside her apart. It was very dark outside. He checked his watch; it said eleven thirty-four p.m. He really wished he could go out to the club or any recreation centre, but Nike had warned him earlier that it could be quite dangerous to go out at night in this part of the country.

He looked at Nike again; he was not sure she had been telling the truth. The lady could be full of mischief. She probably intended to instil fear into him so she would be in control of him throughout their stay in the country. Damning all consequences, he got up from the bed, went to the wardrobe and opened it. Nigeria was a warm country even at night; he decided to change into a light sweater and a pair of jeans. He would go out and explore the city on his own and if ever he got lost, he could always call the hotel and ask to be directed back or, worse still, he could walk into the nearest police station and report himself missing.

Alex's spirit lifted as he got dressed. He went into the bathroom and checked himself in the mirror. Satisfied, he left the bathroom and walked gently towards the exit of the room. As he turned the door knob, Nike asked him sleepily, 'Where do you think you're going?'

Still holding onto the door knob, Alex turned round to face her.

'And where do *you* think I'm going?' asked Alex wryly, but before Nike could utter a reply, he went on. 'I don't like the tone of your voice; you ask as if I'm an invalid. I'm going to look for a night club somewhere; I'm beginning to get bored.'

Nike sat up immediately. She looked furious as she retorted, 'What the hell do you mean, you don't like my tone? This is Nigeria and not the United Kingdom and I'm damned well responsible for you. I brought you here, remember?'

Alex could not believe the cheek of it. Nike was playing mother-hen to him and that did not go down well with him at all. He went over to where she sat and tilted her chin, so that his eyes bore into hers as he said to her in a low but angry voice, 'I chose to come here with you, darling and I damned well can choose to go back to the U.K., should you decide to make this goddamned place unsuitable for me. I am not some stupid bloke that you can decide to embarrass with your madness. Catch my drift?'

Nike caught his drift quite all right. Alex was referring to what she did to Benjamin back in the United Kingdom. She had intended to play the part of a good hostess and be protective of Alex here because she knew her way around, and she knew the people and the culture, but Alex had misunderstood her kind intentions and he had insulted her.

'I catch your drift,' she said angrily.

If Alex noticed her anger, he pretended not to notice it. 'Good,' he said and then he walked out of the room and out of the hotel.

As he walked along the footpath, he thought of their relationship which had always been sort of yoyo. To say he was beginning to get fed up with the relationship would be an understatement. Nike was beautiful; in fact, she was stunningly beautiful and Alex was proud to be her boyfriend. But beauty was definitely not all there was to dating and relationships. Nike had a crazy streak in her; it was as if she had a yearning that desperately sought to be fulfilled; it was as though there was a hollow deep within her that terribly sought to be reached and the more Alex tried to reach it, the deeper it became. Before they came to Africa, Alex had made up his mind to forego Clarida and Alice – poor Alice – and stick with Nike.

Clarida was much too possessive for his liking. She suspected his every move and she made Alex really feel choked. Alice, on the other hand, was too docile, too meek and too naïve to live with a highflying socialite like him. He had thought several times to call it quits with her before it was too late. She was twenty-five and she still had a lifetime ahead of her. Hopefully, she might come across some really nice docile guy like her and they would live happily with each other ever after. But the problem with Alice was that whenever he set his eyes on her, he felt intense pity for her so much that he had never been able to tell her that the relationship between them was over. He had tried to make her see that he was not really interested in the relationship any more by avoiding her, yet, she had not understood. Alex knew that Alice had finally understood when she had fallen victim of Nike's madness the day both of them had seen each other. Alice had stayed away then. A couple of times, he had wanted to call her to apologise for Nike's behaviour towards her that day, but he had resisted the urge to do so. That would make Alice want to come back to his life and the relationship that he had tried so much to douse would be rekindled. He, however, thanked his stars that this time, Alice was not pregnant with his child.

Alex's thoughts reverted to Nike. He tried to be objective about what he felt for Nike. He knew it was something akin to love; he just wasn't sure that what he was feeling for her would suffice enough to endure Nike's eccentricity. Nike was a very exciting lady and she made him laugh most of the time, but would their relationship pass the test of time? Would he be able to stand Nike's inherent madness at old age?

'Alright, brother. You okay?' said a voice behind him.

Alex was jolted back from his thoughts. He looked behind him and saw a young man grinning broadly at him. He made a silent sigh of relief. Nike's fearful warnings had taken deep roots within him. He studied his newly found friend; he was a black man of an average height and he wore a clean white shirt and a pair of blue jeans on a pair of loafers. The young man looked harmless enough. Alex smiled at him and extended his hand for a handshake. The young man took it in his and shook Alex's hand so vigorously that he felt his teeth begin to rattle.

'My name is Gregory; you can call me Greg for short,' said the man very happily as he shook hands with Alex.

'I'm pleased to meet you, Greg,' said Alex, as he gently disengaged his hand from Greg's fierce grip. 'I'm Alex.'

'Alex. Oh Alex. Hi ya,' said Greg as if he was just seeing Alex for the first time after several years. Once more, he took Alex's hand in a handshake.

'Hi,' said Alex wearily. He was beginning to doubt Greg's sanity.

'Alex, you know what? I like you,' said Greg seriously.

Alex looked around to see if there wasn't a mental asylum around; maybe this gentleman had just escaped from there and he was badly in need of his nurse or medication or both. He did not notice any asylum around.

Oblivious of what Alex was thinking, Greg went on, 'You know why I like you?' And before Alex could answer him, he said, 'Because I like white people.' Greg paused for breath and then he continued, oblivious of Alex's weary expression. 'And do you know why I like white people? I suppose you don't. It's because they are so nice, so plain-minded and they spend the hard currency; they spend harder currency than the Nigerian currency. Do you know what I'm talking about, Alex? I'm talking about Dollars and Pounds Sterling. My friend, do you know how I know that *you* white people are plain-minded and nice? Of course you don't; it's because you are…'

Alex had had enough. He yanked his hands away from Greg's grip and hastily moved on. Greg ran after him. Alex pulled out his mobile phone and dialled 999. He put the phone to his ear, desperately willing his call to be answered that moment. After a few minutes, he heard no ringing tone. Then he remembered he was not in the U.K. He probably needed to dial a different code to call the police. He became thoughtful for a while. He looked around; the only being that was near enough to give him a police code was Greg and it would be grossly unwise to ask his *assailant* for a number he could call to get him arrested.

As if he was reading his mind, Greg asked him, 'Are you trying to call the police because of me?' but before Alex could reply, Greg continued sadly, 'You don't need to do so. I've been mistaken for a person who disturbs others several times, but I am really not. I'm just someone who likes helping people. I'm here to help you.'

Alex found his tense nerves relaxing; *maybe Greg was normal after all.* Before he could speak, Greg spoke again. 'Now, where were you going before I saw you?'

'I was looking for a night club,' answered Alex sceptically. He was still not sure he could trust the man enough to divulge any information about himself to him.

'Oh yeah,' yelled Greg; he was clearly back to his enthusiastic self. 'I know a lot of clubs around. I've been living in this neighbourhood since I was very little.' He demonstrated how little he was by bending his knees and taking his right hand low to the ground. 'There's a club I can take you to and you'll enjoy yourself there. Lots and lots of beautiful girls there, you know what I mean?' said Greg, as he winked at Alex and poked him playfully in his ribs. Alex yelped with pain and then he poked him back with intent to hurt. But Greg only rubbed his side and laughed aloud; he was clearly having fun.

While Alex wondered what kind of a *being* Greg was, Greg pulled him towards the direction he was pointing at. Alex followed him sceptically. As he went with him, he looked around them to see if people were close by in case Greg decided to get manic. He saw a few people around and relaxed a bit.

They walked on for about twenty minutes and when they got to a T-junction, Greg turned left and pulled Alex to the entrance of a disco-hall.

Surprisingly, Greg offered to pay for their permits to enter the hall and after the payments were made and tickets given, Greg pulled Alex into the hall.

The disco-hall was filled with men and ladies of all sizes and colour, who were dancing to constantly changing music. Greg led him to a table in front of the bar and bought him a shot of brandy. Alex took the glass of brandy, shouted his thanks above the blare of the music and turned to watch the dancers. Soon, he began to enjoy himself immensely.

Five minutes later, Greg excused himself and went to join a lady on the dance floor. Alex was surprised to see that Greg was a very good dancer. His steps matched the rhythm of the music as he gyrated on the dance floor. Soon, he disappeared among the crowd of dancers.

As Alex downed the rest of his drink, a sexy looking lady walked up to him and pulled him towards the dance floor. Laughing, Alex got up from his chair and followed the lady. While the disco lights changed colours, the lady wound her arms around Alex and wriggled to the music. Alex was drawn into the spirit of the party and he danced to the tunes accordingly.

It was daybreak by the time Alex left the club. As he left, the lady he had been dancing with slipped a piece of paper into his pocket, gave him a very long kiss and waved him good-bye, then she went back into the disco-hall.

Alex did not see Greg after he went to the dance floor; as a last resort, he scanned the hall with his eyes to see if he was nearby. He wasn't. Thinking he could do without the talkative guy anyway, he walked tiredly back to the hotel.

He got to the room he shared with Nike and knocked on the door loudly. Nike opened the door immediately. It was obvious she had been waiting up for Alex. She studied Alex's looks, from his T-shirt, which now had an uneven design of red lipstick, to his legs. She noticed that he was wearing only one sock. She did not need to ask what he had been up to. He had clearly enjoyed himself all night and he had ignored her calls. And she had been up all night worrying over him and hoping for his safe return. Alex was beginning to get on her nerves.

'Where have you been all night?' she asked him contemptuously.

'Never mind. It's none of your business,' replied Alex and without looking at Nike, he hastily undressed and clambered into the bed.

'No, you can't do that,' shouted Nike. 'You're reeking of brandy, or whatever you got drunk on, and cigarette smoke; you should have a bath before you sleep on that bed.'

She ran to the bed to pull him up, but Alex was already fast asleep and snoring heavily. Nike tried in vain to get him off the bed and after a few minutes, she let him be. She looked at the pile of clothes Alex had made on the floor with disdain and shoved it towards the bathroom with her left foot. She determined not to touch his clothes; he would have to sort them out whenever he woke up. However, she noticed a piece of paper peeping out of the jean pocket and she could not resist the urge to pull it out. With hands trembling with anger, she unfolded the piece of paper and read the contents. It contained the name and address of a lady and to rub insult on the injury, the lady had stamped the note with her red lipstick! Nike's fury was immediately brought to the boil. *So Alex had been cheating on her all night.* His first night in Nigeria and he had started cheating on her! She looked at Alex as he slept. They had come to Nigeria with the hope that the vacation would mend things between them but it seemed that Alex was bent on *unmending* things. He had insulted her and he had dragged her pride in the mud by cheating on her on his very first night in a foreign country. Alex's escapade showed Nike that she meant little or nothing to him. Alex had showed her in no mistaken terms that he could do away with her anytime and more importantly, *anywhere* he so wished.

Not so fast, my dear, sighed Nike. *I must show you the stuff I'm made of first.*

As she studied Alex, sleeping and snoring away, the spirit of revenge suddenly entered her and she resolved to make him pay for what he had done to her. She would play it cool with him and pretend that she hadn't seen anything until the right opportunity came.

The next morning, they woke up to a breakfast of croissants, fried eggs and coffee and they had delicious fruit salad for afters.

As they had breakfast in the room at the little dining table made for two, Nike gently told Alex the plans she had outlined for the day. Alex listened as she told him the plans without interrupting her; then he took her hand across the table and tried to apologise.

'I'm sorry I upset you last night,' he began, but Nike quickly cut him short.

'Never mind. It's alright,' she said. 'Let's forget it and enjoy our holiday.'

Alex was pleased to see that Nike was not willing to discuss the matter further; he was relieved that Nike thought that the little argument they had before he went to the club was not worth arguing over; he finished his breakfast happily.

After breakfast, Nike said to Alex, 'I want us to stay in Lagos for a couple of days before we travel to Illudun land to visit my grandfather. I wish to show you around Lagos.'

'Yes of course,' replied Alex. 'But I must go back to work by the middle of next week. Otherwise, Sir Stonewall would be mad and my chances of becoming a partner with the law firm would be ruined.'

'Of course,' replied Nike.

So you had the guts to have a one night stand, she thought angrily, but she was smiling sweetly at Alex, *I'll teach you never to cheat on me again!*

Alex smiled back. He did not know what Nike had in store for him!

Chapter 55

In the lounge of the Sheraton hotel, Mike was attending to two mysterious gentlemen at the reception desk. The one gentleman that really caught Mike's attention was the tall, white, heavily bearded man with a pair of thick, dark sunglasses. Mike knew for sure that his beard was not real. He had been a costume man for ten years and knew a fake beard from a real one. What he wasn't sure of was why the man had to come into the hotel with fake beard; and to cap it up, he had decided to keep those ugly glasses on, even inside the cool lounge of the air-conditioned hotel, which the rays of the scorching sun outside could not penetrate.

Before he started work as a receptionist at the Sheraton hotel, Mike had worked at the circus where he dressed up a lot of circus performers; and the last time he had seen a funny looking man like the gentleman who stood before him was the day he went to the circus to tender his resignation letter.

Mike did not think that the man was there just to make everybody laugh. He had a nagging feeling that he was on a mission and the mission was not a pleasant one. Mike's eyes shifted from the funny looking man to his companion. He noticed his companion was, in every way, different from him. He was a black, stout man with a clean shaven boyish face; and he had a smile on his face. Mike noticed that the only similarity between the two men was that they both wore dark coloured suits. Mike tried to suppress the disturbing feeling as he answered their questions.

'Can we get two rooms on the first floor please?' said the black man.

'Certainly, sir,' replied Mike. 'Single, double or en-suite?'

'En-suite please,' said the bearded man hastily.

'No!' shouted the black man. 'We'll have two single rooms.'

'What the hell do you mean two–,' began the bearded man furiously, but the black man was quick to cut in.

'For goodness sake, will you please allow me to handle this?'

Mike looked from one man to the other, trying to decide why there had to be so much debate over the type of room to secure. Hadn't they reached an agreement before coming to the hotel? And why was there so much tension between them? Besides, Mike thought the two men's faces were vaguely familiar. He tried to remember where he had come across them; he failed totally. He decided to wait for directives from them.

The argument between them was followed by a facial note of warning from the black man and then the two men seemed to reach an agreement.

'Alright, we'll have the miserable single rooms then,' said the bearded man resignedly.

'Right, sir,' said Mike. 'May I have your names please?'

The bearded man started to speak, but he received a poke from his companion. He winced as he painfully held onto his side and gave his companion a dangerous look but he kept quiet. The black man cleared his throat and gave Mike a smile that Mike thought was meant to be pleasant, before replying, 'My name is Silas Mata and my friend's name is Doug Spearson.' Without being asked, he brought out their passports for identification.

Mike knew that the man had lied. Those were not their real names, but there was nothing he could do; he studied the passports they tendered and confirmed the names.

'Sure,' said Mike. 'Your keys are ready, sirs, and do have a pleasant stay here.'

Mike handed each man a key as he tried to study their faces. He searched his mind and made a mental juggle as to where and when he had met them before, but the more he thought about it, the more elusive the answer was.

'Thank you,' replied Silas, but Doug did not utter a word; he was still smarting from the pain that his friend unleashed on him.

As they left for their respective rooms, Mike caught a sentence uttered by Doug and the hair on his neck stood at attention.

'I don't care what happens to Miss World but, whatever you do, make sure that Alex stays alive. Just keep a good eye on them for now; I shall deal with the boy myself!'

Mike suddenly had the premonition that his favourite guests, who shared a suite on the first floor, were in danger. He did not know what prompted his suspicions, but he believed himself to be well gifted in discerning things and this was no different. He felt so sad that the beautiful lady could be the target of a ruthless plan. He had particularly been taken in by her sheer beauty the first day he had set his eyes on her. In fact, after two days of their stay at the hotel, he had come to the conclusion that he was yet to see a more beautiful girl than Nike Adeogun. He knew he had to do something fast – really fast. However, he had to be very careful indeed; those men certainly had a sinister aura about them!

Chapter 56

There was a gentle knock on the door.

'Come in,' mouthed Nike from behind the closed door. She was lying on the bed, having an apple and watching the television.

The door gently opened and a very dark-skinned man in a workman's uniform, carrying a large tool box and a huge spanner came into the room.

Nike sat up immediately. If she was expecting anyone, it was definitely not some repair man. As far as she was concerned, everything in the room was in perfect condition.

'I'm so sorry to barge in on you without previously informing you,' said the man. 'I was asked to come in to check on the air-conditioning system and the refrigerator in all the rooms on the first floor. Some electrical faults were reported earlier on and the hotel management would like to ensure that all electrical gadgets meet our safety standards.'

Nike did not think twice about it. She loved life too much to handle anything that might give her an electric shock. Besides, Alex would be mad at her if he came out of the shower and learnt that she had turned away a repair man for no reason.

'Sure, why not,' she said, 'go ahead.'

'Thanks ma'am,' said the repair man and he set to work.

Silas briskly walked over to the air conditioner and bent over it. As he did so, his eyes darted to where Nike lay. Satisfied that the television had her full attention, he deftly put his hands in his pocket and brought out a small rectangular shaped bugging device. This, he fixed to the wall behind the air conditioner.

It should escape any prying eyes there, he thought.

Silas pretended to examine the air conditioner for some minutes; he hit it a few times with the spanner and after a while, he stood up.

He went to the refrigerator and pretended to check behind it, hitting it a couple of times in the same manner as he had done the air conditioner.

Then he turned around and smiling broadly at Nike, he said, 'Everything is in perfect condition. Do enjoy your stay here, ma'am.'

'Sure, I will,' said Nike without shifting her eyes off the television.

Silas opened the door and walked out of the room. He was very happy with how easily he had accomplished his mission.

At ten a.m., Alex and Nike set out for the national theatre at Iganmu, Surulere. Nike called a cab and in forty minutes they were at the national theatre. Alex admired the sheer magnificence of the edifice. The building was shaped like a gigantic police cap and its environs were lined with different horticulture.

'We cannot go in to watch films today because we have lots of places to visit,' Nike informed Alex. 'But we can take some pictures before we leave.'

They took numerous pictures of each other in strategic places, and they requested passers-by to take pictures of them together. The friendliness of the Nigerian people did not go unnoticed to Alex. They were just eager to please and they proudly explained things about Lagos and the whole of Nigeria to Alex with pleasure. Before they left the National theatre, Alex could not help but fall in love with Nigeria.

Next, they went to the muson centre at Onikan. There, they visited the Muson School of music and the muson cultural centre, which was a beautiful artwork on its own. A tourist guard was on hand to take them around the beautiful complex. There was an array of sculpted musical instruments decorating the walls of the huge complex and the different halls had various décor, peculiar to their purpose. As they went from one beautifully decorated hall to another, the friendly guard explained the origin and purpose of every item displayed. Alex admired everything he saw. As the guard showed them around, he brought out his camera and clicked away.

They spent three hours at the Muson centre and Alex was sorry that they had to leave. He promised himself to come back to Nigeria in the very near future and visit the Muson centre *with or without Nike.*

When they left the Muson centre, Nike called a cab and they headed towards Victoria Island. While seated in the back of the cab, they went on sightseeing to various places ranging from cinemas, well constructed international schools, beautifully decorated parks overseeing the bar-beach and sky scrapers.

The taxi man, having been promised a handsome reward in Naira for his services, eagerly drove them around in his air-conditioned car, while he explained various things to them.

After driving around for two hours, Nike instructed the cab driver to take them to a good restaurant. The driver happily took them to a posh restaurant in Victoria Island and made arrangements to be back for them in an hour.

At the restaurant, they had a mouth-watering meal of fried rice with chicken and seasoned lobster, and ice-cream on cake as desert. While they were at it, a nice bottle of complimentary white wine was brought to them by the staff.

Alex found the meal so delicious that he gobbled up all he was served. At the end of the meal, he was feeling quite sleepy.

After driving around for two more hours, Nike decided it was time for them to return to the hotel. They would continue their tour the next day.

At eleven p.m. that day, Nike woke up with a start. She thought she heard a knock on the door. She looked sideways at Alex, who was snoring away beside her. *Rightfully so*, she thought, smiling. Nike had given Alex the best of her bedroom antics when they got back to the hotel suite earlier and Alex had dosed off, really worn-out. She stretched out her hand to wake him up but she stopped short of doing so. Maybe the knock she had heard had been in her dreams. Why would anyone knock on the door of their hotel suite anyway? The staff could always reach them via the intercom if need be. She must have been dreaming; no one was really knocking on the door. She settled back in the bed and tried to relax. Then the knocking came again; this time a little bit more audibly. Nike sat up immediately. Now, she was very sure she wasn't dreaming. Someone was indeed knocking on the door.

She gently disengaged herself from Alex's grip. Alex mumbled something incoherent, turned to face the wall and snored away.

Nike got up from the bed and hastily put on her house coat, then she tiptoed to the door.

'Who is it?' she asked sceptically from behind the closed door.

'It's staff, ma'am. I've got an urgent message for you.'

Nike opened the door immediately.

A tiny uniformed man carrying a tray of apple juice stood before her.

'You're in danger, miss,' the man blurted out before Nike could ask him what he wanted.

'What!' exclaimed Nike.

'Sshh!' said the man, placing a forefinger across his mouth in a gesture for her to remain silent. He looked around the corridor to see if any one else was around. Satisfied that they had no audience, he pushed past Nike and went into the suite. He had ensured that Silas and Doug had left the hotel complex before venturing into Nike and Alex's suite.

Nike was miffed by the man's sheer audacity. *How could he venture into her room without being told to do so?* The man sure had guts. Nike slammed the door shut then she turned around and marched far into the room, prepared to give the impostor some tongue lashing.

The man, who was already seated on the couch beside the king sized bed with the tray of apple juice by his left foot, stood up as Nike approached him. Smiling nervously, he offered his hand to Nike for a handshake.

'My name is Mike; my friends call me Mickey,' said the man, trying to be as amiable as he could.

Nike did not reciprocate. Eyes blazing, she said tersely, 'What gives you the impudence to venture into my room uninvited and what gives you the audacity to start making preposterous remarks. Your attitude is despicable and I shall invite the police if you do not get the hell out now.'

At that moment, Alex woke up from sleep.

'What the hell's going on here?' he asked as he stretched his torso.

'This impostor here thinks we're in danger and he has decided to play God by coming to rescue us,' replied Nike cynically.

But Mike was quick to answer. 'No, I'm not an impostor; I'm not at all and I'm definitely not here to rescue you guys. I'm here to warn you so you know how to get your arses out of here as fast as you can.'

Nike gave a mirthless laugh.

'Are you for real?' she asked. 'Until this moment, I had never seen a hotel employee who's as mad as you. Now get out of here!'

'But miss…' started Mike.

'Get out I say!' shouted Nike still.

'Now wait a minute,' said Alex. 'I'd like to know what's exactly going on. Turning to Mike, he asked, 'How the hell did you know that we're in danger?'

The man sat down on the couch again before answering. 'Because I heard it.'

Alex was interested now.

'You heard it from whom?' he asked.

'To be honest with you, I do not know their real names; in fact, I do not know how one of the men really looks…'

'See, I told you this man's a bloody impostor, a total nuisance…' began Nike, but Mike went on as if Nike had not spoken.

'I suggest you get the hell out of this hotel as fast as possible. Anytime I see that bearded fella, I get the creeps that something terrible is about to happen.'

'And how do you know that the terrible thing is about to happen to us and not to someone else, Mr *Nostradamus*?' asked Nike sarcastically.

Mike ignored the sarcasm in Nike's question and turning to face Alex. He said earnestly, 'Trust me, young man, your lives are in danger. I heard the fella mentioning your name to his fella and he also had a good description of the miss.'

'How were you so sure it was *me* the fella was describing to the other fella?' asked Nike irritably.

Mike turned to face Nike squarely and without a twitch to his facial features, he said, 'Because he mentioned the most beautiful girl in the whole wide world!'

Thirty minutes after Mike left, Nike and Alex sat in awkward silence on the bed. For the past thirty minutes, they had pondered over what Mike had come to tell them and they had argued at intervals; but Alex was still insistent on their moving out of the hotel.

'Look at it this way, Nike,' he said. 'I see no reason why a hotel attendant would risk his job and come to *us*, out of the whole population of people in this hotel and give us such a warning in the middle of the night. Think about it, Nike.'

'There's absolutely nothing to think about,' shouted Nike. 'The man was simply here to make himself feel important. He just wants to make an impression; can't you see that?'

Alex was beginning to get furious now. 'Why would he want to make an impression on us?' shouted Alex back. 'Are we celebrities or something?'

'We're not celebrities,' said Nike, getting up from the bed to face Alex. 'But it's obvious the guy fancies me. As far as he is concerned, I might just as well be a celebrity.'

Alex chuckled mirthlessly. 'Yeah right,' he said. 'Trust you to believe you're the best thing that's happened to the world, *Miss World*. And just because you *think* a guy fancies *you, that* shouldn't make him cook up stories just so he could have a glimpse of you, dear *miss world*. But one thing is for certain, I'm not ready to get killed in a foreign land because a very pretty arse says so!'

Alex knew that his speech had been edged with jealousy, but he couldn't be bothered. Nike was a very beautiful girl; in fact, beautiful did not even begin to describe her immense *beauty*, but he was sick and tired of being reminded of the fact any time other men saw her. As selfish as it may seem, he was surely not a guy would liked sharing his women, least of all Nike, with other men.

Nike detected the cynicism in Alex's speech and she did not like it. Worse still, he had referred to her as a *pretty arse*. She was pretty, yes, but she was anything but *an arse. Was that how Alex viewed all his girlfriends? Did he normally refer to them as an arse? Or was it just her?* All the anger she had felt towards him since the night he went out and *cheated* on her at the club suddenly came to the fore. Right then, she was just one emotion short of outrightly despising him. She thought of a way to teach him a lesson and she sensed the opportunity staring right back at her; the opportunity lay very much in the situation at hand.

Nike suddenly forced a smile to her lips.

'It's alright, Alex darling,' she said sweetly. 'It's no reason for us to fight. If you want us to move then move, we will.'

Alex felt his tense muscles relaxing. 'Alright sweetie, let's pack and move out of this place; we'll check into another hotel this night and we'll take the next available flight back to the United Kingdom tomorrow.'

Nike chuckled then; she was really amused. 'I never knew you were so cowardly,' she said laughing.

Alex didn't think he was a coward; he just believed Mike. His legal instincts told him to believe Mike.

Two hours later, they were in a taxi heading towards the Grande Hotel in Lekki Peninsula.

At five thirty a.m., exactly four hours after Nike and Alex checked out of the Sheraton hotel, Silas Mata and his suspicious looking friend, Doug, came in.

They both nodded curtly when they saw Mike and without saying a word, they ran up the stairs. Mike stopped studying the computer before him and watched the two men scramble up the stairs like errant rats. The suspicion that he had felt the first time he saw them came back as he saw them again. His heart began to pound loudly as he tried to decipher what it was they were up to. He noticed that Silas had changed into a black T-shirt on a white pair of slacks; but Doug remained as strange-looking as ever. He was still in his dark suit and his beard was still heavy; but the most troubling fact was that Doug still had those damned pair of dark glasses on.

Mike thought of calling in the police but he had no concrete evidence that the men were really criminals. He might have made a wrong judgement about the pair and he could deliberately be walking into trouble should he set the alarm on them.

Maybe Doug was simply trying to be funny; or maybe he had conjunctivitis!

But his mind told him there was more to those two than met the eye.

After pondering the men's motives and meeting a lock-jam, Mike shrugged and turned back to the computer. He had done the best he could by warning his two favourite guests about the danger they might be in; he only hoped *Miss World* and her partner were very safe wherever they were.

Silas looked down the corridor to ensure that nobody was around and then he placed his ear very close to the door. There was no sound of life in the room he had secretly guarded since he moved into the hotel with the Doug.

Although, he was an employee to Doug, he had placed himself in charge of monitoring the movements of their targets. He had monitored them from his room twenty-four hours a day, using the bugging device he had installed in the couple's room.

He had immediately sensed something was amiss when he got back to the hotel with Doug ten minutes before.

After exchanging cold pleasantries with Mike downstairs, Silas and Doug had gone to their separate rooms on the first floor.

Once in his own room, Silas had immediately switched on the transmitter. He listened for a while and to his chagrin, he recognised the voice of the hotel concierge downstairs.

'My name is Mike; my friends call me Mickey.'

'What gives you the impudence to venture into my room uninvited, and what gives you the audacity to start making preposterous remarks? Your attitude is despicable and I shall invite the police if you do not get the hell out now.'

Silas recognised Nike's voice; he was used to it now.

'What the hell's going on here?'

'That must be Alex,' muttered Silas under his breath. He felt like strangling the stupid small man downstairs, right this minute. But he waited and listened.

'This impostor here thinks we're in danger and he has decided to play God by coming to rescue us.'

'No, I'm not an impostor; I'm not at all and I'm definitely not here to rescue you guys. I'm here to warn you so you know how to get your arses out of here as fast as you can.'

Silas snickered. He wondered why Mike or Mickey could not simply mind his goddamned business. He listened with rapt attention and Nike's laughter did not escape his notice.

'Are you for real? Until this moment, I have never seen a hotel employee who's as mad as you. Now get out of here!'

'But miss...'

'Get out I say!'

Silas smiled. 'Good girl,' he said aloud.

'Now wait a minute, I'd like to know what's exactly going on.'

Silas stiffened visibly. He hoped Alex would call Mickey's bluff as Nike had done.

'How the hell did you know that we're in danger?'

'Because I heard it.'

'You heard it from whom?'

'To be honest with you, I do not know their real names; in fact, I do not know how one of the men really looks...'

'*See, I told you this man's a bloody impostor, a total nuisance.*'

'*But I'll suggest you get the hell out of this hotel as fast as possible. Any time I see that bearded fella, I get the creeps that something terrible is about to happen.*'

'*And how do you know that the terrible thing is about to happen to us and not to someone else, Mr Nostradamus?*'

'*Trust me, young man, your lives are in danger. I heard the fella mentioning your name to his fella and he also had a good description of the miss.*'

'*How were you so sure it was me the fella was describing to the other fella?*'

'*Because he mentioned the most beautiful girl in the whole wide world!*'

Silas had heard enough. The stupid busybody downstairs had informed his targets of their intentions.

'Bastard,' muttered Silas. He definitely knew that his targets had slipped through his fingers. From what he had heard, Nike and Alex were no longer resident at the hotel. They had probably relocated to some other hotel.

He surely needed to teach Mickey Mouse the lesson of his life. But first, he had to inform Doug of the latest development. The targets could not escape, otherwise, all hell might be let loose; he might get arrested and he might be made not to enjoy the money Doug had paid him to carry out the task at hand. Silas did not want that to happen; Doug had paid him an amount of money he had never seen in his whole criminal life and the least he could do was to carry out his assignment and enjoy his wealth afterwards.

Silas left his room and ran to Doug's room. He knocked on the door once and the door opened immediately.

Doug did not like being aroused from his sleep. He had gone out with Silas all night and all he needed was to catch a few hours of sleep and here was Silas, barging in on him uninvited.

'What the fuck do you think you're…?' he began, but Silas gestured for him to be silent.

Silas hurriedly brushed passed a very angry Doug and slammed the door shut.

Doug could not bear Silas' effrontery; it was about time he showed him who the boss was here.

'Look here, gentleman,' he started, but Silas again cut him short.

'Our targets are no longer here,' said Silas flatly.

'What?' shouted Doug. 'What d'you mean, man?'

'Exactly what I said,' answered Silas irritably. 'Mickey Mouse downstairs gave us away.'

Doug was doubtful. 'How're you sure of this?' he asked.

Silas looked impatient. 'Because I heard it. Remember I bugged their room?' he asked.

Doug nodded.

'Well my reliable source told me Mr Mike downstairs went to our targets and told them his suspicions about our movements.'

'Oh shit!' swore Doug. He went to sit down on the tiny bed and buried his head in his palms.

'Look, this is definitely no time for time-wasting,' said Silas. 'What we should be thinking of is the next step. If we knew what time they checked out of the hotel, we might be able to guess where they're hiding.'

Doug was thoughtful for a while. For the first time in his entire life, he was at a loss for what to do. Nigeria was a very foreign land to him, and the mere fact of this posed a great limitation to his decisions. Way back in the United Kingdom, he would have just snapped his fingers and a solution would have been immediately proffered. In fact, way back in the UK, his targets would not have escaped under his nostrils like they had just done. Doug was beginning to get sceptical over Silas' monitoring competence.

'What's the next step?' asked Doug; he was feeling very stupid.

'My best bet is they would be heading towards the Grande hotel. That should be the only place the lady would wish to seek refuge at such short notice. My findings told me that the Grande hotel used to be her lodge when she was at the Blueberry secondary school. Posco, my reliable spy is at the same hotel, watching over our dear old man. But first, we'll have to find a way of asking blabbermouth downstairs the time they checked out of the hotel. That way, we can be sure of abducting them before they get to the hotel,' Silas replied sullenly.

'No!' shouted Doug, as he got up from the bed. 'For God's sake, we can't do that; don't you know that by asking the guy downstairs, we would be giving ourselves away?'

'I know how to go about it; trust me,' replied Silas.

Mike was still working on the computer when Doug and Silas came down the stairs to the reception.

'Excuse me, mister,' said Silas, trying desperately to be polite. 'Did you by any means catch a glimpse of the beautiful lady in room 209, first floor?'

Mike smiled nervously and then he pretended to be thoughtful for a while. Silas was impatient; he began to rap loudly on the table.

The gesture did not escape Mike's notice.

After a while, Silas' impatience got the better of him and he decided to help Mike remember who he was referring to. 'You know the black beauty with the white guy; just opposite my room?' he said.

Mike's smile suddenly froze and then it slowly faded. He felt a chill go down his spine. Now he knew these two men were actually after Nike and Alex.

'May I know why you ask after them?' he asked politely.

Silas tried to smile, but it came out as an ugly grimace. He desperately wanted to throw a fist into Mike's face.

'Oh! Nothing,' he said. 'I just seem to fancy the lady, that's all.'

Mike did not believe him.

'I don't know her whereabouts,' he said simply.

'You do not know if and when they checked out of the hotel?'

'No!'

'I see.' Knowing that his conversation with Mike was leading them nowhere, Silas made a gesture for Doug to follow him out of the hotel. Without saying another word to Mike, they left the hotel premises.

Mike watched them leave. He somehow knew that the two men had gotten wind of the fact that Alex and Nike were no longer residing at the hotel. What he could not fathom was how they got to know this so quickly.

Could their room have been bugged? Mike shivered. If that was the case, Alex and Nike would not be the only people in danger.

Mike picked up the intercom and placed a call through to his manager.

'Please I need to go to the hospital now. I suddenly feel sick,' he said. Mike replaced the receiver, packed the few belongings he had brought in a little bag and left the hotel immediately. He was not ready to lose his life.

Nike had deliberately chosen the Grande Hotel as their *hideout*. It was the hotel her father used to lodge her in during the holidays when she was at the Blueberry Secondary School. The taxi stopped right in front of the Grande Hotel gates and the driver said cheerfully, 'Here we are guys. This is the Grande hotel. Hope you have a nice holiday.'

They got down from the taxi and Nike paid the driver. Nike shivered a little from the midnight cold. 'Alex, I honestly don't think this is a good idea–' she began but Alex cut her short.

'We're already through with that, Nike. Whether you think it's a good idea or not is not the point. What we should be thinking of is checking into this hotel tonight, and tomorrow we'll find a way of getting our arses back to the United Kingdom, okay?'

Nike sighed deeply before replying resignedly. 'Okay.'

'Good,' said Alex as he bent down to pick up two of their bags.

Nike carried the third bag and slowly, they walked towards the entrance of the Grande Hotel. As soon as they entered the hotel lobby, memories came flooding back to Nike. They were memories she had thought had been buried and forgotten. They were memories of her stay at the hotel with her father.

She looked around the hotel lobby. Nothing seemed to have changed except for the huge planted tree placed near the entrance of the hotel.

They went straight to the reception and Nike spoke to the elderly concierge who sat looking at the computer with rapt attention.

'Excuse me,' said Nike. 'We'd like to take a room for the night.'

The elderly concierge suddenly looked up and smiled at Nike. 'Certainly, you're…' he began, but then he saw Alex standing patiently beside Nike with two bags straddled across both his shoulders. The elderly concierge looked at Alex for an uncomfortably long moment, his eyes opening wider as he gazed longer. At a point, the concierge squinted and leaned towards Alex as if he wanted to get a clearer picture of him.

Alex and Nike looked at the concierge in total confusion.

Suddenly, the concierge clutched his chest with is right hand and pointed towards Alex.

'It's… it's him,' he croaked in a soft, muffled voice. 'It's the boss.'

Alex was shocked to hear the old man describe him in such a fearful manner.

'I beg your pardon,' he said to the concierge. 'I believe there's a mistake…'

But the concierge was already shaking his head as a tear trickled down his wrinkled face.

'No, I'm not mistaken,' he said. 'You're the boss; because of you, I ran away from the U.K. because of you, I'm here in far away Nigeria and you've come for me. Have you come to kill me as you made me kill your brother?'

The concierge grimaced as he talked and placed his head on the table in front of him. He began to cry.

Alex and Nike looked at each other; they were both lost in confusion.

Alex's heart seemed to palpitate by the second; an instinct told him that he might be very close to the riddle he had been trying to solve. He might be very close to the riddle surrounding his life. He was so sure that this old Englishman crying here was not insane, neither was he hallucinating. He must have reminded him of someone who was responsible for another's death. He remembered that his uncle had told him that his real father had died, and somehow, the mystery surrounding his death had not been unravelled. Could this man have the answer to the unsolved mystery? He tried to calm his nerves. He was determined to get to the bottom of this.

'I'm sorry to have upset you so much,' he said to the concierge, whose head was still placed on the table, his shoulders racking with each sob he made.

'I am definitely not who you think I am,' continued Alex as he dipped his hand into his breast pocket and brought out his passport.

'See, you can have my passport as a proof of identity. I'm sure you'll be convinced that I am a different person from the boss,' said Alex. 'I am Alex Tucker from Great Britain and I am here on vacation with my girlfriend, Nike Adeogun.'

At that moment, the concierge lifted his head from the table. He grabbed the passport from Alex and quickly scanned through it. As he read Alex's full name for the fifth time, he realised that he was not the boss, but he was the little boy that had been the cause of his father's murder twenty-six years ago.

He should have realised this sooner. The boss could not be as young as this at this age. He remembered that the boss had only been a year older than himself when he had made him kill his brother. Of course this gentleman standing in front of him could only be Rory Tucker's son!

Mark had killed Rory and he had never gotten over the guilt. He had run to Nigeria to find succour because he thought Africa was the last place the boss would come to look for him. He had come to Nigeria with the hope of securing a place in an oil company in Nigeria, but things had worked differently from what he had expected.

After being jobless and hungry for two months, he had taken up a job as a farming assistant in a remote village in Port-Harcourt. There, he met and married a lovely young maiden from the village. She had given him two lovely daughters and Mark had woven his world around his family.

Five years ago, they had moved to Lagos city and he had taken up a job as a concierge at the Grande Hotel. He had bought a house very near to the hotel where he worked and he had been happy that Nigeria had provided a refuge for him – a refuge away from the evil boss.

But now, the little boy that Mark found out was Rory's son, had come to Nigeria. Mark knew for sure that the boss would not be far from the shores of Nigeria. He also knew that his quiet refuge was no longer safe for him. He remembered all the hardship he had gone through in a bid the escape the claws of the boss and he suddenly felt tired. He was tired of running away from the boss; he was tired of running all his life. He looked at Alex and decided to spill the beans. If he was going to die, he preferred to die with a clear conscience. But first, he must make arrangements to send his wife and two daughters to his uncle in Great Britain. He knew they would be safe with his uncle. He would also write a long letter to his uncle, explaining how and why he had been in constant fear of even his own shadow. He would explain to his uncle why he had come to live in Africa in the first place.

At some point, Mark wiped a tear off his face with the back of his hand and gazed at Alex. A totally different expression was now registered in his eyes. His expression had turned from that of a frightened man to that of pity.

Mark was certain that if the boss got wind that he had been talking to his nephew and his female friend, none of them would live to tell any other person. As far as the evil boss was concerned, his reputation in the eyes of the public was far more important than any other thing in the whole wide world.

Mark looked at Nike and Alex standing before him, confusion written all over their faces. Then he looked past them at the rows of single chairs which lined the walls of the hotel lobby. Eight single chairs were lined up on opposite sides of the walls leading to the hotel receptionist desk – four on each side. The chairs were empty except for one which was occupied by a gentleman in a cowboy hat reading a newspaper. The man was so engrossed in the story he was reading that his head seemed to be buried in the newspaper. Mark was not exactly perturbed by the man. He had somehow gotten used to him sitting at the reception every night for two weeks, reading a newspaper. For the first three days after the man came to lodge at the Grande Hotel, Mark had been suspicious of his actions, but his suspicions had been quelled as the days passed. Mark thought he was just a bored tourist, who took joy in reading newspapers every night.

Once again, Mark's gaze registered on Nike and Alex.

'You may never get out of Nigeria alive,' he said simply.

Chapter 57

Mark went to the private telephone room of the hotel lobby. He checked to make sure he was alone in the room and dialled a number. He heard the ringing tone and he gently tapped on a table as he waited for his call to be picked up on the other side. After a moment, a sleepy voice came on the line.

'Mathew Franklin's residence,' said the tired, sleepy voice.

'Uncle Mathew, this is Mark. Mark Anderson,' said Mark stiffly. He had not spoken to his uncle in twenty-six years. He only hoped Reverend Mathew Franklin would remember who he was.

Back in the United Kingdom, Reverend Mathew Franklin sat up on his bed; his eyes were now devoid of sleep. He was very much alert now.

'Mark, is that you?' he asked sceptically.

'Yes, it's me, uncle,' said Mark, relieved.

Reverend Franklin could not believe he was actually hearing his nephew's voice after such a long time.

'Where have you been, Mark?' he asked excitedly. 'We thought you were dead.'

'I'm not dead; I'm very much alive in Nigeria,' replied Mark. But before his uncle could ask further questions, Mark went straight to his reasons for calling him. 'Uncle, please I need your help. This is very urgent. My wife and daughters will be with you tomorrow evening. I need you to take them in until I join you all in the U.K.'

Reverend Franklin thought about this for a while; he knew Mark was in no mood for a lengthy discussion. Somehow, he knew that Mark was in some kind of trouble.

'Are you in trouble over there, Mark?' he asked.

'I'm not sure,' Mark replied, 'but I have a mission to accomplish before leaving Nigeria. I have a confession to make. I need to unburden my heart of the guilt I've been carrying with me all these years.'

Reverend Mathew Franklin was all ears; he hated being kept in suspense. 'Perhaps you can start by telling me first,' he said. 'Perhaps I could pray for you.'

Mark was silent for a while; being prayed for suddenly appealed to him. He had never been a religious person, but right now, he thought he needed all the forgiveness he could get from God.

Mark told his uncle the story of his life.

When Mark left the hotel lobby, the man in the cowboy hat, reading a newspaper, took out a cell phone and spoke quietly into it.

'Our targets have finally met with Mark. He's told them a few things. They have an appointment to meet at the hotel lobby tomorrow morning at four thirty a.m.'

Silas listened carefully and after twenty seconds of hearing the message, he replied tersely, 'Right, you hang around there; we'll be there in ten minutes.'

He turned to Doug and grimaced.

'See, I was right,' he said. 'Our targets have lodged in at the Grande Hotel and that bloody Mark has decided to open his mouth.'

Doug lifted up his eyes and looked at Silas straight in the face.

'What do we do now?' he asked. For the first time in his life, he was doubtful of the next step to take. The boy he had loved all his life was involved in this particular saga. But when it concerned protecting his public image, the boss was known to spare no one.

'First, we have to take care of our man, Mark,' said Silas. 'He's been around for far too long anyway.'

The first cock crowed at 4 a.m. the following day. As the cock crowed, the clock on the wall of the hotel suite chimed four times.

Nike woke up and stifled a yawn. She and Alex had hardly slept a wink throughout the night. She looked at Alex snoring slightly beside her. She yawned deeply and exhaled loudly, rousing Alex from sleep.

Alex opened his puffy eyes and smiled weakly at Nike. Nike tried to smile back but her smile faded before Alex could notice it. Alex understood Nike's tension. Today was the day they were supposed to meet with the elderly concierge downstairs. Alex had a nagging feeling that today he would unravel the mystery surrounding his father's death.

Alex checked his watch; the time was four fifteen a.m.

'We had better get ready to see Mark downstairs,' he told Nike.

Nike got down from the bed and went into the adjoining bathroom. She washed her face and brushed her teeth. She came out to find Alex dressed in a pair of jeans and a T-shirt. She quickly changed into a pair of slacks and a top, and with their hearts thumping, they went downstairs.

They got to the lobby and found everywhere deserted. It was still dark outside and every guest in the hotel seemed to be asleep.

They looked around the lobby, expecting to find Mark at the reception desk, but no one was there.

'This is strange,' whispered Nike to Alex.

'Do you feel what I'm feeling Alex?' she asked fearfully.

'Yes,' replied Alex. He was still looking around the hotel reception.

A cold chill suddenly crept up his spine as he saw a foot sticking out from beneath a chair at the reception. Impulsively, he strolled over, lifted the chair and then he froze.

As the chair dropped from his hand onto the floor, Alex covered his mouth to stifle a scream. Nike saw Alex's reaction and ran over to his side. There, she saw what Alex had seen.

Lying on the floor of the reception was Mark's dead body. His eyes were wide open and his tongue stuck out of his mouth, but his pupils had dilated so much that only a little part of them were seen. Thick saliva slowly dropped from his slightly-opened mouth onto his long, white beard. Mark appeared to have been strangled.

Nike screamed. Alex quickly covered her mouth to keep her silent.

'Nike, we have to get out of here immediately,' whispered Alex. 'We don't want to be involved in a murder case.'

Nike allowed Alex to lead her up the stairs.

When they got to their suite, they hastily packed their belongings and ran downstairs. When they got to the reception, they averted their eyes from where Mark was lying dead and they quickly ran out of the hotel building.

'We have to get out of this vicinity as soon as we can,' said Alex. 'I don't like the feeling I am having. I can smell deep trouble in the air. We will get a taxi to the airport immediately. We shall be safe as soon as we get to the U.K.'

Just then, a taxi parked beside them and the driver wound down the window.

'Taxi,' said the driver cheerfully.

'Yes, thank you,' said Alex as he went to the car and opened the door. He quickly threw in their bags and urged Nike to get into the taxi. But Nike was sceptical. They had not called for a taxi and besides, she thought the taxi driver's face was familiar. She tried in vain to remember where she had met him.

But Alex was impatient. He went over to Nike and pulled her into the car. Then he leaned over and shut the door.

'Take us to the airport immediately,' Alex said to the driver.

'Right sir,' said Silas.

Chapter 58

Great Britain, Reverend Mathew Franklin's residence

Reverend Mathew Franklin had not slept a wink since Mark called him the night before.

To say he was surprised to hear Mark's voice after so long would be making an understatement. Mark was the son of his late sister and although he was just eleven and a half years older than Mark, he had always commanded Mark's respect; and Mark and his other nephew who was Mark's late brother had always looked up to him since they were kids. Why Mark had to resort to turning to the evil boss for help when he mistakenly killed his brother still beat his imagination.

However, what beat his imagination more was the degree of evil embedded in Alan Tucker. He had always suspected that Alan Tucker was not what he projected himself to be; he had always known that Alan Tucker was just a wolf in sheep's clothing, but he never knew he was so dangerous; the fact that he managed to carry on his double life for so long depicted an evil ingenuity.

Mathew Franklin suppressed the urge to go and inform the police about his discussion with his nephew. He would wait until Mark and his family were safely on the shores of Britain before he informed the police. Nothing in the whole wide world would give him more satisfaction than seeing Alan Tucker nailed, thereby proving to the other church ministers that he had been right about the pretender. Alan Tucker was a saint in the eyes of the other church authorities and he would let it remain so until the time to give the demon up was ripe.

He remembered Alan Tucker's various charitable actions that had endeared him to all and sundry, especially to the church ministers. He remembered his various donations to charity and he did not forget how he gave generously to people suffering in the third world countries.

Mathew Franklin had refused to be bought over by Alan Tucker's generosity. He had always had his doubts about him. More so, Alan Tucker had always made sure his kind gestures were documented and announced in the church; he would sneer silently at Reverend Franklin each time the announcements were made.

Reverend Franklin was not surprised that Alan Tucker could donate money so generously; after all, he had family money at his disposal. Alan's father and grandfather were business tycoons who invested in landed properties all over the world. The least Alan Tucker could do was flaunt his family wealth in the eye of the public; and what other way could he have done so and at the same time, project an image of holiness and kind-heartedness than give out the money he never worked for.

Reverend Franklin had always known that Alan Tucker was trying to buy his way into the hearts of the church authorities, so that he would eventually be made a knight. In spite of oppositions from the church committee, Reverend Franklin had sworn that Alan Tucker would never be made a knight. Not when he, Reverend Mathew Franklin, was still alive.

The opportunity had now arisen for Reverend Mathew Franklin to prove to the church and to the world that Alan Tucker did not deserve to be a knight. Mathew Franklin was prepared to wait until he set his eyes on his nephew and his family. Then, he would have enough evidence to bring Alan Tucker to book. If he let the cat out of the bag now, who knows, the evil boss might get wind of it in far away Africa and the life of his nephew might be in jeopardy.

Mathew Franklin rested his head on a pillow and counted the minutes until he was ready to hand Alan Tucker over to the police.

Chapter 59

Nigeria, West Africa

Silas constantly looked into the driving mirror at his two guests sitting at the back of the taxi. Each time he looked, he saw how relaxed they were, sitting together, holding hands, and he smiled. The boss would be happy that he had carried out his job perfectly. He only hoped Posco remembered to dispose of his cowboy hat once he had successfully murdered Mark.

Nike tried to relax in the back seat but her instincts told her she was in danger. She looked at Alex, who sat beside her with his eyes closed and squeezed his hand. Alex squeezed her hand back. He did not open his eyes. He was deep in thought, and he did not want to be dragged into any conversations with Nike. He wondered why Mark was murdered and by whom? Definitely, whoever murdered Mark wanted the secret he was about to reveal to be kept a secret. Mark had warned him and Nike that they might never leave Nigeria alive, and Mark had been murdered. That meant Nike and him were in danger.

Alex's heart began to palpitate. All he wanted to do was get to the airport and get the next available flight back to the United Kingdom. What had started out as a nice holiday had turned into a nightmare. He hoped they would be able to get back to England alive.

Just then, the taxi swerved right into a narrow path. The driver pressed on the accelerator and sped through a narrow path with thick bushes lining each side of the road. Nike was alarmed. Her worst fears had been confirmed. She knew that they were not headed for the airport. She knew for sure that they were being abducted.

'Where the hell are you taking us?' Nike shouted at the driver, forcing Alex to open his eyes. 'Will you stop this car at once!' yelled Nike.

But the taxi driver was unperturbed; he remained silent but drove on. For the first time since they got into the taxi, Alex became suspicious of the driver.

'Will you please take us back to the hotel?' he said, trying to appear calm.

'No, I won't,' replied Silas.

'Why not?' asked Alex

'Because I'm taking you to the airport!'

'But this is not the way to the airport,' shouted Nike. She was really agitated now.

The taxi driver stopped abruptly in the middle of the road and got out of the car.

Nike seized the opportunity and decided to get out of the car too. But before she fully made it outside the car, Silas dealt her a punch in the face. Nike was sent flying back into the car. She was momentarily blinded by the punch.

Alex opened the car door and got out of the car. 'Alright fella,' he said. 'Stop fighting a woman and let's take on each other in a combat; let's do it *man* to *man*.'

But Silas shook his head. 'No,' he replied, as he dipped his hand in his trouser pocket and brought out a gun. 'I'm not ready to engage you in a fight. Now get into the car gently before I blow your brains open,' Silas bellowed.

Alex looked around; it was still pitch dark and they were all alone in the deserted road – the three of them. Alex knew he had no way of escape; besides, he could not leave Nike at the mercy of this criminal. His shoulders sagged as he turned and opened the car door.

As Alex got into the car, he felt a sharp pain on his neck. He turned around and was only able to make out the blurred image of the taxi driver, grinning wickedly as he held a syringe in his hand, before he fell into the car and drifted away from consciousness.

Silas bent and leaned into the car. He held Alex's hand up and released it. The hand fell back on the car seat limply. Silas smiled; now he was sure that Alex would remain dumb for a very long time.

Silas went over to Nike's side and pointed a new syringe at her.

'You don't expect me to drive you down to the boss while you can call for help, do you?' Silas asked her menacingly.

Nike shrunk away from him. She cuddled against Alex, seeming to take refuge from his body. A similar scenario suddenly flashed in her mind. She remembered what she and Maxwell did to Mr Dede Cole some years back and she felt a tinge of guilt. Now, life seemed to be playing the same scene again; only this time, she was the victim and Maxwell was not there to tell her a way out. Nike also knew that whatever was in the syringe was definitely not just *pure strawberry juice*. It was the real stuff; it was a *pure, dangerous liquid*.

Nike shrunk further away from the taxi driver; she held onto Alex's body, wishing she could disappear into it.

'Now, don't waste my time,' said Silas irritably. 'I'm not being paid by the hour.'

And with that, he dragged Nike towards him and lifted up her left arm. Nike shut her eyes tightly and screamed as the needle pierced her flesh. Within a few seconds, her eyes closed and she slipped out of consciousness.

Silas smiled and slammed the door of the car shut. He walked round to the driver's seat, opened the door and got behind the wheel. He sighed deeply; he was nearing the end of his assignment. As soon as he delivered the bodies to the boss, he would be out of the picture. He thought of what he would do with the money he would receive as remuneration. He would probably travel out of the country. He would go as far as America, or Canada, or the Caribbean Islands. He would be able to afford all the ladies his eyes fancied. He would live his life to the full. Silas grinned. In a few hours from now, his life would change for the better.

He pressed a button on the door of the car and watched as the tinted windows slowly came up. Satisfied that he would reach his destination without any passerby suspecting foul play, he switched on the ignition and sped towards the east.

Chapter 60

Great Britain; Stonewall and Partners law firm

Sir Richard Stonewall sat in his massive chair in his huge office; his face was a mask of anger. After a while, he rested his head against the heavy headrest and gazed directly at a stack of books which lined the wall opposite him. But Sir Richard Stonewall was not actually seeing any book. What he was seeing were the millions of pounds his firm stood to lose if they lost the Fernando case. He wished that by magic, Alex would appear before him from wherever he had travelled to. For the past four days, he had been trying to get in touch with Alex but all his efforts been futile. He had sent several letters to his house and he had called his mobile phone and left messages on it a million times. But Alex had not replied to any of his phone calls and he had not bothered to show up in the office. He had even sent emissaries to Alex's house on several occasions but Alex seemed to be at large. He could not believe Alex would choose to be this irresponsible especially now that his application to be a partner at the law firm was under consideration.

Sir Richard Stonewall remembered the conversation he had with Alex before he travelled to Africa. He remembered that Alex had asked for five working days off. Now it was nine working days and Alex was yet to be seen around the office premises.

Four days ago, Mrs Ann-Marie Fernanado's lawyers had called to cancel the agreement they had with Stonewall and Partners concerning the divorce settlement. Now they want a higher amount of money.

Sir Richard Stonewall had known all along that Mrs Ann-Marie Fernando would turn greedy along the line and ask for more money and he had tried to persuade Alex against embarking on his damned vacation. But the stupid lad had insisted on going on the journey and he had overstayed.

A meeting between the two law firms had been cancelled and postponed twice just because Alex, who happened to be the leading legal representative in the case, was not around.

Now, a letter had been sent to the firm by the court, requesting Sir Fernando's presence at the court on the sixth of November.

Sir Richard Stonewall opened his diary and checked how many days they had left. They had two days to produce Alex or find another legal representative. He swore and pressed the buzzer. A smartly dressed secretary came in after thirty seconds.

'Have you heard from or *seen* Alex?' asked Sir Richard Stonewall grimly.

'No sir!' replied the secretary.

Sir Stonewall sneered and then he went quiet. 'Mellissa, we have to get Alex this minute; otherwise, things would be disrupted in the Fernando case; do you understand?' said Sir Richard Stonewall angrily after a moment.

'Yes sir!' replied the secretary.

Sir Richard Stonewall thought for a while then his face brightened up as an idea crossed his mind. 'Have you checked him at the airports?' he asked.

'Yes sir!' replied the secretary crisply. In the years that she had come to work for Sir Richard Stonewall, she had learned how to be unfazed and how to behave professionally even when Sir Stonewall was in his most irritable state.

'Have you checked all the airlines?' asked Sir Stonewall.

'Yes sir!' replied Mellissa, still maintaining her efficient, professional demeanour.

'Have you checked all the hospitals?' Sir Stonewall asked.

'Yes sir!' replied Mellissa.

'The Nicon Hotel?'

'Yes sir!'

'All hotels in town?'

'Yes sir!'

'Have you checked the gyms?'

'Yes sir!'

'The prisons?'

'Yes sir!'

'The mortuary?'

'Yes sir!'

'Have you prepared his dismissal letter?'

'Yes sir!... I mean no sir!'

Mellissa had started to sweat now; her professional posture was beginning to wane.

'Then go and prepare it,' barked Sir Richard Stonewall.

'Yes sir!' said Mellissa, and she scurried out of Sir Stonewall's office.

Chapter 61

Nigeria, West Africa

Fifteen hours after Alex and Nike went into unconsciousness, they woke up to the smell of wet timber and dirt. They looked around their abode. It was dark and it had an unpleasant smell. Nike shook her head and tried to adjust her sight to her surroundings. She tried to move but found out she could not. She soon realised that she had been tied to a pole. She called out Alex's name in a tired voice.

'Yes, I'm here,' replied Alex; his voice sounded equally tired.

'Can you move?' Nike asked.

'No, I can't,' replied Alex painfully.

Nike shut her eyes. She could not believe what was happening to her. She could not believe what had happened to her in the last few hours. She wondered what day it was; she tried to remember how they had got here. She only remembered what happened up until they were given injections. How she wished her powerful grandfather was around to rescue them. She wondered in futility, where exactly they were.

'Where are we, Alex?' she asked.

'I don't know,' replied Alex truthfully.

Just like Nike, his body was tied firmly to a pole with a string from his neck area to his feet. Coupled with the smell of wet, decomposing wood and filth, he was finding it more difficult to breath by the minute. Their habitation was too stuffy for his comfort.

Just then, they heard the sound of footsteps coming towards them and they both stiffened.

'You're in the eastern part of Nigeria in a village called Alugu,' said a man as he came to stand before them.

Alex and Nike could barely make out the image of the man standing before them but Alex thought the voice was very familiar. He was sure he knew the owner of the voice very well. What he was not sure of was what he would be doing here in a remote village in the eastern part of Nigeria.

Suddenly, a florescent light flicked on and the room was illuminated.

'Dad!' shouted Alex. 'Dad, what are you doing here?'

Alan Tucker laughed mirthlessly before answering him. 'I'm not your dad, son; and I initially came to take you back to the U.K., but then you were let into a secret you weren't supposed to be let into, so you have to go with that traitor, Mark.'

Alex was flabbergasted; he could not believe that the man he had loved and called Dad all his life – and who had, in turn, treated him like a son – could now be so callous to him. The meaning of the statement Alan Tucker had just made was, however, not lost on Alex.

'Dad, are you telling me that you killed Mark?' Alex asked, wishing Alan would not confirm his suspicion.

Alan Tucker confirmed his suspicion.

'Yes, I'm officially informing you that I ordered for Mark and his family to be killed,' said Alan.

Alan laughed as he saw the shock registered on Alex and Nike's faces.

'And I killed your mother too,' said Alan.

'What!' shouted Alex. 'You bastard,' said Alex as he struggled in vain to be free of the rope he had been tied with.

'And your grandmother too,' said Alan with mirth as he watched Alex writhing and struggling to free himself of the rope.

'I'm going to get you,' groaned Alex.

Alan Tucker laughed all the more, then he became serious all of a sudden. Coming very close to Alex, he said to him seriously, 'I warned you Alex, didn't I? I warned you to steer clear of this bitch beside you.' He pointed to Nike as he said the word *bitch*, then he went on. 'But you would not listen to me, Alex. Now you've come all the way here and you've landed yourself in this mess.'

Alex looked at Alan straight in the face and said to him, 'You told me my mother disappeared.'

Alan laughed, cutting him short. 'Yes I told you that your mother disappeared and could not be found and all that crap. But I told you those lies because I wanted to protect you from the truth, and I wanted to protect you from the ruthless side of me.'

Alex was tongue-tied. He just didn't know what to say to this *demon* he had called *father* all his life.

Alan went on. 'You see, son. I hate to see anybody tarnish my image in any way; and I hate to be betrayed in any form by anybody. Your father Rory betrayed me; he betrayed my trust in him by sleeping with my wife, your mother. You, Alex, are the result of their illicit affair. Of course, I could not take the shame. I could not bear the thought of my wife having a child with my brother, so the traitor had to go.'

Alan Tucker's face became sober and his eyes welled up with tears as he continued. 'Your grandmother, I hated with a passion,' said Alan with eyes burning with the hatred he felt towards his late step-mother, Lady Dorothy Tucker. 'I have hated your grandmother since the day my father married her. The first crime she committed was that she came to take my mother's position,' continued Alan. 'The second crime your grandmother committed was that she made my father disown his own son, Jamie, who happened to be my only full-blooded brother.'

Alan allowed the statement to sink in before he continued. 'The third crime that your grandmother committed was that my brother, Jamie, died as a result of his homelessness.' Alan Tucker sniggered before continuing angrily. 'You see, son, three months after Jamie left home, his girlfriend set him up to be killed. Jamie had offended some people a few months before, but they could not get to him because of the security our father's wealth gave him. However, when Jamie was sent out of our home, he hitched up with his girlfriend who he loved so much. The lady took a bribe from Jamie's enemies and set him up. My brother was killed on his wedding day!'

Alan sneered at Alex before saying tersely, 'My brother died because your grandmother made him leave his home.'

Suddenly, Alan's eyes softened as he made his next statement. 'I loved your mother dearly. I loved Roberta with all my heart, but she threatened to expose me. She threatened to tell the whole world that I killed Rory; so she had to go too.'

Alan Tucker wiped a tear from his face with the hem of his sleeve and sniffed as he said this; then he went on. 'I wouldn't have killed her, you know. But I could not let her blow the trumpet and nip my life-long ambition of becoming a knight in the bud. You know what I mean, Alex?'

Alex did not answer him and he had stopped struggling to be free. He just looked on in amazement. *This man must be sick in the mind*, he thought.

'And now that you know the secret, you have to go too,' continued Alan. 'I can't afford for you to talk to the police once you get to the U.K.; so you and your friend here have to go and join your ancestors.'

Alan Tucker paused and seemed to think about what he had just said; then he said to Alex almost pleadingly, 'I hope you understand.'

When Alex gave no reply, Alan went to stand before Nike and looked at her despicably. Then he spat on her face. Nike closed her eyes to prevent Alan's spit from getting into them. She turned her face to one side. She could not bear to see the pure hatred oozing out from Alan's eyes.

'I hate you,' said Alan suddenly. 'Oh, I hate you with a passion. How I wish I had had the opportunity to kill you before things degenerated to this. I would not have had any cause to kill Alex.'

Nike said nothing. She was too tired and too amazed to say anything. Reverend Alan Tucker was someone she had respected since she met Alex. What she was now seeing and hearing was too much for her to take in. She felt numb and afraid.

'Do you know why I brought you here to be killed?' asked Alan. He was looking at Nike.

Nike remained silent. She looked sideways. She could not bear to look at the *monster* in the garb of a human, who was talking to her.

'It's because I know your background,' continued Alan. 'I know how powerful a King your grandfather is in the western part of Nigeria. I know I may not get away with killing you in Lagos or anywhere in the western part of the country. But your powerful grandfather is the most hated man around here. That's why I brought you here. Killing you here would be a piece of cake. Nobody would be concerned enough to find me out before I go back to the United Kingdom.'

Alan Tucker laughed mirthlessly before continuing. 'You would agree with me that I am a very smart guy. Now wouldn't you?'

Nike looked at Alan and said in a tired voice, 'You'll never get away with this.'

Alan laughed heartily. 'Well we shall see about that,' he said.

Stepping back from the two, Alan snapped his fingers twice. A hefty man in shabby clothes came into the room. Nike could not believe how very ugly a man could look. The man who just came in was not just ugly-looking, he looked despicable with his fat black lips and big, bulging eyes. A scar which seemed to be the result of a knife fight ran across his face from the base of his left eye, across his big pig-like nose, to the right edge of his mouth. The tip of his large ears stood out of proportion to his entire face as if the ears were borrowed from *Spark*. His hair also looked like it had patches of sand in it.

Nike cringed with fear.

'Posco,' said Alan, 'tonight at ten o'clock sharp, I want this hut razed to the ground. Remember, I want no mistakes. There should be no remains of these two that can be identified. Is that clear?'

'It's very clear, boss,' said Posco, standing at alert. 'I shall instruct Jiro to carry out the task to the letter.'

'Remember, do not loiter around the hut until the time to burn it draws near. We do not want to raise suspicions,' instructed Alan.

'Yes Boss,' replied Posco.

At exactly ten o'clock in the evening, Jiro got to the abandoned hut with the bottle filled with petrol. He had been instructed never to venture into the hut. He had no intention of doing that. All he wanted to do was carry out his assignment and lay his hands on the large sum of money that he was promised.

He looked at the hut for a few seconds and pondered within himself, why someone would derive pleasure in burning down an abandoned and dilapidated hut.

Since he came to live in the village of Alugu three years before, Jiro had not noticed any sign of life in the hut, except of course the birds and butterflies that flew in and out of it. He had learnt from the villagers that the hut had belonged to a poor farmer who died long before he got to the village. The farmer had lived alone in the hut after the demise of his wife and two children. The farm land and the hut had been left unattended to because no one had come to lay claims on them – not a single family had come.

Jiro was not bothered about the dead lonely farmer and his miserable hut. He had always thought that the hut should have been destroyed and the farmland taken over by the community anyway. What he did not understand was why the boss had ordered him to burn the little hut with the promise of a handsome reward for it.

As Jiro poured the petrol from the bottle on the wall of the little hut, he began to imagine what he would do with the money he would receive on completion of the little task at hand. He thought about the wealth he would amass; he thought about all the ladies that had formally refused his love advances; he imagined them fighting for his love as he sped past in his huge automobile towards the mansion he would build and he smiled. He was about to be a very rich man and he would soon unleash emotional terror on all the ladies in the village!

When the bottle of petrol was empty, he threw it on the ground and brought out a handful of dry sheaves. He struck a match and set the sheaves alight then he threw the burning hay through an opening in the hut and he moved a considerable distance from the hut. He watched as thick fumes escaped from the hut. He smiled but he was not yet satisfied. The instruction given to him was to make sure that the hut was razed down completely.

Suddenly, there was an explosion and the little hut that used to house the lonely farmer became a burning hut.

A mile and a half away from the burning hut, Alan Tucker watched the whole scene with his binoculars; he was safely hidden in the midst of overgrown shrubs but he had witnessed everything from start to finish. He had witnessed Jiro carry out his instructions with admirable perfection. *The boy obviously deserves an award*, he thought. In roughly thirty minutes, Jiro would be with him to receive his money and that would be all. He would go back to his hideout, take his few belongings including his British passport and the Nigerian passport, and he would take the next available flight back to the U.K. No one would know where he had been and what he had been up to. He would try his best to forget Alex and he would start a new life there as a Knight of John Wesley.

However, apart from Alan Tucker, twenty-one other persons had witnessed the whole episode. As Jiro turned in the direction of the overgrown shrubs, four men came from different angles and rounded him up. Jiro stopped in his tracks. He had been caught. He looked at the four men one after the other. They were all huge, hefty men with mean expressions and they were fast approaching him. He turned back to look at the burning building; it was almost razed down to embers. Jiro imagined his wealth burning away with the hut. He knew that somewhere in the thick of the bush, the Boss, as he had learnt to call his instructor, would be watching everything. He knew that now, the Boss would be trying to escape, to run away with his money, never to return to Alugu village ever again. He was determined not to allow his money to disappear before his very eyes.

As a last resort, he gathered his strength and made to run into the bushes, but it was too late. He was surrounded by his assailants and captured. He struggled in futility to be free from their grip. One of the huge men took a twine and tied his hands behind his back and a crowd began to gather around them.

Alan Tucker did not wait to see if they successfully tied Jiro up; he picked up his binoculars and fled. He ran as fast as he could through the bush and onto the desert land. He saw his car still parked as he had left it and he blew it a little kiss. Then he got into the car and sped off.

Chapter 62

Alan Tucker held his breath as Nigerian immigration officials checked his passport.

'You're an oil worker from Port Harcourt?' asked an immigration official after scrutinising the British passport Alan Tucker had presented for inspection.

'Yes,' replied Alan, trying to sound casual.

'Why are you going back to your country now?' asked the officer.

Damn you, Alan thought. 'I'm on holiday and I wish to spend it with my family and my new born baby,' replied Alan.

The officer looked up then. He looked at Alan for a while then he asked, 'Your wife just had a baby?'

Alan did not want the officer to ask for his wife's details; it might reveal too much. Besides, he had a time constraint; he did not want to be arrested at the airport. So he decided to tweak what he said a little bit.

'Actually, I was told last night that my young daughter gave birth yesterday, but she died right after giving birth to a baby girl. I'm going there to see what I can do for my grandchild,' said Alan as tears welled up in his eyes.

The officer instantly became sympathetic. 'I'm so sorry,' he said. 'Please accept my sympathy.'

'Thank you very much,' replied Alan as the officer stamped his passport and gave him clearance to board the aircraft.

Chapter 63

Nigeria, West Africa

Alex Tucker and Nike Adeogun lay on their beds in different wards in the village hospital. They had been treated for severe bruises. They were both grateful to the young man who had seen them tied up in the little hut like sacrificial lambs, awaiting eternal condemnation to hell on earth.

Nike and Alex had told the man that they were going to be burned down with the hut at ten o'clock. Without wasting time, the man had quickly untied Nike and Alex.

With Alex's hand around Nike, the young man had led them through a bush path to the King's palace.

When Nike and Alex were led into the King's presence, Nike had fallen down from exhaustion and they had both been driven to the hospital by the King's chauffeur.

Back at the King's palace, John Duhu was narrating to the King and his subjects, how he had met Alex and Nike in the abandoned hut:

At eight o'clock that evening, John Duhu, a university student, left his home and went towards the abandoned little hut in the village of Alugu. He was in his final year in the university, studying for a degree in Botany, and he was carrying out research on the effect of sunlight on the activity of auxin in green plants.

For the past three weeks, he had watched his pot of plant hidden under a stack of planks in the little hut. He had decided to use the abandoned little hut for his control experiment primarily because he was aware that nobody entered that hut. He, therefore, knew that his plants would be safe and untouched by any other person.

John had gone to the hut at exactly eight p.m. every night to check on his plant, but as he entered the little hut with his small lantern, he saw two figures tied to planks. He wanted to run out of the hut, but Nike had cried out in pain. That had made him stop and he had cautiously moved toward Nike and Alex.

'Who are you?' he had asked cautiously. 'And who tied you here?'

Alex had replied that his uncle had tied them up, and Nike had informed him that they were to be burned down with the little hut at ten o'clock that day.

John Duhu needed no further explanation from them. If these two people were to be killed in less than two hours, he needed to waste no time before he set them free.

John had brought out a cutlass that he kept as a tool from the base of a plank; he had cut the ropes that were used to tie the two victims and then he had led them to the King's palace.

Chapter 64

United Kingdom, Alan Tucker's Residence

At four a.m. the day after he returned to the United Kingdom from Nigeria, Alan Tucker woke up to the ringing of his mobile phone. He picked it up and flicked the lid open. The caller was anonymous. Wondering who could be calling him at this time of the morning, he slowly put the phone to his ear.

'Hello,' he whispered.

He got no reply.

'Hello,' he said again, this time more audibly.

'Hello,' came the reply.

Alan Tucker recognised the voice immediately. *Why on earth would Reverend Matthew Franklin call his mobile phone, and so early in the morning too?* Reverend Matthew Franklin had never showed any signs that he knew Alan Tucker's phone number, much less that he would call him. The ceremony for the crowning of the knights was the following day and Alan Tucker would not want anything, not even a suspicious phone call from his greatest enemy, to jeopardise his life-long dream of becoming a knight. Reverend Matthew Franklin had been the only one of the whole committee of reverends who had voted against his being crowned a knight; he had given no tenable explanation for his decision and it had been unanimously agreed by the other reverends that Alan Tucker be given the knighthood.

'Hello, Tucker. Are you still there?' Matthew Franklin bellowed into the phone.

'Hello,' said Alan Tucker. 'What a surprise, Reverend Franklin. How nice of you to call me this early morning.'

Matthew Franklin detected the sarcasm in Alan Tucker's voice, but he was undeterred. He had made a promise to his nephew and he was bent on fulfilling it.

He had gone to the airport to pick up Mark's wife and two kids two days before and he had waited for ten hours at the airport without seeing anybody who matched the description Mark had given him. Not wanting to give up so easily, he had made enquiries from the airport authorities and he had been told that Mark's family was not on any of the flights from Nigeria. Reverend Franklin knew instantly that something had gone wrong. He was sure that Mark and his family had not escaped the evil claws of Alan Tucker.

When he got home the following day, he had made a solemn promise to Mark that he would make sure his death was avenged. But he decided to play it cool with Tucker for now. He had to make sure Tucker did not suspect that he knew anything. He wanted to be the first to tell Tucker that the numerous skeletons in his cupboard had been exposed, and the strong hand of the law was fast approaching him. He had to *assure* Tucker that he had no way of escape!

He took a deep breath and tried to suppress the anger that was threatening to explode within him.

'I hope I did not disturb your beautiful sleep this early morning,' he said into the receiver; he was desperately trying to sound as sweet as possible.

'Not at all,' replied Alan through gritted teeth. He was trying very hard not to tell Reverend Franklin to piss off and descend to the pit of *hell*.

'Good! Now I was wondering if I could come over this afternoon for a chat over a cup of tea; or don't you think it would be nice to be friendly with each other now that you're going to be a Knight.'

Alan Tucker was very much surprised. 'Of course, we can meet somewhere…' he began, but Reverend Franklin cut him short.

'I'll like for us to meet at your house… That's if you don't mind. Now that we're friends, we could visit each other's houses,' said Reverend Franklin, laying much emphasis on the word *friends*. 'That's if you don't really mind,' he quickly added.

'Of course I don't mind,' replied Alan. But all he wanted was for Reverend Franklin to leave him the hell alone.

'Good, shall we make it five p.m. later in the day then?'

'Yes, of course,' said Alan much too hastily, then he realised that he had given his consent to the time they would meet absentmindedly; he had been preoccupied with trying to guess why his enemy would suddenly pose as a friend and endeavour to come to share drinks with him in his own house. He had allowed Reverend Franklin to dictate the pace of their conversation. He should be in control of whatever game Reverend Franklin was playing at, so he decided to start by changing the time of their meeting. 'Why don't we meet at…' he started to say but Reverend Mathew Franklin had hung up!

Chapter 65

Nigeria, West Africa

Jiro was under fierce interrogation. He was slouched on the hard, cold floor of the police interrogation room with his back against the wall and his hands handcuffed to his back. His broken nose dripped of thick blood as Inspector Coker stood over him with a heavy booted foot on his left leg. The policeman looked menacing as he asked Jiro for the thirteenth time that afternoon, 'Where the hell is your Boss?'

Jiro opened a swollen eye and coughed loudly. Blood spluttered from his mouth as he coughed, prompting the very angry policeman to kick Jiro in his stomach with his boot. Jiro winced out in pain as he doubled over.

'I said; where is your boss?' asked the policeman once more, his voice failing to manage the loathe he felt within him.

Jiro spoke up in a voice that sounded more like a shrill. 'I do not know. Only Posco would know.'

Inspector Coker was impatient.

'And where the hell is Posco?' he asked, his boot unmercifully grinding into Jiro's flesh.

'N... number 52, Alfred Shinbu Road,' Jiro managed to reply before he passed out.

Inspector Coker swiftly unhooked his walkie-talkie and spoke into it. 'Get some of the boys ready. They should be at number 52, Alfred Shinbu Road in thirty minutes.'

Twenty-five minutes later, four policemen stood outside number 52, Alfred Shinbu Road. After two knocks, a heavily built woman who seemed to be in her thirties came to open the door.

'Is this Posco's residence?' asked one of the policemen.

The frightened woman answered in a shaky voice, her eyes darting from one policeman to another. 'He was sick with fever, sirs. He has been taken to the hospital, sirs.'

'And where might that be?' asked the same policeman.

'Roland hospital, sirs,' replied the woman.

When the policemen got to the hospital, they were directed to Posco's ward by a nurse. They found Posco on a bed with a drip in his right hand.

A doctor checked Posco's pulse with his left hand as he placed a stethoscope on posco's chest.

'We're from the state police command and we are here to arrest one of your patients called Posco,' said one of the policemen to the doctor.

The doctor looked at the policeman; he was totally amazed. Before he could say a word, the policeman who had spoken earlier asked him, 'Is this Posco?'

'Yes,' replied the doctor, but he went on hastily, 'but I'm sorry, I cannot release my patient to you. As you can see, he is down with malaria fever and he is undergoing treatment.'

'I see,' said the policeman scornfully. 'But I insist that Posco must come with us immediately – sick or not. That is the order given from above.' Having said that, the policeman went over to where Posco lay and held his hand that was attached to the drip. In the twinkling of an eye, the policeman yanked out the needle that connected the drip to Posco's hand. Posco cried out in pain as the doctor looked on in horror.

Ignoring Posco's yell of pain, the policeman who had cut off Posco's drip supply, brought out a pair of handcuffs and fastened them securely around Posco's hands. Then he pulled Posco off the bed, leaving the tube, along with the needle, dangling in the air.

The doctor looked on in utter incredulity. He wanted to raise a protest. He opened his mouth but no word came out. He was too shocked to speak.

When he found his voice at last, he said, 'But this is ridiculous. Have you policemen no brains at all? How on earth can you handcuff a sick man?'

The policeman did not answer; he pushed Posco, who was obviously reluctant to move, towards the door.

'You can't do that to my patient,' shouted the doctor. 'I will not allow you…'

But then, the doctor heard the sound of guns unclicking. He turned to face the three other policemen who had remained silent until now. The three of them had riffles in their hands.

'Alright, alright, you can take him,' the doctor concurred as he spread out his hands resignedly and stepped back toward the door. He did not wish to lose his life yet.

'Now, move to the door,' ordered the policeman.

Before Posco took a step, the door opened to let in a short, black, burly, angry woman in native attire. The woman pushed past the doctor and went into the hospital ward. A new policeman in police uniform followed in her wake.

'That is the man who impregnated my daughter and performed an abortion on her,' said the woman, pointing a forefinger at Posco. 'Arrest him!' ordered the woman.

The new policeman shrugged and brought out another pair of handcuffs. Then he promptly bent down and placed the handcuffs on Posco's legs. The policeman clicked the handcuffs shut and stood up.

The doctor's eyes opened wide. He could not believe the drama that was unfolding before him. If he had been watching this saga on the television, it would have been very funny. But this was no TV series; this was happening in real life. He stood, tongue-tied as Posco was led out of the hospital ward by the five policemen and the burly, angry woman.

Chapter 66

Great Britain

At five p.m., the door bell rang for the second time. Alan Tucker knew who it was even before he opened the door.

'Good Afternoon, Alan,' Reverend Franklin greeted stonily as he brushed past Alan and entered the corridor that led to the big sitting room.

'To what do I owe this honourable visit?' said Alan cheerfully, but he was far from being cheerful. He hated Reverend Mathew Franklin with a passion.

'I just felt it would be great for two knights in the making to form an acquaintance before they are crowned,' replied Reverend Franklin as he was led into the sitting area of Alan Tucker's residence.

Reverend Franklin sat down gingerly on a chair as Alan went over to the bar at the corner of the sitting room. He poured each of them a glass of orange juice and strode over to where Reverend Franklin sat.

'Thank you,' said Reverend Franklin as Alan handed him a glass of juice. Reverend Franklin raised the glass to his lips, but he quickly lowered it and placed it onto a coffee table without tasting the juice in it. His action did not go unnoticed to Alan Tucker.

Alan chuckled as he took a sip of his orange juice. He understood why Mathew Franklin was reluctant to taste the drink he had given him; Mathew Franklin obviously did not trust him; Mathew Franklin obviously did not wish to die yet.

Alan watched bemusedly as Mathew looked around the room, mesmerised by the antiques and expensive décor in the room.

'So how have you been?' Reverend Franklin asked at last, bringing his gaze back at Alan.

'Very well, thank you,' replied Alan, smiling cautiously. He was still wondering why Reverend Franklin had actually come to see him. All his speech about wanting to make friends with him did not cut ice with Alan.

'I'm sure you've been very well indeed; especially considering the fact that you've been able to wipe Mark and his entire family from the surface of the earth!' Reverend Franklin blurted out suddenly.

The smile slowly faded from Alan's mouth.

How had Franklin known about Mark?

Alan stared at Franklin in utter amazement; he was oblivious to the glass that had dropped from his hand onto the white, fluffy rug on the floor, spilling the coloured content onto the rug.

'I… I… don't know what you're talking about,' Alan managed to say at last. He averted his eyes from Reverend Franklin as he said so. He had gone through so much stress these past few days, and he was finding it difficult to pretend he did not know what his greatest enemy was saying.

'I'm sure you do not know what I'm talking about,' said Reverend Franklin sarcastically, 'but you will know it when the time comes.'

Alan's face creased into a frown as hot, fierce anger boiled within him. He wished he had his pistol at home; but he kept all his weapons at his secret office. He had always thought his home should be as clean and as holy as possible because this was the home the church and members of the public knew. Now he regretted not having kept a pistol handy. He would have blown Reverend Franklin's brains apart and he would have been able to keep him mute forever. But right now, he needed his privacy; now that he knew his secret was known to his greatest enemy, he needed to think fast. The ceremony for the crowning of the knights was a few hours away and he had to be one of them. He would do whatever it took. But at that moment, Reverend Franklin had to leave his house.

'Franklin,' he said through gritted teeth.

'Yes, my dear Reverend,' replied Reverend Franklin sarcastically.

'Get out!' shouted Alan.

'Of course, I'm leaving your house,' replied Reverend Franklin, standing up from the chair, 'but let me quickly remind you that there's no way of escape for you. Apart from myself, three other gentlemen know your story and the last discussion I had with my nephew, Mark, was caught on tape. But before we inform the police, we want to gather all evidence we can gather to nail you; that should take about an hour and a half. So you see my dear friend, in a couple of hours, the police will be visiting, so I'll advise you to be ready.'

Reverend Franklin got to the door, but he turned back abruptly. 'Let me give you a last piece of advice, Tucker,' he said to Alan coolly. 'Forget about being crowned a knight tomorrow, for you will never become one. I'll try and pay you a visit when you go to jail!'

And with that, Reverend Franklin left Alan Tucker's residence.

Alan Tucker stood rigid for a long time after Reverend Franklin had left. He cursed Alex several times for disobeying him. He reasoned that if Alex had not ignored his numerous warnings over that Nike lady, he would not have had any cause to travel to Nigeria. He would not have met Mark again and his secrets would have been kept from his greatest enemy, Reverend Mathew Franklin.

I should have gotten rid of that Nike lady a long time ago, he reasoned.

Just then, the grandfather's clock on the floor beside the piano chimed six times. At the same time, an idea struck Alan Tucker's heart. He was sure that Reverend Mathew Franklin had not been bluffing when he threatened to expose him. He knew he truly had no way of escape. In a couple of hours, the police might come knocking on his door and his life-long ambition of becoming a knight would never be achieved. Truly, Reverend Mathew Franklin had advised him to forget his hope of becoming a knight, but he could prove him wrong. If the church refused him, he could make himself a knight; he would die a knight before the police came.

Without further delay, Alan left the sitting room and went into his late father's bedroom. He opened a wardrobe and there hung his father's regalia, all complete and unruffled, just as his father had hung it there before he died.

Alan pulled out the knight's clothes and accessories and laid them on the bed. He quickly undressed and changed into his late father's knightly regalia. He stood in front of a mirror and admired himself. He was the exact replica of his late father on the day he was crowned a knight. Alan smiled sadly. Despite all his efforts to ensure he was ceremoniously crowned a knight by the church, he was going to end up performing the ceremony alone, and in the confines of his own house.

But he would end up proving Reverend Franklin wrong; he would not go to jail. He would be the first knight before others were crowned the following day and he would die in his own house.

Determinedly, he went to the sitting room, to the bar area and opened a side cupboard. Inside the drawer lay a cardboard paper and a blue-ink felt pen. These, he brought out and cut a big square from the huge cardboard paper. He left the remaining pieces of cardboard paper on the coffee table and, with the pen, he scribbled a bogus statement on the square cardboard he had made.

Alan Tucker went into the kitchen and found a gum bottle in one of the cupboards. He took the gum to the sitting room and stood on the coffee table on which he had placed the remaining pieces of cardboard. With the help of the gum, he pasted the square cardboard on which he had written a statement on the wall opposite the piano and climbed down from the table. He read the note he had scribbled on the cardboard paper. It read:

Alan Tucker, The First Knight.

'Yes, I am the first Knight,' said Alan aloud as he read his scribble. 'I am the first before others.'

Satisfied, Alan Tucker went back into the kitchen and found a thick rope. He went back to the sitting room and climbing once more on the coffee table. He tied the rope to the base of the chandelier hanging from the ceiling. Next, he tied the other end of the rope around his neck. He tightened it and winced as intense pain seared through his body from the neck area.

Just then, the grandfather's clock on the floor beside the piano chimed seven times.

The two hours of grace Alan Tucker had given himself was up. Any moment from now, the police would come knocking. He had to be dead before they came.

But Alan reasoned that he had to leave a note for Reverend Franklin; he had to let Reverend Franklin know that he, Alan Tucker, had won the battle between them. He had to let his enemy know that he would never stay long enough to be sent to jail. He had to let Reverend Franklin know that he would never have the joy of seeing Alan Tucker sent to jail.

Minding the fact that he had very little time left to write the note to Reverend Franklin, Alan Tucker left the rope that was firmly tied around his neck and bent down to pick up the remaining piece of cardboard paper from the coffee table. But he had no opportunity to write that note to Reverend Franklin. His eyes rolled upwards as his neck bone snapped. Alan Tucker struggled for a while to be free of the rope, but it was too late.

A few minutes later, his hands fell limply by his side as he breathed his last.

Thirty minutes after Alan Tucker died, his limp body was found hanging from the ceiling by the police.

Chapter 67

Nigeria, West Africa

King Igwe, the King of Alugu village, in Eastern Nigeria, paced about his beautiful palace. He was in a dilemma. He had just learnt that one of the two foreigners who were rescued from the little hut was the granddaughter of his arch enemy, King Oba Adeogun.

As far as the two Kings were concerned, there would never be any love lost between them and their generations to come.

When he learnt of Nike Adeogun's family linage, the first reasoning that came to his mind was to eliminate her and send her carcass to her grandfather. But the Queen, a woman who had a heart of gold, had insisted that he sent the girl, along with her friend, back to her grandfather in good health.

The Queen held a cherished place in King Igwe's heart. They had been childhood sweethearts and she had stood by him through thick and thin.

King Igwe would never forget the kind deed of his wife a long time ago, before he became King. He had been hospitalised and he was in need of a kidney transplant. The Queen had willingly given him one of her kidneys and from that day, she had held a special place in the King's heart.

The Queen had pleaded with him to call a truce with the king of Illudun land by sending his granddaughter to him in one piece, but he did not want to project an image of cowardice to his enemy. The Queen, however, had assured him that the long standing strife between the two warring kingdoms would end when Nike was returned to her grandfather.

After a while, King Igwe pressed an intercom beside the royal chair and a guard came in.

'Prepare the two visitors for the long journey to Illudun land immediately,' he ordered.

'Yes, Your Highness,' said the guard and he left the palace.

Nike and Alex arrived at Illudun land the following evening. They were ushered to the King's presence immediately.

King Oba Adeogun was seated in his royal chair when Nike came in with Alex. He stood up immediately and embraced his granddaughter.

Alex looked around the palace. He was mesmerised by the sheer opulence of it. Nike would never cease to amaze him. To think that a girl like Nike came from a very wealthy family greatly amazed him.

'Granddad, meet my boyfriend, Alex,' Nike said.

Alex extended his hand towards the King for a handshake. But Nike jabbed him in the ribs.

'You don't greet a King in Yoruba land like that,' she admonished him. 'You have to prostrate to the King.'

'Oh, I'm sorry,' Alex apologised then he hesitated. 'But how do I prostrate to the king?' he asked.

The King laughed then.

'Don't worry,' said the King. 'You're forgiven.'

'Thank you, King,' said Alex.

Chapter 68

Inspector Coker stood before Posco with his hands in his trouser pockets. Posco shivered as he looked at the huge inspector who loomed over him like a mountain threatening to fall on a miserable squirrel.

Posco was strapped to a chair in the cold, unpainted dungeon that served as the interrogation room. He was tired and weak and famished as he sat in the chair, waiting for the round of questionings to begin.

Posco was not alien to Inspector Coker's brutality when it came to forcing out information from people. Some of his friends had the misfortune of coming under Inspector Coker's interrogation and to his knowledge, only one of them had come out unhurt. The others had either been severely injured in the course of the interrogation or they had died.

Inspector Coker was not one to mourn the death of a suspected criminal. Posco knew that if he died in the hands of Inspector Coker, a certificate of death by accident would be issued in no time and the matter would be buried.

'Posco,' said Inspector Coker gently, 'consider your health before deciding to go through any form of torture.' He paused to let that advice sink into Posco. 'Of course, you may choose to go through a little torture before you talk, or you may decide to talk and remain unscathed,' continued Inspector Coker.

Posco decided to talk and remain unscathed. He reasoned that if he could get a good lawyer to defend him, he could go to prison with his body members still intact.

'I will answer all your questions to the best of my ability, sir,' he said to the inspector.

'Good,' retorted Inspector Coker gladly, 'very good.'

'Now shall we start by knowing who or where the evil boss is?'

'I don't know where he is,' replied Posco honestly.

As Inspector Coker lifted up a huge fist and flailed it in the direction of Posco, Posco continued fearfully. 'I... I suppose Silas would know.'

'And who the hell is Silas?' shouted Inspector Coker impatiently.

Posco fearfully gave the inspector, Silas' address as well as the address of his favourite hotel and his mobile number.

Fifteen minutes later, Silas was picked up from the hotel swimming pool. The policemen who came to arrest him remained deaf to the pleas of Silas' whores as he was led away handcuffed, dripping with water, with only his pair of swimming trunks on him.

Inspector Coker hated the slightest delay in any case he handled. As far as Inspector Coker was concerned, patience was not a virtue!

Chapter 69

Two days after Nike and Alex arrived at King Oba Adeogun's palace, the land of Alugu, in the eastern parts of Nigeria, received an unexpected visitor.

King Oba Adeogun paid his long time enemy a special visit that day. However, his visit to the Ibo land was that of peace and not of war. King Oba Adeogun visited King Igwe to show his appreciation for saving the life of his precious granddaughter.

'What you have done for me is far beyond what ordinary words can describe,' said King Adeogun to King Igwe. 'Apart from coming to show my appreciation for your kindness, I wish to offer my sincere apology for the grudge I have carried in my heart towards the Ibos for so long,' continued King Adeogun. 'Now I believe the strife between us has been totally unnecessary.'

King Igwe got up from his magnificent royal chair and hugged his one-time rival.

There was joy throughout the town of Alugu. There would be no more enmity between the two kings. The hatchet had now been buried and the memories of the civil war of nineteen sixty-seven had been buried with it.

A lavish ceremony was conducted in honour of the two Kings, who had become great allies.

Before King Oba Adeogun went back to his native Illudun land, gifts were exchanged between the two great Kings and a certificate of memorandum was issued, allowing inter-marriages and trade relations between the two great towns.

For the Yorubas living in Illudun land, and for the Ibos living in Alugu land, a new dawn had begun. From now henceforth, there would be peace in the two lands and there would always be peace and love between the two great tribes.

However, in Illudun land, in King Oba Adeogun's palace, in Alex Tucker bedroom, there was emotional chaos going on. Alex Tucker tossed and turned on his huge bed throughout the night. He was tired of sleeping all alone in the big room with the massive bed in it, all without the touch of a woman. Alex needed Nike to be beside him. If he was in England, he would not have minded one bit if Nike was not with him; he would simply have gone out to meet any of his other girlfriends. But he felt somehow trapped here; he could not go looking for Nike wherever she had chosen to hide in the whole palace; he had to wait for her to come into his room. He cursed aloud.

Initially, Alex was dismayed when he learnt Nike would be sleeping in another room, very far from his. Nike had explained to him that her grandfather was opposed to premarital sex; thus, they would never be allowed to share a room in his palace.

Alex had wondered what the King would do to him if he knew how long his granddaughter had been having *premarital sex* with *him*. The king would probably have a heart attack before ordering him to be castrated. Alex chuckled at the thought. But he decided to respect the King's wish and stay put in his room. He would resist the urge to wander into Nike's room for a good *fuck*. However, he wondered for how long this would go on.

Suddenly, there was a knock on the door.

'Come in,' said Alex.

Nike came in holding a couple of wedding catalogues in her hand. She was looking exquisite in a pink and white floral evening dress and diamond earrings. Her long hair was tied in a bun at the back of her head and she wore no makeup save for a slight pink lipstick.

Alex felt a stirring in his loins. He got up from the bed and walked towards Nike.

'I've been waiting for two days, Nike,' he said sultrily. 'Why did it take you so long to come to me?'

But Nike pushed him away and moved back from him. 'Alex, I've told you that there's no room for sex in my grandfather's palace,' she admonished.

Alex chuckled and moved closer to her. 'There's plenty of room here for a long, good *fuck*,' he said to her. 'Look, there's the bed; it's big enough for the two of us.'

Nike pushed him again. 'Alex, I'm dead serious about what I said,' she retorted angrily. 'My grandfather thinks I'm still a virgin and I'll be damned if I do anything to make him believe otherwise.'

Alex laughed out loud then. 'You, Nike, a virgin?' he said laughingly. 'If you're a virgin, then I'll be a goddamned monk!' Alex concluded amidst much laughter and hiccups.

'Shut up,' shouted Nike. 'Don't you know that walls have ears? Someone might hear you and report whatever you say to my grandfather. Now you don't want to go back to England in cremated form, do you?'

Alex shut up instantly. 'No, I don't,' he said seriously. He did not want a repetition of the saga he went through at the hands of his uncle, Alan, and his cohorts. The experience was enough to last him a life time!

'Good,' said Nike. 'Now, I want you to look through these catalogues and point out the suit you would like to wear for our wedding.' Nike threw the catalogues on the bed as she talked.

'Before we came to Nigeria, I explained to my grandfather that you proposed marriage to me back in England. That's the only way my grandfather would understand why I could travel all the way from England with a man,' Nike went on. 'My grandfather is planning the wedding of the century for us and he wants us to get married as soon as possible. I'm sure he'll summon you into his palace when he has fixed a date for the wedding.' And with that, Nike left the room.

For a long time after Nike had left, Alex gazed at the closed door and the catalogues intermittently. He could not fathom how he could be having a wedding without his consent. The King had not even bothered to give him the honour of verifying if Nike had told him the truth or not; he just went ahead and planned a wedding for them simply because he had followed his granddaughter to Nigeria.

Alex thought that Nike might not be the only one in her family who was eccentric. Alex tried to remember the day or the time in memorial that he had asked the King for Nike's hand in marriage and he failed totally. He did not remember ever giving the King an inkling that he was in the least interested in his granddaughter.

While they were receiving treatment in the hospital, Alex had a sober reflection on his relationship with Nike and he had decided that all the major troubles he had encountered in his life had been because of her.

Nike was the one who had insisted he went for a blood test to determine their genotypic compatibility and the result of the blood test had opened up a can of worms. In effect, he had almost died at the hands of his uncle because of his association with Nike. Now, he knew why his uncle had vehemently kicked against his relationship with her. Alan Tucker had desired the father-son relationship to continue and he had foreseen that Nike might compel Alex to seek out who the murderer of his real father was. Now he knew that Alan must have sensed the strong-will and determination embedded in Nike.

Alex was not sure if he should be grateful to Nike for all this or not. He was not sure if he would have been happier for it, had he not discovered Alan killed his father.

Had it not been said that what a man did not know could not kill him?

Now that the mystery surrounding his life had been unravelled, Alex felt that something had died within him. The love and trust he had shared with Alan since he was a child had died and a blank void had been created in his heart. He could not bring himself to admit that he was in love with anyone, much less Nike. In fact, he was sure he did not love Nike enough to want to share the rest of his life with her; the lady had caused him more heartache and unpleasant surprises than all the girlfriends he had in his life put together. All he wanted most in the world was to get as far away from Nike as possible because she would always remind him of Alan's betrayal. They would be better off if they went their separate ways.

Since he came out of the hospital, he had been counting the days until he could go back to England and live his life all over again – without Nike of course! Now, as he thought about what Nike had just told him, he felt that the King and his granddaughter were not only controlling – they were also *insane*!

Alex picked up one of the catalogue lying on the bed and flipped the pages with his fingers, not really stopping to admire the different designer suits advertised in it.

'So the king expects me to marry his crazy granddaughter,' he said aloud.

'Like hell I will!' he exclaimed.

Chapter 70

'The King wishes to see you, dear princess,' a servant said to Nike.

Nike stood up from her bed immediately. In the years that she had come to know her grandfather, she knew that he didn't like being kept waiting whenever he summoned her into his presence. She also observed that the King had been extraordinarily kind towards her; he took special attention to her whenever she was around him. It was obvious to all and sundry that out of all the king's children and grandchildren, Nike was his favourite; and Nike relished every minute of it. Nike felt that the King was trying to make up for the way he treated her father and mother in the past and since she had come to love and accept the old man as the only close family she had left, she had always tried to put up her best behaviour whenever she was in his presence. She had even gone as far as telling him lies when she felt the situation demanded it.

'Here I am, grand-dad,' she said as she entered the King's private sitting room.

'Come here, child,' the King called out to her, beckoning to her to have a seat beside him.

Nike strolled over to where the King was and she sat beside him on the huge leather sofa.

'I have called you for an important discussion, child,' said the King.

Nike nodded and looked at her grandfather expectantly.

'You know I am growing old now, don't you?' the King asked her.

Nike nodded again, but she remained silent.

Then the King dropped the bombshell. 'I've been diagnosed with a terminal cancer!'

'What!' Nike exclaimed. 'How… how come?' she managed to ask.

The King smiled wryly. 'I've been living with prostate cancer for ten years,' he said.

Nike looked at her grandfather in total amazement. She would never have believed that the man who sat beside her had any sickness in him. Since she had come to know her grandfather, he had always possessed extraordinary strength. He was so strong mentally and physically that everyone who knew him thought he was super human.

'I've come this far because there's enough money to keep me going,' the King continued. He looked at Nike for a long, uncomfortable moment before blurting out, 'Nike, I want you to marry that boy and have a son within nine months.'

'What!' Nike exclaimed. She could not believe that her grandfather would force her into a quick marriage just for the purpose of having a son.

And besides, why would her grandfather want a son so fast anyway?

As if reading her thoughts, King Adeogun gave a short, mirthless laugh and said to her, 'I know the question you want to ask me right now is why I want you to have a son in nine months, not so?'

Nike nodded. It was actually so! She wanted to know why her grandfather would want her to produce a child she did not plan for.

'You see, Nike,' King Adeogun began, 'there is a law in this land that stipulates that only a male child can succeed his father on the throne.'

Nike knew that already. She nodded impatiently and urged her grandfather to go on.

'Well,' continued the king, 'you're already aware that I had no other son apart from your late father.'

Nike nodded again, but she remained silent.

The king went on. 'But there's a clause in the law that allows for a grandson or great-grandson to succeed his grandfather after his demise, provided he was born before the king dies, and provided he was born by the first daughter or the first grand-daughter of the king. Unfortunately, my first daughter is barren.'

Nike was very curious now. 'What do you mean *barren*?' she asked the king.

King Adeogun smiled bitterly; he reflected for a long time before answering Nike. 'My first daughter, your aunt, cannot have a child. After many years of trying for a child, she has finally been diagnosed with cancer of the womb.' King Adogun stopped to reflect on this for a moment and then he continued sorrowfully. 'My first daughter, Adebi, will undergo surgery to have her womb removed next week; next week, Adebi will become an empty vessel as far as providing a son to succeed me is concerned.'

The King looked at Nike pleadingly and went on. 'That is why I need you to get married and have a son as soon as possible, Nike. You're my only hope of ensuring that the royal lineage remains in my family after my death.

Otherwise, the crown would be taken away from our family, and it would be given to another family. Now I do not want that to happen. My ancestors were the first to settle in this land and I would be damned if the crown went to another family.' The King looked at Nike almost tearfully and then he went on. 'My child, I want you to secure this throne for our generations to come.'

Nike looked at her grandfather; she was full of pity for the old man. She saw how frail and emaciated he looked now. She resolved to do his bidding. She would marry Alex and have a son that would succeed her grandfather, the King. But two questions came to her mind: *Was she fertile enough to produce a son within nine months? And how could she be sure it was going to be a male child and not a female one?*

For the second time, the King pre-empted Nike's questions.

'I have a family doctor here who would ensure that you're given adequate and thorough medical checkups. He'll also administer medications and advice that would be projected towards you having a male child,' said the king. 'I have briefed the doctor about my plan already.' For the first time, the King's smile had a touch of joy. He picked up a mobile phone and spoke into it.

Thirty minutes later, doctor Wale Macauley came into the king's presence.

Nike almost jumped out of the chair when she set her eyes on him.

Doctor Macauley prostrated fully in honour of the King.

The King stood up and embraced the young, amiable doctor.

'Doctor Macauley, meet my granddaughter, Nike; she's the one I told you about,' said the King.

Smiling, Doctor Macauley turned to face Nike and then he froze. He stood rigid, gazing at Nike as his smile faded to a thin line. His facial muscles softened as the feelings he had tried to suppress over the past few years resurfaced. He remembered those days when Nike was a patient in his care at the school clinic. He remembered the feelings that gradually developed within him as he spent his days, caring for the teenager. He remembered when Nike seemed to have disappeared into thin air and how he frantically searched for her everywhere he could, while being careful not to make the school authorities aware that he had a special interest in Nike Adeogun. He had wanted to see her through school, nurture her and eventually marry her when the time was right. But Nike had left the school clinic without being discharged and he had not set his eyes on her... until now.

Over the years, Doctor Macauley had struggled with his emotions to suppress the love he had developed for Nike Adeogun. Eventually, he had met and fallen in love with a pretty young doctor, who had been transferred to the general hospital in Lagos where he worked before he was fully employed by King Adeogun as his personal physician. And, ironically, they had their wedding fixed for the third Saturday of the month.

Doctor Macauley made a quick mental calculation. *That was sixteen days away.*

He had never for once thought that Nike Adeogun could be related to the great King Oba Adeogun. How Nike could have gone through so much hardship as a teenager, when she was a granddaughter to a wealthy King would forever beat his imagination.

But now that he had set his eyes on Nike Adeogun again, all the feelings he had managed to suppress over the years came to the fore; and the love he thought he had for his fiancée seemed to dim.

'Have you two met before?' asked the King, looking from one person to the other.

'N… no, not at all,' Nike was quick to answer. She had told the King so many lies and she did not want her sordid past to be made known to him. The truth would definitely break his heart. She forced a smile at Doctor Macauley as she extended her hand to him for a handshake.

'I'm pleased to meet you,' she said.

'My pleasure,' replied Doctor Macauley smoothly. But he was still looking at Nike with apparent amazement.

Nike silently wished he would stop looking at her.

Eventually Doctor Macauley turned to the King and smiled. 'Your lovely granddaughter reminds me of someone I went to the university with, sir,' he said.

The King chuckled. 'My lovely granddaughter is studying at the Oxford University in the United Kingdom,' said the King proudly. 'I am sure she's not the one you went to school with. However, I want you to meet Nike officially. I have briefed her of my plans and she's all for it. She's ready to give me a great-grandson.'

Doctor Macauley was silent for a while then he smiled wryly. 'That's good news, your majesty,' he said. 'May I speak with Nike privately, sir?'

'Of course,' replied the King happily. 'Of course you can.'

Nike followed Doctor Macauley to a private lounge in the palace and as soon as they were out of the King's earshot, Doctor Macauley grabbed her by the shoulders and pulled her to himself.

'I have searched for you everywhere, Nike; Oh how I have longed to see you again,' he said, holding Nike in a bear hug.

After some time, he pulled back and asked her the question that had been on his mind for so long. 'Nike, why did you leave the hospital without informing me?'

Nike sighed. She did not wish to remember what she went through at the Blueberry secondary school, but she felt she owed Doctor Macauley an explanation. After all, he was so kind to her back then.

'The principal, Mr Lucas, smuggled me out of the hospital and warned me never to return either to the hospital or to the school again. He actually told the school driver to take me as far away from Lagos as possible.' Then a memory struck Nike's mind. She remembered that the school driver had informed her that Mr Lucas had told him to take her to Illudun land in those days. *Life sure had a way of playing its own games*, she thought. Perhaps, if the school driver had brought her here, she would have met her grandfather and she would have been living in total bliss ever since then. She would not have turned out to be the criminal that she was in Maxwell's house.

'I should have suspected that Mr Lucas was behind it all along,' said Doctor Macauley, cutting into Nike's thoughts. 'How have you been, Nike?' he said after a while.

Nike shrugged. 'I'm fine,' she said. 'I've had my ups and downs in life, but I'm fine now. All I'm now waiting for is for you to give me the all clear medically, so I can give my grandfather his much-desired heir to the throne.' Nike laughed at her own joke.

But Doctor Macauley was not laughing.

'Nike, you can never give your grandfather a great-grandson,' he said quietly.

Nike's smile faded. 'What do you mean?' she asked.

Doctor Macauley looked at her sadly, and then he reiterated what he said. 'Nike, you can never bear a child.'

Nike was still confused. 'I still don't understand what you mean,' she said. 'What makes you so sure of this?'

Doctor Macauley sighed deeply. 'I suppose Mr Lucas did not tell you then,' he said.

'Tell me what?' Nike was almost shouting now.

'Sssh!' admonished Doctor Macauley. 'We need to sit down somewhere and have a deep talk.'

They both went outside to the patio and sat on chairs laid out under a canopy in the garden. There, Doctor Macauley told Nike all about her damaged womb and how they had to remove it to prevent further contamination with other organs.

Nike covered her face with her hands and wept.

Doctor Macauley took out a handkerchief from his breast pocket and wiped her tears away.

'Why… why didn't you tell me then?' Nike asked; but she already knew the answer.

'I was just trying to protect you from more pain,' said Doctor Macauley. Nike nodded. She believed him.

Next week, Adebi will become an empty vessel as far as providing a son to succeed me is concerned.

If Adebi was an empty vessel, then I would be a broken vessel, thought Nike sadly.

'I beg your pardon?' said Doctor Macauley.

Nike jumped. She was not aware that she had spoken her thoughts out loud. 'I'm sorry,' she apologised. 'I was just thinking about my poor grandfather.'

Doctor Macaulay reached for her hand across the table and gently massaged it in his own.

'Marry me, Nike,' he said suddenly.

'What?' whispered Nike.

'I said marry me,' Doctor Macaulay repeated. 'I have been waiting for this moment all my life. Please say yes, Nike. Please.'

Nike looked into Doctor Macauley's pleading eyes and an emotional string pulled in her heart. She liked Doctor Macauley a lot; she was very grateful to him for being so kind to her. However, she was not sure if the liking she had for him could develop further. Come to think of it, she was not sure of anything anymore. So many strange things had happened to her lately that she felt she was beginning to lose her sanity.

She suddenly remembered Alex sleeping upstairs. She had totally forgotten him until now. A couple of hours ago, she had proposed marriage to him. Alex had even travelled this far just to be with her. He had disobeyed Alan by sticking with her and he had risked his own life in the process. It would not be fair on him if she dumped him now.

Nike shook her head and bit down hard on her trembling lower lip until she tasted blood.

'I... I can't,' she said sadly. 'I'm already committed to a man.'

Doctor Macauley sighed. He looked very sad. He had just lost Nike again.

Nike did not sleep a wink throughout the night. She thought of her life; she thought of all she had been through and she decided that telling lies to her grandfather about her medical condition was not worth it. She resolved to tell him everything, right from the beginning. But she could not face him and tell him; she could not watch him as she broke his heart. She would travel back to the United Kingdom and break the news to him over the phone.

Yes, that would be the best idea, she reasoned.

Before dawn, Nike made a resolve to go back to the United Kingdom that day.

'Granddad, I have decided to travel back to the U.K. this morning,' she said to her grandfather, the King, in the morning.

She was in the king's room. She sat beside the King who lay on the bed. King Adeogun could not hide his surprise.

'Why have you suddenly changed your mind?' he asked her sceptically.

Nike was very careful in answering. 'I… I have considered all Doctor Macauley told me and I feel it would be best to go back and sort things out with my school in the U.K. first before Alex and I commence on the wedding plans. Also, Alex would like to personally inform the people in his office.'

The King looked doubtful. After a long time, he said, 'Promise me you'll come back and fulfil your promise to me.'

'I promise,' said Nike as she kissed her grandfather on his forehead.

As she left her grandfather's room, the King knew something had gone wrong. He had noticed the way Nike and Doctor Macauley looked at each other the previous day and he had instinctively known that they knew each other.

He began to experience fear that Nike too might have an infertility problem.

For the umpteenth time, he regretted his decision to disown his late son, Leke before he died. Now he was left with no heir to succeed him.

The king suddenly felt frail; he felt frightened; he felt very weak.

Nike walked into Alex's room and without preamble, she said to him, 'Get your stuff ready. We'll be travelling back to the U.K. in a few hours.'

Alex opened his eyes and stretched his torso lazily on the bed. 'What did you say?' he asked Nike.

'I said get your lazy arse off the bed and start packing your stuff. We're going back to the U.K. today,' Nike snapped.

'Why the sudden change in our plans?' Alex asked.

'Please ask no questions,' snapped Nike. 'Just do as I say.'

Nike could not help feeling irritable. The most recent sad news she had heard was taking its toll on her. She felt sorry for Alex too; she would never be able to give him a child. She had made him go through the blood test for nothing.

Alex packed his belongings and they had a hasty breakfast.

Before they left the King's palace, Nike went to her grandfather's bedroom to bid him farewell.

She opened the door gently and heard his faint snoring. She went into the room and bent to study her grandfather's features. She was sorry that things had to turn out this way.

She bent low and gave the King a kiss on his forehead.

'I'm sorry, Granddad,' she said. 'I'm so, so, sorry.'

But the King did not reply; he was fast asleep.

Nike turned around and quietly left the room. She did not want to disturb her grandfather's morning siesta.

Soon, Nike and Alex were seated at the back of a Mercedes Benz as a chauffeur drove them to the airport.

As their aeroplane flew over the Atlantic, King Oba Adeogun breathed his last.

Chapter 71

United Kingdom

Alex and Nike arrived at Heathrow airport at four thirty p.m. Forty minutes after they arrived at Heathrow, they were out of the airport.

As Alex took his mobile phone to call a cab, Nike asked Alex, 'Are we going home now or do we check into a hotel first?'

Alex looked at Nike as if he was seeing her for the first time in his life. 'What do you mean *we*?' he asked her.

Before Nike could reply, Alex went on. 'Nike, I appreciate all you've put me through in the past few months, but I want to tell you that I do not wish to continue the relationship with you. I have thought about us the last days we spent in your grandfather's house and I am of the opinion that we're not meant for each other. I'm sorry, Nike, but since I met you, I've been through more hell than the angels of Satan. I do not wish to go through any more troubles; with you, I've had one trouble too many. All I need now is a calm and stable life. From now on, let's go our separate ways.'

And with that, Alex pulled his luggage and left Nike standing there, mouth agape.

Nike stood tongue-tied for a long time. She had rejected Doctor Macauley's marriage proposal because of Alex, only for her to be dumped by the same Alex at the airport, with no house to go to. For the first time since she met Alexander Tucker, she truly hated him.

Nike thought she should not let Alex leave her without giving him some headache. She picked up her luggage and made to run after him.

At that moment, her mobile phone rang. She took it out and opened the flip.

'Hello,' she said irritably.

'Hello,' came the faint reply. 'Is that Princess Nike Adeogun?'

'Yes,' replied Nike, a note of alarm began to sound in her.

'Princess, I'm sorry to tell you that your grandfather has passed away. He died in his sleep this morning. Your attention is needed at the palace immediately.'

Nike felt the whole world was closing in on her.

As the cab man drove towards Camden, Alex thought of what Nike had told him at the airport. She had implied that it would not be wise to go home to the house he had shared with Alan Tucker and he thought she was right. Alex was still shocked at Alan's betrayal. He did not think he could sleep in the family house and not experience the anger he had felt towards Alan in Nigeria. Besides, he would never feel safe in that house, knowing fully well that Alan would be lurking somewhere waiting to pounce on him.

He decided it was better if he found somewhere else to sleep while he secured alternative accommodation for himself. He would think of what to do about Alan later.

A name sprang to his mind: Clarida!

Alex remembered Clarida's tastefully furnished apartment. He decided to go to her. He would ask if he could move in with her and hopefully, they could patch things up between them. He gave the driver Clarida's address and soon they were on their way to Clarida's house.

Clarida opened the door on the second ring of the door bell.

Alex was shocked at what Clarida had turned into. He could not believe the sight that greeted him: Clarida had not only gained a few pounds, she had a bulging tummy and she was shabbily dressed; she wore no makeup and she looked much stressed. Alex also noticed that Clarida carried a fat baby in her arm. The baby looked at Alex, wide-eyed as he sucked on a rubber dummy.

Clarida saw Alex and she instantly went livid. 'What have you come to do in my house?' she spat.

'Take it easy, Clarida,' began Alex, but he was cut short.

'I'm not taking it easy,' shouted Clarida. 'I suppose your bitch of a girlfriend has finally decided you're no longer good for her. That's why you've come to me.'

Clarida observed Alex's luggage and laughed mirthlessly.

'You're a fool, Alex,' she said. As she said it, the dummy dropped out of her baby's mouth. The baby whimpered and started crying. Clarida bent down and picked up the dummy. To Alex's great surprise, Clarida rubbed it on her dress, blew on it and inserted it back into the baby's mouth. The baby stopped crying immediately and started sucking on the rubber profusely. Its round, big eyes were once again, curiously fixed on Alex.

'You made me end up like this, Alex,' said Clarida, pointing at the baby.

'When your *bitch* sent me away and you never bothered to contact me, I was in such a hurry to get married and I ended up with a drunkard and a drug addict.' Tears welled up in Clarida's eyes as she continued. 'This is the product of the union.'

Clarida pointed at her baby as if she regretted having him.

'I never wish to set my eyes on you again, Alex,' she said. Then she opened the door, went into her house and slammed the door at Alex.

Alex looked at the closed door for a long time and sighed. This world was truly full of ironies. Never in his wildest dreams would he have imagined Clarida as he had seen her now.

He thought of Alice. He might just as well check her out. Besides, he felt he owed her an apology. He felt the way he had ignored her had not exactly been *fair*.

Alex called a cab and headed towards Alice's residence in Peckham.

Alex rang the bell to the house Alice shared with four other people. He waited for a minute and then he rang the bell again, but no one answered. He decided to call Alice on her mobile; he was told the line was no longer in service. He rang the bell a few more times. Still, there was no answer.

Sighing, Alex turned round and as he was about to leave the front door, Phillippa walked past, pushing a shopping trolley with one hand and holding a cigarette in the other. He noticed her at once.

'Hey Phillippa,' he called, trying to be cheerful.

Phillippa stopped and looked at Alex as if she was seeing a ghost. After a few seconds, her expression changed to one of total disgust. The first words she spoke to Alex depicted that she hated him with a passion. 'Why did you abandon my friend when she needed you most, you arrogant bastard?' Phillippa blurted out.

Alex was weary of Phillippa; he had always been weary of her ever since the first day he saw her. The lady simply lacked polish. She said anything that came into her thick head without thinking of its implications. He sometimes wondered how Alice could get along with such a rough tomboy. However, he had to play it cool with her; he had to find out what the hell she was talking about. More so, he wished to know Alice's whereabouts.

'I'm sorry to upset you, Phillippa, but I'm afraid I don't know what you're talking about. Besides, where the hell is Alice?'

Phillippa laughed scornfully before she mimicked Alex cynically. '*I don't know what you're talking about. Where is Alice? he says.*'

Alex rolled his eyes in exasperation and waited for Phillippa to finish with her irritating rantings.

'Do you think I don't know your games? Answer me. Do you?' Phillippa went on.

Alex was livid now. 'What the hell are you talking–' he began, but Phillppa cut him short.

'Shut the fuck up and listen to me,' shouted Phillippa and then she continued her accusations. 'I've always known you were no good. You've never been any good and I always told Alice so. I'm very smart, you know. I know guys like you. You are too handsome to stay with one lady. That's why I don't go for handsome men,' she said and stopped to puff profusely on her cigarette.

Alex swore under his breath. He looked at Phillippa carefully; she was scruffily dressed and her greasy hair was a mess as usual. She had an ugly scar which ran from the base of her nose to the side of her cigarette-burnt mouth. To Alex, Phillippa was a perfect picture of a junkie.

Alex wondered if Phillippa ever stopped to question herself if *handsome men*, like she put it, would ever wish to have anything to do with her. But he kept quiet. He did not want to upset her further. Phillippa was his only hope of ever setting his eyes on Alice again.

'Poor nice Alice,' Phillippa went on rhetorically. 'Instead of listening to my advice to dump you, she chose to be angry with me.' Phillippa looked at Alex and blurted out angrily, 'You made Alice pregnant and you instructed your black *bitch* to send her away!'

Alex was shocked at the news he had just heard.

Could Alice have been pregnant for him the whole time? Did she keep the baby?

He was now desperate to know where Alice was. If Alice had kept the pregnancy, he may well settle down with her.

'Please Phillippa, where can I find Alice?' he asked pleadingly.

Phillippa scoffed, puffed a little on her cigarette and told Alex, Alice's new address.

'Thanks a lot Phillippa,' said Alex, relieved.

But Phillippa did not answer; she held the shopping trolley tightly and pushed on.

Alex got to Alice's residence late in the evening. He checked the time on his watch; it was ten p.m. He almost turned back from the door, but then, he summoned up the courage and rang the bell. He might as well see her today, apologise to her and see how everything would go between them. He pushed his luggage against the fence and rang the bell one more time.

To Alex's surprise, a tall, bespectacled gentleman, who looked older than him, opened the door.

Could Alice be living with a man? Alex doubted it. He almost laughed for the sheer thought of it. Alice was not capable of being with another man apart from him; that, at least, he knew very well.

Maybe he had come to the wrong address; maybe Phillippa had given him the wrong address to spite him. He remembered that Phillippa had not bothered to check any address book, *if she had any*, before she gave him Alice's address.

'Good evening,' he said to the gentleman. 'Sorry to disturb you this evening. I was actually looking for an old friend, but I think I may be at the wrong address.'

Professor Flanders recognised Alex immediately. He had seen photographs of him in Alice's old abode when they had gone to collect her things shortly before they got married; and he knew Alice still carried a passport sized photograph of him somewhere in her wallet.

'You may very well be at the right address,' said Professor Flanders wryly. 'Were you looking for Alice?'

Alex was taken aback. How could this gentleman know who he was looking for?

'Yes,' he replied. '…Er, do you know her?'

'Of course I do,' replied Professor Flanders. 'Do come in.' He stepped back so that Alex could go into the house. Alex hesitated for a few seconds before he decided to go in, pulling his luggage after him.

Professor Flanders was not exactly sure if he was doing the right thing by letting Alex into the house to meet Alice. But ever since they got married, Alice and himself had never made love. Anytime he made advances to Alice, she seemed to *freeze* in his arms, so he had always stopped at kissing and cuddling her. He knew Alice had not gotten over Alex and he had decided to give her time to heal. He did not want to be a second fiddle to Alex. Several times, he thought he should have gone ahead and made love to her, but he knew Alice would have just done *it* out of duty to him or out of gratitude towards him and she would have simply imagined in her mind that she was with Alex; but that was not what he wanted from her. He simply did not want to replace Alex in Alice's heart. He wanted Alice to love him with the whole of her heart and with the whole of her being, just as he loved her. Professor Flanders was a patient man, so he had decided to wait for Alice to get over Alex.

Alex was led into the tastefully furnished living room.

'Do have a seat while I go and call Alice,' said Professor Flanders gently.

Alex sat down on one of the soft leather chairs and looked around. The wall was painted cream and the soft, blue fluffy rug matched the blue leather sofa in the living room. There were exquisite paintings on the wall and on a corner of the huge living room stood a dining table and chairs. Beside this, there was a little cupboard which contained books and on top of this cupboard was a laptop.

Alex nodded in admiration of the room. He was about to question himself about who the gentleman of the house was, when his eyes were averted to a picture on the wall, adjacent to where he sat. It was a wedding picture. Alex's heart began to palpitate. Impulsively, he stood up and went over to take a good look at the picture, hoping it was not what he was thinking.

It was indeed what he was thinking. In the picture, Alice was wore a lovely pink, flowing dress, she carried a bouquet of flowers and she had a lovely silvery crown on her head. The gentleman he had seen earlier posed with her in an elegantly tailored wedding suit. They both looked very happy.

There was a note written on the bottom of the picture frame. It read:
Happy married life, Professor and Mrs Flanders.
So Alice was actually married! Alex thought he was dreaming.

Just then, Alice appeared on the staircase, unaccompanied by her husband.

'Hello Alex,' she said softly.

Alex turned around and he saw a very beautiful woman standing before him. If he had not known Alice for long, he would have doubted that she was actually the woman standing there. She had shed a few pounds – no! Alice had shed quite a lot of pounds – and she looked regal in her body-hugging little black evening dress.

Alex quickly ran his eyes admiringly all over Alice; from her lovely, brown hair, which fell down to her back, to her beautiful, oval face and her slender, shapely figure and then to her lovely bare feet.

With the same admiration, Alex trailed his eyes back to Alice's lovely face. He never knew Alice could be so beautiful. He had let the stunning, sinful beauty of Nike lead him astray. Now, he had lost a rare gem. Not only was Alice beautiful physically, she was beautiful at heart and she had a calm disposition. That was what Nike lacked. Alex felt like smacking himself a million times and more for letting Alice go.

Alice was watching him with an expression he could not read. He knew Alice had loved him with the whole of her being before, and he had taken the love she had for him for granted. He hoped she still felt something for him; he was prepared to take her back if she as much as confessed to that.

'Why are you here, Alex?' asked Alice.

Although, she had been secretly longing to see Alex, she was surprised that she felt nothing for him now that she had seen him. The burning feeling of deep, ferocious love that she felt for him before had simply disappeared, only to be replaced by nothing. She felt absolutely nothing for Alex. She was not even angry with him.

Alex was surprised at the first sentence Alice made to him after so long.

'Alice I... I... er came to say sorry,' he stammered. He did not know how to explain his behaviour.

'There's really nothing to feel sorry for,' said Alice calmly. 'If you had not left me, I would not have met the most kind-hearted man on earth. And you know what, he genuinely loves me.'

Alex nodded, but before he could ask the question on his mind, Alice answered it.

'And I love him too. I love him very much.'

Alex felt like crying. He had truly lost Alice. He sighed deeply; he looked sad. 'I guess that ends it all then,' he said.

Alice nodded.

'It's nice seeing you again, Alex, but I'd appreciate it if you stopped coming here. I am now happily married to a wonderful man,' she said pleasantly.

Alex nodded again. 'I guess you're right. I think I'd better be going now,' he said, bending to pick up his luggage. Then he remembered something. Standing up, he asked Alice, 'What about... What about the baby?'

'I lost him,' replied Alice quietly. 'I lost him shortly after he was born.'

Alex shut his eyes; he was trying desperately to shut back the tears that were threatening to fall from his eyelids. They fell anyway.

'I'm sorry,' he said after a while. 'I'm truly, very sorry.'

'That's alright,' said Alice. 'Good-bye, Alex.'

Alex turned and without looking back, he left the house.

Professor Flanders had hidden somewhere on the top of the stairs and he had listened to the conversation. He knew it was not right for him to do so, but he had to know where he stood with Alice. He had to be sure she had fallen in love with him; so he had stood and listened to every word. Now that he was sure of Alice's love for him, he was so overjoyed, he felt like dancing on the roof-top.

He came out of hiding and bounced down the stairs. Alice turned around and smiled at her husband. Her eyes were filled with intense love for him. She felt she owed him her life; she owed him everything she had become.

After her baby died, Professor Flanders had done everything in the world to make her happy. He had taken her on holidays to Florida and Brazil and the Caribbean Islands; he had bought her gifts and occasionally, when he was not in a hurry to go and lecture his students, he had brought her breakfast in bed.

Alice had, in turn, paid him back for his efforts by enrolling at the gym and making herself a very beautiful bride to him. But she could not explain why she always froze up anytime they were about to make love. She reasoned that her mind must have been so tuned into Alex that it had to take a strong willpower to tune it off him. Now that she had seen Alex, she wondered how she could have been so blindingly in love with him, when she had someone who was far better than all the Alexes in the whole, wide world. She now had her flesh of her flesh and the bone of her bones. She now had Professor Jeremy Flanders.

Smiling lovingly at her husband, Alice stretched out her arms and ran to meet him. Soon, they were engaged in a passionate kiss.

After a while, Professor Flanders pulled back. He had a questioning look in his eyes. The question in his eyes said, '*Shall we?*'

He held his breath as he waited for an answer.

Alice did not hesitate in her reply. 'Yes!' she said aloud. 'Please take me, right now.'

Her husband let out his breath and picked her up in his arms. He smiled down at her and carried her up the stairs and into their bedroom.

Alex dragged his luggage tiredly along the street. He had gone a little bit further down the road when he realised that Alice and her husband lived very close to his family home. It was actually a walking distance from his home.

Life sure had a way of playing its games on people.

On impulse, Alex led himself towards the home he had shared with his uncle, Alan Tucker, all his life. His heart seemed to palpitate faster as he walked on. He knew how sinister Alan had become; he knew he was threading on the shores of danger as he walked towards his home, but he wanted to find out from his uncle, why he had gone to such lengths to destroy their family. He wanted to know if Alan needed help. Maybe the man had some mental or psychological problems and he badly needed his mind to be restored, he reasoned. Maybe all Alan did was a way of crying out for help.

Even though, Alex failed to convince himself with his own excuse for his uncle's ignoble behaviour, he still felt he had to see him; he felt he had to talk to him.

What if Alan had a deadly weapon at home? asked a tiny voice within him.

Alex shrugged off the warning. Alan, surely, was not expecting him to be alive by now. He must have expected him to be dead, so he could not have been prepared to kill him the second time.

With determination, Alex moved on towards the family house on Goldhurst Terrace, pulling his heavy luggage after him. However, when he got to the house, he discovered that it had been cordoned off with police tape. He stood to gaze at the scenario before him.

Where was his uncle?

Alarm bells suddenly started ringing in his mind. *Could Alan have been arrested by the police?*

Alex moved closer to the house to have a better glimpse of it. As he did so, an elderly grey-haired man with a little walking stick walked past him. He noticed Alex gazing at the tape and he decided to offer him an explanation, albeit unsolicited for. He moved closer to Alex and spoke in a conversational tone.

'I understand that the chap who was living here committed suicide. I also understand the bloke was stinking rich.'

The elderly man chuckled. Oblivious of Alex's bewildered expression, he went on, 'Funny though, why rich folks choose to kill themselves. I don't know what they expect poor people like us to do.' The old man shook his head. 'It's just a pity,' he said. 'A bloody waste of good money.' And with that, he left Alex who stood, rooted to a spot and moved on.

Alex could not believe that his uncle could actually commit suicide. After everything, after all he'd done to everybody's lives, after all the misery he had caused, after all the blood shed he had done, Alan finally decided to take his own life. *It was such a pity indeed.*

Alex pushed his bag against a fence and leaning on the fence beside the bag; he slowly slid down and crouched on his knees. He raked his fingers through his hair in exasperation.

'When will this nightmare end?' he asked aloud.

He got no answer.

Chapter 72

Nigeria, West Africa

Nike arrived at the King's palace six hours after she got on the next available flight back to Nigeria. She felt tired after having travelled such an unexpected long journey. But she had to see her grandfather, the King, immediately. She had to be sure that he had actually passed away.

She dropped her bags in the lounge and ran to her grandfather's sitting room. There, she met several people wailing and mourning and she was convinced that her grandfather had actually passed away.

Nike ran to her late grandfather's private sitting room within the palace. It was so quiet in there. Nike had an eerie feeling standing in the sitting room where she had sat at her grandfather's feet and listened to him as he told her stories that happened in the days of yore. Nike found it quite difficult to realise that the man she had come to know as the only close family she had left, and the man she had come to be so attached to, had died; she was never to set her eyes on him again.

She gently, cautiously walked to her late grandfather's bedroom and opened the door. She peeped into it and found the body of her grandfather perfectly dressed in white and lying on the bed. She tiptoed into the room and gazed at her grandfather's face. It was as though, the old man was sleeping. But Nike knew that the man was dead. She bent down and gave him a kiss on his forehead. As she raised her head up, tears dropped from her eyelids onto her grandfather's face.

Without bothering to wipe the tears off the dead man's face, Nike turned around and quietly left the room, just as she had come in.

King Oba Adeogun was buried two weeks after his death. The burial ceremony was attended by the entire population of the town – both old and young. Many eminent personalities from neighbouring towns and beyond were also present. Throughout the funeral and burial ceremony, Nike felt lonely. For the first time since she lost her father, she regretted not having anyone close to her; she regretted not having anyone she could call her own.

Nike noticed that Doctor Wale Macauley was conspicuously absent throughout the burial ceremony. She wondered why he chose not to come and give the King his last respect. Nike knew Doctor Macauley to be a gentleman, who would go out of his way to make others happy. She knew he would have attended the ceremony if nothing had gone wrong somewhere.

Nike wondered what could have gone wrong to prevent Doctor Macauley from attending her grandfather's funeral.

Maybe he was just trying to avoid seeing her because she had refused his marriage proposal.

Nike regretted her hasty decision in refusing Doctor Macauley's proposal; she had done so, all because she had thought Alex would marry her. But Alex had dumped her like a pile of rubbish; and now, she was left with no man she could call her own. Nike felt a burning hatred towards Alex. Thinking of it, Doctor Macauley would have made a better husband than Alex Tucker. Doctor Macauley was calm and cool and polite and he struck Nike as a one-woman man. He was very much unlike Alex, who could not be trusted to stay with one woman. She made a mental note to call Doctor Macauley later.

The day after the burial ceremony, Nike took a long walk around the beautiful palace. She walked past the large private swimming pool, past the conservatory in which were planted all kinds of beautiful flowers – roses, orchids, hibiscus and sunflowers. She remembered the many times she sat with her grandfather in the conservatory, just drinking tea and talking about everything and nothing. This was where her grandfather had shed tears and begged for her forgiveness. She turned away and walked through the vast compound towards the garage. Because she really had nothing to do, she stopped to count the cars that were packed in the garage, some covered with tarpaulins, others left bare. She counted the cars one by one; she counted twenty-eight. What in God's name was her granddad doing with twenty-eight cars. She remembered the biblical words; *all is vanity and a striving after the winds.*

Vanity; all was indeed vanity. Her grandfather was gone, gone for good and he had left all behind. More saddening was the fact that her grandfather's most cherished crown, the symbol of his royalty, would be taken away from his lineage and given to another family. The old man had fought tooth and nail to ensure that the royal crown stayed in his family after his death, but since he had left no male heir to succeed him, the Adeogun family had to relinquish their rights to the throne of Illudun land.

Nike was not exactly interested in the throne, but she felt sorry for her grandfather, who was known to be a warrior and who had fought for whatever he believed in till his dying day, but who, as fate would have it, had not been able to lay permanent claim to one thing he had cherished most in his life – the Royal crown of Illudun land.

Nike left the garage and walked determinedly towards the little building that housed her grandfather's grave. King Oba Adeogun had, before his death, requested to be buried in the compound of his palace and his wish had been obeyed.

Even in death, King Oba Adeogun refused to let go of power.

Nike opened the door of the building and went in. she was not scared of her grandfather when she was alive and she wouldn't be scared of him in death. She took a look at the grave which would now house her grandfather for eternity and for the first time since her father's demise, Nike wept bitterly.

At ten p.m. the following day, Doctor Wale Macauley's mobile phone rang. He was lying on the bed beside his new bride when he heard his phone ringing. He picked it up and saw that the caller was Nike Adeogun. His heart skipped a beat. He realised he was still very much in love with Nike, despite the deep affection he had for his wife.

When Nike had declined his marriage proposal, he had gone ahead and married his fiancée, Laura, who he knew, clearly adored him; and once again, he had tried to forget Nike and put her in his past. But now that Nike was calling him, he was not sure he would not betray the emotions he felt for her in the presence of Laura, who was sleeping beside him.

Drawing back the duvet cover that was draped over him and his wife, he gently got out of the bed and crept to the adjoining sitting room. At least, he would be sure that his conversation with Nike would be out of his wife's earshot. Doctor Wale Macauley was not someone who enjoyed hurting people's feelings, much less his wife's.

'Hello,' he whispered into his phone as he flicked it open.

Nike was happy to hear Doctor Macauley's voice. His voice gave her an inexplicable inner strength. Perhaps, she could give him the green light and a relationship could start off between them. With time, she would learn to love Doctor Macauley as he loved her.

'Hello,' she cooed happily into the phone, 'this is Nike Adeogun'.

'Yes, Nike. How are you?' said Doctor Macauley uncomfortably. He glanced towards the bedroom occasionally. He did not want his wife to wake up and jump to wrong conclusions.

'Hi Doctor Macauley,' Nike said cheerfully, she was oblivious to Doctor Macauley's discomfort at her call. 'I was just wondering why you did not turn up for my grandfather's burial,' continued Nike. 'Is everything alright?'

'Yes, everything's fine with me,' replied Doctor Macauley, 'and I'm deeply sorry about your grandfather's death. I would have been there, but the burial took place on my wedding day, you see. I… I hope you understand.'

Nike's smile vanished instantly.
Doctor Macauley was married.
Her hopes had been dashed.
Just then, she heard a sweet, female voice in the background.
'Where are you honey? Come back to bed,' said the voice.
And that was all the confirmation Nike needed. She hung up the phone without saying good-bye to Doctor Macauley.

Very early the next morning, Nike packed her belongings and headed towards the airport. She needed to travel back to the United Kingdom as fast as possible and start life afresh. Her grandfather had left her a substantial amount of money in his will to last her a lifetime; even if she chose to live her life as a spendthrift.

Even though, she knew she would be lonely for the rest of her life, she decided to go back to Britain and enjoy her money until her dying day.

At ten a.m., the aeroplane left the Mur'tala Mohammed airport in Nigeria and headed towards the Heathrow airport in Great Britain.

Chapter 73

London, Great Britain

Alex had never felt so alone in his life. He had never felt so shut out from the rest of the world until now.

He had been living in a hotel for the past two and a half weeks. Two weeks ago, he had gone to the law firm where he used to work and he had promptly been handed his dismissal letter.

He had sent out several applications to other law firms but they had all politely declined to give him employment after receiving a bad reference from the highly esteemed Sir Richard Stonewall. Sir Richard Stonewall had written to all Alex's prospective employers and told them that Alex Tucker was an irresponsible lawyer, who deserved to be on a register for the unemployed for the rest of his life!

But his getting sacked and not being able to secure another job was not what was bothering Alex. All the family wealth had been bequeathed to him upon Alan's death and Alex was thinking of setting up a law practice on his own.

What was actually bothering him was that he missed Nike very much. He missed her laughter, her fun and her sharp retort over whatever made her angry. He missed sex with Nike and funny though it may seem, he missed the crazy side of her. He had called her mobile phone several times and he had always been transferred to her voicemail. He had left several messages on her voicemail but his calls had never been returned. He did not know where to look for Nike. The last time he saw her, she had been homeless.

A thought came to his mind; he could go back to Nigeria and look for her. Surely, her grandfather would know her whereabouts. He had not remembered to get Nike's grandfather's phone number or the phone number to the palace, but he was sure that when he got to Nigeria, he would know how to trace his way to the palace. He called a cab and instructed the driver to take him to the airport.

Nike was coming out of the airport as Alex was going towards the departure area. They spotted each other immediately.

Alex spread his arms towards Nike and without hesitation, she ran into them; all the hatred she had felt for him disappearing like a mist. Nike realised that she had missed Alex terribly.

'I'm so sorry, Nike. I've missed you,' said Alex.

'I've missed you too,' said Nike.

Soon, they were engaged in a warm, passionate kiss. After a while, Nike pulled away from Alex. 'My grandfather died,' she said. 'I had to go back to Nigeria.'

Alex was moved to tears. He pulled Nike close to him and cradled her head against his chest.

'I'm sorry,' he said. 'I'll take care of you. I'll always be there for you. I'll never leave you again,' he promised her sincerely.

Nike believed him but she felt she had to tell him what she discovered about herself. 'Alex, I… I can't have children,' she said tearfully.

'It's alright,' said Alex. 'We can always adopt kids. We'll adopt lots of kids. Our house will be full,' he finished, grinning.

Suddenly, he dipped his hand in his trouser pocket and brought out a gold case. This, he opened and brought out the most beautiful diamond ring Nike had ever seen. Alex had bought the ring before they travelled to Nigeria together. Only he had not envisaged that they would encounter any problem that would deter him from proposing to her. But now, his greatest wish in his life was to marry Nike Adeogun.

Bending on one knee, Alex asked Nike solemnly, 'Will you marry me, Nike?'

Nike's eyes shone brightly with tears of joy as she gave her reply.

'Yes Alex,' she said. 'Yes, I will marry you.'

Epilogue

Alex and Nike were married in a low-key ceremony at the registry. Their wedding ceremony was attended by neither friends nor family.

Interestingly, they lived happily ever after!

Lightning Source UK Ltd.
Milton Keynes UK
17 June 2010

155742UK00002B/53/P